Patrick

Daring, adventurous—He sold his ship for a dream of the land and a golden future. He had a vision of what it meant to be a man. He would lay down his life to uphold it.

Mary Frances

A beautiful woman, a gifted artist—She longed for the son who was lost to her and dreamed of reunion. But far more than a mother's hopes would be dashed when she found him.

Elizabeth

Fiery, free—She dreamed of a love as glorious and strong as her own spirit. She was too young to know that such a love could last a brief moment—and cost more than one lifetime of happiness.

The Donovans

Their dreams brought them to Los Angeles. Their destiny transformed a settlement into a city. The unforgettable story of a courageous family in   ,

THE FARTHEST EDEN

The
Farthest
Eden

Louise O'Flaherty

BALLANTINE BOOKS • NEW YORK

For Carl Wilde, my father,
a lover of books

"*El Resentimiento*"	"The Suffering"
Dolores	Of sorrows
Y amores	And loves
Cantemos	Let us sing
Lloremos	Let us weep
Que todo es vivir	For this is loving
Yo quiero	I wish
Y prefiero	And I choose
A estar	To remain
Sin amar	Without love
Ausente	Apart
Sin verte	Not seeing
Ni pensar en ti	Nor thinking of you

By the editor,
Los Angeles Star, 1851

Part One

1851—1852

CHAPTER ONE

"JOURNEY'S END, BETS!" PATRICK DONOVAN exulted, "and there it is at last, girl. California!"

"Not an end for us, Papa—a beginning!"

His daughter, bracing herself at the forward mast, eyes glowing, her body taut with excitement, and her long black hair streaming in the fresh wind, was at that moment like a second and more beautiful figurehead, enhancing the fine symmetry of the sleek and rakish ship.

The tall clipper, with a sailor in the chains throwing lead, was inching under reduced sail toward its anchorage. The shoreline, hilly, barren and dominated by a stark mountain of a peninsula that crouched above precipitous cliffs, was not far distant. But the sun was turning the water, no longer deep, as green as Mexican limes. Still ahead were the treacherous shallows, white-capped and blown with spindrift, for which the San Pedro roadstead was infamous.

The *Elizabeth,* named not for a long-dead English queen, but for Bets herself, was one hundred and one days out of Boston. Surely a fast enough passage, considering the high seas and baffling currents she'd endured rounding the Horn, but nonetheless a matter of great irritation to Patrick Donovan. He was aboard for the last time as sole owner, and the extra days galled him, aware as he was of the record for this same voyage recently set by another clipper ship, the *Flying Cloud.* What he'd have given to beat her time! The *Elizabeth* was fully as fast, and this year, 1851, with any luck at all, should have been his!

But now he was balanced, his long legs apart and firmly planted, gazing at the bluffs, and anticipating with delight the salty, fishy, mud-flat aroma that would greet him ashore, a smell that always meant to him landfall. His disappointment was put aside, for-

3

gotten, along with the weeks of tedium and the brief spells of danger that he'd reveled in. He wore a broad smile, for his plans at last were coming to fruition.

"Ten fathoms ten," chanted the leadsman.

"Papa, where are the houses?" Bets asked suddenly. She was staring at the empty, perpendicular coastline.

The question sobered Patrick, and he was eyeing his daughter as though for the first time realizing what he had done, transporting her so blithely from a quiet home in staid New England to what was really, if one were to be truthful, little more than just another raw little Mexican village.

"Miles away. I've told you all about this landing!" he exclaimed loudly, stilling the uncomfortable doubt. "It's San Pedro and we'll have to take a stage from there to Los Angeles. You didn't expect Boston Harbor, surely?"

She turned, smiling, and he was reassured. He should have known better. His Betsey fearful? She was as eager as he! "Seems to me," he said gruffly, "I've displayed the patience of a saint in answering all your thousand and one questions."

"Indeed you have, Papa—a saint!" With mock admiration, Bets rolled her eyes skyward, eyes which like his, were a deep shade of blue, and the more startling for being fringed with thick dark lashes.

Her aunt, Mary Reyes, standing at the ship's rail, was struck once again by the strong resemblance between father and daughter. The kinship was easily discernible even though Patrick during the voyage had allowed his beard to grow, curly and thick, along the jawline, lending his thirty-eight years an adventurous image. Bets had inherited his black Irish coloring, his straight nose, and his generous mouth. Even their smiles were alike, warm and contagious, although hers had a natural witchery of which, Mary suspected, the girl was not entirely unaware. Yet coquette she was not.

"Your aunt has been teaching you Spanish for the last year," Patrick continued, "and I hope to God you've learned, or you'll be talking only with her or me. In Los Angeles—you do know the full name, don't you?" He rolled out the sonorous words with gusto, *"Nuestra Señora, la Reina de los Angeles, de Porciuncula!* In this town, my girl, the language is Spanish."

"Really, Papa, is it so? I can hardly believe no one speaks English!" They had discussed this before, and the idea, so alien to everything in her experience, intrigued her.

"Oh, a few do, perhaps. Newcomers mostly, like all the rest who haven't gotten past their own German, French, or whatever they were born to. But I don't intend for us to be outsiders, I can tell you! Not for long anyway."

"Si, Señor, yo hablo español," she said pertly, adding, "I do wonder though about so many things! You haven't really described where we'll live, or what you intend to do now that you've sold the ship, or even how we can possibly manage without Aunt Eileen and Aunt Sheila. Oh, I'm going to miss them so! No one can cook like Auntie Eileen. And the cleaning and sewing . . . Doubtless that's why you bought those two slaves in Charleston, although I can't understand you doing such a thing, when you've always said you disliked slavery—"

"Whoa there, slow down!" It hadn't escaped him that she had failed to mention his sister Mary in her speculations about their new household. Bets had been reserved and cool toward her aunt Mary throughout the journey. He supposed, back in Boston, she must have heard those vicious rumors; she could hardly have escaped doing so. But the truth involved a long painful explanation, and that, he'd decided a long time ago, was something his younger sister could only offer for herself.

"Sheila and Eileen were too old to uproot," he said. "Indeed Eileen was far too frail for such a trip, as you well know. As for the slaves, I'll get to them in a moment. Now then. We'll be staying at the Bella Union Hotel until I buy a house, which will be soon. I've been here often enough to know the town and to have some friends. One of them in particular, William Brinkman, is certain to help. And as for what I'll be doing—"

He stopped, feeling once again the surge of excitement that this part of the west had aroused in him at very first sight. Going home to Boston had each time become harder and harder, until finally he had succumbed. The lure had been many-sided, not the least of which was the conviction that there was fabulous opportunity here in the west. Fortunes had been made already, and he told himself there would be many more, one of them his. Throwing in his lot with this sun-baked pueblo was one decision he'd never regret!

"I've great plans! I've been learning all I can about vineyards over the years whenever the ship took me to Europe or here. Now I'm ready to try my hand. And of course I'll raise cattle," he explained. "Do you know, Bets, that more than eighty million dollars in gold was taken out of the Sierra foothills last year? Miners are pouring into those crowded camps, every day hundreds more, and they all need food. The price of beef has gone sky-high!"

He turned to the companionway. "But here's Jeb and Flora . . . I asked them to come up now to hear what I have to say."

The two negroes emerged onto the deck, the woman carrying an infant against her shoulder. At the sight of land, inhospitable as those dry brown hills appeared, their eyes widened with pleasure and their white teeth flashed. Both took deep breaths of the salt air, for its clean freshness was woefully lacking below decks where they had been engaged in packing the Donovan trunks.

"Jeb, Flora, I have something to tell you." He paused, savoring the drama of this moment. "You're a free man, Jeb." He clapped the young negro's muscular shoulder. "You and Flora both are free! I've never been much taken with the idea of slavery, and I'll be wanting none in Los Angeles."

Jeb stared, and a tremor passed through him. His wife's mouth dropped in shock, but then her eyes filled and she began a soft crooning wail.

"Whatever in God's name is the matter?" Patrick, taken by surprise, was shouting. "Don't you want to be free?"

"This ain't no place to turn us out, Master." Jeb spoke quietly enough, but there was fear in his face. "This here's wilderness! Flora and me, we'll most likely starve!"

"Starve?" He was outraged. "What do you think I brought you all this way for? You're going to work for me! For wages!"

"We going to stay with you then? Oh, thank the Lord." Tears now were coursing down Jeb's cheeks as well as Flora's. But there was still less apparent delight in his gift of freedom than Patrick had perhaps anticipated.

"All right," he said brusquely. "Both of you get below and finish the packing. We'll be going ashore soon."

The family's new servants hurried away.

Mary Reyes, who had been listening quietly, said, "They're bewildered. Did you have to wait until today, Patrick? If you'd told them weeks ago, they could have gotten used to the idea."

"I suppose so . . . But as freedmen, Mary Frances, they might have left the ship at any port! I didn't want to take that chance." Actually, such a possibility hadn't occurred to him until now. He'd pictured himself grandly bestowing their freedom upon them at the very end of the voyage, and had given the matter no further thought.

But now his daughter too posed an awkward question. "Papa, when you were buying servants, why did you choose a woman with a small baby?"

Uncomfortable, he avoided her gaze. In fact, he had purchased Jeb without knowing that a wife and child existed. When he learned, the forcible separation was more than he could stomach, and he had no choice but to pay on the spot an exorbitant price for Flora. All of which he had no intention of confessing.

Patrick sought to change the conversation and said instead, "Bets, I've been saving a bit of news for you too. Your Aunt Mary is to be your duenna."

"My *what!*"

"Ha! That stirred you up, did it? A duenna, my girl, is an older woman who looks after you, sees that no man manages to take advantage of you before marriage." He was grinning, but uneasily.

"I know what a duenna is," Bets cried in a fury. "But having one is downright silly at my age—or any age! In New England—"

"We are not in New England, I'll remind you! Far from it. Until a few years ago, this was part of New Spain, and in the society I intend for us to enter, a duenna for unmarried girls is the custom." This was true. She must accept it!

He tried to ease the moment with heavy-handed humor. "Now, daughter mine, I'll grant you that most girls of eighteen already have husbands, thus removing the need for chaperons. And perhaps you too, with just a little coaching from your aunt—"

Bets, with difficulty, was swallowing her indignation. He enjoyed teasing, she reminded herself, and anyway, changing his mind, at least in public, was a virtual impossibility. But coaching from Aunt Mary! Indeed! After the wretched failure she had made of marriage?

"Will you mind doing this, Mary Frances, at least for a while in the beginning? I want you to be happy here." To others this slender graceful woman of thirty, was Mary, or more often Mrs. Reyes. But to her brother, just as she'd been to their parents from the old country, she was still Mary Frances, the much younger, big-eyed, skinny child who'd trailed after him, needed his protection.

"Mind? Oh, Patrick, I'd do anything! I won't deny that I'm glad the voyage is over—" She had been seasick almost continually for weeks, and the gaze she turned on the land was a longing one. "But I'm so very grateful that you brought me! I don't think I could have stood one more day in Boston—the glances, the remarks! I'll astonish you, my dear. I'll be a very good duenna."

"That won't surprise me," he said with awkward tenderness. He was much pleased, having wondered more than once, as she grew paler and thinner in her misery aboard ship, whether she'd made a mistake in accompanying them. But to her, evidently, the long and wretched journey had been worthwhile.

And he was glad for his own sake, and his daughter's as well. Perhaps he'd been wrong not to remarry after Allison died. But he'd loved his wife so deeply, he hadn't really wanted to find anyone to take her place, and he'd argued that a man of the sea, away from home so much, was better off single. Now in this new life he was making, with Sheila and Eileen left behind, he was going to need Mary's help.

Bets meanwhile had turned her back and was squinting through the shimmering brightness of sun on water, pretending to be absorbed in the distant sight of a barely visible ramshackle building and the wharf on which it lay. When she realized that the ship's captain had come to stand at her side, she welcomed the diversion.

Just as he spoke to her, the sailors in the forepeak released the anchor chain, and the words were lost in the loud clanking rumble. The inevitable red cloud of rust rose and was blown away.

"Good morning, Miss Betsey," the captain repeated. He was short, his fleshy middle-aged face being on a level with her own. The yearning in his moist eyes did not escape either Bets or her father.

"Good morning, Captain Warner," she returned. "Are we going to tie up to that little wharf I see there?"

"No, indeed, Miss." He beamed, well-pleased to have her attention, although he was full of his new importance. Once Patrick Donovan disembarked, the ship was virtually his, for Donovan, as agreed, had sold him the majority of the shares. The money he'd saved from a long career at sea had been enough, and at last he would walk the bridge of the *Elizabeth* when she was his own, not another man's! "We must anchor here, a half-mile or so from Dead Man's Island—that's the peak of rock there off the starboard bow. It's low tide so the sandbar is exposed; the water's only about eighteen inches deep near the shore.

"But there'll be a tender coming to take you ashore. See, one's pulling away now from Timm's Point."

He placed a fatherly arm about her shoulders, ostensibly to guide her attention. Yet somehow, perhaps with the sway of the ship, Mary had slipped between them and it was she whom he partially embraced.

"Here, I do beg your pardon, Ma'am," Warner stammered, and hastily withdrew, his countenance an even ruddier color than usual.

"I quite understand, Captain," Mary said. "The ship rolled badly, did it not?"

"If you'll excuse me, I believe I'm needed forward—" He rushed away and was hardly out of earshot when Patrick burst into a roar of laughter.

"Well done, Mary Frances, well done! You'll be a damn fine duenna. I'll wager our young lady here is grateful for your interference . . . That old lecher!"

"I've been managing without help for the entire voyage," Bets said coolly. "He's just being kindly."

"Kindly, is it? He told me last night that now he has a ship, he would be asking for your hand, and did I think you'd care to overlook the thirty odd years between you! The infernal impudence! The man's a fool, and I doubt that I was wise going shares with him on the *Elizabeth*."

Bets was unperturbed. "It's true I wouldn't care to marry him. But if you laughed last night as rudely as you did just now, you've made an enemy, I'll be bound. Oh, Papa, look! All those men on horseback who have come down to the wharf! There are even a couple of padres in brown robes, riding on mules. And what strange carts!"

"Those are carretas, and they are damned uncomfortable with those solid wheels cut from logs. But they're all there is to ride in, except for an old army ambulance stage that will take us into town from here. Can you believe there's not a buggy or carriage in all of southern California?"

But Bets was not listening. Her attention was fixed in fascination on the shore. "Did they all come down to see the *Elizabeth*?"

"When a ship makes port here, it's always an event. We'll be a fine show, too, if the tender capsizes crossing the bar and spills us into the water! But mostly, everyone's eager for the cargo we've brought, the barrels of sugar and spices, as well as the satins and silks and embroidered shawls . . . Jeb, Flora, get topside! We're ready to disembark."

His two newly freed servants appeared with such alacrity that it was clear they had been lingering just inside the hatchway—regarding with wonder and apprehension the desolate, barren coast so different from everything they were used to.

"You'll go in the first crossing with us," Patrick told them. "The trunks can follow along in a lighter."

The negroes advanced to the rail and their eyes widened. For the first time they saw the swaying rope ladder and the boat that bobbed and rolled far below at its foot.

Realizing what was expected of them, Flora shrank back. Clutching her baby, she gazed in mute terror at Patrick Donovan.

"Bets," he ordered, "you climb down first and show them how it's done. Flora, watch carefully! And don't worry about the child—I'll bring her myself."

"No, Master!" Jeb protested. "That's for me to do," and Patrick gave him a nod of approval.

"You're right—it is. We'll tie her on your back. Here, turn around . . ."

After he'd done this, using Flora's shawl, he signalled Bets to go ahead. Two sailors had preceded her, but the girl hadn't needed to watch them. Disembarking at various small ports during the passage had often been accomplished in this manner. Without hesitation, having been assisted by her father over the rail, she groped for a foothold, saying to Flora, "You see? It looks much scarier than it is."

Although the men in the boat below held the rope ends as best they could, the ladder swayed back and forth with the motion of the ship. As Bets clung to the rungs her voluminous poplin skirts swung out like a bell, then were whipped quickly against her by the strong gusty wind. But she climbed down without stopping. Reaching the bottom, she waited until the bosun told her to drop, and then did so. A sailor's arm supported her until she was seated.

Mary, also adept from practice, followed.

But when Flora's turn came she cried, "Cain't do it, Master Patrick! I is going to fall!"

"Flora," Patrick said with unaccustomed patience, "Listen to me! I'll go down just ahead of you, and there'll be nothing to fear. If you make a misstep, I'll catch you. Now come!"

He had swung himself easily over the rail and was waiting. Flora cast Jeb a look of despair, and then trembling, obeyed. Patrick, below her, set her feet on the ladder and they started down.

Once she knew what was required, and had gone a few steps, her courage seemed to revive. Even though the ladder continued its sickening sway, she at length reached safety, and collapsed onto the stern seat.

If this new experience posed any difficulty for Jeb, he gave no indication. His callused bare feet easily found the rungs, and his strength and agility brought him down more quickly than some who were used to the climb.

Jeb seated himself beside his wife and began to untie the shawl.

Bets was sitting alone in the narrow bow of the tender, trying to imagine the details of this new life that would be so different from anything she'd known before. Speaking Spanish, she thought, would be delightful! She'd learned it well and easily—Aunt Mary'd admitted that she had a facility. But a duenna! Whatever possessed Papa? If Aunt Sheila had only been able to come, or Auntie Eileen, they'd have put a stop to that nonsense!

At the thought of the two gentle maiden ladies who had given her such devoted love in the four years since her mother's death, and whom she would probably never see again, tears welled in her large eyes. How lonely they must be now! And how much she missed them . . .

Just as Flora reached to take the infant a large wave hit the small boat tossing it violently.

"My baby's gone! My baby!" Flora shrieked, as the tiny bundle slipped from her grasp into the sea.

Bets sprang to her feet. Others in the boat were crowding toward the stern, and she hesitated, craning to see what had happened, at any moment expecting to hear the shout that the child was rescued.

Jep leapt into the water and was swimming powerfully around the boat, each cry of "There, Jeb, just behind you——" and, "I think I see her!" sending the distraught father in a new direction. But the precious seconds passed. Even though all in the tender were leaning out the sides, scanning the water, the small body had disappeared. The wind had so roughened the surface that there was no clarity, and to make the search more difficult, the child had been naked except for a cotton wrapper that was almost the same blue-green as the sea.

Suddenly the cloth was recovered—empty! As the pathetic, sodden material was handed aboard, Bets started forward in horror, forgetting to hold to the rail. The sea gave a twisting heave, and thrown off-balance, she fell sideways and was suspended out above the water. By the merest chance, she briefly glimpsed a brown, doll-like face.

As quickly as it appeared, it was gone.

"Jeb!" she screamed, but knew there was no time. Without calling further, Bets threw herself over the sloping wooden side and tumbled into the sea.

The water was cold, and she gasped for breath. But fear for the infant drove away any consciousness of the shock.

Where was the little thing? Where? The face had been just at the waterline, and should be farther forward now, just a little—

Seeing nothing, in desperation she searched below the shimmering surface with her hands. And feeling the faint touch of cold flesh, she grabbed, caught hold of a miniature foot, and pulled. The baby slid to her easily.

Then, for the first time Bets realized her own danger. Somehow by dint of constant frantic motion she had managed to stay afloat. But with her arms full, her heavy clothing a binding, dragging weight, she found herself going under.

"Papa!" she sputtered, and the bitter salt water rolled into her mouth.

He was there, reaching down to her. "All right, Bets—easy, girl—"

His hand was like a band of iron gripping her arm, while Jeb swam to her side. Someone else leaned from the boat and relieved her of her burden.

Between the efforts of the two men, Bets was hoisted back over the edge, roughly and in haste, to be left alone sitting on the floorboards, water running from her clothing in rivulets.

As the thundering of her heart lessened, Bets gradually became aware of an ominous silence enveloping the tender. Bets stared back at those who huddled around the unnaturally still baby lying on the stern seat, and at Jeb, standing grim-faced, not knowing or caring that the raw wind whipped through his soaked shirt and breeches.

Patrick was on his knees, pressing the unconscious body in a gentle even rhythm. Bets held her breath as she watched. Seeing that Flora sat rigidly erect, holding her palms together beneath her chin, praying, Bets moved her own lips: "Hail Mary, full of grace, the Lord is with thee—"

Suddenly there was a choking sound, and water gushed from the baby's mouth. It gasped for air, struggled harder, and then gave a tiny yell, furiously angry.

What a beautiful noise, Bets thought as she smiled down the length of the boat at Flora. Lord, don't let me ever forget how wonderful—as Aunt Mary must have forgotten!

Chapter Two

"Not so fast, not so fast," grumbled the sour voice. "I'm drowning in dust. Why must you hurry so?"

True, clouds of dust stirred up by the horses' feet did rise high in the air, but rather less so around the angular figure of the young woman, Felipa Antonia Rodriguez, who was in the lead. Although the costume of her aunt, Doña Ana, had grayed in the hour they'd been on the way, her own embroidered red shirt was still bright, and her stiff, broad-brimmed riding hat remained black and well brushed.

"The ship will already be in," Felipa replied, "and the finest fabrics will be bought at once. You know that."

Doña Ana continued to regard the erect back ahead of her with disfavor. Felipa did ride with superb skill, there was no denying. But it was precisely because Felipa rode well, thought her aunt, that she herself was having to exercise so strenuously in the heat of the day, instead of taking her ease in a carreta and allowing a couple of oxen to do the sweating. Felipa intended to show herself at her best when at length they reached Los Angeles, and Doña Ana was not fooled for a moment by her niece's stated desire to purchase yard-goods for a dress from the arriving vessel from the East. Not for silks and satins had Ana been forced to forego her siesta, or the majordomo of the Rodriguez rancho been pulled away from his work in order to accompany and protect them! Ana only hoped that the real reason for Felipa's eagerness would not be too apparent to all, and shame the family.

The horses topped a rise and there at the foot of the brown hills, lay the pueblo of Los Angeles. The riders could see the unpaved and unshaded streets dog-legging between the rows of low, dun-colored adobe buildings. Occasionally a red tile roof stood out from the other housetops sealed with black tar, lending a spot of color to the vista. A few thick brown spirals in the air indicated the passage of horsemen, for the rains had not yet begun and dust in the rutted streets lay as much as a foot deep.

Felipa had slowed, and was waiting with an air of condescending patience, as though her aunt's tardiness need be excused because of less expert horsemanship, or—and this was even more galling to Doña Ana— because of her advanced age. The older woman was tempted to point out that Felipa's riding ability was merely something she had inherited, and that she, Ana, had once been renowned for this expertise, and not so long ago either! But the day was too hot for argument.

Instead, she whined, "I still don't understand where we're going. The storehouse will be closed now for siesta," and she waited with enjoyable malice for what she knew would be the answer.

"Yes, but look! There's a crowd at the Bella Union. People must still be waiting for the stages to arrive from that clipper ship, so perhaps the cargo isn't unloaded yet. Why don't we go to the hotel ourselves? I always enjoy seeing the finish of a stage race."

"You enjoy encountering Miguel Aguirre, you mean," amended her duenna, but kept the words low enough so Felipa could not hear them. She nodded, and waved a dismissing hand to the majordomo, having decided there would be escorts enough for their return to the rancho. Indeed, Felipa's father was doubtless among those waiting at the end of the stage line.

They trotted their horses along the street toward the Bella Union, Doña Ana wrinkling her nose in distaste. Although a recent city ordinance prohibited filth from being thrown in the zanjas, the open ditches that threaded the town and carried water for all common uses were widely abused. The smell of raw sewage, as usual, was strong in the warm air.

When Felipa reined up before the porch of the hotel, her nervous horse reared—nostrils flaring and front legs pawing the air. Calmly, competently, she quieted him, while the crowd composed mostly of men, watched her.

Doña Ana pressed her own mare closer. "You don't see any women of our circle here, standing about and making themselves common!" she hissed. "Be grateful your father didn't witness that! He and his friends must be inside at the bar, and you will be wise to leave at once."

A younger girl would have been whisked off by her duenna with no argument. But Felipa, at twenty-six, was hardly of an age to be ordered home summarily.

The oldest of Diego Rodriguez' four daughters and the only one still unmarried, she was dangerously close to becoming a maiden aunt herself. Her sisters' children, some no longer very small, made this label painfully apt. She was a spinster; and spinsters, whether beloved, hated, or treated with indulgent contempt, did have a measure of freedom to do as they pleased.

"No, we will wait," Felipa said. "I hear the stages coming now."

"Ears like a lynx," muttered Doña Ana, who was herself a trifle deaf. But she didn't doubt that Felipa was correct, because the crowd's attention was now on the bend in the street. Men had also begun to issue from the double doors of the hotel bar, and a ripple of excitement communicated itself amongst them.

Stately Diego Rodriguez appeared, giving his daughter a brief surprised frown, but the gentlemen with him greeted her with the utmost courtesy.

"Ten to one on Phineas Bishop," suggested Rodriguez to his friends. It was portly round-faced William Brinkman who answered without hesitation, "Done!" With evident and keen anticipation, everyone was awaiting the arrival of the two competing stages.

Only young Lucius Camell—known as Camellito, meaning Little Camel, because of his short stature— sought out Felipa, being more interested in speaking with her than in the betting.

"Will I see you tomorrow night at the party?" he asked.

"Of course." He seemed shorter than ever, viewed from the height of her horse's back, and Felipa's smile held a touch of scorn. She sent a surreptitious searching look through the crowd.

"You'll have an opportunity then to meet our newest hero," Camellito said eagerly.

"This ship owner who arrives today?"

"No, no," Camellito said, "I'm referring to John Carew. Surely you've heard of him?"

"I've heard nothing." She was hardly listening. Where was Miguel?

"Carew arrived several days ago, and since then, every man in town wants to shake his hand."

"Oh? I suppose he's another gold miner who is suddenly rich as Croesus."

"Hardly that. He's a sheep man." Camellito broke into a wide smile. Finally he had caught her attention, and he was clearly enjoying her bewilderment.

"Sheep? Sheep are nothing here. You're teasing me. Come now, who is this John Carew?"

"A sheep man, as I said, but a very brave and clever one. He—"

Camellito's voice was drowned in the sudden roar of the crowd. Two large old ambulance stages, drawn by mules and followed by a pack of yapping, mongrel dogs, swept around the corner.

As the leading coach swayed precariously to the right on two wheels and almost overturned, a thickset, powerful young man could be seen balanced on top beside the driver, shouting the horses on and brandishing an aguardiente bottle. Several seconds before the vehicle was halted, he leaped to the ground, and raced alongside, shouting to its occupants, "You won, gentlemen! Did I give you a race or didn't I? I hope you'll tell your friends about Phineas Bishop's stage line!"

The passengers eased out unsteadily, being somewhat the worse for brandy, as well as a trifle green in color—the result of racing at breakneck speed for twenty miles. But all converged with much hilarity to collect their winnings. The loser in the other coach, Patrick Donovan, paid up with high good humor.

"Hereafter I'll make certain I ride your stage. Never again will I be such a fool as to lay down money against you!"

Bishop, who was assisting Bets and Mary from the high step of the second coach, gave a hearty laugh. "I'm not the victor, Mr. Donovan! To think, I could have ridden inside here, with two such lovely ladies."

Mary seemed not to hear, but Bets acknowledged the compliment with a delighted flash of her clear blue eyes. Patrick slapped Bishop's shoulder, then catching sight of Felipa's father, led his family toward the hotel porch.

"Greetings once again, Don Diego!" he said. "Señor

Rodriguez, allow me to present my sister, Señora Reyes, and my daughter, Elizabeth."

"Señora," acknowledged Rodriguez, bending with his customary grace over Mary's hand, his deferential manner toward both women as flattering as the open admiration of Phineas Bishop.

Mary inclined her head. With the feel of dry land, she was recovering at last from her malaise. Even the careening stage had not prevented the color from stealing back into her face. She had fasted far too often during the voyage, and her thinness was accentuated in her narrow high-bridged nose and the hollowness of her cheeks, but it also brought out the fine grace of her body and the unusual size of her gray eyes. Too, there was a reserve about her, a faint air of aristocratic hauteur that appealed to the Californio men present.

But the real center of attention was Bets. Utilizing a tiny bare room on the wharf after her immersion in the sea, she had completely redressed, and it was the waiting for the trunks to be brought ashore so that she might accomplish this, that had caused the delay of the stages. Once more clad in a fresh dress with ruffle-trimmed petticoat, and soft low-heeled slippers, her lustrous black hair dried by the wind and brushed until it shone, she faced the ring of strange faces with confidence, giving them a radiant smile.

Felipa, watching, felt a stir of envy so strong it was like a premonition.

"Good afternoon, Felipa," said a deep voice at her side, and the newcomers promptly faded from her consciousness.

"Oh, ho! He's here after all," said her duenna, too softly for the man to hear.

Felipa's thin lips curved with pleasure, but she turned with deliberate slowness to look down at the man standing beside her stirrup.

"Miguel! How pleasant to see you. To be honest, however, I'm not surprised to find you here."

"Indeed you're not," Doña Ana mumbled. Felipa hurried to explain. "You would be here, of course, for the finish of the race so as to report it in the newspaper." She was referring to the fledgling *Los Angeles Star,* the town's only newspaper. As a concession to the growing number of Americano immigrants, the weekly was published in both Spanish and English. Miguel Aguirre was editor of the more important Spanish section.

He shrugged. "Yes, for such trifling news is all we usually have available. But in the next edition, there will at least be something of more importance."

"Carew?" asked Camellito, startling Felipa, who had forgotten he was present. She wished impatiently that he would wander away, leaving her alone with Miguel.

To her surprise, Aguirre answered with enthusiasm. "Yes! I've just come from interviewing him. What a fantastic undertaking—and to succeed!" He looked up at Felipa. "Can you imagine driving a herd of sheep—over twenty-four hundred of them—across the plains, mountains, and desert, all the way from Illinois to California? With the help of two partners, he actually did this, even though there was a stretch of about a hundred miles in the Mohave Desert that was totally without water! Men as well as animals almost perished. John Carew is remarkably brave and resourceful."

"But sheep?" Felipa said, perplexed. "The owners of the ranchos, men like your father and mine—they despise sheep."

Miguel paused looking at her for a moment before speaking, "It is not a question of sheep, but of courage."

Felipa bit her lip. "You mean you admire the achievement, although it accomplished nothing very useful?"

"I suspect it accomplished something for Carew," he said drily. "But yes, you might look at it like that."

Camellito broke in. His gentle face was lit with enthusiam. "Please, Miguel, tell us more! I only know what's happened since the caravan arrived here. The two partners have gone on north, and I suppose they'll return in the spring to help drive the flock on to Monterey. By then the grass will have grown enough to graze the sheep along the way. But Carew says so little! He's such a quiet person. I've heard nothing really, and the hardships must have been terrible, especially on the Mormon Trail!"

"He is very reticent," Aguirre agreed. "But as my father has agreed to pasture all those sheep on our land until spring, he was willing to talk with me—"

He broke off, his attention caught by the Donovans who were preparing to enter the hotel. It was easy for him with his slim height to gaze across the heads of everyone else, but Camellito, even stretched up on his toes, could see little. Felipa watched too, resentful of the interruption.

Bets Donovan had just picked up a fold of her forest green skirt and begun to climb the wooden steps. Suddenly Felipa could see the girl as the men must be seeing her. The proud swelling of bosom under the bodice of the New England-style dress, the small supple waist, the flash of a slim and graceful leg only momentarily revealed. But there was more than mere beauty. There was that wide, generous, entrancing smile, and the straight gaze of sea-blue eyes.

"Momento, Señorita Elizabeth!" The booming voice of Phineas Bishop halted Bets and she turned. Tall and burly, he towered above the heads of the slighter Californios.

"My stages were late today, and I never permit that without a reason! Agreed?" He was addressing the crowd, and was answered with noisy cheerful banter. "Then hear my excuse! This little lady couldn't ride to town all dripping wet, so we waited for her to pretty herself up.

"And why, you may ask, did she go overboard into the cold sea? I'll tell you. In order to save a baby from drowning! There you are, my friends. She risked her own life to save a tiny infant, the child of the Donovans' servants. You'll see them soon. They're coming in a carreta with all the trunks, and you'll find them smiling and happy instead of wailing and carrying on as they would have been otherwise. My friends, let's have a cheer for Miss Elizabeth Donovan!"

Bishop's Spanish was awkward, he seemed to translate words just as they came into his head, and a moment was needed for this story to become comprehensible. But then the *olés* rang out, again and again.

Bet's eyes danced and met Patrick's. She could have shouted with the rest from pure exuberance, and knew that her father felt the same. The heat, the odors, even the bloated carcass of a dead dog lying a short distance away in the dry weeds, all had been briefly noted and forgotten. How wonderful was this town and these people who welcomed strangers!

Don Diego waved his hand for silence.

"Beauty and courage can hardly be prized too highly," he said, "and I too would like to express my admiration. Because I am not a master of words, a more concrete offering will have to suffice. I might add that I am doubly happy to take this opportunity to thank Patrick Donovan who has always made every effort to deliver the cargo we needed here when other ship owners looked to larger ports.

"One may know he has not had time to acquire horses, and I have a young filly, spirited yet disciplined. She is called Estrella for the white star on her forehead, but otherwise she is black as a raven's wing, matching the hair of the lovely young woman who will be her new mistress.

"I trust Señorita Elizabeth will accept as a gift . . . my Estrella!"

Again there were cheers, even more loud and enthusiastic as the aguardiente bottle was passing from hand to hand. Through the clamor ripped Felipa's shocked cry: "Father!"

His head snapped around and he looked up at her.

"Yes, daughter? What is it?"

Felipa saw the warning coldness in his eyes, and realized just in time she had been on the verge of disgracing him. She choked back the bitter words of protest, and instead, stammering in her suppressed fury, replied, "It's only that—Estrella's training is not yet completed—not for another month—"

"Of course she must be trained! That's understood. So finish. Then present the filly to the Señorita."

He understood well enough, she knew that he did. She drew in her breath deeply, trying to maintain her precarious control.

"Is that clear?" he demanded.

"Yes, Father. But Father . . . I think if you give Estrella as a gift, the saddle that fits her so well should be given too."

His hesitation was imperceptible, except to her. "Yes, indeed," he said, and she knew that a small revenge at least was hers. The saddle in question was an especially beautiful one that he loved, and particularly because it had often been used by her gracious and charming mother, who had died.

"Shame on Diego!" whispered Doña Ana, leaning close across their horses' necks so that only Felipa could hear. For once she was in sympathy with her niece. "To give away the mare his daughter has raised from a foal—and without a by-your-leave!"

Her backing only fanned the flames of Felipa's anger. She stared with hot eyes as Bets Donovan first protested the lavishness of the unexpected gift then, having caught Patrick's nod, accepted, and thanked Diego Rodriguez. Listening to the warm voice of the girl fashioning phrases of gratitude in classic Castilian Spanish, phrases she herself couldn't fault, and seeing her father's stern features relax with rare pleasure, she was tempted to gallop away, unable to endure the scene further.

"That was a most generous thing you did, Miss Felipa," Camellito said.

She didn't answer, but glanced with sudden hope at Miguel Aguirre. If he too had been impressed, the gift might even have been worthwhile! But no, his back was to her. Like all the others, his attention was on the newcomers who were entering the hotel, the girl laughing, Señor Donovan exchanging boisterous shouts with the onlookers.

Felipa's smoldering gaze focused on the flat-roofed adobe structure, around which there wasn't one tree or a single blade of grass. The Bella Union. Certainly, the best hotel in Los Angeles, yet bound to be an unpleasant surprise for people from the effete East.

She pictured the rooms as she had been told of them, all small, airless, and plagued with insects, particularly fleas, and could not resist saying, "I trust the Donovans will be given one of the better rooms." She knew full well there were none.

Doña Ana snorted; but Camellito replied earnestly, "Oh, Felipa, you are kind! But you must not worry. William Brinkman, like your father, has long been acquainted with Patrick Donovan, and he told me he was offering the hospitality of his home until such time as Señor Donovan finds one of his own. The party is only going inside now to refresh themselves before continuing on to the Brinkman house. And more, I understand that they've been invited to the most important social event of the month—the fandango given by Don Abel Stearns. Rest assured, Felipa, the Donovans will be well taken care of."

CHAPTER THREE

THE WOMEN OF THE BRINKMAN HOUSEHOLD rode to the Abel Stearns party in a carreta, escorted by their men who paced alongside on spirited, richly trapped horses. Handsomely turned out as those riders were, they paled in comparison to Don Antonio Maria Lugo, Judge of the Plains, when he made his appearance at a street corner.

"He's seventy-five!" Señora Brinkman whispered to her guests, Mary Reyes and Elizabeth Donovan. "Would you believe that?"

Don Antonio's age was indeed difficult to credit. No man present sat taller or straighter in the saddle, or was dressed with more splendor. His close-fitting pantaloons, open at the side below the knee, were of gleaming black velvet, and his flat-brimmed hat, also black, was adorned with a silver cord encircling the crown. Under a short jacket embroidered in silver thread, he wore an emerald green shirt, fashioned of the same lustrous silk that formed the wide sash around his waist.

His horse pranced, its neck arched, yet the patriarch's leather quirt and great shiny spurs were never used. He controlled the nervous stallion merely by the pressure of his knees.

Don Antonio was greeted with respect, and he reined his horse next to the carreta in order to be presented to Patrick Donovan's family. After Mary had murmured a conventional acknowledgment, Bets smiled up into the hawk-like face.

"My father has told me how very much he admires you, Don Antonio!"

"He is kind, Señorita! For my part, before meeting his daughter and sister, I was pleased enough that he was joining us here in Los Angeles. Now I am doubly delighted. The reputation for beautiful women that the pueblo already enjoys will be more than secure. May I ask if you both will honor an old man by being his partner at the dancing, some time during the evening?"

"You flatter us by the invitation," Mary told him. After his horse had been expertly spun away to resume its elegant lope, she remarked, as though to herself, "What change occurs in such men between the cruelty of youth and the courtliness of age, I wonder?"

"I beg your pardon," said Señora Brinkman, and Mary started, uncomfortable under the inquisitive gaze of the Californio woman.

"Forgive me . . . I was only thinking aloud," she said, and turned hastily to the young Brinkman daughter, who with her own duenna accompanied them in the carreta. "I did enjoy your singing this afternoon. You have a sweet and very true voice."

Teodocia's round fair face, in which there appeared surprisingly little of her mother's Spanish heritage, lit with shy pleasure.

"I didn't know anyone was listening."

"You sounded so happy."

"Yes, I was! Mama had just given her permission for me to come with you this evening. I haven't been allowed to attend any adult gala gatherings before."

"My daughter is only fourteen," her mother informed Mary.

"Yes, Mama, but Arcadia Stearns was fourteen too when she *married!* And you've said yourself that hers is a very successful marriage, that right from the beginning she was so very poised and mature—"

"Do you consider yourself poised and mature also?" Señora Brinkman asked. Then she relented and patted her daughter's hand. "Doubtless Arcadia was helped to become the grand lady and perfect hostess that she is, in spite of her youth, by being married to a man so much older—as well as very wealthy. Shall we try to find a husband thirty years older for you also?"

"Oh, no, Mama!" Teodocia cried, so horrified that all the ladies laughed together. Bets, smiling at the gentle blond girl, felt the beginning of a protective affection. This was her first friend in this strange new world.

Señora Brinkman had sobered and was now regarding Teodocia with a thoughtful, almost troubled frown. At last, as though realizing her lapse in courtesy, she turned to Mary and resumed conversation.

"Arcadia Bandini de Stearns, you see, was only fourteen, although her husband, Don Abel was forty-four at their marriage. Of course, now ten years have passed, and the difference between them is no longer quite so remarkable. She is an accomplished young woman."

"I look forward to meeting her," Mary replied.

Bets said nothing. She was reminded of Captain Warner's proposal, for he too had been much older. Even had he been strong and handsome and far more intelligent than he was, she told herself, she would never have considered accepting him!

Señora Brinkman must have guessed what she was thinking, because she said, "I was younger than my husband also, though not nearly as much so. And I, like Arcadia, married an Americano, as have two of my daughters. Such mixed marriages have become very popular indeed. It is most unusual today to find a family like that of Diego Rodriguez, where all of the daughters have been chosen by Californio men."

"Not all, Mama," reminded Teodocia. "What about Felipa?"

"Felipa can hardly be considered. After all, she's the oldest and well beyond the marrying age! I might add she has never been a beauty, and since she gives herself very superior airs, her state is not at all surprising."

"Mama, that's unfair!" Teodocia protested. "She still might marry."

"Whom?" retorted her mother. "Lucius Camell? Well, possibly. I've heard he adores her. But he is of much shorter stature than she, not brilliant, and his father was an Americano, after all. We all know Felipa's prejudices, she is so outspoken."

"No, not Camellito. But I think possibly—Miguel Aguirre."

The señora pondered this suggestion, and nodded. "Miguel . . . Yes, I suppose she could have conceived an infatuation for him, handsome as he is and with a profile such as Don Quixote must have had. But being intelligent does not make a man blind—"

"I did not say she had an infatuation!" insisted Teodocia, but was ignored.

"—and if he does reciprocate, it will be purely as a matter of convenience," the señora finished firmly. "Two proud old Californio families tying together. For him to regard Felipa with any passion is most unlikely."

Bets gazed dreamily at the passing scene, the small adobe houses set haphazardly among the dry weeds, and listened without surprise to the conversation. She had heard such idle speculation among mothers and daughters in Boston, and she remembered the talk that had buzzed so maliciously when Mary, young and elegant, returned unexpectedly from Spain. Some of that gossip must have been true, Bets supposed; certainly neither Aunt Mary nor her father had tried to refute or explain it away. But she hadn't enjoyed hearing a member of her family disparaged, and Bets had decided then that she had little interest in most all-female conversations. Watching her father, she wished that she too were riding one of those sleek prancing horses, instead of sitting dumpily in a creaking cart listening to Señora Brinkman dismiss Felipa Rodriguez, whoever she was, into hopeless spinsterhood. It was a relief, therefore, when the carreta rumbled finally to a stop.

As the women were assisted to alight, Señora Brinkman said in a lowered voice, "You see before you the very center of South Coast society, the palace Don Abel built for his young bride! Imposing, is it not?"

"Yes, indeed," Bets said politely, thinking that while this one-story house was considerably larger than its neighbors, by comparison with many homes in Boston it was surely less than impressive.

Once ushered inside, however, she gasped. The *sala grande* was immensely long and luxurious. Obviously, no expense had been spared. While she was admiring the tapestries, hung to protect the clothing of guests from the white-washed walls, she heard her aunt exclaim, "What a magnificent square piano! I've never seen one like it."

Their hostess, gowned in many yards of wine-red Chinese silk and wearing a jeweled comb in her dark hair, drew her slight, erect figure even more ramrod-straight. Her hand briefly caressed the great expanse of gleaming mahogany surface, in which were mirrored the flames of dozens of candles, suspended above in a crystal chandelier.

Smiling graciously, she said, "Yes, Abel ordered it from Steinway and Sons, and had it brought all the way around the Horn, especially for my birthday! It does have a lovely tone . . . But please, allow me to present you, Señora Reyes, to our friends. You too, Señorita—or may I call you Elizabeth? We are much of an age."

"Please do!" Bets said, not disguising her pleasure.

She and Mary, followed by Teodocia, trailed through the *sala,* seeing among the men a number who had been in the crowd at the Bella Union, but who now were entirely sober and accompanied by their wives. The names being pronounced by the hostess were long as well as numerous and Bets found them blurring in her ears. Yet she tried doggedly to remember, for these were the people her father wanted as friends for his family.

Almost around the room, Arcadia paused. Seeing a cluster of men drawn together with their backs turned, a tiny frown touched her face. She approached them in a purposeful way, still leading her guests. The group was so intent on someone in their midst that they were obviously startled when she said, a touch of steel in her voice, "Gentlemen—"

"Forgive us, Señora! We are all so intrigued by Señor Carew's exploits that we have forgotten our manners!"

"I quite understand. I can only be delighted that our guest of honor is so absorbing to you all. Pray continue, Mr. Carew! What were you saying? These ladies, as well as myself, admire daring and fortitude as much as the gentlemen do."

"I assure you, Señora, the story has been greatly exaggerated," Carew replied quietly, his Spanish halting and badly accented.

Bets saw him then. He had come forward and she found herself looking into eyes even more intensely blue than her own. His skin had been baked brown by the sun, but his hair, oddly, had bleached almost white. He was not overly tall, and was of a stocky rather than a graceful build. His deerskin trousers and overshirt were unsuitable for his present surroundings, but the men who ringed him about were clearly deferential. Whatever his exploits had been, Bets thought, he had won their admiration.

"Hardly exaggerated," Arcadia said crisply. "Señor Carew, may I present Señorita Elizabeth Donovan, who, like you, has only just arrived in our pueblo?"

"Welcome, as I have been welcomed, to Los Angeles!" he said to Bets, speaking in English.

Before she could answer, and to her surprisingly sharp disappointment, he had turned away. Arcadia was introducing him to Mary.

"He's the one who drove the great herd of sheep across the country," Teodocia whispered. "Do you think he's handsome?"

Bets studied him. No, not handsome. His nose was

crooked as though it had once been broken. But certainly attractive! His strength, his quiet voice, appealed to her more than perfect features would have done. When at length she turned to answer, Teodocia had wandered away, perhaps to find one of her friends. As Arcadia too had gone and could be seen welcoming later guests on the far side of the room, she, Mary, and Carew were alone, a small island in the crowd.

He was again speaking Spanish, and Bets realized John Carew assumed her aunt was a Californio, not only because of her name, but because of her olive skin.

Mary smiled, which at once softened her thin patrician face into beauty. "May I guess where you're from, sir? Vermont? No—Maine, I think—"

"Maine it is." Then he asked ruefully, "Were you able to guess so easily because all down-easters speak Spanish so badly? That is, if you can find anyone there who speaks it at all!"

"You do yourself an injustice. For a man who is new here, and from New England at that, you speak it very well."

"I'm not really new. My brother and I came out two years ago in the gold rush. We hoped for a strike and we were lucky. We didn't find a fortune by any means, but it was enough to buy our sheep . . . And you? Your English, strangely enough, reminds me of Boston."

"You're right. I'm Patrick Donovan's sister. Perhaps you've met him?"

Oh, why does she monopolize him so? thought Bets resentfully. She was feeling left out, an intruder. She was pleased then to hear Mary say, "You can meet Patrick now. Here he is."

The odd feeling of exclusion disappeared. Patrick's jaunty confidence restored hers, and immediately all four were talking together.

"Now that I have met your brother, Mrs. Reyes, is your husband here this evening also?"

There was an overlong pause. "My sister is a widow," Patrick interjected, his eyes warning Bets to be silent.

"I am sorry! How stupid of me." Carew's voice was still quiet. Bets wondered if it was ever raised in anger or excitement. "I hope, Mrs. Reyes, that I haven't added to your pain."

"No . . . please, let's not discuss it," Mary said. She tried to smile again, not quite succeeding. ·

He hesitated, as though he wished to say something more, but he lost the opportunity, being summoned at that moment by their hostess. As Mary at the same time was distracted by Señora Brinkman who spoke to her in passing, Bets managed to whisper, "Papa, why did you say that? It wasn't true! Isn't Aunt Mary's husband still in Spain with their child?"

"I want Mary Frances to forget and be happy here. I had enough trouble persuading her to agree to this mild deception, so don't give her away!" Patrick responded brusquely.

"But how can she hope to—"

"Hush, girl, there are others who may be listening. Speak of something else . . . Have you noticed the man seated at the piano?"

Bets looked toward the piano, where a dapper young black man was playing a few runs, limbering his hands. Meeting her gaze, he nodded, pleasantly, impersonally.

"That's Peter Riggs," Patrick said. "The local barber and wig-maker. He has a finger, no, his whole fist in a number of pies. Besides acting as master of ceremonies at balls like this one, he is currently exporting stray cats to San Francisco, a town that is plagued with rats."

"Oh, Papa, you're making that up," Bets said, amused, and willing enough to let drop the subject of her aunt's history.

"All true. On my word of honor."

Mary also had heard his remarks. "Patrick," she said, "he's the first negro I've seen here, except for Jeb and Flora. I wonder he isn't terribly lonely."

"Lonely?" It was not a word that loomed large in Patrick's vocabulary. "Don't see why he would be! He's well-liked. Respected. If you're referring to the ladies, I've heard there are one or two of his color, along with the others doing business on the Calle de los Negros. Riggs no doubt visits there now and then."

His sister said drily, "That sort of companionship wasn't quite what I had in mind. But what precisely is this Calle de los Negros?"

"As you suspect, a street of bordellos, gambling dens, and just plain hell-raising," Patrick shrugged.

Mary raised an eyebrow. "It sounds very picturesque. I believe I'd like to see it, perhaps do a painting."

William Brinkman, Teodocia on his arm, had approached, and overheard her. "I assure you, Señora Reyes," he said earnestly, "you wouldn't even want to breathe the air there. Only riff-raff, the scum of society, frequent that street."

Bets noticed suddenly that Teodocia's gaiety had disappeared. At her father's words she seemed to wince.

He finished, "It's no place for a lady like yourself."

"My sister is an artist," explained Patrick.

"Even so," said Brinkman firmly. "Now, may I present to you Señor Miguel Aguirre? He is the editor of our newspaper, the *Los Angeles Star.*"

"Editor only of the Spanish half," protested the tall slender man who accompanied them. "And more of a human ferret than an editor, I'm afraid. I constantly have to seek news." He added, "Even your little Teo has needed to help me at times, giving me advance notice of a party or some other such very momentous event."

The young girl whose eyes had been searching the crowded room, on hearing her name and the irony with which he spoke, responded uncertainly. "But, Miguel, didn't you say any tidbit would be welcome, so long as it hadn't been told over and over by the gossips?"

"Don't be forward, Daughter," admonished William Brinkman. "It's fortunate your mother isn't nearby to hear." His fondness for her, however, robbed the words of any severity, and he continued in explanation to Patrick, "As you are aware, I have no sons, but Miguel is a good friend of my two favorite nephews who consider our house their own. Consequently, she has known him all her life. To her, he's a brother."

Aguirre's brooding, ascetic face relaxed a little as he regarded Teodocia. "And I consider her my sister, as I have none. I assure you, she is never forward, and what she says is only the truth. Even the arrival of the Donovan family was known to all, long before I could print anything about it in the paper. But I am very fortunate this week. First the sheep drive by Señor Carew, with whom I've managed to get an interview, and now the rescue of a baby, by this young lady. May I speak with you about that, Señorita Elizabeth?"

"Yes," Bets said, "although you must not write about it! Saving little Flower was quite accidental. I only happened to see her float by in the water."

His dark eyes approved this disclaimer. "Surely, there was more to the rescue than that?"

"No, truly!"

"Very well. Your modesty does you credit. But I hear the music beginning. Perhaps we can talk after the dance. If I may have the honor?"

She placed her hand on his arm and allowed him to lead her away. In passing, she heard his quick whisper to Teodocia, "He isn't here, dear child! He wasn't invited."

Teodocia nodded, her face averted as though she was close to tears. Whom could she have hoped to meet here, Bets wondered, and felt a growing sympathy with her new friend. Absurd as it might be she herself wished to be dancing, not with Miguel Aguirre, but with a stocky blond herder of sheep, someone of whom she had never even heard before this night.

Arcadia Bandini de Stearns accompanied by the scar-faced, overpowering man she had married—a man almost old enough to be her grandfather, but demonstrating by his proud watchfulness that he was indeed her passionate lover—led off the various dances. There was the traditional fandango, requiring intricate footwork which Bets didn't know but vowed she would learn the quadrille, and even the graceful, beautiful waltz.

All of these were accompanied with dash and fervor by the pianist, Peter Riggs, who also called the turns for the quadrille. But the dance was broken off violently, in mid-chord, and in an instant, what thin veneer of civilization the pueblo of Los Angeles could boast shattered with it.

Bets was facing Miguel Aguirre in the square, his partner for the third time. She had just murmured, "Isn't it warm!" for the densely populated room was oppressively airless, when there was the roar of an explosion, followed by a sharp crash of splintering wood. The house seemed to rock from the vibrations.

Men and women stared into each other's faces, then rushed toward the hall where one of the front doors had been smashed inward.

Bewildered, too stunned to be frightened, Bets watched the men scramble about, cursing and shouting as they tried to find their guns, which in courtesy they had piled in an adjoining room on arrival.

"What is it? What has happened?" she cried, and put out her hand to Miguel as he strode past her carrying a shotgun.

The man's handsome face was cold with anger. "They've shot a cannon ball at us! I wonder if this will ever be more than a miserable, rough little frontier town! It seems not."

"But why? Who would do such a thing?" She looked up. The chandelier was still shaking. Had she really compared this room with a parlor in Boston?

"The uninvited, I suspect. A few disgruntled young men from good families, probably sitting together in the Calle, drinking aguardiente and feeling sorry for themselves. They must have decided to do something about the insult of being ignored, and dragged over an old cannon from the Plaza. There was one there, left from our brief war with the Americans."

Bets was staring at him in disbelief.

"That's crazy. Someone could be hurt!"

"Probably someone will be." Punctuating his words was loud gunfire from the hall. He took her hand in his, and his expression softened. "I'm sorry; I'm frightening you. Wait here—this won't last long."

Before she could assure him that she was not frightened, he was gone.

Behind her, Arcadia Stearns said calmly, "We must all get down below the windows. I doubt if they really mean to kill anyone, but accidents can happen."

Still dazed, Bets turned and saw that others were lowering themselves to the tile floor. She too sank down, next to a young woman who was noticeable for her reluctance to obey, and whose angular body, although seated, was stiffly upright as though in disdain of danger.

"I'm Felipa Rodriguez," she said, just as though nothing unusual was happening. "As soon as Estrella, the horse my father gave you, is trained, I will bring her to you."

Felipa Rodriguez . . . the daughter of Don Diego? Bets had heard so many unfamiliar names in the past two hours that for a moment this one meant nothing more. Then she remembered the conversation in the carreta. This was she, the older girl Teodocia and her mother had spoken of—the one they said cared for Miguel Aguirre.

Uncomfortably aware that the young editor had already danced with her that evening far more than welcoming hospitality required, Bets said, "The horse was far too generous a gift! I am most grateful to your father—and to you, too."

Felipa's long face was expressionless. "You must understand. My father and his friends love the grand gesture. Whatever the excuse, they glory in making a display, the more extravagant the better."

"Oh. I see."

"As for me, any gratitude would be misplaced, I assure you." As though she could no longer endure the ignominy of cowering on the floor, Felipa sprang to her feet.

In the hall, the gunfire had ceased abruptly. "They're leaving! Several of them are wounded, and they've had enough," Abel Stearns was heard to say.

Bets looked around her. Women were rising from

their places, and one, in the shadows, ran furtively toward a side door. It was Teodocia. As Bets watched, the girl gave a quick, frightened glance over her shoulder, and slid from the room.

She had barely disappeared when the men began to return, straggling in, having once again stored the guns. Arcadia went to stand regally beneath the chandelier, and motioned Peter Riggs once again to the piano.

"Resume playing," she commanded, and although her husband was still grim-faced, his eyes rested on her with pride.

As the music began, Patrick appeared beside Bets and threw a jubilant arm around her shoulders. "Best party I ever attended, on my oath! Didn't I tell you, my girl, that you'd love it here?"

"Yes, Papa, and I do—although a cannon shot wasn't necessary to convince me!" And she'd have enjoyed it more, she added to herself, if she weren't beginning to worry about Teodocia, for she could see the Brinkman duenna craning her neck and frowning —and if John Carew would only ask her to dance!

Teodocia returned shortly, as quietly as she had left. But Carew, perhaps because he was a poor dancer, continued to be attentive to the chaperons, among them Mary Reyes.

CHAPTER FOUR

THE DONOVANS' STAY AS GUESTS OF WILLIAM Brinkman was only a matter of a few days. As it turned out, Patrick quickly procured his own home.

The prestigious Sepulveda family, owners of thirty-two thousand acres known as Rancho Los Palos Verdes, had maintained a house in Los Angeles for some years, for the benefit of two elderly relatives who preferred urban living. The building was situated in Sonora, the *barrio* near the Plaza most favored by

Californios and so-named for the state in Mexico from which many of them had migrated. The old couple had died recently, leaving the place now vacant. Since none of the Sepulveda offspring cared to move in from the rancho, Don Jose, head of the clan, was more than pleased to sell this town house for a reasonable price.

But acquiring a rancho was another matter. Patrick spent considerable time deciding on just the right location, a place suitable not only for the cultivation of vineyards, but for cattle breeding as well; and with the further requirement that it be near town. He had watched men like Stearns and Brinkman amass fortunes while rising at the same time to the top of the social ladder, and he had an idea that sequestering oneself in the hinterlands was not the way those things were accomplished.

After a month or so of exploring the rolling plains, all the while trying to dodge the rainstorms of early winter, he had narrowed his choice to two—Rancho Santa Anita and Rancho San Pascual. Then he decided that Santa Anita was too far distant, and from the moment he saw the other one, his heart had been set on owning a part of fertile and scenic Rancho San Pascual.

His decision made, he slogged through the town streets, now ankle-deep with mud, to pay a call on Manuel Garfias, the owner.

The landholder was not at his pueblo home, he was told, but could be found at this time of the morning at the barber's, being shaved and having the sideburns he wore trimmed to the jawline. Patrick issued once more into the mire, this time making his way to the barbershop.

"Good morning, sir. I'll be with you shortly," Peter Riggs said cheerfully.

The one chair was indeed occupied. A hot towel covered the occupant's face.

"Señor Garfias?" Too late, Patrick realized that Riggs was shaking his head.

The covered figure did not respond.

"Señor Garfias don't like to talk—not while he's being shaved."

"Oh, I'm sorry. Then I'll wait." Patrick continued to look at the recumbent figure.

Riggs rolled his eyes. "Señor Garfias don't like being stared at neither."

"Oh, come now," Patrick protested, his own meager patience exhausted. "I'm not talking. Or staring. I'm sitting." He dropped onto a wooden bench. "Surely, when he's here, you often have other customers! I intend to wait, and when he's finished, speak with him."

Riggs shrugged and began to strop his razor. With deliberation, Manuel Garfias removed the towel and sat up.

"Very well, Señor Americano, what is it you want of me? I trust you will be brief."

He was glaring, and Patrick realized his approach to the owner of the San Pascual might have been ill-timed.

He attempted to placate Garfias by coming to the point immediately. "I wish to buy a small piece of your rancho."

"So? And I regret it's not for sale."

"But—" sputtered Patrick, "you have been heard to say, not once but many times, that your property is too big! Also, that having no children, you'd like to break it up."

"It is not for sale." Garfias nodded to Riggs, indicating that discussion was at an end and he was ready to resume their mutual chore.

"But the Sepulvedas, the Yorbas, even the Picos— all are willing to sell a few acres! I don't need a large place—"

"Then your course is very clear to me, as it should be to you. Buy from them. Good day, Señor."

He lay back and shut his eyes, then opened them again. "Still here? So that you will know I mean what I say, I'll tell you that I was cheated once by an Americano. His handshake was only that, a handshake. His word of honor was worthless. In addition, I regret to say that he was a coward. No, I won't sell you a single vara of my land . . . Peter, the towel, if you please. At once. I haven't all morning."

Patrick, speechless with fury, stared into the glittering black eyes until Peter Riggs hastily covered them with the towel. Then he strode from the little shop, giving the door a kick as he went.

Don Antonio Maria Lugo, resplendent as always, sat on the veranda at the rear of his house, and listened with sympathy to Patrick's complaint.

"What was particularly galling, if you understand me, Don Antonio, was that he dared to insult me while he was lying defenceless in a barber chair. As though I'd be afraid to challenge him even then!"

"Stop pacing, my friend . . . I don't understand. Why not take his advice and buy from one of us? There would be no problem at all. Any of us can spare a little. Why, half the time we don't really know what our boundaries are. My own rancho, for example, was a grant for as much land as I could ride around in a day's time. A few acres more or less— what do they matter?"

"No," Patrick said stubbornly, "I thank you. But there's a corner of Rancho San Pascual that I've fallen in love with and must have!"

"Has it a hidden gold mine perhaps?" Don Antonio asked with interest.

Patrick's grin was a little sour. "Do you too think I might cheat? No, not a mine. Although the soil itself is almost gold, for the sort of ranching I have in mind."

"I have found over a long lifetime," Don Antonio raised a hand that was still strong and brown but heavily veined, "that it is futile to lie awake in the night longing for what one cannot have."

"And this I cannot have?"

"It appears that way. Perhaps just as well, too, if I may try to be consoling. The ranch house on the piece of land you covet is too small. It's only a primitive adobe used by the vaqueros during rodeos. Unless you build another house immediately, you'd have to leave your charming ladies unprotected here in town much of the time."

"I suspect," Patrick said drily, "that both of the women you refer to can take care of themselves very well." He saw that Don Antonio was beginning to weary of the conversation, so swallowing the remainder of his angry disappointment, he changed the subject.

"You mentioned that I might be of help on one of the cattle drives north. I'd like very much to accompany you."

"And I issue the invitation. It'll be a long ride, and hard dangerous work, but," he paused with a glint of humor, "I suspect I know you better than Garfias does. We've been waiting for the rains to raise enough grass along the trails for the herd to graze as we go, and another week should see a high enough stand. I plan to leave the pueblo on Monday a week."

"Good. I'll look forward to it. The drive will be good experience, and I thank you."

"Make no mistake, it is I who owe the thanks. Every man who accompanies us means an extra margin of safety for the rest."

"Safety?"

"I use the word advisedly. Many things can happen. The animals may stampede, and in strange territory, rounding them up again is next to impossible. Or we sometimes lose them in the wild mustard which can be as high as a man on horseback. But of course, this early in the season the mustard is no problem, and that's one good reason for leaving now."

Don Antonio leaned back, fingers laced behind his head. He was not an old man who reminisced. He still lived in the present. But Patrick's obvious unpreparedness disturbed him.

"Time was, you see, when a trail boss and his vaqueros could cope with those problems and still deliver most of the cattle, taking a month to make the trip. But those days, I regret to say, are gone, due largely to what I once thought of as riches for California—the gold rush. I now know that the gold that has been found is dross, bringing only slime, hunger and corruption. The changes I see even here in our pueblo sicken me. The desperate miners, the starving men turned outlaw, the waves of new settlers, all eventually will mean the end of our peaceful way of life. Tell me, have you ever seen a mining camp?"

Patrick shook his head.

"They've been romanticized, because a few men, a very few, struck it rich as they say. The rest work in mud, and sleep in leaky cabins or tents, trying to grub out a wretched existence. In most cases, before a lode was discovered there was no town there at all, so food must be brought in by mule-pack and prices are impossibly high. Theft and killings are constant."

"But there are no camps around here," Patrick objected, masking his impatience.

"No. But men must eat, and we take our beef to them. Then they see our fat cattle and our superbly trained horses, and they come to attack us." He shrugged. "It's the old story of haves and have-nots, and the number of bandits roaming California is staggering. Occasionally, they are bold enough to attack outlying ranchos. We've had to post guards." An expression of distaste crossed his face. "The rancho building no longer can be called a hacienda, Señor Donovan; it's a fort."

"I didn't realize the problem was so bad," Patrick said uneasily. To him, any talk of change, when his own dreams were built on the South Coast as it lay about him today, prosperous and serene, was unwelcome. "Haven't you always had to guard against Indian attacks?"

"Yes, and those too have grown worse. Only last year a man named Dalton was ambushed by Indians on the trail, and thirteen men were massacred."

"I heard about that," Patrick said. "I'm prepared to fight Indians."

"Then be prepared also for renegade whites. And in some ways they're worse, to my way of thinking . . . At any rate, you understand now why there'll be five of us, in addition to my trail boss and his men, riding armed and ready."

"I look forward to it," Donovan said again, to which Don Antonio nodded. "And now I'll bid you good day. The mare that Don Rodriguez promised my daughter is being brought to us today. In courtesy, I should be present. Until Monday week, then."

Don Antonio watched him stride away, feeling a small envy because he'd had to push himself very hard of late in order to present that same appearance of vigor and tirelessness.

Alone once more, he leaned back on his bench and looked with pleasure at two young sycamore trees. They were bare now, but in the spring those great green leaves would once again unfurl, providing a shade and beauty that was unique in the pueblo. What native trees there had once been had long since been cut for firewood, and Don Antonio regretted their loss.

He began to doze, as he often did now, and to dream. The dream was of the hacienda of his parents, as he had known it long ago in Mexico. In their patio there had been a fountain and flowers and cool tiles. And always trees, magnificent trees, branching across the sky.

"Oh, Papa, do come and see Estrella! Isn't she beautiful?" Bets asked.

Patrick had been a trifle late and the horse was already in the stable, but he was still in time to add his thanks. Rodriguez' daughter had brought the horse herself.

Patrick took stock of the graceful black mare and approved. She was obviously obedient and well-trained. And not only were her legs and chest good, but she had a steady eye. She wouldn't be skittish or tricky.

He agreed with Bets wholeheartedly. Estrella was beautiful.

Patrick, who ordinarily considered himself an infallible judge of women as well as horseflesh, was less sure in regard to Felipa. She was saying the proper things, expressing the hope that Bets would enjoy riding the horse as much as they, the Rodriguezes, enjoyed making a gift of Estrella. But Felipa didn't smile, nor did her gaze meet his. Unlike the horse, he thought, she hadn't a steady eye.

"Oh, I do love her," Bets cried, "and I can't thank

you enough! Please don't hurry away. I've made some chocolate and I hope you will join us."

"Us? Yes, I see an extra horse is tied there. And still saddled. A horse can become chilled that way, you know . . . It looks a bit like one of the Aguirre horses—"

"Do you mean Miguel Aguirre? Oh, my, no! That's Teodocia's. She's here, and she'll be so pleased to see you."

"How stupid of me. I thought—"

So that's the way the wind blows, is it? Patrick was momentarily amused, not only by Felipa's transparent stratagem, but by his daughter's show of amazement which was somewhat less than forthright. He knew for a fact that young Aguirre had called at least once a week since the Stearns' party.

Cheerful once again, he busied himself removing the saddle and brushing down Teodocia's mare. Already his optimism had reasserted itself. He'd lost the first skirmish. But surely somehow, sometime, Garfias would be persuaded to change his mind.

CHAPTER FIVE

TEODOCIA BRINKMAN HAD BEEN SPENDING A large part of each day at the home of Elizabeth Donovan. The three older Brinkman girls were married and occupied with families, and she professed herself very lonely; and Bets, despite the difference in their ages, was always delighted to see her.

Escorted along the street by her duenna, the fourteen-year-old girl's short chubby figure was always visible at some distance from the house because of her parasol, a necessary adjunct, it seemed, on any sunny day. Californio girls prized untanned skins, and Señora Brinkman was known to view with considerable disapproval the carefree way in which Bets herself went bareheaded.

On reaching the Donovan door, Teo would beam happily, watch her duenna depart, and then insist, fine silk dress or no, on helping with the work of putting the small Sepulveda house to rights for the new owners.

Much change had already taken place there. Although tile floors, such as those in the Stearns' grand house, were a mark of luxury, Patrick admitted to Mary and Bets that he thought them cold, and would much prefer wood planking were it not so rare in this part of the world. When he learned therefore that such lumber was available in San Francisco, he ordered some at once. In only a few weeks, the load of planks arrived, carried down the coast on a sturdy paddlewheel steamboat named *The Seabird;* and the old earthen floors were seen no more.

Meanwhile, Jeb installed the Donovans' treasure, a heavy iron cook stove that had come with them from Boston, into a small alcove on the back veranda. Then he set himself to making shelves. Mary, with the help of a hired seamstress, provided curtains for every room, as well as the many bright cushions needed for the adobe benches built into the walls. While Flora did the daily work for the family, Bets and Teodocia cleaned, polished, and put things away. And as they worked, they talked.

It was not long before Bets learned where her friend had gone with such hurried stealth the night of the Stearns party. Young as she was, Teo was wildly in love with a young man named Garth Peters.

"I've known him all my life," she said dreamily. "Someday we'll marry. He's only seventeen, but when he's older, and has shown my father that he can take care of me, that's the day I'm waiting for."

"Wasn't he one of the young men who broke down the door with the cannon ball?"

"Yes." Teodocia's face clouded. It was a round childish face, so similar to William Brinkman's in its fairness and shape that her duenna was often moved to remark on it to her acquaintances, saying that had

she not witnessed the birth with her own eyes, she
would not believe that blond child could be the
Señora's! "No one was killed, luckily, although a
friend of Garth's was shot in the knee. It was terribly
painful and he'll never walk perfectly again."

"Why did they do such a thing?" Bets was thinking
that Teodocia might have more difficulty than she anticipated in persuading her father to accept such a
wild suitor.

"Garth's mother is a Cota, one of the oldest Spanish
families in Mexico! How does Arcadia Stearns dare
not invite him when she has a party? She deserved to
have the door broken!"

"I've heard that the ones who were left out drink a
great deal, gamble, and do little else, except for going
to cockfights and otherwise amusing themselves."
Garth had, in fact, been castigated in her hearing as
a "worthless young devil."

"Is that so bad? Aren't all young men the same?
Oh, Bets, I do love him so! He's my whole world! I
don't seem to think clearly when it's Garth . . ."

Bets smiled fondly at her. "I can see that. But I do
believe you should be more careful—" She stopped
herself abruptly. She was folding a lace tablecloth that
had been her mother's, and she pretended to be engrossed in getting the corners together exactly.
Teodocia, after all, might not care to listen to advice.

"Careful of what? Please, dear Bets, do go on!"

"I did see you steal out of the house when the
shooting stopped that night. Luckily, no one else
seemed to notice, but I'm certain your duenna would
have been horrified."

"I had to go! When I heard that some men outside
had been wounded, can't you think how I felt? Oh,
Bets, you don't understand—"

"No, I suppose I don't. Did you find him?"

"He was gone. They all were. So I came back in
through the kitchen and no one was the wiser."

Bets studied Teo's open, guileless countenance and
wondered how the girl's parents could be so blind as
not to know the depth of this infatuation. Then, quite
suddenly, she felt a surge of envy. She herself, al-

though four years older, had never known such passion for any man! The first possible stirrings had come when she met that sheepherder, but he seemed to be avoiding her. He had never even come to call! Other men, yes. Almost any unattached man in this town could be hers if she crooked her finger, and most of them had said as much. But not John Carew!

And of course there was Miguel. With no more encouragement than the friendliness she could not help showing everyone, he continued to appear at her door.

Therefore, when Felipa came, herself bringing the horse Estrella, Bets felt an awkward constraint. Her voice was nervously loud as she exclaimed about the horse, and she recognized that she was trying to conciliate Felipa. If only, she thought exasperated, I could tell her that Miguel Aguirre is all hers and I feel nothing for him! That Felipa might find such generosity insupportable never entered her head.

After the mare had been patted and duly admired, Bets succeeded in drawing the tall Californio girl into the house.

Teodocia came running to them, still clutching a feather duster. She was perspiring; and curling wisps of her pale hair escaped from its tight braid. "Flora is bringing the chocolate immediately! How are you, Felipa?"

Felipa replied drily, "Well enough, Teo, which is more than your horse will be, if you are always too busy to rub him down."

She turned and studied the room in which they stood, seeing the pair of glowing silver candlesticks that were placed on the rough-hewn Mexican table. Four carved tulipwood chairs had come round the Horn with their owners and they, like the sterling, should not have fit these plain, whitewashed walls. Yet the soft green of the velvet seats did somehow mingle with the stronger colors of the cushions and draperies, to lend the room warmth and beauty. Felipa glanced briefly at the new, well-oiled planks of the floor, and nodded.

"You've done a great deal. When the Sepulvedas

lived here, the furnishings were like the old people themselves, comfortable and solid, but worn with age. How different it was!"

She looked into the two faces that were according her such attentive, even eager politeness, those two blue-eyed Americano faces. A touch of sadness came into her own.

"Sometimes I think that what has happened to this house is happening to all of us Californios. We welcome strangers as we always have, with all the courtesy of which we are capable, we help them become rich, we let them marry into our families—and we are welcoming our destruction."

The two girls did not reply. Their expressions remained unchanged.

She said uneasily, "Have I offended you?"

In truth, neither of them had grasped her meaning. The impact that a number of foreigners might have, descending on the local society and marrying into the established families, was not a subject they had ever thought about, much less discussed.

"Not at all." Bets was merely pleased that her guest was not being stiff and silent.

But Teodocia said, "My mother, whose blood is as Spanish as yours, Felipa, has encouraged all my sisters to marry Americanos. She says men like Abel Stearns will never give a fortune away for nothing, or let sentiment rule over business sense."

"Exactly," Felipa nodded. "I would expect Señora Brinkman to be one of the first to understand and grasp the advantages."

Teodocia's face reddened. She suspected that Felipa's comment wasn't entirely complimentary to her mother, but she wasn't sure. "Mama married an Americano herself, you must remember."

"I haven't forgotten. As I said, she was quick to see their strong points. Your mother is an intelligent woman."

"Yes . . ." Teo still felt a puzzling doubt.

At this moment, Flora appeared carrying a tray on which were a pot of steaming chocolate and four delicate English teacups.

"Miss Mary be here directly. She say, doan you wait for her."

"Thank you, Flora," Bets said.

The servant hesitated. "Miss Bets, will you be wanting anything more? Reckon I'd best get back to Flower. She plum misable today. Cry all the time, lessen I hold her."

"No, you hurry along. We have everything we need."

Gratefully, Flora left. After the door shut Bets, in an effort to change the subject causing the constraint, said, "Flower is her child. Usually the little thing sits like a rosebud in the sun, doing nothing at all for hours. But once in a while she cries and can't stop, just as though her heart was breaking. Then Flora—"

She broke off. Mary Reyes had entered the room, saying, "Good afternoon, Felipa. How nice to see you!" and dropped her shawl and a sketchbook on a convenient chair. "I'm afraid I forgot the time and missed the noon meal. Chocolate will taste good indeed! Do pour, Betsey, before it gets cold."

Her niece complied, but as she did so, she continued to talk about Flower. "Perhaps one of you might know what could be wrong. Because while I hate to think so, I'm afraid something really is amiss with her. She's so very slow to learn. Don't you agree, Aunt Mary? Surely a child almost a year old ought to be trying to walk and talk, and not be so terribly quiet?"

The older woman was gazing off into the distance, her eyes unseeing.

"Surely there is something that will help! Perhaps an herb of some kind—" Bets was appealing now to the two girls. But she stopped abruptly, seeing their expressions of surprise. They exchanged a glance, and Teodocia said what was clearly in both their minds.

"It is sad, of course, to see a baby that does not grow. But after all, Flower is the child of a servant —not your own."

Bets stared at her friend in shock.

"Teodocia! Can you have said that?"

The young girl glanced again at Felipa. Then she

moved closer to Bets and reached out her hand. "Forgive me, Elizabeth," she said humbly. "I didn't understand. I still don't, but I'll try."

Felipa's lips pressed together. "As for me, I have no suggestions at all. I know more about horses than I do about children."

"Perhaps it would be more pleasant to talk of something else," Mary suggested quietly, "and see, our chocolate is growing cold. Please, Betsey, pass the cups to our guests."

When they were served, she said, "Where is Patrick? I suppose he's dreadfully upset by the news."

"News, Aunt Mary?" Bets was still trying to understand the gulf that had opened so unexpectedly between her and the Californio girls.

"But surely you've heard—" Mary set down her cup and looked at them all in consternation. "No, perhaps not. I was in the Plaza sketching, and everyone there was buzzing with it. So I supposed . . . . The *Elizabeth,* Betsey, encountered a winter storm off the northern coast, and was sunk."

"Oh, no! That beautiful clipper ship—gone?"

"So the men were saying."

"Poor Papa! He'll be heartsick!"

"Yes. Fortunately he still owned only partial shares in her, but he loved the ship and was so terribly proud of her. Parting with his *Elizabeth* was one of the hardest things he ever had to do."

"And Captain Warner? Was he drowned?"

"No. He was saved, although some of the men were lost," Mary frowned. "There's talk about it already. But of course no one knows the truth, and judgment should be reserved. I'm fearful—"

She checked herself, remembering that outsiders were present, but Bets finished the thought for her. "You're afraid of what Papa will say and do? I'm not. Papa will be fair, particularly if he has time to calm down. Captain Warner isn't back yet, is he?"

"No. Perhaps he'll have the good sense to stay away."

"By the time he comes, Papa will know the truth of

it, and then Captain Warner can have no complaint of his treatment."

Mary listened to the confident young voice and spared Captain Warner a moment of pity, regardless of whether or not he had failed his responsibility in the last moments of the stricken ship. To Bets, she thought, everything was black or white, just as it was to Patrick, and it was for this reason that she had never quite brought herself to confide in the girl the whole story of her disastrous marriage.

Even Patrick, much as he loved his sister, had not really understood. His support stemmed from his protective loyalty and devotion, rather than a conviction that she had been right.

Felipa stood up abruptly. "I've enjoyed the chocolate, and must go. Thank you so much."

"It is I who must thank you," Bets responded. "I shall love Estrella always. I already do!"

"I hope so. She deserves it." Felipa's attempt to speak lightly was a failure. Her smile was wooden.

When she had gone, Bets said, "It was good of her to bring the horse herself."

Teodocia shrugged. "Of course she would. She had to be quite certain the mare would be well cared for, although I don't know what she could have done about it, if not. You know, don't you, that she raised that horse from a foal and trained it herself? She could hardly bear to part with her little Estrellita!"

"I shouldn't have accepted. Perhaps I can still refuse—"

"Not without insulting her," Teo interrupted cheerfully. She herself had always found Felipa stiff-necked and haughty. "She'd think you didn't consider the mare good enough and would hate you."

"I'm afraid that she already does. Your friend Miguel has seen to that."

CHAPTER SIX

CAPTAIN WARNER STILL HAD NOT SHOWN HIM-self in town when Don Antonio's cattle drive north to San Francisco began. So Patrick, although raging and vowing vengeance, was forced to depart without confronting the man who, it was now established, had deserted a foundering ship to save himself, leaving three men to perish who were manning the pumps below. That Warner would never again command a vessel, was, everyone said, beside the point.

Once out of the pueblo, however, Patrick's usually resilient spirits began to lift. The cattle drive promised to be one of those taxing, all-male adventures that he so thoroughly enjoyed.

In addition to himself, Don Antonio, and the Lugo trail boss, Toby Bonner, with his vaqueros, four more armed men rode to the sides and rear of the herd. They were William Brinkman, Diego Rodriguez, Manuel Garfias, and Phineas Bishop, whom Patrick knew as the flamboyant owner of the San Pedro stage. All of these held some percentage of the steers, and for the duration of the drive, the five brands would freely intermingle as the heavy awkward beasts, spattering mud and lowing, milled about on the trail.

At the end of the procession six horses pulled a shiny new stage coach, which was empty.

It was evident at once that this was going to be a slow as well as a lengthy journey. The cattle must be prodded along for more than four hundred miles; they must be allowed to rest and crop the myriad green shoots that blanketed the brown hills for so few months; they must be guided to water. Although his rebuff from Garfias still rankled, Patrick told himself that the days ahead would be less difficult for everyone if he and the rancho owner were on better terms.

Accordingly, that first afternoon, he spurred his horse
alongside the magnificent stallion on which Garfias
rode, uttered a greeting, and inquired about the empty
stage coach.

Garfias answered without hesitation and pleasantly,
just as though their earlier confrontation had never
taken place.

"As I understand it, Señor Bishop has plans for a
stage line north. His partners in the San Pedro business
refuse to believe the mountains are passable. So, to
resolve the argument, Señor Bishop has purchased the
coach you see there at his own expense. He intends to
drive it through the passes as we go, and prove the
route is practical."

Whatever Garfias thought of the idea, or indeed of
his questioner, he had replied with courtesy. When
Patrick mentioned this later in the day to Don Antonio, the old man said, "What would you expect?
You are an invited guest of mine."

"He no longer seems angry."

"Angry he never was." Don Antonio's eyes twinkled. "Merely firm. And you may be certain his opin-
ions haven't changed. However, you have my thanks
for making an overture and attempting to ease our
situation."

Progress of the unruly herd was even slower than
Patrick had anticipated. The cattle needed to maintain
both their strength and their weight, and so could not
be pushed too hard. Especially tedious were the days
of splashing through surf, where the cliffs loomed directly over the ocean leaving no beach. At night gentlemen as well as vaqueros wrapped themselves
gratefully in their blankets and slept exhausted by the
fire, knowing that before dawn, after a breakfast of
tortillas and beans, the trek would begin again.

Much of the time on the trail, Patrick enjoyed the
companionship of Brinkman, often discussing with him
the secrets of successful ranching, as well as its pit-
falls, through long desultory hours. The mild Dutch-
man was not only expert—his steers were among the
largest in the drive, and the purple grapes of his vine-

yards commanded extra price for their juiciness—he was generous in the sharing of his knowledge.

As the days passed, Patrick also found himself riding more and more frequently beside Phineas Bishop. This was far from the same Bishop who swigged down vast quantities of brandy and held the stakes for his passengers' bets, while driving the horses of the San Pedro stage breakneck to Los Angeles. Now he showed himself as sober, strong, and as tireless as a young bull. When he was not riding the box of his empty coach, he was scouting the trail ahead or assisting in rounding up strays. In between bursts of activity, he seemed to seek Patrick's company, perhaps he welcomed a chance to converse in English because his Spanish was not yet as fluent as it might be.

Before long he had heard, for reticence was not one of Patrick's characteristics, the story of the older man's career as a ship owner, his succumbing to the lure of California, and his current occupation of buying and selling hides.

"Buying hides, eh? Seems to me, Mr. Donovan, you'd want to own a rancho, to grow your own."

"That will come. You yourself have cattle, I see."

"Only a few."

"Enough to sell up North. Or did you come along just to try out your stage coach?"

"Both. But there's a third reason too. I'm a good man with a gun and Don Antonio expects trouble. I aim to see that this drive gets where it's going."

Patrick realized that the burly man beside him was not being boastful, but merely matter-of-fact; and the same was true when Bishop recounted his past history. He had arrived penniless in Los Angeles only a year or so earlier, and been hired at once by Douglas and Sanford, who were in the business of hauling freight from San Pedro to the pueblo. He had progressed in rapid steps to a partnership, although he still, as often as not, drove the freight as well as the passengers himself. Now he intended to expand the operation up to San Francisco.

"This coach though, will go back with us to San

Pedro, and take the place of the old ramshackle wrecks we've been using." Bishop gave a sudden laugh. "Do you know, Sanford couldn't understand why I wouldn't use one of them for the test, this being such rough country. But I told him I'd really prove my point. I'd bring this brand new beauty—she cost over a thousand dollars!—through without a scratch. And that's what I aim to do."

Garfias had mentioned that Bishop paid for the coach out of his own pocket! Not bad for a young man who had only recently been church-mouse poor. Patrick was impressed, and found he was drawn to Bishop. He liked this kind of man—one who was strong enough, and cocky enough, to bet his money on himself.

Several days later the sea was left behind. Now the cattle were being driven along the steep narrow trails that meandered across the Tehachapi mountains where snow fell. Sometimes the footing was precarious, and one steer, jostled by another, plunged to its death. Bishop no longer permitted a vaquero to spell him on the stage box, although he drove with the same confident ease as formerly. The iron rim of a wheel might well be spinning in space, but he never looked down or back.

He expressed himself as satisfied with the trail as a stage route until on their next to the last day in the mountains, the party came to the top of a long series of switchbacks. Bishop leaped from the vehicle and stood gazing meditatively at the steep grade below him. It was a relatively bare slope, marked only by some straggling pines, sparse underbrush, and the zigzag path down which the cattle and vaqueros had begun to wind.

"Don Diego," he said, turning to the man nearest him, "would you be good enough to tell me—is there a single mark on this coach?"

Rodriguez dismounted, walked around it carefully observing. "Not one."

"Good! Then you'll back me up that I was right. I said the trail's passable. We're past the worst of it, and I proved all I need to. But now—that switchback looks mighty slow! Let's see if there's a faster way down!"

With that, he sprang once more onto his seat. The others gathered on the rim of the incline, guessing what he had in mind and welcoming some excitement.

He lifted the reins, gave an Apache yell, and the harnessed horses raced down the narrow road in a shower of snow. Faster and faster, seeming completely out of control, the stage appeared to overtake the horses, although Bishop was still on the seat and waving his hat with one hand. Then the horses caught up, only apparently to be passed by the coach again. By some miracle of driving skill, the stage remained upright, until it and the horses piled into a white thicket of chaparral at the bottom where the experiment ended.

The other men scrambled apprehensively down the icy slope. Despite finding Bishop scratched and bruised he was otherwise unhurt. While he thrashed about, searching for his hat, the horses stood calmly, and the stage, with a little repair, would be usable, if never again unmarred.

Patrick had reached the scene first. Bishop brushed himself off and grinned. "A beautiful descent! Beautiful! And a whole lot easier than I figured. Yes sir, a stage road through here should be a mighty big success."

Laughing with him, Patrick grasped his hand and shook it vigorously. This is a man after my own heart, he thought. Worth two of that sheep man they made so much of in the pueblo. Phineas Bishop is a man, by God! . . . Worthy of my Bets! I'll have to bring them together.

It occurred to him briefly that his daughter might already have other desires. He had no notion of her growing infatuation for Carew, an innocent passion which, like a jungle orchid, could feed on nothing but air. But he did know of Miguel Aguirre's regular calls and suspected they were not made out of brotherly affection for little Teodocia. Still, he had no qualms about providing the young editor with a rival. The more suitors the merrier! His girl could decide for herself, but he wanted her to have a choice. The widest possible choice!

Back on the trail a little later, he said, "Come and have dinner with us when we return, Phineas. My daughter will enjoy hearing this story, and meeting a man who can drive a six-horse team down a mountain!"

Bishop tipped his head back to watch a hawk circle in a wide, diminishing spiral. "Thanks, friend," he drawled, and more quietly than he usually spoke. "But I reckon I'd better not. I remember Miss Betsey well, and if I get to know her better, I might just find I can't live without her! Mr. Donovan, don't take it amiss for me to say that. I don't mean any disrespect."

"No, I don't think you do. And the name's Patrick."

"Well, Patrick, it's this way—I won't be a marryin' man, not for some while anyway. I can't afford the time, and a woman takes time, lots of it.

"I've got a long way to go, you see. Right now, folks like the Stearns don't invite me to their houses. But they will. They will." He paused, choosing his words with care. "The plain truth is, I refuse to get my heart set on a girl like Miss Betsey, because she'll be married to some other man before I'm ready."

"I understand."

Patrick's genuine regret faded from his mind, as he became aware of a growing edginess among the rest of the party. If outlaws or Indians were ever going to strike, the attack must come before the group left the Tehachapis. Beyond, after Fort Tejon, lay Visalia, Gilroy and then San Jose, reached through open country with little chance of ambush. Now every man's eyes watched as he rode, searching the trees, the rocks, the pristine snow at the top of the hills.

No one objected when the stage coach was abandoned. Having proved the trail passable to his own satisfaction, Bishop lost interest in driving further, and suggested they simply leave the coach and pick it up on their return. The men worked with a will, dragging it off the trail and camouflaging it with snowy branches, because now Phineas would be the freer to fight, ready for whatever happened.

The slopes ahead were quiet. Although the down-hill path ahead offered little visibility as it wound through the trees, it was wider than before. The snow had thinned, showing patches of green, and the cattle were moving faster, as though some signal in their brains promised lush pastures and flowing water far-ther ahead.

With only a few more miles of mountain terrain re-maining, the tension began to drop. Small talk and jokes were heard again. There was a spreading feeling that this time the drive would reach the plains unmo-lested.

Only Don Antonio, the leader, remained grim. He went so far as to caution each of his friends casually, but leaving no doubt of his meaning. To his trail boss, Toby Bonner, he issued direct orders that could not be disobeyed. Lowering their guard could mean death, he said, and Patrick, overhearing, felt his pulse quicken.

Don Antonio, Garfias, and Rodriguez rode at the head, as scouts. Phineas and Patrick were deployed at the sides, ranging backward and forward around the vaqueros who prodded the animals steadily forward. Farthest back were Bonner who watched for strag-gling steers, and Brinkman, his shotgun ready across his saddle.

The first alarm that came was a sharp shot, followed rapidly by another and another.

The cattle, triggered into a panic by the gunfire, surged along the narrow trail, bellowing and pushing, until suddenly they broke ranks and scattered in panic, trampling the brush.

Patrick heard Phineas yell to him above the din, "Back! Go back!" He wheeled his horse, and by cut-ting this way and that, using his spurs unmercifully, he managed to avoid being run down by the cattle, and gained the rear. Together the two men raced back along the trail, their pistols out and ready, while ahead of them sounded a sporadic staccato of shots.

Suddenly the path made a sharp turn. Phineas reined in his mount and slid from its back, and Patrick did the same. They scrambled as quickly as possible on hands and knees to the top of the rise where they dropped flat behind a fallen log and peered over.

Then Phineas began to curse, deep in his throat, and Patrick stared, speechless with shock.

For Brinkman, kind, hospitable William Brinkman, lay not far off, motionless. A lariat, like a vicious snake, was wound around his right arm, pulling it to a peculiar angle. His gun, silent and useless, was dropped by his side; and around his body, blood had stained the snow red.

Nearby, Toby Bonner had taken cover behind a scrawny tree. His back was to them, and as they watched, he leaned out, fired, and then with a gesture of fury tossed away his now empty rifle. He stared with longing at Brinkman's shotgun, so close and yet so far away, but as he hesitated, a fusillade of shots pressed him to keep cover.

Patrick waited beside Phineas, their revolvers braced on the log. The bullets that did not drill into Bonner's meager protection snicked precariously close over their heads.

"The bastards are behind that dead tree on the left," muttered Phineas.

Unexpectedly the firing ceased. The head of an attacker poked out and as quickly withdrew. When it came round again, the watchers had tightened their trigger fingers.

The outlaw must have spotted Bonner's empty gun too, because he exclaimed, "Got him now, Cal!" and stepped out into the open. It was the last move he made. The two guns barked, and he spun, surprise on his face, and fell dead.

Bonner had jerked round at this sudden firing from his rear. "Watch out! There's one more!"

"Not for long there won't be," Phineas promised. Saying, "Cover me," to Patrick, he got to his feet.

Patrick heard the snow crunch as the big man moved off to the side, but he dared not glance in that direction. His eyes felt as though they were glued to the dead tree.

Agonizingly, the moments passed. Once a hand

snaked out, gripping a pistol. Donovan fired and missed.

Then it was all over after another burst of shots. From the side, Phineas had moved into range, and the second wounded outlaw staggered into the open and collapsed into a leaden heap.

Phineas returned, blowing into his smoking gun. As he stepped over the bodies of the ambushers, he said, "Reckon we should have taken 'em alive? Aw, it would have just been extra trouble. And we did these boys a kindness at that, saving 'em from being hung."

He turned with a frown to Toby. "Only two men jumped you?"

"Hell, no!" Bonner said indignantly. "Musta been ten or more. They lassoed Mr. Brinkman, pulled him out of the saddle, and shot him on the ground. But they missed me, so they left them two to shoot it out, and the rest cut out at least half the herd and drove 'em back up the trail."

Patrick was staring down at the body of the person who had helped him so much.

"His shoulder—the arm's torn out!"

"They drug him afore they shot him."

"God!" Patrick turned away, battling against the bile that had risen in his throat without warning. Until this moment, in the heat of the chase and the final shootout, he'd felt only excitement, mixed with outrage that Brinkman, such a good man and a friend, had been killed. But now, standing in a white drift by that mutilated body, it came to him like a cold finger along his spine. All of them might have died today. He, Patrick, might be lying there beside William! In a gunfight, bravery and resourcefulness didn't count for much. One bullet, and it was all over . . .

"Where's your horse?" Phineas asked Toby.

"Bolted. But the othern's over there—grazing."

"Always was an easy-going son of a gun, that gelding. I ought to know, I sold him to Brinkman." To Patrick, his drawling calmness was ominous. It was not difficult to guess what he intended to do next. "Catch him, Toby, and get Brinkman's gun. Let's us go bring back them cows they stole."

Even as he spoke, Phineas had leaped on his horse and set it into a run. Somehow Patrick forced himself into his own saddle while his animal was already in motion, following the lead of the other. When he glanced behind, Bonner too was galloping, beating the gelding's rump with his hat, and closing the distance rapidly.

"Bastards won't be far," remarked Phineas. "Frightened cattle are a handful of trouble."

Patrick couldn't answer. His body was covered with a cold clammy sweat. If he'd had to spur his horse forward, he couldn't have done it. Three men were going alone after the whole outlaw band! There would be another gun battle, and in all probability, he thought, the three would die.

Never in the worst storm at sea, had he truly known what fear was. He did now.

CHAPTER SEVEN

LONG BEFORE THEY OVERTOOK THEIR ATTACKers, they could hear yells and the ceaseless bawling of cattle. Finally, topping a rise they reached the scene.

As Phineas had predicted, the outlaws were hard at work. The animals were no longer stampeding, but were on the verge of doing so again. Milling, bellowing, tossing their heads nervously, they threatened to be off again in a head-long rush. Their captors rode in circles, shouting oaths, and trying to contain the stragglers. The trail, what could be seen of it, was churned with mud.

The noise was such that Phineas did not bother to lower his voice. "Too bad we can't watch this show, but we want to start them cows moving north again. We'll circle around."

Leaving the horses tied, the three picked their way through the snow-covered underbrush, taking a wide circuitous route. With dogged effort, Patrick willed himself to follow the others.

The clamor shifted from ahead of them to the side and then at last to their backs as they reentered the trail well beyond.

"Makin' slow time, ain't they," Toby said with scorn. "Just shows what they know about cattle."

"Later on you can teach them a thing or two," rejoined Phineas. "That is, if they're still alive to be taught, which won't be likely."

Patrick said nothing, only thinking that their own deaths seemed far more probable. He plodded on through the majestic trees and virgin snow, seeing them as if for the first time, and the last.

Only a short distance ahead of the slowly moving herd, Phineas seemed to find what he was seeking. Just past a wide place in the trail, ringed by an almost impenetrable forest of fir trees, there was an abrupt narrowing. This pass had steep sides of slippery shale, topped by boulders.

"See a log around anywhere?" Phineas asked.

The one that Toby found was a trifle long for the purpose, but they jammed it into the pass as best they could, making a barrier to stop the cattle. Then they climbed up among the boulders to wait, Patrick with Toby on one side, Phineas on the other.

"Our turn to set an ambush," Phineas said cheerfully.

Patrick forced himself to grin back, just as he forced himself to climb to this perch. He wondered if he looked as much like death as he felt.

Fortunately, they hadn't long to wait. The noise grew louder, and a man on horseback appeared. Behind him pushed the first steers, now somewhat calmer and quieter.

The man rode into the clearing, then, still unsuspecting, he entered the pass. When he paused at the log, Phineas leaped. The rider was torn from his mount and landed hard on his back. The only sound came when his head hit rock. It made a soft hollow thud, like a rapped melon, and he lay still.

"Pshaw," Phineas said. "That was too easy." He

quickly pulled the victim out of sight, managed to lift the log for a moment to send the horse on, and climbed up to his former position.

The stolen herd halted and two steers advanced to the barrier. They gazed up at the men, fixing them with large curious eyes.

"What the hell is it now?" growled a voice in disgust. The remaining outlaws rode one by one into view. They were working their way among the close-packed animals, and intent on moving them, did not look up. Paying dearly for this lack of caution, three rustlers died, as a trio of shots were fired. In an instant the peaceful, pastoral scene was transformed into raw pandemonium.

Some of the outlaws jumped from their frightened horses, leaving them to fend for themselves among the berserk cattle. They themselves ran for the edge of the thicket.

Most reached shelter and began to return the fire of the ambushers, but not all. The terrified steers charged for the only exit, the trail by which they had come, with the force of a battering ram. A horse screamed as its foreleg was broken in the crush; and the rider was sucked under the sharp hooves, his mouth open in soundless terror.

Over it all, rifles and revolvers flamed, the bullets splattering up among the boulders. Patrick lay flat next to Toby, trying to see the men below without in turn being seen. His Colt was in his hand, and he fired automatically when he could. He no longer was conscious of that lethal lethargy, or indeed of anything except the need to find a target.

"Don't look so good," Toby muttered. "Sometime soon they'll be working their way around the sides, just like Mr. Bishop done before, lessen we can pick off a few. Trouble is, we can't see 'em without getting shot ourselves."

Patrick wasn't listening. He had just discovered that he had just one bullet left. Suddenly that single piece of lead was more important than anything else in the world. He had to make it count. There was only one way, and if he was fast enough, took them by surprise . . .

He leaped to his feet, saw a man at the edge of the tree, and fired at the same instant, while behind him Toby shouted, "Jesus, man, are you crazy?" Then Patrick dropped, still unscathed, among the rocks.

"You're one brave man, Mr. Donovan! But I hope you ain't aiming to do that again."

"No need to worry," Patrick assured Bonner grumpily. "My gun's empty." But he was realizing with surprise that Toby's praise was not unwarranted. As soon as the actual battle had started, his strange, debilitating fear had oozed away and been forgotten. It was gone. He was himself again.

In the end, they were saved by the timely arrival of the others in their party. The cattle had battered a path out of the clearing by then, and the three Californios, dignified and resplendent as always, paced their horses to the edge of the trees and attacked. The outlaws, caught between lines of fire, had no protection. Some brazened it out and were killed, a few managed to claw their way into the thick scrub and were seen no more.

Then an eerie quiet descended. Only the sprawled bodies, a haze of smoke, and the acrid smell of gunpowder remained.

"Are you all right, gentlemen?" called Don Antonio.

The three in the rocks climbed down. Phineas was their only casualty. A bullet had ricochetted and torn a deep cut in his arm. Toby ripped a strip of cloth from one of the dead men's shirts and bound it.

"We've been expecting you," Phineas remarked. "I figured you'd know where we went—after you found Brinkman."

At mention of the name, Don Antonio's jaw tightened. "I only regret I wasn't with you," Rodriguez said softly. "He was my close friend for many years."

Garfias added his own brief epitaph: "An Americano everyone could trust."

"It is some satisfaction at least that most of his killers have paid with their blood," Don Antonio said.

"I am particularly glad to see this one—" He nodded coldly toward a bearded corpse that lay sprawled almost at his feet. "He was their leader. Jose Flores."

"Mr. Donovan did that with his last shot," Bonner told his employer, "and he took quite a chance, making a target of himself the way he did."

Don Antonio's mouth relaxed into a faint smile as he turned to Patrick.

"Well done, *compadre*."

Patrick felt a strong glow of pleasure. Until this moment, he had been Señor Donovan, a friend yet not quite a friend. Now he had been called *compadre*. Close friend.

He was content to stand quietly and wait for whatever came next, and to listen as Don Antonio's deep judicial voice continued . . .

"And Toby, you may take pride in your own courage and loyalty, for which you have my gratitude. I regret you can't rest now as you deserve, but if you don't start rounding up the cattle you saved us, they'll be scattered over the entire mountain. I'll assist you, as will Señor Garfias and Señor Rodriguez."

Patrick and Phineas were left to follow, after they'd removed the guns from the dead. They began their task, dragging the corpses into the underbrush. Neither relished the work and performed it in silence, until Patrick said, surprised, "This one's still alive!"

He pushed with his foot the first man who had ridden into their trap and been jumped by Phineas. The man did seem to be regaining consciousness. While they watched, he moaned, and made a motion as though to sit up. He stared at them blindly.

"He must have a very hard head," Patrick said. "I thought he was killed."

"I suppose we ought to shoot him." His companion spoke without enthusiasm, adding, "I don't really cotton to killing vermin unless they can see me."

"No. Anyway, I think we should take him in."

"Think so? It's a long way back, just to save a man for a hanging." Phineas nevertheless had brightened.

"Wouldn't Don Antonio like to have at least one prisoner? Something to show the town for Brinkman?"

Phineas nodded. With his uninjured arm, he yanked the groggy man to his feet. "Let's go, feller. And move fast if you know what's good for you."

Sometimes falling to the ground, the man staggered ahead of them down the trail.

As Fort Tejon was in sight, and open country beyond, Toby Bonner and the vaqueros continued on alone with the cattle. The others began the return journey, bringing with them the prisoner, stumbling at the end of a rope, and the body of William Brinkman, wrapped in a blanket.

For the first few miles, it was carried tied down across his horse's back. But when the party reached the abandoned stage coach and had hitched up the six horses once again, he was transferred to that more dignified conveyance. Although the seat was too short and his knees had to be forcibly bent, his hands were crossed on his breast and his hat placed reverently over his face.

This silent passenger, ever with them, cast a pall that lasted the four days the return journey took, four days in which they covered the ground it had taken over twenty to do with the cattle. The party rested only a few hours at a time, because even in the cold weather it was essential to bring their friend home to be buried immediately. As it was, throughout the last day, the horses showed the whites of their eyes and were skittish, and there was a sweetish odor of decay that turned Patrick's stomach.

When they rode into the town, people on the street first stared curiously, then backed away as the stench reached them. To Patrick, it was a blurred sea of faces, for he was desperately tired. They all were. When he could spare Don Antonio a thought, he wondered how the old man could possibly endure such grinding fatigue.

Then a shock brought him erect in the saddle. One face, one odious face, watching from the left side of the road, had swung into clarity.

Captain Warner.

Captain Warner who had lost the finest clipper ship

that ever came down the ways, and disgraced her
name in the doing! Captain Warner who had not
fought down his fear but had fled, craven that he was,
and abandoned his men to drown.

Patrick thought of all the things he'd once planned
to say to him should the coward ever dare return to
Los Angeles—and the things he'd intended to do to
him as well. None of them seemed quite right now.
He understood Warner a little better than he had, and
he despised him more.

Diego Rodriguez, riding next to Patrick, said,
"Compadre . . ."

Patrick turned. Their eyes met. Rodriguez' hand
was extended, offering his quirt.

Patrick understood, and he hesitated for a fraction
of a second. He had always had a secret, almost
shamefaced dislike of inflicting pain, and in spite of
his fury, he shrank from meting out so raw and violent
a punishment as Don Diego was suggesting.

But with those black eyes upon him, his choice was
made.

He grasped the quirt and shifted it to his right hand.
As he came opposite Warner, with one strong slash,
he cut downward.

The leather thong split the captain's face from right
temple to chin. Blood spurted like a fountain along
the crevice.

Warner stumbled backward but did not utter a
sound. His palm that clamped against the gaping
wound didn't hide his eyes—liquid black pools of despair and hatred.

Throughout the incident not a gelding or mare's gait
was checked. Nor did any of the riders bother to look
over their shoulders. The small drama had taken place
in complete silence, as though it had not been, as
though to them Captain Warner did not exist.

The entourage came to a halt at last before William
Brinkman's town house.

Don Antonio visibly braced himself for the effort of
dismounting. Slowly, painfully, he swung his leg across
the rear of his saddle, one hand clamped to the horn,

and momentarily balanced himself in the stirrup. Then at last he reached the ground, where he stood swaying like a hewn oak.

The two Californios tensed and leaned toward him, but they made no move to leave their horses. As for Phineas Bishop, he seemed to be studying the distant mountains, and understanding the reason, Patrick too forced himself to appear unconcerned.

Gradually, as the moments passed, the old man straightened. His fingers loosed their hold on the saddle. He brushed the dust from his hat, and placed it under his arm. Then he walked stiffly toward the house, and the woman who must meet him at the door.

They waited, each attempting to conceal his emotions. Patrick remembered the day not so distant, when Brinkman had welcomed the Donovan family so unstintingly to his home. He had been an honorable man, a well-loved man, and now this.

A gelding snorted and shifted its weight, the leather creaking, and Phineas broke the silence to say in his awkward Spanish, "It was a beautiful fight. And by God, I'm glad we got the scum!"

CHAPTER EIGHT

"GRACIOUS, WHAT'S THIS?" MARY, PASSING her niece's door, stopped on seeing the trunk that lay on the bed.

Bets glanced up. "I'm packing. I leave in an hour."

"But where are you going? Does your father know?"

"Yes, of course. I've been invited to spend a week or so with Teodocia at her family's rancho. Her mother still hasn't gotten over the shock of Mr. Brinkman's death, and she thinks that being very busy at the hacienda will help her. The majordomo is ill, you see, and she'll be supervising the entire large household. She wants Teo to learn to give the orders too."

Mary attempted briefly to envisage young Teodocia making out the lists for the day, instructing everyone from cooks to gardeners at their tasks, settling disputes, praising, admonishing, and coping with all the innumerable crises that must arise daily. Her imagination failed her.

"And you? Are you going there to learn also? We do have servants here, not so many of course, but they need guidance all the same."

Bets flushed. However, her sense of justice told her that Aunt Mary had good reason to be speaking a little sharply. Bets had neglected to mention this impending visit, not because she cared whether Aunt Mary knew, but because she wished to avoid even the appearance of asking her permission.

"I'm only going because Teo needs me. All of her sisters are married and there's no one to talk to about . . . that is, the rancho is so far from town."

And so far from young Garth Peters, Mary amended to herself. She wondered if Bets had been allowing the two young lovers to meet here in the Donovan house at times when she herself was out. She hoped not.

Bets carefully continued to fold her dresses and put them in the trunk. "Actually, Aunt Mary, I'm looking forward to the visit. Señora Brinkman has promised we can ride our horses through those great fields of yellow mustard, and take picnic lunches into the hills: their rancho is so large that one can explore all day without ever coming to the end of it."

Mary found something oddly wistful in this enthusiasm, as though Bets, as well as Señora Brinkman, needed to escape from some unhappy thoughts.

"Betsey," she said on impulse, "shall I come with you?"

"Oh, there's no reason for that!" her niece replied. "You may rest assured that being with Teodocia, I'll be well chaperoned."

"I don't doubt that," Mary said evenly. It was only too clear, as it had been for a long time, that Bets regarded her with mistrust. Once again she thought, I should have told her, explained everything, even though it hurts me so to remember. Now, of course, it's too late . . .

"Betsey," she heard herself say, "go on with your packing, or you won't be ready. But listen. I'd like to tell you about something . . . that happened to me."

Bets looked up with that wide level gaze which was so like Patrick's. "Aunt Mary, you needn't."

"No, I must! Don't stop me, or I may never have the courage again. Just listen . . . As you know, I married Francisco Reyes and went with him to live in Spain. His family home was near Sevilla which is very beautiful—"

How very beautiful! Even now, with all that had happened, she could think with incredulity of the myriad brilliant colors, the shimmering heat of the air, the coolness of the fountains, the quick grace of the flamenco dancers.

But the hard cruelty had been there right from the beginning too, and in six years she had never learned to ignore it. The underfed donkeys tied waterless in the field, the great lumbering dancing bear led by a ring in his nose, with spots of wet blood on his brown fur from the whip. She'd never grown used to such things.

Francisco, on the other hand, was unable to see anything amiss, or to sympathize with her protests. After a while she had come to believe that cruelty was a trait in all Spaniards and was handed down from generation to generation, like the love of music, or even the love of love.

Because, he had loved her once, beyond any doubt. He'd been in the official suite of the Spanish ambassador visiting Boston when he met Mary, and the fires of passion that had consumed them both made any sacrifice possible. He would jeopardize his political career by marrying this foreign girl. She would give up family and homeland to live in a distant country she had never seen and could not possibly imagine.

"At first, Bets, everything was like a fairy tale of which I longed to become a part. I learned Spanish. I watched others and learned the customs. I did my best, you see, to become a Spanish wife. And then, gradually, I came to realize I could never succeed because of his mother, who quite simply hated me. It wasn't only that she blamed me for his lack of advancement at court, but he had married without her consent and this she would not forgive. We all lived together, of course, and never a day passed that she didn't let me know in little ways how much she wished I had never been born."

Doña Cesaria's eyes were shiny and inky and prominent. They made Mary think of two black beetles, watching her, always watching her. If Mary was doing tapestry work, Doña Cesaria never failed to point out the crooked stitch, saying, "One must make a little effort, if one wishes to be at all womanly."

If Mary chose a fabric for a gown, it was too gaudy, or if subdued, far too dull.

"You're too young, Maria, to have the taste of an old woman . . . Francisco, perhaps you should introduce Maria to your lovely friend Teresa. She could learn a great deal from Teresa about making the most of herself, don't you think?"

"After a while Francisco began seeing another woman his mother enjoyed taunting me about, later he had others as well. Oh, it was customary; I'm certain all the men we knew did the same. But the others made a decent effort to hide their mistresses from their wives. Francisco seemed to delight in showing me his. He was so blatant about it, so vindictive in his manner, that I should have guessed his mother told him lies about me. I didn't realize, perhaps because by then I no longer cared to know . . . why.

"The only happiness I could hope for was in our child. Jaime was born after I had been there three years, and from the very first he was more his grandmother's than mine. He was the image of his father, a tiny new Francisco, and she doted on him. None of the sins of the mother would be visited on that child. And I might say, he adored her too.

"She used every excuse to keep Jaime with her, constantly. There were long carriage rides in the country, visiting her relatives, seeing where his ancestors had distinguished themselves in battle, or where they were buried. And at home, it was the custom for servants to care for him. I was excluded. He was almost three years old—and hardly knew me."

"I'd like to take Jaime with me today, when I go to paint. He loves to walk and we won't go far—"

"My dear, you get so absorbed, he might just wander away. He's such an active little boy and easily bored. Perhaps Jaime had best stay at home with me. This may be the day his Papa takes him riding with him, on his fine prancing horse. You wouldn't want to miss that, would you, Jaime?"

"No! No!" The little boy ran to Doña Cesaria and hid behind her black skirts, peering out fearfully at his mother.

"There, there, Jaime love." The older woman reached back to pat him. "You and I will have a little party with your favorite cakes . . . Your mother surely won't force you to go with her . . ."

"At last, Bets, I could stand it no longer. I determined to take my child away, which meant leaving Spain. I didn't know how Francisco would react to my going, but one thing I knew for a certainty—he would never allow Jaime to leave, not while he still lived. And my mother-in-law—I shuddered to think what she might do if she guessed what was in my mind!

"But at last I decided to trust one of the servants who had been good to me. I asked him to find out about a ship. He reported to me that there was one in Cadiz that would be sailing soon for America, and he agreed to make the arrangements and then drive me there.

"When the night came, I wrapped my sleeping child in a warm blanket and carried him from his room. Although I was very frightened, I thought luck must be with me, because I saw no one. Francisco was out visiting one of his women—he had told me as much—

and his mother had gone to bed early. Once outside the walls of the estate, I fled to the waiting carriage.

"Huddled on that swaying seat in the darkness, I strained my ears for sounds of pursuit. But none came, and in a few hours we were rattling across the cobblestones of the little seaport town.

"We came to the quay where the ship was tied. I paid the servant twice what I had promised because I was so very grateful that he had kept faith with me. Holding Jaime tight in my arms, I walked up the gangplank, stepped aboard the ship. And then, Francisco came out of the shadows . . .

"It was finished. The servant had betrayed everything. Francisco had known all along and had been simply playing with me, like a cat with a mouse."

He had taken Jaime by force, snatching him out of her clinging arms and hurling her violently against the deck. He handed the boy to the servant who had driven the carriage, then jerked Mary to her feet. Perhaps he would have killed her, if Jaime hadn't waked and asked sleepily, "Papa?"

"Yes, my son. Papa's here. We're going home."

He turned again to her. His hands gripped her so roughly that she cried out in pain. But his hard glittering anger was under control.

"So you would steal my son! Tell me the truth for once. Whom are you meeting aboard this ship? My mother was right about you, wasn't she? Say it!"

"No! Never!"

They had stared at each other in silence. Then he said, "Go, whore. Go back where you came from."

They were abandoning her, stealing Jaime from her, and horror overwhelmed Mary. She grasped his hand, clung to it, pleading, "Oh, please, don't take him from me! I'll do anything you ask, but let me return with you! I swear there is no one, no one . . . I swear I'll obey you and your mother forever! Only please—"

He flung her from him. "This is my country and he is my son. Leave them both. You'll never see Jaime again. I swear it, Maria! I swear it in the name of God."

"Then, when the ship sailed at dawn, I went too. Back to America."

Bets, who had been listening, her azure eyes wide, said in a low voice, "The story was true then! I hoped it wasn't . . . Aunt Mary, I don't want to hurt you, but I can't seem to understand. How could you leave your child? How could you? No matter what your husband was like—or the old grandmother, either—shouldn't you have stayed with him?"

"I couldn't," Mary said coldly, trying to mask the sick disappointment she felt. She'd told the story badly, of course. She could paint pictures with her brushes, but not with words. The anguish she'd endured watching Francisco stride away into the night, carrying Jaime from her, could never be told, but must stay locked inside her always, a great festering sore.

Perhaps Bets had caught a hint of this. "Doubtless you had good reason . . . Aunt Mary, you don't mind staying here, do you?"

"No, I like it here," she replied. "Truthfully, my only reservation on coming was that I'd hate to see you marry a Californio. I admit my own experience has prejudiced me against Spanish husbands."

"You needn't worry about me! What I meant was, you don't mind staying here in town instead of coming to the Brinkman rancho?"

"Oh! No, of course not."

"I do think that will be best. Papa needs you."

Bets returned with ill-disguised relief to her packing.

CHAPTER NINE

THE EASEL WAS TOO LARGE AND AWKWARD TO be carried under her arm. In addition, the footing in the street was hazardous, with deep ruts which had been gouged into the mud during the rainy season and now remained as fixed and hard as fired clay. But

Mary clutched her sketchbook, the box of watercolors and the easel and frequently shifted them around as she walked.

She picked her way along and did not bother to look up when she heard the thud of a horse's hooves.

"Mrs. Reyes . . ."

"Oh, Mr. Carew, good morning." Mary waited, expecting the usual chivalrous remonstrance that she was afoot, instead of riding in one of those creaky, uncomfortable carretas.

"May I carry those things for you?" he asked, dismounting.

Mary knew she looked ridiculous. Unconsciously, she took a step backward, and turned her ankle in one of the ruts. The easel slipped from her grasp and rattled to the ground.

"Please," he said soberly. "May I?"

She watched helplessly as he retrieved the fallen article. "Let me escort you wherever you're going. I shan't stay to bother you, I promise."

"Oh, please, don't make me seem more graceless than I already feel! Of course I will appreciate your assistance."

She was certain that her acceptance of help rather than company hadn't escaped his notice. And she regretted this, just as she had regretted having to be out on the two occasions when he had asked to call.

He held out his bronzed hand for the watercolor box also, but she said, "No, you have your horse to lead. Managing that wretched easel is quite enough."

"As you wish." Her painting stand was nothing under *his* arm, and again she felt foolish. "May I ask where we're going?" He had matched his stride to hers.

"Nigger Alley," she replied, using the common Americano nickname for the street defiantly, and began to walk faster. Now would come the tiresome expostulations: *Calle de los Negros?* A street of ill-repute. Notorious. Nothing but odorous dens of gambling, prostitution and vice! Hardly the place for a lady to be seen!

But when Carew answered, he sounded a trifle surprised and that was all. "You're going there to paint?"

"Paint, yes. But not in oils. I prefer watercolors."

"Watercolor? I know so little about art. All the pictures I've ever seen were portraits, large formal gardens or some very fat angels."

"I am deathly sick of that sort of subject!" Mary exclaimed, pushing back her heavy chestnut hair with an impatient hand. "All those tidy stiff pictures! Ever since I've heard about this terrible street, I've thought ah, now there would be real things to paint." She turned to him, forgetting in her enthusiasm to be distant. "Last year, an artist named Seth Eastman came to Boston. He'd been drawing Indians, and scenes of the wilderness. Everything he did had a freshness and honesty that was breathtaking.

"Since then I've tried to find original subjects of my own. You may be sure, Mr. Carew, that sitting primly on our patio, I don't see a single Indian!"

"I suppose not. But what is this watercolor art you speak of?"

She explained while they walked, not strolling as he might have preferred, but moving briskly toward their destination. She had just finished describing for him Eastman's portfolio of untamed scenery along the bends of the Ohio River, when they completed the few blocks and turned into the Calle de los Negros.

The block-long dusty little street lay before them and Carew watched her face. She could not help but be disappointed, he thought. The scene was not exciting or even interesting, merely squalid.

But Mary had not turned away. She studied the row of shed-like rooms that fronted onto a long, delapidated wooden porch. In the light of day there was no sign of life except for a dispirited sway-backed horse, tethered to a doorknob, and a gray rat that ran suddenly from an open door and scurried into the weeds and trash beneath the planking.

Then as she remained indecisive, a young Indian, dressed in a torn work shirt and faded blue pants which were stained by a dark ring at the crotch, staggered out of one of the doors. He clutched a bottle by the neck, and after shaking his head as though dazed, lifted it to his lips. But the bottle fell from his weak hand. He sank slowly to a sitting position where he stayed, immobile, staring at the empty street.

Mary turned to Carew, aghast.

"Be glad it isn't Sunday," he said. "The vineyards pay their Indian labor in grape brandy on Saturday nights. By Sunday at this time the whole downtown area will be crowded with a mob of drunks, yelling and carousing—not only men, but women and children, often fighting each other with knives. At sunset, the town marshal finally drives them all into an open corral where they'll be held until Monday morning."

"What happens then?" Mary whispered.

"The vineyards pay bail, haul the men away to work, and the weekly cycle begins again. Not very pretty, is it? Not something you want to make a picture of."

"I don't know . . . I don't want to paint just lovely things . . ."

"Shall we go? As you can see, you would be conspicuous setting up an easel here."

"That's true; I hadn't thought it would be so open. But I can make a quick sketch, at least—" Sensing his dismay, she added, "I won't be long. I only want to get an outline, then I can finish it at home."

Her pencil moved across the page of her sketchpad, blocking in the crumbling adobe, the motionless Indian, the spavined horse, and several women, too gaudily dressed for morning, who appeared at the last moment. Then regretfully she snapped down the cover over her drawing.

"There. That should give me enough to do for a long time." A smile quirked her face, softening it. "Hereafter, I'll look for realism somewhere else. Some other street corner will do . . . I must confess, Mr. Carew, that I was brought here in part by simple curiosity."

She was still studying the street and suddenly her smile faded. "Isn't that Garth Peters?"

"Yes."

They watched the youth who had just stepped forth. He stood, gripping a post and breathing deeply, as though he had been running. On a previous occasion when Teodocia had excitedly pointed him out to her, or rather to Betsey, Mary had considered him not handsome, but neatly dressed and attractive.

He looks seedy, she thought. And desperate. "What can be wrong?" she asked aloud.

"You must have heard," Carew said drily. "Gossip in the pueblo misses very little. He's doing nothing but gambling. Already he's lost the land he inherited from his father, and owes quite a bit of money."

"But that's terrible!" Mary was well aware that Teodocia's heart was set on marrying Garth. That Señora Brinkman would ever consent to the union in light of this development seemed impossible.

"Come, there's nothing we can do. No need to make matters worse by letting him see we've recognized him. We'll walk back to your home, and on the way, perhaps you can tell me a bit more about painting. Sheepherders are an ignorant lot."

Although convinced that his questions were put to distract her from brooding about Garth, she answered them, automatically at first and then with animation. For the chance to talk about art was too strong to be resisted. She described the work of Thomas Cole who, as much as thirty years earlier, had set out to capture the spirit of the American frontier. And she told Carew of the Hudson River School of artists who had followed Cole's lead, many of them becoming well-known.

She didn't realize she had given him a glimpse of her own dreams as well, until he said, "And you? Haven't you a portfolio of your own?"

"Oh, yes! I occupied my time in Spain profitably. There was little else for me to do." Her tone was bitter.

They had reached the Donovan town house, and as she turned, intending to say goodbye, he forestalled her by remarking, "I'll be driving my sheep north shortly. I could possibly show some of your pictures to the galleries in San Francisco."

Taken by surprise, she could not dissemble her pleasure. "How kind of you to suggest that! But you've never seen my work. You don't know that it's worth showing."

"Somehow I think it must be. Perhaps you'd help me choose the best samples?"

"Yes, of course. I . . . do you care to see them now?"

She was caught. She hadn't intended to allow him to call. The deception Patrick had insisted upon, putting it about that she was a widow, certainly had smoothed her path in pueblo society and was harmless enough so long as she gave no encouragement to admirers. She was not free to marry and never would be.

He was busy for a moment tying his gelding that had followed them so patiently during the last hour. She studied Carew, noting that he was younger than she (though not so very much!) telling herself that except for the intensely blue eyes, there was nothing unusually attractive about his face with its crooked nose—or about his sturdy body either, that was so different from the lean graceful one of Francisco Reyes.

She was being foolish, she thought suddenly. They were both a little lonely in this alien town, and were enjoying each other's company. There was no danger.

As they entered the house together, she said impulsively, "Mr. Carew, I've been wanting to tell you how much I admired that exploit of yours, bringing those animals safely through the desert. Do you know, a painting of you with the sheep would certainly be the realism I've been looking for. If we found a wild desolate setting for background would you mind very much?"

"Mind? Mrs. Reyes, I'd be pleased!"

"Good." She opened the door. "Do come in."

Patrick, who had evidently been pacing the parlor in an excess of exuberance and impatience, greeted them with the relief of a man who has exciting news and no one to tell it to.

"Ah, Mary Frances, where have you been? I've been waiting for you. Come in, come in. You too, John. This is an important day!"

"I'd never think it to look at you," Mary teased him fondly, "I suppose you've bought a rancho."

Patrick's face fell. "How in the world did you know?"

"Just a guess, considering what could make you so happy. But there, I'm sorry I spoiled your pleasure. Tell me about it. Did you give up at last on the Garfias place?"

"It was only a part of the San Pascual that I wanted," he corrected, "a small part. And as you know, Garfias wouldn't sell. Not to me. He is one of the few Californios who dislike Americans on principle."

"Yes, I know," his sister said. "And why you were so set on his particular rancho I couldn't understand. You could have had others for the asking."

"I wanted that land particularly, because it was suitable for a number of things—vineyards, as well as stock-breeding and grazing. I've an idea a man should have more than one or two strings to his bow."

"I think you're right," Carew remarked. "These are rich times here in southern California, but the price of cattle could fall."

"Oh, I doubt that," Patrick said uncomfortably. He liked John, but he wouldn't want sheep to replace cattle, and what else did the fellow mean? What else would bring down the price?

"I'll grant you it doesn't seem likely. But to have one's fortune tied up in thousands of head of cattle— or any livestock—means taking risks. What happens if there's an epidemic and they all die of fever? Or if there's a year or two of drought and the grass lands dry up?"

"Impossible," Patrick muttered.

Mary gave Carew a silent glance of apology and interrupted. "But Patrick," she said, "you're keeping me in suspense. What is your news?"

Her brother's frown disappeared. "Something I never expected! Do you remember, I told you that Garfias was with us when we were attacked? I haven't seen him since, but today I received a note, saying —oh, here, read it for yourself."

Mary took the square of creamy linen paper that he handed her and read aloud:

Señor Donovan:

    May I express my admiration for your bravery in our recent outlaw encounter? If you are still interested in buying a part of my land, come to see me. I will welcome you as a neighbor.

                                Manuel Garfias

Mary looked up, her gray eyes alight with happiness for Patrick. For herself, the town house was quite sufficient.

"I rode out to San Pascual immediately as you might suppose, and with a shake of the hand, we concluded the agreement. Now I own a tract of about a thousand acres, just west of the huge Rancho Santa Anita. Of course, the main ranch buildings are on Garfias' land and he still occupies them, but I have a few small outbuildings, one of them a bunkhouse that I can use for myself when I'm out there. There'll be time enough later to build more . . . It's beautiful land, Mary Frances."

"I'm certain it is. Does Betsey know yet?"

"I rode to the Brinkman rancho afterward, and told her. Found her out exercising Estrella. A fine little mare Don Diego's given her!"

"A change of scenery will be good for Bets," Mary mused. She was remembering the touch of wistfulness she'd found in her niece's manner. Then, aware of her brother's puzzled frown, she quickly added, "No doubt she'll enjoy the visit. But Bets enjoys everything, doesn't she? Just as you always do."

"Yes. John, will you stay for dinner with us?"

"Thank you, I will," Carew replied, a shade too promptly. "Mrs. Reyes has promised to show me a few of her watercolors."

"Indeed?" Patrick threw his sister a questioning look.

"I'll get them now," Mary said and left the room.

"You seem surprised. Doesn't she usually show her work?"

"Not these. Most of her paintings were done in Spain. There are, well, memories."

"I understand. For a widow, such pictures would

be painful reminders. Perhaps you should suggest that she not trouble herself—"

"No. If she's willing to bring them out, it may be a good sign. Perhaps her feelings aren't so involved anymore." Yet he watched her covertly on her return, and his glance strayed to Carew.

"Will you show them, please, Patrick?" Mary said too quickly. "I must find Flora and tell her that we have a guest for the noon meal."

After she had gone, Patrick removed the pictures from the portfolio. He leafed through them, and with a pretense of casualness replaced several in the case. Then he began displaying the remainder to his guest.

"These are of Spain, John, or at least Andalusia, where Mary Frances lived for six years of her life. The top one shows you Sevilla's cathedral. Wait, let me read what she's written on the back: 'Begun about 1400 after St. Ferdinand delivered the city from the Moors . . . gold interior from Peru, Flemish screens . . . Largest Gothic building in the world.' "

Carew listened courteously, hoping the rest of the watercolors weren't similar in subject. He cared nothing about Spain. What he really wanted was to learn more about Mary herself.

"Now, here's another scene on the patio of the Reyes home." Carew, interested again, moved closer. There was a splashing fountain with nearby orange trees in bloom, their white blossoms drifting down on the blue and yellow paving tiles. "She must have done this one early, when she first went there. In the beginning she wrote home often, telling us how beautiful Spain was."

"Only in the beginning?"

"You know how young girls are. They see the sunshine and listen to the guitars and castanets. When they finally notice the dirt and the beggars, it's a shock."

"You're very fond of her, aren't you?"

"Yes. We have two older sisters, and I myself have eight years on Mary Frances. She was born when our parents were elderly. I've always tried to take care of her . . . I'd like to see her happy."

John nodded, his eyes straying to the pile of water-colors. He pulled out one that had been hidden under the others.

"What an attractive child. Who is he?"

Patrick thrust out his hand to take back the picture, but was too late. "Who is he? Just a child! Now here is the Alcazar, the fortress palace of the Arab kings."

He cut himself off, aware that Carew was not listening, was still studying the little boy. This time Patrick removed the painting firmly from him, and slid it into the portfolio.

"I hear Mary Frances coming, and I'm hungry as a bear. Flora is a fine cook. Shall we go in?"

After Carew had gone, Patrick said abruptly, "I should never have said you were a widow. You do know that you have a suitor, don't you?"

"No!" Her voice was sharp. "I know he is very courteous and helpful. That is all."

"Then you are not very observant. His eyes were on you all the time. He wanted to see those pictures only because they were done by you. Why do you suppose he is so eager to pose with those sheep of his, and ride out tomorrow searching for the right background?"

"Because he's forced to stay in this town awhile longer and even with all the homage he's received, he's lonely, just as I am . . . Oh, Patrick, I'm sorry! I shouldn't have said that, when you are so good to me. But it's true. I do get lonely, and just a little frightened. The isolation of this place is so total, so overwhelming! Do you realize that the rest of the world could be destroyed somehow—everyone die of the pox—and we wouldn't even know? Not for weeks.

"I'm looking forward very happily to tomorrow. Patrick dear, he's young, at least four years younger than I! And there's something else—While Francisco and I are forever parted, and what we shared is colder than ashes, don't forget the sort of lean, aquiline, handsome man who captivated me. You've only to look at Mr. Carew, to see how totally different he is from Francisco in every way! So I'm hardly likely to be attracted. Let me enjoy myself!

"And I promise you—if by any chance you are right, and he becomes interested in me as a woman— I will put a stop to it at once."

CHAPTER TEN

AROUND THE WORN TABLE, FIVE MEN HAD been playing monte. Now their number was reduced to four. The airless room reeked of smoke and unwashed bodies, the forty cards of the Spanish deck were battered and filthy, but the bets, as usual, were made with gold.

The fifth player, who had been included solely on sufferance and as long as his wages from the livery stable weren't exhausted, sat morosely on a broken chair against the wall. He was much older than the others. His face was bisected by a livid, puffily-healing scar that barely missed his right eye and accounted for the indentation in the bridge of his nose.

Garth Peters, who had begun the evening with too meager a stake, and been cursed with consistently bad luck as well, was pondering his next move. The only sound was the persistent coughing of the thin Mexican youth opposite, the only one present who wasn't drinking aguardiente.

The dealer, a recent newcomer from one of the southern states, turned over the pack to reveal a diamond, for him the winning suit. He raked in his money, stacking it into a neat pile, and reshuffled.

His fingers were quick, too quick perhaps, as he had worked for a while on a Mississippi River gambling boat. He handed the pack to Garth to cut, and then laid out four cards face up.

The Sonoran, Juan Flores, wiped his lips on the

back of his hand. "Show us the spade you have up your sleeve," he said softly.

The Southerner sprang to his feet, and the chair fell backward.

"Suh! Ah you questionin' mah honah?"

Flores knew English. He had learned it in a recent period of enforced idleness spent in close proximity to a number of men who spoke the language, not grammatically perhaps, but forcefully. This sentence, however, was incomprehensible to him.

He could guess its meaning though; and when the cheat reached for his gun, he found himself staring into the barrel of a Colt.

"Get out!" snarled Flores.

The card shark hesitated. He was not a coward, and furthermore the seven of spades which had been up his sleeve was now safely on the floor where it could have dropped by accident. But the gun that faced him was unwavering, and he suspected that beneath the Mexican's calm lay a hair-trigger edginess. He reminded himself too that Flores was an escapee from the state prison at San Quentin.

He laid his own pistol slowly on the table; his cigar dropped to the hard-packed clay floor, and he violently ground it out under his heel.

"Let's us get shut of this heah pigsty," he said to his friend opposite, and the two of them gathered up the small amount of coins each had before him. Garth looked at Flores questioningly, but the Sonoran did not interfere. He merely watched them from behind the Colt, until they slammed out the door.

"I should have shot him. I hate cheaters." A sudden fit of coughing raked his body. When it subsided, he added, "Garth, I want to talk to you. I've been watching you play now for several nights. You're in over your head."

"That's nothing to you!"

"No. But maybe this'll make it something to me." Flores, as usual winner for the evening, pushed forward his tall stack of gold until it sat squarely before Garth. The boy stared at the bright slugs as though mesmerized.

"What's that for?"

"I like a man who doesn't quit. Try again, and this'll give you something to try with. That's all."

"That's all!" Garth said with heavy sarcasm. "What are you buying? A killing?"

"I do my own killing."

"All right, but you want something. There's a price to everything."

"The only thing I'm asking," Flores said patiently, "is that you repay me in kind. You're a good enough gambler and your luck should change. I'm betting it will."

"That's all?"

"Yes. Return the gold to me, exactly that amount, a week from now, and we're even."

"And if I can't? Suppose I lose it all? And I will!"

"We'll talk about that then. Don't you figure it's time your luck changed?"

"Way past time. I've lost hope," but Flores noted he didn't push back the proffered advance.

"Suit yourself." The Mexican extended his hand toward the pile, yet he was watching Garth without seeming to.

"No, leave it! Why shouldn't I take the chance? It's the only one I've got left, God knows . . ."

He was talking to himself now, not to Flores. The desperation of these last few months was in his mouth, so sour he wanted to spit it out. How stupid he'd been to gamble away his inheritance! But playing cards was now his whole life. It was hard to believe there had ever been a time when he preferred such innocent pursuits as hunting or cock fighting or serenading girls!

He remembered very well though how it had started. When both his parents died of typhoid, he'd been shocked and lonely. He'd wanted Teodocia, needed Teodocia, and learned that he had to wait. They were both too young, her father explained. His mind understood the refusal, but his body didn't. And to push away his new loneliness and his nagging need, he'd turned to the excitement of monte.

In those days he'd gone to Aleck Gibson's gambling house on the Plaza, a place as different from this filthy den as a lady from a whore. Gibson's was a bright room with a well-stocked bar and half a dozen monte banks, each table having its green baize cover heaped with fifty-dollar gold slugs. The games were honest too, and respectable.

But soon, after a long losing streak, he began to feel uncomfortable there. The patrons were mostly old friends of his father's, and while they didn't rebuke him, some refused to take his money. He'd showed up less and less frequently, playing instead at Calle de los Negros.

He lost, ever more heavily, and in recent weeks he'd had to face the terrifying realization that he had lost his land and probably Teodocia as well. Señora Brinkman would never let her go to such a miserable penniless fool as he!

Oh, Teodocia!

He groaned, "Give it to me . . ." and stuffed the valuable stake in his leather pouch. Without another word to his new benefactor, he staggered out.

Now that the two of them were alone, Captain Warner rose and came to the table. He took the aguardiente bottle by the neck to take a drink.

"Why are you buying him?"

"What do you suppose? I need good men for my Manilas."

"I thought that was it. You're so sure he'll lose all that gold in a week?"

"Sooner." The youth shrugged. "He's one of God's unfortunates."

"You're probably right. But don't you think that gang of yours should be leaving town? It's dangerous to stay so long. Rumors get around and there are rewards offered. I wouldn't trust those two who just left not to turn you in."

"Them?" Flores was contemptuous. "If they did, they'd never leave this street again alive."

"Still, what are you waiting around for?"

"Don't ask me questions!" His anger flicked out like a snake's tongue, and disappeared again.

"Patrick Donovan! That's it, isn't it?"

"He killed my brother, you stupid Americano. I have a debt to pay."

"Then why not pay it?" persisted Warner, emboldened by the brandy. "He rides the streets of Los Angeles every day."

"Probably for the same reason you don't and never will," Flores said drily. "I don't wish to dangle at the end of a rope. No, when I meet Donovan, it will be just the two of us alone, man to man . . . Did you do what I hired you for?"

"Yes, I know what his rancho is like," Warner said eagerly, "I can draw you a map of the trees and hills around the bunkhouse. And there's another thing—his daughter's at the Brinkman place, and they ride every day, she and Brinkman's daughter. Why not pay him back through her?"

Flores looked at him with contempt. "Leave it to you to think of that. I don't fight women. Or did you have something else in mind?"

"I wasn't thinking of fighting," Warner confessed. He licked the scar where it crossed his mouth and smiled, envisioning something. When the younger man didn't answer, he reached again for the alcohol.

Drinking, he studied Flores, marveling again that such a thin, scrawny young man could draw followers as he did. He wasn't even healthy! Even in the candle-light, his lips were an unnatural cherry red; and that coughing probably meant consumption. But in the short time he'd been out of prison, he'd certainly made the Manilas a band to be feared.

"Juan," Warner said urgently, "take me into the Manilas! My God, I'm sweeping out stables! Me! I'm not a peon, I'm a sea captain!"

"You *were* a sea captain." Flores laughed. "See, I know English better than you."

"Since I lost my ship, no one will hire me—"

"Does that surprise you?"

"I'm sick of it! I'd be a good man to have," Warner swept on, unheeding. "Experience counts for a lot and you wouldn't be sorry—"

"Crawl back into your stable muck, old woman." His indifference was more cruel than anger. "Finish the spying I've paid for and then leave me alone. The Manilas are men."

He took his hat from a peg on the wall and left, shutting the door softly behind him. Warner stood gazing at the guttering candle on the table.

For a moment he allowed himself to consider the revenge that had flashed briefly through his mind. That would be something, that would! Bets Donovan was not only beautiful, she was a fighter, and just thinking about taking her by force in some lonely canyon made him sweat. He'd hold a gun on her, make her undress . . .

But then he sighed. He knew the Brinkman rancho and how populated it was, even in the far reaches. Brinkman had believed in running a large number of cattle, which meant lots of men; and he'd bred horses, and grown crops as well. Quite a different place from Donovan's desolate little spread that had been cut out of the San Pascual. Besides, two women together were different than one alone. They might have an armed escort.

Even so, would he really do such a thing? Could he? Suddenly he was horrified.

No! He'd help Flores ambush Patrick, because Donovan deserved whatever he got. But rape an innocent beautiful girl? What was he thinking of? He'd always been a decent man—that idea must have come from Flores. Of course it had! Just what a Mexican outlaw would think of.

He rubbed his face, touching tenderly the ridges of the scar and staring blearily through the haze of cigar smoke that still lingered in the room. How had all this happened to him? He was an expert seaman, the ship shouldn't have gone down. But at the last second he'd panicked, something he never dreamed he would do. And because of that one mistake, after all these years, respected, obeyed—

Look at him now. Begging for work.

His head came down in his hands, and he wept in drunken self-pity.

Here was his explai... his promis... turn to her

CHAPTER ELEVEN

FOR THE FIRST TIME IN YEARS, MARY FACED
the coming day with excited anticipation. She told herself this happy feeling was entirely natural. She was an
artist, and the picture of John Carew might prove to
be her best work. Not only was the subject colorful,
but she planned to try a new technique. She had heard
that Eastman did not first line in his figures with pencil, and she intended to eliminate this step herself. But
painting directly with watercolor meant every detail
must be carefully visualized, and she promised herself
she wouldn't be rushed.

The morning was filled with a bright butter-yellow
sunshine, and such pleasant weather seemed added
promise for success. She and Carew rode their horses
early to the Aguirre rancho where the sheep were
quartered, and he led her at once to the flock.

The first step, she had decided, was to make studies
of the animals, so when she finally set brush to paper,
she would be thoroughly familiar with the shape of
their round white woolly bodies and the thin legs like
dark sticks. As she and Carew approached, the sheep
looked up from their grazing then slowly moved to a
distance. The aloof frowning expression on their tri-
angular black faces put her in mind of a group of
haughty dowagers, and she laughed, Carew joining in.
His laugh was warm, as though he felt an affection for
his charges, even after all he had been through with
them.

Mary sat on a sun-baked rock and lost herself in
sketching. As time passed, she was hardly aware of
her companion who wandered about, silent and seemingly content. Finally, shortly after noon, he apologized for disturbing her, and said that they had been

invited by Sebastian Aguirre, owner of the rancho, to take dinner with him.

Mary remembered that the day before Carew had said he intended bringing a picnic basket, but she guessed at once the reason for the change in plans. He had realized belatedly no doubt, that her reputation might be endangered if they spent all day alone together on the solitary plains. Although touched by his protective considerateness, she felt a twinge of regret as well, for she had looked forward to the sharing of the lunch.

Miguel's father, however, was clearly so pleased by their coming that she forgot her small disappointment. A widower of late middle age, he suffered greatly from a crippling in his joints. He found it very difficult to walk, and spent much of his day in a comfortable chair poring over his accounts and directing from a distance the operation of his rancho. Fortunately, his was one of the largest cattle herds in southern California, and he could afford to keep a complete household, even though his only son lived and worked in town.

Mary was warmly greeted as they entered the cool hacienda. Once Don Sebastian had apologized for not meeting them at the door, but already seated at his large dining table, he did not dwell on his lack of mobility. Instead he began an informed conversation about the famous meal artists of history.

As the meal progressed, and Mary realized how wide his knowledge was of the subject that enthralled her, she was struck by the irony of the discovery. Of all the people she had talked to since returning to America, of all who had tried to be interested—even Patrick who loved her—only this man, a rancho owner of the remote California frontier, truly understood. And he was a Spaniard!

"You are a most gracious host, Don Sebastian!" she said impulsively.

Carew, who had been living as a guest in the Aguirre house ever since his sheep were brought to be quartered there, said, "Mrs. Reyes, it would be difficult to find a kinder or more generous man."

Aguirre snorted. "On the contrary, the advantage

runs the other way, Señora. I live a lonely life here.
There are plenty of people around—the cooks, a
baker, washerwomen, an ironer, a seamstress, and of
course the men who milk the cows, tan the hides, make
butter and cheese and the list goes on. But there is no
one really to talk to. My foreman is good company
when he's here, but usually he's miles away doing the
work this old cripple should be doing for himself.
Therefore, can you imagine what pleasure it is to have
a young man like Señor Carew staying in the hacienda? Or, a beautiful woman gracing my table, although far too briefly?"

"I shall be sorry to leave, Don Sebastian," Carew
said, and paused. "For several reasons."

"I hope sincerely that day will be some little time
distant," responded his host.

"I should be leaving now. The grass is high. But to
tell you the truth, I've come to like Los Angeles."

"Oh?" Don Sebastian glanced at Mary with a faint,
meaningful smile.

Uncomfortable, she concentrated her attention on
the rich beef stew she had been neglecting. The three
of them were alone, and she was suddenly aware of the
deep quiet of the house. Doubtless there were people
about, many servants, as Don Sebastian had said.
But their voices couldn't penetrate the thick walls.
What was needed was family, she thought, men and
women to discuss things with, take his advice—children to run in and out, laughing and making so much
noise they needed to be scolded—a large family, in
such a large house . . .

Reminded of his only son, Miguel, with whom she
had become acquainted in the course of his frequent
calls on Bets, she said, "Señor Aguirre's newspaper is
a great success in Los Angeles."

The hawk-like face tightened. "Success? By what
definition? It prints trivia, and beyond that only ad-
vertisements for those who are in trade."

"But the important news is impossible to obtain in
this very remote area," protested Mary. "He tells us
that he dreams of ways to learn what is happening in

the rest of the world, without having always to wait weeks for mail to be delivered."

"All the more reason I would think, for taking his place in my home, and doing a man's work! Sometimes I find it difficult to believe I have a son. Forgive me, may we speak of other things?"

Shocked into silence, Mary did not again refer to Miguel, but later, as she and John Carew returned to the knoll where the sheep were, she said, "How sad! Don Sebastian is an intellectual himself; he should be proud of his son's efforts to create a newspaper."

"Perhaps he would be, if he had other sons to help him with the rancho. I've been here some time now, and watching him struggle to keep all this land productive when he can't walk, I'm afraid I see it his way. Miguel should consider his father, instead of permitting him to do the work alone."

"I doubt it was an easy decision." Mary ended the discussion. She began again to sketch the sheep, and promptly forgot the Aguirres. Again Carew strolled nearby, leaving her undisturbed.

It was almost sunset when she closed her sketchbook saying, with a contented sigh, "I think that's enough. Tomorrow, I'd like to find a background. Oh, but how tired of this you must be! I've been thoughtless because for me the time passed so quickly!"

"I enjoyed myself," he said. And because she still seemed dubious, added, "I'm the sort who can spend hours, even days, with no company at all. Crossing the country, my partners and I were many miles apart. I would have had to talk to the sheep."

His smile was reassuring, almost brotherly, causing her no alarm.

The second day was very like the first. But instead of sitting on a boulder sketching animals, Mary now wanted to ride her horse through the hills and arroyos of the rancho. She was determined to find just the right setting.

"The spot should be very barren, dry and desolate. I would like anyone seeing the picture to be struck by that, and to know that you were fighting for survival.

Sheep are such peaceful and harmless creatures of a pastoral nature, that we must make the terrain surrounding them appear ominous and dangerous by contrast." She was taking pains to explain her idea to John, because she feared he might become impatient. Having committed herself to the project, she wanted nothing to interfere.

But he seemed perfectly content to ride his bay gelding a little behind hers, ambling slowly across the Aguirre land. Once she turned suddenly and found him watching her intently, so that she felt a flutter of disquiet. But he said only, "I think the horse's girth is loose. Let me tighten it for you."

He did so, then immediately dropped back.

Once again they dined with the elder Aguirre, and afterward, in the afternoon, set off up a dry ravine they had not visited before. She was becoming dispirited because she had not found what she sought.

"Never mind," Carew said. "This may be the place. If not, we'll try in another direction."

"But I must not take up all your time!"

"I've nothing else to do. Until I leave for the North, I'm free. Believe me, Mary, these two days have been the best since I left home."

"I'm glad," she said, aware that he had used her given name, and telling herself that she wished he had not.

He hesitated, his clear blue eyes studying her face. "I've never known an artist before. I'm hoping, you see, that instead of that Hudson River School you told me about, you'll start a new one, say the School of the Far West. You'll be famous, and I'll be able to say that I gave you my time if nothing else."

"You're a dear. And don't think I'm not terribly grateful . . . You say you've not known an artist before. We're even then. I haven't known any sheep men, except for this one, and I still know very little about him."

"That's because we lead dull lives. Perhaps I should list myself as a gold miner, but even then, what is there to tell? My brother and I did make that small strike in the gold rush. Then one night, after we re-

turned to the east, we were having supper with a friend
at the Prairie House in Terre Haute, Indiana. Have
you ever eaten there? Well, take care you don't. The
main dish is fried eggs. They were swimming in lard,
and so bad I remember them yet.

"The three of us were wondering what to do next,
and that was when the idea came of buying sheep as
well as a few cattle and herding them west. To tell
you the truth, we did it more for the adventure than
the profit, although we won't turn that down when it
comes.

"And there you have it—the full story of John
Carew, sheep man."

"Oh, I do envy you!"

"Why?"

She could see he was really surprised and she
warmed to his lack of pretension. "Having the blessed
freedom to do what you like with your life! Let's ride
on, shall we? I see a likely spot at the end of this canyon."

But the site still wasn't right. As they had gone as
far as feasible in that direction, and the sun was low
in the sky, he suggested they give up and try again the
next day. She agreed, and they began the long trip
back to town.

After two days together, she was finding him a comfortable companion. His show of interest in her work
pleased her, particularly when she remembered Francisco's bored indifference, and his mother's outright
scorn.

On the third day, a cold wind blew, knifing through
their clothes. Mary was glad she had already sketched
the sheep, because when she passed the hillside on
which they were gathered, she saw them all motionless
facing in one direction, their hind quarters butting
against the wind.

"What a raw day," she said, and pulled her pale
brown cloak more closely about her. But then they
rounded the brow of a hill, and she saw what lay beyond. Discomfort no longer mattered.

"I think this must be the place," she said. "Yes, see
how desolate it is! Just a little cactus here and there,

and the flat land stretching out to infinity. Please John, ride over there."

The next hour held for her an excitement that was familiar yet always new. She asked him to take the bay farther away, bring it closer. "There now, will you ride toward me slowly along that draw? Thank you, I believe that is what I want!"

She wandered about, seeing the scene from different angles, and she sketched him a number of times, expecting to have more difficulty with the horse but finding the animal easy and the man difficult.

She hadn't realized how broad he was in the shoulders and chest, and how the muscles rippled under his shirt when he moved. Drawing him meant scrutinizing him in an unhurried way and more closely than she had ever studied a man's body before, even that of Francisco, who had refused to be painted. In fact, in their most intimate moments, Francisco had disliked being looked at—

"I love you, Mary."

For an instant she was confused. She had been concentrating so hard. Had she only imagined she heard those quiet words?

"No doubt I sound crazy telling you this so soon, but I've known you were a very special woman since the first time I met you. Go on drawing, pretend you don't hear me. Because I'm afraid if you do, you'll say no—"

Mary's hands had ceased their work. "I do say no. John, you are a fine young man, and I'm sorry, I didn't want this to happen. But I think you must be imagining—"

She stopped. A very curious thing had happened. Studying him as she had been doing—or was it the brief recollection of Francisco's lovemaking? Whatever the cause, she was suddenly suffused and aflame with desire.

The sketches fell to the ground. She took a step toward him, then drew back, covering her face. She was shaking.

"Mary, dearest! What is it?"

"I must go home! Now. Oh, I should never have come out here with you."

"Mary, please . . ."

She forced herself toward her horse, her body filled with lead. Oh how shameless! How depraved! To want, actually *long* to lie with this man, even in the cold mist, on the barren ground!

The horse as she mounted began to walk, carrying her away, and Carew's protest, "But Don Sebastian is expecting us," betrayed his puzzled hurt and stupefaction.

"Tell him . . . tell him I've become ill."

"Ill? You're ill? I'm sorry. I'll take you home at once. But here, you forgot your sketchbook." He reached up, handing it to her.

In fear of his touch, she could not prevent a quick motion of recoil.

She watched his face slowly redden. They stared at each other.

When he spoke, his voice was hard. "I'll tell one of the Aguirre men to escort you."

She nodded, and turned her mare toward the hacienda. He paced his alongside, stiff and silent.

But when they reached the stable, and he had beckoned to one of the vaqueros, he spurred his horse close to hers.

"Mary, I must ask—you did understand, didn't you? I want to marry you! Perhaps you thought—"

"No." It was anguish to get the words out. "John, I am married. Francisco Reyes, my husband, is alive. I left him. Yes, and my little son as well. Didn't you guess? No, of course not. Forgive me. Please—"

"Why did you lie? You said you were a widow! In God's name, why?"

"Because I am a coward, I suppose," she sighed. "They knew the truth in Boston, and I couldn't face that here. Not again."

He spun his bay away, gave the approaching man a curt order as he passed, and then spurred into a gallop. She watched him until he was far away, and then turned slowly toward town.

The trembling had stopped. The strange desire that

had betrayed her was gone. She felt tired and unhappy, sad for him too that he must believe he had been made a fool of.

But as she rode, followed at a respectful distance by the vaquero, she had further cause to be ashamed. For the thought came irresistibly that she was grateful John had delayed his declaration as long as he had. As it was, she had her sketches completed. She could begin to work on the painting.

CHAPTER TWELVE

BETS TETHERED ESTRELLA, HER PULSE QUICK-ening in tune with the holiday mood of the crowd. Most of the population of the pueblo, it seemed, had managed to squeeze into one street intersection and the four surrounding blocks. This was the start of a much anticipated horse race, the course stretching four and a half miles out San Pedro Road and return; and no one who could stagger to the scene with a dollar to bet would have dreamed of staying away. She herself had cut short her visit at the Brinkman rancho pleading her eagerness to see such a grand event.

As she strolled about, careless of the sun on her face or dirt on her shoes, she was greeted warmly on all sides.

"Oh, Señorita Elizabeth, you've returned to grace our town, eh?"

"I'm glad to be back!"

How true that was. At first, she'd loved the long quiet days with Teodocia, but of late she'd been missing all the bustle of the dusty, smelly streets. There was something else too that had brought her back—a restlessness that she couldn't explain, even to herself.

"Elizabeth, will you and your father and your dear aunt come to dinner next week on Tuesday?" Arcadia

inquired in passing. "I'm having a few other people
whom you know."

A few meant thirty or more, a large gay party. Bets
said, "Thank you so much! I'll have to ask Papa, but
I'm certain we'll be there."

It was odd how her heart beat faster at the mere
idea that one of those other guests might be John
Carew! She had been watching for him today, but still
hadn't caught a glimpse of his blond head. However,
she did see her father.

"Papa!" she called. He didn't hear her over the
shouts and laughter, and she stood watching him
fondly. He wore a broad grin, and his enjoyment was
so infectious that she smiled unconsciously. She wondered which horse he favored, and she told herself that
if she were betting, she would be sure to follow his
lead. She had confidence in the Donovan good fortune.

She could see that as yet he had not made his decision. He strode slowly around the big powerful horse
Sarco, owned by Don Pio Pico, and gave a small nod
of approval. Yet when he approached the Australian
horse, Black Swan, bought expressly by Jose Sepulveda
to challenge Sarco, he stared hard at Black Swan's
rider. Don Jose had imported for the occasion a tiny
black man, dressed in jockey silks and seated on a
light English saddle which was entirely different from
the large ornate Californio one that Sarco would carry.
Donovan's lips formed an incredulous whistle.

He turned to find Bets at his elbow.

"Sarco's a beauty," she said.

"Yes, but the weight difference! Black Swan's little
jockey weighs nothing at all. I think too that the
Sepulvedas are very confident. See there? Señora
Sepulveda is whispering to her servants again. She's
been sending them around through the crowd taking
money on Black Swan. I hear she has a regular fortune in gold slugs tied in her handkerchief . . . Still,
I must have another look at Sarco."

He was gone again, and Bets found her aunt standing alone observing the hubbub.

"I hope Patrick doesn't get carried away, Betsey.

He can't afford to lose everything on one race. Such vast sums are being bet, it frightens me."

"I don't think you need worry," Bets returned. She hoped Aunt Mary would not voice these doubts to her father and spoil his pleasure. "He's done very well up to now in this new land, and I'm confident he'll choose wisely today."

"Let us trust that he will. I love my brother, Betsey, but I know his weaknesses. He's generous to a fault but also impetuous. It's a dangerous combination."

Bets looked away impatiently. "I hardly think he'll be foolish. Anyway, the Sepulvedas are friends of ours. He'll feel obliged to support them."

"Oh, that I doubt," her aunt replied. "I said he was impulsive, I didn't say he wasn't shrewd. He'll bet on the horse he thinks will win."

This might be true, but Bets as usual was more than a little nettled by Mary. "How strange! There's Flora, carrying little Flower and running through the crowd. I hope she isn't intending to bet," she turned her back and walked after Flora. But the servant was already gone, lost in the press of people.

Miguel Aguirre however, was nearby, his notebook in hand, interviewing the horse owners and major betters. He looked happy, for this race was genuine news. Bets knew that he would be further pleased if she stopped at his elbow and asked his prediction of the outcome, but he wasn't the one she was seeking. When Felipa joined the young editor, showing him the chamois bag of money she carried, and obviously asking that question herself, Bets was relieved.

Just then someone shouted that the race was about to begin, and a hush fell over the crowd. Bets craned on tiptoe, trying to see, and was suddenly conscious of a prickling sensation at the back of her neck. Someone behind her was staring at her! She was sure of it. The compulsion to look over her shoulder was too strong to be resisted.

Yet when she did turn, it was only to wonder if after all she had been mistaken. She was standing at the outer edge of the crowd, with only a few scattered spectators farther back. Among them, was only one person she could recognize, and he a man she barely knew—Phineas Bishop.

At her questioning glance, he merely waved a large hand in greeting and boomed, "Sarco's a big one, isn't he, Miss Betsey!"

She nodded, feeling foolish. That burning gaze had certainly not come from him!

But there was the signal gun, and she pressed forward with the rest, putting the trifling incident out of her mind. The two horses sprang away down the road, spurred on by a deafening roar of shouts and cheers.

"Miss Bets!" Captain Warner staggered toward her from the starting line, pushing aside an Indian woman, and almost falling himself.

"Yes, Captain?"

She tried not to stare at the livid, puffy scar. She, like Patrick, had loved the *Elizabeth,* and she had wept when news came the graceful clipper was gone. If losing the ship had been the man's only crime, however, they would have tried to find excuses for him, for he had seemed knowledgeable enough as a seaman on that long voyage around the Horn, and it was well known that there could be wicked storms in winter along the California coast. But there was one age-old, unbreakable rule of the sea—a captain must be the last to leave a foundering ship.

And yet, how dreadfully disfigured he was! Bets shuddered, almost disbelieving. Could her father, so kind-hearted under all his bluster, really have inflicted such a punishment?

"Where is he? Where's Donovan?" demanded Warner belligerently.

"Papa's here, I know. Can't you find him?" It was no wonder, she thought, that he hadn't been able to. The poor man was too blind drunk to see.

"He's not!" came with slurred insistence. "Don't you think I've combed this place? If he was here, I'd have found him."

"What is it you want?" She was suddenly curious. What business could this poor wreck have with Patrick? Their association was long over, and the man must feel only fear and hatred for his onetime employer.

A cunning look came into Warner's bleary eyes. "Jest wanna ask him how he bet, tha's all. But have to find him, have to send him to his ranch." He staggered away.

Bets stared after him, and then she too began to scan the close-packed streets. True, the town had turned out en masse; fine silk parasols bobbed everywhere, and would have made Warner's search more difficult. But Patrick was tall, he would stand out in the crowd. And plainly enough, he no longer was there.

"Miss Donovan!" someone said urgently.

Bets recognized his voice instantly, even though they had spoken together so seldom. Never able to conceal her feelings, she replied with especial warmth, her big eyes alight. "Good day, Mr. Carew!"

"Miss Donovan, I need to speak to your father. Can you tell me where he is?"

She drooped with the disappointment of it. She'd hoped so much that it was herself he sought.

"I'm sorry, I don't know. He was making his bet on the race and I talked with him then. But I think now he must be gone, which surprises me, as he surely wouldn't want to miss the start. Besides, where would he go? All the stores, even the bars are closed. Everyone in Los Angeles is here."

Remembering Captain Warner's parting mumble, she added, "It's possible something went wrong out at the Allison, and he had a message to go there."

"The Allison?"

"That's the name he chose for his rancho. My mother's name was Allison. He always liked it."

Carew was frowning. Saying nothing more, he strode away from her.

"Wait! Please, wait! Are you leaving? Aren't you going to see the end of the race?"

He did not stop and she had to run to match his pace. "I'm going to the Allison," he said.

"But . . . do you know where it is?"

"I'll find it."

Her joy at encountering him was all but evaporated. He seemed very brusque, and he hadn't smiled once. Nevertheless, she followed behind until they reached the dusty square where all the horses were tethered together, swishing the flies from their sweat-stained rumps with their tails.

"Has something happened that concerns Papa? I wish you'd tell me!"

"Nothing has happened. I must speak with him, that's all."

"Then I'm coming with you to show you the way. The rancho is not easy to find."

"You will stay here, please." But Bets was already busy, extricating her horse from the muddle of reins and tie ropes. Carew waited, containing his impatience, while the slim figure of the girl insinuated itself fearlessly among the shifting, pawing horses. She wore, as did the younger Californio women when riding, tight black trousers and an elaborately ruffled shirt, this one a deep blue, matching her eyes, but unlike many of her friends, the severe, almost mannish attire became her fully as well as the usual voluminous skirts. She was remarkably beautiful, he realized suddenly, and watched her with more interest, amused to see her carelessly hang the flat-brimmed hat she was carrying, on the saddlehorn. Did she never wear the thing? Probably not. Her lustrous black hair was tied too high on the back of her head to ever fit inside, and her skin, he saw now, was tanned to the lovely color of honey. She had independence then, and spirit —that was obvious in the proud way she walked. If he'd never met Mary, he found himself thinking, he might well have joined the long line of this girl's admirers!

But the reminder of Mary turned him morose again.

"Won't your aunt worry if you leave without telling her?"

Bets led out Estrella. "Oh, no! I'm not really in Aunt Mary's charge, that was just Papa's teasing . . . Will you help me up?"

He did as she bade, while she gave him a sweet

impish smile. He suspected she was quite capable of swinging herself astride the horse's back unassisted.

"Thank you. Now I'm ready." She spurred Estrella into a run while Carew was still on the ground. He sprang into his saddle but only caught up when they were some distance along the road, headed well out toward the Donovan rancho.

The dirt and stench of the town streets were already far behind, replaced by the warm sweet smell of the countryside. Even the wildest shouts of the race enthusiasts had faded, and only the drone of insects disturbed the quiet, until a great flock of geese, honking noisily, flew overhead. The sky was brilliant and clear; and the foothills that seemed to undulate in the distance were verdant with early spring bloom.

"How pleasant to ride today!" Bets exclaimed, "and on such a perfect horse." She found herself wishing she could blurt out the real reason for her contentment. Glancing sideways, she thought, *I could ride beside him anywhere and forever,* and hoped to meet his eyes. But he continued to gaze straight ahead.

"Mr. Carew, tell me please why we are hurrying and why you are so serious! One would almost think you feared for Papa, but that's not possible. He was with me only minutes before the race started." Being unworried, she spoke lightly. It was impossible for her to imagine that anything had happened to her father. As clever and strong as he was, she believed he could take care of himself in any situation.

Carew hesitated briefly before responding. "I have a warning for him," he said finally. "Don Sebastian and I both thought it important."

Her "Yes?" was expectant, and he found he must explain more than he had intended. "Jose Flores, the outlaw leader Patrick killed on the cattle drive, had a younger brother Juan, who is the much more dangerous of the two. He recently made a daring escape from prison and has formed a band of cattle thieves and stagecoach robbers who call themselves the Manilas. This Juan Flores swears that he will get revenge for his brother's murder."

"Murder?" repeated Bets indignantly. "Those men

killed Mr. Brinkman! They deserved to die! But how do you know all this?"

"I learned of it last night. Two of the Indians who herd my sheep, got drunk at Calle de los Negros, and Don Sebastian suggested I pick them up there instead of waiting until Monday morning. As we supposed, they were far too unsteady to ride, so I took them back to the Aguirre rancho in a carreta. They were laughing, babbling. People say Indians aren't used to hard liquor and shouldn't touch it, but who can blame them, with the miserable existence they lead . . . At any rate, it was lucky for us because they were telling each other in loud whispers what Flores had said."

"But surely, an outlaw like that wouldn't have taken them into his confidence?"

"No. And the real secrets of that street are usually well kept. A betrayer doesn't live long. But men will talk among themselves, and sometimes they don't realize that a besotted Indian can hear just as well as whites can."

Her sky-blue eyes widened, and he saw that the color had drained from her face.

"Miss Donovan," he added quickly, "you must not worry. I've already told the Sheriff. He knows now that the Manilas are hiding in the Calle, and a posse will be formed. I only want to warn Patrick—"

"But haven't you thought," her clear voice was high with alarm, "that this Flores and his men may be at Allison! They may be lying in wait for Papa!"

For a second he thought her fear was for herself. But then she kicked her heels into Estrella's flanks and the fleet little mare bounded forward, almost flying down the road toward the rancho.

"Miss Donovan—Bets! Wait!" He galloped alongside, shouting. "There's no reason to think that, none at all! I'm certain the Manilas are still in town."

With her lighter weight and Estrella's strength, she could have outdistanced him, and for a time he thought she would. At last, reluctantly, she slowed.

What other girl would race at top speed toward the spot where she believed an outlaw band awaited her father? His admiration added fuel to the small flame of excitement that had flickered inside of him since they began this strange ride together.

Mary Reyes, not Bets Donovan, was the woman for him, but the abrupt manner in which he had been told of the hopelessness of that love had angered him. What a fool he was, he reflected. Alone in this wild countryside with a girl who would be infinitely desirable to any man, a girl moreover whose glances betrayed unmistakable interest in him, and what did he do but moon over someone who didn't care at all!

"If I had believed there was any danger at your father's rancho, I would have stopped you from coming." One of his warm smiles appeared at last.

"Would you? You'd have had to tie me to a post."

She was intent on hastening, and there was no coquetry in the words, but again he felt that tingle of expectation. "Hardly that, but I'd have managed . . . Are we nearly there? You were right; finding this place would be difficult alone."

"Almost there." She turned her horse into a rutted narrow trail off to one side and they cantered through scrub oak, a small forest of twisted trunks.

Beyond the trees, they came abruptly on an adobe bunkhouse, which stood alone in the mouth of a canyon. Clearly no one was there. No horse was tethered, and the low building wore an air of vacancy. All the same, Carew said, "Wait here."

Dismounting, he walked cautiously toward the door.

As he pressed the latch, she was beside him. He was mildly amused, realizing that his earlier guess was correct; she could easily mount and dismount her horse without male assistance.

The building, as he had supposed, was empty. He glanced into the bunkroom, then returned to the smaller room where Bets waited. This was merely a storage area lined with rough shelves, and containing a chair and a narrow rope bed covered by a striped serape. Undisturbed dust was everywhere. There was no sign that anyone had visited the place in several days, so Patrick must not have left the pueblo after all, and their long ride out was for nothing.

"I asked you to wait. I didn't know what I'd find here."

Bets was at the window, idly contemplating the hills, the oaks, and the cactus, and did not reply. Then, in a gesture that was at once innocent and at the same time calculated, she stretched, her arms raised, hands clasped behind her head. The round fullness of her bosom was outlined beneath the frilly shirt.

John took an involuntary step forward.

She turned, still silhouetted before the light, and looked at him. "Must we go back? I suppose you want to find Papa."

"Yes."

Neither of them moved.

"Why have you avoided me?" she asked in a soft voice.

The arrogance of the question annoyed him, and he made no effort to spare her. "I haven't avoided you. There was someone else."

She didn't seem to hear. Her gaze didn't leave his face.

He was vividly aware of the rope bed set against the wall. The palms of his hands were moist as he gripped them together behind him.

What he knew he wanted was unthinkable! What sort of man was he? This was the daughter of a friend, he reminded himself angrily. She was, in spite of that undisguised longing in her eyes, a pure young woman, good enough for the best family in California to welcome. Any suitor would be honored by her acceptance!

What madness was in him then? He must leave this room, this empty place . . .

Yet, instead he found himself walking slowly forward. Bets came to meet him, glowing and eager with love.

He lay on the striped serape, holding her warm naked body close to his own. John had supposed that once his terrible need was satisfied, the spell would be broken, and he would have to face his conscience and doubtless her recriminations as well. But he found himself reluctant to put her away, and he lay quietly, stroking the silken skin.

At last she stirred, and murmured in a voice that was still thick and dreamy, "Tell me, is there someone else—now?"

Was there? He didn't know. Had he been thinking of Mary the whole time, wishing it was she who was so yielding and passionate in his embrace, imagining that it was she?

Suddenly a bullet shattered the glass window across the room and he was saved from answering.

Donovan! Her father had come!

"Stay down!" hissed Carew, "and get dressed!" Like a character in a music hall comedy, he scurried into his own clothes while crouched absurdly on the floor. He had never dressed so quickly for any reason in his life.

A young male voice shouted from outside, "Donovan! Come out and meet me like a man. Or would you rather die like a rat in a box?"

Carew snatched up his gun. In spite of their danger, he felt like laughing. So the Flores kid had come after all. And he, having forgotten his errand entirely, had supposed he was dealing with a wrathful father!

"Patrick Donovan isn't here! This is John Carew."

"Carew? Are you the sheep man I heard about? But you're lying! I see two horses."

"I'm not lying." He paused, and decided to take the chance. "There's a lady here with me."

"Oh? Open the door and bring her out. Otherwise, how do I know it isn't Donovan?"

"You'll have to take my word for that. My word is good." He rose and walked to the window, making an easy target if Flores cared to shoot again.

Behind him, Bets, in an agony of fear, whispered, "Come back, John! Oh, please come back! You'll be killed!"

But there would be no more shooting yet. He and the outlaw were taking each other's measure. Carew squinted into the sun, at first seeing no one, then spotted a thin figure beside a gnarled tree in the canyon. Flores was alone, as he'd guessed. Flores had come to challenge Patrick by himself.

"Let me see her," the bandit insisted. "I've nothing against you, if what you say is true. I would be ashamed to rob or kill a man when he's making love." He gave a high-pitched laugh that ended in a spasm of coughing.

"Juan Flores—that's who you are, isn't it? Flores, this young woman would be ruined if anyone knew she was here. I cannot allow you or anyone else to see her. But, I can have her call to you. Then you'd know that it's not Donovan. Although I think you know that. Patrick Donovan would never be skulking in a house, out of sight."

"Nor will I!" Bets cried, her clear voice audible. "I'm not ashamed of loving you. Or afraid either! John, I *will* show myself—"

Carew had spun around, holding her tightly, trying to keep her from the window. This was Patrick's daughter, and how better for an enemy to find vengeance than to put a bullet through her? But the girl was totally convinced the danger was to himself, and she struggled with surprising strength.

She had not finished dressing. The black breeches were on again, but not the ruffled shirt, only a thin camisole, tied with a blue ribbon above her breasts. In his anxiety his grasp was awkward, she twisted unexpectedly, and the delicate gauze ripped and fell away just as she stepped proudly into view.

Bets gasped, covering her exposed breasts with her hands.

But the outlaw leader had already turned his back. "To hear her voice is enough. I am a man of honor," he shouted, walking away into the sunlit canyon.

His final words came drifting back less distinctly. "The posse is after my men, and I'm leaving for now. But tell Patrick Donovan to be watchful always. For Juan Flores will not forget!"

CHAPTER THIRTEEN

EVER AFTERWARD, BETS REMEMBERED THEIR ride back to town with a sense of wonder at her own blindness.

John Carew did not wish to linger after the departure of Flores, saying he still felt an urgency about finding her father. She set straight any disorder they'd made in the small room, and smoothed the serape across the bed. Then she rode off beside him, quite lost in a haze of happiness.

Only once did they stop. She had spotted along the roadside, the amethyst-blue blossoms of hyacinth, those hardy, bare-stemmed flowers the Californios called *saitas*. Thinking them the prettiest wild flowers she had yet seen, she delayed long enough to dig up a few of the little bulbs, as she intended to replant them at home, living reminders of this day. She packed them tenderly in the crown of her hat, then hung it again from the saddlehorn. Meanwhile, Carew remained on his bay and watched her, lost in thought.

They reentered Los Angeles on the same street from which they had departed hours before, but now finding it quiet and deserted. The race was long since over, and the crowd dispersed.

Then he broke the silence Bets had been assuring herself was one of intimacy. "I can only ask your forgiveness."

"Forgiveness? Why? John, I came to you willingly! I am so very happy, and proud too."

He leaned across their horses' necks and took her delicately featured face gently between his tanned hands. "Thank you, Bets. You almost make me feel I am still what Juan Flores calls 'a man of honor'. At least, by some miracle, we met no one we know, going or coming, and with any luck your reputation will not suffer."

"What others think of me has never seemed very important," she said, smiling.

"That's perhaps because you've never been criticized."

With his own words, the riddle of Mary Reyes became a little clearer. For the first time, he speculated what it could have been like for her in Boston, a woman reputed to have deserted husband and child. Perhaps she had good reason not to be forthright a second time!

Bets felt impatient. To her, this conversation was merely disappointing. It was dear of him of course, to be so concerned about her good name, but she wouldn't care who saw them if he'd just take her in his arms again!

"Please, John, ride home with me!" she urged. "Surely it can't matter if we meet the whole town now."

"It would matter, so late in the day." He shook his head. "I know there are things you want to talk about, as do I, but I'd still like to find Patrick. If by some chance he's at the house and you see him before I do, will you tell him what I told you? And Bets, you'll hear from me tomorrow. I promise."

He kissed her lightly on the cheek, and with that she had to be satisfied. She rode home alone.

By noon the next day, he still had not appeared. Bets found the morning hours tedious and long without him, and at the dinner table she attempted, as women in love have often done, to introduce her beloved's name into the conversation purely for the pleasure of hearing it spoken aloud.

"Papa, did Mr. Carew find you?" she asked. "He had news for you."

"So I finally learned. How I would have liked to join that posse yesterday! It was my bad luck to be called away, and during the biggest race of all time! I even missed the finish."

"Where were you? I searched for you."

"Here at home, putting out a raging fire in the wood stove, if you would believe it. Flora panicked, I suppose she thought the house would burn down. Anyway, she rushed off and when she couldn't find Jeb, she found me. A fine thing—the servants both see the big race of the year while the master runs home to put out the flames!" He laughed in high good humor.

"That explains it then," Bets said slowly, remembering Captain Warner's fruitless search. But why in the world had that unhappy man mentioned Rancho Allison? Of course he had been very drunk, and he probably didn't know what he was saying. "Something made me think you'd gone to the rancho. So we—I—"

"To Allison? Odd, that's what John Carew thought too. He said if he hadn't found me at last, he intended to ride out there."

"He *intended* to?"

"Yes, and fine of him to make the effort. But it would have been a long ride for nothing, I think. The Flores boy is doubtless too cowardly to challenge me without a gang to back him up, and it will be some time, I imagine, before his Manilas will dare show their faces here again . . . What a race that was yesterday! Were you surprised that Black Swan won? Lucky for me he did, and for you too. We would have lost this house otherwise! It was the lighter weight that made the difference, just as I thought it would. Those horses were perfectly matched."

"You might have lost the house?" echoed his sister. She had been sitting at her place saying nothing, apparently not attending the conversation. But Patrick's remark at last jolted her out of her preoccupation.

"I had no choice, Mary Frances. Manuel Garfias sold me Allison, but he didn't give it to me! I need money to buy cattle, and there was none left. So, I bet this house. Black Swan won, didn't he?"

"Someday you'll lose everything," Mary predicted. Her tone lacked its usual fondness.

"Then what did Mr. Carew say?" put in Bets. She was still intent on being devious.

"I told you! The posse. And he warned me about Juan Flores. But Carew's the one who'd better be careful. I'm not riding a lonely trail up the coast today. He is."

Bets stared at him and her heart seemed to stop. Then it began to beat again, a slow heavy thud against her breast. The first suspicion of abandonment gripped her. She couldn't speak.

Her shock went unnoticed, because Mary, evidently surprised herself, demanded, "He's left for San Jose? Wasn't that rather sudden?"

Patrick shrugged. "Perhaps it was a good time for some of the Aguirre men who accompanied him to leave their own work. And no doubt he felt he shouldn't wait longer. Right now there's plenty of grass."

Bets wet her lips. "Papa, that can't be so! He promised—that is, he told me he would be here today—"

But had he? What had he really promised? She wasn't certain any more. Aware that Aunt Mary was giving her a sharp look, she managed to add, "The grazing must surely be better later on? Every day the grass gets longer—"

"Perhaps it grows, perhaps not. If there's no more rain this season, all the vegetation will simply dry up, and judging by the hot sunny days we've been having, I think he was very wise to start now."

Bets listened, trying to believe that the lack of rain was reason enough for his abrupt departure. But the food on her plate had acquired the look and taste of ashes.

She finally learned the truth late that afternoon, when a note arrived, delivered by Jeb.

The servant came to her where she knelt at the side of the patio, transplanting the hyacinth bulbs she had carried home the day before. Her aunt customarily took a long walk in the cooler part of the day, so Bets was alone.

As Jeb approached, she glanced up at him hopefully.

"Miss Betsey, Mister Carew asked me to give you this here letter, but not 'til I seen you was by yourself."

"Thank you, Jeb." Oh, she should not have doubted!

Here was his explanation, his promise to return to her soon!

She could barely contain her impatience until Jeb had gone and she could rip open the seal. Bets read the message, then read it again in utter disbelief.

I only hope you will find it in your heart to forgive me for taking this, the coward's way, after what happened between us.

I'm leaving Los Angeles, and I won't return. You see, when I told you there was someone else, it was true, and there still is someone else. That being so, I know I could never make you happy. Be happy, Bets! You're too beautiful, too strong and alive, to settle for my poor second-best.

John

She folded the note and put it in the pocket of her skirt. Since one small bulb remained uncovered, she dug a hole with her fingers in the dirt to plant it. She was surprised to see how badly her hands were shaking.

She rose slowly to her feet. Although Bets was all alone inside the high walls, she walked slowly with her head high, back along the tiled veranda.

In the privacy of her bedroom she took the note from her pocket to read once again. Then, in a frenzy, she ripped the paper into smaller and smaller pieces, until at last she flung herself on her bed, racked by a storm of tears.

"Are you sick, honey?" Patrick asked, poking his head into the darkness. His voice was anxious, but he ventured a small joke. "When my girl doesn't come to supper, something terrible must be wrong."

"I'm fine, Papa," she said listlessly. "But don't bring that candle in here. I must have strained my eyes somehow." He must not see her face all puffed and red, or he would demand to know the cause of her wretchedness. He wouldn't rest until he did know, and she didn't want him charging off to shoot John. Not that she'd mind that much, she assured herself, but Papa might end up being hung!

"Come out, darling girl, and I'll tell you a bit of news," Patrick said coaxingly.

"What's that?" She was forced to ask, although she wished he'd go away.

Bets hadn't stirred from her bed but he seemed satisfied. "Miguel Aguirre sought me out today. What do you suppose he wanted?"

"Oh, I don't know. I suppose to interview you again for his paper. Now that you're not only a hero, but rich besides."

Patrick was encouraged because she sounded more like herself. "Even for heroes, one interview is enough," he said. "No, this concerned you. I may as well come right out with it. He asked for your hand."

"Did he?" She pretended interest. "That's surprising. Teo believes he and Felipa have an understanding."

As she spoke, the tall figure and handsome, ascetic face of Miguel Aguirre was clear in her mind. Knowing of the gossip that coupled his name with Felipa's she had regarded him as a friend and even, following Teodocia's example, as an older brother. He had been so courteous, so correct in his manner, that this was easy. And yet, hadn't there been something in the way he spoke to her? And the admiration in his deep-set eyes, the ardor! Could she in all honesty say she was surprised?

If only she cared! Oh, why couldn't this proposal have come from John! If only it was he who had spoken to Papa!

"I can assure you there's no understanding between him and Felipa," commented Patrick. "He is a Californio and has a well-developed sense of honor. He would never give a woman cause to think he cared for her when he did not." Under the cover of night, Bets winced, guessing what her father would say of John Carew, if he knew.

"So how do you feel about his proposal?" Patrick

continued. "Shall we refuse? Or do you want to consider it?"

"It is a surprise—" Bets repeated.

"Oh, come now, Bets. You must have realized. He calls here so often. Anyone reading the *Star* could hardly fail to guess what was on his mind. He's always filled any empty spaces with an essay or his short and really excellent verse, and until now the subject was invariably our wild, remote South Coast, 'the farthest Eden' as he calls it. A very apt phrase too, to my way of thinking.

"Lately, however, he's been writing a flood of love poems, and they're for you. Haven't you even noticed them?"

"Love poems? No, why would I? How do you know they're for me?"

"He admitted as much—told me he meant them as a kind of serenade. Here's the latest one—today's." Patrick thrust forward the newspaper, but then said, "Oh, you can't read it in the dark. Let me . . . Listen, this is called *El Resentimiento,* and begins, 'Of sorrows, and loves, let us sing, let us weep—' "

"It's nice, I'm sure, Papa, but don't go on. Poetry —and so melancholy! What a strange way to court . . . To tell you the truth, Papa, I'm afraid that until now I haven't thought much about Miguel, one way or the other."

"Then you want to refuse?"

Did she? Yesterday, the answer to her father's question would have been an immediate yes. But now her shock and despair were giving way to a deep suffocating anger. If John didn't care for her, someone else did! Didn't it prove that she could have her choice of all of Los Angeles, if the most sought-after bachelor in town proposed to her? She'd like to show John Carew!

"I don't really know," she said. "Give me a day or two."

"Take a week, a month, or forever if you like! A mother would be eager to marry off her daughter to such an eligible suitor, but not a father. I'm afraid I'd miss you."

"Thank you, Papa . . . Are you *quite* certain about

Miguel and Felipa? I wouldn't want to make her miserable."

"I am quite certain."

"Papa, will you ask Flora to bring me a little supper on a tray? I believe I am hungry, after all."

CHAPTER FOURTEEN

"MISS TEO'S HERE," FLORA ANNOUNCED FROM the parlor door. Her formal tone was oddly at variance with her appearance. She wore, as did her mistresses, a cloth wrapped around her hair as protection against the clouds of dust that would presumably be raised in the course of their spring house-cleaning. This chore had been a customary and annual event of Mary and Bets' lives in the east, and they undertook it here without question, none of the three considering that the lack of a hard winter might render such seasonal efforts unnecessary.

"Ask her to come in. And then help me with this rug, please, Flora," Mary said. "We'll take it out to the patio and beat it."

Bets was seated at a table laden with great piles of silver hollowware that she was in the process of polishing. She had agreed with unaccustomed meekness to do a task she ordinarily disliked, because the chance to sit and rest was a welcome one. The hot weather seemed to be affecting her more than it had in Boston. She felt tired and listless.

Teodocia ran into the parlor, tossed her furled yellow parasol into a corner, and at once took up a soft cloth to help with the polishing. But as soon as Mary and Flora had tugged the rolled-up carpet from the room, she stopped and turned to face her friend. Bets saw that she could hardly contain her misery.

"Teo, what is it? Darling, don't look so!"

"How else can I look? Garth is gone. I've lost him."

"Gone? That's impossible, you goose. Garth wouldn't go away. He loves you!" He did, too. Garth wasn't like John, Bets thought grimly.

"He's joined the Manilas."

Bets stared at her, disbelieving and speechless.

"Yes, it's true. He gambled everything away, and then began borrowing from that bandit leader, Juan Flores. When all the money was gone, he was honor-bound to do what Flores wanted, in order to repay him."

"Honor-bound? But the Manilas are outlaws! Is it honorable to become a thief?"

"That's what I asked him last night when he came to tell me. I wept, I—I clung to him——"

"And he wouldn't listen?"

"I don't think he wanted to listen. He's been terribly unhappy lately, and I suppose the excitement of going with Flores—oh, Betsey, if only we could have been married, none of this would have happened!"

"Does your mother know yet? About the Manilas?"

"Everyone knows. How could such a dreadful thing be kept secret? She knows, and I needn't tell you what she said."

"No, I can guess. Oh, Teo, what are you going to do? Perhaps if you promised to run away with him, find a priest to marry you——"

Bets stopped abruptly, wishing she had bitten her tongue before offering such a suggestion. The news of Garth's desperate decision, she was finding, chilled her. Until now he had had her utmost sympathy, as she listened over the last months to the story of his difficulties. She hadn't minded when once or twice he'd called at the Donovan house, just to have a few minutes alone with the young girl he loved. But she'd wondered, even then, how he could simply sit down and let misfortune roll over him the way he did. Surely, with a little gumption, he could have fought back! And now, the suspicion was growing in her mind that he was not just immature and unlucky—but weak.

She was greatly relieved to hear Teodocia's reply, even though the words were bitter. "Run where? Both of us join the Manilas? I thought of eloping with him

once before, and I should have, but we had nothing,
nowhere to live, and before we could leave town
Mama would have sent men to bring me back . . . No,
Betsey, I may kill myself."

"Teo! That's a terrible thing to say!" Bets was
shocked. Even in the depths of her own raging despair,
she had never considered such a measure and never
would.

"Then what am I to do?" Teodocia at last burst into
tears and threw herself into her friend's embrace.

Bets held her tight and tried to console her. "Hush,"
she whispered. "Please, Teo! Wait to see what Garth
does. He may even change his mind. And meanwhile,
you'll find that the time will pass. I'm here, and we'll
be together just as we have been, riding and talking—"

The younger girl pulled away. "But you won't be,"
she said sadly. "I'll be alone and I can't bear it."

"What do you mean, I won't be?"

"You'll be married. Married women do different
things. They run houses, they have children . . . We
will never be the same."

It was a moment before Bets answered.

"Where did you hear that? I mean, that I might be
married?"

"I don't know where. Why do you look so surprised?
Even Mama talked about it this morning when she
was so angry. Why couldn't *her* daughter have attracted a fine young man like Miguel Aguirre? Why
had *she* been singled out to be so accursed?"

"I had no idea there was such a rumor!"

"Isn't it true then? You aren't going to marry him?"

"I . . . haven't decided."

"Well, that does mean he's asked you. Surely you're
pleased! Unless you don't care for him?"

Bets was silent, for this was a question she had not
yet been able to answer for herself. One day she
thought *yes*, the next *no*. Admittedly she liked Miguel
and enjoyed his company. She admired him too for the
way he read difficult books and could talk about things
and places she'd never even heard of. But were liking
and respect enough? Was this caring?

She could not forget the way she had been instantly

drawn to John Carew, as if, from the first time she saw
him, an invisible magnet had caught hold of her and
made her helpless, and in the end sent her running
across the room into his arms. She had wanted him so
much that everything else was blotted out. Would she
ever want anyone else in the same way?

Most of the Californio girls barely knew the men
they were courted by and eventually married, and as
far as she could tell, they seemed happy. So perhaps
that wonderful magic thing that had happened to her
when she and John lay together happened to all married people when they were in bed together, and
would happen with Miguel too! But—would it? Oh,
she was so ignorant! If only she could be sure!

Then, like a dash of cold water, would come the
reminder that John was gone, never to return. She had
best not make comparisons nor ask too much. The
cleverest, handsomest man in town wanted her, he
loved her; and even if her misgivings proved right,
would not half a loaf with him be better than nothing
at all? She couldn't spend the rest of her life pining
for someone who didn't care! She should take Miguel,
and as Carew had advised her in his note—be happy.

But again, there was Felipa. Whenever, as now, she
came to the point of acceptance, a sense of guilt
nagged at her, held her back. Patrick could say there
had been no commitment, and surely there hadn't; but
Bets knew in her heart that Felipa was counting on
Miguel for herself.

It was true, she mused, she owed Felipa nothing.
The tall Californio girl had only given her the horse
Estrella on Don Diego's express command. In fact,
she had never spoken a word to Bets that wasn't tinged
with scornful dislike, nor encouraged her in the least
toward friendship.

And yet . . . Bets admired pride, and Felipa was
proud. She liked spirit—having, she'd been told by her
father, more than enough of her own—and Felipa's
prickly independence engaged her sympathy. Could
she be the one to humiliate this woman, making her
the subject of fresh gossip, while taking the one man
she seemed to care for?

"I hope you don't marry him," Teodocia said after a moment, "because I'll miss you. But that's selfish. After all, as Mama said, he's a fine man." She picked up her parasol. "There now, I'm better. At least I'm calm enough to go home, and I don't want to have to make small talk with your aunt."

There was a coolness in her soft voice Bets had never heard before, as though she was anticipating their separation, and steeling herself to lose still another of those on whom she had lavished her affection.

Bets let her go, knowing that in all honesty she could not yet give reassurance.

The day wore on and Bets felt the unaccustomed lethargy slowing every movement she made. The evening meal revived her a little, but when Mary said, "The servants and I are going to Mass. Don't you want to come?" she refused.

"I'll stay and give Papa his supper when he comes home."

"He should be back soon . . . Aren't you well, Betsey? I don't know what it is, but you hardly seem yourself."

"Of course I'm well." Unwilling to confess any weakness to her aunt, she added, "I'm just lazy. Housecleaning tires me more than riding all day in the countryside. It always has."

"Very well then. I'll tell Flora to leave the stew in the kettle."

The two servants, dressed in their best clothes, came from their quarters, Flora proudly carrying Flower. The little girl's black ringlets were barely visible under a bonnet embroidered with tiny red flowers. Her crisply ironed dress was white organza.

Mary smoothed on her gloves, started out the door, then hesitated.

Bets glanced at her. "What's the matter?"

"I don't know. Do you believe in premonitions, Betsey? I have the oddest feeling—that I shouldn't leave."

"Really, Aunt Mary! Because of me? I'm not a child. I'll be quite all right."

"Yes, I suppose so. I can't explain it, and I've always been cursed with such a wretchedly strong imagination. Well, come along Flora, Jeb."

After they departed Bets sat back in her chair, feeling a new wave of fatigue, so insistent that it stirred in her a vague alarm. There had been cases of typhoid in the town. Could she be ill?

She shook herself. No, this had been a long day, with unseasonable heat. If she could just lie on her bed for a few minutes . . .

But there were footsteps on the porch. Someone rapped sharply. And then again.

"Yes, I'm coming." She got to her feet and went to the door.

Felipa was there, waiting.

"Good evening, Elizabeth. May I come in?"

"Of course. Please come into the parlor. I'm sorry things are so disordered—the rug is still in the patio being aired."

Felipa gave a short nod. She didn't bother to comment. Standing stiffly beside the large table on which silver bowls were laid ready for the morrow's polishing, she drummed the surface with her long restless fingers.

"I saw Señora Reyes and your servants on their way to Mass, and I know your father is with mine at the cockfights. It occurred to me that you'd be alone here . . . and we can talk."

"I'm pleased that you came," Bets said politely. "Will you sit down? I'll get us some coffee."

Felipa appeared not to hear. She remained where she was, and her fingers continued tapping. But she turned her head and her eyes, hot with enmity, bored into Bets'.

"So you are going to marry Miguel."

In her dismay, Bets tried to look away, but Felipa's will was the stronger.

"Well? It's true, is it not?"

"I don't know! That is, nothing is decided yet."

"You mean that *you* haven't decided! I suppose it's fashionable with you Americanos to keep a man dangling. But he has asked you?"

"Felipa, I don't want to talk about this, not with you!"

"Is it true? Has he?"

"Yes."

Felipa took a long breath. "I see."

Bets was unable to endure any longer the anguish so unmistakable in that long narrow face. "You are the reason I've hesitated!" she cried, "I don't want to take him if you care so much, and I won't! Please, I'll tell him—"

"You'll tell him what?" lashed out Felipa. "That you give him back to me? You'll say, 'Go to Felipa! You are not good enough for me'? It's far far too late for that, Elizabeth. If I didn't know, and he had come to me, I'd have married him. You are of course aware of that. But what you don't understand is that I'd have been good for him, better than you could ever be, because we're alike, he and I! We're Californios, and more than that, we treasure the same things— the ranchos and cattle and horses, our way of life.

"But why talk about what might have been! Do you think I'd take your leavings, you conceited fool? He wants you, let him have you, and bad fortune to you both. I wouldn't accept him if you died tonight!"

Long afterward Bets remembered protesting to herself, She's wrong! She must be. Miguel cares nothing about ranchos and cattle or surely he wouldn't live here in town and work so hard to build a newspaper . . .

But then she forgot Miguel, and was conscious only that her sympathy had survived, even though Felipa's scathing contempt roused an answering anger.

"I'm sorry," she said evenly.

Felipa took another shuddering breath. At last, more quietly, she said, "It must be a great satisfaction. You've taken everything."

"Everything?"

"You have Estrella. She too was mine once."

"Felipa, your father gave me Estrella, I didn't take her, as you say. I didn't even ask for her. I didn't ask for Miguel, either."

"No, women like you have no need to ask . . . How is she?"

"Estrella?" Bets felt bewildered.

"Is she well-cared for?" A look of cunning had crept into Felipa's restless eyes. She smiled coldly. "May I see her?"

Bets told herself she should be pleased Felipa's attention had shifted away from her and her marriage to Miguel. Yet she continued to feel uncomfortable, and wary. "If you like. Please come out to the stable."

She took up the candlestick and led the way. When she had opened the stable door and they entered, she set the light on a shelf. Felipa did not stop, but walked past her, going at once to Estrella's stall.

The horse nickered softly as she approached.

"She knows you still," Bets said.

Felipa stroked Estrella's head, caressed her around the ears, all the time murmuring something in a tone that seemed to delight the animal. The sable neck arched, and the velvet-soft nose rubbed against Felipa's hand.

"Estrellita mia!"

Bets watched, wondering why her uneasiness was growing.

Then suddenly, with a thrill of horror, she understood. A lethal gun had appeared in Felipa's hand.

"No! Oh, no!" Bets stumbled forward.

"Stand back! Unless you'd rather I shot you?"

"But why! Oh God, Felipa, think! You love her."

"Yes. But she isn't mine, she's yours. I can't kill Miguel. But I can stop you from having her."

She patted the horse once more, a lingering touch of farewell, and then, taking careful aim, Felipa held the gun against Estrella's white star and fired.

The mare's body jerked once in a violent spasm. Then, for what seemed a long time, she stood, legs stiff, her eyes glazed. At last, with a thud that shook the stable walls, she fell sideways.

Felipa put the weapon back in the pocket of her skirt and walked out, moving stiffly, her head high. Tears were running unchecked down her sallow cheeks.

Bets sank to her knees on the straw covered floor. At once she had decided what should be done, but she couldn't muster the strength even to approach the stall.

She must. And before Papa came home. But the room was spinning around her.

When her vision cleared, she was lying on the floor. She smelled the sweet dry scent of straw, and at the same time she heard her name being repeated in a loud bellow.

"Miss Betsey! Are you all right, Miss Betsey?"

For a moment, she didn't recognize him. Standing over her the way he was, legs astraddle, he looked enormous.

"Mr. Bishop . . . ?"

"Are you all right, Miss Betsey?" His anxiety, she realized, was making him shout.

"Yes. Yes, I am. If I might take your hand . . ." She really did feel very weak. He reached down, and in one movement lifted her from the floor and set her on her feet, where she stood swaying. She would have fallen but for his big hands tight on her arms.

The stall! Seeing it, she remembered, and the dizziness disappeared. She pulled away, trying to speak.

"Easy there. You're not still faint?"

She shook her head. Gesturing toward the silent and apparently empty stall, she forced out the words, "In there—Look in there."

Immediately he obeyed. He picked up the candle and held it over the stall door. After one look inside, he gave a whistle of disbelief.

"Was there something wrong with that little horse?" he asked grimly.

She struggled to answer him. Her throat seemed to have closed, and she knew she was losing control. "No, no, it was—"

She dissolved into heaving sobs, and then as naturally as though they had been friends for years, he took her in an enveloping embrace and held her close.

"There now . . ." One hand was gently smoothing the long tousled hair back from her wet face. She would never have guessed that deep confident voice could sound so quiet, nor his caress be so comforting.

When at length she was calmer, he led her, one muscular arm supporting her at the waist, to a bale of hay. When she was seated, he faced her.

"Now tell me about it, because I'm mighty puzzled. I take it the horse was sound. I can't figure you shooting a fine little mare like that for any cause whatsoever, so it must have been Felipa Rodriguez. When I came, she was running away from here like the devil himself was on her heels."

"Yes, Felipa shot Estrella. But—oh, Mr. Bishop, she had a reason . . . and in a way, I'm as much to blame as she. I . . ." Bets stopped, once more overcome.

"Miss Betsey, understand this—you've only to ask me, for anything. If you need help, I'm here to give it."

Bets steadied her shaking voice and was able to answer. "I do need help. Thank you. You see, she killed the horse because she'd been expecting—hoping, that is—to marry Miguel Aguirre. I'm afraid it was a terrible shock to her when she learned that I'm going to marry him."

Did she see the flash of disappointment that seemed to cloud the rugged face above hers? Perhaps not, because as quick as the turn of a shutter it was gone. He was the same as before, yet not quite the same.

"I can't have heard you right. Are you telling me she gunned down that poor critter just out of jealousy?"

Bets shrank a little from his anger. She said hurriedly, "I guess that explains it well enough. And the problem is that—being to blame—I don't want anyone to know what she did." She paused, not because she was wondering if he could be trusted—for some reason she took that for granted—but because what she was about to ask him to do struck her as horrible. "So it's important that when Papa sees Estrella, he believes she *had* to be destroyed. I've been steeling myself to—oh, but I don't think I have the strength anyway!"

"You want him to think the horse stepped in a gopher hole, is that it?" He did understand, she thought gratefully. "There's no time to lose then, Miss Betsey. Patrick will be coming home any minute. I was to meet him here about getting up a new posse. Go outside. And don't worry, I'll manage it."

She dragged herself to her feet obediently.

"Just one thing I've got to say, Miss Betsey. If someone killed my horse, I wouldn't be covering up for the low-down snake!"

Bets shook her head and didn't answer. Already he was walking toward Estrella's stall, and she was sickened, imagining what would take place. She ran out into the patio.

When she heard the sound, she thought at first it was another shot. Then she realized that it was the clean clear crack of a horse's leg being broken.

CHAPTER FIFTEEN

THE BANNS HAD BEEN POSTED THREE TIMES, each a week apart. Anyone who could show just cause why the wedding should not take place was instructed to come forward. No one had, although Mary ventured once to voice her misgivings.

For the sake of privacy, she asked Bets to come to her room, and the girl complied with reluctance, not knowing how to refuse. She had seen her aunt's latest watercolor on a previous occasion and had no wish to see it again, ever. Unfortunately, the picture had been framed and now hung in full view above Mary's bed.

Doubtless this lowering scene was her best work. Even Bets, shocked as she had been to come on such an unexpected and painful reminder, had recognized its extraordinary power. The sheep as well as the man appeared exhausted and thirsty as they emerged from a vast, gray-brown plain. One could almost feel the dryness of the air, and the bristly touch of the scrubby clumps of brush. Yet the canyon through which the animals slowly plodded had a small growth of chaparral, dusty but green; and ahead, like a breath of hope, was the misty purple sage.

Diffidently, Mary had asked her opinion.

"I—It's very good," Bets had answered through stiff lips. "Has it a title?"

"Yes, *Angels Gate,* the name some of the immigrants have given Cajon Pass. You see, I tried to imagine what it was like for Mr. Carew—and all those brave hardy souls who push across the plains in wagons—to wind down through the pass and see the mountain flanks turn wooded, and the land turn green. To be finally on the doorstep of little Los Angeles, after all the hardships and constant danger, must seem a miracle, don't you think?"

"I suppose so." She had concentrated on studying the sheep, in order not to glance again at John. She would hide her misery from Aunt Mary if it killed her! "I don't see how you can make things seem so real and lifelike, when you don't have a model, or anything to copy. I suppose artists just have remarkable memories for colors and shapes and such. Even for . . . someone's face."

"Yes," Mary warmed to her apparent interest. "But I couldn't work from memory alone. I don't think anyone could. I've had to ride out several times lately just to get the feel of the landscape again. And I did have sketches to work from." She didn't elaborate further, and Bets escaped, resolving never to see that picture again if she could possibly avoid doing so.

Today, entering the room, she studiously kept her eyes from seeking the space above the bed. Instead she glanced about, wondering as she often had before, how a woman so fastidious about her clothing, and so insistent on neatness elsewhere in the house, could surround herself happily with such a clutter of easels, watercolor boxes, tubes of oil paint that she used occasionally, unfinished charcoal drawings, and other paraphernalia.

"You wanted to talk to me?"

"Yes," Mary said. She sounded timid. "Forgive me, but I must ask you. Have you really given enough thought to the difficulties of this marriage?"

Bets was taken aback. "You don't like Miguel?"

"I certainly have nothing against him. Doubtless he's a fine man. Only I'd hoped, as I told you once before, that you wouldn't marry a Spaniard. It's not easy, at best, to fit into a different culture or to understand someone whose background has been so different from yours."

She was of course thinking of her own unhappy marriage, and Bets reminded herself that her aunt could not be blamed for having such reservations. "It seems to me that Miguel is just a man like any other," Bets answered, "and no different because of his ancestry. Besides, he isn't a Spaniard, he's a Californio. Have you forgotten that the Aguirres lived in Mexico for generations before they came here?"

"They lived there. But you'll notice they didn't intermarry with the Indians. It's a matter of strong pride with certain of the families here that the bloodlines are still pure." Mary, out of some memory of her own, gave a little involuntary shiver.

"Come now, Aunt Mary, what do you expect? That he'll beat me?" A shortness of temper, so rare for her until lately, had boiled suddenly to the surface.

"No." Mary sighed, and said ruefully, as if speaking to herself, "Sometimes I think your father's decision not to remarry has been a mistake! Even a stepmother would be more help than I! However, I must try to make you see. Betsey, think what directions your new life may take, how different it may be from anything you've ever known, even in California! Suppose Miguel for some reason gives up his work here in town—"

"He won't! Not possibly. He loves the newspaper."

"Nevertheless, have you considered what living on an isolated rancho would be like?"

"Of course! I enjoyed every day I spent at the Brinkmans'. And this time, remember, I would be the mistress, not just a visitor."

"Oh?" Their eyes met, and Bets looked away, uncomfortably aware that Don Sebastian, even crippled as he was, might or might not turn over the reins of the house to her.

"Anyway, it's all decided," she said, raising her chin, and wishing the picture on the wall had eyes and ears. "Our wedding date is set. So it's quite useless, your trying to interfere."

"My dear, I wouldn't! And probably I'm wrong to worry. Everyone else seems happy enough at the news."

That was true. Congratulations and gifts were pouring in. For unless one or the other of them had a change of heart, she was to marry Miguel.

Leaving Mary, Bets made her way through the sunshine along the tiles of the patio walk. Beside her feet bloomed the wild hyacinth, its hardiness no longer the irritant it had been. Infuriated that the flowers should continue to grow, when her happiness, of which they were to be a living keepsake, had withered, in the early days she had been tempted to pull up the long bare stems and let them die. But somehow she did not, and now the impulse was gone.

He didn't know it, of course, but this was Miguel's gift to her. Her badly bruised self-esteem was on the mend.

Oh, how hot the sun was! Beating down on her unprotected head, it made her dizzy, and she sank gratefully onto the wooden bench before Flora and Jeb's door. The patio shimmered, seemed to rock sideways, and steadied, and she shut her eyes. When she opened them again, Flora was bathing her forehead with a cool cloth, and calling her name anxiously.

"What happened?"

"You done passed out," Flora said.

"It must have been the heat—"

"Ain't that hot," Flora objected, giving her a critical look. "You certain sure you ain't sick?"

Bets shook her head, too languid to answer.

"Maybe you jest tired. All brides is tired jest before they weddings."

"Yes . . . How's Flower?" This question was an unfailing distraction, and as expected, Flora's dark brown face softened. "Flower, she so beautiful! Jeb say she God's own chile."

"Indeed she is." Bets hesitated, and the desire to confide became too strong to be resisted. "Flora, there really is something the matter with me, something I don't understand."

"You doan feel so good?"

Bets did not attempt to be evasive, although she was about to embark on a subject no lady should discuss. She said, "It's my time of month. I'm late—six weeks at least. And I'm ill, I think that's why I almost fainted just now. What can be wrong with me? Oh, Flora, I do feel so miserable!"

Flora eyed her warily. "Lots of things causes a body to be late."

"Lots of things? Like what?"

"This chang'ble weather, maybe. Maybe something you done. Miss Bets, iff'n you was some other girl, I'd say—"

"What?" Bets looked at her curiously.

"I'd say you been with a man. I'd say you was with chile. But Miss Bets, I know you ain't done nothin' like that—"

"Flora, I have! At least, I've done what you mean —once."

They stared at each other. Bets was as shocked as Flora at her confession.

"I didn't know that just once could get you in trouble! I thought you had to be a . . . a loose woman." She blushed. "I suppose it wouldn't have stopped me, but can you believe I didn't know?"

Flora obviously couldn't. Finally she shrugged. "Reckon with no mammy, nobody tole you much. You and Miss Mary ain't close enough . . . What man was it, honey? Mister Michael?" Flora made no attempt to master Spanish names.

"No. John Carew. Oh, I shouldn't have told you!"

"Tole me what? I didn't hear nothin' . . . But why ain't he going to marry you, stead of Mister Michael?"

"Because he doesn't love me," Bets said in a low strained voice. "He's gone now and he won't be back. At least he knows nothing of this. He never will!"

"You shoulda got your pappy after him with a shot-gun," Flora said grimly.

"He cares for someone else." Bets, remembering what Felipa had said, echoed some of her words. "Anyway, if he came crawling, I wouldn't have him! I don't want another woman's leavings."

Flora gave her a shrewd look and said nothing.

"I'm happy enough to be marrying Miguel."

"And soon enough too!" Flora smiled with relief at the thought. "He'll never know that chile ain't his'n. Miss Bets, you one smart young lady."

"A child!" For the first time, the significance of what they had deduced really sank into her mind. "Oh, but I can't! I can't marry Miguel and lie to him! I'll have to tell him."

"Tell him what?" Flower had awakened; they could hear her murmuring inside the room behind them. But this time Flora's attention remained fixed where it was.

"That I'm with child! Because I'm sure now that you're right. I should have guessed for myself."

"You must be crazy, Miss Bets!" Flora dropped down beside her mistress on the bench.

"Don't you see? I must! But who the father is will be our secret, yours and mine, and no one will ever know that it isn't Miguel's. Do you promise? Flora, promise! Swear it! I'd be ruined, if—"

"Ain't I that's goin' to ruin you, miss, it's you. Ain't you lived here long enough to know what Spanish gentlemen is like? They proud! They won't go to marry some woman what's carrying another man's brat."

"Do you *promise?*"

"You can trust Flora." This was said flatly, and Bets knew it was true. So long as Flora retained a memory of anything, she would never forget that Bets had saved Flower from the sea.

But how awful! Overwhelmed by the enormity of what had happened to her, Bets turned and buried her face against Flora's shoulder. A flood of tears stained Flora's dress.

Flora crooned to her softly, just as she would to Flower. "There, there, chile. You be all right . . ."

The parlor was very quiet. Sequestered there, Bets could hear the wedding preparations proceeding apace in the rest of the house. Through the wall from the kitchen came the chatter of the cooks, who had begun weeks before, almost as soon as the banns were posted, to provide a feast for hundreds of people. Flora, aided by the Rodriguez servants, would be re-cleaning the silver and polishing furniture that already shone. And seated around the big dining table would be Señora Brinkman, Teodocia (still pale and haunted), and Aunt Mary, all of them engaged in making *cascarones,* those fragile eggshells, tinted all colors and filled with minute perfumed pieces of gilt paper, that would be broken merrily over the heads of the guests during the wedding dance. Directing every-thing, quietly giving orders and organizing the festivi-ties with the precision of a general planning a campaign, was Arcadia Stearns. Out of friendship and courtesy, she had undertaken to do this, as Mary was unfamiliar with the local wedding customs. Arcadia's voice, from behind the closed door, sounded serene. And why not? Only the two who were alone together in this room were aware that there might not be a wedding.

Miguel seemed a mockery of a bridegroom as he stood at the window in his rich and festive clothing, his blue velveteen trousers embroidered in silver, his white silk shirt and white silk sash. For his olive face had paled, and his slender body was stiff with the shock of what she had confessed.

Bets felt cold fear.

She knew him so little! Gone was the affable, hand-some man, so kind to Teodocia, so flattering to her. In his place was this implacable stranger.

What had she done—telling him?

She realized her hands were trembling and she thrust them behind her. He must not see how fright-ened she was!

But the silence was becoming unbearable. If she could only think of something else, *anything,* instead of waiting to hear the sentence of disgrace she knew was coming . . . Then oddly—because these days even

the thought of eating made her queasy, she found her
mind running over, like a rhythmic litany, the many
varied foods on which the cooks in the kitchen even
now were laboring: barbecued pig, roasted beef,
roasted chicken, tortillas; beans with chili, refried
beans, dark brown bread, flan . . . the list went on,
and was endless and soothing, a little like telling Rosary beads. She would have said the Rosary instead,
but she was beginning to understand that she had
grievously sinned.

Miguel spoke at last, his back to her. His voice was
still controlled and ominously polite.

"May I ask why you have told me this, Elizabeth?
Most women would have gone to their graves hiding
such a secret, especially from a man to whom they
were betrothed. You could have deceived me easily!"

"But I did not wish to lie to you! It seemed that if
we were to be married to each other, the important
thing was not to deceive you. Not ever."

"But you have done so already!" Harsh bitterness
was edging his words. "You accepted my proposal to
be my wife, to belong to me . . . And already there
had been another man!" He swallowed, as though
some bile had risen in his throat. "You let me come
calling, and all the time you were—"

"No! It was not that way! You make it sound horrible, sordid, as though there were secret meetings with
him late at night while I smiled and encouraged you
by day. Oh, Miguel, I would think that a man like
you could understand! It was just a moment of madness that occurred only once! I've tried to tell you that.
And to give you my most solemn promise that such a
thing will never happen again." She paused. "There is
nothing else I can think of to say."

"And if we aren't married? What will happen to
you?"

Ah, that she didn't know! It was a black curtain
beyond which she dared not look. God alone could
predict the outcome! Girls of prominent families, even
in this sun-baked pueblo, simply didn't have bastard
children. If one did transgress occasionally, and common sense told her it was surely not impossible, she
could not imagine how the matter was managed, or

what the consequences might be. All her life, she had been shielded from that sort of kitchen gossip, so to the certainty of disgrace was added the terror of the unknown.

When she didn't answer, Miguel turned, and said incredulously, "You mean you have no plan at all?"

She shook her head. Then, as he continued to stare at her, she said, her voice faltering at last, "I hoped you might care enough for me to understand—to forgive—"

"For the love of God, Elizabeth, I am a man, a Californio! Can you imagine how I would feel if people sniggered behind their hands? They would fall down laughing in the streets to know that my pure little bride is carrying the child of another man!" His restraint had broken and he was shouting. She threw an apprehensive glance at the door.

"No one will know, Miguel, unless they hear us now! Miguel, listen to me. No one knows! No one!" *Except Flora.* Fearful of betraying herself, she turned quickly from the gaze of those tormented black eyes. She had lied to him, after all, but in this one small detail she had no choice. If Miguel should guess she'd confided in Flora, all would indeed be over. He would never endure such knowledge in a member of the household!

But to her relief, his angry thoughts were running along other lines.

"*He* knows." Miguel spat out the pronoun.

"Not about the baby! How could he? It was all over in one afternoon, and now he's gone away. No," she added, realizing what he was about to ask, "I will never tell you who he was! Never! Nothing could be gained."

"You are right not to give me his filthy name! I would have to follow and kill him whoever or wherever he is. But you are mistaken when you say no one else knows." She looked up, startled. "*I* know!

"Elizabeth, when I sent you my wedding present, the satin gown, it was packed in roses. That is traditional, because roses mean 'Thou art the queen of thy sex.' But you are a queen besmirched! Did you think I could look at you in that dress, or lie with you in our wedding bed without remembering? The torture of it! No, until you are delivered of his child, you are his!"

"I see." Her deep dismay was revealed in her blanched face and quivering lips, in spite of her earlier resolution to be brave. "Then there is nothing more to be said, is there? I will tell my father . . . and Señora Stearns."

Suddenly she felt very sick, and thought with horror that she would disgrace herself revoltingly, and in his presence. She must leave at once!

But he was continuing as though she had not spoken. "Although we are to be man and wife, I shall not touch you until after you have been delivered of his child. But from then on, I will try not to hold your shame against you."

Bets froze in mid-step and turned slowly.

"You mean you still want me?"

"Yes, God help me! Elizabeth, we will be married tomorrow as planned. Furthermore, I will give the child my name." He stared straight ahead, as though not wishing to look at her. "But you will forgive me if I am unable to join in the festivities this evening. Make any excuse you like!"

Quickly he strode from the room, averting his face as he passed.

Bets stayed where she was, looking blindly at the sun rays slanting through the window. She was feeling an immense relief. But somewhere in the back of her mind there was also the smallest kernel of resentment. Surely he hadn't needed to torture her so! Had she really wronged him so dreadfully?

Yes, of course she had. She'd hurt him, dealt him a terrible blow, and in the end, he'd been very generous. She must spend her life trying to repay him and make him happy. Ah, she would be a good wife to him!

All the same, for no reason at all, she thought of big burly Phineas Bishop. If it had been he whom she'd been about to marry and to whom she made that confession, what would he have said and done?

Remembering his kindness in the stable, she believed she knew.

Part Two

︵•‹‹•‹‹•‹‹•‹‹•‹‹•‹‹•‹‹•‹‹•‹‹•‹‹•︵

1860—1863

CHAPTER SIXTEEN

DON ANTONIO LUGO WAS DYING.

By his own design, and until the end, no one except his servants knew. Some months earlier, realizing his increasing feebleness, and grimly determined not to parade it, he had toyed with the idea of closing the town house and going to live out his days on his estate. In a casual way, he mentioned the possibility to his bishop, during one of the latter's periodic visits to the pueblo, and was much pleased when subsequently the local parish priest came to call, and place a request. Should such a change be made, might the church perhaps have the use of the house for a school?

"The house is yours," Don Antonio replied instantly. "I give it to you, free and clear. A small donation."

Father Padilla said softly, "I expected nothing less from you, and am very grateful. Having a place already built will save us much time and money. And Los Angeles needs a school badly."

"Yes, it does. This arrangement will be good for me as well, as it forces me to act. You see, now that I've become elderly, I find myself hesitant, less decisive, than I used to be."

Gazing at his host, as always perfectly groomed and ramrod straight, the priest hid a smile. This proud eagle hesitant?

"I've known for some time," the old man continued, "that I should move to the rancho. There are many matters to attend to there, and my duties as Judge of the Plains have multiplied of late. The long ride out and back is really too much for me, but still I've dallied because I am reluctant to leave all this. I will regret not seeing it each day."

The priest realized that his benefactor's affection

was not so much for the simple house, with its utilitarian furnishings, as for the garden. The door from Don Antonio's room stood open, and his chair, as usual, faced the patio. The two sycamores were tall now, and their great leaves, shaped like the hands of a man, shaded the multi-colored tiled walk. In the open spaces were masses of cultivated flowers; marigolds, larkspur, jasmine, roses. Climbing on the wall was a magnificent bougainvillea; the thickly clustered bracts, thin and stiff as paper, made a splash on the dun-colored adobe bricks like spilled red wine.

Father Padilla refrained from pointing out what Don Antonio would not wish to hear, that most people as they became a little feebler left their ranchos for the easier life in town, not the reverse. Instead he said sincerely, "Such a garden, in a town that has so few, will gladden the children's hearts. We will all treasure it."

The patriarch nodded. "Knowing that will make it easier to leave."

"There is one thing that I must tell you," the priest said. "Bishop Amat insisted I do so. The school is to be called 'St. Vincent's' and will be under the direction of an Americano priest, Father Daniel Shaw. He is a fine man, and we of the local parish know that you will be well satisfied with him. But the Bishop worries—"

Don Antonio was glaring in disbelief.

"The Bishop knows me so little?" He drew himself up, his back even more erect. "Surely he did not suggest that I might refuse to give the house if it was to be in the hands of an Americano?"

"Our bishop's hesitation was partly for that reason, yes. As you know, his excellency lives some distance away, in Monterey, and he cannot be as familiar with Los Angeles and the feelings here as he would like. I tried to tell him . . . Unfortunately, there are other reasons, less easy to explain, for your possible disapproval."

"Very well!" Don Antonio's eyes were still frosty. "Send this Father Shaw to talk to me. Your air of mystery arouses my curiosity."

He understood the bishop's point of view better, once he had met the new priest, for at first sight, the man was unprepossessing. Middle-aged, balding, his somber clothing too tight as well as rumpled and spotted down the front, he was hardly likely to appeal to one who was famed as the most immaculate and dashing of Californios.

However, Don Antonio also discovered that Father Shaw was intelligent, patient, and kindly, all desirable traits in teaching children. His jacket was too small because of the strong, barrel-shaped chest it spanned, and the bulging muscles that filled his sleeves. Most important of all, he played chess.

For the short time that remained before the house was vacated, the two played the difficult game every evening, to the particular delight of Don Antonio. And after the old caballero moved to his rancho, Father Daniel rode out frequently on a Saturday night to remain until Sunday. The servants, who revered their master, early learned the visitor's favorite foods and prepared them, and on cold nights put a heated brick in his bed. But the sight of the priest in his worn, ill-fitting clothes, seated across the chess board from their resplendent master, moved them all to private, very respectful laughter.

Father Daniel was the first to be told the end was near. He had not ridden to the Lugo rancho in some weeks because of a bad outbreak of diphtheria in his school. But at length Don Antonio sent him a polite message that put him on a horse the same day. When he did arrive, late in that gray, rainy afternoon, he sank onto a hall bench shivering with cold and clearly exhausted. Although there was a serape across his shoulders, his pants were soaked to the thigh.

The servant who had admitted him was the uncle of three children in the new school and knew what the ordeal had been there with the sick. He did not wait for instructions but went at once to bring heated wine. Then while the priest drank, he slipped away again, to return carrying a pair of Don Antonio's most elegant pantaloons.

Father Daniel stared in a dazed way at the blue embroidered velvet. "I hardly think those are appropriate for me, Pablo. Perhaps a pair of your own instead?"

The servant was horrified. "Would you have the Don throw me out of the hacienda for impudence? Please, Father, put them on! It is what the Don would want."

The priest did so. Indifferent as always to his appearance, after his own garment was deposited in a sodden heap in a basket and removed, he dismissed the matter and asked to be taken to his host.

"Yes, come now please. He is expecting you. He knows you are here, and his strength does not last long."

"He is so bad?" Alarmed, the visitor's gaze cleared. A current of strength seemed to flow once more through the thick body. "Tell me!"

"No, Father, I am forbidden. Please come."

Father Daniel strode along at the man's heels. When they reached the chamber and were told to enter, he pushed open the door, and the servant backed away, leaving him alone.

Don Antonio was dressed and seated in a chair. The bed behind him was smooth. Yet there lingered the scent of illness in the close air, and it was clear to the priest that only an iron will enabled the aged Californio to make this effort. His face was sunken away from his beaked nose, and the veins on his hands stood out like ropes.

Not wanting to betray his shock at the change, Father Daniel hesitated.

But before he could speak, Don Antonio remarked, "I see that associating with me has had a good effect after all. What splendid pants! Now, my friend, a new jacket is also in order."

He was laughing, and his guest, glancing down at the incongruous spectacle he presented, broke too into a delighted roar. "Still I am a priest," he said finally. "I wear the clothing of a Don, but for one evening only. That is all."

Don Antonio smiled at him with affection. "I had not forgotten your occupation," he said quietly. "That's why I asked you to come even though I knew the travail you and your school have endured. To call for you is indeed selfish of me. How are the children?"

"We lost one," was the grim answer. "And also one of the nuns. It was fortunate I had had the disease myself as a child, because we are very short-handed."

"So I've heard. You didn't sleep for many nights. The bishop should be given a full report."

"I didn't labor over my children for the bishop!"

"I realize that well," Don Antonio said in a placating voice. "But all the same he must be told. Because he must never be allowed to replace a man like you. The pueblo needs you too much! And tomorrow—I suppose you will wish to leave early and return to your charges?"

"Yes, although the crisis is past, as you were no doubt aware when you sent your message. I will leave at first light. But I am here now and I think there is something you want me to do for you. Am I right?"

Don Antonio nodded. "We must be honest with each other. As you've guessed, I am finally coming to the end of a long and very pleasant road. And in good time too, because I don't think I would enjoy the days that lie ahead for my people. In my last hours, I prefer not to have many visitors. It is too tiring to make myself presentable for them. But if you could quietly inform my old compadres? Them I would not leave without saying farewell!

"Later tonight, you will be a man of God and give me the last rites, but for the moment, before we are both too tired, shall we have a last game of chess?"

Patrick Donovan was among those few summoned, and to him this was the final proof that he was totally accepted as one of the old guard.

He found the men assembled in the main room of the hacienda, speaking together in low voices befitting the occasion, and each waiting his turn for a last word with the leader they all revered. Manuel Dominguez, Diego Rodriguez, Phineas Bishop, Juan Bandini, Juan Temple—here were all the men Patrick had expected to see. Only one was missing and Patrick assumed that word had reached Don Jose Andres Sepulveda too late, for his hacienda at Rancho San Joaquin was over forty miles distant, and with the runoff from the recent rains, three rivers would need to be forded. Too, Don Jose was a man of over sixty.

The other Sepulvedas however, were present, as well as Manuel Dominguez, and it was a demonstration of the high esteem in which the dying man was held that the animosity between those two families was put aside during this hour. Their bitter land feud was no longer unique in any case. Since the price of beef had been falling steadily in the last few years, and the heavy mortgages which the Californios had put on their ranchos with such carefree abandon in the halcyon days were becoming impossible to pay, disputes were all too common—even between brothers.

This very day, Patrick had heard still another discouraging and far too usual story. A Californio head of family had died, leaving fourteen children, all of whom, under the tenant-in-common system that prevailed, inherited equally. Even in the best of times, any wastrels of such a family, unless bought out by their brothers and sisters, could sell their own holdings to raise money, and more often as not, the best price was offered by outsiders. In this particular case, the rancho was decimated to the point where no one in the family had anything left! Patrick, who was having difficulty himself in paying the heavy taxes, had started to wonder, whenever he saw a rich display of clothing or fine horses, just how much was wealth and how much mere bravado.

"Don Diego, *por favor*," said the servant who had appeared as soon as Manuel Garfias had been ushered from the bedroom, and immediately Rodriguez arose. Garfias, his head bowed in sorrow, strode from the house without speaking to his friends.

With the summoning of Don Diego, Patrick was left alone in his corner of the room, and he moved to the window beside Bishop. Depressed by the occasion of this meeting, he asked too abruptly, "Phineas, I trust your rancho is prospering in these difficult times?"

The answer he received sounded almost indifferent; "Well enough, well enough."

Patrick reminded himself that the Bishop interests ranged far beyond the raising of cattle. In addition to mules, stage coaches, and freight lines, there were such matters as the steam-wagon which reputedly was on its way to San Pedro, the profitable landing at Wilmington, and of course the growing port itself. No, the price of beef would not make or break this young man.

"I can tell you this," Phineas offered, "I'm grateful that when I bought my twenty-four hundred acres of Rancho San Pedro from Manuel Dominguez, he was an even better trader than I. He knew he wanted to sell, and for exactly how much. Some of our friends who have recently sold believe they were taken advantage of, and God knows they were!"

Patrick nodded, but before he could answer, the heavy outer door was flung open and a man hastened in, his clothing drenched with rain. It was Don Jose Andres Sepulveda, come after all, and even now doffing his hat in sorrow.

Patrick was not alone in his surprise. Dominguez, with whom Don Jose was on such bad terms, was frowning at the new arrival with a glint of disbelieving respect.

"We didn't expect you tonght," Jose Loreto, a much younger Sepulveda cousin, said, "Rancho San Joaquin being so far away! How long since you received the summons?"

"Three hours only."

Astonishing as the figure was, they all accepted it as the absolute truth.

"I could hardly loiter along the way," Don Jose pointed out. "I might have been too late."

Forty miles in three hours! Such speed and endurance would be required that it was a wonder horse and rider had survived, but no one remarked on it further. Magnificent, thought Patrick. These tough old Californios did such feats as a matter of course. But they were growing old, dying. Would their like ever be seen again?

His musing was interrupted by the return of Diego

Rodriguez, whose craggy face was bleak as he issued from the sickroom.

"Estimados compadres," he said, "In view of the grief we all feel, I shall postpone my daughter's wedding. This is late notice, of course, but I'm certain you will all agree with my decision."

The others nodded, and then he too was gone, leaving Patrick momentarily distracted. So Felipa, now in her mid-thirties, was going to suffer a further delay to her very late nuptials! But, perhaps she wouldn't really mind. He'd never had the impression that in her self-sufficiency she was panting with impatience to wed little Lucius Camell. Camellito's disappointment was another matter!

"And how is Miss Betsey? Happy in her marriage, I suppose?"

Patrick was momentarily startled. Then he realized that mention of Felipa's wedding must have reminded his friend of that other memorable occasion, Bets' and Miguel's wedding, in the course of which young Bishop had made a legend of himself. The fandango had been well along when he finally arrived for the festivities, bringing as a gift a huge onyx bird that had been carved somewhere deep in Mexico. The figure was so large and heavy that two men should have been needed to carry it, but Phineas had it secured under one arm, a bottle of aguardiente safe under the other. The man whom no one had ever seen truly drunk before, became gloriously so in the course of that night.

"Happy, so far as I know. As you'll discover some day, when a daughter marries she no longer confides in her father to the same extent. Bets and Miguel, living in town as they do, I'm surprised you need ask. Unless for some reason you've been avoiding her."

He was mildly joking, but Phineas did not seem amused.

"As I told you once before, Patrick, socializing is something I have little time for."

"Indeed? I recall a Fourth of July party you gave a few years back when two thousand people came down to that desolate port of yours and celebrated for days! Then there was the opening of your new landing, and just recently a party on Catalina Island that may well go down in history, at least in the memories of the fifty or sixty of us who attended. You say you don't socialize?"

Phineas was staring out of the window, his face set.

"If I've deceived you and the rest, those affairs were a success, and well worth the cost. I like to have people think I'm a lion of a fellow! But you'll notice that while I'm invited to every festive event in town lately, I seldom go."

"That's true," Patrick said after a moment's thought. "I hadn't realized how often you have pressing business elsewhere."

He was studying his friend, and was momentarily disconcerted when he turned suddenly to face him.

"I seldom go," Phineas repeated. "But I assure you, it's not because of Miss Betsey."

"Of course not! I didn't mean—"

"Don Patrick—" He was interrupted by the servant who was suddenly at his elbow, speaking urgently. "If you will come with me, the Don wishes—"

At once Patrick started toward the door, but even so, it was too late. Don Antonio's very elderly cousin, Doña Serina, tottered into the room, tears streaming down her face. She spread her hands to them all in a mute gesture of finality.

Chapter Seventeen

THE ODD LITTLE PROCESSION ON HORSEBACK that Señora Elizabeth Aguirre, weather permitting, headed one day each month through the town and out into the hills, had through sheer repetition ceased to attract attention. Even the presence of an armed Chinese manservant, Adam by name, no longer provoked comment, although the striking coloring and erect graceful figure of the young woman herself, always turned a few heads.

By Miguel's order, Adam rode last, ever watchful and with his shotgun at the ready. Elizabeth, taking her two small sons to Rancho Aguirre to visit their grandfather, Don Sebastian, was thus as safe as one could be, in these rough new times.

Actually, that Adam served as her protector now, was a form of poetic justice, because on the occasion of their first meeting, Bets had been instrumental in saving him from a beating, or worse. Almost two years before, while walking alone past the Plaza, her attention had been caught by the laughter of a small group of empty-handed prospectors who were clustered around some sort of entertainment they found highly amusing.

She could hear the sharp explosive crack of a bull-whip and several times the loud words, "Jostle Lem Perkins, will you? Come on, Chinaman, dance! Let's see you dance!"

Curiosity prodded her to edge closer, until, unnoticed, she could peer between the backs of the spectators. There she had a clear view of the big man who snapped the long heavy whip, and she guessed from his unkempt straggly beard and general grime that he was what her father called a drifter, one of the many unsavory strangers infesting Los Angeles of late.

With this Lem Perkins, and facing him inside the circle, was another man; small, slender and different altogether. He evidently was the "Chinaman," and Bets studied him with interest, recalling how Miguel had remarked only the evening before on the growing number of Chinese who were to be seen in town. Originally brought to California to do the hard filthy labor in the mines, after the lodes played out, they were turned away to fend for themselves, and many were coming here seeking work. This one would appear to have just arrived. A small neat bundle of belongings lay close by.

She was fascinated by his appearance, deciding that his eyes were indeed slanted, and that his skin was not yellow as she'd always been told, but more the color of very old ivory. She barely had time to take note of his clothing, the loose blue cotton blouse and pants, and the soft black slippers, as well as his queue, long and neatly braided, when the crude drifter shouted again.

The lash of the whip slithered like a huge fast snake, striking at the small man's feet, or rather just where his feet would have been had he not leaped high in the air.

Bets sucked in her breath with horror, realizing if the heavy thong had succeeded in wrapping itself around one of those thin slippers, the foot inside would have been torn off at the ankle. But the men around her roared in glee, slapping their hands on their thighs. One of them shouted, "Go on, Lem, cain't you cut off his pigtail? He's got no right to run around like that, not in this here country! He ain't no Injun!"

Grinning, again Lem snapped his whip, and this time must have nicked his victim. The little man was clearly tiring, and hadn't jumped quite fast enough. Bets heard a slight moan that was instantly suppressed.

"Reckon this time I'll larn 'im," the drifter said. He pulled back his arm and the thong undulated behind him as if alive.

"Stop!" Bets screamed. "Stop it at once!" She pushed forward past the onlookers who gaped at her in astonishment.

"Lady, this ain't no place for you—" began one, mildly enough, but backed up a step as she turned on him.

"You men should be ashamed! How can you just stand by and let this ugly bully cut up a defenseless person!"

"I'll be damned! Ugly bully am I?" Lem strode a step toward her, but after a look at her furious and scornful face, broke off the impending argument for a moment.

The man who had spoken first said in a conciliatory tone, "Lady, this is men's fun, and if I was you, I'd just go on home."

"I'll say that too," snarled Lem. "This ain't nothin' to you! Go on, git! Or don't be blaming me if you git cut right along with this here Chink—"

"You touch me and the decent men in this town will string you up," Bets retorted. But the menace in his voice frightened her. She had no doubt that he meant what he said, and unless she removed herself, she too might be hurt. Already he was pulling back the terrible whip.

"Wait! You don't understand," she cried. "This Chinaman has come to town to work for my husband. So I must take him home right away!"

She grasped the man's cotton sleeve as she spoke, intending to pull him along with her from the circle. She could feel the trembling of his arm beneath the thin cloth, but he snatched up his bundle with his free hand, hastening to obey her gestures.

"He's come to work for your husband, has he? Is that a fact now," Lem sneered. "Tell us, what's his name?" When Bets didn't answer at once, he repeated, "I said, what's his name?" giving the others a triumphant grin.

Bets was trying to look haughtily confident, but her heart was pounding. She couldn't think of a single Chinese name, had never, in fact, heard one that she could remember. But she knew she had better reply quickly. Several of the men might be looking sheepish, but fearful of each other's ridicule, they would never speak up on her behalf. Lem's victim would not be allowed to escape without good reason!

Then, like an answer to a prayer, inspiration came. She was not a reader, never had been, but when the Boston newspaper had once run a series of poems by an Englishman named Leigh Hunt, young girl that she was then she'd been much taken with one of them. How did it go?

Abou Ben Adhem (may his tribe increase)
Awoke one night from a deep dream of peace—

"He's called Abou Ben Adhem," she replied with icy assurance. The poet had been writing about an *ayrab,* she admitted to herself, so it wasn't a Chinese name. But what difference did that make?

It made none at all. The silenced group was even

more unread than she. Influenced perhaps by the fact that afternoon mass had just finished and the church was disgorging a crowd of people, many of whom would undoubtedly spring to the aid of this meddlesome young lady, they silently let her pass, and as Bets hurried away, the Chinese was close at her heels.

Once out of sight of the Plaza, he continued to follow and Bets did not discourage him. She had noticed that while his blouse and pants were threadbare, they appeared freshly washed, and the same was true of what clothes she could see in the bundle. His hair too, even though worn in that outlandish fashion, was shining clean. He must have stopped to bathe in a stream before entering the town. But while fastidiousness in a common workman was rare indeed, Bets was impressed far more by his stoic dignity, as evident now as when he faced his tormentors.

She would like to have learned a few facts, such as his real name, but unfortunately he understood not one word she said. Having ascertained this, Bets briskly led the way to her home.

Miguel was already there and she could see from his scowl that he was angry, doubtless because she had disregarded his instructions and gone out alone.

"We've had such a stroke of good fortune, Miguel!" she said hastily, beckoning the Chinese through the doorway. "This poor man is in need of work and you know we've been talking of finding someone to help Tia Pilar."

That was true. The elderly Mexican woman, pockmarked and stringy as tough beef, had helped raise Miguel from a boy, and then kept house for him both before and after his marriage; but with age, she complained of manifold aches and pains, and had become very cross to boot. Even the two little boys did not escape her ill-temper. Only Isabelita, who was the youngest and her favorite, received Pilar's toothless smile, and was permitted to toddle about after her as she prepared the meals. Meanwhile, much of the actual work of the house fell on Bets.

A gleam of interest came into Miguel's face, and the frown smoothed away.

Bets hurried on. "Also, I think he must be a very hard worker, and surely will ask very little."

Miguel stiffened and she regretted raising the subject of their straitened circumstances. He would naturally take it as a reflection on himself, since it was that abrupt decision of his, to leave the *Los Angeles Star* and start a newspaper of his own, that was badly depleting their savings.

Nevertheless, he was still inspecting the Chinese, who stood in patient silence. "He speaks Spanish? Or English?"

"I'm afraid not."

"Then how do you know, may I ask, whether he even wishes to find work or how much he will work for? To say nothing of whether he is healthy and industrious? You don't even know his name!"

"I know all those things," she asserted. "You have only to look at him. And his name—" she hesitated, "is Abou Ben Adhem."

"Now really!" Miguel's lip twitched in the beginning of a smile. He was a voracious reader in his wife's native language as well as his own, and he liked English poetry. Suddenly he was laughing, and she knew the matter was as good as settled. Miguel would want to hear the story (which she would suitably abridge to avoid any question of danger, or lack of decorum), and he would question the man as best he could in sign language. But that would be all. There was a small room presently unused inside the stable, and from now on it would be occupied by Adhem.

In the course of a few days, while old Tia Pilar and the children were getting acquainted with the Chinese servant, his name was smoothed to Adam, and Adam he remained. Although eventually he pronounced for them his actual name, which sounded something like Kwang Pu-Yee, they could find out little else about him, because he made no effort to master the language of his new world. He obviously intended to return to China as soon as his tiny hoard of wages had grown sufficiently, and it seemed likely that far-off as that day be, it would actually arrive before Bets could satisfy her curiosity.

However, she had reckoned without her second son Jose, called Pepe. This child, almost from birth, had shown himself to have an agile, inquisitive mind and a remarkably retentive memory. Unlike his undemanding, more stolid brother Tomas, he asked endless questions and the answers were never forgotten. Months later, he would astonish his father by returning the information almost exactly.

Apparently intrigued by the nasal syllables Adam sometimes murmured to himself, Pepe followed the servant about the house, repeating the sounds and pointing to things as he did so. Something about his eager interest made the Chinese catch fire in turn, and the two spent endless hours together. The high singsong cadences were heard constantly. By the time he was six years old, not only was Pepe, like Tomas and most other Californio children of their generation, fluent in Spanish and English, he had a further, most unusual accomplishment, he could speak the Cantonese language.

At last Bets could learn that Adam did not yet have a wife, but there was a girl waiting in Canton, a city situated on the Pearl River in Kwangtung Province, who would become his bride when he returned there. He had described her for Pepe, and she was surely as lovely as any princess in a fairy tale. When Adam had saved enough money he would return to claim her, and meanwhile, if he felt sadness at the long parting and the hardships he had endured, he made no mention of it.

"How was your visit with Father?" Miguel asked, once he had greeted the children and listened gravely to Pepe's enthusiastic outpouring. He was meticulous about treating the two boys equally, and only Bets, who admitted to herself that it was probably just her imagination, thought she could discern any difference. She was quite sure that Tomas never felt slighted. The ironic fact was that Miguel's true son, the mercurial Pepe, had so many interests and spread his attention so widely, no one person could possibly claim it all, while quiet Tomas quite obviously adored the man he called father.

"The children enjoyed it, as always," Bets answered her husband. "But Don Sebastian wasn't in the best of spirits." She broke off to say, "Boys, Tia Pilar saved you some of the chicken *mole* she cooked for Isabel's dinner. I do believe she's convinced your grandfather starves you."

The two rushed away, Tomas more slowly, perhaps wishing to stay with Miguel.

When they had gone, Bets laughed. "I wish you could have seen all they ate last night and again at dinner today."

"I can guess . . . Tell me about Father. Is he still smoldering because he had to refuse the invitation to Don Antonio's funeral?"

"We didn't discuss it, but I know he is. And after all, who can blame him? There have been some magnificent processions in times past, but that one was half a mile long!"

"Even if it stretched from here to San Francisco, Father was unreasonable. Doesn't he know he is crippled? The road into town that week was only passable on horseback, and barely that."

"It is still bad," Bets said. "Partially washed out in many places. We had to pick our way today, and there were rattlesnakes—Adam shot one that was coiled in the trail. I suppose they've been washed down from the mountains by the recent rain."

"I should have gone with you! But today I—" Miguel stopped, his face grim. "Is Father well?"

"He's much as usual. The servants told me his stiffness and pain are gradually increasing, but of course he'd never mention such things to me."

She picked up from the table the brown sprigged dress she was making for little Isabel. It was finished, except for hemming, and she paused to thread her needle. "He is willing enough to talk of other problems though. His foreman is ill, and he's having to make do with a lazy young scamp—I believe his name is Ramon."

"Ramon is neither lazy nor a scamp," Miguel interrupted. He added thoughtfully, "But he is too inexperienced to be a foreman."

"Don Sebastian was very gloomy about it. I reminded him that the men would probably do what work they've always done, at least for a while. But I doubt if he even heard me." She paused, recalling the conversation with mild distaste. Not that it had been dull, far from it! She would have found Don Sebastian's description of his woes—for he orated dramatically, with a timbre in his voice, and his deep-set eyes, so much like Miguel's, flashing—as enjoyable as she suspected he did himself, were it not for the fact that Miguel's short-comings as a son had figured so largely in his catalog of misfortunes.

She waited for her husband to question her further about the rancho and when he did not, she glanced at him. His set face drove Don Sebastian from her mind.

"What is it? Has something happened?"

"Yes. *El Clamor Publico*—"

"Oh!" It was not difficult to guess what was coming. His new journal had been in financial difficulties for some time, and he had been putting in more and more money, as well as the most desperate effort, just to keep it alive.

She bent her head lower over Isabel's dress, trying to hide her dismay, for she had learned to her cost how prickly Miguel was in matters involving his pride. On a previous occasion, when he had left the *Los Angeles Star* after a bitter argument with the owner over the latter's decision to increase the size of the English edition at the expense of the Spanish, she had been foolish enough to protest.

"But Miguel, isn't he right?" she'd asked. "There are so many more Americanos here now! Surely he wanted you to remain as editor?"

"I did not choose to stay."

His tone was repressive but she failed to notice. "You might have been wiser, then, to keep your temper, at least until you'd talked to the *Southern Californian* about a position with them." She was referring to the rival paper, and remembering, even as she spoke, how often he had disparaged it as poorly written.

"You expect me to go there? I should grovel, ask them to take me in? You must have a low opinion indeed of my abilities!"

"Oh, no, that isn't at all what I—"

He swept on as though she hadn't spoken. "As it happens, I have had another plan for some time. There are several hundred French here now, in addition to all the original Spanish-speaking. I intend to offer a journal that will appeal only to those groups. Let the other publications cater to the illiterate Americanos!"

She had stared at him, trying to marshal enthusiasm, and failing. When, after an awkward pause, she did begin to ask a question, he broke in with a rebuke that silenced her.

"Other wives respect their husband's judgment. I see from all you've said that mine does not! Elizabeth, will you pull down the venture before it starts?"

So *El Clamor Publico* was founded, and for a brief time prospered. The young paper mirrored the interests of the Californios, and they acclaimed it. But then, as the months passed, the journal's popularity began to decline. The number of subscribers dropped steadily, in spite of the endless hours Miguel worked, writing articles, making changes, trying desperately to attract back his old customers—for there were no new ones.

With her husband's initial success, Bets had been wholeheartedly delighted. Later, she prayed that his valiant efforts would stem the inexplicable tide of disaster, and despite what his angry censure of her had implied, could not understand how he could fail. Miguel was a brilliant journalist, the finest in Los Angeles, was he not?

Meeting Phineas Bishop on the street one afternoon, she asked him bluntly for his opinion as to why *El Clamor Publico* was losing ground.

He considered, while Bets thought, he always takes seriously any question I ask. If only Miguel would allow me to speak so freely and honestly!

"If you want me to guess, it's because the town is different, even from what it was last year. More and more you hear English, and there isn't a need any more for a paper all in Spanish."

Remembering her own early misgivings on that score, Bets nodded.

"There's another reason too, Miss Betsey," he went on. "The larger papers have more money to spend in getting the latest news down from San Francisco."

"I thought the appeal of *El Clamor* was based on local happenings!"

"That was so. But the war that's broken out between the states has changed things. I reckon most families here, except for the Californios, have a connection or two back east, and people are hungry for the smallest detail of what's happening. No, local affairs don't hold the interest these days. Not compared to the shelling of Fort Sumter!"

"I see . . ." And deciding belatedly that he must be wondering why she hadn't learned all this from Miguel, she added formally, "Thank you, Mr. Bishop," and went on her way.

El Clamor Publico then, had finally died. Miguel, in telling her, confirmed that Bishop's reasoning had been accurate, although he himself appeared to blame the paper's downfall entirely on his inability to procure the war news as promptly as his rivals.

"To think how I've longed for communication with the rest of the country!" he said bitterly. "How I've fought for it! And now at last a telegraph line actually links Los Angeles with San Francisco—to the ruin of *El Clamor*.

"Last week, the *Star* reported that the South won a major skirmish at Big Bethel, Virginia, while I, on the same day, drivelled on about Juan Temple building a two-story brick building for the town market. A market!"

Bets dared not look at him. Although she ached to go and put her arm around his tall stiff figure, she knew she would only be rebuffed. He would accept no comforting from her until his emotions were once more under control.

"What will you do now?"

There was only one sensible course Bets could think of. But could he ever bring himself to go to the publisher of the *Star* and admit his mistake?

"Elizabeth, the time has come for an important change. My father is lonely, and he needs my help at the rancho."

Bets slowly raised her head. She was so startled that the child's dress fell from her hands, unheeded.

"But—he always has!"

"Are you reproaching me?" Before she could speak, he continued. "Ah, but no more than I reproach myself, I assure you! However, it's not too late. I'm done with journalism! We will go to the rancho to live."

She sat mutely, while he called the household into the room and told them also. Both boys responded with shouts of joy. They loved Rancho Aguirre, and the idea of being there always was clearly the fulfillment of their dreams.

Adam accepted the news impassively, caring little it seemed where they resided, so long as he continued to share their lives as before. Tia Pilar's sharp eyes gleamed in anticipation, doubtless visualizing herself a pampered old servant in a large well-run hacienda.

But Bets, gazing around the simple room, crowded even by the presence of so few, wished she need not leave this house in which she had lived since her marriage. At the prospect of the remote rancho, with its urbane, strong-willed old master, she felt only foreboding.

CHAPTER EIGHTEEN

DON SEBASTIAN PROCLAIMED HIMSELF MOST pleased when told of his son's decision, and Miguel was further convinced the new arrangement would work well. The small adobe in Los Angeles was sold, furnishings and all, and in a short time the family was ensconced at the rancho.

The large, cool, two-story hacienda was undoubtedly more comfortable than their former home. Seeing Miguel stalk about, his black eyes alight as if discovering every familiar corner for the first time, Bets was determined not to harbor any useless regrets for their vanished privacy and independence. She took care to admire aloud the spaciousness of the quarters allotted to them.

She and Miguel had been given an upper room from which, on one side, they looked out through a covered balcony into the walled courtyard; from the other they were afforded a view that spanned the kitchen garden, the vineyards and olive groves, and ended with distant rolling hills, dotted with cattle.

The two boys had their own separate quarters nearby, as did Tia Pilar who shared hers with her charge, little Isabel—an importance causing the old woman to put on unbearable airs. Even Adam, being a house servant, was housed comfortably, having to himself a tiny chamber in one of the thick arms of the courtyard wall.

Gazing down from the balcony, one could watch much of the endless domestic activity of the establishment, for just below, their doors opening in a row onto the covered walk, were all the various workrooms, such as the harness shop, the buttery, a carpenter's shop and the blacksmith's. Scattered out beyond the heavy impregnable gates lay the huts of the Indian workers, situated close by for protection.

Don Sebastian was fond of saying that his orderly rancho was really a small pueblo, self-sufficient, and protected by those walls, capable of stoutly defending itself if the need arose.

Yet to Bets it still seemed far from being a town. She sorely missed the casual meetings on the streets with Teodocia, Arcadia, and her other friends. She missed living near to Patrick, even though she and Miguel, every few weeks, rode in to visit him. Most of all, she confessed to herself, she missed the exhilaration and excitement that life in Los Angeles had offered her.

No matter how often she visited there now, it wasn't enough. She would ride in at Miguel's side, reveling in the familiar noises that assailed their ears, the shouts of Indians selling clean water, the barking and snarling of a scruffy pack of dogs, the creaking of carts and carriages. Even the pungent and unpleasant smells were like a welcome home.

And now that so incredibly, a war continued to be fought within the United States, it was almost an agony not to be where they could hear the news. Memories revived of boys she had known in Boston, and those shadowy names and faces made the distant struggle more real.

If the slowness with which news trickled out to the rancho was a trial to her, it surely must be a far greater one for Miguel, she realized. In years past, hadn't he considered Los Angeles itself too isolated?

How silent and pensive he had been that evening at her father's town house, when the talk had turned to General Johnston's brave band of volunteers! Although then away from town only a few weeks, she hadn't known who Johnston was.

"He's a Southerner, Bets!" Patrick explained, "used to be in charge of the Army's Department of the Pacific, stationed in San Francisco. When war broke out, he left that post immediately and came down here where other sympathizers of the Confederacy were assembling. Now he's led a group of them back east across the Butterfield stage route—"

"A march across the desert?" Bets marveled.

"The only way, Miss Betsey, if they want to get to where the fighting is," Phineas told her, and added with sudden gloom, "Word has just come from San Francisco that three days ago Union troops intercepted them at Fort Yuma. Not all were captured, luckily. Johnston himself slipped through the net and may be with the Confederate Army now."

"Young Bernardo Yorba also," reminded Arcadia Stearns, pride in her voice that a Californio, for no reason at all except love of adventure, had been one of the party. "He escaped too!"

"And Alice Carter's brother, Terrence," put in Mary Reyes.

"That was one of the names, I remember now," Patrick agreed. "Terrence Carter. Who is he?"

"Tell us, Mary; you must know, if you are acquainted with his sister." Arcadia, who was the acknowledged authority on local families, sounded slightly annoyed.

"Why yes, I am teaching Alice to use watercolors! She has a most unusual talent, otherwise I wouldn't have agreed. I'm ordinarily very selfish about hoarding my time."

"You're giving her art lessons then? But who are these Carters?" persisted Arcadia. "Have I met them? They must be new people."

"Five or six years here, I would think. The father's a hide tanner, and a friend of Jeb's."

"Jeb?"

"Our servant! He and Flora brought Alice to me because of her really extraordinary way of drawing animals."

"Ah!" Arcadia murmured, feeling completely enlightened. She regarded Mary with a mixture of amusement and irritation.

Bets, not much interested either in art or the various social strata, remarked, "Bernardo Yorba always was one for dashing bravery!" She was reflecting that young men really did have the best of things, when she heard Miguel speaking to Bishop, and the tightness of her husband's voice drove other thoughts from her mind.

"You say this capture happened only three days ago? How could word have reached San Francisco so quickly?"

Standing facing each other, the two were in startling contrast. Fully as tall but far more slender, Miguel as usual was dressed in the colorful clothing of a Californio ranchero, an open-necked, soft white shirt, a short embroidered jacket, and a wide red sash above well-fitting pantaloons. With his aquiline features and intense dark eyes, he seemed to Bets far the handsomer of the two.

Bishop, broader and sandy-haired with heavy blond brows, looked more Americano than he ever had, chiefly because tonight he was wearing an imposing and beribboned uniform of a colonel in the State Militia. On his arrival, he had explained that he'd come directly from a staff meeting. Otherwise, he laughed, he'd hardly feel justified in wearing military garb as his duties, like the Militia itself, existed mostly on paper.

It was no secret that his only object in joining had been to persuade the Union Army to locate a quartermaster facility at his Wilmington depot. In this endeavor, he met with success, and the arrangement he concluded promised to be highly satisfactory for everyone—himself, the town, even the most ardent southern sympathizers. After all, many local people would be finding work at Fort Drum, and the soldiers quartered there could be expected to spend their pay in Los Angeles!

"The telegraph line is complete, Miguel," he said. "It goes all the way across the country."

He spoke the auspicious words with less jubilation than Bets would have expected, knowing how he too had espoused that particular cause. But then, she realized suddenly, Phineas Bishop in recent years was more quiet about his triumphs. The raw strength and drive hadn't changed, only the expression of it.

"The telegraph line!" Miguel slowly shook his head, his black eyes distant. "From coast to coast at last . . . and I didn't even know."

Everyone present must have understood. For Miguel Aguirre, long parted from the _Los Angeles Star,_ the achievement came several years too late.

The talk shifted, and there was conviviality again, and easy, comfortable mirth. Bets was able to hope that Miguel's dark abstraction went largely unnoticed.

Her own spirits would not flag until the following day, when they journeyed away from town. After the sociability of such visits, the rancho's lonely isolation seemed to her even more pronounced.

Their return was always to be dreaded. Don Sebastian would greet Bets with his usual urbanity, but as soon as he was alone with his son, he would give vent to his irritation at their brief absence, never admitting its true cause, but finding some aspect of Miguel's work to criticize.

"What is it Ramon tells me about your moving a part of the herd?" he inquired on one such occasion. This particular spring day was softly warm, scented with burgeoning spring growth, and Bets had paused in the next room to watch her sons outside, running through the thick stands of purple lupin. They made a charming picture, the two boys trailed by a fat brown puppy so small that most of the time it disappeared from view in the luxuriant growth; but her attention strayed from them as her father-in-law's words came audibly through the half-open door.

"Yes, Father," Miguel answered, "I instructed the men to round up some of the cattle and drive them farther west to graze. After all the rain we've had, the alfilerilla was being trampled into the mud before it could be eaten."

"Ah! And do you know that at least eight head were caught yesterday in a flash flood and drowned? To be frank, while I appreciate your efforts to help I would like to be consulted before any more such decisions are made."

Miguel, stunned by the disclosure, was silent, and Don Sebastian warmed to his subject.

"I realize that an old cripple like myself can hardly be considered competent any more, but you must be tolerant.

"I've run this ranch, badly no doubt, but still I have run it, and for so many years that it is difficult for me to let anyone, no matter how much cleverer, take over."

Bets could imagine Miguel's face turning a dull, angry red, and she realized she had made a mistake by remaining within earshot. Sympathy from her would be as unwelcome to him as the sarcasm of his father.

Coming to live here had been an unhappy mistake. Not that she hadn't had a far easier time than she expected. Women's work, it seemed, was women's work, and while Don Sebastian had been well used to giving domestic orders to his majordomo, he had only done so because of the lack of a female relative to take proper responsibility.

He had at once passed the reins to his daughter-in-law, and she accepted them uneasily, knowing that any mistakes on her part might reverse his decision in an embarrassing way.

Fortunately, she was not ill-prepared for the challenge. In Patrick's household the only servants had been Jeb and Flora, but she had had ample opportunity to learn the ways of both Señora Brinkman and Arcadia Stearns, and the knowledge stood her in good stead. Don Sebastian, almost from the beginning, was treating her with a gratifying respect, but not so his own son.

She heard Miguel say very stiffly, "I am sorry, Father. Moving the cattle seemed the right thing to do."

Then he strode from the room, passed his wife without speaking, and disappeared outside.

There was a creaking sound and Bets realized that the old man was slowly moving his wheeled chair across the floor.

As he reached the threshold, she went to meet him.

"Shall I push you, Don Sebastian?"

"Yes, thank you . . . to the window. I want to see where he goes."

Bets placed the chair where he asked, and glanced out.

Miguel was not in sight.

"You think I'm unfair to him, don't you?" Don Sebastian demanded.

"Yes." She was too disturbed to put a curb on her tongue.

"He expects too much too soon."

"Soon? We've been here close to a year!"

Yes, it was almost twelve months in this isolated place, always under the thumb of this despotic old man, expected to obey him without question!

Oh, how she longed to be back in their little house in town, back where there was friendship and gaiety and life! Aunt Mary had been right when she warned her. Learning to put Miguel's wishes always before her own and *trying* to be obedient—she who always had her own way with Papa—had been difficult enough. But she'd had no idea at all what moving to the rancho held in store.

"It seems less time to me. But I've been alone so long." He glanced at her set face and appeared to abandon the argument. "Elizabeth, out there are those grandsons of mine at play. Always at play! I suspect you are thinking the same as I—that they've had no lessons since they arrived here."

She was still resentful because of his treatment of Miguel, and made no answer. But he was right. Tomas and Pepe were spending whole days in idleness. They watched saddles being made and the horses shod, played games of their own devising, or just hung about underfoot in the kitchen. Such activities had a certain value, of course, but with Pepe's remarkably fine mind . . .

"Miguel used to teach them himself, did he not?"

"Yes, and he was a good teacher! I helped them learn to read and do simple sums, but I'm no scholar like Miguel. He knows history and literature, geography—"

"Yes, he does. But you are intelligent in more important ways. Far more important, I assure you."

It was a compliment, yet one that could not be enjoyed because of the insult to Miguel. How like Don Sebastian she thought, to give with one hand and take away with the other!

"The boys need more of their father's time particularly Pepe, whose quickness is a gift that should not be wasted. Perhaps, if you were to encourage your husband to teach them, even for part of each day, that would relieve me of much of his unwanted advice. I could slowly learn to adjust, and we would all be happier. Will you do that?"

Bets looked into his craggy face dominated by the high-bridged nose. In spite of his serious and troubled expression, she was not deceived. Other older Californios had seemed like eagles in their pride and strength.

This one however, sharp-eyed, or gallant, she had come to think of as a very stubborn and crafty fox.

Still, perhaps a compromise was in order, at least temporarily. The boys would certainly benefit from daily lessons again!

She nodded.

"Good."

"But I don't promise my wishes will prevail!" She took a certain pleasure in adding, "Miguel came here only because he believed you needed him and wanted his help. He is deeply worried about the rancho."

"About my rancho?" The pronoun was stressed ever so faintly. "Nonsense, Elizabeth! He is inexperienced and tends to fret unnecessarily. This has been a winter of floods. Some cattle were drowned, as I just told him. Prices are tumbling because of all the Texas steers that have been brought into California to give us competition. But what is life without difficulties? We will survive. We always have."

Don Sebastian's eyes strayed again to the window as one of the boys shouted in sheer exuberance.

"Pepe does enjoy life, doesn't he? Reminds me of your father—and you too, in that respect. Isabelita has a look at times that brings back my beloved wife. But Tomas puzzles me. So quiet, even when he's happiest. Unlike any of us! I see nothing whatever of his father in him."

"No doubt if we have five children, or ten, all will be different from the others in many ways. Each will be himself."

She was unperturbed. Once Tomas had been born and she had taken her first look at him, she'd known that her secret was safe, and would be forever. His blue eyes were no problem because of her own. What had kept her restless at night for weeks beforehand, was the dreadful possibility that the baby might have inherited John Carew's distinctive white-blond hair. That fear had proved groundless. The thick fuzz of hair on the new infant's head had shown black in the candlelight, as black as her own—or Miguel's.

She found her husband outside the courtyard, pacing angrily among the olive trees, goaded out of his usual reserve.

"Now do you understand why I left home in the first place? Always Father has been this way! As a boy, I was never allowed to do anything without his doing it first and much better. I've tried to make Pepe and Tomas independent for that very reason!"

"You've done a good job of it too," she said warmly.

"Even today he is unable to recognize that I am a man. A man of thirty-eight! He treats me like an incompetent boy . . . Elizabeth, shall I go back to Los Angeles and give this up?"

Her heart leapt with pleasure at the mere suggestion, and it was all she could do to keep from shouting, "Yes, oh, yes!" Instead, she turned her face away and asked, "Do you want to?"

"No." The answer was emphatic. "I've always loved Rancho Aguirre—the hacienda, the land, everything! Even when I was in self-imposed exile I longed to be back here. I have dreamed of taking part again in the big cattle drives and rodeos, riding with the vaqueros through the tall mustard, seeing spring come to these hills in a fiery blaze of orange poppies . . ."

"How mistaken I was!" she exclaimed. "I thought you stayed in the pueblo because you enjoyed your work there."

"My work? Writing about fandangos? Writing notices for tradesmen because there was no real news?" He was scornful. "No! If Father and I hadn't been constantly quarreling, I would never have left this place."

"You two are much alike," she observed. At his startled look, she explained, "You have similar quick minds which Pepe has inherited. And you are both strong-willed, perhaps just a little stiff-necked—"

She only intended to tease, to draw him out of his serious mood. But he replied, "I am sorry you think so little of me."

"Oh, Miguel! I only mean perhaps he needs a little longer to accustom himself to the changes. If you will just be patient with him, in time he'll realize how capable you are."

"That day will never come," he said, but Bets could see that he wanted to be convinced.

"Will you at least try a little longer?" She hesitated, and then, mindful of the love he had just expressed for the rancho, forced herself to lie. "I would be sorry to leave here."

"Yes, if you wish. I think the children too are happy."

"Indeed they are! And Miguel, couldn't you spend a few hours each day with them as you used to? They are running wild, and forgetting all you taught them."

The distant shout of a young voice lent credence to her words.

"Pepe at least has forgotten nothing. He hears us talk of the War between the States, and he asked me last night if it was like the English Wars of the Roses. I had to explain the difference."

Bets, who had never heard of any War of Roses was silent, and in a moment he said, "Nevertheless you are right. Pepe, and of course Tomas too, need the discipline of regular lessons. Maybe soon I will have more time."

She had hoped for a more definite answer, but was not too discontented. The bleak unhappiness had faded from his face, and his walk had slowed to a more amiable pace. She was emboldened to ask a question that had been troubling her.

"Miguel, I've heard so much talk of the ranchos being burdened with big mortgages at high rates. People say that another bad year, with floods such as we've had this winter, might mean ruin for many of them. Does Don Sebastian have a mortgage on Rancho Aguirre?"

"Yes. But I hardly think that is a matter that need concern a woman—" Suddenly he broke off. The shouts outside the wall were clearer now, and they could both hear the unaccountable note of terror that was in the treble voices.

"Snake! Something about a snake!" Miguel snatched up a hoe that had been left leaning against the wall,

and ran out the gate, Bets at his heels. They fought
their way through the thick tangle of weeds and
bushes.

The cries had abruptly ceased. The children were
standing waist deep in lupins, motionless, staring down
at something hidden from their parents' view. Only
when Miguel and Bets were almost there, did they
hear a dry rattling, and then see the small coiled rep-
tile.

Miguel reached for the boys, but before he could
snatch them to safety, Tomas made a sudden dart forward. The snake reared up and struck, falling flatly
the length of its shining, mottled body.

Bets heard herself scream, and Tomas looked
around at her. He seemed dazed. "The puppy,
Mother, the puppy—"

"Are you bitten?" Seeing the snake once more slith-
ering back into a coil, its forked tongue flicking in and
out of its open mouth, Bets rushed to her son, and
pulled him away.

"No, but Pepe and I have been trying to get to the
puppy!" She saw what both children were gazing at
with such anguished eyes. The little brown dog was lying on the ground next to the snake. As they watched,
he tried half-heartedly to get to his feet, and then fell
sideways.

"The rattler was sunning there," Tomas whispered.
"We didn't see it! I almost stepped on the tail, and
then it struck . . ."

Miguel raised the hoe and slammed down with such
savage strength that the sharp edge severed the rep-
tile's body from its head. Then he threw the hoe to
the ground and picked up the puppy.

Although the dead snake continued to twitch and
writhe, no one noticed it further. The two children
waited nervously, while Miguel examined their ominously limp pet.

"I'm sorry," he said at last. "He's been bitten several times, once in the head. He's going to die. There's
nothing anyone can do."

Bets, listening, tightened her arms around her sons.
Warm tears were falling on her hands.

"Such big boys should not cry over a dog," Miguel said, very gently. "I want you to be brave, make me proud of you!"

Tomas sniffled only once more, and his mother felt his back straighten. "I won't cry," he said. Nor would he, she knew. His love for Miguel and the desire for his approval would prevent it.

But Pepe continued to stare at the still bundle in his father's hands, and did not seem to have heard.

Bets stroked his soft hair. "These things happen, darling . . ."

He wrenched his gaze away, and the large dark eyes swimming in tears looked up into hers. "I'm not crying over the dog, Mother! No, it's just that my heart hurts."

"I see."

"Be brave, Pepe," Miguel said again. "You must be like El Cid himself."

His face for once was unguarded, and Bets knew that if it had been possible for him to restore that puppy to life, he would have done so at any cost. For Pepe.

"Elizabeth, you were quite right; I have been neglecting them. The lessons will resume tomorrow."

An uneasiness made her look back at the distant house. She imagined she could see Don Sebastian, still at the window, and he was smiling.

CHAPTER NINETEEN

EARLY ON A PARTICULAR SATURDAY IN THE fall of 1862, carriages and carts from far and wide rolled into Los Angeles. Many were laden with entire rancho families, for weddings were festive occasions at which children were always welcome.

The weather was propitious, not the blistering heat so usual at this time of year, but balmy and delightful. The rumble of a distant war seemed far away indeed, and even the heavy financial worries that plagued so many of the guests had been left at home. Happy anticipation was in the air, for the customary ceremony and the celebrations that would follow, were expected to differ very little from such nuptials of the past, or those still to come in future years. Certainly, few of those lucky enough to be invited imagined that this long-awaited extravaganza of a wedding (which had been thrice delayed, the latter two postponements set by Felipa herself, with no explanations) might possibly be the last of its kind.

Patrick Donovan, like the rest, much enjoyed the sumptuous dinner that followed the rites, although his pleasure was diminished slightly by the absence of his sister Mary. With an airy wave of her hand, she had parted with him and the other emerging guests at the church steps.

She had given him her firm decision at breakfast. "No, Patrick, please let's don't argue. I've sent Felipa my regrets. I do believe that I'm old enough to do exactly what I wish."

"Haven't you always?" he'd growled; but she knew him well, and the depth of his affection.

"Not always. I do not enjoy large, very social affairs, so I shan't go."

He believed he understood why she couldn't feel at ease at such parties, and he felt a familiar touch of sadness. Was she doomed always to live in a sort of limbo, neither married nor unmarried? He'd seen more than once how she was forced to rebuff some newcomer who, struck by the cameo-fine beauty that she had never lost and not knowing her history, began to show her attentions. Coldness wasn't in Mary Frances' nature, but she'd had to learn the way of it!

He'd thought some years back that one man, that sheep fellow, Carew, had got past her guard, and he'd been worried. He didn't want her hurt any more, not ever! But if there had been any danger, it had passed. Carew had left town suddenly, and so far as Patrick could tell, his sister hadn't mourned. She'd simply gotten even more absorbed in her painting.

Thank God she had something like that to occupy her! Her interest in art hadn't flagged with the passing of time, not at all. Something Carew had once suggested must have been buried in the back of her head, because only the other day, evidently after long deliberation and bolstering of her courage, she'd packed up a number of those watercolors of hers and sent them on the boat to San Francisco. To the Gallery Milo, or some such name. She hadn't heard anything about them yet, and maybe she never would. Just because he, Patrick, liked her pictures didn't mean they were anything unusual!

"Anyway, there's one good reason for not going to the wedding feast." Mary broke into his musings with a laugh. "Arcadia is angry with me, and I'd best stay out of her way until she forgets. I refused to accept one of her nieces as a student."

"Good Lord, why?" Patrick was shocked. "Surely, if she asked you to do her a favor—Aren't you teaching that tanner's child? I would think that any niece of Arcadia's—"

"Should have preference? Exactly her reasoning too, I'm afraid," Mary said serenely. "But it was plain to me at once that the young lady has no talent. None at all! I'd have had to insult her aunt far more later on, when she saw the results."

"And I suppose the Carter girl does have talent."

"Yes." His sarcasm was ignored. "Alice has great promise. But right now, she's terribly worried about her brother being a soldier. He's only sixteen. He ran away east with that Confederate mob of Johnston's. Alice says he went with them because it seemed the only way for him to get there, and at least he didn't get captured at Yuma. But it was the *wrong army!* His grandparents are slaves in Alabama today, and Terrence wanted to help free the slaves. He wanted to fight on the *Union* side!" She added more quietly, "I'm afraid the strain shows in Alice's work."

"But Arcadia—to refuse Arcadia!" Patrick swore under his breath. Sometimes he didn't understand his sister at all.

By the time the wedding ceremony was over, and

he watched her walk away from the church, her slim shoulders straight and her head held high, he'd forgotten any annoyance he'd felt.

He called her name and ran the few yards after her. "Mary Frances, are you certain you won't change your mind?"

She shook her head. Then the smile of affection that he cherished transformed her sensitive face.

"Patrick," she said softly, "don't worry so. Go on, enjoy yourself!"

"Yes . . ." He paused, and then he said something he hadn't even known was in his mind. "Why don't you write back to Spain? Find out what's happened. Years have passed, you know. You could write to the priest there. He'd answer you."

She stared at him, her eyes wide and dark. She was as surprised as he.

"I might," she said slowly. "I just might."

The fandango was beginning. Music from guitars, harps, and violins sweetly filled the patio of the Rodriguez town house, and many guests, all of them dazzling in their elaborate satins and velvets, were determined to prove themselves indefatigable. Only the older people were absent, as they wisely took an afternoon rest and conserved their strength for the hours ahead.

A late supper of steaks, broiled by the light of lanterns and the rising moon, would mark the renewal of festivities, planned to continue not just one night, but over an entire week, with horse-racing and cockfighting to pass the daytime hours. Bull and bear fighting had only recently been banned by an outrageous new city ordinance and would be sorely missed; but even so, nothing could quench the high spirits that prevailed.

"Felipa's wedding gown was the loveliest I've ever seen," sighed Bets to her father. "Didn't you think so, Papa?" Even though the tempting music wafted from the interior, she and Patrick were for the moment alone in the large patio, due to their customary disregard for the ill-effects of the afternoon sun. "That brocaded satin was ordered in China especially for her, and the sprays of pink roses on her shawl were embroidered there too . . . Isn't the music grand? I can't seem to keep my feet still! But Papa, where is Peter Riggs? I thought they would have asked him to take charge of the fandango."

"They did, but he refused," her father told her. "He's just opened a new dance hall. A great success, I understand, but it keeps him busy . . . How are you, Bets? I see far too little of my daughter these days."

He wanted to ask bluntly whether she was happy, but the days of her easy confidences were long over and he did not wish to place a reserve between them. Better to pretend he believed all was idyllic. If she had problems, they were hers, and doubtless would remain so.

"I'm fine, Papa." She did look a little wistful. He was pleased when she added. "Do you know, that sounded very good, being called 'daughter' again! I am a wife, and most certainly a mother—words that carry so much responsibility. Just for a little while, I'd like to be a girl again."

"Really now, what else are you? An old woman? If I remember correctly, you've barely reached the ancient age of twenty-nine. Why, our bride of today is past her mid-thirties, yet she must feel very young indeed."

"I wonder how she does feel, Papa."

He gave her a sharp look. Did Bets still worry about Felipa's one time fondness for Miguel? What foolishness! Still, it hadn't helped he was sure, to see what a cool smile the bride had given her bridegroom at the altar when she looked up into his broadly beaming face—or rather looked *down* into it, for although Camellito was known to have increased the height of his heels as much as possible, he was still very short.

"She couldn't have chosen better," Patrick asserted. "Lucius Camell is a fine man, a friend to all of us. He's generous to a fault and hasn't a conceited bone in his body. I think any woman would be lucky to get him. Especially these days, because he has a very promising future."

"Really? I thought all cattle ranchos were having difficult times."

"Haven't you heard? He's starting a bank." At her display of interest, he explained further. "He's in partnership with a man named Isaias Hellman who is very experienced and they'll be providing a service this town has long needed. We must face the fact that the days are gone when a man simply handed over a sack of gold to the owner of the trading post and said, 'Take care of this!' "

"No doubt that's so," Bets said thoughtfully. "But doesn't it require a large amount of money to start a bank? Surely all the rumors can't be wrong! I've heard that some new settlers are contesting the Camells' rancho title, and that there's a question about the water rights as well. Didn't he just recently ride up to San Francisco to appear before the land commission?"

"He did, and you're right; he can't provide much money himself for the new bank. But there's a third partner, his father-in-law. Don Diego has contributed heavily, as has Hellman. And why not? It is a good solid venture! I wish I'd been invited to be part of it."

"I suppose so." Bets found it difficult to imagine Felipa's gentle good-natured bridegroom as a banker. "Anyway, I wish him success. He's a fine man."

"Yes." Patrick studied his daughter covertly. He wondered why, after all this time, he still had reservations about the family's move to Rancho Aguirre. It was probably just that he missed them all; because there was no denying that Bets, while she might seem a little pensive, did look well. Blooming, in fact! Being a lady of leisure agreed with her.

Remembering the days when she had had very little relaxation, he said, "I still wish you had taken Flora and Jeb with you when you married. That ancient Tia Pilar is worse than useless. Flora expected to accompany you, and I think was very disappointed."

"I hope she realized that I wanted her. I would love to have had both of them!"

"Then why didn't you?"

She did not meet his eyes. "Because I thought it best; anyway, Papa, they belonged with you and Aunt Mary."

"Your aunt and I were two adults alone, we didn't need them as much as you. If your man Adam hadn't happened along, I would have insisted. Well, it doesn't matter now. At the rancho, there are all the servants you could possibly want. Will you and Miguel be staying in town a few days after the festivities? We've missed you and the children. I wish you'd brought little Isabel, as well as the boys!"

"Of course we'll come for a visit. Although I shan't be able to drag Tomas and Pepe away from here, so long as anything at all is still going on. They are enchanted, and Pepe, as usual, is beside himself with excitement—

"Oh, Papa, there's Teodocia! Will you excuse me, please? I am so eager to talk to her!"

She was gone and Patrick gazed disconsolately at the small lime and orange trees with which this walled area was planted. Such trees only produced small, rather bitter fruit, and were relics of the very early days. Too bad, he thought absently, that Don Diego hadn't put in the purple-black mission grapes that were so sweet and juicy! He himself had recently planted a vineyard at Rancho Allison, and someday it would bring a good return. But that unfortunately was well in the future, and wouldn't pay this year's taxes or make up for the eroding losses he'd been having lately with his cattle. Perhaps he should be buying sheep. They were the coming thing.

He tapped his feet, but the music had begun to grate on him, and the distant laughter as well. All those tireless dancers reveling away the siesta hour were young people, just starting out in life, full of zest, believing in their own immortalty. Just as he and Allison had done. She'd loved to dance, too. And laugh. What a fine time they'd had together!

Damn it all, Allison, why did you have to die and leave me? I'm lonesome, and a party like this makes it worse. A man remembers so much at weddings!

He wouldn't care to dance now, not with those

youngsters. And siestas were not for him. But he was so restless! Why not leave and come back later? Why not spend an hour or so walking about, perhaps go over to see that new dance hall and saloon of Peter Riggs'?

"Afternoon, Mr. Donovan."

Brash as he was, Riggs was meticulous about using titles, making no exceptions. Patrick supposed the reason was that he had been born in Louisiana and had it ingrained from a child that he shouldn't *presume,* which was an absurd notion here. Los Angeles had no color bar—well, practically none. Riggs was accepted and well-respected; and so he should be! The man's grammar was far better than that used by most of the new whites in town, and except for the Californios he was turned out more elegantly than anyone. He was smart too. Intelligent enough maybe to have figured out that being formal might be a way to raise a fence of his own, keep other people at a distance.

"You've come to see my place?" asked the black, flashing his white teeth.

"Yes." Patrick looked around with frank curiosity, noting the raised platform at one end, with curtains like a real stage, approving the clean new tables, the whitewashed walls, the long, polished bar. "Very nice! And quite a success from all I hear."

Riggs nodded. "I can't complain." He had closed the place for sweeping up, but readily unbarred the door at Patrick's knock. Now he pulled out a chair for his guest. "Have a drink with me? You're way too early in the day to see my show, which is your loss, my friend!"

Patrick laughed. "I expect to be back frequently for that. But not tonight. I have to help Diego Rodriguez celebrate his daughter's wedding."

He seated himself, and Riggs joined him after snapping his fingers to summon the Mexican bartender. When a bottle and glasses were placed before him on the small table, the new saloon owner poured them both a large shot of brandy.

"You should be well pleased," Patrick continued.

"The show here is creating quite a stir. Your Blue Diamond hasn't been open a week and already strangers in town are asking the way."

"To be honest with you, I've been lucky. I've got a girl who would fill a house anywhere."

"Claudine's her name, isn't it? You see, the word has gotten around."

"Claudine, yes." Riggs pondered a moment, giving his visitor an oddly assessing look. "Mr. Donovan, she's planning a new number for tonight. I don't usually let a customer watch the girls rehearse, but for you—Want to see her?"

"I'd be pleased, Peter! Otherwise, for the next few days my curiosity would probably choke me."

"All right, then. Have another drink and I'll go tell her."

He left the table, and Patrick, sitting alone in the quiet room that still smelled of smoke and brandy from the night before, felt a stir of anticipation. He hadn't exaggerated when he spoke of the talk about this Claudine.

A few minutes passed, and then a middle-aged man, looking as though he'd just been waked from a stuporous sleep, his jaws shadowed with a day's growth of beard, slouched in and seated himself at the piano. He began wearily to thump the keys, producing a banal but spritely tune.

After a few bars, two girls ran onto the small platform, just as Riggs returned to the table. The dancers, like the pianist, had a rumpled, frowsy look; yet they were young, and lacked the jaded air of most saloon performers. Patrick could guess that in the evening, fresh from their rest and dressed in provocative costumes, they would be roundly applauded while they sang their bawdy song.

The lyrics were in English. Riggs remarked, not bothering to keep his voice down or avoid interrupting the singing, "I've another one, named Elena, hired especially for my Californio customers. She's popular with them—straight-laced, not at all naughty. But these set the stage for Claudine, a contrast, you might say."

The bouncy little act continued, the girls now and then flipping up their skirts as they kicked their legs, with Patrick grinning back broadly when they gave him a wink, and in no hurry to see it end. But at length the chorus was rounded off with a few exit bars, and the two scampered off.

The pianist now began a different sort of music, more subtle, slightly melancholy, and his air of boredom was gone. Instead of simply banging out chords, he played skillfully.

Patrick watched him briefly, then turned his attention back to the stage. He stiffened in surprise. The woman had appeared as though from nowhere. When he caught a glimpse of small, high-arched bare feet, he still didn't fully understand how she had made so silent an entrance.

So this was Claudine. His mouth formed a soundless whistle.

She was petite, delicately formed. Her flawless skin was faintly brown, yet her eyes shone brilliantly green, set off like emeralds by the long sooty-black lashes. Her lustrous ebony hair was piled high on the top of her head and confined by a narrow gold band studded with pearls. This and similar pearl earbobs were the only adornment she wore, except for three delicate gold chains circling her slim neck.

Other dance hall stars invariably appeared in glittering tight-waisted dresses, the bodice pointed front and back, and the shining satin skirts only serving to direct a man's eye upward to a more than ample bosom. Topping things off might be a large flamboyant hat.

So at first glance, Patrick had thought that Claudine, like the girls who had performed earlier, was not in costume. But the nature of her simple gown forced him to change his mind. It was made of thin lace, and fell almost straight from a very high waistline, suggestive, he thought fancifully, of a nightgown for an empress. While it was cut well away from her shoulders, her high, pointed breasts were shadowed by the lace, which left unanswered the tantalizing question of what she wore beneath it, if indeed she wore anything at all.

She began to sing in French, and unconsciously Patrick leaned forward. He felt the throaty voice slide into him as warm and smooth as the brandy from his glass.

Even with his limited understanding of the language, it was clear enough what the words were suggesting. He was intensely annoyed this time when Peter Riggs whispered, "She speaks English as well, and some of her songs are in English. But French suits her, don't you agree?"

"She's mulatto?"

"Quadroon. Beautiful, isn't she?"

"Very." He said nothing more, wanting to hear the rest of the song uninterrupted. When Claudine finished, and had left the stage without glancing their way, he clapped, hoping to bring her back. He experienced a stab of disappointment when she did not reappear, and then, aware that the proprietor was watching him, said, "Where on earth did she come from? She's hardly the sort I would expect in here." This was so patently true that he meant no offense, and gave none.

"You're right. Well, I suppose I can tell you, but as you'll understand, I wouldn't want the story to get out."

Riggs had Patrick's entire attention.

"She was the star attraction at one of those supper theatres in New Orleans. Very high-class places, as I'm sure you've heard. Unluckily for her, a white man was knifed in an empty dressing room. Claudine was his mistress, so the wife accused Claudine. An ugly mob gathered and the upshot was, she barely escaped the city with her life by hiding aboard a ship."

"A stowaway?"

"Not exactly. The captain had been at the theater himself, and she convinced him of her innocence. The ship was bound for California, so she stayed with him, and finally made San Pedro."

Patrick considered this terse, colorless account, given him by a man well-known as an entertaining story

teller. Riggs obviously found Claudine's history far
from amusing.

"She *was* innocent?"

"As far as I know. But I'm no judge, and in particular, no hanging judge." He gave Patrick a meaningful
look. "I figure what folks were and what they did before they came here is past. It's the same as if they'd
been born all over again. I don't ask questions."

"You're right," Patrick said heartily. "Anyway, a
woman as beautiful as that can be forgiven a few sins."
The knifing already was fading from his mind.

Riggs nodded, although he was still frowning slightly
as if trying to decide something. "She's something special all right, Mr. Donovan, and she knows it. So I want
to do the best I can for her, now she's here. Don't
want her getting discontented." He added finally,
"Would you like to meet her?"

"Very much!"

"I'll tell her."

Patrick poured himself another drink, and after
Riggs had left him, tossed it down. He understood now
why the private performance had taken place. His earlier restlessness was gone, dissolved in a surge of anticipation, and he felt fine.

CHAPTER TWENTY

"I THINK WHAT I MISS MOST, LIVING SO FAR
away on the rancho, is a bit of female companionship,"
Bets said, smiling warmly at Teodocia. "My little Isabel is still too young to be much of a talker."

The two were sitting together again in the cool evening, watching the dancing. Tomas and Pepe, dressed
in embroidered navy blue velvet pants and jackets,
the younger boy thereby looking like a miniature ver-
sion of Miguel, had stayed with them only briefly, then
Pepe, his black eyes snapping with excitement, had

rushed off, shouting the rules of a game he'd just invented, and Tomas followed him happily.

Bets was feeling more comfortable with her old friend than she had in years, which surprised her when she thought about it. One would have expected a wedding atmosphere to revive sad memories of Garth Peters. Instead of being pensive, however, Teodocia wore an air almost of contentment, plainly not unhappy with the current tenor of her life.

"I miss our old talks too," she said. "Betsey, you'll never know how lonely I was after you and Miguel and the children left for Rancho Aguirre. But lately, well, I've been kept so occupied that I haven't had time to think—even about Garth."

"Where is he now?"

"Still with Flores and the Manilas. He remembers me. From time to time, in spite of the risk, someone brings me a note. But of course it's hopeless now. The life he chose meant the end for us. And I've accepted that, except for once in a while when I see someone who looks like him, or I see two people who love each other. Then I weep a little."

Bets changed the subject quickly. "But you say you are so busy. What are you doing that occupies so much of your time?"

"I've been helping Father Daniel with the new school!" Teodocia's round face all at once was aglow with enthusiasm. "Oh I don't teach, I'm much too ignorant for that, but I watch after the youngest children, listen to them say their catechism, and just take care of them. With so many children together, there are lots of runny noses."

"No doubt! And many of them live right there at the school, don't they? Those from the ranchos? I suppose the nuns are close at hand, if some little one should become sick during the night—"

"I live there too! There isn't any proper convent house as yet, so the nuns and I stay right with the children. Father Daniel—such a kind, wonderful man, Betsey, I can't praise him enough! He has a tiny house for himself next door, and his church is just beyond that. It's strange, I suppose, but I am truly happy for the first time in so very long."

Seeing her friend's sudden consternation, she added, "No, you need not look at me like that. I am not thinking of taking religious vows. I love my life there, but not because I want to become a nun. I only meant that I love the children . . . Bets, I do want some of my own, most dreadfully!"

"Of course, Teo. And you will have them."

"Perhaps . . . But I envy you yours! Three, and now another one to be—"

"Gracious, does it show so clearly? I'd hoped not."

"Not so very," Teodocia assured her. "Only a bit around the waist . . . But how wonderful! If it's a boy, I hope he's a lot like Tomas."

"Tomas? Really? Most people never notice him because of Pepe."

"Oh, I know Pepe is brilliant, and charming as well. But after working at the school I've come to love the quiet sturdy ones just as much, maybe even more because they want it more! Anyway, you'll probably have a second girl, and that will be interesting too. Little Isabel is lovely—black hair and blue eyes like Tomas, but really more like you. She's just like you, isn't she?"

"Not exactly," Bets laughed. "She's more obedient than I ever was."

"That's very true," agreed Miguel, who had appeared beside them. Bets could see that he was in an exceptionally fine mood, just as he always was on occasions like this when the graceful Californio customs were being adhered to so meticulously.

"Elizabeth, would you forgive me if I ask Teodocia to be my partner in this dance? We see her so seldom."

"Of course! I must not dance anyway." Just in time she caught his frown. Not only must she not dance and display her condition (he had been somewhat dubious about the propriety of her attending the wedding at all) but just as important, she must make no reference to it yet. Now, for Miguel's benefit, she said to Teodocia, who gave her a suppressed smile in return. "Being an old married woman, I'm expected to take my turn as a duenna, chaperoning all the young people."

Alone, she tapped her foot in time to the gay music, as the dancers formed their squares. She wondered idly why her father had never reappeared for the evening festivities, then he faded from her mind as the music grew louder and faster, and the pace of the dancing accelerated until the men and women were spinning.

Perhaps because she was sitting apart, a spectator, she found herself regarding their wild, gay abandon more thoughtfully, deciding that this occasion differed, and not happily, from those of previous years. How many of these guests had left behind a burden of pressing, even desperate problems! They must be hoping to find in this spacious, familiar Rodriguez house, decorated fully as lavishly now as in years before, assurance that their own difficulties were at worst only temporary, or perhaps didn't even exist.

They would whirl on and on, wrapped in a bright cocoon of forgetfulness, until the music ended. But it must end, sooner or later.

She was watching the colorful, gyrating crowd, her face sober, when she heard, "Good evening, Elizabeth," and glanced up, glad to have her strange musing interrupted.

It was Felipa who sank into the next chair. Beneath her fine lace mantilla, she appeared tired and drawn. Her skin was sallow, lacking the usual radiance of a bride.

Bets, hoping to hide a too observant glance, exclaimed, "What a magnificent dress! All your nuptial gowns have been beautiful."

Felipa didn't seem to hear. She was staring out pensively over the heads of the dancers. "I'm only glad we Californios were able to have this one last traditional wedding. Another few months and it would be too late."

"I was just wondering if that might not be so."

Felipa turned to give her a long cool look. "I think you do understand what's happening. How ironic that it should be you! All the others keep hoping, they keep adding mortgages, they keep on living in the same extravagant way they always have. They—we—

are balanced on a knife edge and one little push will throw us over."

A hint of satisfaction was in her voice as she continued, "Your father, so I've heard, has learned his lessons well in becoming a Californio. Just like us, he's in debt, but still spending as always, and gambling away what's left. Well, there's solace for anything, so they say, in aguardiente."

Bets said nothing, but a coldness gripped her. She hadn't known! Could it really be true that Papa at last was in trouble? Patrick Donovan who always picked the right racehorse, whose judgment as well as good fortune she'd always believed in? Today, he'd seemed himself, self-confident as always, yet restless . . .

She was aware suddenly that Felipa was still speaking.

"I myself am intelligent enough to seek a shelter for when the storm comes, and the best shelter for a woman has always been a man, not just any man, but a someone who will be able to keep what he has. Weren't you surprised that I finally accepted Camellito?"

Taken aback by such a frank question from a bride, Bets said, "Only because you were always scornful about marrying an Americano."

"Quite. However, one must compromise, you will agree, and as his mother's family name was Avila, he is half Californio, after all. You see, Elizabeth, Lucius Camell not only gives promise of having sufficient money, he is the only man who wanted me, though I waited some years to be certain no one else would appear, and even then, I was reluctant. But—" she raised her shoulders, "while in some ways I despise him, I can control him. And I did want the prestige of marriage. My pride wouldn't stand being just a maiden aunt."

Bets was staring at her. "Felipa, why, in heaven's name, are you saying such things? Even if you've thought them!"

The angular, too-old bride appeared amused. "I'll tell you why. I know from experience that you'll never repeat my unsuitable remarks, and I did need to say all that aloud for once. You've known the worst about me from years back, haven't you? A little more can't matter.

"Ah, here come Miguel and Teo! I see that you are as generous as always with Miguel's favors. But then you never valued them highly enough to worry about their loss, did you? Have you been very happy together, Elizabeth? Somehow, I doubt it."

"I don't have to listen to this!" Bets rose, but Felipa too sprang up.

"Do you expect compliments? Do you think I am grateful, because you did not betray me after I shot Estrella? Quite the opposite! Being in your debt is intolerable, the real insult that I cannot forgive . . . Ah, Teo, Miguel—" She broke off to greet them, summoning a brittle smile.

"And here she is, my lovely, beautiful bride!" came a joyful shout. Camellito, beaming, had joined them as well.

For the next quadrille, Miguel asked Felipa to be his partner, and after a slight deliberation, she threw back her head and accepted. Bets was certain she was unable to hide a certain eagerness, which Camellito did not notice. His happiness was too deep to be easily broken.

"Teodocia?" He held out to her his square, stubby hand. "Will you do me the honor?"

It was true then, reflected Bets, her condition was a matter of common knowledge. Gentle, courteous Lucius Camell would never ask one lady to dance, leaving the other without an invitation, unless he knew that the second one was quite unable to accept anyway. Noticing the way he studiously avoided looking at her middle, Bets wanted to laugh.

So once again she was sitting on the sidelines, tapping her feet, and her amusement gradually gave way to irritation. This was absurd! She loved to dance, she was in excellent health, and yet she was supposed to remain rooted here like a crone of sixty!

Then, from across the room, a woman in similar condition beckoned, and she rose resignedly but forcing a smile. What had she expected after all? A mother of three children, she had certainly had enough experience with this particular custom in the past, not to resent it now.

"Miss Betsey, will you dance with me?"

She recognized his voice at once, and wondered with chagrin how long he'd been nearby and whether he'd been able to read the childish disappointment in her demeanor.

"Mr. Bishop! How very kind of you to ask, and how I wish I could accept. But I really cannot."

"That has been the story of my life at fandangos. The young lady refuses! Don't you know that my dancing has improved greatly? Mrs. Stearns was kind enough to take me in hand." Arcadia's sponsorship was not surprising. In recent years, single and successful as he was, Phineas Bishop had not only been welcomed into local society, he was assiduously sought after by all hostesses.

"Therefore when Phineas Bishop says that he is now a fair to middling dancer," he said, smiling at Bets, "you may take his word as gospel truth."

"Oh, I am convinced you are very good. And even if I weren't, do you think I'd refuse you for such a reason?"

"You wouldn't be the first." The gray eyes that looked down into hers held a teasing gleam that she failed to see.

"Surely, you realize why," she faltered.

"Miss Betsey, you don't have to make excuses! If you don't care to dance, that's fine."

"Mr. Bishop!" In her exasperation, she blurted out the truth without thinking. "You must be the only person in this room who hasn't noticed I'm with child! Oh!" She clapped her hand over her mouth, casting a hurried glance around. But no one else was near enough to have heard her crudeness.

He was looking surprised, but not for the reason she supposed. "Sure enough, I knew that. But I don't see that it matters. I would think a healthy woman like you could dance anyway."

Although the impropriety of the conversation made

her nervous, she found herself laughing. "I would think so too, Mr. Bishop! But it's not a matter of health, or my own wishes either. It's a matter of custom. Miguel —our friends, that is, would never approve."

"Good enough," Phineas replied. "Then may I simply keep you company? All the same, I warn you that some time you'll have to help me try out those steps I learned. I worked very hard to master them, and we can't let all that effort be for nothing."

She must have mistaken his meaning. He certainly hadn't taken the time to master a skill she suspected he cared little about, purely for the pleasure of dancing with her. So Bets didn't reply to that. But she did say warmly and a bit defiantly that she would be most pleased to have his company. There was no doubt that to be observed holding a lengthy private conversation with a man other than her husband would be almost as reprehensible as dancing; and this large man, who was really quite distinguished in his crisp uniform, was far from inconspicuous.

As it happened, he did not stay long. He was called away for some social duty by Felipa's aunt, the seemingly indestructible Doña Ana; and then Miguel reappeared and took his place at his wife's side. As both of them watched Bishop's figure threading its way through the numerous guests, Miguel surprised her by remarking, "It's absurd to wear that uniform as often as he does. A colonel indeed! One would think he was battling in the front lines, while actually even the rear lines are thousands of miles away."

"Aren't you being unfair?" Bets responded with indignation. "Mr. Bishop—"

"Capt. Bishop."

"Very well, Capt. Bishop has just explained to me the necessity for wearing it. The militia has a new rule that during the war both men and officers must be in uniform at all times. Anyway, why should what he wears disturb you?"

When Miguel didn't answer, Bets asked, more softly, "What is it? Why are you angry with him?"

"Angry isn't the right word, Elizabeth. At least, I'm

not annoyed with him or his successes, but with myself. He was telling me earlier tonight about the Battle of Shiloh, which took place last April! I was at the rancho all summer, and so I knew nothing. I, a man who was once a journalist! Can you imagine how ignorant I felt? How shamed before my friends? Think of it!"

But he himself chose to live there, Bets reflected. "What happened?" she asked. "I mean, at Shiloh?"

Miguel's mouth tightened, and he looked at her a moment before he answered. "The Union won. The casualties were enormous. From all accounts, it was the bloodiest battle thus far in a war that is horribly devastating. And even out here, so far away in Los Angeles, we don't remain untouched. General Johnston died at Shiloh. You remember, Albert Johnston, who—"

"I remember!" She sighed. "So this is the war that would only last a month or two. Already it's been a year and a half, and there's no end in sight, is there?"

"I'm hardly the one to ask," he said with a fresh spurt of bitterness. "At any rate, this is a wedding we're attending, so let's leave the war and other unpleasantness outside, in fairness to Felipa and Camellito . . . There's Arcadia, and I should dance with her. Will you excuse me?"

The night wore on, seemingly interminable. Miguel was with her much of the time, but when he wasn't, refusing to sit still longer, she drifted from group to group, growing more and more tired. She was far from sorry when at last a servant came to report that little Tomas had been discovered on a bench in the patio, sound asleep. Would Señora Aguirre consent to have him carried to bed?

Rising, she answered that she would tend to the child herself. First, she thought, she must find Pepe, who, like a hummingbird, seemed to sustain his diminutive body on the honey of activity. With good fortune, though, before long she would have both boys bedded down in the small room allotted to their family. Then she too could retire, her defection from the party unnoticed.

But it was some little time before she came upon her second son in the kitchen where, in company with two older boys, he was begging tidbits from the harassed cooks deep in preparation for the feasts of the following day. When Bets called to him, he came at once, taking her hand and giving her the sweet smile that told her he was really glad she was taking him off to sleep. As they walked together toward their room, they encountered Phineas and she asked if he would be kind enough to carry the sleeping Tomas from his place on the bench.

Bishop gently lifted Tomas into his arms and followed. In the Aguirre room, he laid him on the children's bed, covered him with a blanket, and nodding to Bets, went outside.

When Pepe had joined his brother, both breathing evenly in exhausted rest, Bets moved to the small window and stood looking out into the silvery night. The adobe walls of the room were very thick, and she half lay across the opening, letting it support her thickened body. Tired as she was, she was still wakeful. So far, for her, there had been little enjoyment in the festivities, and she was not quite ready to disrobe and retire, playing the role a docile wife should.

How bright the night was! The moon must be full, and she hadn't noticed. She leaned farther out, and then she saw the shadow of a man, motionless, only a few steps away.

Who was he, and what was he waiting for?

The answer to the first question came at once, but the second eluded and intrigued her. She went to the door, and at the sound of its opening, he turned.

"I didn't mean to disturb you," he said quietly. "I'm just not particularly eager to return to the festivities." He added, "I haven't any reason to."

"You didn't disturb me, Mr. Bishop. I was restless." She came out, pulling the door shut behind her. "How beautiful it is tonight!"

Side by side, they stood listening to the music that swelled and filled the patio. Beyond the trees of the large tiled square were groups of dancers who had spilled out of the house, couple by couple, into the pale path of the moon. But in this deserted corner, there remained a peaceful solitude that was only deepened by the laughter nearby.

"When you were learning those dance steps, did you learn to waltz? That's what they are playing now."

"Yes, ma'am. Mrs. Stearns finds waltzes are her favorites."

A silence fell and lengthened. The ochre tile under their feet was smooth and hard, and in between the spot where they stood and the noisy gaiety of the others was the foliage of many small citrus trees, protecting them from view. Bets found herself swaying to the sweet irresistible strains that pulsed in three-quarter time. She looked up at him, temptation growing. What harm could it do? And he would never ask her this second time, no matter how kindly he had been refused earlier.

"Mr. Bishop, we seem to be unobserved here. Would you like to try a few of those steps you've learned?"

His pleased smile reassured her, as he placed his arm around her waist. There was a moment of disconcerted realization when she reflected that she might have been wiser to choose the more impersonal gavotte, then her qualms disappeared in the pure pleasure of waltzing, which she, like Arcadia Stearns, loved so much. They swooped and sidestepped among the small trees, gliding together across the tiles until at last, far too soon, the lovely strains died away.

She stepped back regretfully. Phineas had held her firmly; indeed she had imagined more than a hint of tenderness in his clasp. But of course that was nonsense, and she did him an injustice! He felt nothing for her but the deepest respect.

Nevertheless, there was no question of continuing, even one dance had overstepped the bounds. But, oh, how she had enjoyed that one!

"Arcadia has taught you very well! Thank you, Mr. Bishop."

He bowed in mock imitation of a courtier, meaning

to be humorous. But his powerful body was surprisingly graceful.

"I'm the one to say thank you, Miss Betsey . . . Good night!"

CHAPTER TWENTY-ONE

CONVENIENTLY, BECAUSE OF THE MANY ELABorate changes of clothing needed by the Aguirre family for the wedding festivities, their journey had been made in an old-fashioned carreta, in which there was ample room for the trunks. Don Sebastian did possess a large carriage, but Miguel, indicating one of those preferences that no longer surprised Bets, had decided on the carreta, saying that he rather enjoyed its slowness and discomfort. She was coming to understand that while one side of his complicated nature ached to update and improve the society he loved, the other side clung stubbornly to the old ways.

As they jogged homeward even Pepe was content after those days of ceaseless activity to sit quietly. Miguel had promised the boys they might take turns driving the oxen, but for the moment, lulled by the creaking soporific tune of the wooden wheels, neither was pressing to do so.

Bets sat on the hard seat beside her husband and let her eyes wander over the passing scene. This was the time of year when the countryside appeared to her strange and forbidding, being in its dryness so totally different from New England as she remembered it. Each September and October, after being deprived of rain for more than half a year, the hills and canyons, the great spreads of grasses and dried seed pods, still baked under the relentless sun and seemed in an inexorable process of dying. The myriad small insects that droned and buzzed among the brittle stalks beside the dusty road were like scavengers on a desiccated body.

Bets shivered, and it was as though she herself voiced the thought when Miguel said, "We should have had a first good storm by now."

He spoke casually, clearly unworried. She supposed, because he had lived here always, he had grown used to knowing that the rain would come. Hadn't it always?

But with each year that passed, she had grown to like these months less, and she knew that her father shared this feeling. He'd told her once that when the rains finally began, no matter how cold and blustery the wind, or how unpleasant the mud underfoot, he always felt a thankful relief, knowing for certain the land had been saved once again.

Thinking of Patrick reminded her of their brief visit after the nuptials ended. She hadn't wanted to watch him closely—it seemed disloyal, unworthy of the love and respect she bore him. But Felipa's remarks had lodged poisonously in her mind. Was he in trouble? Was he gambling, drinking far too much brandy?

On the contrary, and to her relief, he seemed even more ebullient than usual. He had greeted the family at the door with bear hugs; then insisted on taking Miguel and the boys at once to the stable to show them a new little filly that he'd gotten by breeding one of his mares to that great horse Sarco. The race horse was now standing at stud, being too old for racing, Patrick explained happily, and while Don Pio Pico was very particular about the mares that were so honored, he had expressed considerable admiration for Patrick's judgment of horseflesh—quite a compliment coming from whom it did!

Instead of accompanying them, Bets chose to run across the familiar patio to Flora's room, throw herself into Flora's arms, kiss her and Jeb, and listen to their news. All the while, she quietly smiled at Flower, who watched shyly from behind her hands, only prevented from fleeing by her mother's firm grasp.

Flower tended to forget who people were when they were absent for any period of time, but it always ended the same. After a little, she would edge closer; and if treated gently would soon be showing the visitor how perfectly she could sweep the tiles, or how she could carry a tray of cups without breaking any. Although twelve-years-old, she spoke like a child of three. She was small and pretty, but her round face was sadly marred by the drooping of her lower jaw and the dullness in her eyes.

"Betsey! Do forgive me, dear, for not being here."

Bets glanced out to see her aunt hurrying from the direction of the house. For a second it seemed to Bets that no time had passed, that she herself was still eighteen and unmarried, because Mary did not change. She ran as lightly as ever, even weighed down as she was now by her jumble of painting materials. Her lovely patrician face with its high-bridged nose was quite unlined, her hair still red-brown. Close to forty-one, she appeared ten years younger.

"Didn't Papa remember to tell you we were coming?"

"Oh, he did tell me, of course. And he was so pleased! He adores all your children. But I was sketching a subject I'm quite excited about, the old trading post on Spring Street. I don't know why I never thought of it before—such interesting characters hanging about—anyway, I got so absorbed I forgot the time. And when I remembered, I ran all the way. I confess that at my age I do get a bit out of breath."

"You needn't have run," Bets said, and realized too late that she sounded ungracious, for the impulsive words seemed to imply that she hadn't cared at all whether or not her aunt had been there to greet them. But before she could say something warmer to this woman with whom she had never felt entirely at ease, Patrick and Miguel issued from the stable and the opportunity was lost.

Pepe was dancing alongside Patrick. "Oh please, Grandfather, please! Say you'll let me be the first to ride her!"

"Well now, Pepe, we'll have to see. Are you a good rider?"

"Oh, yes! Adam says I ride like a young mandarin!"

"Pepe," put in Miguel, "it will be some time before the filly can be trained, you know that. For now, I think you might be less noisy."

His younger son darted up an anxious look, but seeing his father's indulgent expression, cried again, "Please let me!"

"Very well," Patrick said, "but you must promise me something in return."

"Oh, yes, Grandfather! What?"

"You say you ride like a mandarin. Never, never speak Chinese to that little horse! If you do, you'll cast a magic spell, and she'll disappear in a cloud of smoke."

"Then I will never speak Chinese to her," answered the little boy solemnly. "But I must tell Adam too. He's the one who would forget."

Miguel and Patrick laughed.

"Where is Tomas?" Bets asked her father.

"He stayed behind to watch the foal have her dinner . . . What name shall we give her, Pepe?" Patrick reached down and swung the child up to his shoulder. Pepe squirmed about until he was comfortable, riding with his legs dangling down Patrick's chest. They were thin legs, like little sticks. All of him was scrawny, because as Tia Pilar said, he was never still long enough to get any meat on his bones.

All of them, Bets was sure, expected the boy's answer to be something fanciful. Pepe loved listening to stories as well as spinning them for Tomas. The characters, animal as well as human, all had elaborate names, his latest favorite being Rapunzel.

He put his face down close to Patrick's. "Would it be all right," he whispered, "to call her Elisa after Mama?"

"Hm . . . yes, I would think so," Patrick said gravely. He patted a knobby knee near his face. "Wouldn't you agree, Miguel?"

"An excellent name."

In her surprise, Bets was silent. Tomas, not Pepe, was always the one who wanted to be with her and Miguel, who sought their approval. If he had not stayed behind in the stable, he would have been walk-

ing beside Miguel, stretching to match his short sturdy
stride to the man's long one. Pepe, on the other hand,
was like a bit of thistledown, longing to fly to something new, to touch, to know, and then be lured away
again. She had always thought his enchantment with
the whole wide world must mean taking her devotion
for granted.

And now, so unexpectedly, this small impulsive gift.
The joy of it constricted her throat.

After a while in the lumbering carreta, Miguel said,
"Your father is considering raising sheep at Allison."

"Sheep? Good gracious!"

"After all, Elizabeth, it's no secret that cattle prices
are disastrous!"

For some reason she couldn't yet guess, her astonishment had displeased him.

"Phineas Bishop mentioned just the other day, he
expects they'll go lower still. On the other hand, the
demand for wool is tremendous. Do you realize that
most of the people who've had money enough to buy
ranchos away from the old families are sheep men?"

Alerted by his vehemence, Bets was thinking furiously. Was it possible that he too was considering such
a venture? But how could he, when it would mean
flouting one of the most deep-dyed prejudices held by
the Californios? Even if Miguel could bring himself to
do so, Don Sebastian, who made no secret of his dislikes, would never agree!

She said cautiously, "Papa has good judgment. If
he decides it isn't too risky—"

"I don't know what your father will decide, but I've
made up my mind. I intend to buy sheep."

"You? Oh, Miguel!" She was unable to hide her
consternation.

"What's the matter?" he asked grimly. "Do you disapprove again?"

"I couldn't approve or disapprove! I know nothing
about sheep. But have you told Don Sebastian?"

Although he was silent, the answer was in his face.

"Your father despises sheep. He won't even eat
mutton! He'll never allow them on the place."

"Indeed? You can speak for him?" At his tone, Bets

looked away, biting her full lower lip. "Perhaps you aren't aware that Father kept a huge flock for that man Carew. They grazed on Aguirre land for months."

"Wasn't that just a matter of courtesy? Not necessarily a question of liking sheep." Feeling uncomfortable discussing anything to do with John Carew, she tried to dismiss the subject. "I may well be mistaken. No doubt I am. I hope he'll be pleased."

"Elizabeth, why do you always discourage everything I try to do?"

She glanced over her shoulder, but the children were curled up, asleep.

Miguel, reminded of them, lowered his voice. "You didn't want me to start *El Clamor Publico* either. I sometimes think, if I had truly had your support then, I might have succeeded."

She was stung out of the silence she was trying to maintain. "I did support you! I wanted yours to be the most successful newspaper in Los Angeles. You must have known that! Surely it wasn't my fault that more and more English is being spoken—"

"No, that wasn't your fault. But in the beginning, you prevented me from believing whole-heartedly I would succeed, and I think in any difficult endeavor, such a belief is essential. When a man doubts, he hesitates to take the bold steps."

She gazed into his face, her own flushed with uncertainty. Had she really failed him? But the obstacles had seemed so obvious, and she'd only wanted to be sure he saw them too.

"Miguel, I had every confidence in you! I always have!"

"I would accept that, but for the fact that it was you who persuaded me to take a less active part in running the rancho. These last few months may have been pleasant for my father and for you, but not for me. With all there is to be done, I don't give the orders to the men, I sit idly by and teach my sons their lessons!"

"I only thought—let Don Sebastian have a little

time—" She cut off her comments, remembering with guilt how easily she'd been brought to agree that was necessary.

"Time! Those desperate people at the wedding, *my* people, opened my eyes. There is no time! No, Elizabeth." His jaw set and he flicked the whip at the oxen as though now that his mind was made up he didn't wish to tarry longer on the road. "I've had enough of inactivity. My father also wants our easy life to continue, and the only way it can continue is to change the things that aren't important. He'll see that . . . I shall talk to him today."

Sheep, she suspected, were not going to solve his conflict with his father; but mindful of his *El Clamor* accusation, and knowing too that further argument would only anger him, she kept the conviction to herself.

Don Sebastian was adamant. There would be no sheep on his land!

On this occasion, Bets was in the courtyard, giving to Isabel the doll they had brought her, a large one in an elaborate gray ball gown, with a dignified pink smile on its real china face. The raised voices came clearly through the window, deep voices uncannily alike, even though the patriarch's of late contained a querulous tremor that was new.

Miguel, affronted and apparently surprised, demanded to know his father's reasons for refusal; and Don Sebastian, with an aggravating pretense of patience, replied that sheep consumed far more of their fair share of pasturage than cattle.

"You said nothing about that, Father, when Carew kept his big herd here throughout a winter!"

"True, my son. But there were good reasons why I would not object on that occasion. To begin with, I was lonely. My only son chose to absent himself, living and working in the pueblo, and I had no one else. I enjoyed Mr. Carew's company. He was an excellent listener, and bore most courteously with my long and rambling remarks. Even when he brought a charming lady to my rancho, obviously wishing to be alone with her, he was punctilious about the introductions so that an occasional dinner hour might be amusing for me. Yes, I had every reason to accommodate Mr. Carew!

"In the second place, that was a winter of much rain. There was a fine stand of grass, if you will recall. Carew left here just before you became betrothed, and it was that same year that—"

"Just a moment, Father," Miguel interrupted sharply. "You are quite right, Carew left Los Angeles just then, and abruptly too. I had forgotten. Who—who was the young lady?"

"Not so very young," corrected Don Sebastian, "but definitely a lady. I speak of the Señora Reyes."

"Ah," Miguel breathed, but whether in relief or disappointment it would have been impossible to say.

The argument recommenced, but Bets was no longer listening.

Aunt Mary. So it had been Aunt Mary! She had never guessed. Never would have!

John and Aunt Mary!

She watched Isabel hug the doll, and said, "Don't drop her, darling," and all the time, against her will, she was remembering a time she had sworn to forget. When she was racked once again by a spasm of the old anguish and fury, she had to turn away from her daughter. John's *someone else* had a name now! A face. A body. Had he taken Aunt Mary somewhere and lain with her too?

When Miguel came into their room that night, late as it was she was still sleepless. In silence, sore with guilt, she watched him undress, and was touched and made further guilty by the concern with which he said, "You seemed very quiet at supper, *querida!* You're not unwell?"

Love me! she thought suddenly. *Love me enough tonight and I will never think of him again!*

Her husband must have sensed her unspoken plea. He had not yet blown out the candle, and he drew her into his arms. Seeing the eager affirmation in her face, he put his mouth down searchingly on hers, soon moving to kiss her eyes, her throat, while his hands under her nightdress were tight and warm on her breasts.

He threw back the bedcovers and pushed up her gown until its folds circled her neck. Naked and beautiful in his own slim muscular maleness, he straddled her on his knees, and paused, still upright while he gazed with glowing yet somber eyes at the silken curves and shadows and recesses of the woman beneath him. His fingers began to stroke her, lingering at the perceptible swelling that would one day be another of his children.

But almost at once the caresses stopped. His body came down on hers, and in spite of her quickening desire, she gave a small inaudible sigh of disappointment.

She had hoped, as she always did, that this time—this time—he would go slowly, coax her into deeper passion with his voice, his lips, his hands. But he never had, not in all the years they'd been married.

It didn't matter, she told herself stoutly. She was young and healthy and responded easily. Ah, but there were many nights, like this night, when she longed to break through the barrier of his reserve, have him wait, have them both wait, go slowly, touch, savor, simply pleasure each other with love!

Why did he not, she wondered. Could it be because in that long first year of marriage he had at last given in to his desire and taken her, well before Tomas was born, even though he'd promised himself he would not? At the time, foolishly, she'd been pleased, only realizing afterward that he might feel a need to punish himself.

And because she, only that afternoon, had visualized John with another woman, a terrible thought struck her now. Did Miguel, every time he lay with her, see the faceless lover who had bedded her before him? Oh, *surely* not—but if so—

Pity swamped her. She could make him truly happy, and she would! She would now! She clasped him to her fiercely, fitting her rhythm to his, deter-

mined to make him forget everything except his cre-
scendo of aching delight.

Then it was over, and he lay beside her, spent. He
fell asleep, his arm across her, his head on her breast.
But she wished for something more.

CHAPTER TWENTY-TWO

ARCADIA HALTED HER SMART STANHOPE GIG
alongside the rugged light yellow California cart
driven by young Mrs. Elvira McCarty. The latter conveyance was particularly wide as it was pulled by two
horses, and between both carriages, the ladies effectively bottled up Church Street. Neither worried about
it. There was little traffic at the moment, all of it on
horseback, and anyway, being Señora Stearns still carried a certain privilege. Most people surely wouldn't
mind a short wait.

Mrs. McCarty was new in town, and not really of a
class Arcadia liked to recognize so soon. But Lieutenant McCarty had recently been posted to Drum Barracks in charge of provisioning, and while Arcadia,
like most of her friends, was a strong Southern sympathizer, her husband, Don Abel, at a time when he
most needed currency, had been able to sell to the
military base a very large quantity of beef. A certain
courtesy was therefore in order.

The two ladies chatted, first about their carriages,
as Elvira at once admired the elegant Stearns possession. Arcadia secretly had had qualms about its purchase; she didn't even want to think about the cost of
that long passage from England! But she had been
reluctant to discourage Abel out of consideration for
his touchy pride. Knowing better than he guessed what
an extravagance such a carriage was in his present
financial straits, she took little pleasure in owning it,
and would have been happy to drive a common Cali-

fornia cart like Mrs. McCarty's. So her praise of the cart's virtues rang true enough, and she was able to suggest that its bumpiness, which was due to poor balance on the rough streets, could be helped by placing a two hundred pound sack of sand behind the seat.

"I trust though, Mrs. McCarty," she added, "that you are being cautious about driving alone. There is crime in Los Angeles these days, and I myself carry a small derringer."

That had been a mistake. Elvira visibly blanched.

"I don't mean to frighten you! Not at all. In broad daylight like this, you should be quite safe." Arcadia hurried on to a more pleasant subject. "I do hope you and Lieutenant McCarty will be able to join us next Tuesday! I'm giving a small party."

"Thank you, we'll be delighted to come!"

They were discussing the details when Arcadia realized that she had lost her new acquaintance's full attention. Mrs. McCarty's eyes had strayed to the doorway of a small house nearby. Annoyed, she too turned to look, and after a few more words, absently spoken, she also fell silent.

A man and woman had just let themselves out. The unusual appearance of the woman was undoubtedly what had caught Mrs. McCarty's attention. Ebony black hair and faintly brown skin would have presupposed brown eyes as well; therefore the sharp green ones that were clearly visible when their owner glanced out at the street were more than a little startling. The woman's figure, very slender and high-bosomed, was well displayed in a not-quite proper dress, and would have drawn attention anywhere.

In his evident infatuation, the man was oblivious of observers. On receiving a slow provocative smile he swept her passionately into his arms, first raising her mouth to his in a hard, lingering kiss, then burying his face in the shining upswept hair. Still in his embrace, she slid her jade-colored eyes sideways to take in the watchers in the carriages. The slight smile mocked them.

At length the man tore himself away and strode off

down the street. It was then that the woman indulged in a vulgar insolence that turned Arcadia cold with fury. Slowly, with an exaggerated twist of her hips, she strolled back to the door of her house, and at the last instant before she disappeared, she looked back again with that taunting smile, and thumbed her nose. The door swung to, as if in their faces.

"Well!" Mrs. McCarty said. "Uppity, wasn't she?" Receiving no answer, she added, "But those odd eyes! One wouldn't expect a tart to look so—so—oh, what is the word?"

"Exótica!" supplied Arcadia mechanically. She didn't even notice she had lapsed into her own language.

"Yes . . . that." Mrs. McCarty's Spanish was non-existent, and the word's equivalent was not part of her English vocabulary. "Who is she, anyway?"

"I've no idea!"

"You did know the man though, didn't you? I heard you gasp when you saw him."

"Yes, I know him." Arcadia pressed her lips together. For men to have mistresses was hardly unknown; but in her circle, such affairs were handled with a decent discretion. Public demonstrations were tasteless, and this one had been totally the fault of that unspeakable hussy. Anyone acquainted with Don Patrick recognized he was a man of passion, possessing all the transparency of a child and quite incapable of secrecy. So only an evil selfish woman would have permitted such intimacy on the street, encouraged it in fact, and before onlookers. She had made a fool of him, and she would again.

Ah, Don Abel was right! He frequently remarked that the pueblo was becoming infested with rabble, and he'd say angrily that something should be done. But what could anyone do? For crime, there were the new vigilantes. But for insolence? One couldn't even take notice.

A wife—that was what every man needed. Any wife worthy of the name would soon get the whore's hooks out of him.

Thumb her nose at Arcadia Bandini de Stearns indeed!

"Who was he?" pressed Mrs. McCarty, rightly suspecting she had happened on a juicy tidbit.

It would be pointless to try to conceal his identity, for he would be recognized anyway at the Stearns party. Arcadia wished she had never invited this tiresome woman.

"His name is Patrick Donovan." She lifted her horse's reins. "Shall we say Tuesday then?"

But Mrs. McCarty, it developed, was reluctant to drive on alone. "Now that you've told me it's not safe—"

Arcadia sighed, then chided herself. This was as good an afternoon as any to be hospitable, and the duty had to be performed. "I've a suggestion," she said. "Why not leave your horse and cart here? You can send a servant for them later, and we'll ride together. I'd like to show you the Plaza and the church, and perhaps some other landmarks of our beloved pueblo—"

"Beloved?" blurted out the newcomer with a glazed stare. She even made the mistake of wrinkling her nose as a puff of wind blew toward them from a large rank mound of garbage.

"Yes," Arcadia said evenly. "I hope you too will come to find it so after you've lived here a while. Come, I'll help you tie up your horse."

"But won't he be stolen?"

"It's most unlikely. Murderers often go free, but horse thieves are hanged."

Elvira did as she was told, hiding her reluctance. As she seated herself on the fine red leather upholstery of the gig, she wondered if people always obeyed Señora Stearns. All she had asked for was company on the way home. And now the whole afternoon, the one she'd saved for planting some sort of flowers around her dreadful little house, was ruined. Just for some sightseeing! As if there was anything to see in this God-forsaken place her husband had dragged her to!

As it turned out, she needn't have vexed herself. It was not to be a long ride after all.

The ladies had only progressed a short half-block, when they rounded the church, and stopped. Before them was the large open square of the Plaza, in which today a horse auction was taking place. Near by, sitting on the hard ground with her legs crossed beneath her heavy and now regrettably dusty skirts, was Mary Reyes. She appeared to be earnestly exhorting the girl beside her, who was intent on drawing with charcoal. Even from the gig, Arcadia could see the young artist's dark brown hands moving across the white paper.

Arcadia had never quite forgiven Mary for taking this lowly pupil and refusing a Stearns. She was tempted to drive on without attracting her friend's attention, but Mrs. McCarty, making an effort to atone for her earlier frankness, said, "How interesting! And so many horses! I suppose that ring is where they're shown to the men who want to buy?"

"Yes. Would you like to see the sale more closely?"

At that moment, Mary looked up and waved a greeting.

This was far from being the usual happy drawing lesson. They had met at the Plaza, Mary thinking that a horse sale would be a splendid opportunity for Alice to try her skill, drawing many animals in various kinds of action. Alice too, only the week before had been fully as excited at the prospect as one could wish. But now she sketched well simply because it was habit with her. Her mind was elsewhere. Although her eyes were dry, there was grief in them, so much so that it hurt Mary to look.

They sat on the ground together in silence, the one working, the other watching, or pretending to, while full of conjectures as to what possibly could have happened; and finally bringing herself to ask, with dread, "Is it—Terrence?"

Alice swallowed. When she answered, her voice was high-pitched and unnatural. "He's dead, Miss Mary. He was in a battle . . . at a place called Shiloh."

"Oh, Alice, dear Alice, I'm so sorry!" Mary longed to throw her arms around the agonized young girl, but instinct told her such comforting wouldn't be welcomed. Alice had already wept, and now she was steeling herself against the pain. She was stiff and brittle as a dried cornstalk. "But I don't understand! How could you have just learned this? That battle was last April—eight months ago!"

"He warn't killed there," came the toneless reply. "His leg was broke and he was took prisoner. They must not have knowed about it—his army I mean, because Pa wasn't told nothin'. We didn't know nothin'! Then one day a letter come from Terrence, smuggled through the lines. His leg was cut off. There was rats, and not enough food and all, but he was goin' to get home. He'd make it, he said.

"The Army letter finally come yesterday. He died of something called gangrene . . . You reckon he cried, Miss Mary? He never cried at home. Never!"

"No, Alice. No, he didn't cry—"

"Pa and Ma, they figure on bringin' him back here. They goin' to Tennessee to fetch him back."

"But they can't! Good heavens, there's a war going on." She stopped. What a silly thing to say to this child! "Don't you see, it would be terribly dangerous, aside from the hardships of ever getting there? They might be killed themselves! Or somebody might take them for runaway slaves."

"Pa's still got his papers. The ones Massa give him when he tole him he was a free man. So they ain't afeared. And I'm not neither."

All this time the stub of charcoal had been moving with frenzied speed. Three horses were in the picture. They were alive, spirited.

"You? You're not thinking of going with them?" Mary was appalled.

"He's my brother."

"Alice, no! It's wrong for all of you. Why, Terrence wouldn't want you to risk your lives!"

"He lost his'n. Anyways, we got to bring him back."

Mary turned, seeking some inspiration, telling herself that there must be a way to dissuade them. She saw Arcadia then, and not even thinking about her, waved.

Alice saw the gesture, and glanced over her shoulder. The drawing ceased.

"I got to go, Miss Mary. Thank you for all you done. When I come home, I'm hopin' we can get on with the lessons."

"We will . . . but Alice, please listen! I must talk to you! You must not go—"

"Bye, Miss Mary."

She had been gathering her materials together, and she thrust them into Mary's hands. "Keep these for me," she said, and then ran blindly away. At last she was crying.

"Mary," said Arcadia, "allow me to present Mrs. McCarty. She's only just arrived, and has been kind enough to accept my invitation for next week. Her husband, Lieutenant McCarty holds quite an important position at Drum Barracks."

Mary pulled her attention back from the running girl, already small in the distance. She understood all that Arcadia had been telling her in those few words, and regardless of any coolness that might be between the two of them, she must give what support she could.

As cordially as she could manage them, while struggling to put aside for the moment the tragic news that had so shocked and saddened her, the conventional words came. "Welcome to Los Angeles! I do hope you'll enjoy your stay here."

"Thank you," Elvira said. "I'm certain I shall."

Arcadia's frosty expression thawed a little. However, she could not resist remarking, "I trust it wasn't our arrival that sent your very talented pupil skipping away from her lesson, Mary?"

Mary returned smile for smile. "Not at all, Arcadia. Yours wasn't the first interruption by any means. Only a few moments ago Violeta Brinkman passed by and spoke to me." She added, in order to include Mrs. McCarty in the talk, "My niece Elizabeth says that one need only wait an hour or so near the Plaza, to see everyone one knows."

"Violeta is here?" asked Arcadia abruptly. "I un-

derstood she intended to remain throughout the winter
on that rancho of hers."

"She plans to, I think. But some sort of business
came up in Los Angeles. She'll be going back later
today."

"Did she say when, exactly?"

"No." Mary was puzzled. To indulge in personal
conversation of a sort that would not interest a guest
was quite unlike Arcadia.

"I wonder," Arcadia was directing herself to Mrs.
McCarty, "Could you possibly forgive me if I postpone
our tour until tomorrow? There's a small matter, nothing truly important, but still something I'd like to talk
over—suggest rather—to my old friend Señora Brinkman. Today, it seems, will be my only opportunity.
Would you mind very much?"

"Not a bit!" Elvira's reply was a shade too emphatic. "Tomorrow will suit me far better."

"How kind you are! Then that's what we will do . . .
What is it? Is something the matter?"

"We-ell, I am still worried about going home alone.
After what you said."

Arcadia had an immediate solution. "Señora Reyes
is going in that same direction herself. If you'd be willing to share your carriage with her?"

"Of course!"

"Then you'll be safe. Two women together seldom
have difficulty. Anyway, Mary is quite experienced in
getting about—even in the most unsavory parts of the
pueblo!"

Mary repressed a sigh. She wanted so very much to
be alone! Now she must wait still a little longer before
sorrowing for poor young Terrence, or worrying about
his family's pathetic quest, one that must certainly end
in disaster. To think, that wonderful talent of Alice's
might be lost too!

Her assent taken for granted, she found herself
walking the few steps back toward Mrs. McCarty's
cart.

That young woman had been aware neither of her
hostess's odd behavior, nor of Señora Reyes' reluctance. For her part, she was only too happy to have

the afternoon cut short, and she was mulling over what she was going to say to her husband, Roger. The very idea of him letting her drive about this dangerous frontier town with no protection! Such a terrible place. So dusty, and practically no green growing things anywhere. What would her mother say when she wrote that her house, when they arrived, was jumping with fleas?

And she'd expected people to be friendly, to welcome her—after all, the poor things must be starved to see the New York fashions. But they weren't hospitable, not really. Take Señora Stearns. She'd been polite enough, but it was clear that in no way were they ever going to be bosom friends. And this Señora Reyes—she'd said a few kind things, but she was awfully quiet, thinking about something else probably, just as if she was all alone.

They reached the waiting vehicle and were climbing in when Elvira determined to start a cheery conversation. "I'm afraid your friend isn't much of a woman of the world."

She succeeded in astonishing Mary, who said blankly, "Arcadia?"

"Yes. She was shocked, really shocked, by the goings-on in that house there."

"What house?" Thoroughly bewildered, Mary looked where the officer's wife pointed. "What's in there?" she asked, as was expected of her.

Elvira giggled. "Just a love-nest. The woman is beautiful. I have to admit that. But she's only a whore just the same. The man now, he's somebody important."

"Really? If you'd like to turn the cart around, there's room, I think. We must go the opposite way from the church—toward Sonoratown—"

"Let's see, what was his name? Oh, yes. Donovan. I think that was it. Yes. Patrick Donovan. Do you know him?"

CHAPTER TWENTY-THREE

PATRICK HAD ALWAYS ENJOYED HIS OCCASIONAL visits to the vast Brinkman estate. It gave him warm pleasure to view an establishment that was so obviously well-run and prosperous. These days, a large rancho that had not changed hands and still could be so described was a rarity. Also, William's widow had not forgotten how to make a man comfortable, although he considered her possibly the most efficient manager he knew.

He had never come there without experiencing a sense of wonder that Brinkman's sheltered Californio wife, whose sole labor up to the time of his death had been directing a corps of servants, could have firmly grasped the reins that fell from her husband's hands and with obvious relish, driven ahead. As he remembered her from the earlier days, she had been gossipy, more than a little malicious, and intensely ambitious for her daughters. With age, the malice, always laced with humor, had turned from vinegar into a rich dry wine, while her interests broadened and sharpened. Subordinating all else was her fierce dedication to her land.

On this occasion, as usual, she had provided for her guest an excellent dinner, complete with the wines he loved best. Respecting her judgment as he did he found the conversation, entirely devoted during the meal to the continuing lack of rain and her plans should the dry weather persist, diverting and instructive.

"I appreciate this invitation," he said later, as they sat together in the large comfortable courtyard. The droning of the bees among the roses, which for Señora Brinkman were obediently blooming in December almost as profusely as they had in June, the heat of the sun, and the quantity of wine he had drunk, all made him content and a little drowsy.

"It is my pleasure," she responded, and paused. "Señor Donovan, may I ask you an impertinent question?"

"Of course. What is it?" He did not turn his head on which the thick dark hair was now laced with gray, and he answered lazily, but her tone had alerted him, and the languor disappeared. He wondered if this time, unlike all the other occasions through the years he'd been invited here, her hospitality had a purpose.

Even so, he was unprepared for her blunt return.

"You have been a widower for many years. Have you never considered remarrying?"

He could not completely hide his startled apprehension, for his first thought was that she had tired at last of widowhood.

"I have not entirely ruled out that possibility," and without seeming to do so, he studied her. While far from beautiful, her short buxom body was firmer and more limber than most women her age could boast. This was not surprising, he reflected, knowing that she rode the many miles around her rancho daily on horseback, in complete disregard of sun, rain or wind. Her face, although deeply lined and weathered, was certainly more interesting than it had been when she led a life of leisure, and anyway, he thought, all one ever noticed in conversing with her were those shrewd, snapping, black eyes. Yes, a man could certainly do worse if he were interested in marriage. And, if he did not have a Claudine.

To his credit, Patrick did not at that moment remember that she was the owner of a highly prosperous rancho, and that he himself was badly in need of capital.

But while he was phrasing a further noncommittal remark in his mind, she began to chuckle.

"Ah, Señor Donovan, I see by your face that you have reached a mistaken conclusion. You need not be alarmed. We have been friends, if I may be so bold as to use that word, for some years—a highly satisfactory relationship that I would not wish to change. I assure you moreover that fond as I was of my husband, I have created for myself a life that far exceeds in its rewards anything I experienced in marriage. Never again a lord and master for me! I like being free to make all the decisions myself. To tell you the truth, I suspect that if all women could learn what they are missing, the race would die out in a generation."

She was discoursing, he knew, in order to ease his slight embarrassment at having misunderstood.

"Ah, but you see, all women, most women, couldn't learn that lesson. They haven't your energy and intelligence."

"For that I won't thank you," she retorted. "Rather than a compliment to me, it is an insult to the others of my sex. However, I wasn't intending to start a discussion about women. Your intuition was right. Although not on my own behalf, I did have an object in mind when I asked you that question. Shall I come directly to the point?"

"Please do." He was genuinely puzzled.

"Teodocia. My daughter. She needs a husband, and it appears this would be an advantageous marriage for both of you."

To give himself time to think, being totally surprised, he said, "Didn't you just extoll the virtues of the single life? Why would you wish marriage on the poor child? And to a man of my age! You know—of course you do—that I have turned fifty?"

"To answer your first two questions, although I realize they were put facetiously, a woman should have the opportunity to have children if she wishes, and Teodocia does so wish. She is a born wife and mother —sweet, gentle, patient. While hers may be the sort of blond prettiness that will fade, she is very attractive, is she not? She is hardly a chubby little girl anymore. Many people have commented to me on her fine figure."

"She is lovely!"

"As for your age, of course I know it. But with the example of Abel Stearns, who married Arcadia when she was so much younger also, why would I be fearful on that score?"

His mind was racing. He liked the girl well enough, but merely as he would like any friend of Bets'. With Claudine to satisfy all the hunger of his body, and with his sister Mary Frances to be a companion and run his house, he had less need now to remarry than at any time since Allison's death. A child bride would be merely a disruption. As for Teodocia, surely her own happiness wouldn't be served either.

Still, one didn't blurt out such reactions to the girl's mother. He grasped at his last thought, and said, "I could hardly suppose the child wouldn't prefer some-one her own age."

Señora Brinkman sighed. "You continue to refer to her as a child, forgetting that time has passed. She is now twenty-five, and it is because of a misguided preference for a young man of her own age—that miserable Garth Peters, that she is a spinster!

"That episode, and I admit it to you frankly, has not enhanced her reputation, but few of the young men left would be qualified anyway, from my point of view. A callow youth is hardly competent to manage the large dowry I am prepared to give her."

A small spider had been laboriously climbing the leg of the table, and now the Señora took time to flick it away with her fingernail before she resumed.

"The money would be utterly wasted, and as you know me well, you know I could not stomach that. No, I want to be able to hand over Teodocia's assets with no strings attached, confident that they will be used wisely. I've always preferred Americano husbands for my daughters for that very reason, and recent events have borne me out."

He thought at once of his own rancho. In his mind's eye, the vineyards were already covered with beautiful purple grapes, the trees loaded with fruit. Even though he well knew that his cattle, and the new sheep too, were roaming dry canyon slopes in desperate search of a few spears of grass, he envisioned them as sleek, fat, beautiful. Ah, how he loved his property!

And the sickening truth was that Allison might not be his much longer. In times past, if a man couldn't raise a big interest payment just when it was due, his friends who held the mortgage would give him all the time he needed, even be embarrassed that the subject had been raised. But now there was a hard new climate, one he didn't understand. Foreclosure was not a rarity any more! Other men had lost their land. He wouldn't be the first.

He must make that payment, and he needed money. As a husband, that money would be honorably his . . .

But even thinking along those lines was like running after a mirage. Suppose he did agree, suppose by some wild possibility little Teo would agree, by the time the banns were posted and the wedding took place in a seemly fashion, it would be too late. Everything he owned, all could be out of his possession. The dowry might be his, but too late.

"I would want an immediate wedding, soon after Christmas perhaps," the Señora remarked before he could speak. "The priest, I am certain, would be agreeable. I don't like to have Teodocia working at that school! It's degrading for someone of our family's position, also dangerous in these lawless times, for a young woman to walk the streets alone. But my daughter has become so independent, she refuses to obey me when I urge her to come here to live; and with things as they are, I cannot leave my rancho for more than a few days at a time. So, each day that passes, I worry."

Her observant eyes watching him were inscrutable, he realized suddenly, and wished he could know what she was thinking. Could she possibly guess the real reason why he must refuse—Claudine? Because of course she would assume there was a Claudine.

Too bad he wasn't the sort of man to have both wife and mistress! Well, he wasn't. Being a cheating husband had never appealed to him, and if he were married, he would never allow himself to visit Claudine again. Therefore, as he was still enamored, and by no means ready to give her up, he must say at once—

"I imagine you'll want to consider everything at your leisure," Señora Brinkman put in softly. "Being an intelligent man, you don't say yes or no too quickly. Will you dine with me again a week from today?"

He rose at once and looked down at her. "Very well, although I think there can be only one answer and little to be gained by postponing it. I—"

"Please!" She held up her hand. "Humor me by not being impulsive."

"Very well. Tell me, does Teodocia know about this —this suggestion?"

"Not yet."

"I thought not. She would refuse."

"You underrate yourself. Good day, Señor Donovan."

As he rode home, he could not help feeling a faint relief that he had not been precipitous. The idea of giving up Claudine was a little less shocking now than it had been even an hour ago. Forced to consider his mistress dispassionately, he admitted to himself that her demands of late had been growing burdensome.

Keeping a small house just for her was not such an expense in itself, nor was the payment of a few coins for her Mexican maid. But Claudine would eat only the finest foods, many of them imported on ships, and she wore nothing but the most expensive clothes which the Mexican woman stitched from gossamer-like silk. And only the night before, after she had professed being a trifle indisposed, as though noting his disappointment, she had twined her arms about his neck and pressed her body against his, giving herself at last as though she could deny him nothing. Expected to show gratitude, he had promised he would send for the emerald eardrops that she'd admired once in San Francisco and mentioned frequently. Thinking about it afterward, he'd found the scene distasteful.

All the same, these few months had been the most exciting, the happiest in many years, and he told himself that if money weren't in such critically short supply, he wouldn't begrudge Claudine a penny of it!

When he reached his house in town after hours of riding, he was still mulling over the extraordinary proposal of Señora Brinkman.

"Good evening, Mary Frances—"

His sister was seated on the wall bench, industriously

working a square of needlepoint. This was a form of art that she despised, and seemed only willing to pursue when for one reason or another a painting was going badly. Usually serenely absent-minded and happy while her work was in progress, striking a snag could make her almost desperate with anxiety. To doggedly ply the hated needle, as she was doing, was the signal of such a mood, Patrick had learned.

"Trouble with 'the Goose Pond'?" he asked, referring to her current interest in depicting the swampy area where Phineas Bishop some years before had established a new shipping terminal. Lately Mary had turned out several watercolors of the sea, her subjects fishermen and the sailors who worked the lighters and tugs.

"No, why do you think that?"

"The needlework," he explained uneasily. He hadn't been home in several days and he wondered if something unpleasant had happened. She was frowning, and sounded almost flinty. Well, he'd jostle her out of her low spirits, whatever their cause!

But before he could try, she said, "I think I'll go up to San Francisco."

"Oh?"

"Yes." She did not meet his eyes. "One of the galleries there, the Milo, has written me. Mr. Milo says that a show of my watercolors might be arranged."

"Why, that's wonderful, Mary Frances! How pleased you must be! When will you go?"

"At once. Tomorrow. A ship, the *Senator,* leaves in the morning."

"Very well." He added, uncertainly, "A jaunt will do you good . . . But before you go, I've something to tell you. Señora Brinkman and I were talking today, and, well—I might possibly get married again."

"To her?" Mary's busy fingers stopped. Her face cleared. "Why, Patrick, that would be splendid, I think! She's really remarkable, the way she's taken hold at her rancho. And as for being a wife, she did make William Brinkman happy—"

"Not the Señora! Her daughter, Teodocia."

"Teo? That child?" Mary stared at him. She had

paled. "You—you must be crazy! How unfeeling, how selfish and cruel! I would never have believed it of you!"

He was stunned. "Selfish, am I? Cruel? Merely because I am older than she? I am not decrepit!"

"Your age did not occur to me," she said coldly.

"What did then?"

"I'll tell you, as you should have told yourself. She's too young and innocent to cheat."

The ugly word lay between them. She had dropped the needlework, and was standing facing him. "I was told some news by a complete stranger, someone who had no idea I, Señora Reyes, might be your sister. I must have been the last person in town to hear that you've set up a house for a fancy lady. Now that I think about it, you've been going to the Blue Diamond frequently, so I suppose she's one of those easy women who dance there and flaunt themselves."

At last he understood the reason for his cool reception tonight. Even so, the depth of her scorn surprised him.

"You are shocked that I have a mistress? Good God, Mary Frances! What do you think I am, a eunuch? A man needs a woman."

"No doubt." Her distaste was so evident that his anger stirred. "I've been unimaginative, not guessing you had such a problem, and if I had, I still wouldn't expect to hear through common gossip how you'd solved it. . . . But I am being unfair. After Francisco began behaving like a tom cat, I conceived an unfortunate prejudice against men who indulge in cheap whoring—"

"Enough!" he roared. "No wonder you are leaving on the *Senator!* Mustn't stay in the same house with a low fellow like myself, is that it? No doubt you're thinking that I'll be sneaking off to Claudine after I'm married as well as before?"

"Yes." She wavered then. "I don't know . . ." Oh, why had she been striking out at him like this? Her beloved Patrick! It must be her sorrow over Terrence, her heart-sickness that a boy's life had ended so uselessly and caused three more to be endangered, that was making her so shrewish, so unreasonable!

"Thank you for your good opinion! I am flattered! But one thing does puzzle me, sister mine. The idea that my bride-to-be was the Señora somehow met with your strait-laced approval, or so it seemed. It is better to deceive her than her daughter?"

"No, I—it was simply that I thought—" Mary's assurance was demolished. Never before in her life had she had to face Patrick's fury. "The Señora is a woman of the world and she would learn about your mistress. She would make you give her up! So I was glad . . . but little Teodocia, she'd be easily deluded, just as I was—Oh, Patrick, wait, please wait, I'm so sorry—"

He had stalked away, implacable. His back to her, he said in a voice she had never heard before, "Yes, go to San Francisco! Jeb will drive you to the dock in the morning."

CHAPTER TWENTY-FOUR

Come into town for Christmas, please Bets! And bring the children. The house will be lonely with Mary Frances away. Besides, I may have a bit of news . . .

BETS FINGERED THE LETTER AND LOOKED IN puzzlement at Jeb who had brought it to the rancho. "Why didn't Papa just come for a visit and invite us himself? We haven't seen him in months."

Jeb's eyes shifted. "Your Pa's pretty busy."

"I suppose he is spending a lot of time at Allison these days. Jeb, has he bought sheep?"

"Sheep?" Jeb looked surprised and unaccountably relieved. "He done that a long time ago, Miss Betsey. I reckon the rancho does worry him a bit, now you mention it."

"I'm sure it does! Everyone has such troubles! Very well, tell him please that we'll be happy to come. I must ask my husband of course, but he's always loved the Christmas pageant, *Los Pastores,* and all the fun that goes with it. He's bound to agree."

Miguel did assent, but with the grimness that characterized him these days.

"The boys have seen *Los Pastores* several times, but little Isabel never has and she should. The pageant is part of her heritage. Father no doubt will complain bitterly about being left alone over Christmas, but as it will give him a chance to give orders completely unopposed, he'll have difficulty deciding whether to be pleased or furious."

"I hope there isn't one of those great winter storms that day, as there was last year," Bets worried. "Everything was ruined! I'll never forget the currents of water running in the streets and those cold winds blowing a gale across the Plaza."

"I would welcome a storm today."

They were standing together in the courtyard, the afternoon bright and warm with sunshine, just as each day before had been. With his head thrown back, he stared up into that clear cloudless sky and said softly, "Mother of God, make it rain, and soon."

Ever since his confrontation with his father, Miguel had been edgy and morose, and Bets supposed he was still unhappy about the outcome. Don Sebastian had made a show of great magnanimity, saying that if the dry weather ended in time, and there was good pasture, then Miguel might introduce a small flock of sheep as an experiment. He, his father, wouldn't want to discourage any sincere effort, however misguided it might seem to him.

"But that means waiting until spring," Miguel had protested. "The price will have risen before then. Right now, only a few of us even admit sheep might be worth having. Both Pio Pico and Abel Stearns have refused point-blank to lease some of their land to sheepmen—"

"Then don't you think I'm being broadminded?"

asked his father slyly. "Be satisfied. And I will pray for some rain."

Whether or not Don Sebastian bowed his head in prayer, the sun continued to beat down unmercifully, shrivelling the land. Every day Miguel became more short-tempered, as Don Sebastian, ignoring his suggestions, continued to issue all orders to the men.

On Christmas Eve, the family once more journeyed into town in the old carreta. But this time, little Isabel was with them. She sat pressed against Bets, her plump, star-shaped hand resting light as a dove's wing on her mother's arm, her blue eyes wide with excitement.

"*Los Pastores,* Mama?" She licked her lip with her small tongue, as though tasting the unfamiliar words.

"Yes, darling, *The Shepherds,*" Bets repeated. "It is a play."

"A play?"

"She's never seen a play," Pepe put in. "She just can't imagine! I couldn't at first either. Of course Tomas and I are older now. I even know what Papa means when he calls it a survival of a medieval miracle play!" He finished in a rush of breath.

"You do?" Tomas asked in admiration.

"Yes, tell us, Pepe," Miguel said, momentarily diverted from his own thoughts.

His small son's chest puffed with importance. "You say that because *Los Pastores* is the Christmas story. There are shepherds on their way to the manger, and the archangel Michael, and a hermit, and the devil . . . Oh, and the devil has horns and a long forked tail, Isabelita! After the play is over he'll walk right up to you, but he won't hurt you. And someday I'm going to be a shepherd in the play. Did I tell it right, Papa?"

"You described it very well. But I don't believe you explained all those big words you used." Miguel was smiling, but Pepe looked crestfallen.

Tomas said, "I liked the way you told it, Pepe. I'd forgotten about the devil walking about." The smaller boy shot him a look of gratitude.

"But Mama, what's a play?" asked Isabel, having

waited patiently all this time for the answer to her question.

"You'll see, darling," Bets said amid their laughter, "and you'll love every minute of it just as the boys do, and your father."

"Why do you leave yourself out?" Miguel said. He was smiling at her, unable to repress his own keen anticipation. "You are as eager as any of us!"

It was true. She was. Although the previous year, the actors in the little outdoor drama had been driven from the Plaza by a torrential downpour, every previous Christmas Bets had spent in Los Angeles had been rendered more colorful and joyous by the annual pageant.

The performance two years ago had been the finest of all, even though the baby Isabel, seeming a trifle feverish, had been left at home in the care of Tia Pilar. And how young the boys had been! Because he anticipated it would be a long tiring evening for them, Miguel had driven the carreta as close to the Plaza as he could; and then, when the oxen could no longer advance through the densely crowded streets, the conveyance had simply been left, pulled to one side, and the family continued on foot, Miguel at their head, and clutching each other's hands.

"Hold tight!" Bets had cried to Tomas, who was last. "We don't want to lose you."

"Oh, Mama, he knows the way!" Pepe piped in his treble voice that was higher still with excitement. "We both do! You know that."

She did, but she gripped their hands more tightly. There was something about Christmas, she'd thought, that made the children even more precious. How blessed she was, to have them, these two, and the perfect little girl at home!

The play they watched was the same each year, yet always new. All the parts were acted out by townspeople who were, in the spectators' view, far more convincing than any trained actors might have been. The archangel Michael was awesome in his long white robe and halo, although the children loved the devil best with his horns, tail, and cloven hoofs. At the climax,

which was the defeat of the devil at the hands of St.
Michael, the church bells, deafening in their nearness,
rang a paean of triumph.

Soon after the pageant began, Patrick Donovan had
found his grandsons in the crowd, and with the ending,
he bent to ask them, "Do you like it?" His voice
boomed out, even above the noise that was all around
them. "Well, Tomas?"

"I love this night the best of my whole life!"

"And you, Pepe?"

"I too, Grandfather! But, look! Doesn't St. Michael
go back to heaven? He's walking about . . . and with
the devil!" St. Michael did have a careless arm thrown
around the arch-fiend's shoulders, as all of the players
strolled away together.

"They are going now to visit the big houses near
the Plaza," Miguel explained. His own dark eyes were
shining as brightly as the children's. "See, they are
being welcomed at Don Abel's. They'll be given
buñuelos at each place."

Pepe sighed, doubtless at thought of those delicious
fried sweet cakes being offered. "Papa—" That was
when he had put an imploring hand on his father's
sleeve and asked, "may I be a shepherd next year?
May I?"

"Hardly next year," Miguel answered solemnly.
"But as soon as you are old enough, I will see what
can be done."

Tomas too must have been thinking of the
buñuelos.

"I'm hungry!" he said with such urgency that
Miguel laughed.

"Come along then!"

They had promenaded the Plaza where numerous
small booths had been set up. Beguiled by the cries
of the vendors hawking tamales, enchilades, fruit and
candy, even the elders succumbed and bought treats
for themselves until Patrick finally said, with a broad
wink at Miguel, "Perhaps we should go to my house
and rest. If we are all going to Mass at four in the
morning, we'll need to sleep; especially our future

shepherds here, the ones with red candy on their faces."

"Oh, but Grandfather?" This time in his dismay Tomas spoke first, for what was still to come was dear to his heart. "Don't you remember?"

Patrick yawned elaborately. "Remember what?"

"The fireworks," whispered Tomas.

"Oh, the fireworks! Of course. How could I forget?"

How indeed? It seemed every child in the pueblo that Christmas Eve was packed into the south corner of the Plaza, and the anticipation in their faces, alike for wealthy Californio boys and girls, or miserably poor Indians, touched and silenced the adults.

The lavish fireworks began. There were pin wheels, golden fountains, and other wonderful effects that had been brought from China. Best of all, when the show was over, there were sparklers for sale, and Patrick, as was his custom, bought each grandson a package. He bought extra boxes as well and when he thought none of the family was watching, gave them away to the threadbare wistful children who stood nearby.

The walk of a few blocks back to the Donovan house was accomplished in a quiet of contentment, the only sound being the hiss of the lighted sparklers each one carried. Bets had followed behind the rest. She liked to watch the tiny flickering stars that shot off as the little torches were waved in circles and figure-eights. Their own Christmas procession, she thought with a catch at her heart.

So now once again at Christmas, they were entering Los Angeles to the beautiful mellow ringing of church bells. But Bets and Miguel soon were exchanging glances. Dusk had already fallen, and the streets should have been filled with people, laughing, embracing, shouting greetings. There should have been singers and musicians, strolling through the crowd making music, not just Christmas carols, but ballads and tender love songs. Instead there were only a few passersby and theirs was clearly no festival mood.

"Hurry, Papa," Pepe urged anxiously. "We don't want to miss the play."

But Miguel did not move. He was gazing off at the dark Plaza which should have been alight with torches. The children watched his face.

"We were late one year," Pete said. His voice faltered.

"Yes, and I regret that very much! More so now, because we shan't be either late or on time. There is no play tonight, children." He could not hide his disappointment, his tone so bitter that even Pepe was stilled.

When Patrick opened his door to them and saw their glum faces, he said instantly, "I certainly thought you knew! Because of the disaster of the rain storm last year, the committee decided to disband."

Miguel's face stiffened. Bets knew he felt humiliated by his obvious ignorance of the town's affairs. "There have been rains before," he said angrily, ushering his silent family inside.

"Yes, and you're right, the possibility of bad weather wasn't the only reason. The man who has played St. Michael for so many years has gotten old, and too, everyone is a little worried. Work is hard for many to find, and the town itself is changing—"

"I know that well enough! Who better? I've watched the fine traditional customs disappear, one by one. But I didn't expect us to lose *Los Pastores*. Not yet!"

"We will see the play next year, won't we, Papa?" Tomas asked him.

"We won't!" Pepe put in. "That is what Papa is saying."

"No more fireworks?" For once, the older boy's composure was cracking.

"Come along now, both of you," Bets said quickly. "Whatever happens in the future is not for us to worry about tonight. You must be sure to sleep for a little, because the wonderful Christmas Mass is still ahead and you'll be awakened at four o'clock in the morning. Only on a very special occasion do we do that!"

They were nine and eight-years-old and easy to cheer. But lightening Miguel's moodiness when she returned from putting them in their beds was another matter.

Patrick was speaking, trying in his way to erase the disappointment by cheerfully ignoring it.

"Flora is outdoing herself in the kitchen. She's decided to cook a different sort of dinner—one such as she would have served long ago in Charleston. She has been feeding a goose for weeks so that it would be nice and fat, and she'll roast it in the morning. I must say I find a lot of merit in the idea of showing the children a little of the other half of their heritage."

Miguel had been pacing one end of the room, and now he gave a short laugh, entirely devoid of gaiety. "I hardly think you need worry. Unless I am mistaken, that half will soon be all there is to see . . . I am sorry, Patrick, but will you tell Flora I regret missing her roast? My family will stay, but as soon as Mass is over I must return to Rancho Aguirre."

"Oh, Miguel! Why?" Bets cried.

Her obvious dismay that he would be absent must have pleased him, because he reached to take her hand, a simple and for him rare public gesture.

"Elizabeth, there's something I want to say before I leave. I'm afraid I haven't been entirely forthright with you—"

He glanced at Patrick, and the latter rose, saying, "May I offer you refreshment? Coffee, at least? I'll ask Flora to bring it." He sauntered out, not waiting for an answer, and Bets watched him go with affectionate gratitude.

"We are alone now, Miguel. What is it?"

"I decided not to wait until spring!"

"I don't understand."

"One of the big sheepowners was reducing his herd for the year and would sell several hundred head."

"Oh, Miguel! If you buy them, defying your father, won't he be very angry? Please think carefully!"

"I have thought. Do you too consider me no more than a headstrong boy? The price was very low, and such an opportunity may not come again. Anyway, it's too late for thinking! I've paid the money. I have the sheep."

"But when will you tell Don Sebastian?" She wondered why this revelation depressed her so. She knew nothing about sheep.

He hesitated. "Not—at once."

That was just as well, she supposed. Her father-in-law's health was far from good now, and knowledge of this defiant action on the part of his son would undoubtedly throw him into a rage, making worse his spells of dizziness.

"Would a few more months have mattered so much?" She shook her head. "He can't fail to uncover your deception."

Dark color came into Miguel's face at the bald word *deception*. But he restrained his anger. "I have the animals pastured at the southernmost end of the rancho. They won't stray as far as the house, and he doesn't ride out. However, there is always the odd chance—which is why I want to return at once."

He began to pace again, hands clasped tightly behind him. How could he, of all men, have stooped to trickery, she wondered while watching him; and then, in a sudden surge of sympathy, believed she understood.

He must have been desperate to believe in his soul this move was necessary! Until now he had chafed at being unable to act, his hands tied by his father's stubbornness, while the price of beef fell ever lower and expenses soared. When the opportunity came to buy sheep at a price he could manage from his own funds, he took it, hoping to make money for the rancho and accepting as his penalty the ignominy of skulking behind Don Sebastian's back. He was staking everything on this purchase, his self-respect and his honor.

"Why do you think I did this?" Miguel said hotly, confirming her reasoning, "I, who loathe deceit! Because our way of life—the cattle on a thousand hills —is finished. Our people must find a new livelihood, and I believe sheep can make the difference between losing the rancho and keeping it. The taxes, the mortgage, possible litigation to prove the title—oh, why do I discuss this? Again, you are against me!"

There was only one possible answer. Bets quelled

as ungenerous, a fleeting suspicion that once again, blinded by his emotions, her husband had acted too impulsively. In any case, whatever came of this, his inactivity, for which she was too often blamed, was at an end.

"I am not against you, Miguel. No, I'm not! I admire your courage, now more than ever!"

Miguel wanted to believe her. The scowl had lifted a little. But the width of the room was still between them, and Flora came then, bringing coffee.

Before she and the children left Patrick's house, Bets was alone briefly with her father, and took the opportunity to ask him the question that nagged at her mind.

"Papa, I have been wondering, if the price of wool is so high, why would a sheepowner sell part of his herd cheaply?"

"Fewer mouths to feed, I would guess."

"What does that mean?"

"Bets, surely you are aware that as of today, with the year ending, there has been no rain at all, none since the torrents of last February! Doesn't that suggest anything? You have to look ahead to a sparse spring pasturage. It may rain tomorrow and pour for a month, which would prove me wrong. But it may not. I'd hate to bet against the weather."

"You bought sheep yourself!"

"I did, and I'm afraid it won't prove one of my better decisions." He added with an odd smile quite unlike his usual open grin, "I'm not complaining. I have to count my blessings. Why, I might have bought an even larger flock if I hadn't had other uses for my money."

Something in his manner reminded her of the evasive way Jeb had answered her questions about her father. What were those other uses? Something beyond mortgages and taxes? Beyond the needs of his rancho? With a wariness that had never before colored their relationship, she changed the subject.

"What did you mean in your note? You mentioned you might have news."

"Yes, I do." He studied the wide planking in the floor as if he had never seen it before. "I'd prefer that you didn't mention this just yet to anyone, Bets, but I may very well marry soon. Teodocia Brinkman. I've asked her."

Silence fell, broken only by the buzzing swoops of a large blue fly that had become entrapped in the room.

"Well, girl? You're shocked, I suppose."

"No," she replied, although she was a bit, and resentful too of her aunt who, in the most irresponsible way, had apparently taken herself off to San Francisco and left him lonely in the house.

Swiftly, she considered the idea. He was a fine figure of a man still. He was brave, generous, and had a soft heart that he kept well-concealed under a blustering manner that fooled no one. Teo, it was true, was only in her mid twenties, making him twice her age; but in all other respects it was a good match.

There was only one serious obstacle. "Teo still remembers Garth."

"No doubt. What has there been to make her forget? I shall certainly try!"

"Then Papa, I can't tell you how pleased I am!" She threw her slender arms around his neck, his defensive frown vanished, and in a moment they were laughing together, making plans, and arguing about what might be the finest wedding gift ever.

It was ten days later, after Miguel had persuaded her that the time had come to enter her sons in Father Daniel's school, that she too learned of the existence of Claudine.

CHAPTER TWENTY-FIVE

As the carriage rolled into Marchessault Street, Adam looked back at her in a questioning way, as though seeking directions. Bets sighed. He was being deliberately obtuse, of course. Pepe, sitting beside him on the front seat and chattering Cantonese all the way, must have talked of nothing else but the school. Yes, Adam knew where they were headed and was indicating, as strongly as such a loyal and obedient man could, his opposition.

She didn't blame him. Ah, how she herself hated the idea! Although she couldn't yet see Don Antonio's old house, the familiar landmarks were already coming into view around the Plaza, and panic gripped her. She wanted nothing more than to nod to Adam and motion for him to drive home again. Leave those two little boys for weeks at a time in the care of strangers?

And yet she had promised Miguel to at least *look* at the school. He had been persuasive, pointing out what was simply the truth, that he himself was sometimes gone for days, working in the farthest reaches of the rancho.

"But they're so young! Couldn't we wait another year?"

"There are other children from the ranchos there, they won't be lonely. If it were only Tomas, I would be inclined not to insist." She gave him a sharp look, but as he continued, she realized she had read a slight where none was meant. "Tomas is a boy like any other boy, perhaps a little steadier, and he will grow at his own pace with or without school. He could learn all he needs from you and from the daily life here. But Pepe's mind is a sharp knife; it should be constantly honed and used, or it may rust. He is nine-years-old, a time for quick learning, and it is not fair to deprive him of a proper teacher."

"I suppose you're right." Troubled or not, in honesty she was forced to add, "He constantly asks me such questions! He wanted to know yesterday why things fall to the ground, and if some things fall faster than others. I told him I thought they all fell the same, and then he picked up a bird's feather and blew it off his palm. As it wafted away, he grinned at me, that sweet imp's grin, and I wished so much I had the right answer to give him."

"Which Father Daniel will have."

"No more than you!"

Miguel's shoulders sagged a little, and she realized sending the children away could not be easy for him either. So when he replied, with that quick irritability that lay just beneath the surface these days, "No recriminations! I am torn too many ways already," she argued no more. But she did reserve the right to simply bring the boys home again if, for any reason at all, St. Vincent's and Father Daniel did not appear to be far more than satisfactory.

Her plan had been to go at once to her father's home and rest, postponing her investigation until the next morning. But because of the hard dry roads, the horses had moved steadily and quickly, and the sun was still up. She was tired enough! There was an ache in the small of her back, and the baby in her swollen body moved ceaselessly. But both boys were watching her, their eagerness only too apparent. Now was none too soon for them to see this school they'd heard about!

"Señora Aguirre!" welcomed the priest. He had chanced to be repairing a crack in the front wall when the carriage stopped, and he ran over to assist her down. His sleeves were red-brown with adobe dust, but she didn't notice. She immediately liked his strong, gentle hands, and saw that when he spoke to the children, his fine eyes smiled as well as his mouth.

"You must be Tomas; and you Pepe, the one who speaks Chinese. Am I right?"

Tomas, who had been giving him a considering look, said nothing but tendered his own shy smile instead.

Pepe however said importantly, his eyes dancing, "Yes, I can tell Adam what my parents wish him to do. I learned very quickly, did I not, Mama?"

"Yes, darling, but you must not be forward. Tell me, Father, how do you know so much about us?"

"Your friend, Teodocia, who is the sisters' helper and, I may say, quite irreplaceable, speaks of you often. She will be very happy to see you today, but not at all surprised. She expected that you would one day bring your sons to us."

"Oh, but we aren't certain yet—"

"Of course not. Come in, please, Señora. It's too

late in the day for classes. I'm sorry you weren't here a short while ago when I read President Lincoln's Emancipation Proclamation to the children and asked for their comments. The full text has just been received here by telegraph, and I was pleased that they all seemed to understand the importance of it, even though for some the English words were most difficult."

He was speaking easily, leading the way as he talked. Yet Bets had an uncomfortable feeling that she was being tested.

"I'm sorry I haven't had an opportunity to read the speech."

"President Lincoln proclaims that henceforth no man will be held in bondage," the priest said softly. "In every corner of this nation, the slaves shall be freed."

"But there are no slaves here."

"Not slaves as you think of them, no, but there are many in Los Angeles who are in bondage." His eyes seemed to probe hers, seeking a reaction. "Some of the Indians are on an eternal treadmill of joyless labor." He asked abruptly, "Are you aware, Señora, that we have children with us here from all walks of life? Because to us they are equal, as they are equal in the sight of God. Our little Teodocia has said that this would not matter to you, nor even to the Señor, but still I must ask."

"My husband respects learning and intelligence, wherever they are found. Yes, Teo is right. She knows us very well."

"You are speaking of me?" It was Teodocia herself. She had entered behind them, and was smiling broadly. "Do forgive me, Father, if I interrupt, but I thought you might allow me to show my friend the school."

"Thank you, little one. I will then have an opportunity to become acquainted with these lads." He turned and looked down at them with a grave smile. "Tomas, I think you could be of great help to me here. A quiet disposition in a strong body can become the stuff of leadership."

Bets walked away with her friend, but her heart warmed further toward Father Daniel. She had seen the way his eyes lighted at first sight of Pepe, for a good teacher loves a truly apt pupil. But he had had the kindness to speak to Tomas first and not let the older child feel diminished.

"I'm so very glad you're here, Betsey!" Teodocia said, after giving her a warm hug of welcome. "As you can guess, I've been thinking about your father's proposal and wanting to talk about it. I—It's difficult to know what to do!"

"Does he seem dreadfully old to you, Teo? Although he's fifty, to me, he'll always be young and dashing, but then, I am very fond of my father."

Her friend's eyes crinkled in sudden amusement. "Think of it, your father! Would you call me stepmother?" Her smile vanished and she became serious again. "Oh, Bets, you would be related to me and I would see you often, which is the best reason for accepting. That, and the possibility that I would have children. I do so yearn to have a family! I want nothing more than the sort of life my mother had before Papa died, the good life that women are meant to have." She touched her friend on the arm. "Bets, I saw Garth today."

"Oh, no! He is in Los Angeles? He will be caught!"

"He almost was caught. Flores came into town and brought Garth with him. There is so much lawlessness here now, that whenever he wishes, Flores comes to Calle de los Negros for a day or so and no one is the wiser.

"So, Garth sought me out. When I went on an errand from St. Vincent's this morning, he stepped out from between the buildings. He'd been waiting for me, hoping— Oh, Betsey, the sight of him was so unexpected, such a shock, I thought I was dreaming."

"What happened then?"

"Nothing. I couldn't speak. Neither of us did. I think he was going to take me in his arms because he moved to come closer . . . and I too went to him. But then someone walking past in the road recognized him, and shouted. He turned and ran. I stood rooted in that dusty road while the tears streamed down my face."

Bets nodded. "What you are telling me is that you still care for Garth."

"I always will."

Bets found the sadness in the round childish face unbearable, and she could think of nothing to say. She took her hand and squeezed it.

"I wept, Betsey, because I knew then, perhaps for the first time, how truly hopeless it was to love him . . . You asked me if your father seems old to me. The answer is, no more so than Abel Stearns must have seemed to Arcadia when they married, and I've been thinking that if I must marry anyone—which I want so much to do—then someone who is more like a father would be best. A younger man might demand passion in return, and that I can't give, not to anyone but Garth.

"So you see why I wanted to talk to you. If I accept Señor Donovan, as I am now tempted to do, am I being unfair to him? I do love someone else."

"He knows that. Papa—Patrick, that is," a faint embarrassment caused her to change quickly the term of address, "is nothing if not confident. I suspect that he is convinced he can make you love him in short order. And perhaps he can."

"Then you think it is all right? I am not deceiving him?"

"No. But are you truly convinced in your own mind that marriage is what you want?"

"After seeing Garth today, yes. All I want is peace —and contentment, if I can find it."

"Then marry Patrick. He is extraordinarily kind, much as he tries to hide it."

"I will, and the sooner the better. I'll ask Father Daniel to see that the banns are posted. Oh, just making up my mind has made me happier! Will you tell Señor Donovan tonight for me? I can't leave just now, and you will be going to his home."

"I'll tell him. And Teo, he couldn't have chosen anyone I love more!"

Bets had not planned to make an immediate decision about the school, but she was so impressed by all aspects of the small establishment she could find no excuse to delay. The teacher himself was certainly everything one could wish, and the nuns kept the kitchen, the sleeping rooms, even the children themselves as clean and neat as possible. Father Daniel might have grease stains on his coat, but that was only because the nuns' respect for him was so great that they dared not mention the matter.

Most compelling of all was the enthusiasm of Tomas and Pepe, as expressed vociferously by the latter. In those few minutes, with the help of Father Daniel, their sense of strangeness had worn off. They were engrossed in a game of *pelota,* and she found them shouting as loudly as the rest.

Bets called them to her. "We must go now. Would you like to come back tomorrow?"

Although she had guessed that they too liked the school, she was not prepared when Pepe, speaking as usual for both, cried, "We want to stay now! There is to be singing after Vespers, Mama. Many of the others live here and don't have to leave, so why must we?"

There was no good reason. Only—she wasn't ready. She hadn't thought they would be gone from her quite so soon!

"Is it all right, Father?" she asked the priest at last.

He smiled. "I always think if you have to ford a cold river, jumping in the water is less painful than walking in little by little."

"I suppose so . . . Very well then, boys, I'll have Adam bring in your clothes. But you haven't nearly enough for a long stay! I didn't intend . . . this."

"Oh, Mama, what do clothes matter?" Pepe cried. "You can send us everything!"

"Yes, of course . . . and you, Tomas, you're sure? Well, then. I'll come to see you tomorrow, just in case there is anything . . ." Her voice was breaking. She flung herself on her knees to embrace them both at once and held them to her fiercely while she fought away the foolish motherly tears.

"I'll come with you to the carriage," Teo said gently, prompting her, and she had to let them go. It was time to depart.

She and Adam rode to Patrick's house in a silence far more profound than their usual inability to speak each other's language. Adam's shoulders drooped and there was an aura of melancholy about him. Bets remembered with sudden guilt that the boys had not come out to bid him goodbye, and she wished she could explain their neglect was not out of lack of affection for him, but merely thoughtlessness, due to excitement.

Her father at least would have no reason to mourn their absence from his house tonight. How enthusiastic he would be at the news! His grandsons to be permanently nearby where he could be with them frequently! Thinking about Patrick, and eager for someone to approve the decision she'd made, she wished Adam would drive the horses faster.

But to her disappointment, her father was not at home when they arrived. Flora explained he had left only that morning for the Allison, and would be gone for some days.

"Ah, well," Bets said, "at least I won't be lonely. I'll still have you and Jeb and Flower to talk to." And she told them all the details she could remember about the school. Flower, who had never seen such a place, or been one of a crowd of children, or even learned to read the simplest lines, listened with her vacant and entranced face.

When Bets finished, before Jeb and Flora could speak, Flower said timidly, "Tom?"

"Funny what store she sets on that one chile," Flora commented. "Other folks she forgets. But not him."

"Yes, Flower," Bets said gently, "Tomas is staying there too!"

Flower's smile vanished and like a sudden shower of rain, the tears came. Bets hugged her in sympathy, for she herself would have liked to do the same.

Sunday morning, she attended Mass at the old church in the Plaza, just as she had always done until the move to the Aguirre rancho. She was accompanied by Jeb and his family, as Adam, no doubt glad to be out from under the domination of Don Sebastian's cooks, had managed to offer, even without Pepe's helpful translation, to cook the noon meal.

The thick-walled adobe church was crowded as always. Through the years there had been talk of another church, and Bishop Amat, it was known, even had ideas for a cathedral. But as of this year of our Lord, 1863, nothing had been accomplished. All who wished to worship came here.

Bets sat in her old accustomed pew near the back and watched people arrive. She knew most of them, because the Catholic population had remained fairly constant. Newcomers to Los Angeles were Protestant, if indeed they could be said to be anything at all.

She waved to Arcadia who was accompanied by her mother, energetic little Doña Maria Bandini. Stearns himself was in Monterey, deep in litigation.

She spoke to the Sepulvedas as they passed, to Manuel Garfias, and to Felipa and Lucius Camell. Camellito gave her a delighted smile, saying, "Welcome back to the pueblo!" while his wife vouchsafed a cool nod.

"Goodness, Flora, who is that?" Bets exclaimed in a whisper. "I don't think I've ever seen a woman like that! She's like—like an orchid."

"Which one you mean, Miss Bets?" Flora exchanged an uneasy glance with Jeb.

"Come now, Flora, which one would I mean? There. That woman walking in just ahead of Peter Riggs. The one with the lovely toasty-colored skin and the shining black hair coiled beautifully high on her head. She's so graceful, that pale yellow dress just floats!"

"She ain't nobody, Miss Bets. Nobody at all." Flora's mouth shut with a snap. It was clear nothing more would be gotten out of her.

A dancer, Bets guessed, watching the woman seat herself in one fluid movement. If so, and judging by the fact that she and Riggs were together, she probably performed in that dance hall of his.

After another prolonged stare of admiration, because the woman had glanced round at the churchgoers and the flash of her green eyes was startling,

Bets settled back to attend the Mass and wait for the announcement of her father's and Teodocia's impending marriage. Thinking it would be amusing to see the servants' surprise, she had given them no hint in advance. And indeed, when the banns were recited by the priest, there was a stir, not only next to her, but among all the people she knew in the church. Patrick had evidently told no one, and now heads turned, there were smiles and nods. It was clear that this surprise marriage would meet general approval, in spite of the long span of years between the affianced.

Bets turned to Flora, expecting that she too would want to express her pleasure. But Flora and Jeb's eyes were riveted on the place where Riggs and his striking companion had earlier seated themselves.

That pew was now empty. Bets twisted around toward the back of the church and was in time to catch a single glimpse of airy yellow chiffon before it vanished through the portal.

"Whoo-ee," Flora said to Jeb. "Reckon somebody do be mighty put out!"

"Hush, woman!" He sounded angry, Jeb who never chastised Flora.

He gave Bets a sidelong glance, then sank to his knees as the service resumed. Troubled, she too knelt, mulling over what was suddenly clear.

She decided that she was not really surprised. Her father was a man like any other, wasn't he? And the woman had been beautiful indeed, all fire inside, but hard, like a gem stone—an emerald, judging by those eyes. Not one to be lightly cast aside so publicly!

CHAPTER TWENTY-SIX

CLAUDINE WAS ALONE AT LAST. SHE HAD stormed and raged in the presence of Peter Riggs, pacing with the lithe natural grace of a cat the length of the room and back again, over and over. When she threw herself into a chair finally, he believed her fury had abated. He would never have left her otherwise. Although he did not know the extremes she was capable of, he was no fool.

Riggs had never been certain whether or not she was guilty of killing that man in New Orleans, because she had judged rightly that it was not always best to tell him the truth. Peter Riggs might be hard-driving and ruthless in his own enterprises, but he had a very conventional sense of right and wrong, and she understood men well enough to know he wouldn't necessarily sympathize with her point of view. Too much frankness, and she could lose his support, an outcome to be avoided. She needed him, and she rather liked him. They had been friends a long time.

So now she had to convince him that she was badly hurt and insulted, but not coldly, viciously angry.

"To think the great Mr. Donovan would let a woman who has loved him as whole-heartedly as I, learn of his coming marriage from a public announcement! How heartless, how cruel!"

"He's been away the last few days," Riggs observed, "so I doubt he planned it this way." He glanced around the little house provided by Patrick, and gave her a curious look. "You loved him? I had an idea the affair was for you just a matter of convenience."

"I adored him!" she snapped.

"Well, Claudine, there are other fish in the sea, and if I catch one for you, perhaps you'll forget all this. Donovan isn't a bad sort. He didn't slap your face intentionally."

"You think not?" She allowed herself to appear slightly assuaged. "Perhaps you are right. At least I'll give him a chance to explain. Now, Peter, I'm myself again. *Mon Dieu,* it's night already! The Blue Diamond will be opening! Hadn't you better go? I'll come in a while, but I do think I'll rest a bit first. All this has made my head throb."

"Be as late as you like," he said generously. "So long as you come some time tonight, they'll wait."

"Thank you, Peter."

Drooping a little, as though exhausted by emotion, she watched him leave. But after the door shut, she sprang erect. Her eyes narrow, she listened and gave him time to be well away, making certain he could not return unexpectedly. Then she snatched up her fringed shawl and went out the door herself, giving it a hard, savage slam.

"Mr. Warner?"

"Yes, ma'am, I'm Captain Warner." He lurched unsteadily from the lighted livery stable toward her. She had had to wait for some time, before he was in full view tending to his duties with the horses and she could be quite sure he was alone. Waiting had not improved her temper.

"Very well, Captain Warner." She accepted the correction with ill-concealed contempt. "I'm Claudine, from the Blue Diamond. Do you recognize me?"

"Eh?" He came closer to gaze blearily into her face and she forced herself not to recoil from his unpleasant breath. "Why, so you are! I've seen you dance there, and thought to myself how much I'd like to—well, and here you are. I must be dreaming. Come to see the Captain, have you?"

"I've come to talk to you, yes. Is there someplace we can be alone?"

His scarred face split into a leering grin, and she was forced to evade his hands. But the expression on her own face remained unchanged, icily calm.

"There's a little office inside," he offered. "The stable owner won't be back tonight."

"What about customers?"

"Naw. Not this late. And if any do come, they don't go inside there. Come along in, little lady."

One of his moist hands found her waist and she allowed him to lead her through the stable into the small cubicle at the back. Once there, she adroitly maneuvered so that he sat in the owner's chair, and herself opposite, the rough table between them.

"Now then, what can old Captain Warner do for the little lady, besides what he'd like to do?" He laughed uproariously.

She didn't bother with amenities, but came at once to the point. "You can help me punish Patrick Donovan."

Lust faded from his face, to be replaced by brooding sullenness.

"Woman, if I knew how to do that, don't you think I'd have done it years ago?"

"Yes, and I'm surprised you haven't. He told me all about what happened. If I had been you, I'd have made him regret that slash in the face for the rest of his days!"

"Maybe you would and maybe you wouldn't. He's a good shot with a pistol. And he has powerful friends. I'd have gotten far worse than a cut face."

"But you hate him? You'd like to see him hurt?" She leaned forward in her eagerness, and saw his eyes rest on the cleavage and then flick away. She was pleased to realize he had not been distracted, that her question held more interest than her body. For it was necessary that his hatred for Patrick had not dimmed with the years.

"I'd give my right arm," he said flatly.

"Good. Then I think I can help you. And safely too. You won't need to lose an arm."

Suddenly he was less drunk. "Why should I trust you? I know, just like the rest of the town does, that you are his doxy. This must be a trap." His voice had turned ugly.

"No trap, Captain. He's being married. He's scorned me, as though I'm just a cheap whore, or doxy as you so nicely put it. I want him to writhe in hell, and for what I have in mind, I need a man."

"I dunno. As I say, he has friends."

"Suppose I tell you my plan? Then, if you aren't man enough, you can forget it."

"Tell me. I don't promise anything, but tell me."

She began to talk, and by the time she had finished, his hands were shaking with eagerness.

"Do you think you can do it?" She glanced at the half-empty bottle on the table, taking no pains to hide her scorn, and her meaning was clear.

"I can do it! Just you get her outside, with no one around."

"All right. Tell me first, where does she live? I know nothing about her. I'm fairly new in this town, and I don't go around much anyway. The Diamond closes so late."

"Where does she live? Let's see. The old Señora shut the town house and moved to her rancho some time ago. So—"

"Then it's hopeless. A rancho! I've seen those places; they're like forts!"

Again his face was broken by a feral grin. "I didn't finish! Her home is a rancho, but the person under discussion isn't there much. Most of the time she stays at that school, St. Vincent's."

Claudine was not amused at having been misled. "Joke with me again," she said, "and you might get a knife in your ribs. I've got more of a temper than Patrick Donovan has, and don't you forget it . . . A school? That's even better. All we have to do is lure her out. We can't use Donovan's name though, because she must be aware that he's away. Do you know who any of her friends might be?"

"Why wouldn't I?" He was surly under her rebuff. "I've seen her and Donovan's daughter together often enough. Elizabeth Aguirre, the high and mighty Señora Aguirre she is now, but Bets was what they used to call her."

"Donovan's daughter." Claudine laughed softly. "How perfect. Yes, Captain, that will do very well. What else? Think! What else can you tell me?"

St. Vincent's School had closed its door for the night. The children were in bed if not asleep, and three of the nuns and Teodocia, having finished frying *buñuelos* with which to celebrate the birthday of one of their charges on the morrow, were now making the breakfast tortillas in an open space at the rear, a part of the patio that served this old adobe for a kitchen. All were tired; it had been an exceptionally active day, and there was very little talking as they slapped the round flat cornmeal cakes back and forth, thinning them with the pressure of their hands.

Teodocia stopped and absently ate a *buñuelo,* thinking with pleasure about the two little Aguirre boys who had fit so easily into the group. She was proud of them, just as much as if they had been her own. Both were so attractive, so easy to love! The sturdy older boy whose grave manner other children trusted at once, and the bright, spirited younger one with whom no one could ever possibly be bored.

"Sister!"

Simultaneous with the call came a rattle of the rear gate, now latched shut.

The nuns looked at each other. "Who can that be at night?" asked one. "It sounded like a child!"

"Yes." Teodocia picked out an especially large *buñuelo.* If there was a child there, she would feed it. "Don't bother, Sister Barbara. I'll go."

Holding the pastry carefully, she felt her way beneath the tall sycamores Don Antonio Lugo had planted long ago, and skirted the rose bushes that she knew blocked her path. Then she emerged into the moonlight, walking on a paving of red tiles.

The oak door at the end was easily unbarred, for there was little to steal in the small parish school.

"Who is it, please?"

"I have a message for Missus Brinkman," replied a young voice, and Teodocia at once stepped outside.

She was in a wide, weed-choked field, vacant except for a ramshackle shed which jutted up as a small inky rectangle against the sky. This was an area that belonged to the school, and the pupils played here during the day. At night, it was deserted. Even the sounds from Alameda Street was muted, distant.

Facing Teodocia was a child she hadn't seen before, but she easily placed him as one of the many urchins who roamed Los Angeles these days, children of families who having failed elsewhere, drifted in seeking work. She never saw these small ragged figures without a feeling of sadness that their parents refused to send them to school. Yet who could blame such destitute people, she asked herself. The meager pay a child might receive for picking grapes, sweeping out a store, or running errands was far too important for his family to do without.

She smiled down, seeing even in the dimness his dirty encrusted skin and threadbare clothing, and feeling her heart catch with pity. "I'm Miss Brinkman."

"A lady tole me to give you this," he whispered. "She be down thataway. Best to hurry, she say! She cain't tarry."

Teodocia opened the note. Straining her eyes in the moonlight, she made out the words:

> Teodocia, come quickly!
> I have news of Garth.
>
> Bets

"Garth!"

His name fell from her lips in a surprised exclamation. She hesitated long enough to think she should tell Sister Barbara and bring a lamp, then her eagerness ruled out any delays. Bets was waiting! She must go at once.

"Thank you!" She hurriedly proffered the *buñuelo,* and the child snatched it. He pelted away across the waste of weeds, running toward the street.

Teodocia herself had already started off in the opposite direction, the way the boy had pointed. Under her feet was a faint path, one that would lead eventually to Calle de los Negros, and she hurried along it eagerly, expecting every moment to see the figure of her friend, or hear her hail. She didn't question the summons. That Bets had sent for her was enough. It was only when she had almost reached the dilapidated shed, and the lonely vista of the night still remained unbroken, that she finally faltered. How strange! Where could Bets be?

But wait—wasn't that the shadow of someone moving? It was, she assured herself, even though the vague shape had vanished again, merging with the blackness of the structure.

"Bets?"

No answer came and the deep brooding silence for the first time contained a hint of menace. Had Betsey really come to such a desolate place alone? Surely she wouldn't! The boy must have misunderstood. But why, then, was there any message at all?

Teodocia looked back uncertainly at the school. Even from here, above the wall she could see the flickering candlelight where the sisters were working. The distant yellow glow seemed to beckon, more and more urgently, until her instincts suddenly awoke and she knew she should never have left that safe and secure place. Bets was not here! Never had been here!

Frightened now, she snatched up her skirts and started to run. If she could reach the familiar haven that was so close, and yet so far . . .

Much too far! Behind her there was a rustling sound and heavy footfalls. She was grabbed, and a scarf thrown around her head, blinding her. A hand quickly stuffed the lower edge in her mouth.

In a panic that she would suffocate, Teo clawed at the strong silken fabric, and almost pulled it away before her arms were wrenched back and held, cruelly tight.

For a brief odd second, so that it seemed as if she'd gone mad, Teodocia thought she smelled violets. But the sweet scent was obliterated almost at once by hot rancid breath close to her face, and she recoiled, only to be shoved forward again.

In the distance, Sister Barbara, her serene tone unworried, a little chiding, called her name several times. A woman's voice at Teodocia's shoulder commanded, "Hurry, you fool!" She was thrown roughly to the ground, where she lay with legs sprawled, breast heaving, and arms pinioned tight and immobile above her head. Wild with terror, Teo threshed from side to side, as senselessly as a frenzied bird in a net.

Someone with warm sweating hands pushed up her dress and she became instinctively rigid. Her pantaloons were ripped off, her legs pulled wide apart. Just for a moment, fumbling fingers stroked the bare skin of her inner thighs.

Understanding of what was to happen to her, exploded first in her body, then in her brain. In her horror, even without the strangling scarf, she couldn't have screamed. She whimpered over and over again incoherent cries of revulsion and agony, to which no one listened.

CHAPTER TWENTY-SEVEN

"PAPA, IS IT YOU? OH, THANK GOD!"

Bets ran from the dimmed room into the hallway. Her voice rose, in spite of the need to speak softly so as not to wake Teodocia. They had brought her to Patrick's because it was closer than Teo's own home and they dared not let the schoolchildren see the condition she was in.

"Yes," he answered curtly.

"I was so afraid they wouldn't find you! You know —everything?"

"How is she?"

"Not good. But at least now, she's asleep."

She looked into his gray distraught face and her heart ached with pity for him too, she who had thought she could feel nothing more after these hours with Teodocia.

"Who would believe any man could be so vile!" she burst out, unable to contain any longer the anger she had fought back for hours. "Oh, I know you and Miguel have warned us all that the streets aren't safe —but rape! Even the lowest scum that walked could see how gentle, how sweet she is."

He didn't answer. He had thrown himself in a chair, legs outstretched in exhaustion. He stared unseeing at the ceiling.

"Papa, I'm so terribly worried about her! She's out of her head. There are lucid spells, but then it's as though she can't face the memory, and slides away again. If anyone touches her unexpectedly, she goes wild with terror. Do you think . . . oh, is it possible she won't recover?"

"What did the doctor say?"

Bets shrugged. "He was honest. He admitted he doesn't know what will happen."

"Bets, I swear to you by all the devils in hell, when I get my hands on the man who did this, he'll never lie with another woman, good or bad! Fetch me some aguardiente, there's a good girl. I've only a few minutes before we ride."

"Ride where?"

"The aguardiente!"

"Yes, Papa."

She hurried to the kitchen for the bottle and a glass. He drank, tossing it down with a grimace as though it burned his throat. When she saw the color return to his set face, she asked again, "Ride where? Papa, do you know who it was?"

He gave a short nod. "That no-good wastrel of hers. Garth Peters."

"No! I don't believe that!" She was aghast.

"There's not much room for doubt. It was a still night and although the sisters couldn't hear what was said by the child, they think Teo exclaimed 'Garth!' Come now Bets, didn't it have to be someone who knew her well? Even she, trusting as she is, wouldn't have walked off into the dark to meet a stranger! And Peters has been heard to say many times that if he couldn't have her, no one else would.

"At first, the vigilantes couldn't believe he was guilty—the Manilas were working too far away, up north of Santa Barbara, and he's never been known to come into town alone. But almost at once news came that he was seen here in the last week, and the gang itself has just attacked a small rancho near my Allison. Damn their eyes, they killed the owner—a good man, a friend!"

"But Papa, that doesn't prove—"

"The posse is going after them tonight! We'll wipe out the whole band, Juan Flores, his murdering outlaws, *and* Garth Peters." He set down the glass heavily and buttoned his jacket. "I'll be off. Tell her, if she wakes, that she'll be avenged. She has my word on it. Perhaps that will help a little."

"No, wait! I've listened to all you said, and I'm still sure it wasn't—could not have been Garth!"

Patrick hadn't stopped and was already at the door, but he turned and gave her a brief wondering look, as if amazed at her innocence. Then he started out.

"Papa—Patrick Donovan, come back here! You will hear me out!"

It was the first time she had ever addressed him so, and they seemed to become equals then, no longer just father and daughter. Although he did not walk back to her, he shut the door and leaned against it.

"Very well! Say what you want to, but I have very little time."

"I know him! Remember, he often visited our house. And if I say that he is incapable of hurting Teo—"

"That was years ago! He's changed. God, do you credit a bandit with decent feelings?"

"He idolized Teo, and nothing about that has changed. He might be able to kill her—I don't know, he might. But wrap a scarf around her face and brutally rape this girl he loves? Never!"

She had no real arguments, but her complete conviction must have impressed him a little. "I suppose we could bring him back to stand trial. Let a judge decide."

"Decide what? If you bring him back, he'll hang for being one of the Manilas, guilty of rape or not. But he won't ever get here alive anyway, don't try to fool me. Those hot-blooded vigilantes will never take him captive. They'll shoot him down! You know better than I what Sheriff Barton has said. Wasn't it, 'We want no prisoners, to saddle the country with their support for months and winding up with the farce of a trial and acquittal!'?

"No, Papa! Do you want Teo to hate you for the rest of your life? Vengeance, you say! You be the cause of Garth Peters' death, and she'll never forgive you, not to her dying day!"

She saw that at last he was shaken. Clearly, such a

reaction from his own affianced had never occurred to him.

"Does she still love him so much?"

"Probably, but it doesn't matter. I think this is your chance, one you'll not have again. Save him, Papa! Warn him away! And I think you and Teo could well be happy together one day . . . even now."

He didn't answer, but spun on his booted heel and left the house. Still, she was satisfied. Knowing him as she did, she suspected she had won.

But when a small sound came from the room where Teodocia lay, her worried frown reappeared. All very well to promise gratitude from the girl, but a full night and a day had passed and the shock had not lessened. Maybe it never would! Perhaps her mind was permanently affected.

Bets opened the door and looked in. A candle burned at the bedside, throwing tall shadows on the walls. Teo was awake and quiet, but her hands plucked nervously at the coverlet.

Hearing Bets, she tensed at first, then her acute alarm subsided.

"Violets," she murmured.

Thinking that once again her friend's mind was rambling, Bets came to the the bedside and took her hand.

"You want violets, Teo? It's too early, I'm afraid."

The girl shook her head impatiently. Her eyes were wide and staring, but Bets saw with relief that there was sanity in them as well as despair.

"Violets! She smelled of violets. And her voice, when she spoke to him—it was in English, but strange, not Spanish—something else. Oh, Bets, she was horrible! To be so feminine, and still so cruel! The man was dirty and rough and beside himself, driven mad by what he was doing. I can almost understand him—but not the woman!"

"A woman?" Bets repeated slowly. "There was a woman?"

"She helped him! She held my arms. Oh, how could one woman do that to another?"

Bets felt her flesh crawl with disgust. How indeed?

She was possessed by fury, as she gazed down at the white and anguished face of her friend, a face down which tears were slowly coursing.

Yet she must force herself to calmness. A storm of outrage would not help Teo . . . She must think of Teo!

Deliberately, she sat down on the edge of the bed, and managed to speak in a low, soothing voice about nothing at all, just as she had often done when Tomas or Pepe or little Isabel was hurt or sick. And like one of the children, presently Teodocia slept, still clutching her hand.

It was dawn when Patrick returned. Fatigue had made ashen his bronzed face above the dark curly beard. He threw himself down beside the table, his head resting on his arms, and only roused to drink the hot chocolate his daughter brought to him.

When he finished, she could contain herself no longer. "Well? Tell me what happened!"

"I did as you asked, and thank God, because I'm certain now that you were right. When I told him what had happened no man could have pretended grief like that."

"What did you do?"

"I started out with the posse, but I wanted to find him first, decide for myself. I managed to outdistance the rest—it wasn't easy to fool twenty men, but still, it was dark and they were sensibly saving their horses for what might be a long night's work. I wasn't.

"An informer had told us where the camp was, and I got there well ahead. I rode up, tried to hide myself, and yelled out that I wanted to speak to Garth." Patrick gave a faint boyish grin, the first of this long, dreary night. "It was a question whether they'd shoot me first, or listen to what I had to say and then shoot me. Flores has wanted to for a long time."

"Oh, Papa!" Bets blanched. "I didn't realize . . . How very brave of you!" .

"Think Teodocia will be impressed, do you? Anyway, when I made it known that I had news of her, Garth came out alone. He's no coward either, I must say. As quickly as I could, I told him what had happened, and because I knew then that he wasn't the man we were after, I told him the posse was coming and he should try to escape. After that I turned my horse and rode back along the trail, expecting any moment to have a bullet in my back from Juan Flores, or get shot by mistake by my own friends.

"But nothing happened, and shortly, when the posse approached, I was waiting there, pretending I'd been only a little ahead the whole time. If what I did ever gets out, Bets, they'll be wanting to string me up instead!"

"So the vigilantes came back empty-handed?"

"No, because Flores made his first and last mistake. Garth Peters passed on my warning, and then left on the run, but the Sonoran must have refused to believe I hadn't set some sort of trap, and he stayed. Oh, he and his men were careful enough. They put out the fire, and crept further back into the canyon where we could never have found them in the dark."

"But you did? How?"

"Flores coughed horribly. Couldn't control it. Do you know, we found a pool of blood where he'd been standing! The end of it was, he and a few others who lived through the fight were captured. The men were shot on the spot. You were right about that. But Flores has been brought back. The Manilas have harried this coast so long that people will want to see the leader hang. Should be a regular Roman holiday."

This last was said with some distaste. He yawned widely and pulled himself to his feet. "I'd better go to bed. Age is creeping up on me, after all."

"Papa, thank you!"

"For not making a terrible mistake? I'm glad Peters wasn't the man, but now I've no idea who to look for. Never mind, I'll find him. And soon!"

"Yes, I think you will," Bets said. "Teo has told me a few things, and eventually, if we put the facts together—"

"Oh?" Alertness returned. "What did she say?"

"In the morning will do. Get some sleep first."

"No, now! I insist!"

"Very well. There was a woman there too. Teo was talking about a woman, and mentioned a strong scent of violets! And, when the horrible creature said something to the man, she had a faint accent of some kind, not Spanish—something else. And that's all, except that Teo got the impression of great femininity, which makes it all so—so much more unspeakable."

Bets was also exhausted, and she had risen, intending to go to her bedroom. She was startled when she heard his purposeful tread recede across the floor, and a rasp as the outer door was flung open.

"Papa, where are you going?" Stupefied, she saw he had taken his gun from the table, and was squinting through the barrel. The light of dawn, oyster-white now, and ugly in its coldness, streamed past him into the room.

"Some unfinished business," he said roughly. "Watch over Teodocia."

Silenced, she stared after him, knowing that whatever his purpose, he would not be swayed from it this time. Heavy fear gripped her, fear for him.

Chapter Twenty-eight

HE STRODE ALONG THE STREET, NOT HAVING bothered to resaddle his mount. He hadn't far to go, and he wished it was much farther. While he would do what he must do, he dreaded the coming encounter as he had never dreaded anything before.

He realized that he was feeling much as he had on that long-ago day when he and Phineas Bishop and Toby Bonner had pursued Flores' brother's band single-handed, three lone men against twenty or thirty. He remembered his appalling conviction of coming disaster, his sadness that there was no escape, and how he'd looked with fresh aware eyes at his world. Just as the greenness of the pine trees had amazed him then, and the air too with its crisp clarity, now he found he was seeing this rough street in detail for the first time.

As he passed, he noticed the dry weeds, crushed or standing lank and brown between the dwellings. By this time of year, there should be a bright carpet of new growth showing, the young wild oats perhaps, and the first feathery fronds of anise. It was too early for poppies or the purple-blue lupin, but in January, the wild morning-glory should be starting to climb, getting ready to put out its white and rose cups.

Now there was nothing. Only the desolate brittle stems, and the startling leap of a grasshopper, then another, gathering up its long fragile legs and fixing him with saucer-like eyes. So many of them this year! He hadn't realized before, how many. If the drought continued, it might kill the cattle, even the people, but insects would multiply and thrive until they took over the earth!

Then, the pearly dawn changed without warning. The sun rose above the mountains, turning the white to warm gold. The chill disappeared from the morning, but not from his heart.

She lived in a small adobe he'd rented for her down from the Plaza on Church Street. She wouldn't be expecting his visit and it occurred to him to wonder grimly if she might have some other caller—he'd never been entirely sure how faithful she was. But alone or not, she would be there in early dawn. He wouldn't need to wait to have his question answered. He doubted if he could have borne waiting.

He rapped sharply.

Long moments passed, and his temper barely in check, he pounded hard on the timbers.

"Patience," he heard her say in French. The bolt was finally withdrawn, and she stood before him, cool and self-possessed as always.

She was dressed in a red and yellow silk Japanese kimono, nothing else. He could see the nipples of her small high breasts molded by the thin fabric. Her slender legs were outlined by the light coming through a window behind her.

She said in that softly accented voice, "Mr. Donovan." She, like Peter Riggs, always called him that, in spite of their intimacies. While he had never been a man oversensitive to what others might be thinking, the formality from her had always galled him. It was the symbol of an invisible barrier he had never been able to surmount.

He hesitated. Why didn't he simply push past her through the doorway?

"I want to talk to you!"

"Not standing outside, I hope. Please come in."

His money paid for the house, but she always let him know that it was hers, and he was merely a guest.

She had retreated, and stood in a waiting attitude beside the table, on which there lay a bolt of fine fabric, partially unrolled, ready to be cut for another gown. He followed her and shut the door, intensely conscious of the shadowed bed that was visible in the other room, rumpled, and doubtless scented by her body and by violets. The incongruous perfume wafted toward him now, a tiny tendril of remembered invitation.

Her robe had parted in a long revealing line. He stared deliberately then looked away, and as he did so caught a glimpse of her green eyes narrowing.

"I want to know, Claudine, exactly where you were on Sunday evening. A friend, Harris Newmark, stopped by the *Blue Diamond* and hoped to see you dance. You weren't there."

He hadn't seen or spoken to Newmark in weeks, but she couldn't know that. Now, if she was incredulous, if she denied being absent—something that could easily be proved—then he might be wrong after all.

But her lip curled. "That little weasel! I was sick! But I went late anyway. I couldn't disappoint Mr. Riggs."

"You were sick?" His own stomach was churning now.

"I had a chill."

"Indeed? You recovered quickly!"

"One would have to be dying to be excused for a whole evening. What is this about?" She moved closer.

That damnable perfume—how pervasive it was! But not even the slightest desire moved in him now.

"Just this." His voice hardened, as he set a further trap. "If you were home with a chill, my dear, how does it happen that a gold chain I recognized was found in the lane behind St. Anthony's?"

Her hand flew to her throat, where three gold chains gleamed as always against her creamy skin.

"They're all here! What are you talking about?" She snapped the words, but her composure had visibly suffered. Fear flickered in her eyes, as his right hand suddenly clamped on her wrist.

"You were there, weren't you? Tell me, Claudine. Tell me! You took part in that atrocity and you *will tell me!*" He pulled her to him, their bodies pressed together in a travesty of passion.

"I don't know what you are raving about! It's nothing to do with me! You've gone insane!" Her voice, no longer seductive, was high and shrill.

"Have I?" Instinctively, he knew how to subjugate her. With his free hand, he ripped the delicate robe from her shoulders and looked at her long and contemptuously. Stripped naked, her dignity destroyed by his lack of desire, she cringed back, casting a furtive glance toward the bedroom. He tightened his grip.

All at once she straightened and her head came up in a pale imitation of her old manner. "Very well! Yes, I helped hold down your blond wife-to-be, while she learned what bed with you would be all about."

He slapped her hard and ferociously across the face, snapping her head back. The blow released her pent-up, still boiling fury.

"Betray me, would you, lover man? Leave me for some mousy, china-white little girl? I'll see you in hell first. I should have killed her—and you too!"

"Perhaps you should have," he replied and slapped her hard again. "Because I will have to kill you now. Who was the man?"

Her face close, her lips drawn back from her straight teeth, she hissed, "You'd love to know, wouldn't you? Ha! If you'd asked me nicely, like the gentleman you aren't and never will be, I might have told you. As it is, *Mr.* Donovan, you can rot in hell first!"

He didn't let her finish. The last word turned into a screech as he swung her around, pulled her back against him, and his free hand closed around her throat.

The iron clasp tightened. She was writhing, reaching back with blind, clawing motions, and once her long nails raked a bloody path down his face. She kicked, but her bare feet glanced off harmlessly.

"His name! Say it!" Patrick shouted, but his rage had gone out of control with the passing of moments, and she could not have answered if she wished. Her flailings were growing weaker, but his hand around her throat only tightened.

He would have ended by murdering her, if a voice behind them had not said, "Reckon that'll have to do. Let her go!"

Patrick, through a red haze heard, and heard too the click of a gun being cocked. He took a deep shuddering breath, then finally, with effort, loosened his fingers.

Claudine fell to the floor and lay crumpled, gasping in great gulps of air.

Patrick turned, to see Peter Riggs lounging against the wall. In spite of his relaxed posture, his eyes were alert, and the gun was fixed on Patrick.

"Didn't you get a little beside yourself, Mr. Donovan? Claudine couldn't have told you anything, not being strangled that way."

Patrick's eyes went past Riggs to the rumpled bed. But the saloon owner shook his head.

"You're wondering if your woman was having a little romp with your one-time barber? I'm sorry to say, no. Fact is, she was too proud of her Mr. Donovan to share her favors, least of all with a gen'lman of color like myself. No, just happens we've been friends from childhood. I was born in New Orleans too. And she sets store by my advice, so I came over this morning to give her a little of it. You see, I guessed what happened before you did."

"Advice about lying to me?"

"That's right. But now, since she still can't talk, I'll tell you myself what you want to know."

"Do it then! Who was he?"

"Not so fast . . . You always was a one for rushing in. I ain't going to just *give* you anything, I'm going to *sell* it."

"Sell it?" Patrick's surprise was genuine. "I'd have never thought you . . . All right! How much?"

"Not money." Riggs seemed amused. "No, sir. I have more of that now than you do. But I watched what you did to Claudine and I don't want anything to happen to her. If I tell you, you must let her go, forget what she did. Wasn't all her fault, if you think about it. A fine woman naturally sets high store on herself."

Patrick hesitated. He glanced down and saw that already she had recovered. She was breathing hard still, but even now, crouched on the floor, she was pulling the silk robe back around her. Feeling his gaze, her face contorted in a spasm of hatred and she spat, flecking his boots with saliva.

"I can't promise, Riggs," Patrick said. "You'll have to send her where I won't ever see her again! Some other city. Surely any saloon would jump at the chance to get her."

Riggs considered. "All right. She'll leave by stage today."

"Who was the man?"

"That old derelict, Captain James Warner."

"Mother of God! No!"

Patrick, fight his imagination as he would, saw the scene vividly reenacted. The old man, his breath foul with whiskey, pressing his unwashed sagging body on the shrinking girl's and his white fingers, like soft worms—how she must have struggled, her arms held tight and useless by this wretch at his feet!

He reached for Claudine.

Riggs said urgently, "He's in the bar in the Bella Union, Mr. Donovan! Right now! But he was talking of leaving town himself—"

Patrick raced from the house, out into the clean brightness of day.

The Bella Union Hotel was jammed with people, despite this early hour. Passengers ticketed on the steamer to San Francisco were assembling for the coach ride to the dock in San Pedro, and their relatives and friends thronged Main Street and spilled up onto the hotel porch. The bar was open for business.

Patrick shoved his way through the crowd, the faces to him only a blur, and banged back the swinging doors. His Colt was in his hand. The laughter and conversation cut off abruptly.

Captain Warner, standing at the bar, glanced up into the long mirror. His rheumy eyes widened, then flicked from side to side, while men close by him silently faded toward the walls.

"Draw, coward!" Patrick shouted. "First a ship, and then a woman. This time, face someone who can fight back!"

Warner spun around, whipping out his own revolver with unexpected speed and agility. There was a clatter of chairs falling, as the spectators who had remained seated dove to the floor. One jumped through a tall narrow window onto the porch, carrying with him a shower of glass.

The two guns fired simultaneously. Warner's shot missed, and a scream and a curse rang out somewhere in the crowd. But Patrick's aim was truer. One bullet and then another thudded into the captain, slamming him against the mahogany bar.

A grimace, like a wide smile, wrenched open Warner's scarred face. With two bullets in his body, he began, in an odd hitching movement like a crab's, to stagger forward through the acrid smoke.

Hit twice, and still the man plodded on! Still grinned so hideously! Patrick raised his pistol but he was unnerved. The next shot missed, and the big mirror behind the bar broke and fell.

Patrick hardly heard the resounding crash. He was retreating, conscious of nothing but the grotesque mask confronting him. He was out on the porch, which was suddenly vacant, as was the street beyond. A terrified whinnying testified that the only living creatures still in range were the horses tied to posts.

Then Warner came lurching through the swinging doors and Patrick shot, and shot again. Against all reason, he felt the hair rising on his scalp. In this strong light, he could see those bullets penetrate! Was Warner superhuman? Was he some kind of monster who could not be killed, would not die?

But Warner was rocking now. His eyes were glazed. Although he too fired, it was slowly, without aim, the gun seeming suddenly too heavy for his hand. After his last shuddering effort, there were piercing screams from a horse, and at the same time, he pitched forward and slammed against the porch floor.

With that, Patrick was released from his mesmerized horror. While the animal in the background continued its loud agonized keening, he rushed forward and slammed his empty gun down, hitting his enemy across the head.

James Warner seemed finished at last. Patrick stood over him, breathing hard, then goaded by the animal cry that was drilling intolerably into his ears, he strode to the railing.

"Somebody shoot this horse!" he shouted, and waited. The street remained empty. No one stirred. "My gun's empty! Poor devil, his leg is shattered—"

"Look behind you, Donovan!" From somewhere out of sight came the urgent warning, and heart pounding, he spun around.

A ghoulish and terrifying sight met his eyes. Defenseless in the bright sunlight, he could only stand and wait for death.

The ferocious blow had somehow revived Warner, even though the top of his head was a mass of white bone, gray matter, and blood. He'd managed to pull himself to a sitting position, his back against the hotel wall, and now he was raising his revolver with both hands, its muzzle trembling in the effort. From the holes in his body, red streams coursed onto the wooden planks and pooled there. Blood from his scalp ran across his face, but not enough to blind the eyes that gazed blankly.

His finger pulled the trigger. Then at last, slowly, he collapsed to the side and lay still.

Patrick Donovan told himself, surprised, that he'd been kicked in the stomach by a mule. He fell sideways into the dusty street.

CHAPTER TWENTY-NINE

"Señor Aguirre?" The name was badly mispronounced, as it often was these days.

"Yes?"

"You speak English, do you? Good! I'm Roy Sims, Deputy Sheriff. I've a message for you. To tell the truth, Ma'am, I didn't want to deliver it, but a condemned man should get his wish, I reckon. I told him a lady like you wouldn't think of coming down to the jailhouse, but he insisted."

Bets was bewildered. It seemed to her the visitor was making no sense whatever. Still, after so long in a darkened room watching over her father, her vigil only interrupted by efforts to cheer Teodocia, who seemed to dwell in a world of silent despondency, sunlight and the smells of the street seemed healthy and good. She was glad to brace her unwieldy body against the door jamb and linger there.

"I don't understand, sir. Who is it that's condemned?"

"That thief and murderer, Juan Flores. He's to hang at noon today."

"I'm afraid I'd forgotten. My father is so ill—"

"All the more reason why Flores shouldn't have bothered you. I'll tell him, ma'am. Don't worry your head about it. And good day to you."

"Wait. What is it Mr. Flores could possibly want with me?"

"*Mr.* Flores—that's a rich one! Well, ma'am, if you'd believe it, he asked me to see if you'd visit him at his cell. Seems he has a message for you, or for your father more likely."

Bets hesitated. Patrick at last seemed to be holding his own and she could leave him for an hour. Perhaps if she went, she could obtain from the outlaw leader some news of Garth, something that might cheer and help restore Teodocia! To do that, Bets thought, she would talk with the devil himself. And Juan Flores, in spite of his reputation, was not the devil! She would never forget a thin youth with a high voice and a cough, who had turned his back with such absurd gallantry, that long ago afternoon.

"I'll come," she decided. "Just let me get my shawl."

"Are you sure now, ma'am? A jailhouse ain't no place for a lady, and I told him so myself. There's no need for you to go."

"Indeed there is! Please wait here, I'll only be a moment."

Although the jail was small, and most prisoners were confined and manacled together in one large room, Juan Flores, in view of his coming execution, was accorded the dignity of a cubicle of his own. Only his ankles were in irons, and as Bets came down the corridor, he was standing motionless at the tiny window, his eyes fixed on the pale blue square of sky.

Hearing her and the deputy approach, the prisoner spun around but said nothing.

Roy Sims escorted her to within a few feet of the iron-barred door and said, "You'll be perfectly safe out here, Ma'am. Anyways, I won't leave you alone with him."

The bandit's emaciated face was impassive, but Bets sensed his keen disappointment.

"On the contrary, sir," she said firmly, "Mr. Flores asked to speak to me, and I must request that he be allowed to do so privately. Please be so good as to move out of earshot."

"I doubt that your husband would permit—"

"Mr. Sims, it was you, I believe, who mentioned a condemned man's request. Would you take it on yourself to deny this one to Mr. Flores?"

Her will prevailed and the deputy unwillingly withdrew.

"Now, Señor Flores, have you a message for my father?" With Sims she had spoken English, but instinct told her that this man longed to hear his native language.

"Yes, Señora." He paused to cough painfully, one hand pressing his narrow chest. "It is simply—this. My brother met his death at the hands of Patrick Donovan, and for years I wanted revenge. But it is not good for one man to die hating another, so you may tell him I forgive him. He evened the score when he gave us warning of the posse, whether or not I thought he lied."

Bets, at mention of her father's less than forthright treatment of his own vigilantes, had started and glanced nervously over her shoulder. But there was no one close by.

"I would never have mentioned the matter if anyone could hear," Flores said. "You will tell him?"

"Yes." She was puzzled. He had wrapped himself in a mantle of stoic dignity, yet there was something in the intensity of his gaze that made her wonder if he had entirely finished what he wished to say to her.

"Señor," she ventured in the pause that followed, "may I ask, do you know what has happened to Garth Peters?"

He shook his head impatiently. "How could I, imprisoned in this cage? I would suppose he got well away, and will make his way to Oregon."

Bets felt an instant's relief for Teodocia, and then, stealing another glance at the stiff figure behind the bars, forgot Garth. Flores had fallen silent again. Perhaps there really was nothing more, and she had only imagined an entreaty in those deep-set tragic eyes! How could she, a woman who had led a restricted and sheltered life, presume to guess what hopeless longings, or torturing regrets, might lie in the mind of a man facing execution? She should take her leave now, let him return to the privacy of his final thoughts and prayers.

"Before I go," Bets said diffidently, "is there something you need, or something I can do? I would like to be of service."

The brown eyes lit.

"You are indeed kind, Señora, when I am only a stranger who has lived by breaking the law."

"Not exactly a stranger . . ."

She only meant that his name was so well known, but he chose to give her words another meaning. "That's true," he agreed. "We met at your father's rancho, on an afternoon some years ago. You were there with Señor Carew."

She was jolted, and red mounted into her face as she remembered how she had stood at the window, almost completely unclad.

"I didn't think you saw me, you walked away so quickly—"

"I saw. I didn't know then who you were, but later, when I caught a glimpse of you in the pueblo, I asked your name. Oh, you weren't aware of me. I was well hidden in the crowd, being an outlaw leader and having the biggest price on my head in all of California!"

This last was said with a bravado that reminded her poignantly of Pepe, her son, and her embarrassment faded.

"I'm deeply in your debt, Señor, that you have kept my secret. Particularly, when you vowed vengeance on my father."

"As I once told that worm, James Warner," he said with cold contempt, "I don't make war on women. In any event, after what happened to your father's affianced—yes, Señora, that is common knowledge even here in this jail. I can afford at last to pity Patrick Donovan."

Bets had no desire to pursue that subject. "That may be," she said abruptly, "but I am very grateful for your silence. Is there some favor I can possibly do? As I said, I would like to help you if I can."

Her eyes strayed briefly around the tiny odorous cell with its one primitive bucket, and only a straw pallet on the floor, doubtless crawling with fleas and lice. She saw Flores' hands, tight around the bars of the door, and again she thought of Pepe. Suppose that he, with his bright energy and impatience were confined like this, longing to be out in the fresh air! Pepe could never endure captivity, and this man too, while kept here under sentence of death, was in torment. Whatever he had done, no matter how much he deserved being hunted down, in these last days of waiting for the gallows, he had been punished.

"Señora, since you offer so kindly, I will ask. And even though you may refuse, I will understand and not be angry. The favor is this—I have never had the chance, not since I've become a man, to talk pleasantly with a woman. I have never truly known a woman, except for my mother! Now, for a little, I have time. I have admired you greatly. Will you stay, keep me company until I—until noon?"

So there it was, his purpose in sending for her. She had no doubt that Miguel, and her father too, would be horrified that she had come at all, exposing herself to the malice of town gossip. And to linger, to stay for hours?

Nevertheless, suppose it were Pepe? "I will, Señor Flores."

The pleasure which he tried futilely to hide was painful to witness, and she busied herself calling to the deputy. "Will you be good enough to fetch me a chair, Mr. Sims? I shall be here for some time."

Those few hours approaching noon passed far more quickly than she anticipated. At first it seemed strange to be talking through bars, and Bets had tried unsuccessfully to have the door opened. On this point, the jail keepers were adamant. She absolutely could not enter the cell of such a desperate character. So instead, she settled her bulky body on a hard upright chair outside, and listened while he told her of his childhood in Sonora. He only wanted to relive the simple times when he had been happy; he never touched on recent years, nor did she ask. The only interruptions came from his deep persistent cough.

After a while, he drew from his pocket a small volume with a battered leather cover, and handed it through the bars.

"My eyes haven't been good of late," he said, and then was racked by another fit of coughing. Blood gushed bright red onto the straw. Alarmed, she half-rose, but a gesture of his sent her back to her seat. He removed the soaked kerchief from before his mouth and said, "Please, don't waste time calling anyone! There is so little of it left, and I'm to die anyway . . . This is the ballad of El Cid, the legendary Spanish hero, a man I would like to have been. Will you read it aloud?"

She began at once, and was part-way through the book when Father Daniel arrived. The outlaw's disappointment at the interruption was obvious, and she hastened to say, "I will be nearby, and we'll finish this in good time. I promise."

"Thank you, Señora."

Father Daniel, who had evidenced no surprise at finding her a visitor, said, "Kneel, my son, and I will hear your confession. When I have done my best to smooth your way into God's presence, you may return to the inspiration of El Cid. The Señora will wait for us."

Bets stayed on to the end, even the hanging, and was grateful then for the presence of the priest. When Flores was led out to the gallows behind the jail, Father Daniel walked with him, but after his last words of blessing were said, he came to stand beside her, and his calm strength helped her as well.

She had never seen a man die in this way, and at first sight of the dangling loop of hemp rope, she felt her knees start to give way. She fought back her weakness; and managed to remain steadfast through the terrible moment when Flores' eyes, which had clung to hers in a desperation only she could recognize, were suddenly changed to dead stones, staring from a head that lolled sideways on its broken neck.

Until then, she had been oblivious of the pressing crowd around her. But hearing cheers and laughter, she looked up, sickened, to the hillside behind the jail yard. There, women as well as men had made themselves comfortable, some with picnic baskets beside them. And children too; brought to see a famous outlaw meet his just deserts.

The unborn baby in her body gave a sudden violent lurch, and she pressed her hand against her side.

"Are you all right, Señora?" Father Daniel asked worriedly. "Please, lean on me if you feel faint."

She put her hand on his arm and he made a path, guiding her to the front of the building, where blessedly the street was deserted. She sank down on the wooden step, smoothed and worn into a curve by so many feet over the years.

"Perhaps you shouldn't have come," said the priest. "I'm afraid, for a woman in your condition—"

"I'm not thinking about myself, Father! A man has just been cruelly put to death, a brave young man with more sense of honor than many of those who came to watch—and jeer."

The priest looked down at her and spoke sharply. "Make no mistake, my daughter, he was not a good man. He preyed on society. All of us who live and sin have a few redeeming qualities—we could not have a little of God in us otherwise, and Juan Flores was no exception. But he robbed and killed the innocent, many times over."

"He never committed rape!"

"That he did not. Señora, I know you are bitter about what happened to our little Teodocia, and I am glad we have this opportunity to talk. I have something to propose to you, if you aren't too tired?"

"I'm resting now. It's cool here." Bets was not at all curious as to what he might say. The grisly scene she had just witnessed filled her mind. "What is it?"

"First, I must express my gratitude for the way you eased that doomed young man's last hours. I wish you still lived in the pueblo—then on other such occasions we could ask your help. You are a very generous and capable woman."

"Now that I've seen a hanging," she answered drily, "I might be less willing. But I think you wanted to talk to me about Teodocia?"

"Yes, and as you will see, I haven't strayed far from

the subject. Señora Brinkman came to see me. Per haps you've wondered why she hasn't removed her daughter from Mr. Donovan's house and your care, and taken her out to their own rancho?"

"I am surprised, yes, but very grateful that she has not! Teo is my dearest friend, and having her remain with us gives me a little happiness. Every time, I've dreaded the Señora's visit, because I have been fearful she will insist Teo must go."

"Eventually, she will be forced to take her daughter away if the situation is unchanged."

"Unchanged? I don't understand."

"Both the Señora and I believe we see an opportunity for Teodocia to heal herself, to mature, to lay the foundations for a good marriage. To put it simply, your father needs nursing, and she needs to be needed. But so long, my daughter, as you are present to manage everything, she will not pull herself together and face the challenge. She will do nothing! She is too humble and uncertain to assert herself with you."

He paused, his eyes searching her face. "Do I make myself clear?"

"I should leave my own father, you mean? While he is still so weak?"

"Yes. Make an excuse, and go home. Throw his care on Teodocia. In that case, the Señora and I have agreed that the marriage should be performed at once, if Mr. Donovan is willing, and I believe he will be."

"Very well." She was smiling at last. "You do relieve my mind, Father Daniel. I should get back to my husband. Especially as I'm fully convinced now that my boys will be happy where they are, which was another reason of mine for lingering so long in town. Thank you for that too, Father."

He was looking down at her with admiration. "A decisive lady is a jewel. How I do wish I had you to help with the parish work!"

CHAPTER THIRTY

THE LAST FEW WEEKS BEFORE A BABY WAS born were usually tranquil ones for Bets. The waiting almost over, her impatience with her swollen body dissipated into a dreamy languor, and she passed many hours contentedly mending, a type of sewing she ordinarily could not abide. Meanwhile, out of an unacknowledged superstition of her own, she endeavored to keep her thoughts on pleasant things, happy things.

Her father's and Teo's wedding ceremony, for example. Even though Patrick's precarious condition had precluded all but the simplest and briefest rites, and there were no guests at all—just Teo's mother, herself, and Miguel to give the bride away—it had been a surprisingly festive occasion.

Teo, though subdued and drawn, was dressed in her finest silk skirt and chemise, which were of a pale gold color, much like her hair. Her white shawl with long knotted fringe was embroidered in yellow roses, and Doña Violeta, defying the drought in her own way, had been able to bring with her a small basket of real roses, of the same lovely yellow. One was in Teo's hair, and the rest in a vase brightened Patrick's room. Their fragrance was such that the aura of sickness and pain was temporarily banished.

With Teo kneeling beside the bed, Father Daniel had married them, and then she leaned across to her new husband and shyly kissed him.

Patrick's hand had reached for hers, and held it, while he looked into her face.

"I'll have to hurry and get well." His weak voice sounded for the first time like the old Patrick's. "I want to get on with trying to make you happy."

"But I am happy. Already," Teo said softly. Then she turned to the others and her tone firmed. "I see

Flora beckoning, because she's prepared a wedding feast for us. Shall we go in the other room? Patrick needs to rest now."

She and Bets had exchanged a glance and then smiles of understanding. Bets was leaving her father in good hands!

Remembering, thinking of him, led her to worry briefly about his beloved rancho. How was it surviving in these terrible times, lacking his supervision?

Without warning—it must have followed from her musing over the Allison or even from the sad talk with the doomed Juan Flores—the door to the forbidden memory of John sprang open. She had drifted into wondering whether he had found yet another woman, or whether he still pined for Aunt Mary, when she pulled herself up short.

No more of that, my girl! Not ever again. His image was nicely blurred now, had been ever since that shameful orgy of resentment and self-pity she'd wallowed in just after Felipa's wedding. Just a while longer and he would be forgotten.

It was reassuringly easy to distract her mind. There was the important task of listing names for the new baby, and soon she was pleasantly absorbed.

They were, as it happened, all girls' names.

Although she had laughed when Tia Pilar, eyeing her figure, made the prediction, secretly she was convinced.

"Wasn't I right about the others?" reminded the old woman. "And the new Sepulveda baby? I told them it was to be a boy, and a boy it was."

"Yes, but it had to be either a boy or a girl! Perhaps you are just very lucky at guessing."

Tia Pilar pressed her lips together angrily. "I don't guess, I know! Mock all you like, Señora, but I know!"

"I'm only teasing . . . *How* do you know? Please tell me!"

"By the shape, and where the baby lies," the woman snapped. "Girls are farther down, and not in one huge round lump."

"Well, we'll wait and see. Please don't tell Don Miguel what you've decided. He badly wants another boy, and I don't like to see him disappointed, at least not ahead of time."

Tia Pilar, unpacified, gave her a scathing look and did not answer. But from then on Bets visualized the child-to-be as another Isabel and was quite content.

She and her four-year-old daughter took walks together, short ones that suited the child's round chubby legs as well as her own awkward heaviness. The only duties Bets had these days were looking after Isabel and visiting each morning with Don Sebastian.

The elderly man was obsessed, it seemed to her, with the continued dry weather. He had become feeble in the last few months, sometimes looking as if he had aged several years overnight. Without warning, one side of his face developed a droop and he complained that it was numb. He had difficulty eating without choking, and this alone was enough to make him irascible. Yet he did not relinquish his authority. He continued to give orders to the rancho foreman without pretense of consulting with Miguel, and on one occasion also to the majordomo, something he had not done since his daughter-in-law had been in residence. Bets often wished for rain, if for no other reason than it might improve Don Sebastian's temper.

Frequently she would find him staring out his window at the parched and tortured land. By now, the hills should have been carpeted in green, but there was nothing, only a yellowish haze of dust that never settled, but was driven in great clouds by the hot santana winds that blew almost continually.

"This eternal sunshine is a curse on us," he announced when she entered his room one morning. "In all my years, I have never known such a drought! With each day that passes, the chance of a saving storm becomes less and less likely. Our good earth is dying, Elizabeth, and we are doomed!"

With his strange new guttural voice, and his coldly piercing eyes, he looked and sounded to her like a Biblical prophet. She gave a small shudder, disliking him for this talk of death, when her baby's birth was so imminent.

"Surely, Don Sebastian, we will survive this winter,

just as in the past," she remonstrated, trying to speak lightly and not succeeding.

"*We* may survive, yes." He gave her a sardonic nod. "But with no water, and nothing growing on which to graze, the cattle will starve. And without cattle, what are we?"

Surely he exaggerated? Then she thought in alarm, *the sheep!* Miguel's precious sheep needed grass too!

Don Sebastian's grim litany rolled on, growing louder. "Our prosperity, even our livelihood, will be ruined, gone forever! But that is only the beginning. Water is the life-blood of this arid land, and when the land dies, it will putrify. From its poor corpse will come stenches, poison, disease—"

"Don Sebastian!" Her voice was strident. "On the other side of this country, men are killing each other by the thousands. Just because you live far away and in isolation, you can't simply forget them! Here you sit, dramatizing a hardship that in another year will be forgotten—"

"Forgotten?" His lopsided face wore a smile that frightened her, although he spoke more mildly. "You think I dramatize? Believe me, our ordeal has only begun. The streams that run through this rancho are now a bare trickle, and will soon be dry. Los Angeles too will have no water because the zanjas will not be replenished. Go outside, woman. Walk in the hot wind. And see if I exaggerate!"

She left him, but did not go out into the noonday sun. The heat beating down on her head would have made her dizzy. Instead she lay on her bed and wished for rain with superstitious fervor, fearful that Don Sebastian might be right. If only it would end before her confinement, this dryness that hung over the stricken land like a curse!

"Elizabeth?"

"In here." Miguel had returned from one of his rare trips to Los Angeles. She sat up and smoothed her hair, welcoming escape from her dire imaginings.

"Are you all right?" he asked with concern.

"Oh, yes, just an attack of the vapors. What is the news? Did you see Papa, and how is he?"

"He's stronger, but the pain continues to strike him when he least expects it, and is obviously excruciating. I wouldn't have known—he said nothing about it—but I happened to be there when an attack came on. His face turned gray and the sweat started . . . His new young wife tends him like a mother hen, however. Teo has taken charge, so much so that Flora actually seems resentful, and Patrick is amused by that. I never did understand your father's easy-going treatment of his servants.

"Tell me, did Adam go to get the boys?"

"He left early this morning," she answered absently, her mind occupied with worry over Patrick's condition.

"I thought as much or I'd have brought them myself, although it would have meant getting horses from the livery stable. Elizabeth, there is something you should know."

"Yes?" She pushed herself off the bed and got awkwardly to her feet, holding out her hand for his assistance. He stopped speaking, looking at her in a troubled way as though he had just been reminded of her condition.

"What is it, Miguel?"

He busied himself briefly in removing his hat, and the gun he wore thrust through his sash. When he answered, she had a fleeting impression that what he said, startling as it was, was not at all what he had intended to tell her.

"Camellito and Isaias Hellman have had a falling out. They are no longer partners in the bank."

"Good gracious! What happened?"

"Nothing very dramatic, as I understand it. Hellman in his quiet way decided he didn't have enough confidence in Camellito's abilities. Unfortunately, what Hellman told his friend John Downey was overheard, and the remark which is being quoted everywhere is infuriating! His very words were: 'Mr. Camell's only qualification in a borrower was that he must be poor. I saw that doing business on that basis would soon leave me poor also, and I dissolved the partnership.' "

"Ah, poor Camellito!" Bets exclaimed. "But I suppose he really is too kindhearted to be a banker."

"On the contrary," her husband answered coldly. "The bank has been going very well, and is a success! Hellman bought him out and took Downey as a partner, probably for some selfish reason that he doesn't care to mention."

"Miguel! Isaias Hellman is an intelligent honorable man, and John Downey has been the governor of California! To say something like that isn't like you!"

"Be that as it may, Camellito has been far from happy these past weeks. He loves banking and would hate to leave it. So now he's decided to start a bank of his own, one to rival Hellman's."

When Bets said nothing, Miguel demanded, "You aren't enthusiastic? Why?"

She was tempted to reply truthfully, that she still thought Mr. Hellman might be a shrewd judge of their old friend's capabilities, likeable as Camellito was. But she did not want to antagonize Miguel. Instead she asked, "Doesn't starting a bank take a great deal of money?"

"Yes. Once again his father-in-law, Don Diego, is going into the venture with him. But even with the money Camellito received from selling his shares in Hellman, Camell and Company, they haven't nearly enough. I wish I still had a little put away, and could help. It's a good business investment, Elizabeth."

Was it? Her doubts were far from dissipated, indeed they had grown. But what were they based on, after all? Miguel knew Camellito far better than she. They'd been boys together.

"More funds will be needed," Miguel added, "I'm to speak to Ygnacio Sanchez this afternoon. He's one of the few Californios who hasn't suffered much in this drought—he and Señora Brinkman. The Señora was approached, and flatly refused! It's hard to believe sometimes she is one of us . . . Elizabeth, what is the matter?"

"No, Miguel! You must not be responsible for involving Señor Sanchez! He is a life-long friend of your father's, and will not be able to refuse you—even if he would."

There was a short silence while her heart sank.

"I was not asking advice, Elizabeth, I was merely telling you my intentions. As my wife, you must allow me to make the decisions."

' She lay back again upon the bed. Further remonstrance was useless. "I'm sorry, Miguel. I think now I will rest awhile. Will you call me, please, when the boys come?"

She woke to the familiar sound of angry voices.

"You told Arturo to move the cattle to the field near the Santa Anita, Father? I should have been consulted!"

"I was forced to manage for years without the benefit of your advice," returned Don Sebastian. "I feel entirely qualified to determine which part of this rancho is likely to have a little grass left."

"But you cannot put the cattle there!" Miguel's voice rose. He sounded like an anguished boy. "They will eat everything, and there will be nothing left for—for—"

"For what, Miguel?" the old man asked grimly. "What are you saying?"

Bets waited, filled with apprehension. Now, Miguel must confess his deceit.

"I bought sheep, Father. They are grazing there already."

There was a brief silence.

"And none of the men reported this to me?"

"No, I—I ordered them not to."

"I see. My disloyal servants have betrayed me, my son has stooped to treachery. Worse, stupidity. In the face of drought, he buys more animals—to die!" Bets could imagine the old man's eyes boring into Miguel's. "*Caramba!*" he exclaimed in deep disgust. "I have lived too long! Leave me."

Miguel's footsteps sounded, echoing away from his father's room, along the balcony, into theirs. Standing beside the bed, he surprised Bets by saying, "I am both a fool and an ingrate!"

With a sigh, thinking she preferred his wrath to this humility, she pulled herself to her feet. "You did the best you could. Who would have predicted the lack of rain?"

"I should have known there would be a good reason for selling sheep! Some men, my father is one, have a feeling for weather. He guessed what was coming, and I had the effrontery to pit my judgment against his!"

"Miguel, if you made a mistake, it was in good faith. You were only trying to improve the rancho—"

"Why can't you understand?" he cut in, and she braced herself, thinking that once again he would vent his irritation at his own failure by finding fault with her. But he was pursuing a different path, and she liked it even less.

"My sin—yes, sin, I use the word advisedly, is disloyalty. This is my father's property and I have made the men disobey him. He feels wronged! Worse than that, he feels old and alone. I was a poor son to him when I left to work in town, and I am a worse one now I have returned—"

"Stop!"

He stared at her.

"Berating yourself is utterly useless! If you feel so, you should go to him at once, say you were wrong, and ask that he do his best to save the animals. Promise him too that the men in the future will always report to him. But Miguel, please only say these things if you truly believe that feeble as he is, with his mind dimming, he is still more capable than you! Do you believe it?"

"I don't know."

"You must know!" She stared at him, unable to imagine his rebellion having been quashed so easily.

"I have only one course to follow," he answered in a low voice and turned to stare out at the hills. "He is my father. I was taught respect for him. Respect for one's parents is a basic rock of my Californio heritage, and I, who want so much to preserve this heritage, cannot undermine it. I put filial duty aside once . . . I won't again."

Was he dramatizing, as she had once accused Don Sebastian of doing? If so, he had not finished.

"You are wrong when you say I must be convinced he is capable. It is no longer important to me! What is essential is harmony with my father. I have found I can have no peace otherwise."

Harmony! That is an impossibility! Bets wanted to shout, can't you see, he's made you a child! Can't you see?

But she said nothing. He left her, and she went to shut the door. If he actually humbled himself, she did not want to hear him do so.

Instead, she took his place at the window and watched the road which led through a canyon from Los Angeles. Any time now, she should be able to catch sight of the dust cloud which would herald three horses in the distance. Adam had ridden away from the estate many hours before, leading two gentle geldings just as he always did when the boys were coming home for a visit. Soon the three would appear on the horizon.

What was it, she wondered suddenly, that Miguel had intended to tell her earlier before she was distracted by his news about Camellito?

A strange dread rose in her, remembering. He had looked at her with belated apprehension, as though she wasn't strong enough to share whatever it was that worried him . . .

She sat hunched at the window, unmoving, her heart hammering painfully against her side.

She was not truly surprised then to see in the distance only two figures riding, with a horse led behind. The larger figure, Adam, was holding a child before him in the saddle, cradling him in his strong wiry arms.

CHAPTER THIRTY-ONE

MARY REYES, WALKING BRISKLY IN SPITE OF the steep upward slope of the street, glanced at the overcast sky and shivered, then berated herself. How foolish to let the weather seem an augury for success or failure! Even supposing it were one, what kind of day would bring good luck, and what kind bad? Certainly down the coast in drought-stricken Los Angeles, a driving storm would be hailed as the greatest good fortune ever! No, at this very moment, the dealer in art, Vermies Milo, would be judging her picture of the abandoned ships solely on its own merits. If he were to let gloomy afternoons in San Francisco influence his judgment, there would never be another painting or piece of sculpture sold in this city.

All the same she was anxious and therefore filled with scorn for herself. Why hadn't she waited, as any sensible person would, to learn his reaction?

Instead, she'd pushed the painting into his hands and fled, forgetting entirely how he'd encouraged her in advance.

"Ah, Mrs. Reyes," he'd said, "your previous work has been selling so very well! But I do understand your desire to experiment. All good artists must. They change, sometimes they grow. Now you and I recognize, don't we, that Turner achieved exactly that hazy indistinctness you describe? But in oils. In oils. Watercolor is another matter, difficult . . . Still, you've chosen a promising subject. All those hulks left from gold rush days. Imagine the crews just abandoning their ships, running off madly to the gold fields! There is a melancholy about those old boats, some of them sunk, some used as wharves. I'll be most interested to see what you make of them. Yes, by all means, try!"

She'd been fired with enthusiasm, and San Francisco

Bay cooperated, displaying almost every day exactly the misty brooding effect she wanted. She had only to portray what was there.

The work had gone easily and well. To her, the picture seemed good.

But was it?

She hadn't the courage to find out at once. Instead she wanted to walk, to savor the relief she always felt when a painting was finished. The nagging emptiness, the need to return to work, wouldn't come until next week, or next month—sometime just before a new and nebulous idea would be forming in her imagination.

Meanwhile, she was free to see and hear and feel again, and for that purpose, this stretch of Montgomery Street was particularly satisfying. Unlike many areas of San Francisco, in which there still could be found only the hastily thrown together shacks that over and over burned to the ground in the city's recurrent fires, here were solid houses of brick or stone or crafted wood, built meticulously and with love. She could admire their turrets, gables, or ornate carvings while taking guesses as to the previous nationalities of the owners. Each house, it appeared, was a replica, a resurrected memory of a childhood home back in Hamburg or Marseilles, Genoa, Sussex, or even New England, with a very few old adobes scattered into the hodgepodge for leavening; she could savor the saltiness of the air too, and feel the smooth round cobblestones through the thin soles of her shoes.

Did everyone take such intense pleasure in the senses, she wondered, or was it a peculiarity of artists of all kinds? Musicians surely. Singers? Well, perhaps not—but certainly composers! And what about novelists? Goldsmiths? Artisans?

It was an interesting question, but one to which she couldn't discover the answer because she conversed with so few artists. Alone as she was, she behaved very circumspectly, going out seldom in the evening, indeed only twice thus far, once to the Jenny Lind, and once, daringly, to the Théâtre Français. Her pictures paid enough so that she could afford to live in a high-class boarding house situated up on a shoulder of Telegraph

Hill, and sometimes she regretted the privilege. Unlike the denizens of cheaper places, the tenants in her house were dignified, stolid couples, the husband in the city on some business of too brief duration for them to invest in a more permanent home, and not quite important enough to warrant the far greater expense of hotel living. The wives had made it clear at once that they regarded a single woman with suspicion, especially when she supported herself in such a bizarre way.

Mary laughed aloud, visualizing their closed, purse-lipped faces, and then realized she didn't find them funny at all. She was actually lonely.

With this admission, her mind refused to be disciplined any longer and she fell to thinking of Patrick. Parting from her brother in anger had been bad enough, but the realization of how close he had come to dying, and that before she could make amends, frightened her terribly. She would never have been able to resist running back to be at his side, but by the time a fragmentary account of the gun duel reached her, he was out of danger and his quiet marriage ceremony performed. Now he had a wife, and that being so, there was no longer room in his house for his sister.

Homesickness—longing for Patrick and their old life together—swept through her.

"Mrs. Reyes, good afternoon!"

Gratefully, Mary turned, recognizing the little woman immediately although she had only met her once before. It was Mrs. Milo, the art dealer's wife. Mrs. Milo undoubtedly had a given name, but it was never used, possibly because she bore such an odd, indeed striking resemblance to her husband. They had the same small plump stature, and even more intriguing, the same habit of twitching their noses, giving their round white faces the look of inquisitive rabbits. Milo himself had a thin blond mustache that added nicely to the effect. Mary, not very tall, found herself looking down whenever she conversed with either of them.

"I've just come from the gallery," Mrs. Milo told her. "My husband showed me your new watercolor,

Bay of Ships, isn't it called? My dear, he is so terribly excited!"

Mary's spirits bounded upward.

"He likes it? I'm so glad!"

"Oh, very much! He intends to display it prominently and he hopes to persuade you to reconsider and come to our reception tonight. Will you?" She finished in a breathless rush, and Mary smiled.

To her own surprise, as well as Mrs. Milo's, she replied, "Thank you, how kind! Yes, I do believe I will."

"Really?" The little woman beamed. "I suppose we've just caught you this time? Between pictures, I mean."

"Yes."

"My husband will be most pleased. So many of the people who *count* here in the city will be present, and with your promise to come, I'm certain he'll make a feature of your picture. I wouldn't be surprised, not at all, if it sells at once. So you see, putting in an appearance will be all to the good. Shall we say nine o'clock? We'll send out our carriage for you."

Mary went on her way, wondering why she had avoided such gatherings in recent years. She was actually looking forward to this evening! It would be good to talk with someone besides herself. If she hurried, she could wash her hair and while waiting for it to dry could heat up the landlady's flat iron and press the one gown she owned that would be suitable.

Mr. Milo, as promised, sent his carriage, and the coachman drove her in solitary grandeur to the gallery. How different those hushed rooms were from any shop in Los Angeles! Well illuminated tonight by candelabra, as well as by the new but colder gaslight that was San Francisco's pride, they hummed with the murmured comments and tinkling laughter of the fashionable gathering. The gentlemen wore the finest of ruffled shirts, doe-colored trousers and high beaver hats, and the ladies' clothes were the latest to come from Paris, brocaded gowns collared with embroidered tussore silk, the yards of fabric gathered tight at the waist and draped in long folds below. Nothing like those dresses had ever been seen in the southern part of the state!

Then Mary caught sight of her *Bay of Ships,* which stood on an easel in the very center of the main salon where no one could possibly miss it. Her face flushed with delight and gratification.

At length she realized someone was standing just behind her, saying nothing, evidently awaiting her reaction. Assuming it was Milo, she turned, starting to exclaim, "I can't thank you enough—"

But it was John.

Speechless, Mary stared at him, and the murmur of voices all around receded, like gentle surf washing out from shore.

He appeared unchanged despite his thirty-nine years. His stocky figure was still hard and muscular, in spite of gentler living. The thick flaxen hair remained unruly, falling across his forehead, and his eyes, as vividly cerulean blue as if they'd been splashed from a paint tube, held her gaze steadily. With an effort, she looked away, but not before noting a small defect she had long forgotten, his crooked nose. It proved, she thought, a theory of hers that slight asymmetry added to beauty rather than subtracting from it. Remembering how she had solemnly expounded this idea to Alice Carter, she smiled.

"You are as lovely as ever," Carew said.

Alice Carter flew from her mind. "I was about to remark that you hadn't changed. But I am wrong. The John Carew I used to know was not given to easy compliments."

"Neither is this one. I can only state the truth as I see it. How are you, Mary?"

"Just the same." She had somehow told him more than she intended, because he nodded.

"Still alone then. Except for that faraway husband in Spain, of course."

There seemed no comment she could make, so she said nothing.

"I've hoped you would finally come, Mary."

"But I've been in San Francisco for some weeks now," she protested.

"I meant, come here—to one of Milo's receptions."

"You've known I was in the city? You might have paid a call—as an old friend."

"I knew you were here, and also that you were working. You never liked to be interrupted, so I didn't call . . . Milo speaks very respectfully of you, by the way. It seems my opinion of some time ago, that you are a very good artist, was right. That watercolor you did of me—"

"Yes, *Angels Gate*." She was relieved to have the conversation shift to something less personal. "One of the most satisfying pictures—to me, that is. How I wish you could have seen it! I did bring a portfolio of things to San Francisco, but unfortunately—or rather fortunately, *Angels Gate* sold at once."

To her mystification, he seemed amused. "Ah well, I can at least enjoy the one that's on exhibit tonight."

He turned his attention to the watercolor on the easel, studying the ship-filled harbor. Indistinct in the background haze, lofty three-masters as well as a squatty steamer suggested the commerce of the present; but in the foreground were the derelicts, the great sad hulks of abandoned vessels, some sunk low in the water, others serving as convenient moorings for the many fishing smacks. Everywhere, dead spars, denuded of rigging, thrust up through the gray mist.

"Like it?" inquired Milo, coming toward them and beaming widely. He looked from one to the other of them, his button nose twitching.

"Very much!" said Carew.

"But perhaps not as much as—"

"Yes, more." John cut him off. He seemed preoccupied by the picture. "I want to buy it."

"Splendid, my friend! Although you will note I've set a high price. We'll consider it yours, but not for several days. Tonight my centerpiece, my focus of interest must remain where it is.

"Now, I've instructions from my wife to introduce our artist, so you must excuse her while we make the rounds. Will you follow me, Mrs. Reyes?"

She fell in beside the portly little man, at the same

time giving John a smile of apology. Even after she turned away, she knew he was watching her.

For the next hour she slowly toured the gallery rooms, meeting people whose names she had heard more than once, and coming to realize she in turn was not unknown to them. She listened in secret wonder to their compliments. Living as she had in self-imposed isolation, she'd been largely unaware of her own growing reputation in San Francisco's art world. Of course, being sponsored by Milo was a cachet that would launch any artist. All of the critics esteemed his judgment. All the same, one wouldn't be human not to be thrilled by such praise!

At the end, she was sipping champagne and listening to the effusions of Mrs. Milo, who enjoyed these receptions more than any guest possibly could.

"Oh, I am so very glad you came! And did you see how the Governor stood and contemplated your picture for a long time? He's a collector himself! I shouldn't be surprised if—"

"No, Mrs. Milo," said Carew, reappearing beside them. The crowd was thinning now and Mary wondered if he had lingered so long merely to wait for her. Standing close as they were, his hand by accident touched her waist, and a small quiver of sensation passed through her. "That picture is no longer for sale," he continued quietly. "It belongs to me."

Again she felt an awareness. *Belongs to me,* those words spoken firmly, as he looked at her, seemed to carry special significance.

"Splendid!" Their hostess beamed. "You are to be congratulated, Mr. Carew. Shall we have another glass of champagne to celebrate? It's really an excellent vintage, Milo is *so* particular—"

"Thank you," he said, "but I've a table waiting at the Grand Hotel. Luckily, I brought my phaeton tonight, instead of coming on horseback, because Mrs. Reyes has agreed to join me for a late supper. She had no choice, I'm afraid. An artist must be kind and gracious at least once to those who are lucky enough to buy her work."

Doubtless he intended to smooth their exit and avoid

causing comment, for gossip in San Francisco was especially rife. Mary, who had given no such promise, tried not to appear startled, even though Mrs. Milo's rosebud lips parted in surprise.

The dealer's wife gave her one swift glance before replying. "Really, Mr. Carew? Others have tried to convince Mrs. Reyes of this before, with no success. How wonderful! At last she will stop being such a recluse."

"That was a mistake," Mary said, settling herself beside him in his phaeton. "She is very kind and friendly but without much to do. She will make the most of your invitation."

He laughed. "Not my invitation. Your acceptance."

"Which I never gave!"

"Then we're even. I have no table at the Grand either."

"Perhaps one isn't necessary?" she said faintly, "I know very little about the city."

"Are you so hungry then?"

"No . . . No, I'm not."

"Good. We won't go there." He flicked the reins and the horse moved off smartly, his hooves ringing on the stone street.

The short ride was passed in silence, neither asking any of the questions that would have been natural between two people who hadn't seen each other for so long. Mary, under cover of the intimate darkness, studied her companion, comparing the strong young sheepherder of Los Angeles with this polished gentleman at her side. He had been attractive then, his physical appeal further enhanced by the story of his incredible feat of endurance, but the difference in their ages had been enough to prevent her taking him seriously as a man. Or so she'd supposed, until that day at Rancho Aguirre when a strange bright thunderbolt had struck her without warning. He was still muscular, his quiet virility unchanged, but through some trick of the years, now he seemed to be the older. He was in control tonight, not she, and the realization was both pleasant and disturbing.

She was not truly surprised when the carriage was brought to a stop before a small New England salt-box of a house, near the end of Battery Street. Carew tied the horse to an iron hitching post, knowing there was a groom on hand who would take care of the animal, and offered his hand to assist her down from the seat.

"Mary?"

Even then she could have refused, and told herself that she must. Instead, she alighted, and allowed him to lead her up the steps.

His key unlocked the door, and they were inside, standing in blackness.

"Wait here, while I light a lamp—"

"This is your home?" she asked, forced by her trepidation to say something.

He hesitated, then answered, "Yes, when I am in the city."

She didn't notice the pause, nor take much heed of the answer, for with the flare of gaslight, the room's furnishings were revealed. Simple, made of cherry wood, they had clearly originated somewhere in the eastern states, possibly New York. She experienced a moment of relief that they were not Spanish, for it would be appalling, she thought, to be reminded here tonight of her husband Francisco, or even of Patrick, against whose immorality she had been so righteous, such a fishwife—

Then she saw *Angels Gate,* her watercolor of John. It occupied the place of honor above his fireplace.

"I knew we would meet again, and when Milo told me you were to be at the gallery tonight—"

"You bought it!" she cried, turning to him with delight. "It was you!"

"Yes. Can you imagine how I felt when I happened on that picture displayed at Milo's? I knew then, Mary, that I hadn't been wrong about us, that my love for you had not died, never would die . . . I even knew you would come to me."

He stopped, and his eyes held hers so there was no looking away, no escape. Then he touched her face gently and the deep painful longing, stronger than she remembered and more urgent, flowed into her again, torturing her.

"Please—oh, please—"

"Yes, Mary . . . Oh God, Mary! How I've wanted you!"

His arms were hard and tight, straining her body against his, his lips were on her throat, moving downward, pressing the soft swell of breast above her bodice. She gave a little cry of protest when he thrust her away, even though she realized he had only done so to unbutton the fastenings of her dress. The soft folds of fine burgundy silk fell unheeded at her feet.

The first time he took her they might have been former lovers, knowing each other well, finding each other once again. The intense hunger was for both so overwhelming it left no time for tenderness, but reached its hard, almost brutal climax with a hammering force that exhausted her.

But afterward, there was a time of lying in his arms, held close, every inch of her body wanting to touch every inch of his, and then the surge of desire built up again slowly, with murmuring, with kisses and caresses, searing, feathery, demanding, begging, a long slow wave coming in from afar out to break at last just as powerfully as before.

And again, it was all familiar, as though they had done this together many times.

For Mary, it was like coming home, after a long and lonely absence.

CHAPTER THIRTY-TWO

SHE WOKE FIRST, AND WENT AT ONCE TO THE window, as she had done all of her life wherever she was. She wanted to see the grays and oranges of dawn, or if too late for that, the dappling of the streets under scudding clouds, or even the wet shiny pools of rain.

San Francisco was a particular delight because of its variety. Seldom in this city was there bright golden sunshine, yet each day was beautiful, and different from the last.

Today was crisp and clear. Not even mist hung over the waters of the bay, which she was delighted to discover was close by, the view of its activity unimpeded.

On an impulse, she dressed swiftly and made her toilet in the next room, taking care not to wake the man who still slept on the bed, a bare leg sprawled from beneath the blanket, and his fair hair tousled like a boy's. She knew that if she made any sound and woke him, she would be drawn back into his arms, the devastating ecstasy would begin again, and she would be lost. There would be no turning back, no time to think; and she needed to think.

She stepped out into the brilliant clarity of the morning, and closed the door behind her. Her ample shawl felt very good against the fresh wind, and she reflected that it was fortunate she had it with her, not only for warmth, but to partially conceal last night's embroidered silk gown which was far too elegant for morning wear.

She had paused, looking about with pleasure. Before she could step away, Carew appeared in the doorway behind her, hastily shrugging into a dressing robe.

"Don't go!" His intensity startled her.

"I shan't be long."

"There's something I must tell you! Last night—well, talk was out of the question."

"I agree." Being at a safe distance, she gave him a grin, and saw his expression soften.

"Where is it you're going that can't wait?"

"Just to my boarding house. There are things I do need. Another dress, for one! Though what I'm to tell my extremely correct landlady when she wonders where I've been, I haven't a notion."

He leaned against the door frame, seemingly satisfied now that he'd learned her objective. "A tale of a night spent with a sick old lady? Better yet, just give her a haughty look."

"You're very glib. The result of experience I suppose."

"Mary . . ." Suddenly he was serious again. "Hurry back, my dearest. Or I'll think I've lost you again."

"I will run all the way." She turned from him, feeling ridiculously undone, and happy at the same time. "Wait for me, John. We'll breakfast together."

Yet as she walked away, she could not avoid glancing at the adjacent house, the windows like blank eyes, and asking herself who—how many—had witnessed her exit. She believed she knew no one who lived in this area, but still all that was needed was one gossipy acquaintance. She drew herself up short. Did she care so much about her reputation as that? And the need to ask the question considerably diminished the glow she was feeling.

Adultery. She tested the word aloud. She had always been honest with herself, and could not avoid facing the truth now. She, Mary Reyes, was a married woman who had made love willingly—oh, so willingly! —with a man who was not her husband; and unquestionably, were this known, she would be ostracized.

She had been in San Francisco long enough to understand that the city's veneer of sophistication was very new and quite thin. It was only yesterday this roaring gold rush capital had a well-deserved reputation as one of the roughest, most dangerous, most immoral gambling hells to be found anywhere. But vigilantes had reduced the flagrant crime, and civilized settlers from around the world were busily trying to set standards of culture and behavior.

To think that one could sit today in a beautifully furnished establishment on the California wharf—a spot where two years ago there had been only a rough boarding ladder—and drink German chocolate or eat the finest confectionery! Enjoying herself at the next table might well be a former madam, rich as Croesus from having operated a famous brothel, and living a life of the most luxurious leisure, with no lack of broadminded friends. But that woman would not be encountered at the gallery, because she wouldn't be invited there, or even recognized.

Nor would Mary Reyes, should she persist. As an artist, she would be finished.

Mary shivered.

Did she love him then, so much? Physically, yes, she was totally his. His slightest touch aroused desire of an intensity she was convinced she had never experienced with Francisco Reyes, although perhaps it was a mistake to make that comparison. Memories of passion tended to dim with time.

But she also cared about this man in other ways, she thought, trying to disentangle the strands of physical love from simple respect and affection. She liked John's strength, his quietness, his patience. Even in the beginning, in Los Angeles, they had been able to talk or not talk, as they wished. They could be good companions. With him, her loneliness would be assuaged forever.

But love would be bought at what a price! An evening like hers last night, the triumph, the personal fulfillment, would never happen again, not if she stayed with John.

A high price indeed. Could she afford to pay it?

She realized her steps had been carrying her, not toward her boarding house now, but in the direction of the gallery. Did she want to see those elegant rooms once more to bid them farewell? No, not that—not yet! Still, once there, perhaps her own needs and wishes might be clearer. A decision must be made, and after one more day with her lover, it might well be too late. The ostracism would be a *fait accompli,* wish it or no.

She quickened her pace, hoping a visit to the gallery would help somehow to solve her dilemma.

"Good morning, Mrs. Reyes!" Even at this early hour, Mrs. Milo, feather duster in hand, was just inside the open door, bustling about. "After last night's reception, it's rather a task straightening up. Milo likes for me to do the cleaning; servants do sometimes damage things, and breakage is such a tragedy. Have you seen where he is hanging your *Bay of Ships?*"

Disconcerted, for she hadn't expected to meet the

dealer or his wife, Mary murmured, "I thought it was sold."

"It is, but Milo wants to keep the picture here for a few days more, so our other patrons—those who didn't attend last night's showing, can see your work. It is important for you." The short woman stopped what she was doing to give Mary a sweeping look. Did her eyes linger too long on the telltale silk skirt? "My husband has said you have great talent," she remarked, adding, "A gift like that should not be taken lightly."

"I—thank you." Mary turned, ostensibly to locate her *Bay of Ships* which hung on the entry wall in favored splendor.

"Mrs. Reyes?"

"Yes?"

"There is something I think you should know—if you don't, and I think you must not. Although a late supper can be quite innocent, we all realize that."

Mary did not reply. Her gaze was fixed on the watercolor, but she was conscious of nothing except what Mrs. Milo was saying.

"Mr. Carew is a long time friend of my husband's, that's true, but Milo would feel responsible, and he would hate to think anything he did—or didn't—"

She was too flustered to continue.

"What is it you are trying to say, Mrs. Milo?" Mary asked evenly.

The little woman drew a deep breath. "Just this, Mrs. Reyes, Mrs. Carew—his wife, that is, seldom comes into the city; she prefers to stay on that ranch of theirs. She's a mousy sort, dull really and ignorant, but she does exist, oh my, yes, she does exist!"

Mary's hands clenched together tightly, white to the bone, but she did not glance down.

"Does she?" There was the temptation to say more, to deny the existence of a wife for John Carew was of any moment to her. But fortunately, her voice failed.

Mrs. Milo continued softly, "And their daughter is a little darling. Truly! Her name is Ellen. She's seven or eight, and quite adores her father."

Mary could hear the genuine sympathy for herself that underlay this revelation. She had been wrong last night, she thought dully. Mrs. Milo was not a gossip, she was more than merely a nice woman. This warning had not been easy for her to give.

Mary's pride demanded there be no acknowledgment. She steeled herself to make some remark casual enough, but again Mrs. Milo proved herself both perceptive and kind.

"Ah, well, here we stand idly talking, and I know you must be in a hurry. All those splendid pictures waiting to be done! I'm glad you happened by, because there was a letter—"

She hurried away into the nearby office, to return with the missive. She managed to hand it over without looking directly at Mary, who said, "Thank you. I must go now," and fled.

She knocked at the door of the house on Battery Street, far more apprehensive than she had been earlier at the possibility of unseen watchers. She was forced to return because she had left her reticule which contained all the ready money she had. The only alternative, revisiting the gallery and facing Milo, who as a favor kept her savings in his office, was not to be borne. She believed even an unpleasant confrontation with John would be easier.

The door opened. He had dressed during her absence, and his fashionable costume made him seem more a stranger than ever. When he drew her into his arms, she stood stiffly, without response, and instantly he let her go.

She was the first to speak, goaded by her anger and humiliation. "Last night, I mistook you for a young man I have respected and admired. Blunt, unpolished, he even wore deerskins to a Stearns fandango, but he was a gentleman. A man of honor!"

Carew did not answer, but a muscle jumped in his jaw. His eyes, those remarkable cerulean eyes, regarded her steadily. In the lengthening silence, she became aware of the aroma of ham and fresh coffee, and glancing past him, saw he had set a table with a cheerful cloth and bright silverware. The sight did not soften her.

"What is this place? Just a convenient spot to bring your paramours?"

"I told you last night—my town house."

"But not your home! Ah, no, your home is where your wife is." She cried at last, "John, John . . . why didn't you tell me you were married?"

"I intended to, this morning! Last night it—well, it didn't seem important, knowing you aren't single either. Mary . . . dearest . . . yes, I do have a wife, a woman who bears my name. But she means nothing to me. I am in truth no more married than you are."

"Really? I would find that difficult to believe! You live with her, I'm told, on your ranch—for which, Heaven knows, I'm not blaming you. She is your wife! I hear too that you have a pretty little daughter, and for that, accept my congratulations. Now, I'll take my bag and go. Your place, Mr. Carew, obviously is with them."

"Suppose you let me judge my own place and my own marriage! Will you listen, or is this just an excuse to leave me?"

The words were defiant, the tone was not. Sharpness would have driven her away, but the simple wretchedness in his voice made her pause.

"I'll listen, yes." She sank into a chair, her trembling legs no longer able to support her. "Although, you understand, in any case I must go." Her hands, beneath the shawl, gripped the letter from Patrick.

"As you must have known, Mary, I was bitterly disappointed that day at the Aguirre Rancho. You had never even hinted of *your* marriage." He gave her a wry smile, and she reddened.

"Afterward, I might have married someone who did care for me, but regardless of what you think, I do have a sense of decency; and it was clear to me that all I could bring the young lady was unhappiness.

"So I came to San Francisco. I was lonely and resentful, and when my landlady's daughter flirted with me rather timidly, I did not discourage her as no doubt I should have. All she wanted was an advantageous marriage, she admitted as much, and I didn't have to be told she was incapable of love, at least the sort I wanted. But one night, far from sober, I suggested she marry me.

"Like others in my situation, I suppose I was trying to punish myself—and you. Idiocy, of course. You couldn't have known!"

"I hope you have had some happiness," Mary said in a low voice. "I would not wish you otherwise."

"We have a livable arrangement, Emily and I. Which is not to be despised, when we have nothing in common."

"Nothing? I understand you have a daughter."

"Yes, her name is Ellen." For a second the bleakness lifted. "Bless her, she has made everything worthwhile."

"And would you have your Ellen know what happened last night? Ah, John . . . don't you see how everything is changed? You are truly married. I am not. My husband vanished long ago. He is only a shackle that will keep me forever tied. No, my dear, I couldn't let you betray your family, even if I—"

"Even if you—?" The words were sardonic.

Beyond him, in a corner of her vision, Mary could see the bedroom, the rumpled bed. She shivered.

"Even if I could picture myself—just living in a back street, as someone's mistress."

He said quietly, "I don't picture you that way either. Only a mistress? God in heaven, you'd never be that to me!" And the ugliness faded.

"Anyway, I can't stay," Mary said. "The choice is out of my hands. I've had a letter from my brother, asking me to come back. Things are desperate in Los Angeles, not only with the drought, and all the animals starving on the ranchos, but there's a smallpox epidemic. So many people are dying, the undertakers are refusing to bury the dead. People are terrified to leave their own houses! Listen, he says at the end:

I'm asking you, Mary Frances, to go to Bets. Her children are terribly ill, Don Sebastian needs constant care, and her time is near. There is no other help to be had! Most of the servants have run away, basely deserting Rancho Aguirre, and Pilar and

Adam can't do everything, though they try. I curse myself daily that when my child needs me most, I'm a weak husk of a man, hardly able to lift an arm.

"I must go! Surely you agree?"

"I do not. Patrick has the Irish habit of exaggeration. Tell me have you been vaccinated?"

"He mentions earlier in the letter that he is certain I was, in Boston. I—have no recollection of it."

"Then you must not go! But we can discuss all this after breakfast. Smell that ham? I'm a good enough cook—I learned the hard way, over a camp fire crossing the plains. Come along."

He put an arm around her shoulders and this time she did not shrink away. She felt his muscles tighten. He looked down at her.

"Mary?"

"No, oh no, I must not—" But his mouth was on hers, and there was nothing else, no one in the world except him.

CHAPTER THIRTY-THREE

ALTHOUGH IT WAS PEPE WHOM ADAM CARried before him on his horse, both boys were listless and feverish. Tomas rode hunched in his saddle and as they neared the house, he leaned sideways to vomit. Bets learned from him that they had had aching heads the night before, but knowing they were to go home the next day, and fearing they might miss their brief holiday if they were sick, they had told no one.

"Oh, Mother," Pepe moaned from Adam's arms, "I feel so bad!"

"We'll get you into your beds at once, then things will be better." She forced herself to be unconcerned during the few minutes required to settle the two children between clean sheets. But when she returned to Miguel she could no longer disguise her fear.

"Both of them are burning with fever, and their backs ache! What do you think it is?"

"Elizabeth . . ." His eyes were anguished. "I'm afraid—it may be smallpox."

"Oh, dear God, no!"

"That was what I started to tell you this morning—there has been a bad outbreak, not only in the town but on the ranchos. But I decided there was no reason to frighten you, and of course—" he added quickly, "we don't know that the boys have it; we won't know until several days have passed. If no small bumps appear—"

"We must get a doctor at once!"

"Yes, although there is probably not much he can do. The disease has to run its course. *Querida,* have you ever been through an epidemic?"

"No." Here he stood talking when she wanted him to ride at once and bring help! She should be returning to her sons, trying to ease their discomfort.

"If the boys do have smallpox," Miguel continued, "just as soon as the news gets out, the servants will leave, even some of the outside workers, and no one will come near. No one! People will be too terrified. I remember this happening when I was a youth."

"But surely the doctor will come? No one else matters! You know we can count on Tia Pilar, and Adam would die for Pepe willingly. Between us all, we'll manage."

"Yes, we'll manage." She knew he was thinking, with misgivings, of her condition.

"But we must have a doctor! That young German who treated Papa and advised me about Teo. Go to him. He's a good man; he won't refuse."

Miguel gave her a grim smile. "As he's the only decent and sober doctor presently in Los Angeles, he won't be allowed to refuse—if I have to persuade him at gun point."

"Then go at once, Miguel!" she urged.

But watching him ride away, she knew in her heart that she was grasping at straws and he was humoring her. If their fears were truly realized, the fate of their sons would be in the hands of God. No mere human could cure smallpox!

The doctor, when he arrived, confirmed this.

Several days had passed, since Miguel had returned alone yet completely confident that Emil Kramer, who had promised to attend the boys, would keep his word. Late one afternoon, the physician appeared.

At first, when Miguel led the way into the house and pressed on the visitor a glass of wine, delaying briefly his visit to the sickroom, Bets felt angry impatience. But her resentment faded when she realized how desperately tired Emil Kramer was. Observing him, his sunken eyes, his gaunt body, she didn't need to be told he'd had little sleep in days, and that making this long ride to the rancho when he was already besieged by more desperately ill patients than he could possibly see, was an act of consummate kindness.

In only a few moments Bets was leading him to the sickroom. The door was ajar and as they approached, she murmured a few words of apology. No matter how much she and Adam scrubbed the floors or changed the linen, there lingered a pervasive odor of vomit.

The doctor ignored the foulness of the air and walked quietly to the bedside of first one child then the other. His inspection was brief. Tomas looked up at him with dull lassitude, but Pepe, in a voice full of anxiety, piped weakly, "Mother, is today Tuesday?"

"Yes, darling, Tuesday. Why do you ask?"

"Oh, Mother!" he wailed, "I was to tell the other children about Greece today! Father Daniel gave me his own books to read, and I was to report, all about the Spartans, and the battle at Thermopylae." The tears were brimming in his eyes.

"Never mind." She leaned to hug him. "I will talk to Father Daniel, and suggest he let you do it another day."

"Will he, do you think?"

"I promise you he will." She smoothed his blanket then whispered to Dr. Kramer, "I was certain yesterday they were better. Aren't they? The fever is down."

For answer, he took her hand and rubbed it gently across Pepe's face and then Tomas's. The normally smooth skin was nubby. Her small hope died, as her finger touched the many tiny lumps.

"You do feel them?" he inquired. "Come, let's go downstairs and speak to your husband."

Below, Miguel who had been waiting, poured the doctor another glass of red wine. The young man drank before speaking, perhaps wishing to postpone what he had to say.

"Have both of you been vaccinated against small-pox?"

"So that is it, then." Miguel sighed. "I feared as much . . . Vaccinated? I don't understand what you mean."

"I do," Bets said. "When I was a child in Boston I was scratched with a needle, and I still have the scar where it was done. But here, no one seems to know about the procedure! Several years ago, I mentioned it to a doctor who was in the pueblo then, but he just said he didn't have any supplies, nor were there any to be had. Oh, if only I'd asked further!"

"Es hat nicht sollen sein, as my mother in Germany used to say. That meant, 'It was not to be.' " Dr. Kramer shook his head. "You'll need all the strength you have in the days ahead, without wasting any of it in regretting what was not. Think only of what *is.* And I hope that baby of yours doesn't come quite yet. You must try not to tire yourself!"

He turned his attention to Miguel. "Now you, Señor Aguirre, if you've been with the children, you may become sick yourself—"

"No. I had a mild case myself at one time."

"Good! Who else is in the household?"

"My father, an invalid, our daughter who is a child of four. She has not been allowed to enter the sick-room, and will not. She is being watched over by an elderly woman who also had the pox at one time and bears the scars to prove it. Then, there is only Adam left." Miguel's face closed as he thought of the other servants, the ones who, in mindless panic, had vanished from the house. Outside in the small adobe huts were still many workers, women as well as men, but he dared not order them into the hacienda. They too might choose to leave, and he needed them for the manual labor of the big rancho.

"Adam?"

"A Chinese manservant. Unquestionably, we can count on him, unless he too becomes ill."

"If he's Chinese, that's not so likely. Do you know that in China, and many other places as well, the common people for hundreds of years have practiced a kind of folk variolation? They make a powder from the crusts shed by someone who recovered from smallpox, and then induce their children to breathe it, thus bringing on a very mild case of the disease, and future immunity like yours. Eventually the upper classes too realized how effective the method was, and took it up.

"But in our part of the world, which we consider so advanced, it's only been in this century, since Jenner produced his cowpox vaccine, that inoculation has been accepted. Not welcomed, but accepted! Men like Cotton Mather and Zabdiel Boylston realized long ago what could be done to save lives, but they were beaten back by prejudice!"

"Prejudice?" repeated Miguel.

"I refer to a dastardly, incredibly stupid belief, namely, that to prevent a disease, even one that can leave its victims blind, deaf, disfigured or dead, is interference with God's will!" He was forced to pause, hitting one fist into the other, before he could continue. "At any rate, my friends, the practice of inoculation has spread far too slowly, and while it is now common enough in the larger cities, in remote corners such as Los Angeles, almost no one is protected."

Bets was no longer listening. His ringing description of the dread effects of smallpox overwhelmed her with horror. This was the disease that held her sons, her beloved sons, in its grasp! Were they, too, to be blind, deaf, disfigured—or dead?

Only when the young doctor went on to describe the simple care the children should have, and told her what to look for as the symptoms progressed, was she able to think clearly again. She swore to herself that if love and devotion counted, Tomas and Pepe would survive. She would make them live!

Dr. Kramer must have been aware of her determination, because when he left, he paused and looked earnestly into her face.

"I repeat again, don't exhaust yourself! Remember, your midwife may not come, not in these fearful days. And I myself cannot promise to return."

"I've had three other children with no difficulty," she replied. "Right now, I can only worry about the living. Oh, if only I could have had them inoculated! You did say not to dwell on that, but you must understand, it's difficult."

"I understand only too well." He looked off into the distance, clearing his throat. "I myself, as soon as I came to southern California and realized how many of my patients had never even heard of inoculation, planned to send away for vaccine. There is some available now in San Francisco. That was my intention, Señora, but weeks went by because I was terribly busy tending the sick, trying to prevent people from putting filth in the zanjas, yes, even courting a lady.

"I am too late. Before this is over, hundreds may die. Tell me, how would you like to live knowing that?"

He had not expected an answer, and there was none to give. A haggard and driven man, he strode away to where his mare was tethered.

The days dragged on, and for Tomas and Pepe they were filled with pain.

Neither any longer looked up when she entered the room, although both whimpered when they were touched. The lumps under the skin covered their bodies everywhere, and had enlarged and filled with fluid. As the ugly swollen pustules became inflamed and broke open, discharging their evil-smelling, yellow matter, the fever returned and rose higher and higher. Pepe became delirious. Tomas slept, tossing fitfully.

Adam stayed at their bedsides, watching, coaxing

down sips of water, wiping sweat from the hot faces, and only consenting to leave when Bets was present. He did anything and everything willingly, and she realized, when he followed her simple orders for their care, that he had learned more of Pepe's language than even the child had guessed.

Tia Pilar forgot that she was old. She worked in the kitchen, she cleaned, and scrubbed, she washed pus-stained linen. Her beloved little Isabel, after several days had been sent outside to stay with the wife of one of the workers, a childless woman who was willing to care for her away from the stricken house. Each day there was word that she was still all right, that she had not become feverish. and whenever that message came, Tia Pilar's face would clear and her thin shoulders straighten. She worked as though she was forty, not sixty. She was totally unlike the complaining woman Bets had always known.

"Perhaps a little broth, Tia Pilar?" Bets suggested. "They might be able to swallow it today. If you are too tired, I can make it—"

"Too tired, Señora? I am not tired, only worried when I look at you. Go and lie down! That new daughter of yours will be knocking at the door, and I am not a midwife."

Bets went to her and kissed the wrinkled pock-marked face. "I'll be all right, and the baby too. You'll see."

In spite of their prayers for delay, the time came when she knew that with or without help, she must prepare to give birth. The first pain grabbed her low in the abdomen like a giant claw, and made her gasp with its ferocity.

When it subsided, she crept up to her room, trying to tell herself that bearing the other three children had been easy and remarkably fast. Surely this one would be no different! Perhaps by nightfall, even by the time Miguel returned—for he had ridden out that morning to confer with his foreman on rancho matters left too long neglected—she could present him with his new-born child.

But facing what lay ahead, she could not help shrinking with a kind of primordial fear. She was so truly alone! Even if a midwife could be persuaded to enter a house with the pox, Adam should not be sent away for the long hours necessary to bring her. Tomas and Pepe needed him. She must think of them, never forget the heartrending way in which Pepe, delirious, spoke and cried out continuously, with his eyes open and brilliantly bright, yet seeing nothing; and how Tomas, usually so stoic, moaned with the agony of his itching, running sores. For many inflamed pustules had ruptured, and the thick fluid oozing from the soft yellow crusts was a putrefaction only a person with the strongest stomach could see and smell without it churning. Yet Adam remained there, hour after hour.

No, this must be her ordeal, and hers alone. Feeling another sharp spasm take hold, she clenched her hands and set herself to meet it. She had told Tia Pilar that all would be well, and it would be! Countless women had gone this path before her. Hadn't she as much fortitude as they?

But as the hours passed, her confidence ebbed. She had forced herself at first to walk about the room, thinking that such movement might hasten the birth. But as the pains continued, growing in strength, she collapsed back on the bed and lay clutching her abdomen at each shooting cramp, for they were now like knives, twisting and burrowing inside. Her body was drenched with sweat. She had stuffed a cloth between her teeth in order to stifle the groans she could no longer suppress.

And still the child did not come.

She had no idea how many hours had passed. Each minute seemed to drag endlessly, and she was encased in a huge timeless bubble of her own torment. She no longer smelled the horrible smallpox odor that permeated the house. She didn't hear Tia Pilar enter the room and stand staring down, sucking in her breath as she did so. She was only conscious of waiting for the next cramp to send itself inexorably across her body.

"Elizabeth—" It was Miguel now, saying, "Oh, God, will this never end?"

She saw him leaning above her. She thrust the cloth from her mouth and struggled to convey what she had come to fear was the reason for this long torture.

"Something is wrong. The baby can't come—it's caught! Miguel, help me!"

His face in the candlelight looked bloodless. Candlelight! It was night then. The entire day had passed!

"I'll go at once for Dr. Kramer," he said, and hesitated. "Or would you rather I stayed with you and sent Adam?"

"No, no, you must go yourself, and please—oh, please hurry!"

"I will, *querida!* My brave Elizabeth."

He was gone. But now, with the promise of Dr. Kramer, there was a small light flickering at the end of her long, dark tunnel. She fought on, with a surge of renewed strength.

Then gradually, as the hours again passed, and she knew they had by the growing daylight in the room, her resolution flagged. Even though the labor seemed diminished she was no nearer to having the infant than she had been yesterday. Suddenly panic rose in her throat so that she wanted to scream, not with pain this time but with terror. She was caught forever in this gruesome trap of her own body! No, not forever, only until death itself came to let her out. She would *die*. She had heard of women dying this way, slowly, horribly . . .

But again she thought of the sick children, and steadied. She spit out the cloth, spotted with blood from her swollen and bitten lips. A little longer. She must endure a little longer.

Miguel was saying, "She's very weak. It's been going on for such a long time."

There was someone with him, but not Doctor Kramer. She looked up with dull eyes at the fat man who stood beside her bed. He was a stranger, evidently like Emil Kramer a newcomer to the south coast, but there was none of the young German's dignity or spruceness of appearance. This doctor had a straggly beard in which bits of food still clung, and she could smell a sourness of sweat and liquor even before he bent close to press his hands on her abdomen.

She moaned uncontrollably with agony as he did so. Obviously to her writhing, he continued to knead the great swollen mass.

"Is that necessary?" Miguel asked tightly.

"Seems I'll have to go inside," replied the doctor, and ceasing his manipulations, began rolling up his sleeves.

"No, please, no! Miguel, for the love of God, where's Doctor Kramer?"

"He's very ill, Elizabeth, possibly dying. His housekeeper told me that even as a child he had a weak heart. He has exhausted himself . . . But this man assures me he has brought many babies, and at least he wasn't afraid to come."

The doctor said jovially, "Had the pox myself once. Don't you worry, I can do this with both hands tied behind me. Now you, sir, just wait below. I'll call you. Little lady, lie back."

Miguel did not move. The doctor gave him a grin and peeled back the sheet that covered her legs.

"No! No!" she cried, desperately afraid of his rough hands.

"Bend your knees. More—"

"Don't touch her!" a new voice spoke, a woman's voice, and Bets recognized it.

"Aunt Mary," she breathed. "Aunt Mary!"

"Yes, Betsey." Mary advanced into the room, giving the strange doctor a frown of distaste. Clearly she too saw the dirty hands, smelled the brandied breath. "If your baby is to be brought manually, I will do it." She began peeling off her gloves.

"Now look here," blustered the man, "I'm a medical doctor, and this little lady is like to die!"

"You are both dirty and drunk," Mary replied calmly. "You will not be needed."

Perhaps it was the smart San Francisco apparel, perhaps it was her natural hauteur, that silenced him. He turned to Miguel for support.

Miguel asked Mary hoarsely, "You know what to do?"

"By chance, yes." She added drily, "Thanks to my sadistic mother-in-law."

He stared at her, hesitant, while the doctor mumbled, "Don't be a fool, man!" It was Bets who decided him, when she clutched his hand crying, "She knows, Miguel! Please!"

"Very well. Mary, I will bow to Elizabeth's wishes. But the doctor will not leave this house until I am convinced he is not needed. We'll be below."

"Send Tia Pilar immediately, please! I'll need her help. And Miguel—"

"Yes?"

It was in Mary's mind to ask his assistance too, custom or no. But looking into his white, exhausted face, she decided against it.

"It won't be long," she said instead.

Bets heard, and the pain seemed to ease a little. She shut her eyes. Soon then, soon the torment would end.

And indeed, as slowly as time had passed before, it now seemed to race. Mary said, "I need to wash. Tia Pilar, get me a pitcher of water and some soap," and as if in the next instant, the aged woman was back.

"Hold her arms down and try not to let her fight me. I'll be as gentle as I can, but this will hurt quite a lot, I'm afraid."

It did. As Mary's hands groped their way inside of her, and finally, clutching the baby's head, began rotating it, Bets stopped screaming, and slid away into a welcome abyss of unconsciousness.

"It's a fine girl, Tia Pilar," Mary was saying. "Now, I must bathe the little thing. There's still plenty of warm water and soap. Will you take care of the Señora, while I do this?"

Bets felt the old woman's ministrations, but did not open her eyes. She was luxuriating in the blessed absence of torture, a peace that was like a cool and soothing balm.

Then in a while Tia Pilar tiptoed away. Mary too had gone, after giving her a brief glimpse of the baby; and Bets slept.

When she awoke, Miguel was in the room. He was gazing up at the crucifix on the wall, his back to her.

"It's a girl," Bets said in a soft, contented voice. "Shall we call her Maria Rosa after your mother?"

"Whatever you like."

How stiff he sounded! He did not look at her or come to her. Surely he was not angry that the child wasn't a boy!

"How did Aunt Mary happen to be here?" she said uncertainly.

"Your father wrote her, telling her about the boys. He thought we might need her help. She came at once, traveling down on the *Senator,* and Phineas Bishop brought her from the terminal."

"How good of her," Bets said, but she was watching him in growing apprehension, and not really thinking of Mary at all.

"More than just good," Miguel answered, still in that odd tone, devoid of expression. "Patrick thought she had been vaccinated. She had not."

There *was* something wrong! He was saying words, but for him, she was certain, they had no meaning.

"Miguel, what is it? What has happened?"

He turned, and when she saw his face, the awful sorrow in it, she uttered a cry of fear.

"A few minutes ago, Elizabeth—" He stopped, unable to finish whatever he had to say. Then he took a great shuddering breath.

"Pepe died. Pepe is dead."

She only stared at him. It could not be true. It could not! Pepe? The child who was always so alive?

Oh, no, this was only a nightmare. She would wake soon, and go to care for her boys, who would be better, much better.

Then suddenly, Miguel's control snapped, and there was no more escape. He had spoken the truth! Never, in any dream, would he—always so reserved—be shaking his fist at a crucifix and shouting wildly, "I'm glad there will never be another *Pastores!* Glad, do you hear? I couldn't stand it, not when he wanted so much to be a shepherd!

"God! Oh you cruel God! I've lived a little. Why didn't you take me?"

He waited then, in a posture of listening that riveted her. Did he expect an answer?

At length he turned, walked back woodenly, and fell to his knees beside the bed, his body shaking as if he too were very ill.

"La culpa es mia! It is my fault! I made them go away to school, didn't I? Pepe would never have been sick otherwise! Oh, why did I do it? Why? *Mea culpa!"*

She reached out and held him to her, this proud man who had broken. His tears soaked the shoulder of her nightdress.

For a time, her throat was so tight and closed with shock, her mind so filled with the image of Pepe lying dead, that she could not speak. But at last she managed to say, in a halting whisper, "No, Miguel, don't blame yourself . . . you couldn't have guessed this would happen . . . Nor I . . . we loved him so terribly much!"

He did not answer, but she knew he heard. His body stiffened, as though his soul had returned unwillingly to it.

Then she let him go, and lay back, staring into the heavy silence of the night. Silence. The terrible silence that would always be with them.

Pepe, ah Pepe! Never again to hear your excited childish voice, or see your sweet funny little face break into that grin of delight . . . never again . . . never . . . again.

Her own tears came, quietly at first, and then in sobs of wrenching anguish.

She was hardly aware when Miguel's arms at last embraced her.

Chapter Thirty-four

THEY STOOD IN A SILENT ROW AT THE GRAVE-side, Miguel, Bets and Mary. Beside them, rigid in his chair, was Don Sebastian, and beyond him were Tia Pilar and Adam. All were waiting for Father Daniel, who even now was approaching from the direction of the barn, the cassock he wore for the occasion crumpled and dusty from his long ride.

"Elizabeth?"

It was Don Abel Stearns, behind her, and although his expression was as dour as ever, his voice was gentle. She was relieved that he had spoken, so that she could, if only briefly, look away from the newly-dug excavation, the nearby mound of hard, raw dirt, and the pathetically small pine box, already nailed shut.

Pepe. Oh, Pepe. She clutched her trembling hands together and forced her face not to crumble.

"Elizabeth, your father asked me to tell you that I am here as his representative. He regrets, more than anything in his life that he is still not able to ride—even in a carriage."

Don Abel was flanked on either side by Teodocia and Arcadia. Although steeped in her own unhappiness, Bets, glancing at Teo, divined that Patrick's wife would have preferred to tender this message herself.

"Thank you, Don Abel. I deeply appreciate your coming." She turned to Teodocia. "And how is Papa?"

Her friend gave her a smile that warmed her a little. "Difficult! As Don Abel says, he wanted so much to be here. He said, 'All our friends will attend and wonder where I am!'"

All our friends. They—the Stearns, Teo, and Phineas Bishop, were the only ones who had ridden out today! Yet the absence of all others was not surprising, in view of the despair that still gripped Los Angeles. In a town of less than five thousand, as many as fifteen or twenty were dying each day of the pox. The constant tolling of funeral bells had finally been forbidden by the Council. It was well known that the dead were simply piled like cordwood on rough carts and hauled away to be disposed of in a common grave, or burned. Pepe could not even have a proper funeral Mass because to bring his body into town would mean too great a risk of contamination.

"You are fortunate this rancho has a small burial plot of its own," Arcadia remarked, not being cruel in her reminder, but matter-of-fact; and Bets could only agree. Still, the spot was so dreary and desolate, particularly today with a hot santana wind blowing, and everywhere grasshoppers jumping in the dry brown weeds.

But now Father Daniel had taken his place. He began to speak the time-honored words that solemnized death, so that she was forced to attend to them and think—and remember.

This was really so! Pepe, their much loved child, the thin-legged and never quiet, the mischievous, the angelic. He was in that box, and forever stilled.

"I am the resurrection and the life . . ."

Her hand sought Miguel's arm, but dropped away again when she felt the unyielding tension of his muscles. He was aware of nothing except that small casket. He had not spoken since they entered the graveyard.

Only at the end, when Father Daniel, with a glance at Miguel said, "I will lift up mine eyes unto the hills from whence cometh my help," did he seem to hear. He turned his head and stared off fixedly into the seared, desolate canyons that were his land.

The rites were over. Father Daniel paused. He put his hand on the pine box and patted it gently, and the whisper Bets heard was from himself, the man and the teacher, not the priest.

"Farewell, dear blithe little spirit."

Now the casket was being lowered into the hole, the ropes held by six men belonging to the rancho, one of them Adam. She saw that the ivory Chinese face was wet and for a moment she stupidly wondered why, until she realized her own was also drenched with tears.

That dark hole. How he hated the dark. Always.

At the priest's direction, the first clod of dirt dropped, hitting the wood with a thud. Miguel started violently. He extended his arm, as though he would stop the burial, then his hand clenched and fell to his side.

Neither he nor Bets saw when Father Daniel in compassion beckoned them away. They stood rooted at the graveside, listening to each shovelful, until the work was done.

"Is it over, Mother?" Tomas asked her. On their return to the house, she had gone to his bedside immediately.

"Yes, darling. Yes, it's over."

"I should have been there." His weak voice was fretful. "Pepe would never have let me have a funeral without being there himself."

For answer, she lay down beside him on the bed and lifted his head onto her shoulder, oblivious of the festering yellow sores that were only now beginning to dry a little.

"I did feel well enough," he persisted.

"You are weaker than you think." She was grateful he had not been present to hear the soil falling on Pepe's body. "Besides, people are so afraid of the sickness that if you had come, none of the men would have been willing to carry the coffin."

"Except Adam."

"You're right."

"Will Father come in to see me soon?"

Would he? Bets didn't know. Miguel this day had buried his only son.

She said cautiously, "If he does not, you must understand that he is not himself today. Just now he went off on his horse. Perhaps he needs to be alone for a little . . . Oh, dear, I must go—"

She had felt the spurt of warm milk inside her

chemise. It was time for nursing little Maria Rosa, and her body, having its own clock, knew nothing of death or burials or comforting a young boy.

She stood up and looked down at her first-born. His blue eyes were on her face, and from them, slow tears trickled across his mottled, disfigured cheeks into the pillow.

"Don't cry, Tomas. We must all be brave," she said helplessly. Although she did not glance down, she knew the milk was making dark circles on her dress.

"Mother, do you remember what Pepe said when the puppy died?"

Her throat closed and she could hardly answer. "He said—something like—'I am brave. It's only that my heart hurts.' Does your heart hurt, Tomas? Is that why you're crying?"

"Yes," he whispered, and brushed the back of his hand across his eyes, dislodging one of the ugly crusts as he did so.

She went away, not daring to ask whether his heart hurt more for Pepe, or for the father who did not visit him on such a day.

Mary sat with her while she nursed Maria Rosa. They were alone, the guests and Father Daniel having departed shortly after the burial. There had been profuse apologies, not from Father Daniel, whose services were urgently needed elsewhere, nor from Phineas who appeared at Bets' side when she was momentarily alone and surprised her by talking, not of Pepe, but of a new business venture that he hoped would be of interest to Miguel.

Her husband, she knew, would have been incensed by the brief conversation, thinking this long-time friend —and herself too—unfeeling. But she welcomed the distraction. Anything, to have her mind taken off what she had just witnessed. Unnoticed by the others, she moved a little away from them so as not to be overheard.

"Those kettles you bought must be enormous," she said in a low voice.

"As they each cost sixteen hundred dollars—yes. They are the largest you have ever seen. I buy from the ranchos any cattle my friends can't sell elsewhere. The animals that are hopelessly lean and starved, and won't last much longer anyway, without forage. We stew the meat in my kettles right out on the range, and sell all of it to Drum Barracks. As many as two hundred head can be processed a day."

Bishop glanced across at Miguel. "Miss Betsey, what is your husband doing with his cattle?" he asked. "Has he been able to move them north to where there's pasturage?"

"No. Don Sebastian was opposed to the idea earlier, and then when it was clear that they should go— well, it was too late. With the smallpox epidemic there weren't enough men. You ask what Miguel is doing? When the cattle die, he skins them for the hides. That's all the money a steer brings in these days. Being so shorthanded, he works with the men, and it's a dreadful task. The stench of the dead cattle hangs over the whole hillside."

"You might ask him later, if he wants to sell to me. I take anything that's alive. Of course he won't get the price cattle should be worth, but he'll have the hides too this way."

"He'll be very glad to sell," Bets said gratefully. "I'll ask him, but I'm quite certain—"

Was she sure, she wondered with sudden misgivings? He would consult Don Sebastian, and who knew what the patriarch would say!

But a new stubbornness crept in, making her straighten her spine and look Phineas in the eye. Things had clearly come to such a pass that Rancho Aguirre might be lost to the family for good. Wasn't that what was happening elsewhere?

She had been a submissive Californio wife until now. She had allowed her sons to be sent away, allowed sheep to be bought with precious funds, allowed her husband to bow his head to a tyrannical old man whose mind was growing senile.

She still had three children who would someday inherit what was left.

It was time to fight.

"Miguel will send you word in a few days," she said.

He nodded solemnly, but there was the same glint of admiration she'd seen in his eyes once or twice before.

"I expected I could count on you."

"Did you? I understand this—that such a kind offer cannot possibly be profitable! All the old compadres— do they realize how you are helping them, saving what you can of their cattle?"

He bristled, as if she had offered him an insult. "Miss Betsey, I couldn't stay their friend if I gave them anything. If I even tried, they would refuse. No, don't ever say that, or think it. The business is profitable!"

Arcadia had approached then, and the talk ended. But he had given Bets something she could think about, something besides Pepe, and in the future when she looked back on this day, she would thank him most of all for that.

Arcadia, announcing her departure, had been as usual entirely forthright.

"Don Abel is not as young nor as strong as he used to be, Elizabeth. To be quite frank, I would have stopped him from coming at all today if I could. I had a mild case of smallpox many years ago, but my husband never did, and that disease, as we've seen over and over, is no respecter of a gray beard! So you will forgive us if we do not enter the house at all on this visit. He's angry, of course! He says we're flouting the traditional customs, leaving you without even the comfort a funeral dinner can give."

"Forgive you? More than that, I am truly grateful, Arcadia, that he would come near us at all! I only hope you get home safely."

"Thank you, Elizabeth. It will not be an easy journey, nor pleasant, especially through the streets of Los Angeles, where more than once lately I've seen bodies left to rot by the wayside. Do you know, I wanted to leave our town house for the time being and retreat to the rancho? We could have had vaqueros posted day and night to warn off strangers, as many others have done. But this is a time when no words of mine will sway him. He is too proud to run from danger."

So they had gone, upright Don Abel, grimly protective between the two women, his wife and Teodocia, the latter worried and anxious to return to Patrick, even though Flora and Jeb had been left to care for him.

As the carriage rolled away, Miguel, who had through sheer will responded to the courtesies, saddled his horse. He mounted at once and galloped off into the lonely reaches of the rancho.

The child at her breast, Bets stood by the window watching the diminutive figure that was her husband, still visible at such a distance, and still riding hard away. She felt forsaken.

Mary, the never-finished mending in her hands, glanced over at her. "Remember what Father Daniel said? 'I will lift up mine eyes to the hills from whence cometh my help.' I think Miguel is hoping to find comfort out there, and perhaps he will. If so, you wouldn't begrudge it to him."

Bets felt a touch of the old resentment Mary had often aroused in her and she said a trifle sharply, "And what of me? Where is my comfort?"

Mary didn't answer at once. She seemed preoccupied, although her eyes were on the tiny baby who sucked fiercely while Bets cradled the downy head against her exposed full white breast. Then she said, "The baby helps, doesn't she?"

"Yes," Bets admitted. "I suppose it's because she forces me to think of life, not death, when I feel the strong flow of the milk. Just now I've begun to plan what to tell Isabelita, and to think of tomorrow. She does make me forget—for a little."

"How well I know."

Bets glanced at her aunt and said, more gently than was her wont, "Your child must have been a comfort to you too."

"Yes—when I was allowed to see him."

"Aunt Mary, have you thought—I know how bitter you are—but have you thought that I must owe my life to your having been in Spain? That's true, isn't it?"

"Yes, some good did come from one terrible night there, so long ago."

"Would you tell me about it? I'd like to know."

Mary gazed out at the clear sunshine, unseeing. "I think I can, now. For years I shut away the memory, hating it as a particularly ugly cruelty because it involved someone other than myself—an innocent servant girl.

"It happened shortly before my own child was expected, and on the night of a festival. All the servants had been given the day and the evening too, to participate in a procession, otherwise things could never have happened as they did. I was left alone with a girl in labor—her name was Elena . . .

"Doña Cesaria must have known there would be difficulty with the birth and she should have sent for the midwife well in advance. But in her sly way she ordered me to the girl's room, telling me that caring for the servants was the duty of any woman who ran a household, and I should sit with Elena, keep up her courage, until the midwife arrived.

"The hours went by and the girl was in torment. She tried bravely to stifle her moans, but I needn't tell you what she was suffering; you know well enough. I mopped the sweat from her face, and held her hand even though the nails gouged bloody holes in mine. All the time I listened for the coming of the midwife, but there was nothing, and at last I understood. If she was coming at all, it would be later, much later. Doña Cesaria was prolonging this girl's ordeal in order to give me a distorted glimpse of what my own birthing might be like.

"Things didn't turn out as she expected, however. Elena, as I've said, had courage. Whispering and gasping between convulsions, she made me understand that she had had this trouble before, and she knew what must be done, if I would do it. I told her yes, anything! Although when she explained, I admit I quailed. I knew nothing, nothing about the inside of my own body or any woman's, and I was afraid. I thought I might even kill her, doing what she begged.

"But finally, I couldn't endure any more! I thrust in my hands while she screamed and heaved herself about. The baby's head was jammed tight against a sort of hard round ridge, and I thought for several desperate moments that I could never get past it. But when the pressure eased between spasms, my fingers slid in and although the muscles clamped down again, squeezing my wrist and almost breaking it, I had a firm grip and I turned the head.

"That was all there was to it. I pulled away my hands and the baby came sliding after them. Bless Elena, she didn't faint; I suppose she was too frightened that I wouldn't know what to do next. She instructed me, and I did it all, until finally I had washed the little thing and put her in Elena's arms.

"I was sitting beside them, exhausted and elated and too relieved to speak, when Doña Cesaria finally arrived with her midwife."

"That's wonderful! What did the old witch say?"

Mary noted that Bets' eyes had lost, at least temporarily, the flat dullness shock and sorrow had lent them.

"Nothing. For once there was nothing she could say. No little barbs, nothing. Later she suggested, with sarcasm, that I learn more midwifery, as it seemed to be my sort of skill, and I surprised her by agreeing."

"Elena must have been very grateful to you!"

"Yes. I thought her husband was too—it was him I counted on to help me escape when that time came. But I suppose fear of his master and the Señora was too strong, stronger than any debt he owed me."

"Well, I at least am grateful! I was terrified at having that drunk, dirty old man touch me."

"With reason, I think. Perhaps it is only an old wives' tale, but I've heard that filthy hands make childbed fever."

Bets shuddered. "I haven't really thanked you before for having the courage to come here. I hope you are taking care—staying away from Tomas, for example."

"I've no reason not to be sensible. That Adam of

yours is most capable and needs no help with Tomas."
She tossed the mending on the table and jumped to her
feet, as though in the course of their talk she had come
to a decision.

"Betsey," she said, "I should tell you that I won't
be here at Rancho Aguirre much longer—only until
the servants come back. I've done a good deal of
thinking in the last hour, ever since Teodocia brought
me a letter that had come to Patrick's house. It was in
answer to one I wrote many months ago, to a priest
in Andalusia.

"My life has reached a crossroads. I can't say yet
what direction the new turning will take, I only know
there must be one. And just now, talking to you about
Spain, being *able* to talk calmly about it, I was thinking and wondering about my son, something I've never
allowed myself to do before . . . Jaime is a young man
now. Do you suppose—if we were to meet—he would
remember me?"

"Aunt Mary, what has happened?"

"I was informed I'm no longer a wife, I am a
widow. My husband, Francisco, who always rode
horses as though the furies were after him, was killed
in a fall."

Bets gave her a long look. "Then you are—free."

"How oddly you said that! Yes, I suppose I am.
Free from grief, free from the vows I failed to keep.
Yes, I am free."

Part Three

1865—1869

CHAPTER THIRTY-FIVE

PATRICK'S SATISFACTION ON ATTENDING THE Temple Theater was, as always, diluted by irritation.

On the one hand, that the town finally could boast such an amenity, even though it might be situated rather prosaically on the upper floor of the city market, was a source of pride. For Juan Temple, the building's owner, in this initial toe-dipping in the waters of culture, had provided most generously. There was a real stage, some forty-five by twenty feet in size, and in addition to comfortable arm chairs in the parquet, each side wall boasted a prominent private box, zealously vied for by every Los Angeles gallant. All this was attractively arranged, and the stage was well equipped. Even now, through the partially opened curtain, Patrick could see a large painted backdrop; and it was this vista of a formal Italian garden, together with a seascape less frequently displayed, that for five years had annoyed him.

At the time the theater was first planned, Mary Reyes had been invited to paint the scenery. But when courtly Juan Temple approached her on the subject, she had not even taken time to consider!

"I am flattered, but I must refuse," she said. "Exceedingly large landscapes or views of interiors require a special skill, one I have never tried to develop."

"Oh come now, Mary Frances," Patrick had protested, "I'm sure you can figure out the way of it."

When she shook her head, giving him a rueful smile, Temple asked, "There's no use then in my trying to persuade you?"

"None, although I do thank you for offering me the honor. Unfortunately, not only am I not the right sort of artist, I can't suggest anyone who is. Perhaps if you inquired in San Francisco . . ."

That had been done. And as a consequence, Patrick would enter and take his seat, then study the backdrop with disdain, growling under his breath, *"to think, instead we could be enjoying the work of Mary Frances!"*

But after a while, as always, he forgot the matter, too occupied with talking to his friends, and waiting with pleasurable anticipation for the show to begin.

And why hadn't it begun, he wondered tonight. They must be running a half hour late already! It was to be hoped that the great and famous Shakespearean actor who, enroute to visit a sister in San Diego, had graciously consented to declaim a few choice scenes from *Hamlet* and *Othello* did not believe that because this was a small frontier town he could treat his audience in a cavalier fashion. If he did—Patrick grinned to himself—Arcadia Stearns, whom he could see in the row ahead already looking tight-lipped, would set him straight!

Patrick's smile faded, watching her. She was dressed as elegantly as always, her spine was stiff and straight. But there were none of their friends who weren't aware that Don Abel, a stalwart honorable man who should be enjoying his old age, was battling for his very life against the wolves who would confiscate his lands. He was not here this evening—doubtless away somewhere protecting another exposed flank.

Patrick had just leaned forward to speak to Arcadia, when Mrs. Temple bustled onto the stage. Doña Maria was almost as elderly as her husband, Don Juan, but the two of them continued to enjoy this enterprise, their theater, with boundless energy and enthusiasm.

She apologized for the lengthy delay, admitting she was unable to account for it, as she had sent her carriage round to the actor's hotel some little time before, and he should have arrived by now. "However," she continued, giving a nod to the pianist who tonight, in honor of this special occasion, was Peter Riggs, "shall we pass the minutes that may remain, in singing all together some of those splendid partisan songs so popular during the war? For five days now, that terrible struggle has been at an end, and we can show our gratitude by refusing any longer to take sides—"

"Bonnie Blue Flag, please, ma'am!" shouted a Confederate sympathizer in the gallery; and at once, a strident female voice on the other side of the house responded. "For shame, sir! Will you be guilty of treason?"

The rebuke was over-strong, and there was a scattering of laughter. The protest came, of course, from Elvira McCarty's mother, for that formidable woman had, in a short month's visit, made herself well known. She was an outspoken and long-winded admirer of Abraham Lincoln, not because her son-in-law was a Union officer, but because she herself had been one of the countless supplicants to the President, asking for mercy for her son, Elvira's brother, who was under sentence to be shot for some military dereliction of duty. His life having been spared, now her entire conversation consisted of laudatory anecdotes about President Lincoln, and as most people considered him an opportunist, and a crude and unmannerly one at that, she was only listened to as a matter of utmost courtesy. One of her stories did stick in Patrick's mind, however. A member of the French legation was supposed to have remarked, "He seems to me one grand *gentilhomme* in disguise," and Patrick had wondered privately if that assessment might not be the true one.

Doña Maria meanwhile was dealing firmly with the question of the first song. The Union having won the war, she refused to be drawn into offending the scattering of Fort Drum officers in her audience.

"We will begin if you please, Mr. Riggs, with *The Battle Cry of Freedom.*"

To support Doña Maria, Patrick sang with gusto. He was in fine humor, having been reassured to hear that the great actor had at least reached his hotel. Too many times, promised performers failed even to catch their ships for Los Angeles, and tonight, at least, the audience would not go home disappointed.

At first, few others joined in, majority sentiment having been for the other side. But the tune was catchy, and feelings hadn't run as high as many loved to assert. Before the last "rally 'round the flag, boys!" the hall was resounding satisfactorily.

Bonny Blue Flag was next, followed by *Tenting To-night,* and then the war songs were abandoned for the sweet and haunting *Listen to the Mockingbird;* and still there were no introductions from the stage. The April night, beautiful outside, was becoming close in the packed room.

"You see, we are not too late, Miguel!"

Patrick, much pleased, turned to greet the new arrivals, and watched his daughter move gracefully along the row of seats, smiling, nodding to the Camells. Extraordinary, he thought, how her beauty never dimmed. That sweeping dress of her favorite color—larkspur blue, like her eyes, and worn with a fine white embroidered shawl, was well chosen; and her lustrous black hair was magnificent, piled high and caught with a Spanish comb. But the secret of her allure, that which turned the heads of men and women alike, was her unquenchable vitality. Even now, she was excited and eager, and Patrick chuckled to himself, knowing how limited her interest in drama and poetry really was.

Miguel, now, his anticipation was another matter! It was rare to see him so animated and sociable. His thin intense face was relaxed, his dark eyes alight.

Camellito was giving them a wide smile, and Patrick watched the young banker a little sadly. Camellito was incapable of dissembling, and he was trying to appear unworried—clearly an impossibility.

There had been not one year of devastating drought, but two, the second administering the death blow to the cattle economy. At last, this winter, normal rainfall had returned but its longed-for relief came far too late for most Californios. Their taxes were too high to be paid, and their debts were so staggering even the friendliest merchants refused credit. Bank loans made to them were uncollectible, and consequently, notes offered by the bank, even bearing heavy interest, were being peddled at fifty cents on the dollar, and finding few takers.

Camellito must have felt Patrick's gaze, because he glanced over and called out, above the singing, "How is your handsome little Brian?"

Patrick grinned. "What can I say? He's a Donovan! Fast learning to walk, and slow learning to talk."

"Isn't Teo here tonight?"

"She's with Dr. Kramer. One of the saloons had a donnybrook, there was gunplay, and even some women on the street were injured. The doctor asked her to help him, and well, she couldn't refuse."

Felipa gave him a sharp glance, but Camellito responded, "She's right, bless her. We all need Dr. Kramer, and he's frail, no doubt of it. If Teo can save him a little of his strength, it's all to the good."

The small cloud that had been hovering over Patrick lifted. He hadn't been pleased when Teo had insisted—apologetically, but firmly—on acceding to the doctor's last-minute request.

Not that he didn't trust them both! He knew Teo's loyal nature too well to doubt her, even if he hadn't another, less happy reason to be complacent. But the fact remained that she'd agreed not to assist the doctor at night, and he was irritated when a true emergency tempted her to do so.

This wasn't the first time, since the terrible *Ada Hancock* disaster of two years ago during which his wife by chance had discovered her aptitude for nursing the sick and injured, that he wished she had never happened to be on the wharf at Wilmington during the explosion. But his mild resentment never lasted. He liked too well to see Teo happy.

Cheered by Camellito's matter-of-fact comment, he relaxed, no longer caring to sing, but enjoying himself. However his contentedness did not last long. Small at first, just a tendril of discomfort he could almost doubt was there, the pain began.

Not in this public place! It had been a month now, and he'd hoped, never again—but no, an attack was really beginning.

The spasm ballooned into a ball of agony. It grabbed his abdomen, twisting, turning, until he needed every ounce of strength he had to keep from yelling aloud.

"Papa!" Bets leaned above him, her worried face swimming in his consciousness. "Oh, Papa!"

Then strangely, she fell silent. Her hands still clutched his shoulders, but he sensed her attention had been abruptly caught by something else.

Another voice was speaking—Doña Maria's it must be, although unnaturally high and thin. There was no other sound. Not a cough, not a foot scraping.

"I repeat, Mr. Edwin Booth regrets he cannot be with us tonight. It is the only time in his many years on the stage, I was asked to tell you, he has ever missed a performance. But he is prostrated! Word has just been received, over the telegraph, that his brother, John Wilkes Booth, has shot Mr. Lincoln!

"The President is gravely hurt, but still alive, and has not yet been moved from the Ford Theater in Washington, where this dastardly attack took place, which is all we know as yet.

"Therefore, I ask you, my friends, to be understanding, and to forgive Mr. Booth—Mr. Edwin Booth, that is! I doubt if any of us, no matter which side we favored in the war, can find an excuse for the dreadful crime John Wilkes Booth has committed . . ." She faltered, then added tremulously, "Good night, dear friends."

Was the pain easing a little, perhaps sooner than usual, because of his utter astonishment? His arms were still clenched across his belly, the sweat still poured from him, and Bets was needed to support him upright in his chair. But the unendurable peak was passing.

He was aware once more of other people, those clustered in little knots, talking excitedly, those walking from the hall in silence. Peter Riggs, at the piano, had begun to play *Battle Hymn of the Republic,* a song, it was said, the president loved.

Riggs sang the words, slowly, somberly, as if they were a dirge, as if President Lincoln had already died.

He has sounded forth the trumpet that shall never call retreat,
He is sifting out the hearts of men before his judgment seat;

Oh be swift my soul to answer him, be jubilant my
feet!
Our God is marching on.

In the beauty of the lilies Christ was born across the
sea,
With a glory in his bosom that transfigures you and
me;
As he died to make men holy, let us die to make
men free
While God is marching on.

It occurred to Patrick that never before had he
heard Peter Riggs sing, and he straightened his sorely
aching body in order to peer through the crowd at the
clever black man whom he'd been acquainted with for
so long, but still did not understand.

Then he caught his daughter's whisper to Miguel,
complaining, "She should be here to help Papa, not off
gallivanting!" and he was able to feel a certain amusement. To Bets, the distant travail of a president would
inevitably take second place to a loved one's suffering,
plain before her eyes. He knew too her disapproval
was not for Teo, but as always (though less undisguised now, because of that heavy debt of gratitude)
for Mary Frances.

And with good reason this time! Mary Frances had
no business being on a ship alone, bound for Panama,
en route to Spain. She wasn't even sailing in a clipper,
but on one of those hazardous steam-driven ships that
so frequently exploded. The *Ada Hancock* was only
one instance, there'd been many many others. Why,
the *Independence,* plying its way between San Francisco and Panama—the very run Mary was taking—
had burned to the water's edge, costing one hundred
fifty lives!

Also, and quite aside from the dangers of the voyage, at this very moment, Mary Frances, bless her, undoubtedly was seasick.

Chapter Thirty-six

MARY, IN SPITE OF HER UNIFORMLY MISERAble experiences at sea, was always surprised by the persistence of her queasy discomfort.

This time, there had been the short voyage to San Francisco on the *Senator,* necessary because ships for Panama only cleared from the northern port; and now thirteen more days on the *Nebraska* had elapsed. Fortunately there had been no storms, but even with the sun shining and the sea almost glassy, she was still nauseous. The only consolation was that in this large ship, which was both under sail and powered by paddle wheels on either side, she would complete the journey far more quickly than in the fastest clipper.

Lying in a deck chair, she averted her eyes from the horizon, which swung high in the air and back again. She tried not to remember that after the short train ride across the isthmus, yet another long passage by water, this time on the Atlantic side, awaited her.

Oh, this was a foolhardy expedition anyway! Now that she was so far committed, she had to be honest with herself. Suppose she did succeed in making her way to Spain, what then? Old Señora Reyes doubtless was still alive, still hating her malignantly, and ready to do everything in her power to prevent her grandson and his mother from meeting. But of Jaime, there'd been such a strange absence of news in that one letter from the Spanish priest! He wasn't dead, surely that would have been stated, but of his health, his activities, his happiness—nothing. This silence, as much as anything, had decided Mary. She had to learn the fate of her son.

The plan conceived, she would have liked to set forth at once. But the situation at Rancho Aguire had not permitted her in good conscience to leave, until this last winter when with the blessed rain and the end of a second outbreak of smallpox, the hacienda was no longer shorthanded.

While he still lived, she had been kept busy by the many irascible demands of Don Sebastian. Even in his final extremity, he had despised pity, and Mary could somehow make him feel less angry, and, though helpless, a man of undiminished dignity.

Thinking of Miguel, and Mary was doing so with determination, for the ship had suddenly encountered a series of rolling swells, she wondered again what had made strife between father and son so inevitable. The memory of Don Sebastian's death scene, although less vivid to her here in this bright harsh sunlight so far away from the gloomy chamber at Rancho Aguirre, revived her indignation. Had the man been taking revenge for some fancied slight, or did he merely feel driven, as always, to assert his dominance?

The window of the invalid's room had been kept shuttered to protect his eyes, the only part of him still under his control, for he lay board-stiff, except for the muscles of one leg that twitched and jerked for no reason. For days, he had passed very little urine, and the useless body was bloated and yellow. The truly horrifying aspect of his paralysis was that the dying Don clearly knew all that was happening, and when asked to blink his eyes would do so, thus indicating approval, and expressing his wishes. Even to the last, it seemed, he would remain master of his own destiny, and the household's as well.

She had happened to be there, in the background, folding fresh linen, when Bets and Miguel came to stand together at the bedside.

Bets, in an apparent effort to reassure her father-in-law that everything was as usual, enumerated the chores and menus for the day, all of which he acknowledged by blinking. She then fell silent and Miguel, clearing his throat, began to speak.

"Father, there is something I wish to say before it is too late. I do not believe we should try any longer to deceive each other, or hold out false hope. For me, this is a very solemn and sad moment, in which I must bid you farewell."

Mary glanced down at Don Sebastian. Was it possible she had detected a flicker of annoyance on that stony misshapen face?

"We have had our differences in these past years, you and I, but I trust you have confidence now in my stewardship of our rancho, and can therefore meet God content, knowing I will follow capably in your footsteps."

Miguel stopped, waiting for the eyelids to close and open again, signalling approval. But the pause lengthened. Don Sebastian's eyes were still fixed on Bets, just as they had been during her housekeeping account. They did not shift to Miguel.

Miguel's face and figure grew almost as stiff as his father's, while his skin slowly turned red with humiliation. He made one last attempt, and Mary was able to guess what it cost him to do so. He leaned closer to the man on the bed, and said in a low voice, "Father, look at me, please!"

Still there was no response.

Miguel shrank back, then rushed from the room. Bets whirled to follow, and Mary was left alone with Don Sebastian. A few minutes later, he who had resisted so stubbornly, made a sudden gurgling noise in his throat, and died.

Going to inform the family, Mary came upon Bets just outside the door, her face tear-streaked, not from sorrow but from anger. When told, she only nodded, saying, "I wasn't able to stop Miguel, he's ridden away to be alone.

"Aunt Mary, what can I say to him when he returns? He's convinced his father was deliberately shaming him, even trying to tell us he wanted *me* to run the rancho! It did seem almost—but no, how could he? That would be too cruel a way to use his own son!"

But certainly not impossible, Mary reflected. Ever since Pepe's funeral, Bets had been putting forward suggestions concerning the cattle and sheep, and more than once, to Miguel's evident chagrin, her ideas were approved over his own by Don Sebastian.

Witness the desperate problem of finding food and water for the sheep during the second dry winter. Bets had somehow managed to lease pasturage in the mountains, and Miguel's subsequent "failure" in attempting to drive the animals there had no whit diminished what Don Sebastian mentioned all too frequently as "Elizabeth's accomplishment."

"What can I possibly say to Miguel?" Bets cried again.

"There is a very simple explanation," Mary answered calmly, "Don Sebastian lost control of his eyes at the last. Poor man, what a torture it must have been for him, not to be able to express confidence in his son."

"Of course! Why didn't I think of that? I suppose I was too convinced Miguel had gotten his father's back up with that frank mention of death. Don Sebastian would never admit the end was coming, and preferred to have us all pretend he would surely recover and go on ruling us until the end of time. He was a tyrant, with no human feeling for his son!"

"I wonder," Mary said. "How can one know how much or how little he cared for Miguel? There are so many different ways of caring."

Bets shrugged this aside. "But was it so, then?" she demanded. "You tried to speak to him before he died, and he didn't respond?"

"Yes . . . It was quite clear to me he wished to answer Miguel and could not."

Mary waited until Bets had gone to apprise the household of the death; then she returned to close Don Sebastian's eyes, unable to enter the room without a certain trepidation. No one but she would ever know what had actually happened after Miguel and Bets had rushed from that room. No one but she had seen Don Sebastian blink at her with such joyous, malicious rapidity! All the same, it was not good to lie about a dying man's wishes.

As it turned out, her kindly-meant falsehood was all for naught. Miguel did not permit himself to be deceived.

That he had not, became evident when the matter of further schooling for Tomas arose.

At last on the way to recovery from smallpox, the boy had grown stronger quickly, and was one of the fortunate survivors. The only reminders of his ordeal were the pitting of his skin, not nearly so disfiguring as they'd feared, and a subdued but resentful bewilderment. Never before had he been forced to arrange his entire day himself. It was clear he missed terribly Pepe's endless inspirations and plans, his easy talk, his ready laughter.

Mary often noticed Bets watching her son, perplexed by his new brooding reticence.

"If only he would confide his troubles," Bets said to her, shortly after Don Sebastian's death. "He must be so very lonely! I've been putting off even thinking about St. Vincent's, but maybe he would be happier in school with other boys."

However, when she broached the idea to Tomas, he answered flatly, "I don't want to return to school. Why must I, Mother? Father was teaching me this past year, and now he has more time than before."

"Oh, I hardly think he has more time," Bets replied. "The rancho still has so many problems, and with your Grandfather gone . . ." She turned to Mary, remarking, "It seems to me Miguel is always in that office of his, poring over the records!"

At this moment, the three of them were outside in the hot sunniness of the kitchen garden, gathering tomatoes and green peppers. Mary, knowing something of Miguel's true activities, said quickly, "This earth is so hard and scorched, I'm surprised anything grows! Has the cook been throwing the washing-up water here, as you told her?"

Before Bets could answer, Tomas said, "No Mother, that isn't so. Father always finishes the livestock records quickly. It's his history of Mexico he's working on . . . Need I go back to school?"

Bets was frowning. "I thought you liked St. Vincent's, darling," she said absently.

"I did, when Pepe was there with me," he answered in a low voice. "But being at school was never like being at home, no matter how good Father Daniel and the nuns were to us. I would miss everything here. Finding miner's lettuce the way the Indians do, or watching the foals be born, or just being able to see the hills. I would hate school!"

Bets looked away, and Mary could guess what she was thinking—that they all, perhaps because they'd been dwelling so much on the boy who was gone, had failed to help the one who remained.

"Go find Isabel, please, my son, and bring her here. I think the three of us should look for miner's lettuce together this afternoon."

But when he had gone, her resentment flared. "You knew about this!"

"About Miguel's history of Mexico? Yes. He asked me about illustrations. It will be a good book when it's finished, Betsey."

"I don't care how good it is! A history of Mexico— when we are in danger of losing our land! I wouldn't be surprised but what this foolishness is all Don Sebastian's fault. Even after death, he makes trouble! I told Miguel what you said, but I thought then he wasn't convinced and I see I was right. So now you must tell him yourself, make him understand his father didn't turn against him—oh, come on! I am so furious!"

Bets, in grasping her aunt's arm, took little care to be gentle, and Mary realized that a part of her niece's wrath was directed at her, for knowing something about Miguel which she, his wife, had not.

Bets rapped on Miguel's door, calling his name sharply. He did not answer, but after a long moment, they heard the bolt of the door withdrawn.

He stood before them, courteous but distant. Behind him on the table, lay a notebook, the open pages covered with his meticulous, elegant handwriting. Spread out nearby were some parchment maps.

"Have you come to discuss my book, Elizabeth? Please, both of you, come in."

"Miguel," Bets cried, "you must listen to us! Wasting time in this way, when we need you so, is unfair to me and the children. Do you want to lose the rancho? Oh, it's cruel to be so stubborn!"

Mary, feeling awkward, had turned from them and was pretending to be interested in a row of heavy volumes on a shelf, their elaborately tooled leather bindings dark and mouldy with age. She winced at the bald accusation, wishing Bets had chosen her words more carefully.

Miguel however ignored his wife's outburst and said to Mary, "Those are treasures of mine, found in Mexico City, and dating from the Conquest of Cortez. One is actually an eyewitness account by a monk in his train! I've had them stored away for years, waiting until the time when I could begin my history—"

"You say, 'until the time you could begin your history' " Bets broke in. "Is this the time, Miguel? Is it? Oh, Miguel, Don Sebastian is gone, and you must take his place!"

"No, Elizabeth. That honor was bequeathed to you."

"It wasn't!" Her anger dissolved into dismay. "Tell him, Aunt Mary!"

But he put up his hand, effectively halting them both. "Nothing Mary can say would alter my conviction that the rancho decisions are to be yours. And do you know, I believe my father was right. You will succeed, just as you did in finding pasturage for the sheep."

"Oh, Miguel, please." Bets suddenly was weeping. "I cannot. I cannot."

"If any special knowledge I have can be of use to you, I shan't withhold it," he said with unusual gentleness. "And of course, I will not embarrass either of us by totally withdrawing. We'll maintain a facade for the servants and vaqueros. But otherwise, Elizabeth, you must manage, and you will. Now, ladies, if you'll excuse me?"

And, Mary reflected, looking back, Bets had man-

aged. She had worked hard, yet not made herself conspicuous in the doing. Some of the men, particularly
the foreman Ramon, had at first displayed a certain
curiosity, but as they were told again and again she
was merely relaying orders from her husband who was
too busy at present to ride with them on the range, the
situation was accepted. If Bets in her desperate struggle had changed a little, and like Tomas, grown a
shell of her own, it was understandable.

The slap of the *Nebraska's* paddle wheels slowed,
and forgetting her resolve not to look at the water,
Mary glanced out. Land! Mirrored in clear turquoise
water was a lush green mountainous land—too green
perhaps, too packed with vegetation.

This must be the Bay of Panama!

Her heart beat faster and she gazed avidly. How
different this was from previous landfalls; Manzanilla,
with all its bright gay Mexican colors, or Acapulco,
the coaling station! The latter, seen at night, had been
unforgettable because of a mountain fire raging in the
background, and while the ship was there, she'd spent
feverish hours trying to capture the excitement and
beauty of the flames.

For a moment, she studied the panorama of jungle
growth, finding to her surprise she was made uneasy,
even a little frightened by its rank luxuriance. Then it
occurred to her that precious time was passing. Her
seasickness had subsided in the sheltered water, and
she must not waste this opportunity.

She dragged her drawing materials from beneath
her chair and set to work happily. If the long voyage
bore no other fruit, she resolved, she would at least
have a portfolio to send to Milo.

CHAPTER THIRTY-SEVEN

A PRELIMINARY SKETCH HAD BEEN COMPLETED by the time the anchor chains rattled down. During the last few minutes Mrs. Margaret Cullinan, an elderly shipboard acquaintance, had stood nearby at the rail, not speaking or otherwise distracting her, but when Mary put her charcoal aside, she said, "What a splendid talent to have! I know you aren't nearly finished, but may I see what you've done? . . . Ah, yes, Taboga Island does jut up, does it not?"

At Mary's puzzled glance, she explained, "That's this bit of land we've anchored by. I once heard it called, the Island of Flowers."

"Yes, I suppose it might be. I think even from here I can make out some wild orchids. But it doesn't strike me as a *flowery* place, all the same, does it you? Magnificent, no doubt, in a wild, flamboyant sort of way, but not flower-pretty, not at all! Oh, it's difficult to explain, but ever since I began that drawing, I've felt somewhat the same as I did toward a certain beautiful but malevolent horse my brother Patrick once owned. I could feast my eyes, but I didn't want to get too close."

Mrs. Cullinan, who was small and spare, with a plain topknot of iron-gray hair, a weathered face, and an air of calm tolerance, had been studying the sketch, and said, "I think from this I do understand what you're saying."

Mary turned to her impulsively. "I can't seem to get out of my mind what you'd started to tell me yesterday, before the dinner gong interrupted. About the journey you and your husband once made across this isthmus. I keep wondering how it all ended because now that we're actually here, it makes me shiver to think of that desolate river winding through the rain-forest jungle, and you, for days the only woman in a crowded, flat-bottomed barge—what did you call it? —a *bungo?* After such an experience, I wonder you could bring yourself to return!"

"My dear! That was twenty years ago. When Henry and I came through then, going in the opposite direction, of course, it was all quite, quite different. The little railroad they have now didn't exist, and one had no choice but to set out by *bungo* and finish by mule or even afoot. But those days are past."

When Mary said nothing, she added, "Some of the natives must regret all the change, however. They poled the barges and charged a good price for doing so. It was very hard work actually, but they made it as easy for themselves as they could, taking frequent stops and splashing in and out of the water." She laughed suddenly, remembering. "Do you know, they didn't wear a stitch of clothes! Henry and I were younger then, and just starting out as missionaries. I was shocked, I may tell you. But of course, I saw much worse afterward, and learned what was important and what wasn't. Through the years, Henry and I had a wealth of experiences."

"Indeed you must have!" Mary said. She had come to like this capable, unpretentious widow, as well as feel gratitude for her company. Mrs. Cullinan, who had been the wife of a medical missionary, sent by the trading companies first to Hong Kong and then Canton, was taking this long route back to England because she planned to visit her sister, living in New York, on the way. Except for herself and Mary there were no women travelling alone aboard the ship, even in steerage. Mrs. Cullinan, because of her age and circumstances, had been accepted, if a bit patronizingly, by the other stateroom passengers. Mary had not, being far younger and an artist as well.

The Englishwoman's smile faded, as she gazed with musing reminiscent eyes at the land nearby. "You are right. I might have been very hesitant about coming back this way again after our previous experience, if the railroad hadn't been built. Henry and I escaped whole once, and there's no use tempting Fate a second time, is there? Riding on a train, you and I will reach the other side in a few hours instead of taking a week or more. So we shan't be ashore long enough to be fearful."

"Fearful of what exactly?"

"The diseases, my dear. Cholera, malaria, especially yellow fever, which is a dreadful scourge here. But gracious, parts of your own country suffer from it too! A missionary we met from New Orleans told us that in his home city many people plant a lemon in the front yard—trying to ward off Yellow Jack, as they call it. Superstitious nonsense, of course, and it amused Henry very much."

"I should like to have known Mr. Cullinan," Mary said.

"His faith was remarkable. A calm and confident man, and a tower of strength to me here, just as he was in China and all the years we were together. Even floating on that sultry river, where it seemed one could almost breathe in some dreadful perhaps fatal disease, he remained serene. Our fate was in the hands of God, he said, and it would be ungrateful of us, as well as useless, to worry."

"Then you didn't worry?"

"I'm afraid I did a bit, yes . . . since you've asked me, I will go ahead and finish the story, even though it's a rather unpleasant memory . . . As I told you, there were five of us white people as passengers in the boat—Henry and I, and the three strangers on their way to the gold strike in California. They had been delayed in the little village of Chagres at the mouth of the river for over a week, having to wait until a *bungo* was available. Two were brothers, the third was a giant of a man who eventually surprised us very much. Somehow one doesn't expect such a big man to be a coward.

"During our Chagres River journey it was so uncomfortable. Worst of all was knowing the tropical jungle was so very close on both sides of us. A dense rain-forest smells oddly, almost sweet, like warm rotting fruit, and the very damp heat presses down on one, day and night. There are incessant noises, the

screaming of the howler monkeys—there! Do you hear
one now, in the distance?—and bird calls, and the
clicking of beetles . . . Well, before long one of our
party became ill.

"Even before the poor man began to vomit black
blood, which is a sure sign of yellow fever, violent
arguments had begun. The giant, refusing to sit anywhere near his friend who was shaking with fever,
declared he was afraid of contagion, and when the
telltale vomiting started, he insisted the sick man be
put off the boat!

"To do so, of course, what with the alligators in the
river, as well as the bushmaster and fer-de-lance
snakes in the swampy brush—both so terribly poison-
ous—would have been just the same as murder!
Henry refused, naturally. But it was the sick man's
brother who prevented it."

"What did he do?" Mary, mindful that she herself
would shortly be traveling through the same primitive
wilderness in which this had all taken place, was listening with fascinated horror.

"He pulled his gun first, and forced the big man to
drop his overboard. Through the remainder of the trip
those two watched each other, one afraid to shut his
eyes in sleep, the other driven insane by fear, and
waiting his chance. Meanwhile, with the sick man delirious Henry and I had our hands full, caring for him.
And all the time, there were the noises that got on
one's nerves, and the unwholesome smell . . .

"At last, after six days, we reached a tiny village,
just two or three huts. It was Cruces, where we had to
leave the boat and go on foot. Usually, there were
mules to ride, but by bad fortune, another party had
arrived a day or so sooner and taken them all.

"The old road to Panama City is now just a rough
path, although once it was a wide, cobblestoned road,
built with slave labor by the Spanish conquerors who
needed a way to transport their gold and silver treasure from Peru across to the Atlantic, where it could
be shipped to Spain. The jungle is always ready to re-
claim its own, and by the time we'd arrived, three
hundred years later, the road was in miserable condi-

tion. The cobblestones in many places were rutted out, leaving great holes, and even where paving remained, the walking was little better because the stones were so hot to the touch. My shoes wore out in the first mile, and then my stockings. I walked barefoot the rest of the way.

"In Cruces, we had managed to procure a rough sort of litter for the sick man, and our natives were paid to carry it. The rest of us had our own luggage to manage . . . Mrs. Reyes, by the time we had straggled that twenty-eight miles to Panama City, sleeping on the ground as we went and with nothing to eat, I had almost given up." She chuckled. "I was something to look at, I'm sure. Filthy, slimy with sweat, covered with insect bites, and my feet bleeding.

"I remember being almost at the breaking point just before we reached the outer limits of Panama City. It was then that Henry turned to me and said, 'Margaret, you are an admirable woman.' I was encouraged, just enough to go the remaining mile . . . Henry was like that.

"Ah, well," she concluded, "I have tried since to be what he expected, without needing compliments . . . I see some of the passengers are already climbing down into the launch to go ashore. Shall we join the line?"

Mary nodded, and slowly gathered her belongings together. Having journeyed thus far, she told herself, she had little choice but to go on, whatever her misgivings. Then, all of a sudden, she was swept by the sharp clear memory of another disembarking. How much more confident, how adventurous, she'd felt that day! But the difference wasn't really surprising, she reflected. She wasn't a woman of much courage, and when she'd climbed down the swaying ladder of the clipper *Elizabeth* to face the unknown in California, Patrick and Betsey had been beside her.

The two women were fortunate to find seats on the small train, for there were over three hundred passengers from the *Nebraska* who required transportation across the isthmus. In the end everyone got aboard; although it seemed impossible to breathe in the stagnant tropic heat, and with so many crowded together. The train was expected to move at any moment, but nothing happened. The engine remained dead, and the temperature inside the little cars rose steadily higher.

Those who had no seats to lose, soon climbed out in search of information, while the rest continued to swelter. Departure time was long past, and no one was able to discover what if any difficulty existed. Mary, for the first time in her life, fought against fainting.

After two hours, the engine at last was stoked up, then without warning began to move and those passengers still strolling beside the track were forced to scramble aboard at some risk. The resulting circulation of air made the heat drop a trifle and become bearable. Mary at last could rouse herself and speak to her companion who had been sitting quietly, fanning them both with an ivory and silk fan produced from her bag, and not appearing unduly distressed.

"Mrs. Cullinan, I must say, for a time there I actually envied you your passage by river! But I suppose we can console ourselves that the train will at least take us across quickly. Oh, my word, do look! That glorious butterfly must be at least six inches across!"

"Yes, it is beautiful."

"You said that oddly!"

Mary was silent a moment, as they stared out the window at the moist vegetation, so thick and close they could have stretched out a hand and grasped fronds of huge, bright-green leaves.

"Henry was much taken with this country. Perhaps because he could see so much that needed doing. If we hadn't already been committed to going on to China, I am certain he would have remained. Several times we spoke of it."

Mary shook her head in disbelief. "It seems impossible, especially after all you've told me!" Feeling just then another small rivulet of perspiration course down her back, she added, "Even in Panama City, or this town we're going to—Aspinwall, the climate alone would be unbearable."

"Oh, my dear, climate is something one gets used

to. I venture to say, after a month or so, you'd find the excessive heat unpleasant perhaps, but easily ignored."

"I'm only happy I won't have occasion to find out! Our ship for New York, the *Ocean Queen,* is waiting for us, and seasick or not, I will be very happy to go aboard at once."

Disappointingly, the *Ocean Queen* was not waiting when they stepped from the train in Aspinwall. The only ship anchored out in the swampy bay was a squat ungraceful steamer, badly in need of paint and showing, as it rolled sluggishly in the surge, a thick growth of barnacles. When word passed among the *Nebraska* passengers that their intended transportation, a large comfortable American paddle-wheeler, was overdue to the extent it was a matter of some concern, there was a rush to procure space on this vessel, the *Santiago de Chile.* Mary watched with dismay the pushing shouting men who stormed the small shipping office.

"We'll never procure a cabin!" she said to Mrs. Cullinan.

"I'm certain that's true. Even steerage will be overcrowded. However, it may be a blessing. That ship doesn't look very seaworthy to me. Surely the *Ocean Queen* will arrive in a day or so, and I suggest we make the best of the situation and get ourselves a room at the hotel."

Even Mrs. Cullinan's composure was shaken however, when they entered the only hotel, the Washington, and dragged their valises through a lobby jammed with people. The desk clerk, even then, was turning away importunate groups of travelers, pointing out what was obvious, that the establishment was already filled to overflowing.

"What on earth shall we do?" Mary asked. Her face was white and clammy, and Mrs. Cullinan studied her with concern.

"I don't really know. The important passengers will doubtless become guests of local officials. The rest will have to sleep here on the floor—the chairs, you see, are already taken." Mary, feeling exhausted, gazed with envy at the fortunate occupants of the furniture.

"I wonder though," the Englishwoman continued. "The owner of the hotel is someone we knew long ago in Panama City, a fine man. It was he who urged Henry so strongly to stay! A few years ago, we heard from him again, when he wrote to say he planned to build a hotel here. Even though this was at the time, only a remote village on a swamp, it was the spot chosen for the railroad station on this side, and he was convinced Aspinwall, which was the town's grand new name, would grow, right along with the railroad.

"Come with me. Mrs. Reyes! My Spanish is poor, so perhaps you'd ask that young clerk, for me, if by any chance Mr. Bertram Cox still resides in Aspinwall?"

Mary hastened to the desk, where temporarily there was a lull. The slight, brown-skinned young man waited for her to finish speaking, a courteous refusal already on his tongue. He obviously considered her question merely another of the many demands he'd already had to speak with the hotel's owner.

"Señor Cox is not well today." He shook his head, his lugubrious expression intended to discourage these foreign ladies. "I would not dare disturb him."

"Oh, I am sorry." Mary turned away, but Mrs. Cullinan, who understood Spanish better than she spoke it, intervened.

"Do you mean Mr. Cox lives in the hotel itself?"

The clerk's dark eyes stared at her blankly.

"Ask him, please, Mrs. Reyes."

Mary did so, and was told reluctantly that it was so.

"Then tell him, please, that the widow of Henry Cullinan wishes to pay her respects." She added, in an aside to Mary, "If Mr. Cox is too ill or suddenly too old to remember me, which I doubt, then at least we will have tried."

The clerk sighed. "Very well," he said, "I will deliver the message, although there may be a delay as I must find someone to take my place here. We are so very busy today. Will you wait?"

"We will be outside on the veranda," Mary replied, and feeling her strength give out, she hastened away to the broad shaded porch, where there was a faint breeze which revived her a little. Sinking gratefully onto the wooden steps, she said to her companion, "That was good of you! I suspect, if you were alone here, you would have made do, without asking favors. Am I right?"

"Perhaps. Certainly I have slept many nights of my life without a bed. However, I can assure you I had planned, if we were here more than even a few minutes, to call on Bertram. Henry liked him so much. And I know he admired Henry."

"That being so," Mary said hopefully, "surely he will reply to your message if he can."

Another hour passed, but when the hotel employee sought them out there was a new and genuine respect in his manner. "Señor Cox will see you at once, Señoras."

"Thank you . . . I'll go alone, my dear. I hardly need an interpreter with a fellow Englishman." She hurried away, and Mary settled herself to wait. She was more relieved than surprised when Mrs. Cullinan returned after a short time to report good news.

"The hotel, as we've observed, is completely booked, but my friend offers an immediate solution to our problem. He hasn't been well it seems, and in order to oversee the hotel with less effort, he's living here temporarily. I confess he appeared in excellent health to me, and I did sense there might be some other reason for his occupying a hotel room, but that is none of our concern and we can only be grateful, as his own house is vacant. It is a small but comfortable place, he says, and insists we would be doing him a favor by staying there and providing a little work for the cook and houseboy."

"What a kind way to offer rescue!"

"Indeed yes, and typical of him, as you will see when he joins us for dinner. And now, his carriage is coming for us; and the young man, I see, is bringing our valises. Our situation here in Aspinwall is somewhat improved, wouldn't you say?"

Riding in the carriage, which was driven by a very dignified, very black man, wearing the briefest of pants and nothing else except a large, carefully tied neckerchief, and a shining tall silk hat, Mary, bemused by the strangeness of everything she was seeing, inquired, "How did your friend Mr. Cox ever happen to locate in such an out-of-the-way country?"

"Bertram was—is—a remittance man." Seeing Mary's lack of comprehension, she explained, "That means someone who lives abroad, often for many years or even a whole lifetime, subsisting on an allowance from home. Such men sometimes are rascals of one kind or another, but in Bertram's case, it was nothing like that. He was the third son of an earl. When his eldest brother inherited the title and estates, and also married the girl Bertram had been courting, rather than hang about in England, he requested a remittance, and shipped out with the idea of seeing the world.

"Actually, I believe he did see most of it—he gave Henry some helpful bits of advice about China, when we met. But then his ship came into Panama, and as he told us, he stepped ashore and never wanted to leave, formidable as this country is. It wasn't even the highlands, which can be quite pleasant indeed, but the jungle itself that fascinated him. Not every man's cup of tea, but it was his . . . and I often thought, through the years, it might have been Henry's."

Mary smiled politely, feeling the heavy sultriness with every breath, her clothes clinging to her stickily. But Bertram Cox and his decision became slightly more comprehensible when they reached his home. For the house, in contrast to the steaming hotel lobby, presented a welcome illusion of coolness. There were shuttered doors opening off on all sides to admit the prevailing sea winds, the furniture, being wicker, was airy and inviting, and on all sides, looking out, one could see the glossy foliage of tropical plants, not thick and impenetrable, but artfully arranged. Shading the roof and patios were luxuriant tulip trees in full bloom.

"How lovely!" Mary exclaimed, "and we're to stay here? Mrs. Cullinan, I can't tell you how grateful I am."

"Nonsense," the older woman said briskly. "Don't you think I'm delighted to be comfortable too? And I wish, as we've been thrown together in this small adventure, you'd call me Margaret. Will you?"

"Thank you. My name is Mary."

They smiled at each other. But soon after, Mary went to her bedroom window to gaze pensively at the smoke-encrusted funnels of the *Santiago de Chile,* visible through the palmettos that lined the bay.

A small adventure? Perhaps. But unaccountably, she found herself wishing she had taken whatever passage there was, in order to leave this exotic, cruel and alien land.

CHAPTER THIRTY-EIGHT

BERTRAM COX SENT A NOTE APOLOGIZING, BUT postponing his visit to his home, a delay that disappointed his old acquaintance, who several times said in a puzzled way, "Quite unlike him. Quite!"

Mary, however, was not displeased. An additional day of unbroken leisure would be welcome, giving her more time to adjust to the enervating heat. Having servants to care for all their needs, the two women were free to take a long slow saunter through the dusty streets, observing the small Indian shanties, scanning the horizon fruitlessly for sails, and strolling on Front Street in and out of the open stalls stocked with baskets, pottery and other wares intended to tempt travellers. Throughout the squalid town, the flamboyant colors were startling and lent even the poorest areas an air of unreality. It was difficult, Mary decided, to picture someone dying of disease or starvation while at the same time one was being amazed by a scarlet trumpet vine that covered all of a mouldering wall, or admiring the many trunks of a great, spreading banyan tree. Even the insects seemed too large and garish to be believable.

Dressed in lighter clothing and no longer compelled

to lug a valise about with her, Mary was finding the climate somewhat more bearable. The first night, accustomed to the coolness that descended on California after sunset no matter what the heat of the day had been, she had felt oppressed by the mosquito netting with which her bed was provided, and a number of times, half-asleep, she kicked it aside. The penalty of bites on her exposed feet and ankles put an end to her carelessness.

On the morning Bertram Cox was expected, there was a rash of activity on the part of the dignified woman cook—an Indian—and the gangly houseboy, an amalgam of many races and colors, who until then had been goodnaturedly averse to moving at more than a snail's pace. Unsmiling, intent on her work, the cook labored from early dawn in her kitchen; the boy meanwhile mopped all the stone floors of the house, and placed large bowls of vivid flowers in every room. All of which made Mary wonder if the owner of the house might be a stern taskmaster, feared by his servants.

But no. When Mr. Cox arrived, the houseboy opened the door with a welcoming grin that almost split his face from side to side.

Mary, having had reason to expect their host to be in poor health was forced to abandon that notion also. He was far from young, but his step had the same spring it must have had more than half a century earlier. While no taller than the houseboy, he was just as slim, and held himself straighter. He wore no jacket, but his elaborately ruffled and embroidered shirt, and spotless white trousers, were as elegant a costume as Mary had seen since leaving Los Angeles.

He greeted Margaret Cullinan by taking both her hands in his and saying, in his clipped voice, "A happy reunion, indeed! If only Henry were here with us."

Then, introduced to Mary, he studied her a moment, before giving a precise nod. "You failed to mention, Margaret—if your friend will forgive a personal allusion—that she walks in beauty like the night."

"So I did!" She smiled at him. "But neither did I warn her that you can quote every English poet who ever put pen to paper."

"I can and do, unfortunately." He added, to Mary, "Forgive me, Mrs. Reyes, if I embarrassed you."

Mary, however, was amused and pleased. "Lord Byron?" she hazarded.

He nodded, his sharp eyes commending her.

"How does the rest of it go?"

"It was really the end of the stanza that occurred to me as apt.

> She walks in beauty like the night
> Of cloudless climes and starry skies
> And all that's best of dark and bright
> Meet in her aspect and her eyes.

"Ah, well, we old men can still dream. Having no facility myself for creating, I try to content myself with collecting the finest work of others."

"Mr. Cox is being quite modest," Margaret said. "He is known as an expert, not just a collector. And not only of poetry, but many other things, such as the native folk art. I haven't pointed out your beautiful treasures, Bertram, those on the curio shelves and throughout the house even though Mary's been admiring the appliqued wall-hangings! I wanted you to explain everything to her yourself."

"You know me well, do you not, Margaret? What exquisite pleasure it gives me to lecture! But at this moment, I see dinner waits. I look forward to introducing our guest to a few of our local gastronomic delicacies, and I shall be disappointed if my cook hasn't outdone herself."

He was not, of course, disappointed. The meal had scarcely begun when Mary exclaimed, "Such delicious soup! Even better than yesterday's, which was a sort of fish stew—very hot tasting—"

"*Seviche,* no doubt. Corbina fish flavored with tiny red and yellow peppers, and onions sliced thin?"

"Exactly. And this one is chicken perhaps?"

"The base of *sancocho* is chicken, but plantain, yucca, coriander and various vegetables have been added. Enge will be most pleased to be told you like it, Mrs. Reyes . . . Reyes? That is a common name in Spain, I suppose?"

"Fairly so. I've met others, not related to my husband's family."

"I ask, only because as long as I've resided in our very small Aspinwall, not one person of that name has chanced to come; and now, by coincidence, there are two."

"Oh? Who is the other?" Mary, faced with a large bowl of rice, topped with mounds of coconut and tiny dried shrimp, was wondering how she could possibly do it justice.

"One of my desk clerks. Usually I hire only native-born, as I have an idea that in his own country a man should be given first opportunity for advancement. But in this case my sympathy was aroused on learning the new arrival was a remittance man like myself. Again, like myself, he is a third son and without inheritance. Reflecting on how good this country has been to me, I felt I could hardly refuse another in my same circumstances his chance also. So, there happening to be an opening, I took him on, and thus far I've had no reason to regret it. In fact, I wonder if perhaps I've persisted too stubbornly in my allegiance to the natives."

He fell silent, and Margaret Cullinan gave him a sharp glance. "You sound discouraged. Has something happened?"

"Yes. A matter of business, really, but I may as well explain. No doubt you thought it odd I would be pleading illness?"

"I confess I did. You seemed as well as ever to me."

"I am. But I needed an excuse to remain at the hotel day and night. Someone has been stealing, not only from the hotel guests, but from the till as well. I find this so very disturbing because theft, in Aspinwall, is not at all usual."

"Not usual?" Mary put in. "I'm sorry, of course I know nothing about your town, but people on the ship were speaking as though one must constantly beware of pickpockets, both here and in Panama City."

"We are infested with vermin of that sort!" Mr. Cox said furiously. "They come here from all parts of the world and feed on the passengers and anyone else who is foolish enough to permit it.

"But the natives would touch nothing not belonging to them—at least in the past. Honesty and honor were the same word. Oh, they've become greedy, their palms are out, but they do not steal, as yet. Or so I believed. I thought them all like Enge and Justo. Surely you noticed the small but choice collection of gold artifacts that I keep openly displayed in the house? It includes a large, fairly valuable gold pendant of the Coclé style, in the shape of a crouching jaguar, something only too easy to sell here. But I assure you neither of the servants who work for me would think of taking it or anything else."

"But one of your native clerks has succumbed to temptation?" Margaret inquired. "You are convinced the thief is a clerk?"

"I'm afraid so. At first, I would not believe it. I told myself some of the riffraff constantly passing through here must be guilty. But I had to admit finally, that was not possible. And now I am spying on men I have considered my children. On Monday, when I so rudely cancelled my engagement here, I thought I had caught the thief, but he slipped through my hands . . .

"Oh, well, let us speak of something else! Mrs. Reyes, please, tell me something about yourself."

Mary hesitated, and Margaret said to her, "Don't be modest, or I shall have to speak for you! She is an artist, Bertram, and a good one. I hope she'll show you some of her work."

"I should like to see it very much!" He spoke perhaps a shade too heartily, and Mary understood exactly what he was thinking. It was often difficult, when you yourself had an understanding of art, to be forced to inspect and praise the work of someone who in all probability was only a talented dabbler. Ill at ease, she hoped the matter would be forgotten.

The remainder of the meal was occupied by their host's urbane comments on this country he had chosen for his own; and with his enthusiasm, Mary's concept of La Grenada, as the province was called, was further influenced and enlarged. There was still the forbidding jungle, a confusion of brilliant flamboyant colors and hidden danger. But the impoverished people who dwelled in its shadow became flesh and blood.

Enge no longer appeared just a stout, unsmiling woman, whose dark-skinned strangeness was emphasized by the wearing of a small gold ring in the end of her nose. She was a Cuna, one of the few willing to leave their San Blas Islands to work on the mainland, and it was the special pride of her people, the mola cloth work, that decorated the walls of this house. On festive occasions, like this, she wore a blouse she herself had made from a number of different colored pieces, stitching them together in layers to form an intricate design—in this instance, that of an eagle with a human baby clutched in its claws. Her pleasure in Mary's understanding of her artistry transformed her usually plain, stolid face.

Justo, meanwhile stood by grinning without comprehension while his master explained the mola needlework. But Bertram Cox next addressed him in Spanish, and he hurried away, to reappear with a crude musical instrument, made of seven short lengths of reed lashed together. This too was Cuna, and Enge had taught him to play. Bashfully, he did so. The music of the pipes was high, almost tuneless, and Mary found it haunting.

Mr. Cox then conducted his guests about the house, lifting his treasures lovingly from their shelves, and then replacing them exactly where they had been before. If he became a trifle pedantic in his explanations of the pottery, gold sculptures, even of the bowls made from gourds of the calabash tree, neither of his listeners minded. He was a man who had taken pains to learn a great deal about his adopted country.

After they completed a slow tour of the little house, he turned to Mary. "I have dominated the discussion long enough. You promised to let me see a little of your work?"

"Yes—" She hesitated, as always, when placed in this position, her confidence ebbing away. Forgotten were the triumphs of San Francisco. The sole reality was here and now, when a new critic, one who had never even heard of Vermies Milo, would form his own opinion.

Nevertheless, she went out and brought her portfolio, placing it in his hands. Then she said, "Excuse me," and went to walk in the garden.

It was some time before the two elderly people joined her where she sat on a bench beneath a tulip tree.

Bertram Cox came first, the sheaf of watercolors and sketches held carefully in his hands.

"I must apologize," he said, "for being so ignorant of what is going on in the rest of the world. You are a professional, are you not?" Although phrased as a question, it was actually a statement of fact.

"Yes," Mary agreed. "My work is sold through a gallery in San Francisco."

"It is evident. These are beautiful, quite uniquely so. There was a time in my life—long past, fortunately for my peace of mind—when I would have given my soul and reckoned myself the richer, to be able to create a picture others might wish to look at, day after day. I have consoled myself by collecting instead. I hope you realize how fortunate you are?"

"Sometimes I forget," Mary confessed. Then smiled. "But not for long."

"As Keats said, 'Beauty is truth, truth beauty— that is all ye know on earth, and all ye need to know.' That has been my credo too, and I am not ashamed of it. This one," he was turning over the drawings, searching. He extracted Mary's favorite—a drawing she had made in Acapulco of a small boy, squatting on his heels in the dirt street and gazing raptly at a lizard that returned his scrutiny with trepidation, eyes bright and body pushed up on its short front legs. One could almost see the tiny breast pulse with rapid breathing.

"You like it?" Mary asked.

"Very much," he said with respect.

"Then I hope you accept it as a gift. Please! You have been so very kind to us."

"Thank you, I will treasure it." His pleasure warmed

Mary. "Margaret, why didn't you tell me about this remarkable young woman, give me some warning?"

"Bertram, I know what I like, and I like Mary's work," she replied comfortably, "but I understand very little about pictures."

They were strolling back into the house, and Margaret continued, "I've been thinking about your problem at the hotel. What disturbs you particularly is that one of the Indians may be stealing?"

"Of course. And speaking of the hotel I must leave now to return. I intend to count the receipts before each man leaves his post. But what is it you wish to say?"

"Suppose this new clerk, this Reyes, is the thief. Wouldn't that be preferable?"

"No. Worse, I think." His enjoyment of the afternoon had evaporated. He looked older, and tired. "I have accepted Jaime as a younger me. Almost as a son. It's difficult to put into words, but if he proves false, my faith in myself, and in my judgment, is false also."

"His Christian name is Jaime?" Mary asked slowly.

"Yes . . . Ah, I must leave, ladies! And I thank you for a most enjoyable interlude."

Jaime Reyes, she mused. Reyes wasn't unusual, and Jaime must be one of the commonest given names in all Spain. There was no possibility of this being her own Jaime, for this young man was a third son, and penniless.

But merely hearing of someone with the same name as the boy from whom she'd been separated for so many years—he'd been three, then, and he would be almost nineteen now—set her thinking about him with desperate longing. If only the ship would come!

Chapter Thirty-nine

"Good morning, Mary. Would you like a mango?"

"Not just yet, thank you." She sat down, surveyed the breakfast platters with distaste, and gazed out the open shutters into sunlight that was already baking the patio tiles with especial virulence. The air was very still.

"Are you feeling all right, my dear? Your face is flushed."

"Oh, yes. It's just so terribly hot today!"

"No more so than yesterday, surely."

"It seems so. And it makes me listless." Actually, Mary's head was throbbing too. But she had spent a very restless night, which would account for her malaise, and in the long hours she had done too much remembering.

"Margaret," she said abruptly, "I'd like to catch a glimpse of this other Reyes who has come to Aspinwall."

"Do you think you might know him?"

"I doubt if he's anyone I've ever met. But I am curious, all the same, and he may be someone who can give me news. Also, I want to go to the wharf and find out if there's any word of our ship. You must be eager to get on with our journey?"

When her friend didn't answer, Mary glanced at her. "Aren't you?"

"No. To be truthful, I'm traveling back to England merely because it's the thing to do, now that Henry's gone. I have an idea, once I reach London, I'll be wishing I had somewhere else I need go!"

"I see." After a moment, Mary inquired, "Have you thought of remaining in New York with your sister?"

"I couldn't. My sister's husband dislikes me."

"Dislikes *you?* That's impossible!"

"Thank you, my dear. But it's true. So I shall only stop briefly in New York to see my sister once again, then be on my way."

She sat in silence for a moment, and then said, "However, I do understand your eagerness. And of course we will go to find out about the ship. You seem tired this morning, Mary! It's unfortunate you refused Bertram's offer of the carriage, when he made the suggestion yesterday."

It was true the idea of riding seemed much more attractive this morning than it had then. But the town was so small, to walk everywhere was entirely feasible, and being driven by a black coachman in such an outlandish outfit had struck her as a bit pompous. Not wishing to offend Mr. Cox, who was being so very kind, she had insisted that she loved walking.

"I'm quite all right. And I'm ready to start out as soon as you are."

But as they walked, the distances seemed endless, and strangely everything seemed to shimmer. Mary fancied she could see waves of heat rising from the street, and when at last they reached the harbor, the brilliant sheen of the water burned her eyes and reached searching fingers back into her head, accentuating the throbbing.

She squinted out. The squat smoke-blackened steamer was no longer riding at anchor, and except for an occasional small fishing smack, the smooth green surface was empty, all the way to the horizon. They were saved walking to the end of the wharf by a passerby who informed them there was still no word of the *Ocean Queen*.

With that, Mary's disappointment was so great she had difficulty in restraining herself from weak tears. She became conscious that Margaret in concern had grasped her arm, and she was grateful, for her legs were trembling.

"I think we should return to the house at once, Mary." The words sounded queerly muffled, as though they came through a thick curtain.

"No! No, I must go to the hotel! Mr. Cox said this Jaime Reyes was the morning clerk, didn't he? I must see him!"

"Very well, then, but I will insist on getting the carriage to take us home."

They progressed slowly, Mary leaning heavily on her friend. This terrible heat, she thought. So enervating! Could it be making her ill?

Fortunately, the hotel was nearby, and they were soon climbing the steps to the veranda, then entering the lobby.

Briefly, her view of the reception desk was blocked by a group of travellers; then they moved away. She stared with aching eyes, and the image that had tended to move jerkily up and out of sight, steadied. *Francisco!* It was Francisco himself, standing behind the counter, his attention on the big ledger. Francisco, *who was dead!*

Her bewilderment turned to disbelief. She must be delirious from the heat! Suffering prostration perhaps. This man was young, very young, and Francisco Reyes had been even older than she! If he were alive now, he would be in his forties . . . But the same face. The same expression. How odd. How very odd.

She must be quite ill.

She murmured, "I would like to go back," and found herself outside in a chair on the veranda.

Margaret left, but she soon reappeared, accompanied by Bertram Cox. Their faces, neither of them smiling, swam in and out of her consciousness.

"The carriage is coming," she heard Mr. Cox say, and saw Margaret nod.

"I don't want to be any trouble." She spoke apologetically to those shifting disembodied faces.

"No, no trouble at all."

Then Mary was in the carriage. Ahead of her loomed the large bare black back, and above it, the stovepipe hat. The harness jingled as the horses started to pull.

"Wait, please! Mr. Cox—"

The vehicle halted. One of the horses pawed the ground restlessly.

"Will you ask your clerk, the one named Reyes, to come to your house when he is free today? I must speak to him!"

"Yes." The surprise in his voice was courteously suppressed. "Of course, Mrs. Reyes. I will tell him."

Mary was arguing wth Margaret, who insisted she should lie on her bed and rest, until the fever abated.

No doubt about it any longer. Not just too much hot sun, but a high fever. Her forehead was burning to the touch, yet she shook as though with the ague.

Her teeth chattering, she said, "I do feel horrible, Margaret! The climate must not agree with me. Now I have a chill."

"Please, my dear, do go to bed! You'll feel better lying quietly."

"Not yet! I must wait. It's almost noon and Francisco will be coming."

"Francisco?"

"Yes, he's my husband."

Margaret was frowning, but she said nothing more. She settled Mary on a wicker lounge, and tucked a blanket around her, although she herself was filmed in the usual perspiration from the heat of the day. Enge brought in a cup of tea, and held the spoon as though feeding a baby. The hot liquid failed to warm Mary, and after a few sips she refused to take more.

Leaving the room with Enge, Margaret asked, "You will doze a little, won't you? And Mary, don't count too much on that young man from the hotel coming today. Bertram would have had to warn him you are ill. Europeans seem to take diseases here so very easily."

"Diseases?" Her vision steadied, and for a moment her mind was clear. "What do you mean? Do you think I have malaria—or yellow fever?"

"Probably not," Margaret soothed. "But we shouldn't admit Mr. Reyes until we are certain."

"Oh no! No!"

Yet moments later, alone in the room that was so quiet except for a parrot cawing somewhere outside, she had forgotten the scrap of conversation completely, and returned to her puzzled expectation. Francisco was coming—a man who was dead was now alive, and youthful again. How could it be?

She must have slept a little because she awoke with a start. There were voices in the room beyond, one determined, the other protesting.

"She asked me to come, and I am here!"

"But Mrs. Reyes is ill! There is danger of contagion."

"I am not afraid in the least." The speaker was male and young. Confident. "I insist you permit me to pass."

"Very well." The Englishwoman's voice was stiff, unfriendly. "I am an elderly woman and cannot stop you. Through this doorway . . . Mary, your visitor is here."

She heard the door close as Margaret left them alone. Then she opened her eyes and looked at him or his ghost, hoping the delusion was gone.

"Francisco?" Mary shrank against the back of the settee, and added in Spanish, "Is it you?"

The ghost gave her husband's smile, not the genuine joyous smile that in the beginning of their relationship had charmed her, but the later one, mocking, with a touch of cruelty.

He said in a wondering tone, but without warmth, "So you really are my mother!"

"Jaime!" she whispered. She should have guessed! If she weren't feeling so wretchedly dizzy and ill, she would have understood at once. Doña Cesaria had remarked so often, and with such triumph, from the day the baby was born, how much he resembled his father. "All Reyes!" the vindictive woman had crowed.

Jaime, her own son, was saying, "I wondered, when I was told to ask for you, but I decided the idea was foolish. How many women named Maria Reyes must there be? I told myself too, I wouldn't know my mother if I saw her. After all, she deserted me at such an early age. And the oil painting of her my father commissioned when they were first married Grandmother destroyed. She ordered it first slashed, then burned. So I cannot imagine my mother, except as a vague memory—

"I came anyway. And now you call me by my father's name, which not a soul here knows. I must admit you are she, and the incredible has happened."

She was shivering so violently the blanket shook. It was difficult to see him properly because the light came from behind him and hurt her eyes. Even so, the image of this slim young man, handsome, graceful, was imprinted on her brain, and even if Mary never saw him again he would not be forgotten in any detail.

"I'm here, because I was coming to Spain to search for you!" she said with weak eagerness. "I couldn't, before. Oh, Jaime, I can't tell you—"

She stretched out her hand to him. Tears were coursing down her face.

But he did not move. When she realized he had ignored her hand, she let it fall back heavily, the shock of his coldness so great that she couldn't speak. He had been a loving little boy, and always she'd remembered him that way. Never had it occurred to her, not once in the countless times she had imagined this meeting, that he would reject her!

"You hate me?" she murmured at last.

"Is it surprising?" He still was studying her, with dispassionate eyes. "Father was right. He said you had an odd sort of beauty that was half hauteur and half glow . . . He said you were a witch."

"He meant by that, I suppose, I was a bad woman?" She could still summon a feeble anger.

"No, although he thought so, for a long time. In later years, and at the end, he said he might have been wrong. But my grandmother never changed her mind. She told me all about you, all about you."

Was he really repeating, or was her mind spinning again? If only she didn't feel so terribly ill! Every bone in her body ached.

She turned her head restlessly. The gleaming gold jaguar caught her eye, and she concentrated on it, trying to keep from slipping away. She knew there were things she should ask him, important things, but she couldn't think what they were.

"I'll come back another time," he said.

She managed to nod, and then he was gone. She could resist no longer, and gave herself up to the chill that shook her like an aspen leaf in a high wind.

At the end of three days, the fever abruptly dropped, and the dreadful aching subsided. Although very thin, and too weak to raise her head, she supposed she was on the mend. She lay with half-shut eyes while Enge tried fruitlessly to tempt her with minute sips of a rich broth.

Margaret's spare figure was moving quietly about the room, straightening, dusting. The shutters had been thrown partially open, admitting the scented air from the garden but diluting the light.

"I see you've never really unpacked, Mary. You're like a bird of passage, poised to fly on at the first opportunity. Most of your clothes still neatly folded in your valise, and your reticule hanging from the bedpost, doubtless with the passage money all counted out and ready to be paid!" Then she came close to the bed and the lightness left her voice.

"My dear, I should tell you the *Ocean Queen* finally arrived yesterday, and sailed this morning. It's better you know, so you'll be content to rest, and not worry when the fever returns."

The *Ocean Queen?* Mary, whose memory had been slowly clearing, realized Mrs. Cullinan did not know, had no way of knowing that her reason for going on to Spain no longer existed. Even with this good-hearted friend, Mary had been reticent about her unhappy marriage, and she shrank now from making the necessary explanations. She said reluctantly, "Margaret, the hotel clerk, Jaime Reyes, is my son."

"Your son!"

"Yes. Don't look at me so. I'm not delirious now. He was on his way to California to find me." That *was* true, wasn't it? "And I to Spain to find him. By lucky chance we are in Aspinwall at the same time!"

She could see the puzzled frown on the older woman's face, and continued, as brightly as she could, "Not so surprising, really. You've been telling me this is by far the best sea route between Europe and San Francisco."

"But my dear, three sons! Why haven't you ever mentioned them? If I were you, I would be so proud—"

Three sons . . . There it was, incomprehensible, but nevertheless a fact, and Mary's body stiffened with the shock of it. A third son and a remittance man—so Jaime had presented himself to Bertram Cox!

Why? Why? There seemed no possible reason, good or bad, for such pointless lies.

In any case, harmless as they might be, they had deceived a man who was unfailingly kind and generous to her as well as to Margaret, and he must be told.

Still, she thought wavering, Jaime would surely have an explanation. Shouldn't he be heard first? He'd promised to return for another visit.

"I can't talk—not now," she said weakly, and her sudden overwhelming exhaustion was genuine. "Oh, Margaret, I'm so desperately tired."

"Of course you are, poor lamb! And here I keep you from resting. Let me bathe your face with this cool cloth, and then you nap a little, build up your strength—"

"Margaret, what did you mean—'when the fever returns'?"

"Only, that it's likely to. That is the course the disease usually takes."

"What disease, Margaret? Tell me, please, I want to know."

"You have yellow fever."

CHAPTER FORTY

"No, JAIME! STAY AWAY!" SHE CRIED THAT AF-ternoon when she heard her son's voice again outside.

But he ignored her and walked in, to stand at the foot of the bed.

"How yellow your skin is!" he observed.

"Yes. I have yellow fever, and you are not brave but merely foolhardy to come near me!" She was feeling much stronger, however. Could Margaret be wrong? Perhaps the worst really was over.

Her son grinned, this time with a touch of friendliness. He must not despise her completely, she thought, or he would not have taken the risk of returning.

"Not brave nor foolhardy," he contradicted. "I shall be greatly surprised, mother dear, if I become ill. One of the best surgeons in Spain spent considerable time in this part of the world, and I've heard him express the opinion, while a guest at Grandmother's dining table, that yellow fever is not contagious."

"Indeed! How else can one get it?"

Her son shrugged. "Who can say? Perhaps, like malaria, from breathing the bad swamp air. I've come to see you again, because I'm still curious."

"About what?"

"About you. Natural, isn't it? My loving mother left, apparently without a backward glance, so I wonder where she's been, what she's been doing. For example, who was your lover?"

Mary started. After a pause, she said evenly, "I shall answer you this once, and then the subject is closed. My lover, as you put it, was merely a fabrication of your grandmother's. She hated me from the beginning, turned your father against me, and succeeded in separating me from my child. No doubt she has indulged you all your life—she certainly did when I was present—so you must feel affection for her, and for that reason, I won't go on about her as I am tempted to do."

Again he grinned. "Grandmother and I understood each other."

"Now you've asked a question, and in fairness it's my turn. Why have you left Spain, and why did you lie to your employer?"

"That's two questions, Mother dear. However, I'll answer them both—but only in confidence. Is the old woman away? The servants let me in."

"If you mean Mrs. Cullinan, yes, she's gone out for an hour or so."

"Good. The servants understand Spanish, but not English, so we will converse in English. I speak it very well, do I not?"

"Not like an Englishman, perhaps, but well enough. Now Jaime, please explain! I can conceive of no earthly reason for your deceptions."

He looked puzzled, for she had spoken too rapidly in the unfamiliar tongue. But then he shrugged. "Listen, then. My grandmother and I argued. She was very angry with me! She said, 'I will give you money. I want you to travel and become a man. When you are one, return and take your place here.'

"So, I went to North America first, to the state of Massachusetts, because I was curious about my dear mother. But she wasn't to be found in the city of Boston. I met someone who said she was in California, and I took a ship to go there, and on the way came to Aspinwall. Here I met with true misfortune—is that the right word? At the hotel, my money was stolen! There is a thief. No one knows who he is. I owed for my account, also, so I wanted to work for Mr. Cox to earn the money, but everyone said he would hire only Indians. Therefore, I learned all I could about him, and said what I thought would please him. What is the harm in that?"

Mary was much dismayed. "What is the harm? Jaime, you are accepting his kindness under false pretences. It is dishonest!" At his blank look, she switched to Spanish and repeated the words, ignoring her son's jutting jaw and narrowing eyes. "You will have to make this right! Tell Mr. Cox the truth and I'm sure he will be lenient. Would you rather I told him?"

"No! You will not!"

An odd expression crossed his face, one so sly its very childishness disarmed her. "I will, myself."

"I mean it, Jaime. You must! Have you no sense of honor?"

"As much as you!" he retorted angrily. But then he said, "That was ill-mannered, and I apologize. I have said I would tell him and I will. But only *after* he finds his thief. Otherwise he may decide it is I who cannot be trusted, and therefore I am the thief."

She considered this, and decided the brief delay could do no harm. Still, she was not happy with him and the bald story he had told her. They were speaking Spanish again, and she reflected that this cool stranger who was her son would not be able to hide so easily behind Spanish words.

"May I ask what you and your grandmother quarreled about? I can't imagine her banishing you for anything short of murder."

"That's a third question. How greedy dear Mother is! But, I have nothing to hide and the answer is, I was gambling too much!"

Gambling? Francisco had loved gambling, and Doña Cesaria had never objected.

"I must go now, Mother dear, but I'll return in a few days."

"One favor then, Jaime. Don't call me that!"

"You don't want to be called Mother? I'm disappointed."

"You know what I mean!"

He laughed, and giving her an airy wave, went out through the doorway.

Mary followed him with her eyes, pleased when he stopped at the curio shelf where she could gaze at him unobserved and remark to herself how straight-backed and handsome he was.

Jaime called back to her, "Someday you must tell me what all these things are," and his voice was no longer sardonic. He was genuinely interested, she thought. She could tell.

"I'll be happy to!" Forgetting her illness, she cried, "Come again soon!"

Yes, he had been badly hurt by her apparent desertion. He cared nothing about her, that was clear, but in time, given a chance, she would put things right between them!

He did come again. But the fever, as predicted, had risen even higher than before, and now there was vomiting, so frequent and prolonged it seemed the lining of her throat must be torn out with the dry heaving. Much of the time, with only occasional intervening periods of lucidity, she was out of her head, thrashing in the restlessness of her heated blood, and moaning with pain. Finally, there was only torpid semiconsciousness, when she lay as if already dead.

It was then that Jaime returned and stood by her bed for what seemed a long time. She knew he was there and imagined she spoke to him, but the silence remained unbroken. She lay curled on her side beneath her netting, her eyes shut, sensing he had come to the head of the bed and was peering down.

The house was totally quiet, no voices from the servants doing their work, not even a birdcall. Was this death? she wondered. This stillness, and Jaime pondering without love the face of the mother who had left him?

But he shifted position, and his boots scraped ever so quietly on the tile floor. There were other small new noises too, what, she neither knew nor cared. He was alive then, and so was she! She wanted to hold out her hand, call him by name, but was too weak. Once again the comforting waters of unconsciousness closed over her.

"I think the crisis is past." A man's voice. That of Bertram Cox.

Then a cool, dry hand pressed against her forehead. Margaret's. She easily recognized the touch, for this action had repeated itself many times over. "Quite

right—she's out of danger," Margaret said. "Oh, thank
the Lord!"

"Yes, we should. This woman still has her beautiful
work to do . . . See, she heard me! I saw a smile. Go
back to sleep now, Mrs. Reyes."

Awake again. Mary was aware of their subdued
voices in the next room. The sound of a cup placed on
a saucer, a spoon rattling; and she knew it was a meal-
time the two older people were sharing there.

Tentatively she turned her head to watch for a time,
and with deep pleasure, the pattern of gold bars the
sun made streaming through the shutter slats.

She was better. No doubt of it. So weak she could
barely shift her body, but cool. She could feel the netting, see the gold pattern, hear the human voices. Better!

She lay quietly, drinking in details of the room, and
deciding from the slant of the sun it was early morning. Then she realized Bertram Cox, by being there at
that hour, must have moved back to his home. She
called out in a whisper.

At once chairs scraped and the two entered the
room. Again there was the testing of her forehead, and
a satisfied nod between them.

"Welcome back!" Mr. Cox was wearing his precise
smile, yet to her puzzlement, it seemed a little forced.
His shoulders, usually carried so jauntily, were
stooped.

"It is you who should be welcomed," she said, each
word an effort. "You've come home then?"

"Yes."

"You found your thief?"

"I did." His lips pressed together and she saw him
exchange a quick glance with Margaret. "Later, when
you're stronger, I'll tell you all about it. For now, the
important thing is to rest and eat a little. Enge has prepared a chicken broth, truly fit for the gods, and is
waiting to bring it to you."

Mary nodded, telling herself she was only too willing to be cosseted, and that her brief impression of

unhappiness on his part must have been only a delusion, natural enough after such a severe illness.

Thinking Enge was coming then, she let her gaze wander to the doorway, and, as it had so often, fasten on the curio shelf in the next room. Something was different there but in her lethargy it was a moment before the explanation came and she gasped aloud. The centerpiece, the gold jaguar, which had been like a talisman to her during those long delirious days, was gone!

"Where is the jaguar?" she asked sharply.

Cox, who was preparing to leave the room, froze. "There's nothing to worry about! I sent it out to be repaired. A hair-line crack, one I hadn't noticed."

Mary heard Margaret Cullinan give a small sigh.

She had only to study both their faces to have her suspicion confirmed. "Who was the hotel thief, Mr. Cox?" she asked quietly.

There was another exchange of glances, and then he said, "I suppose you will guess, if you haven't already—although we did intend for a few days to spare you . . . He was your son."

"Dear God." After a moment she said bitterly, "He took the jaguar too?"

"Yes. The last time he was here. But stealing something of that sort was only a greedy impulse, I imagine. The servants were temporarily in the garden, you were unconscious so far as he could tell, and therefore he had an opportunity he could not resist. It was his undoing, of course. I was totally convinced Enge and Justo were beyond suspicion, and we knew he had called here. So, I returned to the hotel and set a trap. I caught him pilfering the cash box."

Mary was unable to speak. She lay very still, unaware that one hand was working spasmodically at the edge of the thin sheet covering her. As Bertram Cox continued, his dry, unemotional voice was steadying.

"I've since learned he was a gambler. In a village this size, such activities should have been easily discovered, but he confined himself to the high-stake games of the travelers passing through. It seems he was a plunger, and an unlucky one who often lost.

Such men, you must understand, cannot stop playing, and they become desperate for money."

Mary recognized the kindness that prompted this explanation. Mr. Cox was helping her, and himself as well, to find an excuse for Jaime. But she was remembering, so clearly she could almost hear his strong young voice, how Jaime had laughed and said, 'I have nothing to hide, I was gambling too much.' She'd been surprised then at the idea of Doña Cesaria becoming so angry at her beloved grandson she would banish him, and merely for gambling. The truth was, of course, she hadn't. He'd been a thief in Spain as well as in Aspinwall, and that was the sin the old woman had not tolerated.

So Jaime had lied to her, his mother, as readily as he'd lied to Bertram Cox!

Anger, Mary was finding, was a strong restorative.

"I'm sorry! So terribly sorry—and humiliated! I can't tell you how I regret my part in all this. That tale he spun of being a third son should have put me on guard, I should have told you at once it was untrue. But he made me believe he would confess his deception. He convinced me!"

"He convinced us all. Don't blame yourself."

"But I do. I must. Oh, what shabbiness! To think you have been so good to us, when all the time—"

"Mrs. Reyes, I insist you stop this at once. You will make yourself ill again." He gave a small eloquent shrug. "We must be philosophical. Permit me to slightly misquote Sir Francis Bacon, and say that when one has children one gives hostages to fortune. You cannot control fortune, you know—nor a child, once he has become a man."

"Where is Jaime now, Mr. Cox? What will become of him?"

He shook his head. "I've no idea where he is. He left Aspinwall, and has not been heard of."

"He left?" She stared at him. "I don't understand. You mean you let him go?"

"There seemed little point in calling in the authorities. The money was spent. And the local jail is far from pleasant."

"I see." Mary murmured, knowing he would not care for any expression of gratitude. At length she asked, "Did he start back to Spain, do you think?"

"Possibly. There was a ship in the harbor. But the train to Panama City runs daily, so he may have chosen to escape in that direction, headed for China or even California. We'll probably never know. At any rate, it's all over. You should rest, so we will leave you now, and send Enge—"

"Wait, Bertram." Margaret came to the bed and took Mary's trembling hands firmly in her own. "Mary, I know you wish to be alone for a little, but there is something I should tell you first, something I wish you would consider."

"My own situation has changed, due, I'm afraid, to someone else's sad misfortune. Until recently, a doctor and his wife were stationed in Aspinwall. But it seems a month ago, there was an emergency at an inland village, and they were called. As well as they knew the surrounding jungle, coming home they lost their way. They wandered, and were not found in time. There's no use dwelling on their tragic end, I'm only telling you about it now to explain, because their dispensary is still here, and until another doctor can be persuaded to come, I've been asked to, well, do my best. The shipping company has offered to pay me a small salary.

"Now, it occurred to us, Bertram and me, since you probably won't be going on to Spain, you might consider staying here for a bit, to help. You told me once you understood midwifery, and with your fluent Spanish—"

"No! Oh no, Margaret, I cannot!" Stay on in this scene of her heartbreak? "You are good to want me, but I must leave!"

Although she was clearly disappointed, the older woman did not protest. She went from the room then, with Bertram Cox, saying only, "Rest now. Remember, you are far from recovered."

Mary knew this was good advice, but waiting for Enge, forcing herself to swallow the nourishing soup, and afterward lying sleepless on the bed, she contin-

ued to turn over alternatives in her mind, concentrating on making her plans and trying not to dwell on
Jaime's perfidy, or let herself wonder where he was, or
how he was. Her son, whom she had found only to
lose, did not bear thinking about, now.

She had about decided to go on to Boston, where
she could visit her ailing elder sister Eileen, when
Justo, beaming, brought her a letter. At once she pored
through the pages covered with Miguel's distinctive
graceful writing, devouring every small detail about
Brian and Maria Rosa, Bets, Patrick, and the rest, seeing in her mind's eye all the dear familiar faces.

She knew then that Boston for her was not the answer, not the place she longed to be. Never mind that
she hadn't a proper niche in Los Angeles society. The
people of whom Miguel wrote were the ones she loved
and missed and should return to. Patrick! She'd find a
small house of her own near his, and she'd try to atone
for the years she'd stood aloof from the activities of
his friends. Francisco no longer bound her, she was
free, she might even remarry . . .

However, there was one great obligation she had.
Whether he wished it or not, Bertram Cox must be repaid the amount Jaime had stolen. There wasn't a
great deal she could give him now, the savings she'd
piled up with Milo having been greatly depleted during those months in Los Angeles when she'd been un-
productive, and occupied solely with Miguel's book.
But there was still enough to make a start and show
her good faith before departing, and it was all here,
hanging in the needlepoint bag just over her head.
She'd take out her passage money and a little more to
travel with, then insist, absolutely insist, on Mr. Cox
accepting the rest. And as she earned more, she would
send him more.

She reached above her head and brought down the
reticule, opening it eagerly.

Then she stared inside, and searched frantically
with her hands, even while knowing the bitter truth.
Those small furtive noises, Jaime staring down at
her . . .

CHAPTER FORTY-ONE

MIGUEL SAID, "I'VE HAD A RATHER DISTURBING letter from your sister."

Patrick tried to conceal his alarm—yes, and annoyance. Why should Mary Frances be writing to Miguel and not to himself?

Miguel smiled slightly, understanding his father-in-law very well. "It seems I am the only one she knows who is willing to write long detailed letters, telling all the news about the family. I relish such a task, and she encourages me by sending an occasional answer."

This was true, but hardly the entire story. In the months Mary had lived with them at Rancho Aguirre, while she catered to his father's wishes, and also took such a sincere interest in his book, providing all those beautiful and invaluable illustrations, they'd become close friends. He was surprised how much he missed her!

On her departure, they'd made a pact.

"I'm more than a little frightened, Miguel," she confessed. "The journey will be so long, I'll be so far away! If I ever reach Spain, I want to be able to visualize just what my family here is doing, the little everyday things as well as the big. All that will bring them closer. Miguel, will you write to me?"

"I would enjoy doing so. But you must reciprocate."

"I promise!"

So he kept his word, taking time from his book to tell her all he could remember—not only of the delightful absurd antics of Brian and two-year-old Maria Rosa, and such good tidings as the fact that the sheep were prospering, but also including a description of the beautiful spring that had burgeoned in the hills after this, the first normal winter of rain. And most important, a cheerful, carefully-shaded account of her brother's state of health.

Until now, he'd had only one note from her, and that just a few lines long, sent chiefly, he decided, to give him a mailing address.

This time, however, there was a real letter which he was requested to pass along to Patrick, so he took the first opportunity to ride into town.

Patrick, somewhat mollified, said, "I'm glad some-one has heard from her! Then she must be all right. And I suppose she's reached Boston by now. She was looking forward so much to a visit with our older sister. Odd, isn't it? Eileen, who was much the frailer of the two, is still living, while Sheila the robust one is gone. But perhaps Mary Frances has already left there for Spain?"

"No, as a matter-of-fact she hasn't gotten to Boston. Here, you'd better read it for yourself."

Patrick started to ask a question, then seeing Miguel's expression, he opened the letter.

Miguel, dear:

I am still in Aspinwall, and have read and re-read your so welcome letter. I cannot describe my pleasure in receiving such a happy account of my loved ones! How strong and beautiful little Brian must be! I pray his Papa's malady will continue steadily to improve, as you assure me it has been.

Patrick shot Miguel a quizzical glance before reading on.

Please tell Patrick I do miss him terribly and will surely write to him too, as soon as I find an extra hour, and feel stronger. You see, I have had yellow fever. I hasten to assure you I'm completely re-covered, and am doubly fortunate now in that I cannot contract the disease again. That fact, com-bined with a tragic event I shan't touch upon, has brought me to what you may all consider a strange decision. For the time being, I intend to remain in Aspinwall.

There is desperate need here for medical help and I feel it my duty to do what I can.

As you know, I am not unskilled in midwifery. A friend here spent much of her life in the Orient with her husband, doing similar work, and she has a rudimentary knowledge of surgery; but her Spanish as yet is not good enough, so she needs my help. There is a dispensary available to us, praise be, and it is well-stocked.

I confess I am not convinced I will ever feel at home in this country. We are now in the rainy season; it's both wet and very hot, which I find quite oppressive, unbearably so at times! Yet my need to paint is stirring again. The brilliant colors of the rain-forest excite me, there are mangroves brooding all along the shore—

"This is crazy!" Patrick shouted. "Stay there? Yellow fever has affected her mind!"

"No," Miguel said quietly, "I think not. She's been made tremendously unhappy for some reason, and I would guess cannot find any reason either to go on or come back. So she's caught there. I wonder what the tragic event was."

"Probably some baby dying of malaria," Patrick snapped. "Mary Frances is too easily affected by some things and not enough by others. What are we going to do about this?"

Miguel looked at him, surprised. "Do? Nothing! What can you do?"

"I cannot allow my sister to throw her life away!"

"Patrick, your sister has been a grown woman for a number of years," Miguel said. A wry smile touched his mouth. "The women in your family, I've found, do not take kindly to having decisions made for them."

But Patrick was not listening. He sat glaring angrily at the letter he'd crumpled in his fist. "If I weren't such a feeble old crock, I'd fetch her back! But the way my midriff behaves, if I went, I'd just be someone else for her to take care of. Captain James Warner, damn his eyes, must be laughing in hell at the state he left me in! Sure and what a brown day this has turned out to be!"

"Brown?" repeated Miguel, puzzled.

"Oh, just something Mary Frances used to say as a child. Funny, I haven't thought of it in years." His face softened as he remembered. "She meant the sort of day it was shaping up to be—successful, or dismal, or sad—whatever it was would have a special color. A really grand morning, a parade, say, or a wedding, with the sun mellow and the breeze blowing, would be pink—although she couldn't say why, because she disliked pink, never used any shade of pink in her pictures. A day almost as good would be yellow, a quiet one blue, and so on. A really bad day was a dark muddy brown, she said, and once the color was set, there was nothing to be done; it stayed the same 'til night. Just a notion, but I don't know but what there was something to it. Today was gloomy enough, even before you brought that letter."

Miguel said nothing. He did not welcome personal questions himself, and therefore never asked them. But Patrick went on to explain. "Just more bad news about Abel Stearns! It's no secret, everyone in town knows."

"I don't."

"Eh? No, I suppose you wouldn't, living out on your rancho. Abel's in very deep financial trouble that's been building up over the last few years. Like a lot of others, he's got far too much land and after those two years of drought no cash at all to pay his debts. A few weeks ago, one of his own lawyers threatened to sue him, to collect a bill of eighteen hundred dollars! Then there was a note for thirty-five thousand dollars, owing a man named Parrott in San Francisco. Parrott got a writ of attachment and forced a sale of livestock at such low prices, one of Abel's foremen said publicly he doubted if anything could be saved, either for Don Abel or his creditors! What is so infuriating is, time and again, he's reduced to selling land at public auction just to meet some niggling sum. Fourteen dollars and seven cents lost him Rancho la Habra!"

"And this morning's news?" Fury was growing in Miguel's black eyes.

"The worst! Rancho Alamitos is lost. Magnificent Rancho Alamitos."

Silence lay for a moment between the two men. Then Patrick added, as if to himself, "Don Abel, the strongest of us all! I can only be thankful I have but one modest stretch of land, with not too large a mortgage, and that I've started a vineyard . . . But Don Abel . . . Ah, well, the grim old wolf fights on."

"And Arcadia?"

Patrick broke into a brief but genuine laugh. "As you would imagine! Every inch the lady, head held higher than ever, composure untouched. She makes it clear Don Abel may be ringed about by dogs, but will never be pulled down! Her friends admire her more than ever."

"I wish I could help!"

"As do we all. But any pittance which either of us could spare would do no good. Even the bank can't help him further. Camellito's loaned him far too much now.

"Ah, well, Miguel, no use brooding over what can't be mended. Come out and see what a fine mare my Elisa has become."

But Miguel refused, his face closed, and Patrick, further distressed that he had thoughtlessly reminded Miguel of Pepe—for it was Pepe who had once given the filly the name Elisa—watched his son-in-law gallop furiously away, as though driven by a devil.

Alone again, Patrick returned to mull over the disturbing letter. The familiar round hand, careless yet graceful, set up a sharp longing to see his much-loved Mary Frances. If only she still lived here in his house! How he missed her prickly independence, her spirit, her odd way of looking at things . . . and her devotion, her deep, loyal devotion to himself. If she were here now, the house wouldn't be lonely!

For it was lonely. The Mexican nurse had taken Brian for a week-long visit to his grandmother's rancho, and while Teo never missed having noon dinner with him, she was gone all the rest of the daylight hours.

Not that he grudged her the time away! He'd made a bargain and he'd stick to it. She was happy, just as, at their marriage, he'd sworn to her she would be. But he could still wish she was working at Father Daniel's school, as she'd intended.

Unfortunately, there'd been changes there. Some time ago, it must have been four or five months after Brian's birth, the overworked priest had received an apparent bonanza. A large group of nuns came from Ireland to assist him, and their superior at once showed herself a woman of great energy and ability, so efficient in fact that she quickly earned the nickname of "the sergeant major." Father Daniel must have fervently wished himself alone again, and overworked!

Poor little Teo had chosen that time to return to her duties, and found herself pushed, kindly but firmly, to the side. At the end of only one day she had left, barely able to hold back the tears. Father Daniel looked grim and regretful when he spoke to Patrick about it, but being an honest man, he admitted the new regimen was benefiting the children, and that, after all, was what counted.

So now Teo assisted Dr. Kramer on his rounds instead.

Which was all right, of course. Kramer was known to be a fanatic in his devotion to his work, and except for music, cared for nothing else. He seemed a nice enough fellow, if rather too formal and not much of a conversationalist.

Patrick had seen a good deal of him during his own precarious convalescence, and considered him a good doctor. So when the time came he had himself asked Kramer to deliver Teo's baby. Not that there was anything to worry about with Teo, she was young and physically healthy, but a husband wanted to be sure. And too, there was the baby. He hadn't thought he'd care so much, but he did. Although a little shamefaced about it, for he was over fifty—a ridiculous age to become a father again, he was delighted.

And Brian's birth did prove uneventful. Most births were, Patrick suspected, when attended by a man like Emil Kramer whose hands had coaxed the infant into the world skillfully, gently, and with a minimum of pain. The doctor had a good manner too, addressing Teo as Mrs. Donovan, even when he was elbow-deep in doing things that could hardly have been more intimate!

Ah, that had been a pink day! He couldn't remember it often enough . . .

When Kramer was gone, and Flora and Jeb and Flower had come in to admire the red wizened little gnome who was Brian, and then they too were gone, there'd been a fine and perfect moment for him with Teo and the baby.

It had been so very many years since Betsey's birth, he'd forgotten how a man felt, gazing down at a new human being he'd helped to make. He'd never had a son before! The love that awoke in him at first sight of the child was so strong it was like a bright silver cord running between him and Brian.

Then Teo reached across and pulled him down to sit on the bed, the baby lying between them. Her warm hand fleetingly caressed his face. It was a simple, affectionate gesture, but that was all, and he was conscious of a familiar disappointment. Telling himself to count how lucky he was, he caught her palm against his mouth and kissed it.

"I just want to thank you, Patrick," she said huskily. Tears were brimming in her eyes.

"What? Teo, my dear, it's I who thank you!"

"No. I've been wanting to tell you, but I never had the courage before—" Red suddenly suffused her face and neck. "Betsey said you were kind, and you are. I do know you expected, and wanted, more from me than I've been able to . . . give. But inside me there is only a numbness, and has been, ever since that terrible night—"

She had turned away in her embarrassment. He gently brought her back to face him.

"It's all right, Teo! My dear girl, I'd rather have you, frozen like ice, than all the torrid purple passion of every bawd on Bath Street!"

"Truly?" She had to laugh, and the constraint was broken.

"Truly!"

"Patrick?"

"Yes?"

"I am free of Garth Peters! I can tell you that, at least. He's gone and everything I felt for him is gone too. I've borne your child, and I'm free of Garth. Oh, I do care for you very much!"

"And I love you, Teo."

He loved her too much, in fact, to let her know later on, how much he wished she'd be content to stay home, to care just for Brian, and for him.

CHAPTER FORTY-TWO

BETS HAD VIEWED THE ADVENT OF A BABY HALF-brother with two, quite different emotions. Brian, in looks, was another Patrick, and therefore to be loved by her instantly and completely. But there was no denying, a son and heir for her father meant that no longer could she count on, some day in the distant future—the more distant the better—having his rancho Allison bequeathed to her and her children. She dismissed the ungenerous thought from her mind. She was no whit less delighted to witness her father's happiness in this child of his late years, but her determination had hardened. Rancho Aguirre must be kept safe for Tomas, Isabel and Maria Rosa.

It was in this mood, some months before Don Sebastian's death, that she had overheard talk of fertile meadows in the San Bernardino mountains, lush stretches of greensward lying among the ponds of Bear Valley. The land was owned by a man called 'Lucky' Belknap, who had ringed the area, so it was said, with men carrying shotguns. Intruders were not made welcome!

Bets listened avidly. She had come to Arcadia's party alone (the Stearns still entertained, though less lavishly than formerly), as Miguel, at the last minute, had ridden out with his vaqueros on a futile errand ordered by Don Sebastian, moving the few remaining cattle from one arid spot to another just as barren. Seated in the Stearns' smaller, more intimate sala, Bets was giving every appearance of listening to an elderly Sepulveda lady bemoan the dire effect of this second year of drought on Rancho Los Palos Verdes; but actually she heard none of the familiar complaints. Her mind was occupied by the conversation just behind her.

"You'd be wasting your time, Loreto," a man was advising. "I tried six months ago to get him to lease that land to me. How do you suppose I felt, knowing all that fresh green grass was going to waste, while my cattle starved? But all Belknap would say, in that cold way of his, was, 'No, sir. I have no interest.' I wanted to kill him!"

"He had no use for the grass himself, yet he refused?"

"Yes, and there was nothing personal between us. Other men I know have approached him too. But that's the sort we're getting in Los Angeles these days, tight-fisted devils who care for no one but themselves—"

Bets had heard enough. "Excuse me," she said to Doña Dorotea, and went in search of Phineas Bishop. When she could speak to him alone, she lost no time in asking whether the vacant meadowlands did indeed exist.

"You must mean that property of Elias Belknap's," he said, and Bets realized from his restrained tone the depth of his dislike for the man. "My guess is he smelled gold there, and didn't want anyone else nosing around. Sheep herders might be curious."

"That's his business—mining? What sort of man is he?"

She must have spoken too eagerly, because the bushy eyebrows drew together in a frown.

"His actual business is speculating. Other men do the work. Lucky Belknap is one of the richest men in the state while only in his mid-thirties, chiefly because he sold his holdings in the Ophir mine of the Comstock at just the right time.

"As to what sort he is, the best word maybe is ruthless. He's not one a woman should have any dealings with—if that's what you have in mind."

She stared at him in astonishment. "Phineas!" (During their lengthy dealings in cattle hides, she had suggested, considering their many years of acquaintance, the use of Mr. and Miss might perhaps be dispensed with; and he had agreed, but with reluctance. He still forgot, much of the time.)

"Oh, I'm not saying you can't bargain as well as anyone, Betsey. I'm the one who knows best you can." He smiled, and then it faded. "What I'm saying is, Belknap has a rotten reputation. He's divorced his wife, but long before that he was taken to court several times, charged with such matters as seduction and paternity. I'm told he has a particular liking for young girls."

There was such distaste in the last words that Bets took care answering. She said lightly, "Then if I ever meet him, I shall be quite safe, being thirty-three years old and usually found in the company of three children."

She was thinking however, that even without the children for protection, doing business with a man who fancied himself a seducer would not worry her in the least. So far as she had been able to discover after her years of marriage, love-making was pleasant enough usually, and on occasion could be far more. But never had the bitter-sweet ecstasy of that afternoon long ago with John Carew been repeated, and she was inclined to believe now her youth and inexperience had lent the day a rare but fraudulent magic.

She was tempted to murmur something like, "Miguel may wish to approach Mr. Belknap himself," but did not. She could not have met the gray eyes watching her.

Instead, because she had been reminded of her girlhood lover and believed her sentimental memories of him were now reduced to the commonplace, she remarked, "Speaking of sheepherders, Phineas, whatever became of that man, John Carew?"

He professed surprise that she didn't know. "There's been so much talk about Carew lately! John Downey will need help from the northern part of the state to win his election for Governor again this year, and San Francisco's vote is critical. The population there has been exploding crazily ever since the gold rush. It makes us look like a sleepy little village! At any rate, Carew is prominent now in those parts and Downey has appointed him his aide, so for the time being he's in Sacramento as a political advisor."

"How interesting . . . Did he ever marry?"

"Yes, although I've never met her. It's said she's a shy little body. Won't be much help to him if he plans to enter politics."

"I suppose not." Bets reluctantly dropped the matter. She had too much respect for this good friend's perspicacity to delve further.

Instead, because she had always found his driving ambition and the methods he adopted for assuaging it totally fascinating, she asked him about his rumored plan for pushing through a railroad from Los Angeles to his dock in Wilmington. She was not surprised to learn that although there were problems, for even a rail line only twenty-one miles in length would require a state charter as well as a large government subsidy, he was as usual confident. Phineas had a faculty she much admired, of using patience when it was needed. The charter might be difficult to get? Then if necessary he would run for the state senate, from which vantage point a franchise should be obtainable.

She enjoyed the conversation, and only ended it regretfully.

"Goodnight, then," Phineas said. "Oh, and Miss Betsey, if you're planning on riding into the San Bernardino mountains in the next day or so, don't bother."

Startled, she looked up at him.

"No need to go so far. Lucky Belknap is staying here in Los Angeles, at the Bella Union."

"Thank you, Phineas." She was greatly pleased. He

had warned, he might disapprove, but he had confidence in her!

Whatever she had expected in the way of a mining speculator, rich but of unsavory reputation, it was not the man who approached briskly to where she was seated in the hotel lobby, bowed, and said, "How interesting, Mrs. Aguirre, that you would ask to speak to me. Why you, rather than your husband, I wonder?"

Taken aback, Bets studied him. For a roué, he cut a strange figure, being dressed entirely in black—his well-cut trousers, long frock coat, even his neckerchief, thin as a string and tied in a bow. His hat, still firmly on his head, was flat-crowned, broad-brimmed, and black. This ministerial appearance, so in contrast to the local fashion, was belied by his eyes, frankly assessing, and by the two shiny pistols tucked carelessly into the pockets of his coat. He was only a little older than she, and he walked and held himself in a way that told her he was both muscular and arrogant. Under one arm, he clasped a flat tin box.

She recognized at once that he was different from the other men she knew, but she wasn't certain where the difference lay. Whatever it was made her uneasy.

"My husband is not in town at present, Mr. Belknap. I may as well come to the point at once. You own some mountain meadows, good grazing land covered with thick fresh grass."

She had determined to maintain a dignified, cool demeanor. But speaking those words, she could not avoid the thought of stricken Rancho Aguirre—the cracked and dry water holes, the sparse brittle remnants of weeds almost hidden by great swarms of voracious grasshoppers, and wandering the barren hills, Miguel's sheep, slowly, slowly dying. Oh, if the wretched animals could only be permitted to reach that luxurious green forage, those clear ponds of water!

She must have betrayed her hungry longing as clearly as one of the Indian children who watched tortillas being cooked in the Plaza. She realized her mistake when she saw a thin-lipped smile flicker briefly across his craggy face.

"I have, at Bear Valley—and I've turned down higher offers, Mrs. Aguirre, than I'd guess you can possibly make. See this box?" He snapped open the lid. "Look here. I'll be buying some land with this cash later today. You could hardly add much to that, now could you?"

She glanced at the many large bills crammed inside, then forced herself to look into eyes that were amber, flecked with yellow. Mountain lion eyes.

"Not much, no. But surely something is better than nothing! Of course I knew you'd refused other offers, but I hoped—"

"I did refuse other offers, but they were made by men." His bold gaze swept over her, lingering where it would. "I have a weakness for beautiful women and their sad stories. I think you know that, or you would not have come."

At the confident accusation she felt her face flame. How dare he! She had come because once told of the meadowlands she wanted them so much she could not have slept again if she'd done nothing to get them. Hadn't she as much right as any man to have a business proposal taken seriously?

Anger loosed her tongue. "On the contrary, sir," she snapped. "The gossip I've heard would not encourage the use of any feminine wiles from me. You are notorious, true, but only with innocent young girls!"

He gave a mocking sigh. "That is the trouble with gossip, it's so often wrong! Extreme youth is appealing, I admit, but hardly essential . . . Elizabeth—pardon me, Mrs. Aguirre, I do not like hotel lobbies! I suggest we go elsewhere and discuss what you wish to propose, over a glass of wine, and in comfort as well as privacy."

By chance, they were at that moment alone in the small lobby, for even the clerk had gone outside to wave farewell to the coach passengers leaving for Wilmington. Bets was only too aware of Belknap's gaze, which now openly rested on the curve of her bosom.

"This is quite private enough," she said curtly. "I see I was a fool to approach you. There is really nothing to discuss, is there?"

"As it happens, yes." He allowed the silence to lengthen, before remarking in a mild tone, "If you are going to do business with men, dear lady, you should learn there are no holds barred. I am not the only man in town who would want to find out whether a woman who was forward enough to propose our meeting, might not also be, assuming her wish was granted, generous in return. I wonder—would she?"

"If I understand you, sir—no, indeed! I trust I've satisfied your curiosity, and I bid you good day!" She had sprung up and started toward the door, but his austerely-clad figure barred the way.

"Wait!" he commanded, and reluctantly she halted. "Very well. I consented to meet you, not only because I'd heard of the beauty of the lady who was Bets Donovan, but also because—whether you are generous or not—I intend to grant your request."

She stared at him dumbfounded, her indignation evaporating.

"You said . . . you intend—"

"I do. After a number of wasted months in Bear Valley, I've come to the conclusion there is certainly gold there, but merely as a minor strike—one that can wait. You will understand that while I was prospecting, I didn't want strangers wandering about. Nor do I now, but the situation has changed. I need to move my men elsewhere, and still keep the area protected until the day I'm ready to mine." He shrugged, as though the matter was of no importance. "Therefore, if you wish to drive your cattle up, you may."

"These are sheep."

"Sheep, then!" He spoke with revealing curtness.

Earlier, Bets would have felt a small satisfaction at his annoyance on being even so slightly misinformed, but she was now too overjoyed, her jubilation marred only by regret that this unexpected piece of good fortune hadn't come a few months earlier, when the cattle too might have benefited. Alas, however, the once great herd was decimated. The few steers left, destined to be slaughtered for Bishop's stew kettles, were too starved and weak to stand a long drive into the mountains. Only the sheep would be saved.

Ah, but she must not count on anything yet! Not until this unpredictable man named his fee for the pasturage. Rancho Aguirre's money was in short supply.

Her heart beating wildly, although she tried to conceal her anxiety, she asked the question.

"There will be no charge."

"No charge? But that is too kind! I cannot—" She stopped in confusion, seeing Belknap's upraised hand.

"Wait. No charge in money. There is, however, one condition."

"Yes?" In spite of her efforts, her voice trembled. Had his offer been only a cruel joke after all, and he was going to suggest . . .

But no. His answer was straightforward.

"As I say, I have use for my men elsewhere. If you use my meadows, I will want your vaqueros, those who drive the sheep up, to remain, and I want them armed. They will not only tend the sheep, but be watchdogs for me. Can you spare them?"

"Oh, yes!" she cried eagerly. "There is little for them to do now anyway, with our cattle dead and dying. Is that all?"

"That is all. You accept?"

"Indeed yes! You are most generous to suggest such an arrangement."

Again she saw the thin smile. "Not generous, Mrs. Aguirre. You won this time, because it suited me. Another day, when I hold all the cards, I will name the meeting place—and you will come."

"There will not be another day," she said, and left hurriedly, fearful that he might change his mind.

Driving the emaciated sheep many long miles to their new pasture would be a difficult undertaking that could well end in disaster. A load was lifted from Bets' mind when Miguel offered to head the drive.

She had told him, with some trepidation, of her talk with Elias Belknap. But Miguel, in following all Don

Sebastian's erratic orders, spent much of his time on the range and had not been in Los Angeles in many weeks. Fortunately, therefore, he had heard none of the rumors about the speculator's reputation with the opposite sex. The frown he wore when his wife told of sending a message to a strange man, and then worse, meeting with him at the Bella Union, smoothed away as she related the outcome.

"Elizabeth, how splendid!"

"Yes. Mr. Belknap was generous."

"I don't know that I'd say *generous*. Any Californio who could spare a meadow would have given it to you without question, and put you under no obligation. But, he is Americano, and a stranger to our ways. Fortunate, wasn't it, you asked just when you did! Earlier, you'd have received the same refusal as the others. Later, and someone else's stock would already be up there, growing fat again on that beautiful pasture . . . I'll drive the sheep myself."

"Oh, would you, Miguel? I'd be so relieved. It's such a long distance with no water or feed. How many men will you take? And how long will you expect to be on the trail?"

Miguel's dark eyes were on her, but she knew he was seeing only the parched trail eastward and a flock of tired, thirsty sheep.

"Fortunately, from here we are well on the way. It's not much over fifty miles. Four men, and I would hope to make it in about three days. There used to be a spring along the way, but it's probably dried up now, so I shall have to press on and give the animals very little rest."

"The sooner you go the better, I think," she ventured.

"At once. Tomorrow morning!" She had not seen him so happy, so hopeful, in longer than she could remember.

CHAPTER FORTY-THREE

THE FOLLOWING DAY, LONG BEFORE DAWN Miguel had already been out, putting the men to rounding up the sheep, and himself assembling the few necessary supplies for the drive to the mountains. Bets, hearing his movements, and the click of shotgun shells, the sharp clang of heavy spurs, threw a blanket around her and went to give him what help she could.

She was not the only one to have awakened.

"Father?" Tomas stood quietly in the door of his room, holding a lighted candle. His hair, matted in sleep, spiked up into an absurd cockscomb, but there was nothing ridiculous about the tense posture of his sturdy body, or the anxiety in his face. "What has happened?"

"Nothing, Tomas," Miguel answered. "Go back to bed. It won't be daylight for some time."

"I can't sleep," the boy said, but obedient as he always was, drew back. Miguel however, as though the child had suddenly pierced his preoccupation with the task ahead, said, "Wait, Tomas. Perhaps I can use your help after all. I want to start this sheep drive as quickly as possible. Will you run to the stables and see that my horse is saddled?"

"Oh, yes! Yes, Father!" The boy, still in his cotton nightshirt, leapt down the shadowed stairs.

"That was good of you, Miguel," Bets said. "He's so terribly lonely! I tried to persuade him to move to another bedroom, but he would not. It's too bad, as he doesn't sleep well in the room he shared with Pepe. When I suggested changing, he said a very strange thing. He said, 'If I leave, my brother will be gone from me altogether.' "

Miguel did not answer, but strode rapidly down the

staircase, while Bets reproached herself for mentioning Pepe. She knew better. It was always the same. Miguel seemed to curl inward at any reminder.

Not that she blamed him! For her too, the memory of their much loved son remained raw and painful. But it was a matter of sorrow to her also that Miguel did not attempt to comfort Tomas or return his love.

That he never would, had been impressed on her with finality the night after Pepe's funeral. Miguel, riding the hills in his angry unassuaged grief had not returned home until almost dawn.

She had said to him then, "Miguel, Tomas has been waiting for so very long, and he is stunned with grief. He's asked for you many times tonight."

When her husband did not reply, she pleaded, "Won't you go to him?"

"Now? He wouldn't be awake."

"What does that matter? He will want you to wake him."

But to her great disappointment, he shook his head. "I cannot." He'd walked close to where she lay in bed and stood looking down in the thin darkness. "You don't understand, do you? I would do anything, *everything* . . . if he were truly my son. But he is not."

You have two daughters still! The protest rose to her lips and was repressed. He loved them both, possibly as well as she, but they were no consolation to him.

He rasped suddenly, "How I wish I had never known!"

"I should not have told you?"

"Eh? Of course you should! Do I want to be deceived?"

"But—"

"Let's not discuss it. Not tonight of all nights." He threw himself fully clothed on the bed beside her, where he lay tense, hands clasped behind his head. After a while, he said with indifference, "Don't worry about Tomas. Tomorrow I will be kind to him. After all, none of this is his fault."

And he'd kept his word.

They reached the lower floor, to find Tia Pilar dressed and already preparing a morning repast. She scurried about, moving the heavy pots with unnecessary noise as a small protest against the hour, but there was no audible grumbling. Miguel's dish of *pinole* and a cup of chocolate were waiting for him.

He ate hurriedly, telling Tia Pilar between mouthfuls exactly what provisions he wished to take. She obeyed his orders silently and with the respect she always accorded him.

When Miguel went out to the stable with the laden saddlebags, Bets followed, wishing the impossible—that she too was to have a part in this sheep drive, so important for the rancho. Instead, she would have to endure the torment of waiting.

"We'll expect you back in about four days?"

"I can't say exactly. One never knows . . . Tomas, where is my horse?" He was peering into the gloomy stable as he spoke. Beyond the adobe structure, the sky was now orange-gray. The two cottonwoods that grew beside what in other years was a small stream, but now was only a dry gulch, loomed overhead, their heart-shaped leaves rustling with faint ghostly music in the light wind.

"Coming, Father," called Tomas, and the Indian stable boy led out Miguel's gelding, saddled. Just behind came Tomas himself, fully dressed for riding, and leading his own mare, also ready for the trail.

Miguel started. Bets quickly put her hand on his arm before he could speak.

"Careful," she murmured.

"What is this?" Miguel asked, his impatience to be away sharpening the words.

"Please, Father, may I come with you? I'm ten, soon to be eleven!"

Bets remembered with sharp pain how Pepe would have pleaded, the words tumbling out. He'd have had ten good reasons for being included. Not "I'm ten soon to be eleven," but "I can help you, Father! I can ride all day, I'm never tired, the sheep are used to me—they trust me. Oh, please Father, let me come!"

Though for Tomas to have thrust himself forward

at all must surely sway Miguel. Could he sense the hope and longing in the inadequate little speech?

Evidently he could. He sighed, no doubt wondering how much so young a rider would slow the drive, and said brusquely, "Very well. But there will be no stopping, understand? Not until I order a rest for the good of the animals."

It was an unnecessary admonition. Tomas would die before he displayed weakness or discommoded Miguel.

He said with assurance, "I won't want to rest!" and jumping onto the horse's back, he guided her into place behind his father's mount. Bets had no need of dawn's light to see the boy's shining eyes.

She would have liked to run to him, hug him, say a few motherly words, but recognizing his new adult status she contented herself with waving to them both, and then turned quickly toward the house. She could hear the thud of their horses' hooves, as they rode into the distance where the vaqueros awaited them with the flock.

Already visions of outlaws, murderous fiends who would have no compunction about killing a child, were racing through her mind. There would be little peace for her in the next few days!

She went indoors to tell Miguel's father what had been undertaken.

"They're gone, are they?" Don Sebastian was just asking Mary, the words slurred yet harsh, and difficult to understand.

So he knew! Bets hid her irritation. She watched her aunt plump up the pillow behind his head and begin to spoon the cut-up bits of tortilla into his mouth. Mary was the only one of the household able to feed the tyrant without adding to the fury that possessed him most of the time because of his growing immobility. Tia Pilar and Adam were permitted to perform more menial services; but eating, to him, had always been a dignified, highly formal ritual, and Mary, even though he must be agape like a hungry baby bird, somehow kept it so.

He swallowed the tortilla impatiently, and added, "I know everything that goes on on this rancho still, don't think I do not. The sheep go to the mountains!" He gave a little crow of triumph at his omniscience.

Mary said calmly, "That's true," but Bets, turning her face from him, continued to frown. They hadn't intended telling him about the new pasturage until the drive was under way, in case, as was most probable, he chose to be contrary and disapprove. But one of the range bosses must have visited him the night before, and had the information skillfully extracted. She prepared herself for Don Sebastian's reproaches.

"It is the only possible way to save them," he commented, surprising her. Then he further threw her off balance by surmising, "Elizabeth, you arranged for the pasture lease, I suppose?"

"Why would you think that?" she countered, but a second too late. His mouth twisted into what passed for a grim smile.

"My son has many talents, but the ability to negotiate with a man like Lucky Belknap is not one of them."

"Bets needed to do very little negotiating, as I understand it," Mary said. "You are full of surprises today, Don Sebastian. When did you hear of Mr. Belknap?"

"I have not always been bedridden," the old man said, affronted. "Nor a man of small consequence. Back in '59, long before Miguel saw his duty and brought his family here to live, Belknap was one of the first to appreciate what a bonanza of silver the Comstock was going to be. He wasn't wealthy then. He was just a shrewd, eager young man, and he needed partners. But I was already too crippled to ride, and I was also averse to taking a stranger's word for mines I hadn't seen and wouldn't see. Beyond that, there was another reason for refusing. He wasn't the sort I wanted for a partner. He was too coldblooded, too singleminded . . . Still, my caution was a mistake. I admit that now."

Bets left him brooding on his lost opportunity, and went to tell Adam his master was ready to be bathed.

In the night there was a small earthquake, nothing of any consequence, and hardly noticeable compared to the destructive and terrifying heaving and buckling that had taken place in '55 and again in '57. But as always, when the bed shook ever so little, Bets came awake instantly. Her first thought was to go to Tomas, but as the sleepy confusion cleared from her mind, and she remembered the boy was away on the trail with Miguel, she lay back, her pulse still pounding. Would another shock follow?

She had been more frightened than she cared to admit during her first earthquake, which had occurred when she and Miguel still lived in Los Angeles, and been so severe that afterward scarcely a dwelling remained undamaged. Patrick's town house was left with great cracks in the walls, and their own small box of a house, hers and Miguel's, lost its chimney and parts of the roof. But oddly, it was a harmless manifestation that had most terrified her. During the first rolling shake, which came at about eight o'clock in the evening, before Miguel came home from work, she had stared in disbelief as the floor seemed to rise and fall, pictures fell from the walls, and dishes rattled and smashed in their cupboards. Running wildly toward the door, infant Pepe at her shoulder and small Tomas gripped by the hand as he stumbled along beside her, she happened to glance at the water barrel. The unnatural sight of water bubbling and splashing and running over the sides was far worse to her than the shaking floor. Nausea rose in her throat, and she and the children fled outside.

But on this occasion, there was at the most one sharp tremor, and nothing more. As the minutes passed, her fear subsided, and she began to wonder if she alone had been awakened. No sounds came from Don Sebastian's room, and she concluded that the elderly Californio had lived through too many such disturbances to notice anything so minor. Mary, on the other hand was awake. Bets could hear the soft sound of her bare feet pacing the wooden floor. But then that too stopped.

No need to get up, Bets thought, drowsiness returning. The quake was gone, and for once it had done no harm.

How wrong that conclusion was, she was to learn when five days had passed and Miguel returned, later than he had calculated, by at least twenty-four hours.

He and Tomas came in alone, the other men having been left on guard in the mountains, in accord with the agreement with Belknap. The two riders approached slowly, their horses walking in a dispirited, tired shuffle, and the first words Miguel spoke were to the stable boy who came running.

"Rub the horses down well before you give them water, but do so as quickly as possible! They are tormented with thirst."

Tomas slid from his mare, but did not go immediately to be embraced by his mother. His eyes were on Miguel, and the anxiety in them warned Bets that something was amiss.

She and Mary had been outside gathering vegetables from the garden when they saw the dustcloud that at last heralded the anxiously awaited arrival. So both stood waiting with smiles of welcome that concealed relief. The chance of outlaw attacks had been very real, especially with such a small number of riders going out, and even fewer on the return—just a man and a boy! Bets feasted her eyes on Tomas and held herself back from running to him. It would not do, she thought, to let him know she'd worried. He had done a man's task and should be treated on his return as a man. Goodness knew, he would be a child again soon enough!

Miguel swung down from his horse, his face gray with a patina of fatigue.

"Tomas, ask Tia Pilar for food for both of us. Then when you've eaten, go to bed at once." In explanation to the two women, he added: "We've hardly stopped at all coming back. I knew you'd be worried about him, as late as we are."

"Worried about both of you," Bets intended to say, but his expression kept her silent, frightened her. He wasn't thinking about himself, or her.

"Yes, Father," Tomas mumbled. He was clearly on the verge of falling asleep in the yard. Stiff and sore from the long ride, he stumbled over a rock as he started away.

Miguel put a steadying hand on his shoulder and said, "You were a help to me, Tomas."

The boy flushed painfully and his bloodshot eyes shone. He turned away and ran toward the house.

"Thank you, Miguel," Bets said.

"What?" He stared at her uncomprehending. "Elizabeth, Mary, I must tell you what happened."

Bets could only imagine that the worst had occurred, to cause him to look so. "The sheep are dead?" Her voice rose in her consternation. "Surely you couldn't have—"

"Not all. No." He seemed unable to continue.

Mary, with a glance at Bets, said, "Don Sebastian has been asking to see you, Miguel, as soon as you came. But he's asleep, so if you and Betsey would like to talk privately—"

He gave her a brief grateful smile that faded instantly. "No. I'll go to him now. Please come with me, both of you. Then I can confess my failure and not have to relive and endure it—twice."

He strode away toward the house. Mary turned to follow, but Bets held her back, saying, "Why did you stop him? Why not let him tell us what went wrong? If the news is so bad, I don't care to hear Don Sebastian rant and gloat. The sheep are the important thing—"

"No, Betsey, Miguel is. I know you're on edge from the waiting, but can't you understand how he must feel? Let him tell his father and you together, and get it over! Then he can rest."

Bets, already tasting her bitter disappointment, did not answer.

"I see by your face the drive did not go well," Don Sebastian said at once.

"No," Miguel replied grimly, "I lost a part of the flock."

"Indeed. If you'd troubled to ask my help before you went, I'd have told you where there's a good water hole. A drive like that is too long for animals already badly weakened, to go without water. But of course no one, least of all my son, would think of consulting me, a cripple."

Miguel answered in a tired voice, "The sheep did not die for lack of water, Father. I knew where the hole was, and as it wasn't completely dry, we camped there. No, what was disastrous was the earthquake."

"An earthquake? When was there an earthquake?" rasped Don Sebastian, temporarily put out of countenance.

"In the night, Wednesday, when we were in the foothills. Didn't you feel it? Maybe not, because it was very mild. Still, for us, it was enough. The movement of the ground terrified the flock and at once they went crazy. Berserk. Running mindlessly in all directions.

"Had we been on horseback—or even able to see! But no, it was the middle of the night and no moonlight at all. The men were asleep on the ground, wrapped in their blankets, and we were taken by surprise. By the time we saddled, the sheep had scattered, stampeding through the rocks and the pines and chaparral . . . We spent the remainder of the night trying to find and gather them together, all of us working, even Tomas, shouting to each other in the darkness . . ."

He paused, his thin face mirroring the frustrations of those long hours. His hands clenched together and unclenched.

"There was no moon, but you might suppose the white blur of a sheep would be easy to see, and we did locate a number of them fairly soon. But what appeared to be a sheep would be a big rock. Or what moved, with a scattering of pebbles, was another animal altogether, a deer, a startled hare, or a coyote. The task after a few hours had elapsed became difficult, almost hopeless—"

"I sympathize, as do the ladies," Don Sebastian cut in. "But I for one do not care to hear more excuses. How many of these valuable sheep did you fail to retrieve?"

"Six," Miguel said. His exhaustion had turned his voice hoarse. "And two more were found dismembered. One had been killed by a bear, and the other by a wildcat."

"But Miguel, out of three hundred-odd sheep, that is nothing!" Bets exclaimed. In her relief, she was delighted. "Only six lost!"

"Eight," corrected her father-in-law. "And kind as it may be to reassure your husband, even you must see that a proper watch should have been set. Then those eight would be safe still."

"I don't agree with you," Bets said, setting her chin. "I'm sure Miguel was prepared for anything except an earthquake. And who would have expected that?"

"For a leader, being on guard against all unexpected things, Elizabeth, is the first step beyond mediocrity. I'm sorry, my dear, but I doubt if Miguel wishes commendation when he deserves none. Nor does he need to hide behind your skirts. Am I right, my son?"

Miguel returned his father's stare with dead eyes. How exhausted he was, Bets thought, and in her indignation she would have spoken out again, had her husband not answered first.

"Yes, you are right, Father. I cannot accept a woman's defense, but only I suspect, because I am not man enough to be humble. In time, who knows? Perhaps I will learn better."

He had learned better, it seemed, after Don Sebastian suffered his final paralysis, and at the moment of death was either unwilling or unable to indicate confidence in his son. Giving way only once to an outburst of incredulous and bitter anger, Miguel had chosen to believe his father indeed had bequeathed the responsibility for the rancho to Bets. He withdrew into his study, began to write his history of Mexico, and never again, so far as anyone knew, permitted himself to agonize over the problems of the estate.

CHAPTER FORTY-FOUR

TEO WAS FINDING HER WORK WITH DOCTOR Kramer the most satisfying thing she had ever done.

How odd it was, she often thought in simple wonder, that something so very important could result from a friend's casual request, one too minor to think twice about. For it had been just such a plea by Elvira McCarty, that placed her on the Wilmington dock the one night in her life it would matter.

Elvira was not a close friend—Bets was Teo's only really close friend. But Elvira's company helped her over a hard time. She and Patrick had not been married long, he was still an invalid from his gunshot wound, and she herself was little better, trembling at any startling noise, and fearful of sleeping because of the dreams. It was pleasant to spend a frequent hour or two with someone like Elvira who said funny, even irreverent things. With her, life was less serious.

Arcadia Stearns had introduced them after a talk with Teo in which, unbeknownst to Elvira of course, she had pleaded, as much as Arcadia ever did, for Teo's help.

"I'll tell you frankly, Teodocia, Abel is worried that Lieutenant McCarty may ask for a transfer back to the East, and his departure would be, well, a difficulty, as Abel still does business with the Army. The Lieutenant's young wife is restless, I've heard, and bored. It's very worrisome."

"Perhaps I could help to entertain her," Teo suggested timidly.

"Would you? Just for a while?" The offer was not, obviously, unexpected. "You two are the same age and should have a few interests in common—certainly more than she and I have! Although even you may find her a trifle . . . Well, dear, these difficult times of war place burdens on us all.

"Let's see . . . you might invite her for coffee and some of that light cake your Flora makes, doubtless similar to what Elvira was accustomed to in New York. Then, if nothing else occurs to you, ask her to go with you to Drum Barracks to see the camels. They're the one thing that seems to interest her here. I've heard her remark tactlessly, at least a dozen times, how odd it seems for camels to be anywhere in the United States, even in this *very odd* California."

Arcadia was referring to an acquisition by the local military establishment of a number of camels, ordered there by Jefferson Davis, Secretary of War, on the theory the animals would be excellent supply vehicles for use on the deserts of the Southwest. Occasionally, a train of them lumbered through Los Angeles, carrying supplies destined for Tucson and Fort Mojave, and causing a sensation in the town. The goggle-eyed crowd of spectators was not confined to children.

Teo, not averse to seeing camels herself, did as requested, and after that, there were other frequent excursions. She was particularly grateful for Elvira's company a few months later, when she was stronger and might have returned then to St. Vincent's, but discovered she was with child. The heavy labor she'd done before at the school was not to be thought of, and considering Patrick's needs, it seemed best she remain at home. Thrilled as she was at the prospect of becoming a mother she dreaded the long months of inactivity ahead, and enjoyed Elvira the more.

So, when Lieutenant McCarty was ordered to San Francisco for a week on Army business, and Elvira suggested Teodocia accompany her to Wilmington to see him off, Teo at once agreed. She would enjoy the bustle of the departing passengers, and be able to imagine a happy day in the future when Patrick, well once more, would take her north on a ship to see the city she had heard so much of, and never seen.

They arrived at the wharf a little before five in the evening, after a pleasant drive in an official Army carriage. Lieutenant McCarty kissed his wife and boarded the small steamer *Ada Hancock* which was at the dock, puffing smoke, all ready to carry its second and final load of passengers out to the *Senator*. The larger ship lay at anchor down the bay, out of sight behind Dead Man's Island.

The two women stood watching the travelers stream aboard, most of them with laughing excited faces. There were a number of families, but Teo, because of her own happy secret, followed with her eyes most avidly a young couple with a child of about six months. Their obvious absorption in the baby pleased her, and she fell to wondering whether her own would be a pretty little girl like this one, and if so, what her name should be. She felt disappointed when the little family disappeared into the cabin of the ship, but then she caught a glimpse of Phineas Bishop. When she waved, he walked over to them.

Teo introduced Elvira, and busy as he was with the loading at his docks, Bishop doffed his hat and greeted her with his usual respectful courtesy, remarking truthfully that any friend of Miss Teodocia's was welcome. If the facilities of his wharf could be of service to either of the ladies, they had only to ask.

As he too was sailing that evening on the *Senator,* he could not remain longer with them, and indeed his burly figure was the last across the gangplank before the sailors were throwing off the oil-stained lines. The small steamer, chugging a cloud of black smoke, backed away, turned, and headed out toward the choppy water of the roadstead.

Teo was quiet, thinking again how exciting such a journey must be, as she watched the *Ada Hancock* steam away. After a while, afar off, she could see the vessel begin to career from side to side as it encountered turbulence, and she started to remark on this to Elvira, but the words were never uttered. For at that moment there was a distant boom, and then an orange ball seemed to envelope the steamer.

Before their disbelieving eyes, the *Ada Hancock* disintegrated, blown apart, with timbers flying in all directions and minute doll-like figures of people propelled into the air, into the water, some still moving, some already limp in death.

Thin screaming began, distant and faint, but audible.

"Oh, God—" Elvira cried, her hands hard against her open mouth. Everyone staring from the wharf appeared likewise paralyzed by shock.

Then a tall gaunt man whom Teo recognized as Frank Lecouvreur, Phineas Bishop's bookkeeper, came running from his office, waving his arms and shouting to the dock workers to hurry—to jump down into any small boats they could find, and row out—and suddenly there was a spate of activity, and the spectators were pushed aside. Some of these had just put relatives and friends on the *Ada Hancock* and they shrieked anguished questions to which no one knew the answers. Their own eyes could tell them there was death out on that water, but not how many were still alive, nor who. Yet the piteous inquiries continued.

Teo, her arms around the sobbing Elvira, murmured soothingly, "He's all right, I'm sure he is, we'll know soon—" But she wasn't sure. She really hadn't much hope. They could only wait to find out.

At last several small boats had reached the hotly flaming wreck and were circling; the dock men could be seen hoisting bodies in over the bobbing gunwales, usually with difficulty because their burdens were inert. Teo was haunted by the memory of the faces she'd seen lit with anticipation only minutes before.

Several grotesquely laden skiffs soon started the long row back, and Teo suddenly wondered, with horror, what would happen when they landed. The dead didn't matter now; they were beyond suffering, but the burned, the wounded—

"Wait here a moment, Elvira! I'll be right back."

Hardly hearing her friend's protest, she ran to the entrance of the large warehouse.

"Mr. Lecouvreur?"

The bookkeeper, his wire-framed glasses askew on his nose, was engaged in hauling boxes of freight off the low platforms that occupied much of the floor

space. He glanced up at her frowning, while his hands
and back continued their steady work.

"Forgive me, but I wondered—is a doctor coming?
One will be desperately needed, and very soon. The
first boat is landing now!"

"I sent at once to Fort Drum, Miss. Doctors and
soldiers too will be coming—as well as help from the
Senator—they'll have heard the boom of the explosion."

He turned his back to hoist a crate, but he must
have realized she was staring at him in wonderment,
because he said, "These loading stands have to be
emptied. They'll be useful—to lay out the wounded."

"Yes." She fled back outside where the first boat was
tying up.

Then, like the others waiting there, she could only
stare in stricken horror. For only one of the injured
was able to climb out unassisted. His face blackened,
a bleeding arm held across his chest, he moved slowly
and wearily. It was Lieutenant McCarty, but Teo had
no eyes for him. She was rivetted by the remainder of
the boat's contents. Bodies of men, women, children,
some with missing limbs, their festive clothing torn and
burnt, lay on the floor boards and across the thwarts.
Even the badly burned made little noise, apparently
too shocked by the enormity of what had happened to
feel pain. Only one victim moaned loudly, a young
woman who was sitting bolt upright, clutching the
bleeding end of her leg from which the foot had been
torn away.

The rowers sat dazed at their oars, as though now
they had ferried this grisly cargo ashore, they were at
a loss what to do with it.

Teo stood aghast as well, until she came to herself
with a jolt. That red pool beneath the seat of the girl
with the severed leg was fast widening! Blood spurted
down to it in a fountain.

She caught up a coil of light line from the dock and
threw it down to the oarsman nearest her.

"You must tie the stump," she cried, pointing. "And
tightly, at once, or it will be too late!"

Then behind her, Lecouvreur appeared, barking

commands, and the spell was broken. She stood back while the victims, living and dead, were manhandled onto the dock. The task needed to be done quickly as other boats were arriving, and as soon as one of the injured was swung up onto the wooden planks, he was carried by a workman or one of the arrived soldiers, into the warehouse.

A very large middle-aged man required the help of two, one grasping his shoulders, the other his feet, while he sagged, unconscious, between them. A child of seven or eight, crying softly, with flesh torn from his leg in a strip and still hanging, ran along at the side, his hand clenched tightly on the man's sleeve.

The crying woman was now ashore, still in an upright position, still clutching her leg. The stump had been tied, but too loosely, and Teo knelt beside her. She tightened the slimy wet line, while the once-pretty face, now visibly graying, gazed at her sightlessly.

"That's right," said a man's voice. "And perhaps you'd best stay with her, Mrs. Donovan, in case the jostling dislodges it."

She glanced up, to find Dr. Emil Kramer, hands in tight fists, surveying the scene. She, like Patrick, had confidence in him as a doctor, and if asked, would have described him as sober and calm. But observing his posture and expression, she realized she had not, until now, known him at all. At this moment, gazing at the carnage before them, he was clearly consumed by rage.

Abruptly he turned on his heel, as though forcing a lid down on his emotions, and gestured for a soldier to carry the woman away.

Teo scrambled to her feet to follow, and all at once caught sight of a baby lying nearby, the same child she had admired in those happy minutes of embarkation. The little thing was alive, and apparently, by some miracle, uninjured, not even crying. It lay like a stranded beetle on its back and was trying in happy absorption, to catch with one tiny hand a waving foot still encased in a neat white stocking. The other foot was bare, the covering having been blown off in the blast.

As the infant was in imminent danger of being crushed by the boots of those rushing past, Teo snatched it up. Then she looked around her, searching the confused scene for the parents, and finding them almost right away. The drowned father looked peaceful in death, but the mother had met a more violent fate, and Teo averted her eyes after a single glance. Carrying the child, she ran after Dr. Kramer and the woman she'd been told to watch.

Afterward, she could remember mercifully little of the long hours that followed. The dead were laid in neat rows outside, because there was only room for the living in the warehouse, and some of those cases were so clearly hopeless, she wondered if she would ever blot their agonized faces from her brain. But they were so many, they tended to merge, leaving only a confusion of disjointed memories.

In the first few minutes, Elvira had edged into the building, vast relief on her face at finding Teo so quickly, and said, "Goodness, what are you doing in this dreadful place? Roger's alive—merely a little hurt. We're going home! Hurry!"

"I can't leave yet. You go, it will be all right."

"Oh, don't be silly! You'll just be in the way here. Why on earth—"

Dr. Kramer, from somewhere several platforms away, called, "Mrs. Donovan, if you'll just hold this man still for me . . ."

Teo said firmly to Elvira, "No," and started away. Then remembering the baby still in her arms, she thrust it at Elvira. "Take this child away from here. You can do that! Take her home with you and feed her."

"I don't know anything about babies," Elvira wailed.

"Take her!"

Later, there was the moment when Phineas Bishop was brought in, unconscious and apparently more dead than alive. But after the first ripple of dismay had gone through the room, for most of those there knew or worked for him, there was a shout of, "He's all right.

Just a blow on the head and he's coming round." And attention returned to the seriously wounded.

From time to time, trailing after the doctor, she heard snatches of meaningful words . . .

"The boat careened and cold water run into the engine room, and the boiler blew! God! Ripped her apart to the water line! Them what got off was lucky—"

Lucky? Teo stared down at a woman whose arm, the bone sticking out whitely, the doctor was just then amputating. Lucky, yes in one sense, for at this moment she was unconscious.

Others were not. There was a harrowing din of screams and moans. Although an Army surgeon had also arrived, many of the injured had not yet received any of the blessed, pain-numbing laudanum, or even been examined. Of the fifty or so who had ridden out on the *Ada Hancock,* only four walked away from the wharf afterward, and between thirty and forty people lay on the hard platforms, some of them now very still, as still as their friends placed side by side beyond the door. The pretty woman with the stump of a leg was one of those.

Teo in these early months of pregnancy had been fighting nausea. But oddly enough, here in this scene from hell with the smoky light of lanterns, the screams of pain, and the smells of vomit, urine, blood and human terror, she felt no queasiness at all. She found herself doing exactly as ordered, with no quivering of the hands or averting of eyes. Outside of giving her a sharp glance or two in the beginning, the doctor seemed indifferent to her feelings, and as she continued to be of use, her tasks multiplied and became more responsible. Even after men trained in nursing arrived from the army base, the two worked on together.

Eventually, the long night ended. By dawn, there was nothing more the doctors needed to do desperately and at once. The Army took charge, just as though this wharf had been a battlefield and they were caring for casualties. Teo was idle for the first time, and she who had never really thought about war and its aftermath,

imagined it now. Overwhelmed, and longing for the
fresh air outside, she walked wearily toward the door.

A middle-aged woman was just entering, and she
said to Teo, "I'm Mrs. Johnston. Please tell me—
would you know, is my son all right?"

Teo, made slow-witted by exhaustion, gaped at
her. She recognized Mrs. Albert Sidney Johnston, the
widow of the General Johnston who had died at Shiloh, a woman who in other circumstances would have
greeted her by name, but at this moment had no
thought for anyone except her missing son.

"He's outside on the dock, Mrs. Johnston," Dr.
Kramer said quietly from behind Teo. "Ah, here's Mr.
Lecouvreur . . . Frank, will you take care of Mrs.
Johnston?"

Lecouvreur offered her his arm and the two passed
from view. Suddenly there were piercing cries from
the dignified, usually stolid woman. Teo started to go
out to her, but Dr. Kramer put his arm across the
doorway.

"No," he said, and she saw he was supporting himself with that arm against the frame. His face in the
morning light was drawn with fatigue. "There will be
many others like her, all day. It is only beginning.
Come, you must go home."

She did not protest. In fairness to her unborn child,
she needed to rest, and she knew it.

They walked out silently to his worn black phaeton.
The only thing he said on the long drive back to Los
Angeles was, "Mrs. Donovan, you are a natural-born
nurse."

She didn't see him again until the night of her
baby's birth. She was quite unafraid, even when the
spasms were acute, being convinced he would see her
safely through it. They worked together as they had
on the wharf, he knowing what was needed, and she
obeying his orders exactly. After her last gasping effort had produced the baby, she felt a warm glow of
accomplishment, and gratitude as well.

He, however, became very polite and quite formal.
He said to Patrick, who was admiring Brian with un-

concealed joy, "I've been intending to apologize to you, sir. I had no idea your wife was with child when I permitted her to spend so many hours tiring herself, during the *Ada Hancock* disaster."

"Eh?" Patrick glanced up at him in surprise. "No, I never supposed you did. No doubt you had other things on your mind that night."

"Yes. However, I appreciate your understanding . . . My congratulations on your son, and now I'll bid you good night." He nodded to Patrick, intending it seemed to say nothing to her. But then he halted at the door and looked back toward the bed.

"What became of that infant?" he asked. "The one you found on the dock?"

"The McCarty's kept her," Teo answered. "Elvira didn't want to at first, and we put notices in the newspapers, here and in San Francisco too, for relatives, although it was hopeless from the start. We didn't even know the names of the parents! Then, after a while, even though we were expecting a child of our own, Patrick and I offered to take the little girl. But Elvira surprised us. She wouldn't give her up."

Dr. Kramer smiled at Teo, and she realized it was the first time in their sporadic meetings he had ever done so. "I wondered. Thank you."

He placed his worn, broad-brimmed hat on his head and departed, and Teo forgot him in the ecstasy of admiring her son.

She had once told Bets, and believed it to be true, that all she desired in life was husband and child. So for a number of months she lingered without regret in a state of near idleness, Brian demanding very little of her except nursing and love. Then one morning it struck her as absurd, even wasteful for one tiny baby, no matter how beautiful, to have two capable women like herself and Flora waiting on him so slavishly. Patrick could be counted on in a pinch, and even Flower liked nothing better than to sit, holding Brian, in the same simple rocker Jeb had made so many years before for her own babyhood, and crooning to him in exact imitation of her mother. Flower's eyes, on those occasions, were less vacant than usual. They shone with love.

Teo hesitantly suggested to Patrick she would like, just for a few hours a day, to help out at St. Vincent's, and he agreed. If there was any hint that he might not really be enthusiastic, and was answering so quickly to avoid any thought of keeping her home out of duty to *him* she failed to recognize it, and went off happily one morning to her former work.

The day was a deep disappointment, even though Sister Barbara and the other older nuns were so pleased to see her. By afternoon, she knew there was no longer need for her there.

Father Daniel, whom she had seen little of during the day, appeared as she was leaving, and accompanied her out the door. When they were a little distance away, he stopped. She noted without enthusiasm his clean coat and spotless collar.

"My child, I see you are disturbed."

"Yes, Father. I love St. Vincent's . . . and now there's no place for me."

He said wryly, "I sometimes wonder if there's a place for me! But the children are plainly benefiting from the additional supervision, which is what matters. They will miss you, you know. They all loved you."

Teo said nothing. He was frowning as though trying to make up his mind, and at length said, "I wonder . . . I've known you a long time and I might offer a suggestion. Yes, I will. Teodocia, Dr. Kramer told me how splendid you were the night of the ship disaster."

"He mentioned me—to you?"

"He said you were of great help. Now, perhaps you don't know this, but he is not at all strong. His heart is damaged, and it is only a miracle of the good God's that he survived the last epidemic. Yet he works harder than three other men, and always alone."

The priest paused, and Teo asked, "He has no wife?"

"No, unfortunately. When things were so very bad here during the drought, the young woman he was beginning to care for insisted he must return with her to a more comfortable life in New York, and when he

refused, she wept but departed with her parents . . .
Teodocia, the doctor has little money, not enough to
pay a nurse, even if one were available. If you want
to devote yourself to good works, why not assist him?
Take some of the load from him?"

"But I know nothing! Oh, Father, how could I help
him?"

"One learns by watching and doing. Tell me, that
night—did he ask you to do anything beyond your
capabilities?"

"No . . . Nothing was too difficult."

"Many women would have found just being in that
charnel house intolerably difficult," he commented.
When she did not answer, he asked, "May I suggest to
him you would be willing?"

Teo looked up then at this good man whom she had
revered so long, and the respect for herself she could
detect in his face brought tears to her eyes. Gladness
welled inside her.

"Yes, Father," she said, "I would like that. Oh, I
would!"

So the matter was arranged.

Dr. Emil Kramer called the next evening and clos-
eted himself with Patrick. In a short time, both men
came into the parlor where she sat with the baby.

The young doctor said to her, "Your husband has
given his permission for me to train you as a nurse,
and at the same time have the benefit of your services.
Naturally, with a young infant, you won't want to
spend more than an hour or so each day. Shall I call
for you about nine o'clock tomorrow morning?"

How stern he looked! Had she once imagined she
saw him smile?

"Well, Teo?" Patrick said. "Do you want to? Or
have you had a change of mind? You may refuse if
you like, my dear."

"Certainly, she may," the doctor said stiffly.

"No," Teo rubbed her finger softly against little
Brian's cheek. "I will be ready at nine."

CHAPTER FORTY-FIVE

BY THE TIME DON SEBASTIAN HAD BEEN DEAD almost two years, Bets was lulled into believing the fortunes of the rancho were secure. Then, without warning, the frightening truth emerged.

Her father-in-law, shrewd as he was, had been no different from other Californios in his approach to finance. He too had borrowed on his land during boom times, perhaps for additional herds of cattle, perhaps to support his enormous household of servants, perhaps merely for a luxury that caught his eye. After all, saddles owned by all the compadres were trimmed with solid silver, and spurs were gold. Their ladies wore tortoise-shell combs as costly as jewels, and silk gowns trimmed with intricate foreign lace.

The lending of money in the days before the first bank appeared, was the function of the local merchants, and interest rates were often enormous. The old Don had not played the fool as badly as one fellow Californio who mortgaged seventeen thousand acres at a rate of five percent per month; but Rancho Aguirre's debt was respectable, all the same.

Miguel tried to explain this to Bets when, white-faced and shaken, she came to find him in his study. The mortgage holder, a Basque named Gaston Larronde was even then waiting below, apologetic but firm. He wanted his money.

"But this can't be!" Bets stammered to Miguel.

Rancho Aguirre in trouble? How was it possible? Had she become careless? No, far from it. Phineas, visiting with them on his way back from one of his numerous swings about the state, had only this morning complimented her on the fine condition of the rancho!

And she'd been happy. After she strolled with him a

little distance out to see the fat, healthy sheep, then the three of them, Phineas and Miguel and she had enjoyed a delicious noon meal together while Phineas brought them up to date on the news. Sad news, as it happened. An opulent Sacramento River steamboat, the *Yosemite* had blown to pieces under way, killing forty passengers and maiming many more.

"Sometimes I think your father is right, Elizabeth," Miguel had observed. He too, she could see, was savoring this small party in his own gracious dining room. "Patrick hates modern ships—says they are dirty and dangerous—and dangerous at least they're proving to be. I would guess at least ten of those river boats have been lost in the last fifteen years, wouldn't you say, Phineas?"

"Yes, but it's not the fault of the ships. The captains are to blame! The fools stoke up the boilers to top speed, and race! As for dirty—you could hardly say that about the *Yosemite*. She was a real beauty—with red plush upholstery, marble-topped tables, gilt mirrors, and the like. All the politicians liked to travel on her—going from San Francisco to the capitol. I've done it several times myself, and when the casualty list comes out, there'll be friends of mine on it, I'll be bound.

"Ah, well, let's not talk about it! On such a fine occasion, we can find a happier subject."

"Tell us about the transcontinental railroad," Miguel suggested. "Ever since '62 when President Lincoln signed the bill, I've been waiting to hear work has been started. There've been so many rumors."

"It's more than rumors now! Union Pacific tracks are inching westward from the Missouri and at this end crews have started the nearly impossible task of finding a way through the steep Sierra Mountains. The Big Four of the Central Pacific—Stanford, Huntington, Hopkins and Crocker—are as tough as any men I've met, and if anyone can succeed, they will."

Phineas chuckled suddenly. "I must tell you something! As you know, I'm waging my own little battle for a local rail line. So last week I visited in the home of Charles Crocker, who is responsible for actually getting track laid, and the one who was shrewd enough to recognize the industry and endurance of the Chinese. After his own workers—and who could blame them!—stayed on that miserable job only long enough to get stage money for the Nevada silver mines, he recruited two thousand Chinese to do the hard pick and shovel work—using one-horse dump carts and black powder to blast through solid rock walls. There'll be more of them too, as ships loaded to the gunwales have begun to arrive from Hong Kong.

"But what I wanted to tell you about, was in his house. He was once a dry-goods merchant in Sacramento and doesn't lack in any way for money. Now are you prepared? In the place of honor in the parlor, over the most immense fireplace you ever saw, is a large watercolor by Mary Reyes!"

"Wonderful!" Miguel said, his eyes glowing. "I'll have to write and tell her. Which picture is it?"

"As I remember, it was called *A Street in Aspinwall*. Crocker bought it from Milo Gallery and paid a pretty penny, so he said."

Seeing Miguel so drawn out of himself, Bets had thought complacently that their lives were at last on an even keel, and from now on could be enjoyed without worry. Occasions of this kind enticed Miguel from his seclusion, and she must try in the future to have more of them.

And now this! Not more than an hour after Phineas's departure.

She stared at Miguel, who was speaking with an unnatural calmness that further frightened her. "Gaston Larronde has finally come, has he? Ah. I'd hoped, as we missed the interest payment last year and he said nothing, he might have decided to wait for his principal until we were able to pay. I see now such forbearance would be too much to ask of anyone—"

"What do you mean—we missed an interest payment? I didn't find any note of money due on the books! In God's name," she burst out, "Why didn't you tell me of this?"

But he refused to respond to her agitation. "Father and he had an informal agreement, whereby Larronde bought hides from us and simply deducted the payments as they were due. An excellent plan, until of course there were no more hides! I didn't tell you because, as I say, I hoped it would not be necessary. But you've managed very well, and why frighten you, when there was nothing to be done? Five thousand dollars is impossible to raise."

"So much! Oh, Miguel! How could your father have borrowed so much?"

Miguel shrugged. "He was not alone. And if the price of cattle had held, there would have been no problem. Who could have guessed the halcyon days would end! Do you know, I would enjoy seeing and talking to Larronde. It's a pity I shan't, because he's an interesting fellow, one whom others would do well to emulate. He came to California about fifteen years ago. His wife took in washing and he delivered the clean clothes. They soon saved enough to start a business in which the hides were put to use, and—"

"Miguel, stop! Do you think I care a fig about the life of Gaston Larronde? Where are we going to get the money to pay him, tell me that!" Suddenly she realized the significance of what he had said. "What do you mean, it's a pity you won't see him? He's below now, and asking for you!"

"No, Elizabeth." He shook his head. "Tell him anything you like, tell him I'm sick, tell him I've gone away. But this is one of the things Father left in your care—his debt." He added courteously, but leaving her in no doubt he meant what he said, "I have no solution. My talking to Larronde will solve nothing, and I certainly will not lie to him and say he is soon to receive his money. So, being without inspiration, I am content to leave the matter with you."

Already he was retreating into his sanctuary, shutting her out.

She stared in disbelief at the closed door, wanting to pound on the carved panels and scream her protests like a fishwife. Only the knowledge that a raised voice could be heard below stairs restrained her.

She was to soothe Larronde? Or was she expected to

lie because Miguel himself was too honorable to do
so?

Bets clutched the stair rail and took deep breaths,
trying to regain some measure of calm. Then, because
she had no choice, she slowly descended to the parlor
where the rotund Basque was waiting.

"My husband is unwell, Mr. Larronde! He sends his
apologies."

"I am sorry to hear that, Madam." The humble
expression on the plump, middle-aged face, hardened
into a dogged determination that she understood. He
would have no mercy, and why should he? A man who
had risen, by dint of hard thankless labor, to being rich
enough to lend money!

She had intended to try persuasion, to point out that
the rancho in another year or so would be solidly productive again, thanks to the sheep and to a small grove
of walnuts which seemed to be doing well. But instinct
told her now that any pleading, no matter how reasonable, would be a mistake.

"Does Señor Aguirre understand the situation? The
note is due. I let the interest date pass, out of consideration, but my wife is not well, and I need the money.
If I am not repaid completely in seven days, I shall be
forced to foreclose."

Foreclose. The ugly word, pointing up the reality
of her family's peril, started a film of sweat on her
palms. But the clenched telltale hands remained hidden
in the folds of her multicolored skirt.

"I do not like to do this, madam. I am not a hard
person, but every penny I have was earned by my own
aching back and that of my wife. I will not give money
away!"

"I understand." Bets was surprised herself at how
calmly she said, "Mr. Larronde, I wish to tell you, the
money will be sent to you in time. We appreciate the
additional week's grace."

Her assurance gave him pause. "Señor Aguirre is
able to pay? Frankly, I'm astonished. I know the condition of most of the ranchos hereabouts, and this one
had the same hard times as the rest. Worse possibly,

because of its location. If he is counting on obtaining a bank loan, there are none available."

"Where he procures the money is surely of no interest to you?"

"No, and I will be pleased if he finds it. I do not want to see him lose his land! But I *will* be paid."

"Yes, you will. You—you have my word on it!"

"And that is good enough," he said politely. "Very well, I will take my leave. Pray tell the Señor I hope his health improves as rapidly as his fortunes seem to have done."

Alone again, Bets stood irresolutely at the foot of the stairs, trying to find an excuse for not telling Miguel without delay what she had done. Might he not be engrossed once more in his ancient tomes, and only look at her blankly if she disturbed him? No, that was foolish! In a matter of such importance, even if he would not admit his worry, it was there, eating at him. She must go up, confess the sorry truth—that she had given her word, doubtless construed by Larronde as Miguel's word, to an outright lie.

And it was a lie, she well know, now that she could think more clearly, which her husband had never intended. Being human, he had insisted that she, having been designated to authority by his father, should be the one to utter the heartbreaking final words of defeat, thus placing their much loved land on the block. She was to have spared him that odious task, but done that and nothing more. Five thousand dollars might not be the largest sum in the world, but it was just as unobtainable as twenty thousand or one hundred thousand.

Or was it? The possibility ran through her mind. Patrick's fortunes seemed to have improved. Wasn't Allison becoming productive again? Or there was Phineas Bishop, who had always been willing to help her. He had, with his various successful ventures, enough money surely! But perhaps he was one of those men who never let cash accumulate, but poured it immediately into something new. She didn't know, and if that were so, if she asked his assistance and he couldn't give it, she would have further humiliated Miguel, and for nothing.

Just above her head, she heard the door open, and the prospect of an immediate confrontation decided her. She fled through the hacienda, calling to Tia Pilar to tell the Señor she had gone to Los Angeles, and beckoning Adam to accompany her.

Throughout the long ride on horseback, she was silent, indifferent even to the spectacle of a great golden eagle spiraling overhead, a majestic sight which ordinarily would have given her a thrill of pleasure. So much hung, she was thinking, on a simple yes or no from her father, or if necessary from Phineas. Suppose both answers were no? Ah, they must not be! What would follow was unthinkable!

On arriving at last, in the late afternoon, in the familiar streets of the town, she awoke to the exhilaration of coming home, and her natural optimism began to prevail. She turned her horse toward Patrick's house, telling herself that somehow, somewhere, she would raise the money.

And her father's shout of welcome seemed a good omen. It had been so long, he was so dear, and he was so glad to see her!

"Where's Teo?" she asked, as he helped her dismount.

"She'll be back any minute now. Bless her heart, she's never out late with Dr. Kramer . . . Adam, you look so wiry and strong, I'll expect you to be working soon for Charles Crocker on the railroad."

Adam, baffled as always as much by Patrick's jovial humor as by his phrasing, merely smiled toothily and bobbed his head, whereupon Patrick laughed, clapping him on the shoulder. "Never mind. I know you'd never leave Bets and Miguel."

"Oh, Papa, how are you?" Bets cried, quickly adding, "You look fine," although absorbed as she was in her own problem, she'd noted with a pang the deep lines pain had etched in his face. She didn't wait for his answer, knowing it would be a hearty denial of the truth but after signalling Adam with a glance, giving him leave to go and care for the animals, and unable to endure the suspense longer, she commented, "I noticed all the new vineyards as I came into town. I suppose yours are producing well too?"

As she hoped, he didn't notice her abruptness.

"Yes, I should have a crop this year. Finally the vines are bearing. I'll tell you frankly, though Bets, it will be a near thing. Between the sheep and the grapes, I should get out of debt at last, and a tremendous relief it will be. Living on a knife edge taught me one lesson —no more borrowing!"

"You too! But I would have thought— Surely Doña Violeta, being Teo's mother—she wouldn't have stood by and watched you go under?"

"Wouldn't she? Perhaps not in the final extremity. Ah, but I'd have hated to need ask! She has refused to throw a life line to everyone else, no matter how close a friend. And do you know, I admire her more than ever. She's tough, she has had to be to survive, but she's clear-eyed. She knew such loans as she could make would be useless sentimental gestures, and no real help. She'd have only sunk herself as well."

"I suppose so." Bets looked once more at the fact that her first and easiest prospect had faded, and then dismissed the disappointment. Tomorrow she would approach Phineas. He would not fail her.

Phineas did fail her, without ever knowing that he had.

When she and Adam arrived at Wilmington the following day, she approached the warehouse confidently. Bishop, it was well known, habitually spent his mornings there conferring with the bookkeeper, Frank Lecouvreur, about his growing skein of transportation enterprises.

A slender, olive-skinned young man, strikingly handsome, stood by a high table in Lecouvreur's office, adding a long column of figures. He glanced up at her entrance, and flashed a ready smile.

"Señora? Might I be of assistance?"

The question, in English, betrayed an old-world Spanish accent, and she wondered briefly who he was, as upper-class newcomers from Spain, like those from Mexico, usually found their way into Arcadia's graces. However, her mind was filled with the need to speak to Phineas.

"Señor Bishop, please. Will you tell him it's Señora Aguirre?"

"Oh, I am sorry, Señora! He is not here today." He could hardly have helped noting her expression of dismay, she may even have paled, because he added with an air of concern in which there was also curiosity, "Perhaps some one else can assist you? I myself?"

"That's all right, Mr. Real," Lecouvreur, who had just entered, said sharply. "Get on with your work. I will take care of any visitors . . . Madam, please come with me." He offered his arm, and as he guided her out onto the wharf, muttered, "I prefer not to discuss anything before that young man. We know nothing about him, but almost at once, from the day he stepped off a ship from Panama, he's been on the rise. Even Phineas likes him and has made him my assistant. It is possible, I say, to be entirely too trusting."

"Mr. Lecouvreur, is it true Mr. Bishop is away? I have an important business matter to discuss."

"Then I am sorry to have to tell you this. When he returned yesterday there was an urgent message waiting and he left at once for the north. He'll be gone most of the month and I can't even say where he is, as he's travelling about the state, drumming up support for his own Wilmington-Los Angeles rail line. But in another several weeks, you can reach him in Sacramento."

"Sacramento?" she repeated, thinking how little several weeks sounded, when by then for her it would be far too late.

"He's a state senator now. Had you forgotten?" Crusty Lecouvreur actually smiled, inviting her to share his pride in his employer. "Even our Mr. Bishop does have to spend time in the state capitol on occasion!"

"Camellito, I must speak to you privately!"

"Bets! Fine to see you! Of course, dear friend, come

this way. I have a small office I used to occupy frequently in making loans, but of late it's only gathering dust. Here, please sit down. Tell me, how is Miguel? And the children?"

"All in good health, thank you. But Camellito, I've come to you in desperation. Gaston Larronde has given us just seven days to raise the five thousand dollars we owe him, and if we cannot, we lose the rancho! I trust the bank will lend us the money?"

His broad smile had faded, and his eyes failed to meet hers.

"You too?" he murmured. "Bets, you must know, if I could possibly help you, I would. But I haven't been able to make a loan in months! The bank has no liquidity."

"Liquidity? What does that mean? I thought, if I could show you just how we intend to repay the money next year, when there'll be wool to sell, it was the business of the bank to assist us—"

"No liquidity simply means there is no cash to lend." Camellito sounded very tired. "We have none, Bets. Not at present. The truth is, I gave far too many loans far too easily—to friends just like you and Miguel. Many have not been repaid. So, the money simply is not here."

"Five thousand dollars is not a large amount, not for a bank—" Bets argued.

"No," he agreed. "Not large at all. Yet I can't even lend it to you personally. I hope you believe I would do that if it were possible."

For a moment, she was silenced. Through the open door, if she turned her head, she could see the bustle of activity in the next room, the appearance of prosperity. Yet there was no doubting Camellito's word. She had known him too long.

"Yes. I am disappointed, that's all." She tried to keep the despair from her voice. "Have you any suggestions then?"

"Only a dangerous one." He made a rueful grimace, so very different from his beaming gentle smile of old. "Perhaps Lucky Belknap will make the loan, since you have collateral. He carries enough currency in that tin box of his to save Rancho Aguirre on the spot! But Bets, if Miguel approaches him, he should be certain he can repay the money promptly. Belknap is a hard man. He wouldn't give you the extra time Larronde has!"

"He was reasonable enough when he leased us the meadowland."

"I didn't say he wasn't reasonable. But he only deals when it suits him, and he takes what is his—without pity."

"We'll remember that," Bets said, "and I thank you for the idea. I wouldn't have thought of him."

This was not true. She had thought of Belknap, but as the very last resort. "Would you know where he can be found?"

"At the Cerro Gordo in Inyo. There's been a big silver strike, and he's one of the major speculators. Miguel can ride up there and back easily, in the amount of time you have."

He was supposing Miguel was here in town with her and could start without delay. Even so, if she and Adam returned at once to the rancho, there should be time enough. She thanked Camellito, and hastened away.

But passing the cashier's counter, she heard her name called and was forced to pause. Felipa, she remembered now, was working in her husband's bank.

"What is it?" In her overpowering anxiety, she found it impossible to be less than brusque to this woman who had never made any secret of her hostility.

Felipa glanced around, as if to make certain no one was close enough to overhear, and said, "I can guess why you've come, and I want you to know just why Camellito refused you a loan. Elizabeth, it would have worked a hardship on us, but we do have enough money personally to have helped you."

"Indeed? Knowing him, I find that difficult to believe! He's always been the most generous man in Los Angeles."

"Exactly. So I persuaded him some time ago to put all our property in my name. I told him it was only right and just, I should have the security, and if he didn't, I—well, it doesn't matter how I persuaded him. I had to stop him somehow from giving everything away to our impoverished friends, and I succeeded.

"Why do you look at me like that? I only took a leaf from Señora Brinkman's book, and no one criticizes her! Don't think I've liked seeing so many ranchos lost. I've agonized over each one! But I refuse to go down with them."

Bets said nothing, unable to disagree. The minor amounts the Camells could have contributed would, in most instances, have been money down a rathole.

Felipa, who had been watching her, added, "I expected to enjoy telling you this, letting you know it was I you had to thank. I find I do not, because— simply because I am weak enough to wish there was some way to make an exception for Miguel. But after the things I said to Camellito, it's impossible . . . I've trapped myself. Will you tell him I pray he succeeds elsewhere?"

Bets thought, I should hate her for this, but I don't. How can I? My life isn't barren like hers, yet I too hang on like grim death to what is mine!

Trying to hide the wild hope that had sprung into his dark eyes, Miguel agreed at once to the long ride to the Cerro Gordo. Bets settled back to wait his return, taking the two girls for long walks, and inspecting with Tomas the young walnut trees and a field of alfalfa he'd recently planted. Her son had begun to take more and more responsibility for the rancho, and as he spoke of the crop, his enthusiasm overcoming his reticence, she listened bleakly, trying to tell herself there was no danger he would not see his walnuts mature, yet knowing somehow, in her heart, what the outcome of Miguel's errand was to be.

Miguel arrived home again, grim and angry.

"He would accept the rancho for collateral, Elizabeth, oh, yes! But he wanted an interest rate that was unbelievable, far higher than any ever asked here, if you would credit that—and the principal due in only one year! For me to have agreed would have simply meant losing the land by inches, because with the heavy interest, we'd never save enough to pay off the loan.

"To tell the truth, I took such a dislike to him, if we must lose Rancho Aguirre, I'd rather it be now—at the hands of Gaston Larronde."

"So you refused?"

"I did." He added with a rare humility that touched her, "Was I wrong?"

"No. Even though we've come to the end, and there is nothing more we can do."

Yet when Tia Pilar brought her a sealed note the following day, saying it had been delivered by a stranger at the gate, even before she opened it, she realized her answer had been premature. There was something more after all, if she could bring herself to do it.

The note was terse, yet left little to her imagination!

Bets,
    By four in the afternoon on Monday, I will be waiting at a table, fifty feet to the left of the statue of Adam, in the Garden of Paradise. Come alone.
                                        Elias Belknap

CHAPTER FORTY-SIX

THE HOUR OR SO A DAY TEO ORIGINALLY PROM-ised to assist Dr. Kramer, had expanded to absorb most of her time and energy. She found that the sur-prising composure she'd displayed when faced with the shock of the *Ada Hancock* disaster did not desert her on closer acquaintance with illness. In the various crises befalling the doctor's patients, she remained calm and levelheaded, and took modest pride in knowing she was more than a little help. Women clutched her hand for strength, men were grateful for her gentle-ness, and sick children were less complaining when she soothed them. She was very happy.

Inviolate agreements, both spoken and unspoken lay between her and Dr. Kramer. The spoken one was that she would not be asked to enter a house where there was a sickness dangerous to Brian or Patrick. Unspoken, but equally well understood was the rule she would never, outside of the worst emergencies, be available in the evening. And important to Patrick, although it meant inconvenience for the doctor, she did not allow herself to be absent from the traditional noon meal at home.

In the beginning, she had been puzzled and hurt by Emil Kramer's reserve, as they sat side by side, not speaking, in the phaeton. He held himself so aloof from any suspicion of camaraderie that she decided forlornly he must for some reason dislike her. He was so very different with the patients!

But when it was necessary, as it often was, to explain to her what a medical procedure would entail and what her duty would be, he unbent, and gradually evolved the habit of using the sometimes lengthy rides for this purpose. Her interest and comprehension pleased him, and he could not help commending her when she guessed at once what he meant to do.

As time passed, she found herself more and more curious about him—what his childhood had been, what Germany was like—for she could not even imagine such a far-away, mysterious place. Why he had left home in the first place. *She* would never venture away from Los Angeles, the dear familiar town, the people she loved, the great rolling ranchos!

Teo longed to know the answers to these and many other questions but could not bring herself to ask them. If he wished to talk about himself, she thought, he would!

She had begun to despair that such a day would ever come, when by chance a call on a patient unlocked his tongue.

It had been a sad call, for the aged woman they went to see was beyond hope. Her breasts were hard and enlarged in a way Teo had never seen before. They looked like sacks full of round stones. While Dr. Kramer did briefly examine them and replaced the empty medicine bottle with a full one, he had confided to Teo ahead of time that all this was only for reassurance and could not help, except possibly to diminish the pain a little.

The reassurance, Teo saw at once, was more for the husband than for the patient herself. Standing in the small dim room at his wife's bedside, the old man looked frightened and already very lonely. When Dr. Kramer finished giving him careful instructions for administering the medicine, he put a trembling hand across his eyes and mumbled forlornly in German.

His wife reached up and took his hand. She began to talk. The doctor nodded, and all three, for a long time, conversed in what was to Teo an incomprehensible tongue.

Then at last the visit was over. Out into the sunshine and the blessedly fresh air, Teo and the doctor went, leaving the sadness behind, yet taking it with them. For a few minutes they rode in silence in the carriage, hearing the dull clop clop of the horse's feet in the dust of the street, watching the people pass along the wayside.

Teo's mind was occupied still with the long desultory talk she had just heard and not understood. What impressed her was the lack of haste with which it had been conducted. Dr. Kramer had been so patient, listening to those long guttural sentences spaced with many pauses, just as though he hadn't another thing to do and wasn't an hour behind schedule already.

She stole a glance sideways at his pale thin face and then down at the sensitive hands holding the reins, and she heard herself ask, "Whatever did they talk about, for such a long time?" She wanted to add, "You were so good to them!" but did not dare take the liberty.

"I'm sorry. It was a long time for you, I know, not understanding the language."

"I didn't mind!" Teo said quickly. "I wondered, that's all. Several times I thought I heard Hamburg. That's a city, isn't it? In Germany?"

Emil Kramer turned his head then, and smiled at her, as one might at a child. "Yes, a very large city. You've lived here always, I believe, so you can never have seen any place remotely like it. Herr and Frau Fiedler and I were talking of the old times. They lived most of their lives there, and I was born there."

"Oh." She spoke very softly, hoping he would continue if she remained very quiet.

"Yes, and I still love Germany. Odd, I never dreamed of leaving my country until almost the day I boarded ship. I had just obtained my degree in medicine and gone to Berlin because there everything was happening. Oh, Teodocia, you cannot imagine the excitement, the beauty of Berlin! The Tiergarten alone, the most celebrated Park in all Prussia—that would astonish you, but the city dates from the thirteenth century, and consequently there are also such beautiful boulevards lined with great old trees. There's the Brandenburg Gate, modeled after the Propylaea in Athens and so magnificent. And the palaces, ach, the palaces! But how can I describe to you great stone edifices, I wonder, when you have seen nothing but these simple adobe buildings?"

His use of her given name had not gone unnoted. Feeling more mature, and delightfully more equal, emboldened her to ask, "But if it was all so beautiful, why did you leave?"

"It was not all so beautiful," he said, sobering. "Many people were oppressed, and the states of Germany were constantly at each other's throats. We—a group of radical young men, Frank Lecouvreur was one of us. He came from Alsace and joined us as we schemed and fought for German unity. We almost succeeded. But the king of Prussia, because he hated revolutionaries, refused to become emperor, and the dream collapsed. The old regime came back to power, and we had to flee. I was able to escape to America, as did Frank, but some were not so lucky and they died martyrs. They were my friends."

"I'm sorry." Teo had followed little of this, but she understood the sorrow and anger he still felt. Trying to distract him to more pleasant memories, she said, "Tell me about Hamburg."

"Hamburg?" His eyes twinkled. "How can I? That grande dame is more ancient than Berlin."

Teo did not answer, and his amusement disappeared.

"Never mind," he said, "I've just had an idea. We must do much riding around daily in this ramshackle carriage of mine. There is one thing I love, one subject I sorely miss discussing, and that is music. Suppose, to pass the time, I tell you about the great composers of Germany? For in music, Germany is the home of the masters. All the great ones, or nearly all, were my countrymen. Would you like that?"

"Yes, please!" Her obvious sincerity pleased him, and he cleared his throat.

"Very well. Let us commence then. I shall begin with Georg Friedrich Handel, who was a rascal and an opportunist. But he did compose splendid oratorios! For the *Messiah* alone, all else should be forgiven."

He continued to talk, while Teo listened raptly. The teaching intonation she recognized at once. Except for Emil Kramer's German accent, Father Daniel had sounded much the same when he told his classes stories from history. The doctor then not only adored music, he also loved to teach, and there would be no more awkward silences. She settled back, giving a small sigh of contentment.

From time to time during the months that followed, Emil—for now she thought of him thus and had even on one or two occasions impulsively so addressed him —suggested it might be pleasant for them, with Patrick included of course, to have a musical evening together. She at first supposed he wished to attend an old-fashioned Californio fandango, should one be given. But when he made no reference to dancing, it seemed clear he intended merely to *listen* to music, perhaps at one of the minstrel performances, occasionally presented in an empty store on Aliso Street. She finally asked if such an entertainment was what he had in mind, and he gave himself up to one of his rare outbursts of laughter, explaining at last that he had at his home a treasure, a genuine Chickering piano, on which he would play for her and Patrick. Some Chopin perhaps. Certainly some Brahms.

The verbal music lessons by now had progressed to Johannes Brahms, a favorite of his, not only because the composer was an exact contemporary, but his birthplace also had been Hamburg.

"Then you grew up with him as a friend?"

"No, I met him later. You see, he was born in a tenement in the brothel district, and before he was ten, he played piano in the bawdy houses to help support his family. My mother would not have permitted such a companionship."

Teo was never sure when he was joking. Often, when he must be laughing at her, he was solemn as an owl.

She said with unusual boldness, "I don't agree with your mother. Surely one couldn't blame an innocent child for doing what it was told!"

He did not answer, but merely looked at her for a long moment, while her face grew warm. She knew however that he was not displeased.

After that, she felt a genuine regret that she would probably not have the pleasure of listening to him play the work of the little brothel child, because whenever the proposed musical evening was mentioned, she found herself making an excuse.

She was not entirely clear why this was so, but she did feel a strong reluctance to bring the two men together any more than necessary. She loved Patrick, of course! He was kind and good to her, and so gentle and patient when—she blushed thinking about it— they went to bed, she felt an especial affection, even tenderness toward him.

And Emil she revered. For how could one help admiring (from a distance and very properly) a man who was afire to help others, who wasted his meager strength and resources without a thought for himself, who was so educated, so wise . . .

No, there was no *reason,* but she knew she would be uncomfortable, alone in Emil's small house with both men present. The musical evening was not to be.

However she hated to refuse and it was just after she had done so again, that the carriage, proceeding along Spring Street, happened to pass a pair of picket

gates, above which huge cactus plants reached out
bulbous spiny arms. Emil abruptly reined the horse,
and as the clanking of the harness stopped, Teo could
hear the cheerful beat of a piano accompanied by
several fiddles. There was no sign on the gate but she
knew where she was—the entrance to a popular
pleasure-resort, one respectable enough although
scorned by the Californios, a place named the Garden
of Paradise.

Teo had heard, from her friend Elvira, glowing re-
ports of extensive well-shaded grounds, discreetly
placed tables, a peculiarly-shaped but fascinating building called the Round House, a large bar, and a framework supporting some swings called "Flying Horses."
Above all, Elvira had said, there were flowers and
many trees, lovely bowers of them.

Teo looked around again at Emil. A small vein was
throbbing in his temple, but he spoke very calmly.

"If you must refuse, always, to let me play for you,
there's music here. May I buy you a coffee, or a
chocolate?"

Teo hesitated, sorely tempted.

"It's quite a nice place," he added. "I like it particularly, because it reminds me of beer and wine gardens
back in Germany."

The touch of wistfulness decided her.

"Very well. Yes, thank you, I would like some refreshment."

"Good." He came around and assisted her down,
and they entered the picket gates together.

Strolling beneath the trees past small tables tucked
into secluded corners, with beds of cultivated flowers
on both sides, and gay music welling toward them
from the balcony of a structure still largely hidden
from view, Teo exclaimed, "Isn't this delightful!"

"Yes. There's far too little greenness in Los Angeles. I cannot understand a town with no trees! I've
plated some pomegranates and figs around my house
in Sonoratown, and I'm sure the Californio neighbors
consider me crazy."

"I doubt if anyone thinks any such thing!" she said
indignantly. Then, "Oh, goodness! What is that?"

"The heroic statue? It's presumably Adam, and the other is of course Eve. But look, Teo, at the amusing house! It used to be round but George Lehman added the six-sided framing on which to hang all those trumpet vines . . . Teo?"

She was not looking at the Round House, but instead was staring it seemed at something beyond. At his questioning tone, she spun back and clutched his arm.

"Oh, Emil—I find I am awfully tired, after all! We did so much today. Please, let's leave, quickly."

"If you wish," he said a bit stiffly, and led her without argument back toward the entrance.

As they emerged on the street, she said, "I hope you're not angry with me! I wanted to stay, and perhaps tomorrow—"

"Teo, it is you who should be angry. If you knew what I—" He broke off, then asked, "Are you all right?"

"Yes, oh yes. Simply tired."

No, she decided, he hadn't seen Bets sitting at one of those intimate tables, deep in conversation with that man whom Patrick and Phineas made no secret of disliking. What was his name? . . . Belknap! They called him Lucky Belknap.

She wouldn't want Emil to have noticed and he surely would have, if she hadn't hurried them both away. She wouldn't want Bets to know either, that she had seen her.

Not that there was anything wrong in their being there. Bets, dear Bets, would never do anything wrong! Even a married woman could encounter a masculine friend by chance and accept a glass of wine . . .

Yes, Bets who never drank wine, had had a glass of it on the table before her! And the man—Teo hadn't liked the expression she'd caught on his face. Not at all. It was a cold face, she thought, and yet his eyes had been shining with a kind of nasty triumph . . . And she'd seen Bets give a little shiver, as though the Garden was chilly, which it certainly wasn't.

What reason could Bets possibly have for being at the Garden of Paradise with lucky Belknap?

Teo pondered the question and then firmly put it out of her mind. Whatever the answer, whatever her dear friend was doing, she trusted Bets and always would.

Even when some time later Arcadia said something very odd, that Teo was fairly certain was not so, she refused to speculate any further.

"Isn't Elizabeth fortunate to have the father she has?" Arcadia had remarked.

"That's true, she is," Teo laughed, much pleased. "But what favor has Patrick done her recently?"

"You know very well! And Abel and I do, too. We had wondered how Miguel ever was able to pay off the Larronde mortgage on Rancho Aguirre when loan money is so dreadfully hard to get, and yesterday Abel asked him, point-blank. Of course, it was Patrick who had saved him, although Miguel said he could only guess how the money was raised. Probably by Patrick, he thought, breaking one of his stricter rules and appealing to your mother to break hers, although I am really surprised dear Violeta would agree to relinquish one single dollar, even to her son-in-law! No doubt begging money from her must have been most distasteful, and explains why Patrick insists on hearing no more about it from anyone—as Elizabeth, who dealt with her father, reported. Even Miguel is absolutely not to mention it to him.

"You look surprised! You knew nothing of it, Teodocia? Truly? I had no idea. Then you must promise me you'll say nothing to your husband—or anyone, just as I assured Miguel we would not. It is a matter of our honor!"

"I won't say a word," Teo replied firmly. And she never did.

CHAPTER FORTY-SEVEN

EVEN PATRICK, WITH HIS PROCLAIMED DIS-
trust of the iron horse, could not resist celebrating,
along with the rest of the town, the day that Phineas
Bishop's own short line, the Los Angeles and San
Pedro, having persevered to triumphant completion
over endless difficulties with charter and funding, finally drove its last spike and began operation.

"But Patrick," Teo teased, "you can't mean we're to
ride on a train! I remember last May when the transcontinental tracks were joined in Utah, and the newspapers talked of nothing else but how historic it was—
the two locomotives meeting in some wild spot called
Promontory, you said anyone crazy enough to buy a
passage would be taking his life in his hands!"

"That he would, my girl," Patrick said darkly.
"Those trestles and tunnels through the Sierras will be
breaking down any day, mark my words. But there
are no trestles or tunnels between here and Wilmington. Not one!"

"Oh trestles! And all this time I thought you expected the boilers to explode."

"That too. But it's not likely Phineas would allow
such a disaster to happen on his line! No, Teo, I have
every confidence. We'll all go, even Flora, Jeb, Flower
—all of us!"

The ride under discussion was one a large share of
Los Angeles would experience that very day. For
Bishop had issued a blanket invitation to the entire
town for free round-trip trips to the Wilmington wharf,
and in order to accommodate everyone, the small train
would spend the entire day chugging there and back.
Nor was that all. In the early evening, he would be
giving a select celebration dinner for close friends at
the Lanfranco restaurant, and later the same night he

had scheduled a grand ball, open to anyone who wished to attend (about two thousand guests were anticipated), at the new town depot. It would be a day to be remembered!

Teo, recognizing Patrick's keen anticipation, had told Emil Kramer she would not be making rounds with him that day, and she too tried to share the general holiday feeling of the household. A ride on a train was a novelty she looked forward to as eagerly as everyone else; it was only the destination that frightened her. Although at the time she had somehow remained as calm as the doctor himself, the suffering she had witnessed during the *Ada Hancock* disaster had been so hideous, so heart-wringing, she had never revisited the shipping wharf and dreaded doing so now.

However, the morning's outing began joyously. For the short distance to the depot, all of the family crowded with goodnatured laughs into the carriage. Brian considered himself a big boy, and he squirmed a little in protest when plunked down on Flower's lap; but he always loved riding on the high coachman's seat, watching Jeb handle the reins, and in no time at all, he too was caught by the excitement of the crowded streets. He was further entranced by the spectacle of a snarling snapping dog fight, viewed in perfect safety from his perch.

"Alameda and Commercial Streets will never be the same," Patrick predicted with glee, as the vehicle, having neared the corner where the depot stood, inched its way through a tight jam of horses, rigs and pedestrians. "Think of it, every steamer day there'll be a crowd like this!"

"Not this bad, surely! I think everyone in Los Angeles is here," Teo replied. She was keeping watch for Phineas Bishop, who had privately suggested they take the earliest trip, assuring her he'd make certain Patrick wasn't caught in a long queue. Standing for hours in this milling assemblage, with the intensely hot September sun beating down, would hardly be advisable for a man who wasn't strong.

Phineas, thoroughly occupied as he was, did somehow find them, after they'd alighted and after Jeb had put the carriage in the care of one of the ragged boys hovering about for that purpose.

"This way, Patrick," said the triumphant owner of the shiny new railroad, shepherding them all along the platform past cars already loaded with people who hung out the windows, gesticulating, shouting, chattering.

"I've saved a private car at the front . . . Yes, of course, Miss Teo, there's plenty of room for Jeb's family too."

Already they could make out in the first car, Arcadia and Abel Stearns, Arcadia clearly delighted to see them. They climbed aboard, all but Patrick, who must first walk farther ahead on the platform and inspect the small locomotive that was puffing clouds of black smoke from its high round stack, as if it too was impatient to be off.

Phineas, oddly, was not encouraging too protracted admiration of this iron toy of his, and Patrick at once discovered why. On the tender, the manufacturer had been guilty of a misspelling, and the name Los Angelos appeared in large letters. Patrick pretended he hadn't noticed, and saw his friend's frown smooth away. Phineas then went off to roam the train, welcoming his multitude of guests, while Patrick rejoined Teo in the first car.

Here there were a number of empty seats, as most of those especially invited had chosen to travel later in the day. Aboard however was an official dignitary, the governor's representative, who walked back to speak to Abel Stearns and Patrick Donovan.

"John Carew! What a fine surprise!" Patrick exclaimed, while Don Abel too extended his hand cordially. "Here, John, will you sit beside me and tell us what you've been doing? Teo won't mind moving across the aisle."

No, she wouldn't mind! She didn't want to listen to dull political talk, when the open countryside was already flying past, the train's motion creating a strong wind and swirling eddies of dust through the windows. Why, they must be going at unbelievable speed! She changed places happily, going to sit beside Brian, as wide-eyed as he, while the men's conversation went unheard.

For a time, the discussion did center around the political situation in Sacramento, and Patrick was able to satisfy his curiosity about some of the new bills being introduced in the legislature. Stearns might have been expected to take this opportunity to complain about taxes, but he remained dourly mute. Patrick was surprised at this, until he remembered he'd heard something about a land syndicate, the formation of which was in some way expected to solve the old Don's difficulties.

When there was a pause, Patrick said, "How is your wife, John? Is she with you? If so, I trust you'll permit us to entertain her—"

He stopped, because Carew was shaking his head, mentioning the explosion of the river boat *Yosemite* a few years back.

"John, do forgive me—I had no idea! You mean your wife was a victim of that terrible catastrophe?"

"Yes. You see, we'd continued to live near San Francisco, because Emily cared very little for politics and entertaining, and liked to make only brief visits to Sacramento while I was there. When she did come, it was by river boat, and the *Yosemite* was her favorite."

"But the published lists—her name wasn't—"

"She wasn't killed, not at once, although her injuries were grievous. She lingered on as a hopeless invalid, until recently."

"How tragic! You have my deepest sympathy."

"Thank you. But it was our daughter Ellen who carried most of the burden—and suffered greatly. She and her mother were very close."

Oddly put for a grieving widower, Patrick thought. His own wife Allison had been dead many years now, but he remembered vividly his rebellious, disbelieving sorrow. But when he said, "Tell me about your Ellen," he was rewarded by an immediate smile. No doubt about the man at least loving his daughter!

"A fine girl, Ellen, and she shows promise of being pretty as well. She has my coloring, but luckily otherwise looks like her mother. Now that Emily's gone, I intend to drop out of politics soon. I'm so busy I can't have a day to myself, and I'd like to be more of a father to Ellen."

"What will you do, instead of politics?"

"I was a sheep rancher before, and I can return to that work and be happier than I am now . . . But enough of me. I haven't congratulated you on your lovely wife and that fine boy! You are a lucky man."

"Yes, indeed!"

"And your sister, Mrs. Reyes? How is she? I thought she might be with you today." This last was said in an off-hand manner, Carew having begun, it seemed, to take an interest in the sparse dry landscape rolling by.

"I only wish she were!" Patrick's indignation at his sister's decision was as strong now as the day Miguel had brought him that surprising letter. "She's in Central America, in New Grenada—Panama—living in a wretched little town called Aspinwall."

Carew abandoned the scenery. He stared at Patrick. "Living in Aspinwall? Good God, why?"

"She started off for Spain, with the idea of searching for her son. Then something happened, we don't know what, and she just bogged down—didn't go on. She's made a place for herself in the village, helping out as a midwife, and I suppose, hard as the life there must be, it is an adventure of sorts."

He paused, not having thought before of that aspect of his sister's decision. Suddenly he was remembering himself, captain of a clipper ship, young, strong, whole, pacing his canted deck in a driving storm. That had been adventure! All the world his horizon!

Well, yesterday was gone. Today, his horizon was shrunk to the walls of his house. Adventure meant only a short ride on a train, under the watchful eye of Jeb.

"I've written Mary Frances time and again," he said, shrugging off such useless regrets, "telling her to come home, and sometimes she says she will, soon. But she doesn't."

Carew said thoughtfully, "Of course, she's painting well, and that must be part of the reason she stays. I know it's good work—I've seen some of the Panama pictures. From them, it was clear she'd been there, but I had no idea of this!"

It occurred to Patrick to wonder why a man whom he himself hadn't encountered in a number of years should be so interested in his sister, and knowledgable about her too. Then he remembered. The fellow had briefly been a suitor, calling at the house, escorting Mary Frances out to paint! Perhaps he'd even cared for her.

Pleased to be able to air his grievances to a sympathetic listener, he plunged on. "I wouldn't object, understand, if I thought Mary Frances was happy, but there's a sadness creeps into her letters now and then. And her health does worry me. She was all right for a time after the yellow fever, but lately she's had malaria. Still, I tell myself there's nothing to be done. When her mind's made up, it's made up."

"How very true!" Carew spoke with an emphasis that turned Patrick's head around to him in further surprise. "True of all women," he added quickly. "Haven't you found them so?"

And Patrick, reminded of Teo's devotion to her nursing work, could only agree.

"Have you thought, by the way," asked the politician, "what will be the effect of the new transcontinental railroad—on Panama? Travelers certainly won't continue to make a long journey by sea, down and back, in order to cross the isthmus, when there is now a much easier and faster way from New York to San Francisco. Aspinwall is finished, which may bring your sister back sooner than she intends."

"I do hope so." Patrick had brightened briefly, then looked dubious. "With her, one never knows."

Mention of the Pacific Railroad, however, had introduced the ever-popular subject of how track had been laid through the formidable Sierras. Carew confirmed that Chinese laborers had needed to blast tunnels through granite walls so hard the powder charges often backfired out without even cracking the surface. Discussion of these hardships and difficulties happily occupied the remainder of the time to Wilmington. Patrick courteously offered the hospitality of his home for that night, and was told, with regret, the governor's party would be sailing north again in the late afternoon. Then the train slowed, pulling up to the Wilmington platform which proved to be nothing more than the old shipping wharf. Beyond lay water, and to the sides rocks and tidepools, the shoreline of the estuary.

"Another time, when I bring Ellen with me—" Carew began, and was interrupted by a squeal of delight from across the aisle.

"Papa! A ship!"

Patrick excused himself and went to his son. Looking where the small finger pointed, he expected to see another of those ugly steam vessels. Instead, lying at anchor in the near distance was a schooner, her naked spars slim and graceful against the sky.

"Come along, Brian! Let's go outside where we can see her better." He reached for his son's hand, and the child eagerly pushed past his mother. "Remember, I told you all about Papa's own ship, the *Elizabeth?* She was larger, and—"

"The train will be leaving soon, Patrick," Teo called after them. "No one else is disembarking!" but they were already on the steps and clambering down. She gazed after them, troubled, but when Jeb rose to follow, she said, "No—let him go alone, Jeb! We can watch. Let them be alone."

Nevertheless, she wished the two were back in the car and the engine was pulling them all away from this place. She hadn't looked out the window at all, not since the heavy iron wheels had come to a screeching stop here. Even so, in her mind's eye, she was beginning to see again those ghostly passengers of the *Ada Hancock,* happily hurrying aboard their ill-fated ship, blind, as she was not, to the horrors that awaited them.

"What's the matter, Miss Teo?" Phineas Bishop exclaimed. He had finally returned from his jaunt

through the train, and was standing beside her seat.
"You look pale."

"It's only—" She stopped, unable to put her apprehension into words.

"She's anxious, naturally," Arcadia said. "Patrick has taken Brian for a stroll, and they might overstay."

"And why not return later?" Phineas suggested easily, his eyes still grave as they rested on Teodocia. "You too, Miss Teo. It's a fine place for walking! You'll catch sight of every kind of shore bird there is, and Brian can wade in the tide pools. Do you have to return just yet? Remember, this train is going back and forth all day, and the front car will still be reserved."

"But Brian will need his noonday meal," Teo said desperately.

Phineas gave a laugh. "I'd be greatly surprised if my facility here can't put together a picnic for you. Why don't we go along and ask?" He turned to the Stearns and invited them also, but Don Abel emphatically was not a man for picnics, and so Arcadia declined.

Unable to think of any more excuses, Teo rose, gathering up her shawl and Patrick's broad-brimmed hat. Then she realized the family servants were preparing to leave the train with her.

"Oh, no, Flora, Jeb! We all noticed how much Flower loved the ride, and look, she can't wait for the train to start again. You must stay aboard."

"But you might need me," Jeb protested, uneasily, avoiding his daughter's childlike look of entreaty.

"I'll manage and there's help here if I need it."

While she was speaking, she'd stepped from the car to the wharf, and now finally she was forced to look around her.

In the water, just beside where she and Phineas now stood, had been tied the first boatload of burned and maimed people! Almost at her feet had been laid the pathetic dead, arranged in mute rows. And just there, the pretty girl with the missing foot had bled and bled . . .

But the images did not grow stronger as she'd

dreaded they might. Instead, as though weakened by the bright sunlight, they gradually faded. For there were, after all, no grim reminders. The empty clear water lapped gently around barnacled pilings, and just ahead, on the pier's rough planking, a glittering-eyed seagull strutted in arrogant unconcern.

When the train's whistle suddenly blew, she was able without regret to watch the cars start, jerk back, and then, gathering speed, noisily roll away, Flower's entranced face pressed against a window.

"Hadn't you better come with me and tell my cook what you'd like, Miss Teo?" Phineas suggested after a moment.

"Oh, yes . . . And thank you!"

As they walked on together, because she felt greatly relieved, and because she had always been at ease with Phineas, she said, "You are so truly kind! I'm surprised some fortunate young lady hasn't persuaded you to marry her, long since."

"I don't recall many trying!" His brief jocularity disappeared. "All the same, I have come close to marrying, and more than once. I'll tell you the truth: whenever I think of settling down with some good woman, knowing it's for life, I back away."

She realized, to her surprise, he was speaking seriously of himself. Conscious of the compliment he was paying her, this man who was well known for being voluble on business matters but exceedingly close-mouthed on his personal life, she asked quietly, "I wonder why that should be so?"

He was silent, slowing their pace as they neared the building, then he said, "Because, long ago, I lost my heart to someone! Miss Teo, if you'll forgive me for mentioning a man you doubtless don't want to talk about, I can make myself clearer. I think you must have felt the same way about marrying anyone else, anyone at all, so long as you cared for Garth Peters."

"Oh . . . Yes."

"Well, there's always been only one woman for me, and nothing has ever changed my mind—even though she doesn't need me or want me, not in that way! Never has."

"You are quite sure? You've asked her?"

"Asked her? Oh, I couldn't! There would be no use in it!"

Teo decided, from his vehemence, that the lady he cared about most probably was married. She wondered briefly who it might be, then dismissed the matter. Phineas would never divulge that.

"I'm sorry! Sorry I asked too, if I've caused you pain."

"No, don't be. It's eased my mind to tell someone, just once. Will you wait here while I find the cook?"

He went inside, and Teo stood gazing out at the lovely ship that lay so peacefully beyond, in the reaches of the bay. She was still thinking about Phineas, and it struck her that he'd understood quite well her reluctance to return to this spot, and had taken care to vanquish her fears.

Was anyone ever as considerate of him? Looking back, it seemed to her that they'd always taken for granted his great strength. He was successful and self-sufficient, and he wore his assurance like a suit of armor. In all the years of their acquaintance, today was the first time she had been made aware his armor had a chink, and now she'd looked through and seen Phineas Bishop, the man, as he really was. The knowledge of his loneliness, his carefully hidden longing, saddened her.

But then, in the distance, down among some big rocks, she caught sight of Patrick, and saw him pointing her out to Brian. When her little boy waved and called to her, love for them both, strong and protective, washed over her.

Did Patrick too, beneath his bluster and easy laughter, have a core of unhappiness? Perhaps so, because if she was being entirely honest, she would admit he had come to love her in too many ways that could not be returned. She was not satisfied just to be with him. By her own choice, she was gone many hours a day, uncertain what more she wanted, yet seeking more all the same.

But today they would be together, unhurried, free

to walk side by side on the rocky shore and show the sea to Brian. She must go to them quickly, her husband and her son, make certain they both had a perfect day, one to remember always.

CHAPTER FORTY-EIGHT

ONCE A YEAR OR SO, MIGUEL HAD OCCASION to enter Camellito's bank. Originally, he had enjoyed those brief sporadic visits, liking to see his boyhood friend bustle about, full of importance and manifestly happy.

But in late years, the pleasure had diminished, simply because Camellito himself no longer wore the same air of joyful self-confidence. Miguel, used to brooding about the direction his own life was taking, seldom felt much curiosity about other people's, but even he had noticed the change in the rotund banker.

This time Miguel was greeted warmly. But Camellito could not disguise a certain wariness, and Miguel guessed that even now he winced every time one of his Californio friends entered the bank, fearful he would be asked to make a loan. Not that he was often asked any more. For most of those whose affairs had been shaky, time had long since run out. During the past few years there had also persisted a number of disquieting rumors: that the bank itself had been in difficulties not once but several times because of its president's open-handedness; that Camellito, by order of his wife, could no longer give either banking or personal loans; and that each refusal resulted for him in a spell of illness. None of this however had been officially confirmed.

As the two men talked together on this occasion, and it became clear Miguel had only stopped in for social reasons, Camellito's manner became easier.

"Ah, Miguel," he said, "Have you greeted Felipa

yet? She still insists on keeping her position as cashier in the bank, although I— Felipa!" he called, "See who's here, after so long!"

Miguel had failed to notice her, seated on the far side behind the counter, and he told himself his lapse was understandable. The change in her appearance shocked him. In her late twenties she had been, not handsome certainly, but possessing a certain mettlesome spirit he found attractive. Now, well past forty, there was apparent only a cold aloofness, and what little femininity she'd had was gone. She was lean as a coyote and had a dusting of dark mustache on her upper lip.

Juiceless, he thought. *All the vigor has been dried out of her.* By disappointment? Or simply by time itself? For no reason he could think of, he felt guilty.

She had looked up, frowning, at her husband's call. Taken by surprise, a flush stained her sallow neck and face. "Miguel!"

"Good day, Felipa! How pleasant to see you. Are you and Camellito attending the festivities at the Lanfranco tonight? I hear Phineas has taken over the entire restaurant just for his guests."

"That one always has something to celebrate, doesn't he? Yes, I suppose we'll be there, although why anyone would choose to pay for food at such a place is beyond my comprehension. Obese old French Louis drinks claret before, during, and after all the meals he serves."

"He also cooks with it," Miguel said. "Very successfully too, to my taste."

"Our Californio way of cooking is good enough for me!"

"There's another cause for celebration," Camellito put in. "Don Abel's problems appear to be solved at last . . . Yes, Jaime? What is it?"

He turned to speak to a tall handsome man who had appeared at his elbow, and Miguel too glanced round with mild curiosity. Camellito seldom acquired new assistants, for the ones he had, remained loyally attached, year after year.

"About Mr. Robinson, sir. He came in earlier, seeking you. He is at his tailor's, down the street, and asked me to let him know just as soon as you returned from your dinner."

"Then do so, Jaime!" Camellito beamed. "It's essential I talk with him. Go at once!"

"Yes, sir." The assistant hurried away.

"Who is your new man?" asked Miguel.

"Jaime Real, from Spain. He's been working for Phineas at the warehouse, but wasn't too happy there because Frank Lecouvreur as we all know, can be cross-grained at times. Frank would give him no responsibility, actually seemed to dislike him! Well, as this fine young man told me, he's always wanted to be a banker, so I took him on and I haven't regretted it. . . . Isn't this paperweight of mine attractive? A solid gold jaguar! Real presented it to me at Christmas. Seems he bought it from an Indian down in Panama.

"But what I wanted to tell you concerns Mr. Robinson. With a little technical advice from our bank, I believe he and a group of San Francisco investors are going to make Don Abel solvent once again, perhaps richer than before. The Stearns holdings have always been land-heavy, with no cash to pay expenses. This syndicate plans to take over all Don Abel's remaining ranchos on the South Coast, giving him in return an eighth interest in the trust. Then the land will be promoted, developed, broken up into parcels, and sold.

"With a transcontinental train to bring settlers west, and a sales program drummed up by the Robinson Trust, I wouldn't be surprised to see our little pueblo suddenly expand like one of those gas balloons . . . Ah, here's Robinson now! Excuse me, will you, Miguel?"

He hurried away, his enthusiasm, for once, more than a pale imitation of what it had been in former days.

Felipa sighed. " 'With a little advice from our bank,' he says! I really believe he's convinced himself that is so. These men must have a bank or two available in San Francisco, so if we're involved at all, it will only be for a pittance. Can't he understand that?"

Miguel said uncomfortably, "The syndicate is all San Franciscans?"

"Oh, not all. Or they weren't at first when Elias Belknap was included. But there was some nasty business involving the wife of the chairman, and he was bought out. That Belknap! I'm surprised someone hasn't shot him. He does favors for women he wouldn't think of doing for their husbands, and there's always a price. Always!"

She was interrupted by the entrance of Patrick Donovan, leading by the hand his small son. In the background, watchful and trying to be inconspicuous, was Jeb.

Miguel, as he stooped to greet the little boy, felt a familiar stab of jealousy. Patrick's *son!* What a beautiful child he was too, sturdy, handsome, with Patrick's black hair and blue eyes and that same wide smile of pure enjoyment.

"Brian, Teo and I have had the grandest day together," Patrick confided. "And I knew it would be! You remember my telling you how Mary Frances used to give a special color to a day? Well, blood will tell—or as my sister Sheila used to put it, 'apples never fall far from the tree.' Brian actually ran to me this morning and said, 'It's yellow today, Papa!' What's more, he was right, it was a very yellow day, train ride, picnic, and all. I keep asking myself, could anything in this world have been finer?"

Could anything have been finer? Miguel stared out through the doorway at the dusty street, wondering if he, in all his life, had ever asked that question. For him, whatever happened, the cup was more than half empty, while for Patrick it was always more than half full. He, Miguel, had *never* experienced a perfect day! What a sad thing for a man to acknowledge.

Patrick gave a little laugh at himself. "Forgive me, am I not a typical father? After all, sunshine is yellow, and the boy probably only—"

He stopped abruptly. With no warning, he seemed to become smaller, fall in upon himself. Sweat started on his forehead and pain made an ugly rictus of his mouth. He uttered no sound, however, and people a little distant continued to conduct their banking business, unaware.

Jeb was at his side in an instant, supporting Patrick, an arm under his and across his shoulders. Jeb cast a worried glance at Brian who had cried out, "Papa!" but Miguel, seeing the child's frightened stare, had quickly grasped his hand.

"Its all right, Brian," Miguel said in a low voice. "Come along, Jeb is bringing Papa."

Out in the street, Jeb swept Patrick up in his muscular arms and deposited him, writhing in torment, on the seat of the carriage. Then he picked up Brian, and swung himself and the child to the driver's seat. Brian clung to him, face averted, all the joyousness gone.

"Doan worry, Mister Michael," Jeb said to Miguel. "He be all right. This ain't nothin' new. Brian, he used to it."

"You don't need me, Jeb?"

"No, suh. Mister Patrick be fine 'fore we gets home. He feeling better already."

It was true, Miguel saw with relief. Patrick's face was still shining wet, but he was no longer driven to agonized movement. Instead, evidently conscious of his son-in-law's concern, he had begun muttering in a thin but angry voice, "I'm all right . . . God, Warner should have killed me! What an old crock I am! Worthless!"

Miguel well understood the lacerated pride that prompted this outburst. He had not missed the anguish with which Patrick, even racked with pain, had reached futilely for his small son. His was a heavy burden to bear—not to be able to walk confidently with his child and show him things! Always to fear an attack that would terrify Brian!

For once, Miguel's reticence was forgotten. He leaned in and put a sympathetic hand on the older man's shoulder. On impulse he said, "Hardly worthless, old friend! Doesn't it count for anything that you saved Rancho Aguirre for us?"

Patrick stared at him. With the receding of the sharp

stabs, his eyes were losing their dullness. "I? What are you talking about?"

"Oh, I know Elizabeth asked me not to thank you, so all this time I have obediently refrained from mentioning the matter. But I've decided I had to let you know how exceedingly grateful I am—and always will be."

There was a pause before Patrick said gruffly, as though in fact he did not like to be reminded, "Let's not speak of it! Such things are best forgotten. Will Bets be coming in yet today? Phineas is expecting you both at his party tonight."

"Yes, and she's bringing the children in too, hoping to be in time for a late train ride as well as have a visit with you. They're all very excited—even Tomas."

"Good!" Patrick managed a grin. "I can't wait to see them . . . You can drive home now, Jeb."

That night, which promised to rival in festivity some of the sumptuous gatherings of the past, Bets had looked forward to eagerly. She liked the Lanfranco, which was the first establishment in Los Angeles to make any pretence of serving high-class food, and as always, a party given by Phineas was certain to have no effort spared.

Fat Louis had hired two cooks for the occasion, both, for once, sober. This freed him to wander about among the guests, claret bottle in hand to assure that all the glasses remained full; although, often as not, he would step behind a convenient screen and when he returned again, the level in the bottle had dropped. His dewlapped cheeks became ever more florid as the evening progressed, and his remarks, to himself at least, more uproarious. The jokes may well have been too raw for such company, but no one could be sure, for what little English he had was obliterated by a heavy French accent.

Placed on the street, because the restaurant's interior was completely filled with guests who milled about among the tables, was a piano, and skillfully playing it was the same accompanist who for years now had been a mainstay at the Blue Diamond. Peter Riggs

himself, occupied with his various lucrative enterprises, no longer obliged.

Bets had wandered outside, on the pretext of listening to the music. She should have been enjoying herself immensely, but she was not. The visit in town,
culminating at this party, had since her arrival at Patrick's been a disappointment, and she still was mysti-
fied as to the reason. Miguel, she'd discovered at once,
was sunk in moody silence. More surprising had been
the reserve apparent in her father's welcome, although
he swept Tomas, Isabel and Maria Rosa into his usual
embrace, exclaiming over Tomas's added height, and
making such extravagant compliments regarding the
girls' hair, eyes, and general beauty that elfin Maria
Rosa crowed with pleasure, and Isabel, who at ten was
a little pudgy and, if one were truthful, not at all
pretty, hugged him with passionate love, her arms tight
around his waist.

Jeb had already taken Bets aside and told her about
the attack Patrick had suffered publicly at the bank,
but she suspected uneasily that even the degrading
humiliation, for such he would consider it, did not account for the somberness of his gaze at her when he
thought she wasn't looking.

So, delightful as it was to see her old friends now,
and to know that for Arcadia, the hard times would
soon be over, Bets continued to feel dispirited. Even
in her planned reunion with Teo, she'd been disappointed! Her old friend at the last moment had gone
out on an emergency call with Dr. Kramer, and so
Patrick and she had not yet put in an appearance.

"Ah, Miss Betsey!" It was Phineas. "Listening to
the music? Some of these new songs seem downright
silly to me! *Sweet Genevieve*—or that sugary one that
just finished, *Her Bright Smile Haunts Me Still!* Everyone else loves them, or I'd ask for Strauss waltzes
the whole evening."

"I wish you could too!" She was surprisingly glad to
see him. "My, Phineas, we haven't met for a very long
time." Trying to remember just when the last occasion
was, her welcoming smile wavered. She hadn't seen
Phineas since before she'd gone seeking him at the

Wilmington warehouse. If only he'd been there that day!

"Betsey, is something wrong? You look as if you'd seen a ghost."

"How does one look then?" She managed to sound amused. "No, there's nothing wrong. I was just reminded of a day that's best forgotten . . . Phineas, I've been wanting to tell you all evening, the children and I loved our ride on the train."

"Did you? Good! Then I've a favor to ask of you, Betsey. Will you christen the locomotive for me? I'd be honored if you would."

"Why, I'd love to!"

She felt a rush of gratitude. He was lifting her spirits, as always. Dear Phineas! How often had he appeared at her side when she needed him?

She looked up at him and started to say, almost with her usual gaiety, "If I'm to christen her, I must know her name," when she became aware that Felipa had appeared behind them, and was waiting with an air of urgency.

When Bets fell silent, Felipa said, "I'd like to speak to her alone, Phineas."

"Only if she wishes," he answered, and Bets realized he was remembering the wanton killing of Estrella. He did not trust Felipa and her enmity.

"Yes. It's all right," Bets told him.

"Very well. I'll return in a minute or two."

When he was gone, Felipa said, "This has been a day for uncovering the truth, I'm afraid."

"What do you mean?" Although the soft playing of the piano continued, and merry-making could be heard, she and Felipa were alone in their dark corner of the street. The uneasiness that always assailed her in this woman's company was stronger tonight, more of a foreboding. Whatever Felipa was going to say, she did not want to hear it, and she wished she had urged Phineas to stay.

"Only what I must tell you. Elizabeth, all of us knew you were in danger of losing Rancho Aguirre some time back, because of the mortgage Gaston Larronde held. Then the debt was miraculously paid, and at a time when bank loans were desperately hard to get!"

"I know all that!" Bets said sharply. "Why do you want to—"

"People are curious! Miguel refused to divulge anything—except to Don Abel who is like a clam himself, so no one knew the answer. Some said your father raised it for you, while others thought you might have begged it from Phineas, and I myself leaned to that explanation. He's always been so soft where you're concerned."

"We will not discuss Phineas and I see no point in listening any longer!" Bets this time took a step away. But Felipa still continued as though she hadn't spoken. "The trouble was, none of us actually *knew,* so just now, when Miguel asked me a searching question about what loans Lucky Belknap had made through our bank, I wasn't prepared. After all, such matters are confidential, as Miguel well knows. Men in trouble don't interest Lucky Belknap, and women—" She stopped. Her long fingers were weaving together with painful force. Bets sensed that Felipa herself was frightened, and her own undefined apprehensions grew stronger.

There was a movement behind her, and she gave a quick glance back into the shadows, realizing Phineas had returned. Yet she made no effort to stop Felipa's revelations. She could not. She had to know the rest at once, appalling as it might be.

"Yes?" she whispered. "And women . . . ?"

"I said, 'Any woman he lends to pays in other coin.' After what I'd told him earlier, in the bank, well . . . He will guess the truth, don't you think? Just as I did . . . Oh, Elizabeth, how I truly regret this. Not because of you, God knows, but because of him! I would not willingly hurt or shame Miguel! You know that, don't you? You've always known—how much, how terribly much—"

Suddenly she spun away and ran into the restaurant, disappearing into the noisy crowd of celebrants, while Bets stood numbed, absently hugging herself against the coldness that was filling her body.

"Betsey." His strained voice cut through her lethargy. "Good God, Betsey!"

"You heard." Her own shock was too great to give any thought to his.

"So it was Belknap!" He groaned. "Oh, Betsey, *why* didn't you come to me for the money? I'd have given you anything in the world you wanted! Anything! And so gladly!"

He was endeavoring to keep his voice low, but the anguish in it finally caught her attention, and she looked up at him. Was it only the night shadows, she wondered, that made his eyes shine so? No, it was anger.

She managed to summon up a smile, although it was small and sad. "You'd gone up north, Phineas. Frank Lecouvreur didn't know where . . . I did go to you first of all, after Papa. You know I would."

"Thank you for telling me that anyway. Even though I will never forgive myself for failing you . . . Betsey! Are you all right?" He had put out his arms in sudden concern, and clasped her. She was swaying, and she clung to him.

"Are you faint?" he demanded.

She did feel dizzy, as though she'd been struck hard. It was the shock, the sudden devastating shock, she thought hazily. After all this time, after she'd believed the brief sordid episode could be safely forgotten, Miguel might—no, he probably would—find out! And forgiveness for cuckolding him was not possible! She had sworn to be faithful, she had broken her vow, and no matter why she had done it, he was dishonored.

Her safe secure world was going to crack wide open.

Her children—would they be disgraced?

Distraught as she was, she was still surprised on hearing a torrent of words, low and passionate and oddly broken, from the lips pressed against her hair.

"Hold onto me, my dearest! I won't let you fall. I wouldn't, ever! Ah, God help me! If I'd only had the right to help you, keep you from harm—If I'd only had the right—"

Her head was clearing. She pulled away a little and straightened, and the voice stopped.

She must leave at once. She needed time alone, to think.

"Will you do me a kindness, Phineas? Will you bring your carriage and drive me to Papa's?"

"I will, Miss Betsey, of course."

She glanced up at him, noting absently that he was again as always, bluff, respectful, and her good friend. Had she imagined those tortured words of endearment?

Even in the darkness, his gray eyes were flinty, and it seemed wise to add a word about Belknap. "Phineas, listen to me. Please don't add to my troubles by seeking him out. Fighting him won't help! Heaven knows I don't wish him well, I'd like never to hear his name again, but it was—only a business transaction, don't you see? He had something to sell . . . and I chose to buy. So let it be ended! Will you promise me?"

He hesitated. "Certain that's what you want?"

"Yes."

"It's too bad, because if I ever got my hands around his neck I'd kill him! . . . Very well. You have my word."

CHAPTER FORTY-NINE

MIGUEL DID NOT RETURN TO PATRICK'S HOUSE at all that evening. Bets set herself to endure the long hours, both expecting and dreading his accusation. Once she asked herself how often she'd waited alone like this, while he outrode his devils of fury or grief, and the number of times seemed beyond counting.

Still dressed in incongruous party finery, she stayed huddled in her room until she heard her father and Teodocia come home and make their way to bed, then in the darkness she slipped quietly into the parlor.

There she paced the length of the moonlight-illumined room, until her restlessness at last gave way to exhaustion, and she could sit, stiff and wakeful, in her father's chair. A soft patter of rain had begun, ordinarily a lulling and comforting sound, but all she could think, hearing it, was where was he now, out in the wet night?

She must have drowsed a little, because she started, taken by surprise, when a yellow light flared just above her. Had he come at last? But no, she saw it was only Patrick, his blue eyes narrowed as he adjusted the wick of a coal oil lamp. The flame steadied, and he turned from it, to frown at his daughter.

"Papa, did I wake you?"

"No, I knew you were out here, but I wanted to be certain Teo was deeply asleep. Betsey, girl, you're your own woman, long gone from me as a daughter, and you can refuse to answer. But I must ask you anyway. Where did you get the money to pay Gaston Larronde?"

"Ah, you too! I should have known there was something on your mind when I had so cool a greeting from you today." Today? Was it only that afternoon she'd come? The hours since had been so long.

"Unfortunately your husband was moved to thank me for my help in paying the debt. He wouldn't have mentioned the matter, as you evidently tried to prevent him, but I happened to have one of my attacks in public, embarrassing myself and frightening poor little Brian. In Miguel's sudden pity, he spoke before he thought."

"What did you tell him?"

"Nothing! Do you take me for a fool? But Bets, how do you answer me?"

Nothing? Perhaps not. But his surprise had certainly set Miguel thinking, and then, with Felipa's indiscretion—

"It's as you guessed," she said dully, gazing at the floor. "Elias Belknap lent me the money. If you want the details, he gave me a long-term loan at low interest. And it's not—" She forestalled the question, "being paid back through Camellito's bank. To avoid questions, he placed it in San Francisco."

She was surprised by her own composure. Those

many months ago, when she made her decision at the Garden of Paradise, she'd felt cold dread at the possibility of her father, as well as Miguel, learning the truth. But now, so much worse would come when she faced Miguel, that telling Patrick left her with a feeling almost of indifference.

Her father still wasn't certain what had happened, or chose not to admit he was. "You might as well have bargained with the devil!" he rebuked her. Then remembering the sleeping household, he slightly lowered his voice. "The man has a filthy reputation, don't you know that? People will talk, if this is ever known, and you may be sure they'll believe the worst—that you paid his price!"

"They'll be right, Papa. I did."

She expected an explosion, but none came. Patrick stood stock-still, glaring over her bowed head, with his hands balled into fists and his jaws clamped hard together.

How badly had she shocked him, she wondered worriedly. She might even cause one of his attacks!

"Are you terribly angry?" she whispered. "Of course, I know you must be disappointed in me!" She was finding she did care what he thought. She cared very much!

"Am I angry?" He found his voice again. "Damned right, I'm angry! I'll never forgive myself for not having the money to offer you. That my Bets, my own daughter, should have to sell herself like a whore—"

"Papa, no!"

"Didn't I hear you say you shared that lecher's bed?"

"Once! Just once! To save Rancho Aguirre. Does that make me a whore?"

She had sprung to her feet, for a frightening span of time believing her father no longer loved her. Then he looked in her stricken face, and he was completely undone. He held wide his arms and she flew into them, as eager for their shelter and comfort as if she were a child again.

"There now, little love, there now." He smoothed

her shiny hair, pressed her soft wet cheek against his. "It's no blame to you, Bets, don't ever think it is."

Then after another long moment, "Come to think of it, my girl, I wouldn't be surprised but what you got the best of him, at that."

"Him?"

"Belknap."

"Whatever do you mean?" She pulled back to look up at her father.

"That fellow's got an ungodly high opinion of his attraction for the fair sex, wouldn't you say?" Patrick chuckled, low in his throat. "I've no doubt he figured after the one time he got you to bed, you'd be back again on your own accord—and eager, too. Am I right?"

She thought about it, and nodded.

"You probably are, Papa. When we parted, he told me what day he'd be there the following week. I wasn't really listening, I just wanted to get out of that house of his and reach my own home safely. I didn't find him irresistible. Not at all!"

Patrick chuckled. "Can't you see him waiting in vain then, the next week? He probably went specially to the barber, maybe even bought some silk nightclothes, because I'll wager he doesn't wear that black preacher's coat when he's debauching someone's wife. Tell me, does he take his tin box into bed with him?"

Bets had begun to smile, but the words *debauching someone's wife* brought the mantle of bleak unhappiness settling back over her.

"Don't, Papa. It isn't funny!"

"I know . . . You're thinking about Miguel?"

"Yes."

"I've only one suggestion then, Betsey, girl, and it's this—that you consider very, very carefully, if it's a confession you have in mind. What might seem reasonable to you and me, is different to a Californio. You saved his lands and that's a fact. But your husband considers his honor to be beyond price."

Miguel did not return until the following day at noon, and she never did learn where he'd been. Jeb later could only tell her the horse he'd ridden was thirsty and stumbling with fatigue.

When he walked into the front room of Patrick's house, she was not waiting there alone. Her own children were out in the stable, deep in some secret preparations for Patrick's birthday, but Teo was with her, having only minutes before alighted from Dr. Kramer's carriage; and she herself, trying to distract her mind, was seated on the floor with Brian, teaching him to play jacks.

At the sound of the familiar footsteps, she dropped the small rubber ball and got to her feet. She had been anticipating his return for so long, in her ache of tiredness there was little left to feel but relief.

The cold anger she expected was in his face. So she was dumbfounded when he thrust forward a news journal and, addressing both her and Teo, demanded, "Have you seen this? Surely not, or you wouldn't be so calm, so unconcerned—"

"What is it?" Teo asked, startled.

"Here—read the *Star,* and the *News* has the story as well. There's an embezzlement at the bank. One of the tellers, a young Spaniard named Real, has stolen over fifteen thousand dollars! The loss was discovered early in the evening, which is why Camellito never came to Bishop's party—"

"But Felipa was there." Teo sounded bewildered.

"I suppose he couldn't face telling her." Miguel brushed the interruption aside impatiently. "The newspapers found out, and published an account this morning. Already there are people in a panic the bank will fail. They're demanding their money, and by tomorrow—"

"But I don't understand," Teo persisted. She alone was answering Miguel. Bets was unable to speak. "Why is anyone worried? Fifteen thousand dollars isn't so much for a bank to lose, is it? Even such a small bank?"

"I'd like to hope that's true, Teo, but I don't know! The bank has been on shaky ground for a long time. Even though Camellito stopped lending, the depositors have no confidence. And now this abominable thief!

He's escaped, and probably won't be caught, so the money's gone . . . Teo, where is Patrick? The calls on the bank have been heavy, and far more cash is needed! All Camellito's friends will have to help—Patrick too."

"He's out at the stable. He bought a new pony, not for Brian's birthday but his own, because he said, on *his* birthday he wanted to give his son a present. Oh, dear!" She looked with pretended consternation at the little boy who had leapt to his feet, eyes shining. "Now I've given away the secret!"

"Let's go to see the pony! Please, Mama!"

"All right, darling. It was all your Papa could do, to wait until I got home—"

"Teo!" Miguel's imperative tone stopped her. "Give me five minutes alone with him, first!"

Even before she could agree, he was gone, running out the back and through the patio, while Brian tugged disconsolately at her hand.

Teo turned to Bets. "But surely it will all come right? Everyone loves and trusts Camellito!"

"Our friends do, yes," Bets answered her dully. "But there are so many others, new people who don't know him. Times have changed." She wasn't really thinking about the bank, but about Miguel. She'd been reprieved for the time being by this embezzlement, and until the bank's danger had passed, he would have no time for suspicions and accusations. But she felt no relief. Sooner or later, her husband would have to be answered.

The beleaguered bank's destiny continued uncertainly, although the initial run on deposits was brought to a hesitant halt through the loyalty of the Californios. Every one of them contributed at least some small sum. Even Señora Brinkman, this time, gave adequately if not generously.

The sturdy old lady arrived at her daughter's house on horseback, having ridden in that fashion the long distance into town from her rancho, and when Teo expostulated, she replied in an offhand way that she felt more at home on a horse's back than she did in a carriage.

Patrick noticed Teo's willingness to let the matter drop. The Señora's other daughters were wont to regard their mother with continued incredulity, as though, with her brisk energy and independence, she might well have dropped from the moon. But not Teo. Since she had been working for Dr. Kramer, she had changed more than a little herself.

Señora Brinkman accepted a cup of chocolate, settled comfortably, and said, "Indeed I do intent to help the bank. This occasion is different. No doubt I've been criticized in the past for my harshness, but I could not rescue every rancho that fell on evil times. How was I to choose among them? The only course was to say no to everyone! But as a child, Camellito was a favorite of my husband's, and naturally, in his memory—" Her astute eyes softened, as though she cast a dutiful backward glance into the past, then closed the door again, respectfully.

"It seems to me also—wouldn't you agree, Patrick? —that it is important for us all that the bank survives. These new people, with their hard work and penny-pinching—I've seen them look with scorn at the carefree, prodigal ways of the Californios. They say we've been like grasshoppers, playing, jumping about, never giving a thought to tomorrow—"

"Not you, Mama," interrupted Teo, laughing.

"Not I, no. But unhappily, I'm an exception. So like the righteous everywhere, they haven't been sorry to see us meet the ruin we so richly deserve. The bank however, is to our credit. Managing a bank takes intellect, it's believed, and for one of us to do some work besides running cattle and breeding beautiful horses— Yes, Teo, Camellito is recognized as one of us, even though his name is Lucius Camell. His mother, after all was an Avila, and he is a distant cousin of the Palos Verdes Sepulvedas—"

"I love Camellito as much as any of you," Bets protested. "But I've never thought of him as intellectual!" To her, that word was reserved for Miguel.

"Of course not," Señora Brinkman said impatiently.

"We know that, you and I. But all the new settlers, the farmers, the shopkeepers, they take a banker at face value. Therefore the rest of us have a little reflected glory—no, not glory, but respect. And that is important."

Patrick, leaning against the deep adobe window sill, agreed with all she said. But he was a little amused; he had been expecting her for some time, and had no doubt that contributing to Camellito's cause was only an excuse for this visit.

Naturally, she wouldn't ask him bluntly about Teo and Emil Kramer! There would be suitable regard for his dignity, and apology for even hinting at the matter. But Teo was, after all, her daughter, and she'd add, if there was any cause for alarm . . .

He would then assure her there wasn't, and say it firmly, although he would not tell her why. Not even to Teo's mother could he disclose her unfortunate lack.

An unpleasant analogy came into his mind. He'd heard once, and doubtless it wasn't so, that Arabs had a practice of cutting their young daughters in such a way that when they grew up they had no pleasure in love-making. Thus a man could be sure his wife wasn't tempted to steal into a neighbor's tent.

Teo was like an Arab girl. What had happened to her, the horror of being raped, had driven away all physical feeling. She was loving and sweet, she kissed him, and she never refused his advances; but in spite of all his effort and skill, she remained as free from desire as the day he married her.

Yes, she was safe with Kramer, and he wished to God it wasn't so!

As promised, Señora Brinkman gave adequately, if not generously, and the bags of money, some large, some small, piled up at the bank. A statement, signed by Camellito and his assistants, was issued, saying, "We have in our vaults fully as much coin as is needed in the transaction of our business."

Miguel was on hand to watch what transpired the following day and he reported events back to Patrick. Riders on horseback and in spring wagons arrived, crowding the streets. They gathered on corners and in nearby saloons, exchanging rumors and reading to each other the widely-distributed statement. Gradually, however, and in spite of the official reassurance, ominously long lines formed at the cashier's window. As they grew even lengthier, horsemen galloped away to inform the others who were still indecisive, and they too came.

At that point, the emergency plan Miguel had conceived was brought into play. The sacks of money, painfully collected from old friends, were ostentatiously carried in through the front doors for all to see.

The withdrawals continued, but more slowly, and the bank remained solvent until closing time. After that, in the privacy of the empty rooms and with the doors safely barred, Camellito admitted to Miguel he could not reopen on the morrow.

"Not, and last one hour!"

"Then do not open. Announce a moratorium."

"That will finish it." Camellito's pleasant face was shrunken, beaded with sweat.

"Not necessarily. There's no one in town who doesn't know you have trouble, but many hope it is only a passing squall. Besides," Miguel pointed out, "what choice do you have? This will at least give you more time to borrow. Enough money, and you can weather the storm."

"Borrow from whom?" Camellito asked bitterly. "I've exhausted the resources of everyone I can possibly beg from, and anyway, there isn't enough gold among us all put together to save me."

"You can go to San Francisco."

And Camellito went. He argued his case desperately, and his father-in-law, Don Diego Rodriguez, deeply involved himself, brought to bear all the influence he had. But the bankers and investors in the north knew enough of the situation to refuse point-blank.

The days passed and the bank's failure loomed. Miguel, who had been responsible in the beginning for the raising of investment money from his father's old friend Ignacio Sanchez, spoke and thought of nothing else.

CHAPTER FIFTY

ON HIS RETURN FROM SAN FRANCISCO, Camellito sought out Lucky Belknap.

The two men met at the closed bank, which already
exuded a dreary mustiness. Camellito in his eagerness
arrived first, although Belknap, true to his reputation,
was prompt. Admitted by the banker, he strode in,
and his eyes gave the room a slow methodical inspection before he spoke.

"Mr. Camell," he stated, "you have need of my
assistance." The tall, austerely clad figure towered
over Camellito, who wet his lips, almost afraid to
hope, after all the discouragement he'd already met.
He stared in fascination at the famous box resting under his visitor's arm reputed to contain all the money
anyone could wish.

"I don't know why you hesitated so long in coming
to me," Belknap said with a thin smile. "We both
know you are desperate. And I'll tell you, without
keeping you in suspense, that I'm willing to make you
a large loan."

Camellito, to his shame, found himself sinking onto
the hard wooden bench beside him. He felt a tight
pressure in his chest, a sensation he'd had before, but
never in such intensity.

It would pass, it always had, but he despised himself for succumbing to weakness before this erect vig-
orous man.

Belknap, however, was choosing to ignore the banker's hunched-over posture and labored breathing.
"There are two conditions," he continued, meanwhile
standing at the window and looking out, as though,
Camellito thought, he was studying the buildings opposite with a view to purchase!

"Yes?" It was difficult to answer, he was so short of breath.

"First, I will advance you the two hundred thousand dollars you've been seeking elsewhere. However, you and your father-in-law, as the major partners, must give me a blanket mortgage on your combined real estate."

Camellito gazed at him in anguish. He had every confidence in his beloved bank. Given the chance, it would survive and be stronger than ever! But how could he tie up Don Diego's possessions in the bargain? His father-in-law had already invested so much —been so generous—

"For myself, of course! But not Don Diego!" He wanted to spring to his feet in protest, and could not. He was like a vaporish woman, he thought with self-loathing, giddy just when he should be strong and resolute. "Surely, he need not be involved!"

"Yes, Mr. Camell," Belknap said coldly. "The security must include the Rodriguez property also, or there is no loan. Of course, if you object so strongly, you are free to take your business elsewhere." He placed the black felt hat on his head, clutched the tin box more firmly, and looked toward the door. "In that case, I'll bid you good morning."

"No!" Camellito fought back a wave of nausea. "Very well, I'll ask him. He'll agree—what else can he do?" Now words came in a rush. "Let's proceed with the loan as quickly as possible, sir! Every day that passes makes it more difficult to win back the confidence of my depositors."

"I have the money ready," Belknap said, giving the box a sharp rap. "But you are forgetting. I said *two* conditions. You've heard only one."

"Oh, God!" Camellito murmured to himself, and then realized he might have uttered the despairing words aloud. He didn't know if he had or not, he felt so miserably sick.

"I shall also require your other large contributor, Ignacio Sanchez, to include in the mortgage two thousand two hundred acres of his prime land—that is, the pasture land lying nearest the San Gabriel mission."

Camellito was speechless. Then a glow of anger percolated through his miasma of queasiness and pain.

"Well?" Belknap was asking. "Can you persuade him or not? Make no mistake, I will not back out or change my mind. I've wanted that particular land for years but Sanchez would never sell to me. Of course," he added, "should you succeed in your efforts to save the bank, then I will be disappointed. That should please you."

Camellito, listening to the dry mocking voice, was unable to answer at once. He was finding himself tempted to abandon everything he had worked for all these years, just for the pleasure of flinging this cruel demand back in the teeth of the sharp greedy man who had made it. The unfamiliar taste of hatred was steadying, enabling him to forget temporarily, his physical weakness.

"If I had a choice—" he began, but was interrupted.

"Of course you have a choice! Never let it be said Elias Belknap forced anyone into anything. To my mind, business is like a woman. I want her to come to me willingly or not at all."

Liar! thought the banker, but the word remained unspoken; and Belknap continued, "This is a fine little bank. Surely keeping it in business is worth a little unpleasantness? If so, Mr. Camell, unless you have some other source of funds, you'd best deal with me. For if you don't, these doors will never reopen, and neither Rodriguez nor Sanchez, for whom you seem so worried, will see a penny's worth of their investment again. On the other hand, with the aid of my money —as well as the very expert management of yourself and your assistants—the bank could well survive. Then all your problems will disappear, will they not?

"Ah, I see you are undecided. I am a reasonable man, so I shan't press you. Take a day. No. Take two days! If in two days, you come to me with the written agreements of both Diego Rodriguez and Ignacio Sanchez, I will hand over the money on the spot. If you do not appear, I will understand you have gotten your help elsewhere. Now, could anything be fairer than that?

"Until then, I'll be staying at the Bella Union, and will be looking forward to our meeting there. Good day, sir."

He strolled out. The door had barely shut behind him when Camellito rushed into the back room and retched into a bucket.

In the end, it was Diego Rodriguez who was forced to speak with his old friend Don Ignacio. Don Diego was deeply reluctant to do so, but his son-in-law being so obviously ill, he feared the outcome of the interview might be jeopardized by Camellito's poor appearance. If the bank were to be saved, continued confidence in the strength of its president was a necessity.

Don Diego, still straight and tall in the saddle was, at seventy-three, uncannily like his daughter, Felipa in both figure and manner. He too wore haughtiness wrapped about him like a cloak. Yet when he returned from this errand and had dismounted, he appeared stooped, and years older.

"Well?" Felipa asked. Camellito sat in an iron garden chair a little distance away and did not rise. He was fighting for breath, but trying to conceal from his wife his painful efforts. To his bewilderment, this illness had not passed off with the rapidity of previous attacks.

"I have his promise," Don Diego said shortly. "But I'll tell you this: I would have released him from it then and there, were it not for you, Felipa. I kept reminding myself—I can't have my daughter made a pauper."

"I won't be penniless, nor will you. Nor Don Ignacio," she said. "Have you lost confidence in the soundness of the bank? We all agreed, enough new cash will stave off the withdrawals, and then all will be well again."

Felipa had not mentioned her husband or his abilities, and Don Diego did not even glance at the supine figure in the chair.

"To tell you the truth, daughter, I don't know

whether I've lost confidence or not. But I heartily wish I, as well as Ignacio, could back out. That splendid old friend! His courage and generosity deserve better than what he fully expects to happen."

"What does he expect then?" Camellito croaked.

"He said to me, *'No quiero, morir de hambre!'* Does that sound like confidence to you? Well, I too, do not wish to die of hunger!"

"Father!" exclaimed Felipa.

"Yes, you'll see, all will come right!" Camellito assured them earnestly, yet he could not help panting as he spoke. Don Diego threw him a contemptuous glare before stalking away into the house.

Felipa moved to follow, then turned back to stand above her husband, her long shadow falling across his face.

"Do you call yourself a man?" She gave a short, scathing laugh. "This was your opportunity to show Father, to show them all! Instead you lie prostrate and let others sweep up the pieces of what you've broken. Lucius Camell, I despised you always, and I was right. I should have been thrown from a horse and died of a broken back, before ever I agreed to marry such a weakling!"

CHAPTER FIFTY-ONE

THE REOPENING OF THE BANK WENT SURprisingly well. This time, as the long lines formed, Camellito himself, sweating and pale but grandly attired in a new frocked coat and tall silk hat, stood by the counter, and the stacks of gold pieces at his elbow towered taller than he was. Settlers still swung from their horses at the door, but at sight of this truly opulent display, some halted, shamefaced and indecisive, others backed out. The run on the bank was stopped before it started, and that afternoon there were even a few new deposits.

Convinced his crisis had finally passed, Camellito was jubilant, and his indisposition subsided accordingly. He personally called on the many friends who had helped him, thanking them and inviting them all to a celebration party.

Miguel was one of the very few who declined, telling Bets he did not agree with Camellito's confident view.

For the first time since the bank had faltered, he had sought her out, rather than Patrick, to confide his continued worry, and that he would do so now made her uneasy. She sat quietly, head bowed, for she was mending Patrick's clothes, a chore Teo had little time for, and she was grateful for the busyness of her hands. The long wait for Miguel to raise the subject of Lucky Belknap had told on her. She felt tired and listless, even to the point of no longer feeling dread. The uncertainty had become intolerable.

Her eyes on her work, she said, "I understood the bank was saved."

"I wish I could believe it is. But I can't help thinking, the farmers and other new depositors are simple people, easily overawed by the sight of so much gold. They are also cautious and careful, and after they've had time to consider, some of them may decide to cache their money at home, or in another bank, and take no more chances. That, Elizabeth, is what I am afraid of."

"Then let us pray you are wrong."

"Elizabeth . . ."

Her heart turned over. Was this the moment? But no, she decided, looking up, his expression was not one of impending accusation. Not yet!

"Suppose I am not wrong! Suppose the bank fails, and Ignacio Sanchez loses everything he has . . . Then I think we should sell Rancho Aguirre."

The sewing dropped from her hands. She could only stare at him.

He continued, speaking awkwardly, and now it was he who looked away. "Don Ignacio will be a pauper, and through no fault of his own. An old man—with nothing. He will blame me, and rightly so, for having involved him against his inclinations. If I—if we— were to sell our land, I could partially repay him. But I would want your agreement—"

She had sprung to her feet as he was speaking. "Miguel, you have three children! Will you make beggars of them—and us?"

He managed a thin smile. "It wouldn't be that bad. There might be enough left for a small house in Los Angeles, I would work again at a newspaper—"

"No! No! I didn't save the rancho only for you to throw it away!"

Silence fell between them. He nodded, as if this was the answer he'd feared, and a muscle jumped spasmodically in his cheek.

Bets however was experiencing doubts. Wasn't what he proposed exactly what she'd always thought she wanted—to return to town, to see him established again as a respected newspaper editor?

Then why hadn't she seized the chance? Was she so enmeshed in her long bitter fight to save the rancho that she would not abandon it, not for any reason?

Perhaps. But, she reminded herself, it was Miguel who had originally spurned their life in Los Angeles, unhappy, and refusing to humble himself even a little in order to regain his old position as editor. How much more difficult after all these years would it be to find such work now? And if he did, he would truly have to demean himself! For he would not be returning with prestige. He would be just a sour, middle-aged man, forced to take orders from youngsters. And for that narrow unrewarding life, he would give up the freedom of Rancho Aguirre, the wide lands he had loved passionately all his life?

He would not, she decided with sudden conviction. He would not!

Then what would have happened, she wondered, studying his averted face, if she'd agreed to the proposal? Why, nothing, of course. Not even realizing it himself, he had banked on her refusal. He'd offered to help Don Ignacio—she'd refused—and so a little of his guilt was eased. Wasn't that the way it was?

Very well, if it would help him, she would gladly take on her own shoulders some of his burden. All the same, it was disquieting to realize how very deeply his peace of mind depended on the precarious affairs of Camellito!

Unhappily, Miguel's fears for the bank were soon borne out. Withdrawals quietly began again, and each day the trickle grew larger, until it became a flood. In a panic, Camellito applied to Belknap for a further loan, which was granted.

The nature of the security the banker gave Belknap this time was not disclosed, but whatever his sacrifice, it was in vain. The new money melted away even more quickly than the first, and there was no further reprieve. One morning, without fanfare, the Campbell and Rodriguez Bank closed its doors for good.

Inside the deserted rooms on that final day, Camellito paced alone for hours. Only a crippling shortness of breath sent him out and home at last, to face the recriminations of Don Diego and Felipa.

Miguel accompanied his family back to Rancho Aguirre, and there, in the room they had shared so long, he finally asked his wife the question she had been expecting.

"I had almost convinced myself I should not probe into the question of the mortgage money," he began. "After all, what good would it do? But now that everything else in my life has fallen apart, and I am a pariah among my friends for ruining Don Ignacio—"

"That's not so, Miguel!" she cried, exasperated. "You encouraged him to invest his money, true, but it was Don Diego—"

A gesture silenced her; and he continued. "Even my rancho, as I tried to tell you, is no longer a pleasure to me, because were I to give it up, I could save him. But I understand your refusal, Elizabeth, and I cannot truly blame you. You are a woman and a mother. No, the blame is mine. I should not be weak enough to let you sway me . . .

"No matter. Don Ignacio is finished, and he is only one of many, for the day of the Californio has passed. Perhaps you remember—ah, you would not, you are far too sensible and level-headed to care for fancy words. But I used to call this rich, much-loved land of ours, 'the farthest Eden'. Now it is no longer so very far, nor, alas, for me an Eden, as a new and different time has begun. Each day, dusty little Los Angeles becomes less of a pueblo, more of an American town, while the cattle grow ever scarcer on the hills, and the great spreading ranchos look to their end. Well, these changes, as any impartial observer would tell you, are not wholly bad. The breakup of the great landholdings, an event I personally abhor, will mean a multitude of small farms and homesteads, and opportunities for many. The new people, crude and ignorant as they are, deserve their chance, and I wish them good fortune with what once was ours.

"The dispossessed however, pose a problem. So long as they remain, they will continue to mourn for the old days—for extravagance and generosity, for courtesy, leisure, beauty. And I, I am one of them. I will not, cannot, adjust to any other mode of life.

"I see by your expression you do not understand. Let me just say then, as a reason for this rambling speech, that having no other cause for satisfaction, it would make me happy to know my wife has not been unfaithful to me. Wait! Before you answer, I must tell you I have been tortured by doubts, knowing in this too, I was at fault. Wretched, despicable Belknap! Had I been acting the part of a man, running my rancho instead of sulking in my room like a boy scolded by his father, I would have recognized him for what he was. It is far too late now, but I apologize. I am deeply ashamed for having exposed you, my wife, to his attentions.

"Elizabeth, he must have tried to seduce you! Did he succeed?"

Until this moment, she had not been certain what answer she would give. During the long weeks of waiting, it had seemed impossible she should lie, deceive him further. But listening as he bared his tormented uncertainty, she wondered what in his heart he really desired. She was remembering how he had once cried to her, about Tomas—*I wish I had never known!*

Truth, she was thinking sadly, was more precious than she'd dreamed. It was a luxury one could not always afford.

"No, Miguel, he did not!"

Her husband studied her face, then he slowly let out his breath.

"Thank you. I should have known. Indeed I did know, because before we were married you told me you would never be unfaithful, and you are not a woman to break your word. I'm sorry I needed to ask; it was an unworthy suspicion, but I wanted to be told. I wanted there to be something left of which I need not feel ashamed. . . . Elizabeth, *querida,* why are you weeping?"

"I think—for the girl I used to be—and for so many wasted years. Miguel, you haven't called me *querida* in so long! But everything is all right now, isn't it?"

He shook his head, as if in wonder. "All right?"

"Yes." She spoke with a kind of forlorn eagerness. "Our property is growing prosperous again! Our debts are paid and the price of wool is rising. Because of you, we are fortunate enough to have sheep instead of cattle. Phineas says cattle will never be important here again. Oh, Miguel, don't brood any longer about the bank. You did all you could! Nor about Don Ignacio—"

The expression on his face, the sadness, puzzled and frightened her. She went quickly to him, laying her cheek against his, pulling his arms around her. When his embrace tightened in response, she felt immense relief, and an easing as well, of the secret guilt that filled her.

She hadn't lied, she told herself. She hadn't been unfaithful—not in the true sense of the word. Nothing of Miguel's—none of her affection, certainly none of her passion, had been given to Belknap. She had paid a debt as required, and only that.

She could still make Miguel happy! Tonight he must forget all his recent disappointments, his worries. She would make him forget! They would relive an earlier time, when he had faith in himself, when his fierce pride was still intact. Tonight would be another beginning!

Making her believe he shared her optimism, Miguel bent his head and kissed her. Soft at first, then more urgent, his mouth searched and lingered, and little flickerings of desire flowered inside of her. As she watched all he did, her blue eyes dreamy, the fringing ebony lashes half-closed, he undressed her, and afterward himself, but slowly, seeming to savor every motion, postponing his pleasure and hers in the way she had wanted, but he'd never done before.

He knelt then at the bedside where she lay ready, welcoming, and began to whisper words of love and to touch her body intimately, and the tender caresses of his hands and lips were like strokings of fire, making her reach for him, making her cry out repeatedly.

Only when neither of them could endure waiting longer, did he come to her. There was barely time for the brief bittersweet reflection—*this is how it could always have been with him,* then all thought was wiped away, her body arched to meet his, and she felt her unbearable need balloon and explode, bringing aching, sweet fulfillment.

She awoke at dawn, and found herself alone. At first, still drowsy, Bets lingered happily in the memory of last night's love-making, so unlike anything ever before between them in its closeness, openness, Miguel's unrestrained giving of himself.

But gradually, an apprehension that she didn't understand replaced her contentment. She wondered where he'd gone, and then as time passed, and she went to search for him throughout the house, a fearful suspicion overcame her.

Had he truly been convinced the future could be faced?

Or had he, in the best, most articulate way he could find—bidden her farewell?

CHAPTER FIFTY-TWO

"WHAT A SPLENDID HAUL OF MAIL WE HAVE!" Margaret Cullinan said. "Here's a letter for you, and Bertram's beloved literary magazine has come from England as well. It seems I'll have the *Aspinwall Courier* all to myself for once! My word, Mary, isn't this the perfect day for you and me to be truants! And so beautiful outside too."

She smiled gaily at Mary, who was sitting at the breakfast table, watching through the open door a glistening green hummingbird dart among the scarlet hibiscus blossoms, probing in them with his long slender bill, and hovering, his wings beating so rapidly they were almost invisible.

It was exquisite outside, sunny but slightly cooler than usual. On the spur of the moment the night before, the two women had tacked a notice on the side of the clinic, announcing: *Closed Tuesday*. Actually, this was not as irresponsible an impulse as it would have been a few months earlier, as only two patients had appeared there during the entire previous day. The completion of the railroad across the United States was already having its effect. The flow of travelers had greatly diminished, and many natives, no longer able to find work in Aspinwall, were returning to their villages.

Mary at once abandoned her contemplation of the hummingbird and tore open the envelope addressed to her in Miguel's distinctive script. Tidings from Los Angeles!

But with the first lines, her heart constricted, and her pleasure in the day of freedom vanished as though it had never been. For with the first words, she understood this was no ordinary letter, and was frightened.

Mary,

It is almost dawn. The news yesterday was so devastating I am hardly able to put pen to paper. My beautiful Elizabeth has too much courage to understand my despair, but I confess to you, dear friend, I am weeping as I write.

Camellito's bank has failed, bringing ruin to him and many others.

Mary must have exclaimed aloud, because Margaret was gazing at her in alarm. "My dear! Is the letter bad news?"

"Yes—wait, let me read on."

I have seldom wanted to kill a human being, but I think, if a young Spaniard named Jaime Real were to come within reach, I would shoot without compunction. It is he who betrayed Camellito's trust and brought him down, and Real's Spanish blood shames all of us who share it!

Who is this Real, you ask? He arrived in Los Angeles two or three years ago, totally unknown, but possessed of a charming persuasiveness that quickly opened doors. He worked for a time under Frank Lecouvreur at the wharf, and Lecouvreur commended his diligence and ability. However, that shrewd man has since admitted that for no reason at all he didn't trust his young assistant, and therefore gave him little access to the books, which was doubtless the reason Real eventually left there.

He next applied for a position at the bank, giving Camellito to understand he had always had a longing to be a banker, but the friend of his father's, for whom he'd expected to work back in Andalusia, had backed out, claiming he preferred someone with less of an ear for those in trouble. Hardly for most bankers the best recommendation, would you say? But the tale bore an uncanny resemblance to Camellito's own history, and our old friend hired him at once.

All went well, indeed the young man was given a raise in pay and highly commended. Then one day he disappeared. At first, foul play was suspected; but when the bank books were examined, the true answer came to light. Real had embezzled close to $15,000! Immediately, on the following day, a number of depositors, whose confidence in the Ca-mell and Rodriguez Bank was already low, began withdrawing their funds, and the fatal landslide was set in motion.

Aside from my pity and concern for my boyhood companion and the many who lost their savings, I carry an intolerable burden of my own. I met Ignacio Sanchez on the street yesterday. He saw me, but passed by without speaking.

Mary, her hands trembling, folded the sheets of fine linen paper and laid them on the dining table. She had not entirely finished, and now perhaps she never would. Miguel had unknowingly brought her pain as intense as his own.

Jaime Real. Real had been the family name of old Doña Cesaria. And from Andalusia? Ah, Miguel's description was too close for coincidence! There could be no doubt at all.

"What in the world is it?" Margaret was asking in alarm. "You're so dreadfully white!"

"It's—I've just learned of the bank failure in Los Angeles."

"Yes, a sad occurrence," Margaret agreed, continuing to watch her with puzzled concern. "The *Courier* carries a mention of it today, I see. Did you have savings you've lost?"

"No, nothing like that. But—Lucius Camell was a very dear friend."

They were all her friends! Camellito, and Don Diego. Miguel. Even elderly Don Ignacio. All, all victims of her son's perfidy.

She went on numbly, "There is no way I can help . . . but I must go home."

"Bertram and I have hoped you might consider this your home."

"You have become family to me, both of you," Mary responded, and forced herself to put aside for the moment her bitter abstraction. She managed to give her friend a faint smile of genuine affection before adding, "Even before this happened, Margaret, I confess I was thinking of leaving."

"Because Bertram has asked me to marry him? We're old people, Mary! We don't have to be alone together. You know how much I enjoy your company, and as for him, I think he's as proud of your artistic success as any father could be. You surely don't feel shut out?"

"Of course not!" Mary assured her, although the truth was, she already did feel slightly uncomfortable, foolish as it seemed when the three of them had lived in the same house for more than three years. When Margaret began to protest further, she added, "The clinic will be having fewer patients—already we see a great difference. I shan't be needed much longer."

Margaret nodded reluctantly. "It will surprise me if the natives do not continue to get sick, although perhaps not with so many foreign diseases, but you are quite right. I will be able to manage alone." She reached across the table and gave her friend's hand a brisk pat. "Bertram and I want you to be happy. If going to California is what you wish, he can easily arrange for your passage. Doubtless the next ship north from Panama City will have a stateroom available."

"Margaret, you are so good to me!"

"Anyone would be. You're the sort who gives more than she takes. Wouldn't you like a cup of tea?"

"Yes, please."

"Oh, and here's the newspaper. Perhaps you'd like to read the account of the bank failure for yourself, although, as I say, it's too brief to—Yes, Enge?" The Indian cook had appeared in the kitchen doorway. "Oh, very well. Mary, the fishermen are here with the lobsters. Excuse me for a moment."

Alone, Mary sank back and read through the terse and highly critical article. Poor unfortunate Camellito, she reflected. In addition to being made virtually without funds, he was now being publicly castigated, when, in fact, the true villain was the man who had brought the depositors to a stampede, Jaime Real. Real, who was almost certainly Jaime Reyes, her son!

She was about to throw down the newspaper in a surge of indignant anger, when a familiar name in an adjacent column caught her eye. She sucked in her breath, and as she began reading, once again her dread turned to horror.

NEW VICTIM OF LACHENAIS

A prominent member of the Californio community has been found shot to death in a remote corner of his rancho. The body of Mr. Miguel Aguirre, a former editor of the *Los Angeles Star* was discovered after Mrs. Elizabeth Aguirre asked a family friend, State Senator Phineas Bishop, to conduct a search.

According to the Senator, there is not the slightest doubt that the notorious bandit, Michael Lachenais, who only the previous day had murdered his own partner in crime at a site a few miles distant, shot, then robbed Mr. Aguirre. The outlaw's capture is believed to be imminent.

Mary snatched up Miguel's letter, and read the last few lines. Then she tore the pages and threw them in the refuse basket, before hurrying from the house.

The door slammed behind her. Even though the window shutters were open, she did not hear Margaret's surprised call. She managed to stride along briskly, as though she had an imperative errand, but her briskness this time hid only despair.

Miguel!

She must escape from herself, from her thoughts, and there was no escape. None! The planned for, dreamed of, return to California was impossible now. Face Patrick and Bets, when she knew where the blame lay for Miguel's death? Were Miguel still alive, she might have helped him, eased his unhappiness. But dead—and by his own hand!

Beyond any doubt he had killed himself. Phineas knew that too, of course. He must have found Miguel's gun and gotten rid of it, deciding with grim practicality that if Lachenais was doomed to hang for several murders anyway, one more wouldn't matter. And Bets! How Betsey must have agonized over calling for help before finally turning to her old friend and praying he would find Miguel before the ranch hands did, or the Sheriff's posse, out seeking the bandit.

All this, because *her* son Jaime had cast a stone into their lives, and its ripples continued on and on. Miguel, gifted, moody, and so very-dear to her, was dead. Ignacio Sanchez and Diego Rodriguez were ruined. And Camellito—didn't he wish he too had died, rather than suffer such disgrace?

Her son Jaime had done all this.

Miguel's condemnation would be written in her mind forever, and in crimson letters:

"It is he who betrayed Camellito's trust and brought him down, and his Spanish blood shames all of us who share it."

Aspinwall was not large, and she came quickly to its edge, where the dirt road petered out and jungle began. She walked on, following a faint Indian path, not slackening her quick steps. For once, she was blind to her surroundings. A brilliantly-hued red, yellow, and blue macaw perched just over her head, and on another day she would have stopped short, oblivious of all else, to absorb with deep sensual pleasure his flashing colors. Now, although the bird chattered to her angrily, his jagged beak clicking, she did not even glance up.

Farther along, a harmless-appearing young snake slithered across her path, its small sleek body undulating curves of velvety brown and gray. She almost trod on the tail of a fer-de-lance, and never knew.

The heat was, as usual, intense, and the air was heavy with moisture. Even living in Panama as long as she had, she always suffered from a sense of clammy oppression when she ventured into the green rotting world of tropical jungle. But not today. Today she was oblivious of discomfort, as well as beauty, or danger.

So this was what despair meant, she was thinking. This was how it felt not to care any more whether one lived or died. She could understand completely how Miguel had embraced death as a friend! He'd found death a good friend, one to be cherished, one who brought forgetfulness.

She ran on. The small path, barely discernable, crossed another, and still further, branched and branched again. Then, in a tangle of thick vine trunks, it disappeared entirely.

She swung around, searching. Where had she entered this shadowy glade? She was ringed with trees, covered with great parasitical growths of fern and orchid. The opening, and there must have been one, had vanished into the untraceable lushness.

Suddenly her heart was pounding, and she was wrenched with fear—not only of the jungle itself, for the green swampy wilderness posed immediate danger, but also of what had been in her mind. She had come this way of her own volition! Could she have been seeking the same solace Miguel had found?

She had always known how easy it was to become lost here. So easy, and so fatal. If one were rash enough or foolish enough or unhappy enough, one blundered into this steaming morass without a guide —and one did not return.

Was that *why* she'd come this way?

No, never! No matter what happened! And with that determination, in spite of her perilous situation, she felt better.

But the deadly peril remained. With the sun overhead, she didn't know one direction from another. Where *was* the path?

Unbidden, tales of people lost flashed through her mind. People like the poor young Army Lieutenant, Isaac Strain, who some years back in seeking a route for a canal across the isthmus, had led his men to slow agonizing death. He'd simply taken a wrong turning, and then in desperation doggedly followed a river that wound nowhere, while all the while, a situation of terrible irony, he and his little band were only a day's march from a settlement.

That mistake could be hers . . .

She spun around, her eyes and ears no longer dull, but sharper than they'd ever been before. She could hear a veritable cascade of sounds, the howling of monkeys, the clicking of cicadas, a sudden harsh birdcall, and the distant roar of a jaguar; she could see all the menacing fecundity of the twining vegetation, the creeping, clinging tendrils that seemed to reach for her hungrily, like tentacles.

In terror, she broke from one small glade into another, pushing her way wildly through the tangle of growth, until at last, feeling something feathery on her bare arm, she glanced down. A six-inch-long centipede lay there, its legs rippling on either side of its reddish segmented body like living fringe. She cringed, screaming, and jerked to dislodge the giant insect, but the thing clung until she brushed her arm hard against the rough bole of a palm. Her skin tore, she felt a sharp stab of pain, but the creature fell wriggling to the ground, and vanished beneath some rotting leaves.

She stood still for a moment, rubbing with repugnance at the spot on her arm where the creature had rested, and shivering. How many other horrible things —tarantulas, scorpions—might even now be finding the haven of her long skirts and starting to climb the undersides?

The ugly notion sent her running again, beating her way through the damp growth until every breath was drawn with deep shuddering effort. Her panic grew, for wasn't the underbrush thicker now, almost impossible to get through?

Then, unexpectedly, she stumbled onto a path. Narrow and dim, but still a path. She gazed at it in perplexity. As best she could tell, it was going north and south, and she needed, she felt almost certain, to go west. Didn't Aspinwall lie to the west? But west was not possible! On that side lay a great fallen log, filled with swarming ants, and beyond was an impenetrable thicket of vines.

There was nothing to do but go forward, and remembering Isaac Strain, sobbing in her weariness, she plunged ahead.

The ordeal ended as abruptly as it had begun. She rounded a turn, and off to the left she heard voices. Laughing, chattering, young Indian voices. The foliage thinned, and she pushed through, scratching her hands and catching her dress on a protruding branch. She jerked the fabric free, ripping it, and then she was out, standing at the edge of a small street in Aspinwall.

The two Indian girls, dressed in bright cottons, their long sleek hair neatly plaited, had fallen silent and were gaping at her. Shaken as she was, she realized what a startling figure she must present, bursting from the jungle, her white blouse wet with perspiration, her chestnut hair torn from its pins and hanging wildly, her skirt dirtied with bits of lichen and moss. No doubt too, her eyes were staring and frantic.

She turned from them, and with trembling hands, brushed some of the jungle debris from her clothing. Then she walked slowly away, toward the house of Bertram Cox.

She was alive, and what a fool she'd been to play with danger, to have rushed blindly into the jungle, even to imagine that death might be welcome! It hadn't been, and she would never in her life again make that mistake.

Terror, she supposed, had acted as a catharsis, because she could think clearly now, and face the future. Life, though it must be lived forever in Aspinwall, was still for her poignantly sweet, and love of it pulsed in her veins. She had learned that much about herself.

She entered the house, her head high, although she felt a little feverish, and very tired. The centipede must have bitten her, she thought calmly, noting how the sunlight that slanted in the windows shimmered and wavered. She'd be sick for a bit, it was inevitable, but a small price to pay. Smaller surely than death.

"Mary! Good, here you are at last! My dear, you have a guest—" Margaret's voice changed, filling with alarm as she started toward her, then stopped. "What has happened?"

Bertram Cox, who was drinking gin and bitters, ejaculated something and set his glass down so hard the liquid splashed out on the rattan table. Only the stocky fair-haired man at the far end of the room was quiet.

Her eyes, still not adjusted to the dimness after the brilliant sunshine of the street, widened as she stared at him. She must be a victim of hallucination, she told herself, but the small core of gladness that had flamed up at sight of him grew larger.

Although his gaze did not wander from her face, she bethought herself of her disheveled appearance, her torn clothing, the grimy wetness beading her forehead; and one hand crept up surreptitiously to smooth away a loose strand of hair.

"John . . ." she whispered. "Is it really you?"

"Yes, my darling."

He came to her then, and knelt, brushing a clinging bit of moss from her cotton skirt.

Then he stood again, and they faced each other. When he spoke, it was brusquely, as though he anticipated argument, and this time would have none of it.

"Mary, I have come to take you home."

Part Four

‹◊‹‹◊‹‹◊‹‹◊‹‹◊‹‹◊‹‹◊‹‹◊‹‹◊‹‹◊‹‹◊‹‹◊‹

1871

CHAPTER FIFTY-THREE

"TOMAS, THE PARADE IS COMING! I CAN HEAR it!" Maria Rosa cried. Her hand clutched her brother's even more tightly in her excitement. They had not been quite early enough, so they had missed being in the front row of spectators crowding the favorite vantage point before the new Pico House; consequently she was stretched up on her toes as high as she could go. She was eight years old, with very large dark eyes, small-boned and delicate. A noisy, self-possessed, wisp of a child.

Isabel, her older sister, exclaimed suddenly, "Oh, no! Those Pike wagons have stopped just in the way of the marchers!" and her indignation was echoed by others. For two big wagons, both loaded full of the feckless, gypsy-like families known as Pikes, had pulled to a halt, partially blocking a side of the street. The bearded men knew what they were about, too, Tomas thought. They held loaded shotguns in the crooks of their arms, some of their ragged, dirty-faced children were shouting taunts, and their packs of mangy dogs had settled down to scratch fleas.

But if the Pikes thought they'd made for themselves a fine high seat from which to view this long-anticipated Fourth of July parade, the very first since before the war, they had misjudged the jovial temper of the crowd. It wasn't half a minute before a press of angry men surrounded the wagons. They fired pistols and whipped up the horses, sending the poor, overworked beasts off at a plodding but determined run. Even bare-ribbed and spavined as the animals were, it would be a long while before their owners got hold of them again.

There was a lot of laughter, and yelling, and the smell of gunpowder was acrid in the air as haphazard shooting continued from sheer high spirits. And then the first small group of marchers passed. They were Scottish men, seeming outlandish to the Aguirres because of the short plaid skirts that displayed their knobby knees. One was skirling out an ear-piercing tune, from a contraption that appeared to be nothing more than a number of polished wooden rods, sprouting from the leather water-bag he held beneath his arm.

After that, to everyone's delight, came a brass band leading a contingent of Mexican War veterans. The same band played regularly at the Garden of Paradise, and all the musicians were cheered vociferously by their friends. They responded with grins and a rousing rendition of *Yankee Doodle*.

Maria Rosa had begun to tug at Tomas's hand, wailing, "I can't see!" At eighteen, he was broad-shouldered and strong, so he caught her by the waist and in one easy motion swung her onto his shoulders. The wail turned to a squeal of delight.

Isabel meanwhile had been craning her neck from side to side, and now she asked him, having to speak loudly to be heard above the music and shouting and gunfire, "Where can Mother be? She's missing all this!"

"I haven't seen her yet."

His sister sounded anxious, and Tomas wished she hadn't asked. He didn't want her guessing his uneasiness about Mother. It was all very well for Mr. Bishop to occasionally give the family his advice, such as where and when they should sell the sheep, or the walnuts, honey, and lemons. He'd been a great help, no doubt about that, especially in the difficult days after their mother became a widow.

But lately, whenever they came to town like this, Mr. Bishop had fallen into the habit of asking her to accompany him, not only to committee meetings concerned with his many enterprises, but to social events, and for Tomas who treasured even the smallest memory of Miguel, her casual acceptance of such invitations was a disagreeable shock. This very morning at Grandfather's house, Mother had told them all she would look for them at the middle arch of the Pico House portico, and they should go on ahead because she wasn't quite ready, and then she'd added that Mr. Bishop was calling for her in his carriage. For Tomas, the pleasure of the long-awaited day was at once diminished.

He was bound to feel a certain sadness anyway, standing here watching the parade and listening to the music, because he could remember so well how Father had loved such celebrations, and how fiercely he'd hated to see so many of them change from being regular customs to being abandoned and forgotten.

Oh, if only that outlaw Lachenais had been caught a few days earlier! If only, when the vigilantes had hauled him screaming and crying, to be hung at the Tomlinson and Griffith corral, it had been before he'd gunned down the finest person who ever lived. If the posse had been quicker, Father would still be alive, taking part today, perhaps even being the Grand Marshal! And Tomas would be riding beside him, also mounted on a prancing Aguirre horse . . .

"Tomas! Isabel!"

It was their Aunt Mary, calling and beckoning, a stocky stranger close at her side. So with Maria Rosa riding high in the air, and Isabel following behind, he threaded his way to where she stood, her arms outstretched. Even Maria Rosa, leaning forward precariously from her perch must be kissed. Tomas was very glad to see his aunt again, and finally to meet her new husband. She'd been living in Sacramento since returning to California, only coming to Los Angeles for occasional short visits, and each time alone. John Carew's business with the Governor had until recently prevented him from accompanying her.

So Tomas studied with curiosity the man Aunt Mary had married so hastily in Panama. A man about the same stature as himself, but deeper-chested. Strong looking, the teen-ager thought. His own eyes being blue, and his mother's also, he didn't find that ice-blue color of Carew's eyes remarkable, but he was surprised by the white hair and brows. The man didn't appear to be old in any other way!

"Isabel dear, this is our Ellen," Aunt Mary was saying, so Tomas too turned politely to be presented to John Carew's daughter.

His first feeling was one of surprise. So Carew's hair hadn't turned white from age! The girl had it too. Her hair however was very long, and the shining beauty of the thick braids that reached far below her waist astonished him.

"And this is Tomas, Ellen." Aunt Mary gave him her generous smile. "Oh, Tomas, at last we've come back to Los Angeles to live! John has bought the Roja place. Doesn't it adjoin Rancho Aguirre directly?"

"On the west corner," he mumbled, not really listening. He was looking into wide-set eyes that were not blue as he expected, but dark gray. He thought of the still water in a shaded canyon pool.

In spite of her demure air though, her tilted chin hinted at independence. She evidently had a mind of her own, something he approved of in girls. And how pretty she was! Sturdy like her father, yet also petite and graceful, and her face was unblemished, not even slightly pock-marked like his own. Smooth and soft.

He might have gone on staring, not realizing he did so, but John Carew said to him, "I believe I've bought good land, Tomas, although most afternoons, they tell me, the wind blows a gale there. Didn't I hear that you instructed your foreman to plant eucalyptus as a windbreak?"

"Yes, sir." *You* instructed *your* foreman! Tomas straightened, oblivious of Maria Rosa, bouncing on his shoulders.

"Have the trees helped?"

"Yes, and they grow very fast too." Then reluctantly, because his eucalyptus seeds had been part of a packet William Wolfskill, a business associate of Phineas Bishop's, had received from Australia, he added, "They were General Bishop's suggestion, but I've another kind of tree you might think about. The mulberry. I've started a grove to raise silkworms."

"Is that so?" Carew laughed in an interested way. "Somehow the production of silk seems more fitting to the Orient."

"Not at all," Tomas said earnestly. "Mulberries are being planted all over this area, and the cocoons do so well there's even a demand in Europe now for our California worm. Father Daniel has planted two young trees next to the church door. He says if silk-making is so profitable, he'll let the nuns try their hand at it, to fatten the poor box."

He became conscious suddenly that Isabel was staring at him, her mouth slightly open; and realizing the reason for her astonishment, he reddened. He didn't often talk so much, it was true, and certainly not to a stranger. He'd been carried away by the heady compliments of being treated as a grown man and being asked for his advice as well.

Nevertheless, his expansiveness was cut off. He busied himself swinging Maria Rosa down and giving her into the care of his aunt who had a good view of the street. Because now, two magnificent, high-stepping horses—Californio of course, he would have recognized them even without knowing their riders—were pacing past, caparisoned in the traditional heavy trappings of ornate silver. Who would have guessed at this moment that of once vast Rancho Palos Verdes nothing remained except a few paltry acres! The two Sepulveda men, splendid in their satin jackets, velvet pants embroidered down the sides, and wide, flat hats with silk tassels swinging round the brim, were eyed with envious wonder by most of the spectators, themselves dressed in calico dresses or old brown trousers and heavy boots. Tomas felt a surge of pride that he, like those skilled riders, was a Californio!

"Where's Grandfather?" Isabel asked their aunt, no doubt hoping she would tell her and Maria Rosa the secret Tomas had managed to keep from them. Grandfather had promised a surprise for today, the only hint being that it was something Adam had had to procure for him. But Aunt Mary must not have known either, because she said, "I can't imagine why he hasn't come yet! He's always been like a boy himself about parades—"

She was interrupted by a young man shouting a spiel to the crowd as he bestowed balloons upon their children. Maria Rosa, who had never seen such a wonder before, held tightly to the string of her tugging red sphere, fearful it would escape into the sky.

"Note the climate here, friends!" declaimed the man loudly. "A climate unsurpassed anywhere, with breezes equal to the most benign zephyrs of Italy, and soil so bountiful it will grow any and all crops!

"Ask yourselves why a colony from Denmark has purchased five thousand acres to be subdivided into small farms, why an English gentleman has been seeking one hundred thousand acres for fellow settlers from the British Isles, why the Germans hope to establish another outlying community like Anaheim, as rich and successful as the first.

"Then, ask yourselves whether ten dollars an acre for such fertile land is not truly the bargain of this or any other century!"

"Sounds enticing, does it not?" Arcadia Stearns had joined them, and she gave a contented little laugh.

"One of Don Abel's ranchos?" Mary asked her.

"Probably, although one can't be certain. The Trust has grown so large. Our South Coast is having what Abel calls a boomlet, although he says the area can never really develop until the railroad brings people directly here instead of into San Francisco. All the same, there's been a surprising demand for homes and small farms."

Tomas could see how attentively John Carew was listening to Señora Stearns, and his respect for the judgment of this new member of the family continued to climb. His father had always admired Doña Arcadia greatly, and he did too. For everyone knew how undaunted she'd been when time and again her husband was within a hairsbreadth of ruin.

Don Abel was said to be arguing with the Robinson Trust, chiefly because, as Grandfather explained, he'd been his own master all his life, and a driving, domineering one at that, so he simply couldn't adjust in his old age to accepting the decisions of others. Only last week, while he was getting rich again and all due to the Trust, he'd gone ahead and given out grazing leases on thousands of acres, this, though he knew as well as any man alive, how hard sheep were on the land, leaving it scrubby and unattractive, without a blade of grass. Scarcely the rolling green countryside to appeal to purchasers! As a consequence, today he was in San Francisco answering an angry complaint from Mr. Robinson, who headed the trust!

Yet none of these ups and downs were visible or ever had been in the demeanor of his wife. Even at the worst time, when their income had fallen to less than three hundred dollars a year, she held her head high. A great Californio lady!

All the same, Tomas, like Miguel before him, didn't like to think about land sales. If he had his choice, every rancho would have remained intact, and all of them just as they were in his childhood. So he turned his mind away from the conversation and let it drift pleasurably to the afternoon's events.

First there would be Grandfather's surprise, and after that, in the Plaza, a number of speeches delivered from the red, white and blue bunting-draped platform set up alongside the new fountain. No fear either they'd be more than short, rousing speeches! There were barrels of beer waiting in the shade of the saplings Mrs. McCarty and her friends had planted to hide the unsightly water tank, and no boring orators would last long in such an atmosphere!

Then, as a climax to the day, three or four Californio families planned a picnic at Eaton Canyon, with a punch of fruit and brandy, and a stew of wild game. Having contributed three tender young cottontails to that stew the day before, Tomas was prepared for it to be the tastiest he had ever eaten.

He surprised himself by asking abruptly, "Miss Ellen, will you and your father be coming to Eaton Canyon?"

"I haven't heard. Will we, Papa?"

She had a pleasant voice too, Tomas thought. Softer than Isabel's.

"I'm afraid not, Ellen. I promised the governor I'd stay all afternoon at the Plaza festivities, to get some idea of how the new settlers think politically."

Ellen's gray eyes turned to Tomas and he could see

that they were laughing and rueful, just as though he and she were life-long friends. He wracked his mind for something further to say, but without success; and then Maria Rosa called out shrilly, "Grandfather's coming! Here's Grandfather!"

There he was, bringing up the end of the parade in style, driving his new burgundy-red brougham pulled by a fine matched pair of sorrels. Loud cheers and shouts from the spectators accompanied the carriage, then, as it came abreast, the reason for all the commotion was apparent.

Patrick and Teo with Brian between them were all together up on the coachman's seat, and Adam was clinging to one door, standing on the small footstep, because, there was no room inside the cab! The entire seat and boot were filled with fireworks, hundreds of bright red and yellow paper cylinders heaped high, as festive a sight as anyone could wish.

Chinese firecrackers! Tomas had never imagined he would be so excited by the sight of his grandfather, bringing the finale for this Fourth of July parade. He forgot his reticence and cheered loudly, while Patrick, catching sight of him, grinned and waved his hat.

But even as he was shouting in delight, Tomas became aware that not all in the crowd were similarly pleased. He could hear a few angry mutterings, an oath or two, and the words *yellow peril*.

Falling silent, he listened, trying to understand. He knew there was wide-spread antipathy toward the Chinese. Phineas Bishop had remarked only the evening before on what he explained was the root of the problem, which was that the many Orientals who had worked so hard pushing railroad track through the Sierra were arriving lately in the cities, and were obtaining work that less enterprising people believed should be theirs.

But surely these hecklers couldn't resent Adam, who had been an Aguirre servant, as good as a member of the family, since before Maria Rosa was born?

The question was answered, when a poorly dressed man on the opposite side of the street bellowed, "Take that, John Chinaman!", ran to the back of the brougham and tossed something inside.

The tiny missile was only a lighted match. But a firecracker at once caught fire and exploded, and with that there was a stuttering series of loud bangs, a roman candle arched up, and skyrockets began to whiz in all directions. The crowd pressed back, screaming in fright. Smoke curled skywards, and in the space of only a minute the carriage itself was a ball of flame, erupting like a miniature volcano.

The first firecracker had barely sizzled into life, when Tomas sprinted across the street, side by side with Carew. The older man leaped for the heads of the rearing, terrified horses, while Tomas reached up his arms to Brian and swung the little boy quickly away. Patrick, just as though he were his former strong self, lifted Teo bodily and handed her too down to Tomas, before jumping out over the wheel.

By this time, others had come forward to help with the frenzied animals which, at last unbuckled, were being led with the greatest difficulty, plunging and snorting, mad with fear, away from the acrid smell and continued explosions.

"Adam!" shouted Patrick, "Where are you?"

That was when Tomas realized his mother had finally arrived. He found her standing in the middle of the street, not nearly far enough away from the carriage and its missiles. She was holding a cloth to Adam's cheek, while the little man, appearing dazed, patted smoke from a charred hole in the sleeve of his blue blouse.

"He has some bad burns, Tomas," Bets said, filled with seething anger. He could see that the cloth she held trembled, although it touched Adam's face with tenderness. "I want to take him home. Also your grandfather, if he will agree to come. He *would* drive for himself today, and the excitement will surely make him ill! You, of all of us, can persuade him, so please try!"

"Yes. Mother," he burst out, "the man who threw the match should be caught and punished! He's destroyed Grandfather's carriage and hurt Adam! How could anyone hate Adam?"

Bets gave a meaningful glance down, and Tomas saw the bewildered expression of the Chinese servant. "Oh, I doubt very much if harm was meant." she replied. "Probably it was some thoughtless merrymaker who's had too much brandy . . . Now, Tomas, let's not waste time talking. Please bring Grandfather."

Persuading Patrick to leave the scene was, as to be expected, far from easy. He hadn't yet had an attack of pain, and his brougham was providing a spectacular bonfire. Not until the town's two pumpers had come racing up, bells clanging, and trailed by a pack of yapping dogs, would he consent to being seated in Phineas's big carriage. He was driven slowly away, one arm around Teo, the other waving to every friend he spotted in the crowd.

"Don't be late at Eaton Canyon, young man," he shouted to Tomas. "I'm leaving Brian in your care!"

"I'll bring him, Grandfather, don't worry! We'll all be there, waiting for you."

But after Patrick had gone, Tomas morosely watched the dying flames and nursed the soreness in his heart. That someone had wantonly set fire to his grandfather's beautiful gift, sending it up in a dangerous burst of explosions, and merely out of hatred for an inoffensive Oriental he couldn't possibly know personally, bewildered and angered Tomas.

No one else seemed perturbed, however, and the incident was over. The firemen were milling about, drinking beer and joking, having assured themselves there was no danger to nearby structures. The crowd, heading for the Plaza, was dispersing. But he could not look away from the hot carriage body, its framework showing dark through the red flames, reminding him of a burning animal carcass.

"Tomas." John Carew appeared at his side, the girl Ellen a few paces back. "I've been thinking about your silkworms. I'd like to experiment with them myself, as well as plant some crops, but the only thing I really know anything about is sheep. Could I ask you to stop over soon and give me a few suggestions?"

"I'll be happy to!"

Tomas didn't look at Ellen, but his despondent cloud had lifted.

CHAPTER FIFTY-FOUR

THE SUN WASN'T UP WHEN TOMAS, ALREADY dressed, wearing a particularly fine white silk shirt and his best claret breeches, appeared in the kitchen for breakfast.

Early as he was, he had not avoided Tia Pilar. Now that the rancho was fairly prosperous again, she no longer cooked, but instead had appointed herself majordomo of the house. If it hadn't been for the frequent intervention of her mistress, she would have made the lives of the servants under her intolerable, constantly fussing at them all in her shrill voice. She was, in short, enjoying her last years to the fullest. And one of her pleasantest duties, which was no hardship to her as she slept poorly at best, was stationing herself in the kitchen shortly after sunrise in order to scold the cook and maids for their slightly later rising.

Although with Tomas's arrival she scurried about, muttering the usual dire imprecations on the heads of the absent servants while she happily prepared his tortillas, she still had time to give him sharp inquisitive glances, having doubtless noted he was overdressed for riding the range.

"You are up earlier than usual, Tomas!"

"Yes." He continued to eat, and there were no more comments, although her unsatisfied curiosity pursed her mouth and made her bang the iron pots with unnecessary violence. She called all the Aguirre children by their first names and used the familiar *tú*, as was only fitting for one who had cared for them since birth. But Tomas, being the son, and grown now into a young man, merited respect, and in the last year their relationship had changed. She could no more have asked him directly where he was going than she could have asked Miguel. In her mind, Tomas had now taken Miguel's place.

For his part, he had no intention of enlightening her. The quiet thoughtfulness of the boy had developed, in the young man, into habitual reticence. He had come to treasure privacy. But he was fond of Tia Pilar, and when he finished eating and was ready to leave, he said, "I'll be here for the evening meal as usual, although late perhaps."

He was rewarded by a fleeting sardonic smile. Now she had a smattering of information on which to be mystifying, if she wished. His mother and sister had stayed several extra days in Los Angeles but were due back today; when they asked for him, Tia Pilar would not need to betray how little she knew.

He had made an early start because, while the ranchos adjoined, the houses themselves were a good three hours ride apart. That meant, with the time spent going and coming, he'd have only a short visit with the Carews, which was just as well, as John Carew hadn't said just when to come, and perhaps only three days after the invitation was issued was too soon. Doubtless he'd be asked to spend the night, hospitality would demand it, but with his words to Tia Pilar he'd deliberately closed off that possibility. He didn't want to appear too eager. Not like a callow youth of whom no one had ever asked advice before!

Besides, he admitted to himself, as the horse picked its way among the rocks of the canyon floor, it wasn't just to Mr. Carew he wanted to appear mature, dignified, well-mannered. There was the girl, Ellen.

He fell to daydreaming, which was foolish when he'd only met her once. But suppose she was at home when he came. Suppose her father and she happened to be talking together, as he rode up, and then she was invited to walk around the rancho with them. He wouldn't be alone with her, of course. Many girls still had duennas, and even in his own family, girls were carefully protected. There was no duenna for Isabel —Mother laughed at the mere idea—but he'd noticed that Isabel and little Maria Rosa never went anywhere by themselves. Adam, or some member of the family, invariably accompanied them.

Still, if Ellen was present, he could at least see if she was really as pretty as he remembered. They wouldn't need to be alone for him to determine that! And perhaps she'd smile as she did before, and they'd exchange glances . . .

In a sudden burst of high spirits, he spurred his mare up the steep shale hillside, an ascent more suited to a goat than a horse. With a clattering of stones, they reached the top, and he continued on, more sedately.

Threading his way through a grove of scrub oak, he gave himself up to the pleasure that always filled him when he went his solitary way through the hills. Not that he was truly solitary! There was plenty of life. Jackrabbits abounded. More than once, with a loud whirr, a bevy of quail rose fast and suddenly across his path, and he stopped to marvel at the thread-thin anchoring of their delicate top-knots, which were shaped like small apostrophes. Then, pausing at the edge of a clearing that lay beyond—an old, well-loved retreat of his, because while still close to home it was totally secluded, totally secret, he spotted a fox. Thinking itself unobserved, the animal had poked its long inquisitive face around a twisted tree trunk, and was staring at him, motionless.

"Don't think that meadow is yours," he told the fox amiably. "It's my special place, so beware."

The fox disappeared but without undue haste, and Tomas remained for a moment, remembering how often he'd come running to this little refuge—after Pepe died, after Miguel died. He had wept here, and found his own comfort.

He listened to the myriad familiar noises of wilderness, and then reminding himself he had barely started for Carew's rancho, rode on.

"Then you don't think this would be a good spot either?" Carew asked. He and Tomas had walked together to several different locations which the new rancho owner was considering for his mulberries.

"I doubt it, but I don't know," Tomas said, and regretted he hadn't a positive, authoritative answer to give. But it worried him that even on a day like this, still and almost sultry elsewhere, there was a strong cool wind funneling across the wide-open expanse. "I've never heard whether wind is bad for the trees or the worms either. Even if you plant windbreaks, I'd not want to take the chance."

He added, after a moment, "The soil seems to be deep, and if that's so, walnut trees would do well. You'd not only have a harvest of nuts, you'd have shade for the buildings."

"Yes, that's something to consider," John said.

It being time for the noon dinner, the two walked back to the house, Tomas thinking ruefully that he hadn't acquitted himself very well as a consultant. All he'd said was, *I don't know!*

He was cheered however to find Ellen Carew already seated at the table. He greeted her awkwardly, and turned with a certain relief to Aunt Mary who was obviously delighted to see him so soon again.

He had no need to worry about remarks to make, because his aunt, it appeared, was well accustomed to living with a demure young girl and a man who was less talkative than most, and she proceeded in her own way to put her nephew at ease.

After reminiscing about the pleasanter aspects of rancho life as she recalled them from her months with his own family, she at length remarked, "You've been in this house before, haven't you, Tomas? When it belonged to the Roja family?"

She paused to serve him a large helping from the platter of roast lamb, and he said, "Yes, once."

"It seemed depressingly dark so I've made a few changes. John was good enough to have his men enlarge the windows of the front room, as you may have noticed."

He hadn't, but when he turned obediently to look,

he saw she'd altered more than just the windows. The adobe walls, which to his recollection had been left their natural color by the Rojas, the brown deepened and streaked by grime and soot, were now white. The old Mexican-style furniture was still there, but cleaned and polished, and all of the pillows and the serapes across the tables, instead of being many-colored stripes, were a solid, bright yellow. Yellow too were the long draperies suspended loosely by their rings on the dark wood poles at the ceiling. The room was a sunny melding of dark woods, yellow and white.

"This is something new for me, decorating a house," his aunt said. She sounded unsure of herself, and he hastened to say, "I'll tell you how I remember it here —as a kind of cave. I like what you've done. Don't you, Miss Carew?"

To his surprise, the girl hesitated before answering a bit defiantly, "Yes. It's lovely."

Perhaps she had never admitted as much before, because Aunt Mary smiled at her happily. "I'm glad! You see, Tomas, the house I lived in in Aspinwall was treated this way. Of course, wicker furniture has a different look altogether, but there was the same cool effect of using only one bright color."

"What was Panama really like, Aunt Mary?" Tomas, who all his life had simply accepted the existence of this aunt of his mother's, was suddenly curious about her. Why had she lived for so long a time away from her family and friends? And how could she have brought herself to do so? He would never think of leaving Rancho Aguirre! He loved his own land too deeply. It was in his blood, just as, he often thought with secret pride, it had been in his father's before him.

She chose however to answer his question only in a general way, telling him a bit about the Indians and the still-primitive town. When he asked about the jungle, she said, "If you want a description, I'd rather you looked at one or two of my pictures, although I must say I've never been very pleased by the wild animals I drew, especially the ocelot and jaguar. Mediocre work, I'm afraid."

"You're being far too modest," her husband protested. "I like them. More important, Milo does."

"Thank you, darling, but I'm not modest, only honest. I had a student once whose work with animals was extraordinary. Rough, but extraordinary. I wish she could have sketched one of those jaguars—running or pouncing. You'd have seen the difference."

"Who was she?"

"Her name was Alice Carter. She went back south, with her family, during the war and never returned. They shouldn't have gone, but her brother'd been a prisoner of war, and died . . ."

Her gaiety had disappeared. "So many people were like that," she continued. "During the war. They vanished, never to be seen again. Fine people, talented people. One of the frightful prices to be paid."

Tomas exchanged glances with Carew, and the young man said, "I would like to see your jungle pictures, Aunt Mary! Panama is so far away, and I'm curious."

"Very well. I am better with a brush than with words."

"You do well enough with either," her husband put in. She laughed, but their eyes met, and the brief look of intimate understanding they exchanged, roused a small quirk of envy in Tomas.

"No," she insisted. "I discovered just how inadequate my feeling for words really is when I helped Miguel with his book. What happened to his work, Tomas? Was it finished?"

"Yes, just a few weeks before he was shot by Lachenais." Again, there was an exchanged glance, and he wondered why, but did not question them. "My mother has taken the manuscript to a printer, now that we have more money. It will be ready for binding soon—in the best red morocco leather—but I wish Father could have seen it for himself! His finished book . . . He'd have been . . . ."

He was floundering. He almost never spoke of his father, fearful of the pain. This time he had plunged in without thinking, and to his shame he was in danger of being overwhelmed.

His aunt put her hand on his arm. All she said was, "I am very eager to have a copy. Very eager!" Then, "John, dear, aren't you expecting Congressman Houghton this afternoon?"

"Lord, yes! To talk about that huge appropriation for a San Pedro harbor. The Governor's for it, luckily, although most people will say the country must have a great deal of money to waste if it can spend so many thousands on a useless mudhole like the Wilmington Lagoon . . . But I am disappointed, Tomas! I shall have to wait here for Houghton, and I did want to show you around, and consult you on other locations for trees. Also, there's the possibility of bee-keeping, which my daughter has suggested. You have some hives, don't you, at Rancho Aguirre? Tell me, how much does honey bring?"

"The price is over a dollar a pound," Tomas said. To his relief, his voice was steady again.

"That much? Excellent! Next time you come we must plan for some bees."

"Surely someone else, John, can walk about with Tomas today, and ask him a question or two," Aunt Mary put in. "I'd love to myself, Tomas, but I've just begun a new picture, and I'm at the dreadful stage where I can hardly take time out for meals, without being disagreeable. Maybe Ellen could act in John's place . . . Will you, dear?"

Tomas held his breath. Surely, her father would object! But neither he nor the girl appeared to find anything remarkable in the suggestion.

"I would like to!" Ellen said.

"Fine." Her father agreed heartily. "Then that's settled. Mary, where did I put all those figures Phineas Bishop provided on the projected cost of the harbor? Oh, it is too bad. I'd hoped to get away from all this and back to ranching!"

They walked together slowly through the stable yard and around the small Indian huts. Neither spoke for some time. Tomas was interested in the way the rancho had been laid out, but he was also intensely aware of the close proximity of the fifteen-year-old girl. Just being alone with her was strange and exciting. Even better, he found to his dismay he was not made uncomfortable by his lamentable lack of conversational skill, as he certainly would have been if others had been present. He was used to silence and he guessed Ellen was too.

"About the bees," he said at last, and only because he had just noticed a likely spot to put hives. "Your father said you suggested them. Are you thinking of bee-keeping yourself?"

"Of course." The gray eyes regarded him with amazement. "Why shouldn't I?"

"No reason. I just thought—my sisters are afraid of bees."

"I'm not. Although I wouldn't want to be stung."

"You may be. But I could show you how to be careful. And I can bring you a swarm if you like. I think this is a good place for them, with a garden nearby . . . A rose garden! I never would have guessed Señora Roja grew flowers."

Ellen too surveyed the small garden. "The Señora didn't," she said evenly. "My stepmother brought these bushes from your grandfather's patio and planted them here, just as soon as Papa bought the land. I—don't care for roses very much, but no doubt the bees do. Have you a swarm to spare?"

"No, I meant I'd find you one. Wild swarms aren't hard to move. I'll make you some frames too—like the small ones I use in my hives. The bees build honeycomb in them. It's interesting work, bee-keeping."

"It seems so!" She asked him a question or two about the gathering of the honey, and they discussed other details of the project for some time.

At last he said, "I'd better start home. They'll be expecting me," and realized from her expression that she was as sorry as he to have this companionable visit come to an end.

"Tom, I want to tell you—"

Tom. At any other time, if he'd asked himself whether he liked this short American form of his name, he would have answered promptly that he did not. Tomas was a good name, just as it was; his favorite, in fact, except for Miguel.

But hearing it now on the lips of this diminutive girl at his side—why, her head barely reached his shoulder, making him feel older and protective and very capable—he savored the word. *Tom.* It was all right. It fitted him.

"Yes, Ellen?" All afternoon he had been calling her Miss Carew, but the time for that, he realized happily, was past.

"I will tell you!" she decided. "It's just—I'm glad you came. Being with you is the very first time I haven't been homesick for San Francisco. And I didn't hate my stepmother as much today, not when she talked to you as kindly as she did."

He stared. "You hate Aunt Mary? How could anyone? She *is* kind! More than that, she's well, she's good. I can't tell you how much she did for my Grandfather Sebastian, and my father too. And for me, after Pepe died—"

He caught himself abruptly, realizing what he had said. He'd spoken Pepe's name, and the old misery hadn't rushed in!

He tried it again, carefully. "Pepe was my brother."

"I know. She told me once. She seemed sad when she spoke of him."

"Then what do you mean, Ellen, about hating her?"

The girl reached down, avoiding the roses and picking instead a small bedraggled white daisy, from a clump growing wild outside the garden. She turned it round and round in her fingers while she spoke.

"I'm shut out now—Papa used to love me so! After Mama died, there were just the two of us and no one else. I want him to be happy, truly I do—" She looked beseechingly at Tomas. "But I always thought he'd choose a wife who'd look after him as Mama did, not be wandering off all day! Oh, that doesn't matter, I suppose—"

She started again. "I wanted him to marry, and I expected everything to be the way it was with Mama. He was fond of Mama, at least—he must have been, mustn't he? But, I don't know, they weren't at all like

Papa and Mary are. You saw them together just now, you must have seen how for him there's only one person in the whole world. It makes me sad somehow, for Mama! And for me too, because I'm all alone."

He was silent, possibly too long, trying to sort out what she'd said in the burst of unhappy, incoherent words, and she added uncertainly, "I've never told anyone this before. But I thought we were friends."

He found he was feeling much as he did when Maria Rosa would fall and hurt herself and cry. But this was a stronger emotion, different in a way he didn't understand, and not so simple to act upon. He couldn't just put his arms around Ellen Carew!

"We are friends," he said earnestly. "If you want, the next time I come, we can ride into the hills—I'd enjoy showing them to you. Would you like that?"

"Yes . . . oh, yes, Tom, I would! And you'll see too —I'm a good rider." It was like the sun coming out, when she smiled. "Well, there, that's over! I won't talk about it again, I promise."

It seemed he had helped her a little, even without holding her as he did Maria Rosa. And remembering how he had said his brother's name, a thing he hadn't done willingly for eight years, he told himself that in some mysterious way she had helped him too.

It was past time for him to leave, but he didn't mind going. There would be other days. The future stretched ahead, the long, long summer, leisurely and golden.

"I'll be watching for a bee swarm. I may not find one right away—but shall I come tomorrow?"

"Yes." She added firmly, "But tomorrow, come sooner!"

CHAPTER FIFTY-FIVE

TOMAS HAD NO INTENTION OF MENTIONING HIS day's expedition to the family, and if there were any questions he was determined to be his usual laconic self. He was fond of Isabel. They were companionable, not as close as he and Pepe had been of course, but never arguing or being selfish with one another. But he didn't want any probing fingers, no matter how gentle. He wanted to think the day over quietly, by himself.

He need not have worried, however. He came home to find his sisters in a glow of excitement, and his mother, although trying to maintain her composure, was hardly calmer. Her eyes sparkled in a way he had seldom seen before.

As soon as he'd entered the house, she rushed to him and began talking, insisting he sit down and listen while she told him all about the remarkable honor that had been done her. In the last year or so, as doubtless he was aware, Mr. Bishop had entrusted a few, very minor, negotiations of his business to her, because he had confidence in her judgment. Now there was this possibility of a harbor development, which if it were to come about would be of paramount importance to Mr. Bishop. And he had—oh, dear, she was so pleased she could hardly think, perhaps she would ruin everything, but she did believe she must try, as he'd asked her—

"Asked you to do what?" Tomas asked warily.

"Didn't I say? To serve with Congressman Houghton and Benjamin Wilson, on a committee which will appear before the River and Harbor Commission of the United States House of Representatives! We are to make certain a large appropriation for the harbor is approved. I wonder what those two gentlemen will say when they hear they have a woman working with them!

"I'm going back into town again as soon as we can get ready, and stay at your grandfather's for a month or so, for I must be really well acquainted with all the ins and outs of the project as it is now. Then I make the trip to Washington. Think of it!

"And best of all—" She beamed at Isabel and Maria Rosa. "The girls are going with me!"

Little Maria Rosa, caught up in anticipation, began dancing about the room on her tiptoes, and Isabel was smiling, a dreamy expression on her face. Tomas wondered if she visualized herself becoming overnight one of those sought-after southern belles—she a girl not yet thirteen!

When Tomas said nothing, his mother looked at him more closely. "Do you mind our going without you? I thought it best for you to stay here on the rancho, in case any problems arise. And too, it's always easy for a man to make a journey alone. You'll have many chances, while this may be the only opportunity your sisters will ever have to visit our nation's capital."

"No, Mother," he assured her. "I promise you, I don't mind at all." Any other time he might have. But not now!

The trunks stowed in the boot, and the girls, dressed in their best figured-cotton dresses with three-tiered, ruffled skirts and more ruffles on the sleeves, already seated in the carriage, Bets gazed up at the coachman's seat in exasperation. She had planned to have one of the stablemen drive them, with an extra horse on a lead rope for him to ride home again. But here was Adam all ready to go instead, and as always, when he didn't care to understand her orders, giving her a blank look of incomprehension. Meanwhile not swerving an inch from his intentions.

The truth was, after the frightening episode on the Fourth of July, she didn't want him to leave the safety of the rancho. The temper of the crowd that day, the ugliness of the shouts of *yellow peril* had shocked her.

Then afterward, in the evening, Patrick had confirmed that in his opinion the igniting of the fireworks had been more than just a drunken joke. There was a sullen chorus of resentment against the Chinese, he'd said. Just as long before, when the novelty of a lone Chinaman's queue would single him out as a fit object for torment, now their growing numbers, and unchanged alien appearance, made them the butt of every petty bully's wrath, or quarrelsome drunk's crude humor. Bets, having heard all this, did not want Adam to go into Los Angeles.

But the argument ended, as the rare disagreement with Adam always did, with the servant getting his way. He had clearly no intention of permitting some untrained lad from the stables to escort and protect her. He seated himself, his face impassive, in the driver's position, and she could only surrender and allow the disappointed stable boy to assist her up to sit beside the girls.

As they drove away, she pondered his stubbornness, wondering just why he had insisted on coming. Protection for her and the girls? Times had changed since the hanging of the last notorious bandit, Michael Lachenais, but it was possible Adam did not realize that. Or was he perhaps simply exhibiting his own inconspicuous brand of courage? He must have sensed, even remotely situated as they were, the tide of ugly resentment. That might be; yet he had always been a sensible man, hardly the sort for bravado. It almost seemed he must have some reason of his own for going into Los Angeles.

Despite her misgivings, there were no unpleasant incidents on the journey, and in due time, Bets and her daughters were greeted with enthusiasm by her father and the servants. Flower alone seemed less delighted than usual, but Flora in a whisper suggested the explanation. The girl who was now a woman grown, being over twenty, doted on Master Tom and had expected him to come too. She was a little disappointed, that was all. And indeed, in a few minutes the sulkiness cleared from Flower's face.

She had acquired a small vocabulary, and it was Flora's joy to show her off to the best advantage. So in addition to allowing her to help unpack the trunks, simple conversation was expected.

"How are you, Flower? I'm so glad to see you!" Bets said.

"I'm fine. Thank you." Flower carefully hung a dress in the wardrobe.

"My room looks so lovely and clean!"

"My mother and I work together."

"I know that, dear. You are a great help to her. She loves you very much, as we all do."

"I love you. I love Tom!"

"He is nice, isn't he?" Bets put her arms around Flower and hugged her. "Oh, it's good to be in this house again!"

"Mister Phineas here, Miss Betsey," Flora announced, entering the room and smiling as she always did on seeing her daughter loved.

"Tell him I'm coming—oh, and Flora, when there's time, ask Isabel to recite some of the poems Miguel used to write for his newspaper, the simpler ones, about California. She might even let you hear one of her own, too, if nothing much is made of it. She is so much like her father! Anyway, Flower always liked rhymes, I know, and she'd enjoy a poem or two."

"I'll do that, Miss Bets. Oh, it's fine to have you home!"

Phineas appeared glad to see her also, although he at once explained that he always welcomed her level-headed advice on some of his ventures.

"Also, do you know Frank Lecouvreur's gone back to Germany on a visit, and I'm trying to find someone I can trust to keep an eye on the warehouse books. Ever since that Jaime Real affair, I've been more careful. Too bad you're going to be so busy on the Harbor Committee!"

"You're teasing me, of course. I know nothing about bookkeeping, and you know it."

"True. But the thing about you is, you are capable of learning almost anything. I've been very impressed. Always was, in fact."

"Thank you."

His carriage, she noted suddenly, was proceeding toward Wilmington, and she said, "I thought the meeting was at the Pico House?"

"It's been postponed until tomorrow, so your committee will be visiting my wharf today to review a few of the figures ahead of time." He cleared his throat, for no reason she could see, ill-at-ease. "Miss Betsey, would you like—that is, I would be honored if you'd care to see the house I've built in Wilmington."

"A house! I didn't know you were building one."

"Didn't you? That's the trouble with living out there on Rancho Aguirre. I've been the talk of Los Angeles for months." He gave a short bark of a laugh, quite unlike his usual roar. "You know how I am. Once I get my heart set on something, I don't let go. Even if years go by, even if it's hopeless, I never forget. This house is just part of some impossible grand plans."

"I didn't know any of your plans were impossible," she said. "Just difficult. All of them seem to work out in the end."

"I hope you're right," he said fervently, but with a finality of tone that told her he didn't intend to explain.

She was further puzzled when the horses swept at last into a long wide driveway, and were reined to a stop before the steps of a tall, imposing white house, built of the most costly material possible in those parts —wood. Clearly no expense had been spared. A series of peaked roofs reached back and back, and there were spacious covered porches across the front on both the first and the second floor.

"So large! Why, Phineas, it's a mansion!"

"Thirty rooms is all," he said with false modesty.

Bets pointed up to the large square cupola that crowned the highest point. "Oh, I like that! You can even see the ocean from there, I suppose?"

"The ocean, as well as my wharf, and the great new harbor to be."

When Bets said, "It's a beautiful, beautiful house, I've never seen a finer!" pleasure softened his square rugged face, making it almost handsome.

"It's finished, but still empty of furniture for the most part. And the gardens are all planned, but as yet they're nothing but tilled ground. But come inside. Let me show you."

They crossed the porch to the heavy beveled-glass door, and he ushered her in with a sweeping, courtly bow. He laughed as he did so, but she was thinking the flourish suited him better than he knew. It reminded her, too, of the time they had danced together at Felipa's wedding.

"Now here, on the left," he announced, "is the front parlor. Imagine it, a front parlor! There is also a back parlor. It's strange, I've lived here for many years and been a Californian in every thought and aim I ever had. I say Californian, Betsey, not Californio, because the word means all of us now, not just our friends who are of Spanish blood, but the new settlers as well, the farmers and small shopkeepers who've come out here to stake their savings and their hopes, even their lives, on this wild, fertile, beautiful South Coast. This is our land—theirs, and yours, and mine, and God grant we use it wisely!"

His voice had begun to echo in the great, high-ceilinged room, and he stopped abruptly.

Bets said, "I've never heard you speak so!"

"No, and I'd better get out of the habit. I've had to make so many speeches in the State Senate, I've been shouting them out in my sleep. What was I saying? Oh, yes—Even though I'm a Californian, I get a hankering now and then for an occasional look back to Delaware where I was born. And that explains this house. It's a Delaware house.

"Come along, Betsey. I want you to see everything!"

His pride and pleasure were understandable, she thought, observing the fine craftsmanship of the banister as she followed him up the staircase. She was so engrossed in the house, that when they reached the large front bedroom he'd clearly designed for himself and had in fact already sparsely furnished with a brass bedstead and a gigantic wardrobe, she failed to note the diffidence with which he said, "Well, that's all of it . . . Betsey, haven't you wondered why I built this house?"

"*Why* you built it?"

"Yes. I'd hardly need so much room just for myself."

"Hardly! But you said it was something you'd wanted for a long time."

"Not the house, that wasn't what I wanted. The house was just to be a gift for someone. I've tried to make it perfect, good enough for the woman I'd like to bring here."

Seeing her bewildered stare, he hurried on to say, "I've been afraid to ask, but I remember a talk I once had with Miss Teo, and I've been telling myself, if I don't at least try, I'll always wonder if I shouldn't have . . . Miss Betsey, will you—do you think you might possibly be willing to marry me?"

She was silent, never having envisaged this. He was her close friend, and perhaps she should have guessed she meant more to him than just that, but she hadn't!

He had turned away, and she studied him where he stood at the window, not pressing her for an answer, but gazing out at the winding channel to the bay.

She had always admired him, enjoyed his company, felt comfortable and free to be herself with him. Was that all? She remembered again the night they had danced together at Felipa's wedding, all alone in the moonlight. Hadn't there been something between them then, something she had refused to recognize?

"Phineas—"

He turned at once, but did not approach her.

"First, I must tell you how very honored I am that you would ask me to be your wife."

His face stiffened, as though he had feared a refusal couched in just those words, and she realized she had seen that flash of disappointment sometime before, though she couldn't at once think when. Then it came to her. Phineas had looked so, long ago on a night in her father's stable, when she had told him she intended to marry Miguel. Had he loved her, even then?

"No, wait! Oh, Phineas, dear Phineas, I'm not refusing—at least not yet. Please understand, I haven't thought of you in this way, and I need to imagine how our lives together would be, and well, just look at you in a new light. Before I marry again, I want to be very sure of my feelings."

"I want you to be sure! Betsey, there's something more I have to say. I care for you so terribly much, I couldn't stand it if you came to me—if you were lying in my arms—and still you were thinking of another man. You must say no, rather than that."

He took a deep ragged breath, and she could see how he forced himself to ask, "Is there such a man?"

He was not, she sensed, referring to her memories of Miguel. Rather, he must have known long ago that there was a girlish infatuation. He may even have guessed that Tomas had not been fathered by Miguel. And now he was asking her, *was it ended?*

She had believed it was. But John Carew was in Los Angeles with Mary, and she had thus far avoided an encounter. Was it because she was afraid, because she couldn't really trust the indifference she told herself she felt toward him?

"I don't know."

Phineas nodded heavily. "I thought as much."

"Will you give me a little time?"

"Why not? For me, an indefinite answer is certainly better than a firm no. At least for a while. However, it won't be pleasant." He grimaced. "I hope you can decide soon, Betsey. You are a woman who needs a man stronger than herself. That's the truth, and you'll find it out one day. But don't keep me waiting too long, or I'll be so weak-kneed I won't be worthy of you. Hah! Don't laugh!"

"I'm not laughing. Oh, Phineas, I am so very fond of you!"

"That's a little to the good, but hardly enough. So for now, we'll pretend this talk never took place, and make things easier for both of us. Can I expect an answer by the time you return from Washington?"

"Oh, yes, I would think so!"

. . . But you could know now, she was thinking. If you had less foolish respect, if you would simply take me, with love, here in this beautiful quiet house, we would both know at once.

She was seized by the temptation to make the first step herself. But she hesitated, and the opportunity passed. Phineas walked to the door, and about him there was no longer the naked vulnerability of a man who has confessed to love. He was himself again, and she dared not.

CHAPTER FIFTY-SIX

THE WEEKS PASSED, WITH BETS ABSORBED FOR long hours in acquainting herself with the entire harbor situation. She bobbed about in a small boat, studied pages of figures on shipping, listened while it was explained to her how tides could be harnessed and used to dredge out a channel. To stop up the tidal 'leaks', she was told, and so concentrate the flow of water for the necessary scouring action in the shipping channel, a sixty-seven hundred foot rock and timber wall, running along part of Rattlesnake Island and connecting seaward to Dead Man's Island would have to be built. A bold and expensive concept, and one she must completely understand in order to promote.

Meanwhile her daughters, for the first time in their lives, were becoming thoroughly acquainted with Los Angeles. With so much to see and do, there was a friendly tug-of-war each morning, to decide the outing of the day.

Maria Rosa, surprisingly, liked to call on their parents' friends, and only her sister knew it was because of the huge outlay of sweets which were invariably presented. As their hostesses eyed her slight, elfin form in disbelief, the little girl would literally stuff herself, chattering cheerfully all the while. Isabel, however, found social conversation difficult, and preferred, so far as Jeb would permit, to explore the streets, wandering in and out of the small shops, watching the towns-people, and listening to the shouts and talk, some of which was undoubtedly far too rough and colorful.

Isabel would never forget for the rest of her life the sight of a fourteen-mule team rolling down Spring Street, hauling three great wooden wagons laden with silver ingots from the Cerro Gordo. The mule skinner, a great bearded man caked from head to foot with the burning alkali desert dust, snapped his long blacksnake whip alternately at his mules and at stray dogs along the way, and casually, with his other fist, handled a jerk-line through the harness rings. He knew he was the center of all eyes, and he winked broadly at every girl on the street—including her!

So day after day the two youngsters rode about, escorted by Jeb, or on occasions when he was occupied elsewhere with Patrick, by Adam. There was no dangerous incidents, although Isabel told her grandfather she'd seen sullen faces when Adam was spotted driving such an expensive carriage and carrying a gun. Once a laborer had spit tobacco, missing his target but spattering the driver's seat with ugly brown droplets.

"By God, Isabel," Patrick roared, "I wish I'd been there! He'd have had trouble chewing his tobacco for a month!"

"I wish you had been too," she agreed, but she was wondering if the grandfather she loved so much could possibly realize how frail he looked these days. The strapping man who had been Patrick was shrunken, his body seemingly eroded by his attacks.

She added, "There's a silly song called *John China-man* that you hear everywhere! It goes: *I thought you'd cut your queue off, John, and don a Yankee coat—*"

"Don't!" Patrick interrupted sharply. "I've listened to that more than I care to, and I wouldn't want Adam to hear you and think we have any use for such sentiments."

"No," Isabel agreed contritely. She had forgotten Adam's presence in the house, but trust Grandfather to remember! She ran to his chair and threw her arms around his neck.

"You're a good girl, Isabel!" he exclaimed. "Now tell me, what are you going to be when you're grown up?"

"Be?" She sank to the floor at his feet and looked up at him, puzzled. Tomas had done her an injustice when he suspected her of hoping to be a belle. To the contrary, she was convinced she was doomed to be homely. No one exclaimed now that she was the image of her mother! The raven-black hair was the same, yes, and the sea-blue eyes and dark lashes. But where was her mother's shapely figure? Her grace?

No, she was not to be a beauty, but she had never envisaged any future for herself except as a wife and mother.

"Yes, *be*," Patrick said testily. "Good gracious, girl, you've a lot of your father in you, including his brains. I'd like to see you use them! You could be a doctor, say, like Emil Kramer. Or a teacher. Or write for a newspaper as Miguel used to!

"What made me think of all this, I've recently had a letter from a friend of mine back in Boston, a lawyer named Henry Durant. Says he's turned to God for consolation after losing first his baby daughter, then soon after that his little boy—to diphtheria, and one of the things he's going to do with his money is found a college, to be called the Wellesley Female Seminary. Do you know, Isabel, later on I'd like to see you go there and study! Henry's a fine man. What would you think?"

"I only know the things Father taught me. I haven't been to school," she answered thoughtfully. She was going around the idea, like a mouse nibbling at cheese.

"You've still time. If you want, I'll speak to your mother, see what she says."

They were happily discussing his idea, making plans that both knew might never come to fruition, when Bets returned to announce in some trepidation that the federal hearings had been moved up a week, and therefore the time had come to start their journey. From Sacramento, they would take the long train trip to New York, and after a night spent there, go on to Washington.

She and the girls must be ready to sail for San Francisco in the morning!

Patrick had intended accompanying them to the Wilmington docks, to see them off, but a last-minute attack of pain left him dazed and weak. Phineas, believing the departure was the following week, was still away on his own business in the village of San Bernardino. But Teo for once was free—Emil Kramer having had no calls that morning, so she rode along on the small San Pedro train, chatting happily with Bets about all the wonders which would be seen on her lengthy journey.

Wonders, and discomforts and dangers too, Bets thought but did not say. There was no sense causing apprehension in her daughters when the stories she'd heard about the transcontinental train ride might be greatly exaggerated. However the descriptions of crossing the Sierra mountains were undeniably sobering.

Luckily for them it was August! In winter, there would be a good possibility of freezing to death, should the unheated coaches break down indefinitely. But at any time of year, the unreliable brakes were a serious problem on long downgrades and some of the curves.

Still, Bets could not feel anything except joyous anticipation. This was an adventure, hers and Isabel's and Maria Rosa's, and even if they never had another, it would be remembered all their lives!

A small steamer was waiting to transfer the passengers out to the ship, which this time was the newer and more comfortable *Oriflamme*. Goodbyes were quickly said, for Isabel and Maria Rosa could hardly wait to get aboard and take their seats. Even Bets was too preoccupied to linger, Teo noted with a twinge of sadness. It was always she who waited on the dock, waving a handkerchief and smiling. It was always someone else embarking for San Francisco—and this time for even more distant and exciting places beyond.

As the boat steamed away, remembering the *Ada Hancock,* she waited, soberly watching until it was out of sight before turning away to return to the train.

"Boarding now, Missus Donovan?" The elderly conductor made a point of knowing by name all the passengers who rode in the front car. "We won't be leaving for another twenty minutes or so."

"It doesn't matter, I may as well . . . oh!" She had just caught a glimpse of Emil Kramer disappearing around the corner of the shipping office. And there beside the wharf was his familiar phaeton, the ancient horse patiently standing, head down. Had there been a drowning here? Or a fisherman hurt or ill? "Thank you," she said hastily, "I'll be back later."

She hurried after the lanky figure of the doctor, thinking absently that should she be needed, she was most inappropriately dressed in apple-green brocade.

Rounding the corner of the building herself, she found he was well ahead of her, striding along the deserted shore. A heron, startled by his approach, flew up and winged away over the water.

She called, "Emil!" but he didn't stop, and realizing the wind was blowing against her and he would be unlikely to hear, she did not try again but instead began to run.

Where could he be going? There was nothing out here—no overturned boat, no supine figure—no one at all in sight anywhere, except the doctor himself.

His purposeful stride checked after a while and he stood gazing out, apparently watching the small surge suck in and out amongst the rocks. Teo, panting hard, her dress snatched up out of the way but her light shoes uncomfortable and heavy with sand, ran to him.

"Emil!"

He spun around. Caught unaware, he had no defence, and she saw in his face what could not be mistaken, what he had hidden from her successfully for so long, his yearning hunger.

They gazed at each other in consternation.

"What are you doing here, Emil?" she managed to ask. "I was afraid—that is, I thought something had happened—"

"Nothing has happened," he said impatiently, then angrily, "I come here often! Whenever my love for you, Teo, becomes too unbearable . . . Yes, this once,

I will say it! How do you think it is for me, being with you, listening to your voice, touching you in passing, every day, month in, month out? And knowing, *knowing,* you belong to another man!"

He wrenched his gaze away and stared in stony desperation at the water. "I come here to be alone, to look at the sea, and to tell myself how unimportant I am. The surf will be here, these little sandpipers will still be running, the gulls will swoop and cry, whether I am happy or unhappy. Whether I have you or not!"

With that, his restraint was broken, and he turned to throw his arms around her, pull her close.

"Once, I was almost tempted to try to win you." His face was pressed against her blonde hair and she could feel the warmth of his breath. "It was the day we went into the Garden of Paradise. Remember? But Teo, I spoke to Father Daniel that night. I confessed my sin—that I coveted a woman who is the wife of another. He told me I must stop taking you on my rounds with me, but the idea of not seeing you each day was so frightening, and I was convinced I was strong enough—I swore I would be—

"But I am not strong enough! Oh, Teo, beloved!" He began to kiss her, gently, almost reluctantly at first, then with passionate insistence.

Suddenly she heard the hoarse words, "Teo, please! There's no one here!" and he was undoing the bodice of her dress with the skillful fingers she had seen work miracles so many times. Now, though, there was no sureness in them. They trembled against her silky skin.

At the pressure of his lips on an exposed breast, Teo's dulled eyes flew open.

"Oh—oh, no—"

"Yes! Oh, Teo, I see the joy in your face. How can you deny me, dearest, most beautiful Teo—"

"No!" But her hands were as heavy as the wet sand. They would not lift to push him away.

It would have ended exactly as Emil wished, she admitted to herself afterward with remorseful honesty, had not a skiff carrying fishermen appeared just then around a point. Emil, although blinded by his passion, could not help but hear the cheerful voices which still at some distance carried clearly over the water.

Slowly he pulled away from her, his face like a mask. Left to herself, she turned from the view of the distant boat and began mechanically to rebutton her dress.

After a moment, he said in a low voice, "I am myself again. You need have no more fear of me. We'll go on working together as though this never took place."

"Emil . . ." Teo was filled with desolation. "We can't! I must not go with you, or help you again—Oh, Emil!"

"Why not?" he asked with bitter anger. "Yes, I know, I swore once before—to myself as well as to Father Daniel—and I broke my word! But I've learned now, we cannot be alone in such a place. Teo, *liebchen*, I promise you, you will have nothing to fear from me, ever again. Nothing!"

"Not from you perhaps . . ." Slowly walking away, she forced out the shameful words. "But I have something to fear from myself. I never thought I could feel so, but I do . . .

"Goodbye," she whispered, almost too softly to be heard.

One of the fishermen called to him then, "We have fish to sell, Mister!" but there was no answer from Emil.

She was weeping. The rest of her life loomed ahead, one day just like the other, dismal, repetitive. Yet mixed with her desolation was wonderment. She was no longer frozen, as Patrick had said. She had felt her body quicken, actually burn with desire!

How could this have happened? Was it because she had been so taken by surprise she hadn't had time to be fearful? Surely she didn't love Emil! That would be wicked, married as she was to Patrick! She'd idolized her young doctor, yes, but only as a distant god, one far above her.

Just one thing was clear, had been clear at once. She could not go with him again on his visits.

So, she must give up her beloved work. No more

climbing in the carriage in the morning, hurrying to help the patients, knowing a warm glow of accomplishment when some sick person patted her hand and said, "I do believe I'm better."

Never, never again!

In spite of her resolution, as the days passed it might have been impossible to hide from her husband her confusion and despondency, had not Abel Stearns died suddenly and alone at the Grand Hotel in San Francisco.

For all the Californios, there began a period of stunned mourning, longer perhaps than usual because an immense tombstone, carved by a famous artisan there, had to be completed and sent down before the funeral could take place. If Teo's eyes were sometimes red with weeping, people might be surprised, for Don Abel, admired as he was, had been a dour and aloof man; but they concluded that tears of grief, even for him, were only natural in someone as loving and kindhearted as Teodocia.

CHAPTER FIFTY-SEVEN

DON ABEL'S FUNERAL WAS THE TALK OF LOS Angeles for many years afterward. Not because it was particularly elaborate or well-attended—many previous such occasions in the Californio heyday had been legendary in such respects as the length of procession —but rather because of a macabre mishap which occurred at the cemetery.

All had gone routinely well at the church. The bishop, who had travelled down from Monterey, was elderly, but still leonine and majestic in his gold-threaded miter and robes; and he concluded the service with a eulogy so fulsome all present found it adequate, even for the man who had been the most powerful personage on the South Coast for over three decades. Don Abel's widow listened from the front pew where she sat as straight-backed as ever, garbed in rich, rustling black silk and lace, her mantilla pulled forward to shield her face. She professed herself satisfied.

Following the funeral, there was a brief lull while the many guests spoke together in somber tones and then repaired to their carriages. For the various long-time servants who had crowded into the rear of the church but would not be going on to the burial, these few minutes were always the most interesting. Such a splendid gathering of Los Angeles society provided food for conversation for months.

Jeb and Flora were present, dressed in their best, for they as Donovan servants had been well-known to Don Abel. Today they had been forced to leave Flower at home under Adam's watchful eye, because she was suffering from a temporary catarrh, and even her mother had to admit the constant coughing would have disturbed the assembled company. Their pleasure in being included therefore was somewhat diminished by regret at her absence.

"Flower, she'd of loved getting to see all these fancy dresses," Flora mourned. "How nice that Miss Anna Dominguez do look!"

"I see Master Tom's here," Jeb remarked.

"Where's he at?" Flora craned her neck.

"Yonder. With Miss Mary and her husband."

Flora's gaze followed his pointing finger, and her eyes narrowed. Without thinking, she said, "Wooee! Miss Bets not going to like that!"

"What won't she like?"

"Him—Mister Carew—being so friendly with Master Tom."

"And why not?" Jeb asked her indignantly. "He's Miss Mary's husband, and Mister Patrick thinks a lot of him. Miss Bets'll find it right courteous he invited her son to share his carriage. They all had a long ride into town this morning, remember that."

"I remember." Flora continued to frown, but Jeb's attention was elsewhere.

"Look there!" he went on. "Miss Ellen's come too.
I ain't seen her before. Pretty young'un! Looks a lot
like her Pa, don't she?"

Flora didn't answer. She had given the girl sitting
beside Mary a cursory glance, but she was far more
interested in the two men occupying the facing seat of
the large expensive vehicle. She couldn't hear the
words, but she could see Master Tom speaking in his
slow measured way. She'd never known him to talk so
long at one time! Something about the rancho, she
guessed. He did know a lot about livestock and crops.
More'n most folks gave him credit for.

But watching those two side by side and so friendly
together made her uneasy. Father and son, and they
didn't know it! She was the only one in the whole
world outside of Miss Bets to know . . . Not Mister
Carew himself even! Why couldn't a man just guess a
thing like that? If it was Flower, she would know her
anywhere!

"I should be the one driving Mister Patrick today,"
Jeb was saying, reverting to the grievance he'd been
harping on all morning. "What if he has one of his
spells and I'm not there to take care of him? It's too
bad! But when Miss Teo's mother asked the two of
them to ride with her or she'd be all alone, saying she
hated funerals wuss'n anything but this was one she
couldn't very well miss, he went right ahead and said
yes—you know Mister Patrick! Wonder if I shouldn't
maybe take you home, and drive on out there just in
case."

Flora agreed, although she hadn't been listening.
She gave her head a hard shake as she often did when
trying to get a worry out of it. "Let's go home," she
said. "I seen too much already. More'n I like to."

When the cortege had wound its long slow way to
the cemetery, and come to a halt opposite the open
grave where the great granite monument loomed, the
mourners grouped themselves at a respectful distance
from Doña Arcadia and her closest friends. Another
somewhat shorter ceremony was conducted by the
bishop, and following the conclusion of these rites, at

considerable effort, the shiny metallic coffin, weighing over eight hundred pounds, was hoisted out on ropes, to hang suspended above the freshly dug hole.

The priest was making the sign of the cross and intoning a last blessing just as the sorely strained ropes suddenly gave way. Don Abel in his casket plunged with a clanking thud against the hard dirt floor of his grave.

Doña Arcadia shrieked, and shrieked again. The two piercing cries were followed by appalled and universal silence.

Patrick, standing next to the stricken widow, at length ventured, "Arcadia, I've an idea your husband wouldn't be entirely displeased. It isn't every day a man's wife buys him a casket so magnificently heavy it breaks the ropes!"

"My opinion is still stronger than Patrick's," Señora Brinkman, flanking her on the other side, said calmly. "I am convinced that right now Abel, wherever he is, is highly amused. Although he was not a man much given to humor, as the good Lord knows, still, startling everyone would have suited him perfectly."

She paused to bestow on the surrounding monuments a glare of deep distaste. Then she continued, "As he will expect you to act the composed hostess as always, and these many guests will soon be appearing at your house for refreshment after their long ride, I suggest we leave here at once. No, we are too late! The bishop is approaching to offer his commiserations, and listening to them will take considerable time. Suppose Teo and I go on ahead to make sure all is ready at your house, and Patrick can follow, with you. Is that agreeable?"

"Excellent, Violeta. Thank you."

"Teo!"

"Yes, Mama, I'm coming. But need we hurry so? This is such rough ground."

"Nonsense! The sooner away the better. Just watch where you're walking. The bishop is a bore, and I cannot abide cemeteries."

Patrick, unobserved, had also started back toward

the row of waiting carriages. After standing for so long in the hot sun, he was feeling undeniably weak. He'd done his duty for his old friend Don Abel, and now he would find Violeta's rig and sit in its shade until the others came. Teo, in trying to dissuade him from riding out to the cemetery and then going on to Arcadia's, might well have been right after all.

"Patrick, wait for me."

"Mary Frances!" He broke into his wide smile, but she noticed his shakiness at once.

"Let me walk with you," she said quickly. "My new kid shoes with these funny heels aren't much good for walking, and I'll feel safer taking your arm."

"I'd be pleased, you know that!"

She tucked her hand into the crook of his elbow, feeling his thinness and wondering to herself if she could possibly support him were he to collapse.

He looked so very white and frail! He was dying, she realized with sudden awful conviction. Slowly, little by little, dying! Her brother, whose presence in her life she had always taken blithely for granted, loving him so much and being loved in return, was not immortal after all. Perhaps even by this time next year—

"You're stumbling!" he said. "Those damnable shoes!"

His concern wrenched at her. She forced herself to walk more steadily, but the touch of his warm living arm under her fingers had become infinitely precious. She dared not let him see her face.

As she turned her head away to the side, she caught sight of John approaching with Ellen, and she gave him a quick shake of her head. Bless him, he understood at once and halted, briefly gesturing with his hand. He would know she wanted the privacy with Patrick.

"I see far too little of you these days, Mary Frances," her brother was saying. "Pleased as I am you've come back, my one big regret is that you don't live nearer to me."

"Oh, that is my regret too, Patrick—" She made a quick decision. "I'd really rather not go on to Arcadia's. I'm still the same Mary Frances with no talent for small talk, and these affairs with large groups of people make me uncomfortable. Also, I'm a bit tired."

None of this was true. Ever since she'd remarried and found her role clearly defined once again, she'd come to rather enjoy attending social functions. While John had made it clear he expected no support of that sort from her, she knew he had been handicapped in his political work by one over-retiring wife, and she was determined not to be another. Mustering her courage, she had made it a point while in Sacramento to accept all invitations, even do some entertaining herself. It had all been far easier than she expected.

Now that she had her emotions under control and could look at him, she saw with relief as well as sadness that he was only too willing to be deceived.

"Why don't I escort you to my house then?" he suggested at once. "John can pick you up there afterward."

"But I hate to keep you from seeing all your friends," she murmured.

"Are you joking? I'd much rather have a few hours with you! I can't think of anything finer!"

"In that case, just let me tell John that you and I will be taking his carriage."

"Will he mind riding with someone? Oh but wait. It won't be necessary." He was looking down the long row of horses and rigs, and had spotted among the coachmen a familiar charcoal brown face. "There's Jeb! Strange, he must have misunderstood me . . . No, on second thought, he probably didn't!"

He shouted, and Jeb, with no show of surprise, waved in acknowledgment.

Watching while his own horse was guided through the jam of equipages in the road, Patrick realized that his heavy pall of fatigue was lifting, all due no doubt to this unexpected gift of an afternoon with Mary Frances. Now he'd be able to reassure himself about her. The stricken look she'd had on her return from Panama had faded, and what its cause had been he would never know. He'd not been able to ask—it was too plain, on the few occasions he'd seen her, that there was a raw wound she wanted to hide, keep to herself, and share with no one, he suspected not even with John.

Today, she was still too thin, but her husband said she was painting again. Watching her at the church where she sat beside John, he'd thought she seemed actually happy despite the occasion.

There was only one possible worry he could foresee for her now. Carew's daughter had appeared to stand a little away from her and closer to Tomas. So, being a stepmother might be proving difficult. One never knew why exactly, but children seldom did take to stepmothers! He might have imagined the coolness in Ellen, and she could have drawn close to his grandson for another reason entirely. She was young, but not too young to be taking a good healthy interest in Tomas!

This reflection reminded him that in missing the gathering of friends at Arcadia's, he would lose his chance for the casual talk he'd planned to have with the boy. Tomas had never before been left in total charge of Rancho Aguirre, and Bets had especially asked her father to watch for problems and be ready to offer advice if needed.

Well, there'd be another opportunity to find out how rancho affairs were going. And if not, in a few days he'd make one!

CHAPTER FIFTY-EIGHT

"MY DEAR TEO!" PATRICK SAID IN MILD EXAS-peration, a week or so later, "If you are determined to stay at home, then let us put the additional time together to some use!"

Ever since Don Abel's funeral, he had been exceedingly puzzled by his wife. While he had been pleased by her unexpected decision to give up nursing, it seemed illogical—their son being at school a large part of each day now—to insist, and so abruptly, that Brian needed all her attention. But having made the choice, why must she mope about, refusing social obligations she had always looked forward to, and pretending to enjoy every minute household chore, even those he knew made her restless!

A possible and pleasant explanation for this moodiness, so unlike Teo, had occurred to him. Could she be with child again? In that case, another recent change in her that secretly hurt him—her avoidance of intimacy by such transparent stratagems as feigning sleep—would be natural enough!

But when he'd asked her, his hope was promptly dashed.

"Of course not!" she'd snapped, and then apologized contritely.

"I am sorry, Patrick! How could I speak so?" Teo felt, for her part, a pang of guilt that was becoming more familiar each passing day. Her confused unhappiness was surely no fault of his! She was finding it more difficult to conceal from him than she had ever imagined. Lucky Emil, she thought again. Lucky, lucky Emil. To be every moment so totally absorbed in his work he need think of nothing else!

"What would you like to do?" she asked her husband, and tried to appear interested.

"I've been wondering, now that the funeral is over, if we shouldn't drive out to see how Tomas is getting along. I feel neglectful, although Bets did instruct him to consult me, and he's yet to come once."

"Perhaps Adam could drive us, if we're going to Rancho Aguirre," she said, beginning to think through the possibilities. "You might be able to persuade him to stay. I know you've been uneasy about his being here in town so long, what with all the nasty talk and dislike of the Chinese, and the bullying we hear about. In that case, we'll need to take Jeb too, to drive us home again."

"I can drive us," Patrick said jauntily, just as though Jeb hadn't held the reins for the last two years, while the only time Patrick himself had done so was for the few blocks of that momentous Fourth of July parade.

"Anyway, taking Adam home would be useless. He wouldn't stay!"

"Why ever not?"

"He confided something to me recently, but I doubt if he'd object to you knowing. Haven't you wondered why he goes so often to Calle de los Negros where all the Chinese have been settling? It's because he intends to marry soon."

"Oh, I'm glad! But who? There are many Chinese men here certainly, but I've yet to see a Chinese woman."

"Nor I, but he assured me there are five or six recent arrivals. They're kept jealously guarded in their houses."

"Guarded! In those wretched little hovels?"

"They're no longer so wretched inside, I've heard. There are tales of Chinese wool carpets, and vases, even treasure! None of it's true probably, but no outsider can say. At any rate, there are two rival societies—tongs—and Adam has already paid a great deal of his money to his group, the Hong Chow. When he has paid enough, he will be given one of the women in marriage."

"He's buying a wife?" Teo was aghast. "I remember Betsey once telling me his dream! How he would some day return to China where a beautiful young girl waited, by a river—"

"That's all he had, I imagine, just a dream," Patrick said gently. "A man alone and miserable in a foreign land needs some sort of vision to keep him going. Why Teo, he's been with us more than twelve years! Don't you suppose if such a girl existed, by this time her parents would have found her a husband? No, this is really what he's been waiting for, and he's greatly pleased."

"I see." Teo was finding she was glad enough to end this talk about useless dreams, and she dismissed the subject of Adam. "Very well then, Jeb will go instead. What about Brian? He's always begging to stay at St. Vincent's overnight like many of the children, but he's so very young—"

"Brian comes with us, of course. I wouldn't think of

leaving without him. Also, Teo—if Jeb goes, why not Flora and Flower? They haven't been to Rancho Aguirre in years. It will give Flower such pleasure to be near her adored Master Tom. More important, she and Flora can make themselves useful. With us as guests, Tia Pilar may be grateful for help."

Teo was not deceived. Tia Pilar needing help indeed!

"You have it all planned, haven't you? It's to be an outing for everyone." She was smiling at him at last, if a bit tremulously.

The Aguirre carriage Bets had left with them was large; but with Patrick, Teo, and Brian inside, the three servants had to crowd together on the coachman's seat, rather ludicrously, as they were not small people. However, half-way there, time was taken for a picnic where there was a view of the distant ocean through the hills. With Brian's excitement at spotting a deer and Flower's simple pleasure in gathering large basketsful of the scarlet Indian Paintbrush still blooming hardily at the end of August, the hours passed quickly enough. No one except Patrick was tired when Jeb reined the horses to a stop before the hacienda.

If they had come especially to find Tomas, they were lucky. He was just leading his mare from the stable, holding in his free hand several small wooden frames of a sort Patrick had never seen before. Hearing the shouts of the visitors, he tossed the reins to the stable-boy and ran to the carriage.

"What are those?" he was asked by his grandfather after all the greetings had been made.

"They're for bee-keeping," he explained. "You can put frames like these in the hives, and later on the honeycomb will be easy to remove."

"You have new hives then?"

Tomas answered readily. It was one thing to be evasive with Tia Pilar, quite another not to answer his grandfather's questions. "No, but Mr. Carew has. I finally found a wild swarm for him, and now I've made these frames and am just taking them over. With all the rancho work here, I couldn't get away yesterday, and I've promised . . . I hope you're planning to stay?"

"For tonight, at least."

"I'm glad! Let me run inside and tell Tia Pilar, so she can give the cook her orders. Then if I hurry, I can easily be back in time to eat with you."

"By all means, a promise is a promise! But surely, you can't ride all the way to Carew's house and be back by evening?"

"Oh, no! I've not got very far to go. Someone is meeting me to—to pick these up. I promise you, I won't be late."

"Fine, then!" Patrick said heartily. "We'll look for you at supper. Meanwhile, I'll walk around and see what changes you've made in your mother's absence." His tone removed any suggestion of criticism from the words, as already he was delighted with the well-kept look of the stable yard and what garden and fruit trees were in view.

"But Tomas, if you're going in the house to talk to Tia Pilar, you might ask Flower to go in with you." He lowered his voice, "It would give her pleasure. Although she's a grown woman, as we all know she still has the mind of a child, and I think she's a little confused about you. You're either a favorite brother or her son, I don't know which, but certainly not a whit less important."

Tomas turned at once and called to Flower, who was standing by the carriage, her eyes on him. "Come with me, Flower! I must give orders for supper, and I don't know what foods the family would prefer. Will you help me?"

Her delighted smile was his reward. They went toward the house together, and her parents looked after their girl, beaming as they always did when she was happy.

Then Patrick offered his wife his arm, and the two of them wandered toward the vegetable gardens which he thought she might like to inspect. Jeb was busy unharnessing, a task he always preferred to do himself, but he was encouraging the help of Brian who at this stage of his life loved horses above everything; and Flora was idling about, giving their daughter a few precious moments of responsibility in the kitchen before she herself went in and quietly held a conference with Tia Pilar.

There was an old bench in the midst of the tomato plants, and Patrick, more tired by the journey than he cared to admit, was grateful when Teo said, "Why not sit for a little?" He was not really surprised when she remained by his side only long enough for him to settle himself, and then began to pace back and forth along the path by the wall. He leaned back and watched her for a bit, perturbed by her restlessness. But the sun was warm and comfortable on his shoulders, and without intending it, he fell asleep.

He roused to find Teo shaking him, crying, "Patrick, wake up! Wake up!"

"Yes. What is it? Have I overslept?" He squinted at the sun. It was close to the horizon, but not low enough surely, for suppertime. He still felt groggy from the heat and his exhaustion.

"Patrick! Something has happened!"

He drew himself erect, the mists dissolving from his mind. "Not Brian?"

"No, it's Flower! We can't find her. She isn't in the house, and we've called and called. Flora is beside herself with worry. We can't think where she would go. No one saw her leave. Oh, if she becomes lost in the hills, and night falls, it will be dreadful! She'll be so frightened!"

"We must send out a search party at once! Tomas isn't back?" Tomas knew every nook and cranny of this great spreading rancho.

"No!"

"Very well, tell Jeb to gather together all the stable hands and any vaqueros who are nearby. They must be ready to ride."

He hurried to find Tia Pilar, hoping to hear from her a calmer story than from either of the parents. Even she, however, was shaken out of her usual complacency.

"Señor Donovan, she was here in the kitchen, when Tomas came to tell me there were guests. I let her talk awhile, even asked her a question or two—I am an understanding woman, Señor! But then Tomas left, and I did also, going to seek out that lazy good-for-nothing cook who would siesta until sundown if I didn't watch. When I returned, the kitchen was empty. I supposed the poor girl had returned to her mother and I thought no more about her—except to feel pity for the parents of such a one!"

Patrick said grimly, "So you don't even know in what direction she went?" The aged woman raised her hands in an expressive gesture. "Then question all the house servants again! Quickly! Someone may have been looking out of a window. If there is any information, come and tell me."

He rushed away, this time to the stable, preparing to organize a search in which he placed little faith. The area was so vast, the men would have to fan out through such rugged territory—and all before dark!

In the stable yard there had been a flurry of activity. Each man of the six available had led out a saddled gelding, and now they awaited his instructions. Jeb, standing alone to one side, on seeing him coming, sprang forward and called out, "All them little huts outside the walls—think she could be hiding from us, Mister Patrick?"

Patrick went to him and threw an arm across the strong broad shoulders that were so stiff with fear. He said, "One moment—then you and I will look through each one again," before he began speaking to the riders, describing Flower and what she was wearing, and assigning each man an area to cover.

"There's little use going east or south," he said, "because in those directions is only open country. Someone would have seen her. But to the west is heavy brush, and northwest and north are the hills. Divide up, and only fire a gun if you find her! That way, we'll all know."

"Yes, Señor!" They had caught his urgency, because this uncharacteristic quiet forcefulness was more telling than his shouts would have been. All of them flung onto horses and galloped off.

Then he turned to the women. Teo, who clutched Brian to her tightly as though she feared her treasure too might disappear, and Flora, who stared at him wide-eyed, a trembling hand pressed against her mouth.

"Flora, they'll find her!" He hoped to bolster her courage, but the assurance only seemed to confirm for her the very real possibility of disaster. She collapsed against her husband, weeping aloud in an abandon of hopelessness.

"Hush, woman!" Jeb said, holding her. He added, without conviction, "We'll get her back."

When his wife did not respond, he said, his deep voice loud over her wailing, "Sun's almost gone, Mister Patrick! Trouble is, Flower—she ain't like other girls! She can't take care of herself."

Flower was twenty years old, and this was the first time either of her parents had ever admitted she was different in any way. Patrick saw Teo's face crumble in pity.

He didn't want to have heard this humble admission either. He said firmly, "She will be found! Jeb, you and I will go through every building on the place again, and after that, we ride out too. I know the area fairly well, even if you don't, and I understand—God knows I do understand—how you feel. A man has to keep searching for his daughter!"

It was another two hours before the suspense ended. As no gunshot had been heard, Patrick, although gray with fatigue, had just told Jeb to saddle up for both of them. Night had fallen, and he stood with Teo and Flora in the stable yard awaiting the horses. The air was turning chilly, and the sable sky was already a glittering panoply of stars, tonight only to be noted and cursed for being moonless.

Flower simply appeared, walking toward them from the perimeter of darkness.

The first the others knew of her return was Flora's wild scream of relief and joy. Jeb sprang to the stable door, lantern in hand, as Patrick and Teo started, uncomprehending, and looked toward the distraught mother. Then they too saw her in the yellow lantern light.

Flora went running, crying, "I was afraid! I was so afraid!" She clutched her daughter's shoulders and gazed at her avidly.

"Afraid?" Flower repeated.

Patrick, only half listening as he battled his exhaustion, wondered at the blankness of her answer. Didn't she understand the word, or was she thinking in her own way, of something else entirely?

"Where you been at, honey?" Jeb had gone to her too, and was holding up the lantern, peering in her face as though he couldn't really believe it was she, their Flower, back with them and unharmed.

"I follered Tom—out there." She pointed to the hills. "I seen—I seen—" There was a long pause, then she said flatly, "I forget."

Had she? Her gaze was vague, but she was smiling, a new, sly sort of smile.

But Flora by now had recovered sufficiently to hug her close, rocking her in a tight embrace; and Patrick shook himself. At last it was over!

At that moment, Tomas, riding fast, issued from the cottonwoods beyond the stable. He reined the mare short, and showing his surprise at finding them all outdoors so late said, "I'm sorry, I was delayed—"

"Have you a gun, Tomas?" Patrick interrupted, his voice harsh. He was beginning to feel the hated twist in his abdomen, and he knew in a very few seconds the pain would be tearing at him with its probing iron fingers. "Fire into the air at once! It's the signal. Jeb, oh Jeb, come quickly!"

Jeb was there, easing him to the ground, placing his back against the stable wall. Then Patrick, even through his agony, was conscious of surprise, for Jeb's clasp gave way to Teodocia's, and it was her arms that went around him, and as the spasm racked his body, offered support and comfort.

"He's better," she said at length, and again there was a departure from what had become custom in these crises of his, as she added, "All of you, please go on to the house. We'll come shortly. Yes, Jeb, I can manage."

The minutes passed. They were sitting together on

the dusty ground, the two of them alone, and his strength, with the cessation of torture, was slowly returning. Each time the recovering took longer and was less complete, and one day, he supposed, he would not escape at all. But feeling Teo's soft arms, the forbidding thought faded.

"All right now?" she asked, and disengaged herself in order to study him critically.

"Yes, but not ready to walk yet, I'm afraid."

"There's no hurry." She sounded as though she meant it, and he glanced at her, remembering her restlessness of the afternoon, and marvelling at the quiet way she sat now.

"Not for me," he answered. "I'm content just to sit here with you."

"Patrick." She gave a vehement shake of her fair head. "I'm very proud of you!"

"Eh? Whatever for?"

"You wouldn't know, would you, my dear! Why for the way you took command! Tired as you were, you were able to keep us all from panic—even Flora, and you were so careful of Jeb's dignity, when he could do so little to help. Oh, I wasn't that frightened I didn't watch you, and we—none of us—could have asked more of any man! I was proud, and I was content too, though it seems strange to say it—just as I was the day you and I and Brian spent at the shore.

"What I'm trying to tell you is—I've discovered I love you. Very much. I'm terribly proud to be your wife."

He didn't trust himself to speak, but reached for her hand, taking it gently in his.

After a moment she said, "Another thing, although it doesn't seem as important as it did before, I'm fairly sure I'm not—frozen any more."

"Oh?" He started to ask a question, then refrained, and instead said carefully, "No, it's not terribly important, you're right. But I'm very glad. You will be too."

"But you'll have to teach me—everything."

Her eyes were crinkling, laughing at him, and he

was astonished. His shy little Teo speaking so openly of such matters!

"It will be a pleasure," he said, and decided this might be a favorable time to mention what had been troubling him. "About the nursing—I thought I wanted you to give it up. But these few weeks have convinced me I was wrong. You should do the work you have a talent for and which makes you happy. Brian doesn't need you all the time, you know that. Why not tell Dr. Kramer you'll continue?"

Teo considered. "Yes, I think I could go with him now," she said.

"Good."

They sat close together against the wall, her hand clasped in his until Tomas, sounding worried, called to them from the house.

Chapter Fifty-nine

Bets and her daughters still had not returned when Adam, in early October, won his bride. His plan, as he managed to make clear to Patrick, was to take her with him eventually to Rancho Aguirre. But for now, they would remain in the house he had acquired near Calle de los Negros.

The morning after the Chinese wedding took place, he appeared at Patrick's door and with dignity invited the Donovans to go with him, that he might have the honor of presenting to them his Almond Leaf, as her name translated into English.

"We are eager to meet her," Patrick responded. "But we'd hoped you would bring her here to us."

Adam shook his head. "She not leave house. Not custom. Also, maybe, not safe."

"Not safe? I don't understand."

"Tong of Nin Yung angry." Adam shrugged.

"Leader wanted Almond Leaf for self. You come please?"

"Yes, of course. Bring the carriage around, and you will drive us."

Perhaps it was his long acquaintance with Adam that caused Patrick to note, whenever he rode through the streets, how many more Chinese had established themselves in the town. There were laundries, tiny shops, truck gardens, all along the commercial streets; and wherever field or manual labor was needed, there too one saw the familiar ivory faces and long black braids. It was not surprising, he often thought, if less enterprising men, finding themselves without work, felt resentful. It might have helped had the Orientals made the slightest effort to conform to the customs of their new land—simply learning English or Spanish would have eased their way. But most of them did not.

Just how alien even their own Adam still was, was borne in on him today at the conclusion of the short ride, when they reached his adobe shack. It was a corner house, no better and no worse in external appearance than the others of the burgeoning Chinese settlement. Its only distinction was a scraggly red geranium plant beside the door. But when they entered, the sweet aromatic smell of incense was strong in the air, and a brass statue Patrick supposed to be that of Buddha sat alone and in honor on a low table.

Both he and Teo looked around them with curiosity, wondering if any of the tales of hidden opulence were true. Not, apparently, in this house. Here were no oriental treasures. This small room was furnished merely with rough chairs of the sort to be found in any workingman's home. They were however cushioned with tasseled pillows of scarlet silk, fittingly exotic.

After he had carefully barred the outer door behind them, Adam clapped his hands, and an opposite door opened. A girl entered, taking very short tottering steps, and swaying with each one. Teo caught her breath. "How young she is!"

Patrick wasn't sure this was true. It was hard to

tell, he thought, taking as much time to openly admire Adam's bride as he felt was expected.

She was very small, and her figure, childlike, seemed underdeveloped. Also, her face was not truly pretty—the cheek bones were too flat, and there was a fleshiness in the lids of the upslanted eyes, possibly the explanation for her having been sent to this far country in search of a husband.

Nevertheless, he understood at once Adam's intense satisfaction in his wife. The turquoise robe she wore was of the finest brocaded silk, her lustrous black hair was elaborately coiffed, and even in her silent obeisance there was dignity. Patrick knew enough about the Chinese to understand the significance of that swaying, actually painful walk. She had bound feet, an ancient custom restricted to higher-class women.

Adam saw his glance at the tiny feet, which, wrapped in white cloth, were only a few inches long. He said, "Lotus feet. She not a peasant or *amah!* That why Nin Yung angry."

"She is lovely. I congratulate you. She speaks no English?"

"No, she just come from Kwantung." He turned and spoke to her in their own sing-song language, and she replied, eyes downcast modestly. Then she knelt, placing her forehead to the floor several times, before she rose and hobbled from the room.

"She bring refreshment," Adam explained, and motioned his guests to be seated on the scarlet cushions.

He himself did not partake of the tea and small cakes she served, properly mindful of his own status with the Donovans. Instead he stood close by, watching his new wife serve, and apparently not finding the stilted conversation at all awkward.

"The tea was very good, Adam," Teo said, rising after a few minutes. "Will you tell Almond Leaf so, and thank her?"

"Yes, Missy."

"And Adam, Mr. Donovan and I wish you so very much happiness!"

"Thank you Missy, Master. I drive you home now."

Teo glanced over her shoulder as they left the

house. There was no doubt Adam had only the rosiest anticipations for the future, but she wondered about the girl-bride, whose face, throughout the visit, had been that of a porcelain doll, wearing a painted, demure and meaningless smile.

Almond Leaf, the teapot in her hand, was gazing after Adam, and the smile was gone. Caught offguard, she looked lonely, Teo thought, and frightened.

As it happened, Teo and Patrick were again discussing Adam's marriage, when Phineas Bishop came during the afternoon to bring worrisome news about the Chinese quarter.

Teo had just been speculating as to what could have alarmed Almond Leaf, for surely she wasn't fearful of her husband! And Patrick agreed, but more cautiously, reminding her what a shock it might be for a young girl to be married to a stranger, with no regard given to her own wishes. Teo, who hadn't understood this was the case, was mulling it all over and feeling pity for Almond Leaf, when Phineas arrived.

"Trouble is brewing, and amazingly it's among the Chinese themselves," Phineas said. "The Hong Chow leader was shot at and wounded an hour ago. Members of the rival tong are said to be bitterly angry because some woman was given in marriage without their leader's consent."

"Ah! Then she was afraid for Adam, not *of* him!" Teo exclaimed, causing Phineas to look at her in some perplexity. "I'm glad!"

"*She* being Almond Leaf, who has married Adam," Patrick clarified, his eyes smiling at his wife.

"Adam? Miss Betsey's servant?" Phineas was startled. "I'd hardly expect that quiet little man to cause a tong war! I hope he's staying out of harm's way. Shouldn't you have sent him together with his bride out to Rancho Aguirre?"

"One doesn't simply send Adam anywhere," Patrick said drily. "He would only pretend he didn't understand what you say. Anyway, I'm not much worried, not when it's his own people he faces. He's an excellent shot, and he's sensible. I imagine he'll remain prudently indoors with Almond Leaf, until all this blows over."

"If it does just blow over. There are a lot of people in this town who'd like nothing better than to see the two sides massacre each other. And if our own hot-heads get involved—"

"We hope they do not!"

"We do. But I've come by also to give you some other, more welcome news. Miss Betsey and her girls have finally arrived back in Oakland, and they'll be taking the first boat down from San Francisco, getting in late tomorrow. Patrick, your daughter did a fine job in Washington! The River and Harbor Commission listened to her and to Houghton and Wilson favorably, and have recommended the appropriation. I've no doubt our harbor will be approved by Congress."

"*Your* harbor, Phineas! Think of it, your muddy, shallow, little 'Goose Pond' is to be a real harbor! With some deep water channels and the protection of a breakwater, ships will be able to deliver their freight without lighters, and Los Angeles commerce will boom. It's tremendous! I'd like to see a lighthouse built on Point Fermin tomorrow, as a symbol of what's to be."

"I'd like to see something else—Lucky Belknap's face when he hears! I didn't tell Miss Betsey, didn't want to fluster her, but this will be the biggest setback that scum ever had. And she was the one who did it!"

At the grim fervor in the big man's voice, Patrick darted him a quick glance. Surely Phineas didn't know about what had happened between Bets and that devil? No, of course he didn't! It was no secret in Los Angeles that any time Phineas could hand Belknap a hard business slap he did it, but in spite of Belknap's many unsavory fights, he and Phineas had never tangled physically. Doubtless there was just a long-standing dislike between them.

"You mean, because of San Diego?" he surmised.

"That's it. Belknap thought he was mighty clever, speculating in land down there, figuring with that tre-mendous natural harbor, San Diego couldn't help be-coming the water gateway to the southwest."

"Not an unreasonable assumption, either," Patrick observed.

"No, in fact it seemed a sure thing. And now, after this appropriation, San Diego along with Belknap must wonder what hit 'em. As you say, it's Los Angeles Harbor now!"

"My congratulations too, Phineas," Teo said warmly. "You must be feeling on top of the world!"

"I'm pleased, I can't deny it."

"Are you, Phineas?" she asked, taking him off guard. "Somehow, you don't really seem so."

"I don't, Miss Teo?" His gray eyes met hers. "Well, to tell you the truth, I've another matter hanging over the fire that's even more important to me, and I've been waiting a long time for a yes or no decision. Too long. I'm pretty well convinced I've lost that one, and just have to be told—be put out of my misery!"

"First time I've ever heard you give up on anything, especially ahead of time," Patrick said uneasily.

He didn't answer, and Teo chided herself for having drawn out this unguarded confession which he might already regret. Guessing he didn't wish to explain further, and attempting to cheer him, she asked, "Is your beautiful new house finished yet? Everyone talks about 'Bishop's mansion', but no one has been inside, they say. Absolutely no one!"

He responded as she hoped, even though his jocularity was a little forced. "Now that's a broad enough hint, Miss Teo! I'll have a party soon and show it off to you and the whole town. Yes, it's built, but as yet I've only got a few sticks of furniture. Just enough for me to live there. I moved in a week or so ago, and I'm finding it's a mite large for one person."

Patrick said drily, "No doubt it is. A house that big must be roomy enough for a family with ten children!"

Without a smile, Phineas acknowledged this was so, and then, saying he would be meeting the travelers at the train station the next day and would bring them home himself, he took his leave.

"Well!" Patrick said to Teo. "I've never seen him edgy before! What do you suppose that was all about?"

His wife, who belatedly thought she could guess, did not answer.

Flora, after admitting Mister Bishop, had returned to the bedroom wing where Jeb was whitewashing walls, and resumed her ruminating on the worrisome subject of the change in their daughter.

"Can't figure it out!" she said. "That girl's been acting so shifty—ever since she got lost."

"She warn't lost," Jeb corrected stolidly. Flora's complaint was not new, he'd been hearing it many times in the last month. So far as he could tell, Flower was only behaving more the way other girls her age did. A little silly. In a way, he was glad to see it.

"I'm not talking about that," Flora persisted. "I mean the way she do with her hair, pulling at it to make it straight, and saying why ain't it a pretty white color! And asking me, is she pretty too? What do she mean *too?* Pretty like who? Miss Isabel? Miss Isabel, she is smart enough, and she is good to her Ma and little Mary Rose, but she ain't what I'd call real pretty."

"I reckon Flower don't mean Miss Isabel," Jeb said. He was painting the bedroom Miss Mary used to have, the one that was now a guest room, and he wanted to finish and have the walls good and dry before Miss Betsey's daughters came back to use it. He wished Flora would stop talking and let him get on and not have to think about anything else.

But Flora had her own work done, and was in no hurry at all. Any subject she got her teeth into, she liked to fret over, like a dog with a bone.

"I sure wish I knowed what happened when she went out there, follering after Master Tom. She seen something! She told us that. But what was it? And how come Master Tom didn't catch her, sneaking along behind him?"

"Flower does that sometimes. Hides and watches. You know she do."

"I certainly do know." Flora sighed. "But what was you saying about her not meaning Miss Isabel? Who else can she be thinking of?"

"You said she wanted white hair. So maybe Miss Ellen?"

"Why, sure 'nough! Miss Ellen! I remember at the funeral, you pointed her out to us and said she was a right pretty young 'un."

He stood back, to see whether he'd left any streaks on the wall. "No, Flora, you done forgot. Flower was ailing that day. She warn't there." He paused, brush in hand. "That is peculiar, ain't it? Flower ain't never seen Miss Ellen. Oh, but she must of!"

"That's right, Jeb . . . She must of!"

Flora abruptly ended the conversation by running from the room.

She hurried along the hall, seeking her daughter. And found her in Bets' old room, smiling at herself in the big, walnut-framed mirror the family'd brought with them when they came west.

Suddenly the girl leaned close and kissed the lips of her reflection, a long tender caress that lasted while Flora stared. At length Flower must have felt the gaze from the doorway, because she turned around and gave her mother the quick sidelong glance Flora had come in late weeks to dislike thoroughly.

"You enjoying that—that kissing?" Flora asked, trying to hide her dismay.

"No." Flower sounded downcast.

"Then why you doing it?"

There was no answer. The girl had resumed her position before the mirror and was studying the image she saw. Her expression was a mixture of puzzlement and disappointment, and distraught as Flora was, her mother's heart ached with pity. The cold mirror. Poor, poor child!

"You seen folks kiss like that, I reckon, and you figured to try it?"

Flower's continued silence confirmed the suspicion.

"You doan need that—not ever, honey! Your Pa and me, we love you more'n anybody else could."

Flower's face still held a hint of sadness, and on any other occasion Flora would have rushed forward and hugged her fiercely in consolation. This time, however, Flower's problems would have to wait.

She tried to speak slowly and softly, knowing if she did not Flower would retreat at once into a vacant stare.

"Was it Master Tom you seen kissing?"

Flower's head bobbed slightly.

"And who else? Who you see?"

Flower only picked with her fingers at a small rough knot in the weave of her skirt.

Flora swallowed. She said, "You doan know her name, is that it? Tell me, was the young lady—did she have pretty hair, almost white?"

The girl nodded, and suddenly words were tumbling out. "Them two dint see *me!* They act like they was blind and deef." She tossed her head angrily. "She dint have her dress on neither!"

Chapter Sixty

BETS COULD NOT FAIL TO NOTICE THE ABNOR-mal quiet prevailing around the depot on Alameda Street when she and her daughters stepped down from the train. Usually at midday both Alameda and Commercial would be aswarm with people, not only the passengers and those meeting them, but touts for the hotels, gambling houses and whorehouses, as well as numerous street vendors, hawking their wares of fruit, peanuts, tortillas and the delicious chicken and shredded beef they had cooked over charcoal braziers. Drunks would wander past from nearby saloons, and a policeman would be in evidence, watchful for disturbances and doubtless seeking a lad or two who intended leaving town without paying his bills.

Bets had always liked the crowds and the excitement, not minding at all the reeks of horse manure and human sweat that intermingled with the pleasanter odors of cooking food.

Today, those who had come to meet passengers

were fewer, and mysteriously, the hangers-on, the vendors, even the policeman, were absent. There was a dull orderliness about the emptying of the train that disappointed her, and caused her to greet Phineas in an abstracted way and with less warmth than she might otherwise have displayed toward him.

"How good of you to meet us—but gracious! Have I been away so long I've forgotten what Los Angeles is really like? The town used to be so exciting—like a tinder box. But the streets are positively peaceful!"

"Not peaceful enough, I'm afraid," he answered. His eyes had been studying her quizzically, but now he turned away, pointing out to a porter the trunks to be sent to Patrick's. At that moment, a loud burst of gunfire sounded in the next block. "You can't see Calle de los Negros from here, but you can hear it. There's bad trouble, and it may spread. The top men of the two Chinese tongs are fighting each other. So far their brawl hasn't sparked the rest of the town, but it might at any time. As you say, like a tinder box."

"I'm sorry," she said, reddening. "My words were badly chosen."

"You didn't know." Still he didn't look at her, and his voice lacked its usual warmth. "Here we are. Maria Rosa, would you like to ride up with me as I drive?" He added in an undertone to Bets, "I think it's best to take you all to Patrick's at once . . . Unless, is there anything else you had in mind for the afternoon?"

"No, nothing. Doubtless it would be best to stay off the streets."

"Doesn't Mama look beautiful?" Maria Rosa asked him, squirming her weightless body sideways on the seat and turning her large brown eyes gleefully on his face. "She bought so many clothes in Washington!"

"I had to have them for the meetings!" Bets protested.

"She wore the prettiest dress of all to come home in!"

"Oh? Did she?"

"Yes, she said she wanted to surprise Grandpa. I do like blue, don't you? It's just like her eyes. The other ladies there wore hats all the time, but Mama wouldn't. But she *is* wearing a bustle."

"Hush, you little tattle-tale," Bets said.

"I don't like bustles," Isabel whispered to her mother. "I think they're silly."

"So do I," Bets agreed.

"Doesn't she look beautiful?" Maria Rosa demanded again.

"She always does," Phineas replied shortly, laying the whip on the horses and putting them in a fast pace.

Yes, Bets decided, he was definitely in an ill humor, and she herself had somehow brought this about. Her reply to his question concerning the afternoon's plans must have further displeased him, but she couldn't think what else she should have said. Hadn't he himself suggested it would be wise to go to her father's?

It occurred to her that she had promised, on her return from Washington, an immediate answer to his marriage proposal, but surely that was not the root of his grievance. He could hardly have expected her to blurt out an acceptance then and there as she stepped from the train accompanied by the two girls . . . Or had he?

In light of the constraint that had so suddenly arisen, it was something of a relief when on reaching the house, he refused to come in, saying he was needed back at the Plaza where a citizen's group was keeping a watchful eye on the Chinese.

"But will you be back to see us this evening? Phineas, I do want to thank you—"

"For meeting the train?" He gave a short laugh. "Please don't, Miss Betsey."

"No!" She had never before known him cool and distant—not toward her! "I meant for sending me to Washington. And also, for all the many other things you've done for me . . ." Even to her, it sounded so like a farewell that she stopped.

She would have tried again. She wanted to let him know somehow—difficult as such a conversation was in the presence of her daughters—that the situation hadn't changed, that her affection for him was undiminished, and that even in these months away in Washington, as occupied as she'd been, she'd thought about him, missing his support and companionship.

Perhaps he knew all this, and it wasn't enough. Already he had swung back up behind his horses, giving the girls a wave of his hand. Uneasiness, strengthening into a premonition, swept through her. Had she, by her casual greeting, her silence, made a decision she never intended? He in his way was as proud as Miguel, and if he believed he'd been refused, he wouldn't ask again. No, he would simply leave her, go out of her life . . .

She started to call him back, almost did. But then Patrick threw open the door and was welcoming her exuberantly. When she looked again, Phineas was already far down the street. The carriage swayed around the corner on two wheels, and he was gone.

"Miss Bets!" hissed Flora from the hallway.

Bets glanced out. She had spent a somber half hour, because after an initial close look at her father, Phineas had been driven from her mind. The change in Patrick frightened her. But she put on the best face she could, and tried to be suitably animated while reviewing for him and Teodocia as many details of the Washington trip as she could remember. Responding to his eager interest, she told of the hazardous and exciting train ride, the committee meetings, even her impressions of Washington itself, especially dwelling on the austere beauty of the Capitol building, with its recently installed cast-iron dome that weighed almost nine million pounds.

"Must be magnificent!" Patrick exclaimed. "How I would like to see it!"

"I wish you could, Papa. But Teo—" Her friend looked a trifle peaked. Poor dear girl, she too must wish sometimes she could make a journey! "You would have hated the weather there. In August and September the heat was horrible, and the damp air made it so much worse."

But Teo smiled, and surprised her by replying, "I wouldn't want to travel now, anyway."

"Miss Bets, I got to see you!"

Flora had hardly given her time to answer before repeating the summons more urgently.

This time Bets rose, saying calmly as she left the room, "Papa, let Isabel describe for you the very pleasant boarding house we stayed in. And Maria Rosa, tell them about the woman who made ice cream for you every single week."

Once out of sight, however, she ran swiftly back to her bedroom and faced the agitated Flora, demanding, "What is it? I've never seen you look so upset!"

"Oh, Miss Bets, oh Miss Bets—"

"Flora! For pity's sake, stop that and tell me! If you're trying to say Papa's worse, I'd have to be blind not to see it for myself."

"Mister Carew done come back! Him and Miss Mary, with Miss Ellen, they is living out near your land—"

"I know they are. Surely, that isn't why you called me back here—"

"No'm! Miss Bets—Master Tom and Miss Ellen is —Oh, they doan know no better, but they is—"

"Tomas and Ellen are what?" When Flora only shook her head, tears rolling from her eyes, Bets grabbed her by the shoulders. "They are *what?* You will answer me!"

Then abruptly her hands dropped and she stepped back. The two women stared at each other.

"Never mind, I can guess!" Bets drew a deep breath and turned away. "I won't ask if you're certain. You must be. How long has this been going on?"

"Doan know, Miss Bets. I jest found out. Jesus God, I like to died!"

"Flora, you tell Jeb to harness the horses, have my carriage ready at the door. I'll go out there—today— to talk to John! Somehow, I have to persuade him to put a stop to this—this youthful romance—for that's all it is, surely. They're both just children, after all! He'll have to forbid Tomas the house, tell him something—anything!"

"Maybe he won't. Him and Master Tom is good friends."

"Are they, indeed! Then if I have to, I'll tell John the truth, although I swore all those years ago I never would." She had been pacing as she talked, but now she stopped and looked at Flora. "Strange, isn't it? After all this time! As they say in church 'the sins of the fathers.' I only hope Tomas doesn't have his heart set on this girl too much."

"Oh, Miss Bets!"

"Well, go on! Tell Jeb. And meanwhile I'll explain to Papa that I'm so eager to get home, I want to find out how my son is and how he's cared for the rancho, I won't be staying here tonight, although Isabel and Maria Rosa can visit him for a few days yet. He may think it's odd I'm in such a hurry, but if I sit and talk with him a little while longer, it will be all right."

And Patrick, after expressing his disappointment, had become somewhat reconciled to her departure. For one thing, he was easily tired; but also he was nervous about the Chinese situation, and it distracted him from dwelling on her own plans. Sipping chocolate, she forced herself to listen to the account of his and Teo's social call on Almond Leaf, and it did occur to her to wonder if either Adam or his new wife could be in danger. However, her father, it appeared, was not alarmed in that respect.

Adam was, as Patrick said, a sensible and peaceable man. His marriage might have been the cause of the present dissention, but he was not one of the leaders, and he had never taken an interest in tong affairs. He would hardly be out with a gun, sniping at men with whom he had no quarrel! No, and Bets agreed, only too willing to be persuaded, he would doubtless remain prudently under cover until in a few hours the disturbance had quieted.

But as she and Jeb rode along Plaza Street from Sonoratown, the comfortable assumption that today's fracas was a minor one, soon to be over, was proved wrong before their eyes. As they drew near the Chinese settlement, a gang of Orientals surged into view in the next block, circling one another with brandished knives, firing pistols sporadically, and all the while uttering high nasal cries as they grappled with each other in bizarre looking, but highly effective physical combat.

Jeb, without realizing he did so, let the horses slow to an amble, while he and his mistress stared in amazement. Both, like others calmly loitering in the Plaza to watch, felt no sense of personal danger because the spectacle, what with the foreignness of the adversaries, their incomprehensible yells, and their odd circling movements, seemed to have little more reality than a battle acted out on a stage. It promised to result in more noise and fury than actual bloodshed.

However, a mounted policeman emerged from a side street, and spurred his horse headlong into the thick of the struggle. He intended, it was clear, to drive the Chinese mob back into the Calle, and at first he appeared to accomplish this aim with ridiculous ease. Still fighting, most of the little band of men retreated out of sight around a corner. But not all. One of them, perhaps confused by the attack, scurried instead through the doorway of a dilapidated old building.

The policeman at once dismounted and gave chase, disappearing inside as well.

Then shockingly, there came a sharp staccato of gunshots from within the adobe. And after a long moment, the law officer staggered out, dripping blood with every step.

One of the crowd of spectators, a burly man dashed forward to aid the wounded policeman. There was another shot, and he too clutched his chest and spun half around, then fell heavily to the ground.

With that, the remaining watchers in the Plaza sprang to life, aware at last of their own peril. Scattering in all directions, they were speeded away by the wild shooting of the Chinese who had reappeared. Around the square, shop doors slammed shut and men poured from the saloons to form clusters in every doorway. Grim-faced, they began returning the fire from the Calle.

"Drive on, Jeb!" shouted Bets, and the horses raced away from the Plaza at full gallop, not being slowed until they reached the edge of town.

There Jeb pulled up. He turned to ask, "We going

around, Miss Bets? Coming back in from the other side?"

"What? No! We're going on."

"We ain't going home—after that?" He stared at her in disbelief.

"No." Was there really a reason for her not to continue on to John's rancho? She briefly considered, and decided there wasn't. She could only pray that Adam would manage to stay aloof from the rioting. But if he didn't, there was nothing she could do to help him. Nothing at all.

Jeb broke into her thoughts, saying worriedly, "Don't you reckon them John Chinamen'll get to Mister Patrick's street?"

"Jeb! Knowing Adam as well as you do, you can't believe his people want to massacre strangers like us?"

"They killed that man back there," Jeb said sullenly. "He was dead."

"But the policeman drove his horse at them and they lost their heads! Perhaps if they'd been left alone to fight it out, nothing like that would have happened! It is a tong war."

"Mebbe so. But it looks like big trouble for ever'-body."

"Yes, I'm afraid so. Jeb, you're right, the family should know there's a riot starting. We aren't really far from the house now. You'd better walk back and tell them."

"You mean, leave you to go on by yourself?" His disapproval of that solution couldn't have been plainer. "Mister Patrick'll have my hide!"

"Then he'll have to have it. Go on, Jeb! I'm telling you to!" She watched him, grumbling, swing down from the carriage. "I'm safe enough. Times have changed and you know it. The dangerous place now will be in town, so be careful!"

He trudged away without answering, so she picked up the reins and drove on, her mind already on the interview ahead. She dreaded encountering John Carew again in such circumstances, knowing she would have to fence with him about Tomas, and finding herself still unable to muster any telling arguments.

But apprehensive as she was, she was even more fearful she might not find him at home.

He was there, however. When Bets was at last before the covered veranda, he had heard the jingling of the harness, and thrown open the door.

"Bets!" He hesitated almost imperceptibly, then strode down the steps to her.

A stable boy had come running, and she relinquished the carriage, instructing him not to rub down the horses but merely to walk them, as her visit would be very brief. Then, there being no further excuse for delay, she turned to Carew; and in spite of her pressing anxiety stood looking up with deep curiosity at the man who had long ago, for one blissful, clearly remembered afternoon, been her lover.

CHAPTER SIXTY-ONE

ALTHOUGH OLDER, JOHN LOOKED VERY MUCH as Bets remembered. He had been rugged rather than handsome then, and he still was a stocky, strongly muscular man. Today his clothes, even for rancho work, were a far cry from the worn deerskins in which he had first appeared in Los Angeles, but such a superficial change made little difference. He was like a stone polished by the water of a stream. His surface had been smoothed, but there was no question he was rock-hard underneath.

Yes, he was virtually the same, yet for her, some unique quality was missing. He was shorter than she'd pictured him. The gaze of his blue eyes was merely thoughtful. The smile he'd produced at her unexpected appearance was courteous enough, surely—but where was the magnetism she'd found so irresistible? Had she really cared so much, so terribly much, for *him?* That passion suddenly was inexplicable.

"Good evening, Bets." He was trying to sound

pleased, but he was doubtless wondering why she had come at that hour and alone. Perhaps he sensed she brought trouble.

Was it evening already? Could it be so late? She was tired, and a little dazed, but he was right, the sun had sunk below the horizon. She had arrived, probably, just before the evening meal, hardly the best time to speak with him in private.

"Won't you come in? It must be Mary you want, and she will be very pleased. She was hoping after you returned—"

"No, not Mary," Bets said impatiently. "It's you I came to see. I must talk to you, John!"

"What is it? Is something wrong?"

"Yes, I'm afraid so. I've discovered—I'm sorry, but it's quite important that we are alone. Is Aunt Mary in the house? Or your daughter?"

"Not now." He was frowning, wariness in his voice. "Mary is sketching, and she's never back until the light is completely gone. And Ellen is outside somewhere, probably fussing with the new bee hives. Did you know your son found a fine large swarm, and brought it to us? He is certainly a credit to you, Bets."

"Yes . . . Tomas is the reason for this visit."

"Oh? Well, please come in. The parlor is more comfortable than standing out here, and it's turning cool."

She hadn't noticed the chill before, but now she found herself shivering. She followed him through the doorway and into a shadowed room, where at his gesture, she sank onto one of the cushioned chairs. John said nothing while he busied himself lighting a lamp, but when it flickered into life, he turned to face her.

"Well? I gather from the way you spoke, you are somehow disturbed about Tomas. I want to say that I'm equally sure he's done nothing to displease you. He's not the sort, and you wouldn't be coming to me if he had. So, I am at a loss. Just what is the trouble?"

There was always the faint possibility that Flora's information had been in error. Bets said cautiously, "I believe he spends a great deal of his time here?"

"Indeed he does. And he's welcome. He's intelligent and capable, and he's been helpful to me. In fact, we've become quite good friends. Surely, you can't be objecting to that? Good God, Bets, too many years have passed!"

"No, I don't object to that, John. He can choose whom he pleases as his friends. But he must not come here, ever again. I have to ask you to forbid it."

"And why?"

"I can't tell you why! It's—won't you simply believe me, trust me, when I say it's necessary?"

Carew's eyes had narrowed, and his chin jutted forward. "No. I'm sorry, but you'll have to give me a reason, and a good one otherwise I certainly refuse. He's been welcomed here, and will continue to be. As I've already said, I like him. He's even the sort of man I'd approve of for my Ellen, if some day they should come to care for one another."

"But that is just it," she cried in desperation. "They already have come to care!"

"Indeed? I didn't know, and frankly, I wonder how you do. But supposing it's true, and I'd guess that it is, is that so bad? I've said I would welcome him as a son. I'm wondering though, now that I think about your coming here—" His voice, already scornful, hardened. "Perhaps I do understand! Is it possible you object to my Ellen, a girl you have not even met?"

"No!" Bets sprang to her feet. "How can you think that? I've not the slightest doubt she's a fine girl! Although they must not be allowed together, should never have been, the reason is not that I disapprove of her— not in any way!"

"Then what is the reason, may I ask?"

"They're—far too young."

"He's eighteen, isn't he? Ellen is several years younger, but that's as it should be. Aren't you being overly concerned?"

His annoyance had faded, but he was making little effort to hide his distaste for this conversation, and for her. Undoubtedly, he saw her now as a domineering mother who believed no wife could possibly be good enough for her son. A woman like old Señora Reyes, who had rejected Mary, hurt her so deeply.

Bets knew then, as she had really known all along, there would be only one way to reach John Carew. She would have to share with him the secret Miguel had expected her to keep, that she had sworn to keep.

"Very well," she said dully. "You force me to tell you, and I hope you will not have cause to regret being so unbending . . . You say you'll welcome Tomas as your son? John—he is your son."

"Yes, I'd—" He had not grasped her meaning instantly. But then he did. The words she had spoken hung almost visibly in the air, and they struck him dumb.

At length he shook himself. He walked to a cupboard and removed a bottle of brandy. As he did so, there was the sound of footfalls in the next room and Bets started. But he said brusquely, "Only my houseman. He doesn't understand English. Even if he did, I would think you'd have had enough of secrecy . . ." He paused to pour them both a glass of the brandy. "Perhaps you don't drink this often, but now, if ever, is the occasion. Take it. We need to be calm, both of us, to discuss what should be done.

"Bets, by God you should have told me! Don't you realize how I've been cheated? To think of it—Tomas! All these *years* and I didn't know I had a son!"

"A son! A son!" she echoed tiredly. "It seems to me that's all you men care about."

"Tomas was mine. You should have told me!"

"I'd have died first, believe me. Was I to drag you back, force you to marry me, just because by some improbable chance I became with child? I wouldn't abase myself so. And you should be glad I didn't. Even then you wanted Mary—"

"Yes, even then. And always. But it wasn't up to you to solve that problem for me, was it? I was a grown man, I should have taken as much responsibility as you, and he is my child as well as yours."

"Brave talk!" she snapped. "And what was to be the happy ending?" But her old resentment had died, and she did not wait for an answer. "Let's not waste time arguing about what is long past. Now that you do know, and can understand why he and Ellen must be kept apart, what is to be done? What can we possibly tell them, I wonder!"

"I would think, the simple truth."

"Tell Tomas that Miguel wasn't his father? Never!"

John Carew studied her with cold eyes. "What happened to the girl you once were? That free-spirited, free-thinking girl? She wasn't afraid of truth. Nor am I. Nor, I believe, would Tomas be. Your son—and mine—is entitled to the facts of his parentage."

"You fool! You don't know him at all! Haven't you any idea how much he adored Miguel?"

"That may be. And I would hope from now on I can help fill the void. At any rate, as I see it, we have no choice."

"No, you haven't. I only wish you had!" The deep young voice was outraged, tragic. Tomas stood in the archway, and beside him was Ellen.

Bets would remember only Tomas. No longer for her, after that first moment, was there anyone else in the room. Ellen, staring at her, white-faced, was a stranger for whom she realized she should feel pity but did not. Carew was only someone from the distant past. They faded from her vision, but to the day she died there would be her son, his eyes, voice, face—accusing her, with the words, "You deceived my father!"

"No! Oh, no, Tomas! Before Miguel and I were married, I told him. He knew you weren't his son."

"That's a lie, Mother! Because he couldn't have known. How could he—and still love me? He did love me—or do you deny that? Tell me the truth!"

The truth? How much talk there'd been of truth! And once again, as when she faced Miguel, she could not pay its price, knowing how Tomas would suffer.

"Miguel loved you. Yes."

"And I loved him—best of anyone in the world after Pepe. So now you steal him from me, tell me he wasn't my father! You've stolen everything from me—including Ellen—"

She could no longer bear to look at him. There were tears coursing down the face of her reserved, self-contained boy. She hadn't seen him weep in many years, not even when word came of Miguel's death and he, anguished, too quiet, had gone off alone to battle his grief in some hidden and solitary place.

"To think—" He finished with such bitter contempt that she shrank back, "I once loved and honored you!"

John, with an uncomfortable glance at Bets, said, "You're being unjust, Tomas, even cruel. Your mother —and I—did nothing dishonorable! We harmed no one."

"No one?"

"It seemed so, then. Tomas, my son, I hoped you would be able to understand."

The two looked into each other's eyes, two men so much alike, who had begun to be friends, but were now divided by a gulf that was uncrossable.

The younger one shook his head. He appeared somewhat calmer and again in control of himself. But to Bets, his air of grim decision was more ominous than tears.

"You see, Mr. Carew, you and my mother do not matter to me any longer. I don't care to understand why you would love and yet not marry, and I've no wish to know what happened afterward. I only know what is *now*. Ellen, you tell me, is my sister . . . My *sister!*"

He paused, pondering, then he resumed stonily. "I am not your son. Never think that I am. All my life I have been the son of Miguel Aguirre, and I shall continue to be.

"As for you, Ellen—" He turned to her then, and his voice gentled. "I believe I would have liked being your brother—if we'd been brother and sister from the beginning! But it's too late now. You know that, don't you?"

She nodded, her head bowed. He put out his hand and with unashamed tenderness raised her face so she must look at him.

"I'm saying goodbye to you, because I must. There can be nothing for us, and so I am going away."

"Going away?" Bets asked sharply. "Where?"

His eyes did not leave the girl. He might not have

heard. "I'll think of you always, Ellen—and envy you, living here in this land I've . . . loved so much—"

His young voice broke. He rushed from the room. Those he had left heard him run across the veranda and down the steps, while they stood transfixed, each separate from the others, each encased in the prison of his own grief. Shortly, there was the sound of creaking leather, and then a drum of hoof beats, loud at first but growing softer in the distance.

Ellen said in a clear voice, "He's gone. I won't see him again, ever . . . But neither will you, Señora Aguirre!"

CHAPTER SIXTY-TWO

TOMAS, BETS THOUGHT, MIGHT BE FREE TO seek forgetfulness in some new and faraway place. She was not. She walked out to the stable yard where the horses, still in harness, waited, heads down, half-asleep, and seating herself in the carriage, nudged them into life. Then she began the long tedious hours of retracing her way back to town.

Oblivious of the jouncing on the rutted, rock-strewn road, Bets sat stiffly erect as she drove. She gazed at the changing moonlit vistas of scrub oak, cottonwoods, or wide empty plain, and saw only the face of her son as he denounced her.

He was gone. Perhaps for the rest of her days he would be gone, living a life she'd know nothing about, in some different place she'd not even be able to visualize. Could she bear wondering about him, always?

Doubtless he would find a measure of happiness. He was young, and some other girl, in the course of time, would take Ellen's place in his heart. But would he ever stop dreaming of his rancho, he who had loved it so deeply? No. Such forgetting was not in Tomas. He would always be a man in exile, and thus for him who was blameless, there would be punishment also. And all because of the loves that should never have been—his mother's, and his own.

Oh, Tomas . . . Tomas, forgive me!

It was a relief to enter the town at last, and be struck through her preoccupation by the strange and frightening stillness. The downtown streets, normally so busy and noisy, especially in the hours approaching midnight, were completely empty! Her horses' hooves thudded loudly as the carriage passed along the dark, deserted Plaza.

Then abruptly, she came upon a sight so appalling that the reins dropped unheeded from her fingers.

"Dear God!" she murmured aloud, and sat staring. The moon shone on a large Conestoga wagon which stood abandoned in the street. Its canvas cover was gone, and from the high hoops of the frame, four Chinese men hung by their necks on hempen ropes. Their bodies were limp in death.

"How horrible!" she breathed, her stomach churning. Frantic to escape the grisly scene, she laid her whip on the tired horses. But at the corner by the church, her flight was stopped by a shouted order and a man in sheriff's uniform, who had evidently been keeping watch unnoticed in the Plaza, came pounding toward her.

"No one's allowed through here now! Don't you know that?" Then the curt tone altered. "Sorry, I didn't see there was a lady driving. Why, it's Señora Aguirre! Remember me, Ma'am? I'm Roy Sims, the sheriff now."

"I do remember." His peculiar mispronunciation of her name had jogged her memory. "Sheriff, what terrible crime did those poor men commit, to deserve hanging?"

"Hanging's not the word. They were lynched! To tell you the truth, Ma'am, people went crazy in this town for a while. Why, this lot ain't all. There's six more dead Celestials swinging from a wooden awning on Los Angeles Street, and another five at the Tomlinson and Griffith corral. And besides the lynchings, there was bull-whippings, shootings, houses looted, and some fires. What with all the smoke and blood and yelling, until about an hour ago, it was pure hell around here, if you'll excuse the word. Just in China-town, I mean, of course! Nowheres else. Still, to-night's work sure wasn't something to be proud of."

"Proud of? I should think not! A cruel massacre like this—we may never live it down! Have you ar-rested the people responsible?"

"Reckon we have, a few. The trouble is, Ma'am, it warn't just the ignorant Pikes or that thieving scum from around the Calle. A great many worthy citizens were out here tonight, and only a very few of them stayed on the side of the law. Them I can just about count on one hand; Mr. Bishop, Judge Widney, and your father, Mr. Donovan, and, let's see, there was Cameron Thom—"

"My father? But that's quite impossible! He's far from well!"

"He looked well enough, the once I caught sight of him, raging like a lion and cutting down some poor devil they'd strung up. Likely saved his life . . .

"Anyway, it's all over now. When we finally got the upper hand, and a hard fight it was, us being so out-numbered, all the spirit went out of the mob. Some of 'em looked downright ashamed, and they went home nice and quiet."

"And the Chinese—who weren't lynched—did they go home nice and quiet also?" Bets asked bitterly. She was thinking of Adam now, desperately afraid for him. Gentle, capable Adam who had nursed Pepe and Tomas through smallpox without a thought for him-self! Was he one of the many pathetic corpses?

"Far's I know they did. Must of took their wounded along with 'em too—there wasn't a one left out on the street. And now it's all over, Chinatown is so quiet I'd bet it would be safe there all night, even for a woman alone!"

"I'm grateful to hear you say so." She flicked the reins. "I'll be going. Good night to you, Mr. Sims."

She had been tempted to tell him what was in her mind, and suggest he accompany her. But almost certainly he would object, and she was in no mood for delay and argument, even if by avoiding them she forfeited the advantage of his protection.

Instead she waited until she was well away from the sheriff's surveillance, before turning left at New High Street. Although she didn't hesitate, she could not help glancing from side to side fearfully. This wasn't the way home—as the horses told her by their laggard reluctance, but led instead to the Tomlinson and Griffith corral. She would never forgive herself for her cowardice, if she failed to search for Adam! She must find out if he'd survived this senseless slaughter of his people; and if he wasn't one of the poor unfortunates hanging at the corral, she told herself, she would have to go farther still, to Los Angeles Street and the gibbet there.

So she drove from one of the make-shift gallows to the other, and at both, encountering nobody and very conscious of the ominous quiet, she stopped long enough to satisfy herself that none of the victims was Adam. At the corral, this meant leaving the carriage and walking closer, as one dead man, having the same slight figure as her old servant and a particularly long thick queue like his, hung with his back to her, and only by circling the gently swaying body could she be certain. It wasn't Adam.

But in spite of her relief, she felt a nagging dissatisfaction. Not all the dead had met their end this way! Some had been shot. Could he be lying wounded, alone, needing help? She must see him, talk to him, know he was really all right. *Where* was he?

Hurriedly, not giving herself time to think, because driving through the unsavory area was dangerous at any time, and to do so tonight was a rashness no sensible individual would undertake, she determined to return to the Plaza by way of Calle de los Negros. Hadn't the sheriff stated that it would be safe there all night? True, he was making a small jest and exaggerating, but having nothing better to sustain her, Bets repeated his assurance, fearfully aware even of the sound of the carriage wheels creaking in the menacing, empty streets.

The Chinese quarter was very quiet, just as Sheriff Sims had described it, so unnaturally it might have been without life. All the doors were shut tight, and not a drunk or whore was in evidence. A dog barked, briefly disturbing the uncanny stillness.

She found herself listening hard, conscious of all the various missing sounds, and remembering suddenly a scrap of conversation between her father and Jeb.

Jeb had happened one evening to ride through the Calle, and he'd remarked afterward on the noise of "all the tiles aclacking."

"Tiles?"

"Them ivory tiles—what John Chinamen gamble with."

"Oh, yes," Patrick had said, enlightened. "Mah-jongg! They do love the game. The whole quarter plays every night!"

But not tonight it seemed. What were the people in these dark hovels doing instead? Cowering in fear? Mourning their dead?

A high shrill scream of agony sliced through the night, then cut off abruptly. The wounded! There must be many of them, dragged here to be tended furtively behind closed doors and in darkness.

Living, breathing, suffering people were close by, almost near enough for her to reach out and touch. And Adam, was he here too somewhere—injured, in pain?

She dredged the recesses of her mind for the few details her father had mentioned in his description of Adam's house. *On a corner. A scraggly geranium plant.* It wasn't much to go on, yet as she approached the beginning of Aliso Street and looked searchingly at the first small adobe house, she saw beside the door something growing that looked thicker, larger-leafed than a weed. Were there a few flowers? She couldn't be sure.

This might be Adam's house . . .

And if it was, what was she to do? She could hardly leave the carriage and rap on a Chinatown door at this hour! Especially this night, after what had been done to these people—by her people!

On the other hand, was she just to give up, drive on home? No!

The house window was very close and the shutter was open. On an impulse she instantly regretted, she called out: "Adam!" and cringed at the sound of her voice. She was already poised to whip up the horses, when a hoarse, weak voice answered.

"Bets?"

Astonishment held her motionless for an instant, then she was out of the carriage.

"Papa! Where are you?"

The door opened. A pale hand beckoned, and without hesitating, she ran inside.

Moonlight flowed past her. She could see, where it fell in a silver oblong, a small Chinese woman standing at the foot of a pallet placed on the dirt floor. But Bets had no eyes for her, because on the rough straw mattress lay Patrick.

The front of his shirt was dark in a large circle, the stain growing larger even then, and Bets caught her breath in shocked consternation, recognizing that the spurting wetness was his blood.

She flung herself on her knees beside him.

"Papa!"

He was terribly weak. She could see how painfully he collected his strength to speak. Then he answered, the words rattled by his hard breathing, but although death must have hovered only a pace away, his strained voice was filled with gladness.

"I saved Adam, Bets! I was worried and I went . . . I cut him down!"

"And they shot you! Oh, Papa, where is Adam now? You need Dr. Kramer at once!"

"He's gone to bring him . . . although I think . . . I know . . . Bets, there's no use."

She swallowed hard, trying to open her throat. She mustn't break down, not when he was so pleased with what he'd done! But when she spread one hand across her face, the tears trickled through her fingers.

"Papa, I am so proud of you," she managed. "That was a good thing—to save Adam."

"Yes. Oh, it was good . . . once more . . . to be a

man!" He stopped breathing for a moment, then resumed with a rasp that shook his body. "Will you say goodbye? To Teo—and Mary Frances? Ah, but it's hard to leave now! Teo and I . . . have been so close . . . the last few months have been . . . and tell her I'm glad! . . . Bets?"

She took his hand and held it tightly between hers, while she sank lower, close beside him, and put her drenched cheek against his face. She did not know he had died, until the Chinese woman came to kneel there too, and gently patted her shoulder.

When she returned to her father's house, Jeb was waiting, leaning sleepless against the stable wall. He came at once to help her from the carriage, then he began unharnessing the horses. Bets stood in the darkness watching, guessing from his manner he had something he hated to put into words, just as she did.

"Your Pa ain't here, and I doan know where he's at. He *would* go. Told me I had to stay home, case the trouble got here, but later on I went looking anyway, cause Miss Teo was beside herself she was so worried. Didn't find him nowhere! Miss Bets, I—"

"Papa's dead, Jeb. I found him."

"Oh, Miss Bets!" His hands stopped their automatic work. His face was hidden by the night shadows, but she could feel like a palpable thing the sorrow they were sharing.

"Doan know what I'll do without him," Jeb said, his voice thick.

"I don't know what any of us will do."

Silence fell heavily, until Bets said wearily, "I hate to tell Teo, but I must. It's surprising she didn't hear my carriage."

"She fell asleep a little bit ago. Didn't mean to, I reckon, but she was wore out, crying, walking around, and feeling real poorly too. She told Flora just tonight, there's going to be another chile."

"Oh!"

"Said she just found out. You reckon your Pa knew?"

"I hope so. But, yes—" Bets was remembering

Patrick's gladness, and her grief lifted for a brief moment before settling back. "Yes, I do think he did."

"You going to wake her?"

"I suppose so." But she did not move toward the
house. Besides Teo, there were Brian, Isabel, and
Maria Rosa to be told, and Flora. The difficult task
loomed like a mountain to be climbed. And she was
tired. So very tired!

She tried to steel herself and go in, but her exhaustion held her rooted where she was. All of them would
grieve, and all of them, the servants too, would expect
her to be strong, to be calm. Even Teo, his wife and
the mother of his unborn child, being ill, nauseated,
would look to her for strength. She would have to
make decisions, be strong for the rest of the family.

And she would be. Patrick's daughter surely had in
her some of his blithe fortitude.

But not tonight! Ah, not tonight.

One such blow as she'd had, she could sustain. But
two, her son and her father both taken from her, and
she was undone, all her courage sapped.

"No," she said aloud. She started to ask Jeb to bring
out a horse for her, because she knew suddenly what
she wanted to do, must do, and there was time yet.
But a movement caught her eye, and when she heard
the soft rasp of leather against leather it seemed a
good omen, the first of this terrible night. Her father's
gelding, the one he'd ridden out so bravely, had wandered home at last, and was standing by the half-door,
waiting to be found.

"Help me up, Jeb," she said, ignoring her cumber-
some attire. Her tone was such that he adjusted the
stirrups and did as she asked without question.

"Dr. Kramer won't be bringing Papa's body home
until tomorrow morning, so you go to bed. I'll be back
in time to tell them all."

"Yes, Miss Bets."

She kicked the big horse with both heels. Her shoes
were soft but he made a lackadaisical circle, and
reluctance headed away.

She gave him more kicks, and he began to lope.
Soon he was galloping, while she clung to the large

saddle, her skirts hiked up above her knees and her shining hair loosened and streamed behind.

It would be a long hard ride to the big house in Wilmington, but there, oh, he must be there, she would find Phineas.

CHAPTER SIXTY-THREE

WHEN THE WILMINGTON HOUSE, TALL, SOLItary, and lighted only by moonlight, loomed into view, despair swept her. He was not there after all! This long long ride had been for nothing, and she was so tired, so prostrated by shock and grief, she could barely stay in the saddle.

But then she made out a faint silhouette moving high in the silvery shadows of the cupola and as she drew nearer, it became a broad-shouldered figure wearing a sea cape, stalking back and forth. He was not only home then, but awake, keeping some kind of watch—perhaps for an overdue ship.

The carriageway skirted the house, so she pushed the gelding into a canter, then reined him just below the wide porch.

"Phineas?" Her voice was hoarse, and against the strong wind, little more than a whisper, but hearing the drum of hoofbeats, he had already come to the parapet and looked over. He could not possibly see into the well of darkness below, but after she called, he disappeared. Evidently he'd recognized her voice from the single word, and guessing he was on the stairs, she stiffly dismounted. Almost at once the front door was thrown open.

"Miss Betsey!" He seemed as surprised by her unexpected appearance as John had been earlier, and she imagined she heard the same hint of reserve in his welcome.

"Is there trouble, Miss Betsey?"

Yes, she had been right about the coolness. Of course, she told herself, he couldn't know why she'd come seeking him in the middle of the night. He would have to suppose some emergency had arisen.

When she didn't answer at once, he added, still remote, "If you need my help, you know you've only to ask."

Suddenly she was smitten with self-reproach. Had she always sought him before only to beg his help? It seemed so, remembering. She'd wanted his advice, his backing, and even once—his money. Now again, she needed him, if only in a different way.

"But forgive me," he was saying, "I'm afraid I'm being discourteous. Won't you come in? Leave the horse where he is. I'll have him looked after—"

"No, wait. Please—" Her hair was being whipped in long strands across her eyes, and she held it back with both hands, feeling at the same time through her light cloak, the chill of the wind off the sea. "I won't come in until I've said what I came to say . . . Phineas, two terrible things have happened tonight . . . Oh, Phineas, Papa is dead!"

"Ah, no! Why, I caught a glimpse of him during the worst of the fighting, and he was giving a good account of himself! Was he killed, then?"

"Yes . . . saving Adam."

"I will miss him! He was always a good friend. Betsey, I am so very sorry!" He came to her then and took her in his muscular arms, holding her close and secure, just as he had done more than once in her troubled life. Although she sensed he was offering her comfort and nothing more, she leaned against him, grateful for his strength and warmth.

"And the other terrible thing?" he asked. His deep voice had gentled, doubtless with pity.

"It's Tomas . . . He—" Phineas waited in silence. After a moment, she felt his hand lightly smooth back her wildly disordered hair, and remembering that same tender gesture from the long past, her sadness grew.

"Go on. Tell me."

"He's gone," she said. "And I can't even guess where. He was angry, and told me he would never return . . . Oh, how can I endure it? Never knowing—years of never knowing—"

"Tomas is a grown man, my dear. I could find him for you, but it would do no good."

"No, and I didn't come for that." She straightened a little and looked up at him, hesitating. But there was no roundabout way to tell him what she wished. She had always been forthright with him, and she must be now.

"You asked if I needed you, and yes—I do! That is why I am here at this late hour . . . Do you remember when you said a time would come that I'd need someone stronger than myself? I didn't truly believe you, because for years I've been struggling to keep Rancho Aguirre, fighting every battle myself, and winning. But tonight—oh Phineas, tonight is that sometime! My dearest dear, it's you yourself, not what you can do for me this time, or what you can give me, but just you! You to hold me, love me, keep me steady. I want to be able to weep tonight—and not be alone—"

There was so much more she should tell him! All the thoughts she'd had as the rawboned horse pounded through the night carrying her here. For it was clear to her at last, who and what she wanted.

She'd been homesick in Washington, but it wasn't just untamed, uncouth little Los Angeles she'd missed, it was this man. Phineas. Honorable, powerful Phineas. A man filled with restless vigor, striding along into the excitement of the future. She wanted to be with him and go with him, because California and Phineas and the future were all twined together in her heart and mind, and for her they could never again be separated.

"Let me stay with you tonight," she pleaded.

A tremor passed through his big rugged body, but he slackened his embrace deliberately. "Just tonight? No, Betsey, I think not. I'm expecting a ship. When the cannon fires, it's the owner's signal, and I'll be going out."

"Oh." She shut her eyes, defeated.

But then at last his control snapped. The passion he had held contained for so long exploded in a fiery shower, and he was shouting at her, wildly, like a madman.

"You ask for tonight? Will you torture me? Good God, woman, don't you know I could not bear it if you stayed once, and left me! I have so much love for you I'd need a hundred nights, a hundred years of nights—and then I'd have only begun! I've offered you all that I have, all that I am, and you dare to suggest to me—to *me*—a single night?"

"No, no, not just tonight!" She was shouting too, trying to stop him, and she was feeling joy again, she who hadn't imagined she could. Life was flowing back into her in a rushing torrent. "All the rest of my life. Phineas, listen to me! I want you for all the rest of my life!"

His arms had gradually tightened again until she could scarcely breathe, and when he fell silent, she could feel the pounding of his heart so close she thought it was her own. Perhaps it was.

He had heard her. He threw back his head and gave a roaring laugh of pure exultation.

From somewhere at sea, a cannon boomed. Neither of them listened or looked back, as he carried her into the house.

ABOUT THE AUTHOR

LOUISE O'FLAHERTY is a transplanted Mid-Westerner who only married a southern Californian, but then, like the members of the Donovan family, fell permanently in love with the wild and beautiful South Coast.

After graduating from Wellesley College, she became a wartime Navy cryptographer, during which time she met Joseph O'Flaherty. While their three children were growing up, she continued to write, most recently two romantic suspense novels set in the Los Angeles locale. Encouraged by her husband, an author of several histories of the region, she became fascinated by the moving story of the Californios after the gold rush. The result is *The Farthest Eden.*

NEW FROM BALLANTINE!

FALCONER, John Cheever   27300 $2.25

The unforgettable story of a substantial, middle-class man and the passions that propel him into murder, prison, and an undreamed-of liberation. "CHEEVER'S TRIUMPH . . . A GREAT AMERICAN NOVEL."—*Newsweek*

GOODBYE, W. H. Manville   27118 $2.25

What happens when a woman turns a sexual fantasy into a fatal reality? The erotic thriller of the year! "Powerful."—*Village Voice.* "Hypnotic."—*Cosmopolitan.*

**THE CAMERA NEVER BLINKS, Dan Rather
with Mickey Herskowitz**   27423 $2.25

In this candid book, the co-editor of "60 Minutes" sketches vivid portraits of numerous personalities including JFK, LBJ and Nixon, and discusses his famous colleagues.

THE DRAGONS OF EDEN, Carl Sagan 26031 $2.25

An exciting and witty exploration of mankind's intelligence from pre-recorded time to the fantasy of a future race, by America's most appealing scientific spokesman.

VALENTINA, Fern Michaels   26011 $1.95

Sold into slavery in the Third Crusade, Valentina becomes a queen, only to find herself a slave to love.

**THE BLACK DEATH, Gwyneth Cravens
and John S. Marr**   27155 $2.50

A totally plausible novel of the panic that strikes when the bubonic plague devastates New York.

**THE FLOWER OF THE STORM,
Beatrice Coogan**   27368 $2.50

Love, pride and high drama set against the turbulent background of 19th century Ireland as a beautiful young woman fights for her inheritance and the man she loves.

**THE JUDGMENT OF DEKE HUNTER,
George V. Higgins**   25862 $1.95

Tough, dirty, shrewd, telling! "The best novel Higgins has written. Deke Hunter should have as many friends as Eddie Coyle."—*Kirkus Reviews*

LG-2